Leonid Leonov

The Russian Forest

A Novel

Fredonia Books
Amsterdam, The Netherlands

The Russian Forest

by
Leonid Leonov

ISBN: 1-4101-0341-2

Reprinted from the 1966 edition

Fredonia Books
Amsterdam, The Netherlands
http://www.fredoniabooks.com

CONTENTS

CHIEF CHARACTERS OF THE BOOK

AGAFYA, a peasant, Ivan Vikhrov's mother.

BIG KOSTROMA, nickname of Cheredilov.

CHANDVETSKY, a Colonel of the Gendarmes, officer of the tsarist secret political police.

CHERNETSOVA, Varya, a school-teacher, friend of Polya Vikhrova.

CHERNETSOV, Pavel, Varya's father.

CHEREDILOV, Grigory (Grisha), son of a profligate priest, one of the 'Musketeers" (which see).

GIGANOV, Mikhail, an agent of the secret political police.

GRATSIANSKY, Alexander, son of a wealthy Professor of Theology, once a school friend of Ivan Vikhrov and then an insidious enemy. A professor of forestry.

KALINA, Timofeyevich, an old forester on the Yenga.

KNISHEV, a lumber magnate, a merciless despoiler of Russia's forests.

KRAINOV, Valery, a Soviet diplomat and an old friend of Prof. Vikhrov. One of the "Musketeers".

KOLYA, see Lavtsov.

LAVTSOV, Kolya, a work-mate of Sergei Vikhrov.

LENOCHKA, see Vikhrova, Yelena.

MARK, see Vetrov.

MATVEI, a peasant, Prof. Vikhrov's father.

MORSHCHIKHIN, Pavel, a Party worker, friend of Sergei and Ivan Vikhrov.

MARIA YELIZAROVNA, a squirrel, so named by Kalina.

MARIA VASILYEVNA, head nurse in a military hospital.

"MUSKETEERS," the school-mates Ivan Vikhrov, Grigory Cheredilov, and Valery Krainov.

OSMINOV, Pavel, Prof. Vikhrov's favourite pupil.

RODION, Polya's boy friend.

SAPEGIN, Ilya, a rich landowner on the Yenga.

SAPEGINA, Sofia (the "Lady-Ox"), his wife, a German.

SAPOZHKOV, Secretary of a Komsomol local in Moscow.

SEMYONIKHA, see Vetrova.

SERGEI, the son of Demid Zolotukhin, adopted by Prof. Vikhrov.

SLEZNYOV, a friend of Gratsiansky.

STRUNNIKOV, Professor, an army surgeon, chief of a military hospital.

TAISA, the hunchback sister of Prof. Vikhrov.

TIKHODUMOV, Rodion (see Rodion).

TIMOFEYEVICH, see Kalina.

TITOV, an old engine-driver.

TRINITATOV, a rural clergyman.

TULYAKOV, a Professor of forestry, Vikhrov's teacher.

VALERY, see Krainov.

VARYA, see Chernetsova.

VETROVA, "Semyonıkha," a villager, mother of five sons famed on the Yenga.

VETROV, Mark, her son, an active village Communist.

VIKHROV, Ivan, a forest scientist, son of a peasant.

VIKHROVA, Yelena, his wife.

VIKHROVA, Polya (Apollinaria), his daughter.

YELENA IVANOVNA, see Vikhrova, Yelena.

YEGOR SEVASTYANICH, a village feldsher (doctor's assistant).

ZOLOTINSKAYA, Natalya, the woman who shares Varya's flat.

ZOLOTUKHIN, Demid(ka), son of a village shark, a boyhood friend of Prof. Vikhrov. Later a village headman under the Nazis.

The train arrived exactly on time, but Varya was not on the platform. Polya dumped her luggage a little to one side of the crowd, and stood there for a long time looking out for that kind punctilious soul, the dearest in the world to her after her mother.

Clearly, something must have happened to detain her—some trouble or illness perhaps—but what could befall a student in the Soviet state, where youth itself was a safe-conduct, as it were, against all ills? And what illness could attack a girl of twenty who not so long ago had put the shot farther than anyone else at the inter-district sports meet? Probably she had forgotten to set the alarm clock the night before and was now charging down the station, jostling passengers and other people's relations, in order to throw herself upon her friend's neck. But the stir and bustle attending train arrival had subsided and still there was no sign of Varya.

Polya decided to venture forth on her own in search of the address, which she had written down on a slip of paper. Having subdued the suitcase, the handle of which had come off one of the rings, she found that she did not have hands enough for all the bundles and packages. That is always the case when four people see you off and none comes to meet you. She would have lost half her belongings had not a sooty-faced youth with a Komsomol badge on his overalls—obviously not a porter—dropped down on her from somewhere above. Shouldering her bag and the cross-strapped sack containing her winter coat, he caught the suitcase up under his arm and started off down the deserted platform in such a matter-of-fact way that one would think he had been doing this kind of thing every day of his life. Accustomed

7

by now to having these pieces of good luck attend her all the way from the Yenga, Polya accepted the miraculous intervention without a word.

Her benefactor was taciturn to a degree. In a way that was not so bad, because miracles always tended to lose their lustre through explanations; on the other hand, the least he might have done out of mere civility was to ask her name or the object of her visit to the capital city, all the more as she was simply dying to tell someone about her plans of life for the next century or two ahead. She caught up with him and apologised for the kettle tied to the bag, which was bumping against the lad's knee and rattling its lid, blabbing out all its provincial news, but the young man coolly reassured her that in the old days as well rustic grandmothers used to travel to Moscow with their samovars. Coming out into the street in a decided perspiration, he enquired whether it was a portable load of firewood or squared stones that she was lugging along as a gift for her Moscow aunt. Before Polya could recover sufficiently from his impertinence to think of an annihilating retort they had already reached the trolley-bus.

Now the miracles came so thick and fast that you could not make out where one ended and another began. A shiny blue vehicle on aerial wheels, with doors invitingly wide open, was waiting for Polya at the stop. No sooner had she stepped in and paid her fare than she found that her luggage had deposited itself inside, and that overcrowded though it was in there, a seat had been made available for her by the window, which was lowered on account of the heat. Polya did not want to go away without settling accounts with the young man, and the trolley-bus authorities obligingly gave her time for the quick performance of that operation.

"Excuse me, but how much do I owe you for your ... well, your chivalry?" she asked through the window, rummaging about in her mother's shabby old purse with an air of studied preoccupation.

The lad looked up, and for a moment Polya was struck by his remarkable resemblance to Rodion—the same grave greenish eyes with the mischievous twinkle in their depths, and the same engaging habit of looking you squarely in the face when speaking to you. True, this one was younger and not quite as tall as her friend; it was the soot and his work clothes that made him look older, but given a scrub he wouldn't look more than a year older than Polya—a mere boy, in fact, and one who had apparently made up his mind through sheer swank never to be caught smiling. No, this one was not a patch on Rodion. Rodion would never have been so rude as to make fun of a girl the first time he met her, a girl somewhat awed by happiness, as anyone would be when one's fondest wishes were coming true.

"Nothing at all! Curiosity is the blight of my young life. Just that, and a compassionate heart, as I watch the distressed go by from the window of my cab ..." her benefactor answered imperturbably. "I'm a fireman on the engine that brought you to Moscow."

At this, unable to think of anything more scathing, Polya advised him to hurry back before some railway thieves ran off with his poor little engine while he stood there getting off with strange young ladies, and he'd have his pay stopped for thousands of years to come. Head cocked, the young man nodded sympathetically at her feeble efforts at retaliation, until he had her blushing with impotence and annoyance. Luckily, the driver managed at last to swing the overhead trolley back into place—it had jumped the wire—and the bus moved off smoothly. The sunshine, the wind blowing in her face, and this foretaste of all the fascinating adventures that lay in store for her, made Polya suddenly feel happy and light, and her heart sang a little tune to the words of her favourite saying, which she had used as an epigraph for her diary: "A tiny leaf caught up in the rushing river."

All at once Polya became aware that her new fellow-passengers were all smiling with that queer light upon their faces which people have when listening to the calls of the early birds in a forest still wet with morning dew. No one was looking at her directly, but they must all have become aware of her happy state and noblest of intentions, all the more enviable in that she had everything before her. Apparently all of them, from the conductress to the grave-looking gentleman with the long moustache, who was wearing a cloak and an old-mannish black hat—a professor at the very university she was going to enter for all she knew—felt flattered that such an attractive girl as Apollinaria Vikhrova was henceforth to become a resident of their excellent city, and would start mastering the various useful sciences to the joy of her mother, the Lenin Komsomol, and all their great Homeland. Scarcely, therefore, had Polya breathed an inquiry as to the whereabouts of Blagoveshchensky Alley, where Varya Chernetsova lived, when all of them began to explain to her how

9

to get there, almost falling over each other and even quarrelling a bit in their eagerness, and by a happy coincidence that caused general satisfaction two of Polya's neighbours happened to be going to the same new big building, because they worked in a sewing workshop in the yard of that very house No. 8a, while the professor, who turned out to be a watchman at some place or other that was within an ace of being a military works, even lived there in a wooden house just across the yard. In short, nearly everyone was going Polya's way that morning.

All four got out together and started off down the sunny side of the street, with Polya's personal effects conscientiously distributed among them. Overwhelmed by the splendour of the Moscow street, Polya walked in the middle, treading gingerly as though afraid to cause damage to the national property, and trying to memorise the details for her evening report to her mother at Yenga. A dazzling militiaman held up the stream of traffic while the procession crossed the road at the corner; the handsomest buildings in the world towered on either side, and from all the open windows floated triumphant radio music that could possibly have only one name—*Invitation to Life*. What's more, there were flowers galore that summer; stacks of them, wrapped in clouds of sweet morning fragrance, with the undried moisture still on their cut stems, were being sold on every corner from kiosks, trays and wicker baskets. But for some reason Polya always hurried past them, jealously pressing to her bosom a small package in grey paper, the only piece of luggage which she could trust to no one.

The black-hatted professor, who proudly headed the procession, turned right, then right again into a cool grassy lane with little houses standing under lazy sprawling trees of the kind that are supposed to grow only on the outskirts. The poplar fluff was dancing merrily here—that spring blizzard was late this year—and the little local inhabitants, tipful of excitement, were trying to catch that weightless fairyland snow, while the gentle wind puffed it off their trustful childish palms, and it was perhaps the very meaning of life to them to give clamorous chase to those elusive flakes again and again. If not for the children the place would have been quite deserted, and a cyclist passing down the alley with a flash of glancing sunbeams would have been considered an event. Reared over this quiet backwater of life was an eight-storey block of flats, finished in the rough. Polya looked up anxiously—her friend Varya lived right at the top—but crowning all miracles was the discovery that the lift, after a prolonged period of idleness, had started working again that morning of all mornings.

"Thanks awfully!" Polya said to her companions at parting, and bowed to them with special regard, as if it was not just fellow-passengers standing there before her, but the confidential agents of a wise and benevolent humanity. "We're neighbours now, we shall be seeing a lot of each other now ... shan't we?"

The flat was unlocked, but nobody peeped out to see what the noise was about when Polya dragged her belongings piecemeal into the hall. She took breath and listened. From somewhere within came the low whistle of draughty air, and the tinkle of dripping water. Several doors, some of them padlocked, gave on a dim passage. Polya knocked at random on the first door on the left, and a woman's voice called out to her to come in.

The tidy half-empty room was on the sunny side, and through the wide-open window it was all flooded with the hard quartz-like brilliance of the sky. A woman was sitting on a child's stool mending a silk stocking which was drawn on her hand. A tumbled heap of knitted wear lay on a plywood worktable before her right at her feet. The work was tiring and the woman no longer young, but she liked her trade because there were lots of customers, and besides a living it gave her a sense of being useful, and that was necessary to give meaning to one's existence. She had been good-looking once; tight braids of almost white hair coiled round her head in the old-fashioned style crowned a large bulging brow. Polya had a feeling that she had met this woman before in the company of similar old folk, all as prim and grey-headed as herself—in a pack of cards probably.

"Ah, I remember, a gentleman's pullover—your father's?" the woman said, pushing up the cardboard eyeshade over her forehead and peering near-sightedly at the visitor. "Yes, I've looked it over and am still of the same opinion. There's no flying from fate. It has had its day, and the only thing is to undo it for wool."

The hard finality of the diagnosis overruled all questions and objections, and although it was obviously a misapprehension, Polya for some reason felt a twinge at her heart.

"There is a mistake, I'm afraid. I've only just arrived. I am looking for Varya Chernetsova," she explained with lips that had suddenly gone dry.

The woman looked up from her work again.

"I know. You are that girl from the provinces—sorry, the periphery," she corrected herself after the fashion of the age, which strove to level all citizens so that none feel offended. "Comrade Chernetsova will soon be back—she has been urgently called out to the district committee of the Communist Party," she added. Coming from her, this sounded rather impressive and odd. "Sit down, if you have time to spare. I'll show you in a minute where she hides her key ... I don't want to drop this loop."

"Yes, of course. I have all the time in the world!" Polya smiled engagingly. Indeed, the first impression she gave was that of having brought fresh cool air and heaps of cheap outdoor time with her, the way people bring butter or unbleached peasant linen up from the country. "A hundred years is nothing to me!"

At that the woman asked Polya to move up closer.

"How young you are!" she observed casually.

"Oh, no, I only look youthful," Polya protested, blushing. "I'll be eighteen soon."

"How soon will that be?" the woman asked slowly, regarding her closely all the time.

It turned out that Polya would be coming of age within two hours, nine minutes and—here Polya consulted the silver wrist-watch her mother had given her for a present on finishing school —and three seconds. She tried to prove that eighteen was no small age—why, Darwin at her age had read a scientific paper, while Herostratus.... According to her, that ancient philosopher could only discover his great Truth in childhood, in his barefoot rambles over the pebbly bed of an ancient Greek rivulet, whereas she, Polya, for all the rambling she had done in the forests, where she had purposely gone deep into the thickets, had discovered nothing worth mentioning yet. Hence, it followed that she had a great deal to do yet to live up to her country's expectations and add her bit to the treasury of human knowledge, which, she hinted, was in a rather neglected state thanks to world capitalism.

"I suppose you mean Heraclitus?" the woman with the stocking tactfully remarked.

"Yes, of course ... I always get them mixed up a bit. There was a Herodotus, too, wasn't there? Which of them burnt that temple down? I'm sorry, I keep interrupting your work." Polya looked disconcerted and began to apologise for her misplaced chattiness.

"Oh, no, all this is very interesting and very important," the woman said gravely, looking as though she were pleased, if anything, at the interruption. "Please continue."

"I've finished," Polya confessed in a very small voice.

It was some time before the woman bent over her stocking again; she looked as if she could go on listening without end to the naive and contradictory music of Polya's prattle.

"If you find it dull talking to me, take a book off the chest of drawers, my child."

"That's all right, I'll just sit around. In any case I have to put my ... well, my thoughts and impressions in order, you know," Polya whispered.

After the oppressive heat outside, the alpine breezes of the eighth floor were pleasantly refreshing. Sitting down on the edge of what served as an armchair, Polya took stealthy stock of her surroundings. The central piece in the room was a child's cot of sterile cleanliness with a bedside table on which, in addition to a half-finished cup of milk, lay three wooden nesting dolls on their sides, all in the order of rank and all shining from much fondling. All the other essentials of life and livelihood were piled together in the right and much smaller side of the room behind a Chinese screen, among them a dressmaker's dummy reflected at full length in an ancient looking-glass between two carved columns. Ever since it had been split down the middle by a deep irreparable crack, this thing ranked as a family relic rather than a piece of furniture.

Leaning slightly forward, Polya peered into the greenish tarnished glass, and understood what it was she owed the good luck and the miraculous coincidences of the last few days to. Gazing at her out of the oval walnut frame were two funny provincial girls of about fifteen each, with shining eyes and a skin so deeply tanned by the Yenga sun that their faces were the same colour as their coffee-coloured frocks. Obviously, a creature like that could not take a step in such a wide-awake city as Moscow without being noticed. So all those people who had been so eager to share their lunch baskets with her in the railway coach, who had run to fetch boiling water for her tea at the way stops lest she should be left behind, who lent half a dozen pairs of hands to drag her luggage into the trolley-bus and afterwards saw her home to Varya's alley—all of them were just being sympathetic with that peculiar, inoffensive, even somewhat egoistic sympathy by which simple people try to fill a bitter gap in their own cheerless childhood.

"Is this your first visit to Moscow?" the woman asked, without looking up from her work.

"I was born here, but they took me away to the forest range when I was four."

"Is your father in the forest service?"

"No, he's working here, he's ..."—Polya hesitated for some reason—"well, he's a forestry professor."

"Then you don't live together?"

"Mamma parted with Father when I was little. He's fairly well known as a matter of fact, he's done a lot of research, only he turned out to be a bad person."

"Who gave you the story of the family troubles—your mother?"

"Nobody."

"Then what makes you think he is a bad person, my child?"

"Because ... because Mamma is good!" Her voice rose.

After that she couldn't stop until she had emptied herself of all that had settled like silt upon her soul. It came to this—his science was as dull as dishwater, and he was probably not much of a professor either; no wonder they blew him up like that in the forestry magazines because he couldn't see the wood for the trees. Thank goodness her girl friends didn't read those articles; they'd have teased her to death, wondering in what old dust-hole she had picked up such a parent.

"His name is Ivan Vikhrov—maybe you've heard of him?" Polya came out with it at last, looking up with timid eyes brimful of hope.

Judging by the flicker of interest in the woman's eyes, the name was apparently familiar to her. Yes, in her young days in St. Petersburg she had met a taciturn student by that name, for she only remembered him because he was said to be a cook's son. She mentioned also in a light casual way so as not to hurt her young visitor's feelings, that she had heard about Vikhrov's reverses from another acquaintance of hers of those St. Petersburg days—a forestry scientist, too, but a much more successful, she would even say flourishing one. Here a cloudlet of unwelcome reminiscence crossed the face of the woman with the stocking. Unlike Vikhrov and despite Polya's damning opinion of the forestry profession, that man, she said, possessed a singularly lively albeit somewhat embittered mind, which gave special brilliance to his universally recognised gift of ruthless analysis. But apparently the age needed such men, seeing that it put him in charge of the critical reviews in forestry publications in which he made policy statements, and denounced the heresies and fallacies of his comrades.

"That man is a professor, too, and, as far as I remember, he told me something about Vikhrov. But I am a stranger to all these forestry affairs and quarrels," she wound up reticently.

"You can be frank with me. I hate my father. What was it he said?"

Irremediable grief shone out of Polya's eyes. You could not help feeling sorry for that gentle provincial creature, who was being made to pay for the sins of her parents, but on the other hand, it would have been worse to offend her by an untruth.

"I make it a rule never to lie to children. I don't want to pain you, my dear, but ... it was not a very flattering opinion, it was a harsh one if anything."

"I know, I have seen some of his articles," Polya said, with the air of one fully resigned to her fate. She knew the name of her father's celebrated critic without being told.

"If I were you," the woman with the stocking continued kindly, "I would find comfort in the knowledge, first, that you still have your mother, and secondly ... that your father must have accomplished a great deal in life to have drawn down upon himself the pen and wrath of such an eminent scientist. You must not give way to despair, my dear—we can't all be talented, and, judging by your domestic affairs, this Vikhrov is a bit eccentric too."

There it was, the same dark suggestive hint, which Polya had so often come across between the lines of the reviews on her father's books, which, despite the different signatures, and sometimes just initials, clearly revealed a common authorship—so uniformly sharp and acrimonious were they. No matter how one accounted for Vikhrov's existence in forest science, whether by the generosity of the age, or, on the contrary, by a lack of interest in forest affairs, this verdict was now settled irrevocably and not subject even to discussion, and it was only through naiveté of heart, through poverty of imagination, or ignorance of the stern conventions of the age that one could still count upon mercy.

"But ... this acquaintance of yours—did he also live a long time in the forest?" Polya asked thoughtlessly.

"No, he lives practically all the time in town on account of his delicate health; he needs constant medical attention."

"Then he is ... he is devoted to the forest from a distance, he writes books himself, I suppose, if he is such a fine specialist as that?"

The woman with the stocking on her fingers was constrained to explain the seeming contradiction.

"Well, you see, my child, he is not exactly a forest man. I'd call him simply a distinguished figure in that field. Generally speaking, he is a man of very tragic destiny, a man of the most versatile genius. In his youth he gave promise of becoming a poet or a musician. Ah, you have no idea yet, my dear, what tricks fate sometimes plays with all our plans! No, I wouldn't say that he was a great lover of the forest, although he did wander about the park for hours when he came down to our estate.... It was quite a small place, though, just an old-fashioned little house with columns," she added quickly, noticing Polya's watchful and jealous curiosity. "Besides, a talented critic doesn't have to know or to be able to do everything himself—his business is just general observation. At any rate he has sufficient taste and culture to judge other men's activity—the good or bad of it. For eight years now all kinds of public responsibilities have prevented him from finishing a research—I don't remember on what subject exactly—but it's something very fundamental. I have rather a bad memory for that kind of thing, I'm sorry to say," she added by sudden afterthought, refusing to pass final judgement, as it were, on problems so complex and confused.

"Isn't this man a relation of yours by any chance?" Polya asked quietly with a peculiar emphasis.

The question was obviously an unpleasant one. No, he was no relation of hers. Once, in their youth, they had simply taken passing notice of each other for a time. What's more, their friendship, if you could call a fleeting relationship of thirty odd years ago by that name, broke up before the revolution, and now they met only rarely, usually in the street, although Destiny, the old mocker, had placed them in the same block of flats in their old age—true in different sections of it and on different floors. Seemingly the years, while preserving all his other virtues intact, had made a rather cold retiring person out of this once impulsive sociable youth. Polya was struck by the alternate shades of bitterness, admiration, and resentment with which this woman spoke about her father's chief judge, as though she were at once accusing him, defending him, and cursing him for some unpardonable offence.

"Won't you tell me his name?" Polya asked once more.

"But you told me you know who it is."

"I just want to be sure, if it isn't a secret, of course."

"There is no secret about it at all. The whole country knows him," the latter answered reluctantly, though not without pride. "Well, Gratsiansky ... why?"

"Oh, nothing. It's just what I thought," Polya said, smiling disarmingly.

Both the elderly woman and the young girl were silent for a while. It was just like a meeting of two people in the Yenga wilds in the old days, when they would warily steer clear of each other, trying to fathom each other's designs. Meanwhile the woman with the stocking had recollected some of the details of the now so elusive circumstances under which she had first heard the name of Polya's father. Oddly enough, before calling up the image of that man, now somewhat blurred by distance (she had met him only once), she first recollected a large portion of raspberry ice-cream between wafers, which had tasted so delicious in the heat, and then the elongated field of the Kolomyagi racecourse in St. Petersburg flooded with a gay throng, over which a little cloud of tragedy had hung like a passing drizzle. And nothing more, except perhaps an aching sadness half-melted in the mists of time. Later in the day, round about six o'clock, the celebrated aviator Matsievich had crashed—he was the first victim of Russian aviation—and an hour before that Gratsiansky had introduced to her, Natasha Zolotinskaya, then a girl of eighteen, his three chums—the Three Musketeers—one of whom had brought the ice-cream to the stand in which they were sitting. It must have been Vikhrov. His comrade, a lanky deep-voiced young man, was called Big Kostroma for some reason. Like a grain of sand or the stirring of a breeze in the mountains, the nickname touched off the thawed avalanche of ageing memory.

There was something she had to make sure of first, it was most essential that she should.

"Good God, Vikhrov, Vikhrov! Why, I was just about your age at the time. Your father studied in St. Petersburg, didn't he?"

"I don't know. He was already a professor when he married, and I was born later still. He is lame."

"Now that I don't remember. I don't think there were any lame ones among that trio, but ... wasn't he arrested afterwards and exiled to the North?"

"I never asked Mamma any questions about Father so's not to hurt her. Only once I asked her just casually ... it upset her, and she said—some day you'll find it out for yourself ... you'll see him and understand."

"How is it your mother never mentioned anything about it, if you lived together all the time?"

As it happened, they hadn't been living together *all* the time. Polya went home to the Pashutino Range, where her mother's little hospital was, only during the summer holidays. The last three winters she had been living in the home of Varya Chernetsova, whose father, Pavel Chernetsov, a former Urals partisan, was now employed as a vet at the D.E.C.* The trouble was there was only a seven-year school at Shikhanov Yam, not far from the forest range, and so Polya finished secondary school in the little town of Loshkarev, which stood at the point where the fussy little woodland stream Sklan joined the Yenga. Like Shikhanov Yam, it had been just a rich Raskolnik** village before, but with the textile mills put up there after the revolution it had been promoted to a township, and there had been some rumours about a cinema-film factory going up there too, but they must have found a better place for it. It was a one-horse little town, no patch on Moscow, of course. Grass grew in the streets, and the buildings were smaller, but then the air—why, you could have it barrelled and shipped for export!—and the boundless water-meads beyond the Yenga! When the sweep of sky was reflected in them upside down during the spring flood the tugboats with the rafts looked as if they were running about among the clouds. And there were elk and badgers in the forest, and people had come across the lynx, too, and not long before her departure those smart local peasants from Vasilyev Pogost had marched in with a real live Bruin slung on poles. They had got him drunk on honey vodka from a *duplyanka*** which they had put on his favourite trail the night before. "First he'll knock the lid off with his paw, then roll over the ground, growling, the way he always does to crush the bees, even though there aren't any, and after that he'll settle down to the feast. That's when they take him, sleepy and tipsy, and he lies trussed up, bewailing his plight with human tears." And Polya herself had heard say that in the old days, before the birchwood on the south side had been cut down, the place was

---

* D.E.C. (District Executive Committee)—local governing body.—*Tr.*

** Raskolnik—member of a schismatic sect which arose in Russia in the 17th century.—*Tr.*

*** *Duplyanka*—a stump—a hollowed out beehive.—*Tr.*

so chockful of nightingales—they used to fly through the windows straight into the housewives' soup! The old geezers still bragged about the wonderful full-grown pines that used to grow along the high bluff in the days gone by, which they said stretched for at least a hundred and fifty, if not four hundred kilometres—in any case, not less than eighty—almost all the way to the Dvina marshes. Why, even now, in a thunderstorm, it was amazing the way those Yenga pine forests would let themselves go, how they'd start creaking in the hug of the wind, and let loose such a scorching blast of July heat that your pillow would smell of hot strawberries and pine needles for three days afterwards. That's what our Yenga is like!

Varya was a long time coming, and you could not very well break off in the middle of your talk, no more than you could break off a song on a high note, for it was comparable only to the trilling of a bird, was the sound of Polya's pretty voice.

"No, we can't complain about our town. We have a stadium you can run about in, and a palace of labour at the tannery, and in the town library you will even find the correspondence of Michelangelo. We took an oath in the seventh form, that when we made good we'd never forget our home town, and would send one book a month there at least. Our Komsomol there are a disciplined, friendly, educated lot. True, everything's made of wood there so far, it's all forest land, you know, we couldn't even find the bronze for a statue of Lenin, but then what a park we laid out in his honour! It's murmuring over our heads already, our own park: never mind the bronze, we'll have that too. When we planted it there were only about twenty leaves on each sapling, and now.... We're always talking about the Future and our Country as if they were something a long way off. But if everyone went about the job seriously within a radius of, say, ten paces around him"—Polya with half shut eyes, figured out the area of the circle—"and tidied up those three-hundred and fourteen square metres as he would his own room, his work-place, or the table on which he eats, and if he were to tend it properly, or at least plant a cherry-tree on it, even if it was only one in a life-time—whew!—you'd be surprised what a hundred thousand hands can do in one hour! I was thinking of writing a letter to the whole Komsomol to take an example from us Loshkarev boys and girls. D'you think they'd publish it in the papers? They wouldn't think it cheek, would they?" she enquired in a confidential whisper.

Was it because she knew too much about life and about Gratsiansky as well, that the woman with the stocking could not bring herself to look into Polya's eyes, the unclouded eyes of youth? Bending over her work, she was thinking that never, perhaps, had there been such a wide gulf between the two generations in Russia.

A minute later she had overcome her inexplicable confusion.

"Your name is Polya, is it not? Mine is Natalya Zolotinskaya. You are a good, warm-hearted, clever girl, and I am glad to have made your acquaintance," she said almost drily but with deep emotion, while Polya listened flushed and expectant, feeling that she was going to hear words that are not uttered twice. "Remember what I am going to tell you. If there is anything you don't understand now, you will later on. When life burns down it leaves a last golden spark in the ashes. It quickens, and goes out, and then comes the cold. . . . It is this last spark that holds the entire experience of a lifetime. Here is my golden spark for you. People demand of fate happiness, success and wealth, but the wealthiest are not those who have received a lot, but those who have most generously given of themselves. Personally, I discovered that truth too late." She looked up questioningly. "I see that you don't agree with me."

"Please don't be offended, but it wouldn't be honest of me to keep silent about it now. You've put it very well . . . that about the . . . well, the golden spark. But today you have used the word *fate* three times. We had a full-dress debate on that subject in Loshkarev, we talked our heads off for two days and in the end we decided that this was a harmful word of the weak, which expressed nothing but frustration. So there's no such thing as fate, there's only iron will and necessity."

Madam Zolotinskaya smiled, her first smile since their conversation had started.

"It all depends from which point you look at a person's biography, Polya—from the beginning or the end. At your age we also dreamt of doing big things, we read serious books, toyed with dynamite, argued ourselves hoarse, and this is where I am now, thirty years later, mending someone's unwashed stocking to buy milk for my granddaughter. Mind you, I was once on top of the world. And, frankly, I am not a bit sorry that life has degraded me to the ranks, made me just one of the people. How it happened I don't know. It's the way of a human being to give the measure of his surprise the name of fate, that's what it is.

But you are right in the sense that one's youth lasts as long as one has not uttered the word *fate* in application to oneself." The woman laid aside the finished stocking. "If you'd like a wash after your journey, it's the second door on the right down the passage. Turn the light off after you."

A lifetime conscientiously lamented was contained in her brief, very calm confession. Polya felt sad and disquieted and was drawn towards the window. She went over to it and looked out—and, unaccustomed to such heights, she felt dizzy. What she saw there was a lot of sky with occasionally an imponderable bit of poplar fluff sailing through it. Straight below lay Blagoveshchensky Alley with its tumbledown little church buried among the trees. There, on the grass-plot, children were dancing and singing in a ring, and judging by the way that lively circlet contracted, sank down with a low curtsy, then spread out with a lifting of arms, it was the favourite game of "Bake-me-a-loaf". Snatches of their song reached the eighth floor through the steady hum coming from behind the nearest chain of buildings, where "the river of life was rolling its stony waters". Polya liked that phrase culled from the future letter to her mother. Then she looked up, and the immensity of what she saw took her breath away. Before her lay Moscow.

All was wrapped in a tremulous noonday haze which shaded away through blending colours into a spectral blue. Only the eye of an artist could have embraced that balanced multitude of diverse buildings which seemed to flow in the heat blur. The crude massive tones of the materials that go to make up the modern cityscape were still distinguishable in the foreground: the almost undiluted madder lake of the old mellowed concrete deepening to purple in the shadows, or the pale green of the foliage with a dash of cadmium in it—because it was the height of summer—or the sienna brickwork, pinkish with distance, of the new municipal buildings pushing their way terrace-like through the old town quarters, or the breath of the city's industry iterated a hundredfold in the smudges of factory smoke painted with sooty black upon the gigantic canvas of the sky. All this was pressed together, rammed one into the other, reduced to model scale so as to fit into this overcrowded spaciousness.

Farther stretched miles of roof in a gleaming jumble of facets, a sea of roofs, covered, if seen through narrowed eyes, with a dazzling opalescent ripple—a real sea, but for the delicate touches of a water-colour brush which had painted into that

21

flowing landscape the threadlike structures of radio masts and power lines, the high-peaked roofs of railway stations resembling the keels of capsized ships, the faded old-world charm of Moscow's belfries, left marooned in the stormy wake of industrial progress, and the façades of the public buildings marshalled in semicircles and intricate curves, which, like dotted lines on a chart, marked the outlines of the embankments or the main thoroughfares. In a gap between them glimmered the river with a bluish glint of nickel—naturally the most beautiful and brimming river in the world, for was it not Moscow's. One degree farther up, on a distant knoll near the horizon, as if at the base of snow-capped mountains, divined by a quickening heartbeat rather than by a silhouette that had been familiar since childhood, rose the most famous architectural creation of the Russians—the Kremlin, that majestic geometric bulk with a gigantic white stone column in the middle devoid of both the fanciful refinements of the West and the contemplative indolence of the East. Something glinted on the golden cupolas, which were slightly flattened as if by the weight of the sky—probably the undried dew of history, as Rodion had cryptically expressed himself in one of his poems. A slender yellow wounding ray from there entered Polya's heart through her dilated pupil and beckoned to her, and she stepped, invisible, through the ancient gates, where the cold of eternity touched her with a momentary chill. Mentally she went round the collection of masterpieces and sacred relics, those stone amulets, which, regal though they were, looked plain in comparison with the deeds of the ancestors upon whose breasts they had been hung at the outset of their career. Holding down the little straw hat on her head, Polya gazed up at the ruby stars on the spires, which resembled the heavenly ones in being visible from all points of the planet; she tried to count the enemy cannon ranged around the Petrine arsenal, and respectfully touched those things she knew so well from the pictures—the great bell with the chipped-off piece, and the most peaceful cannon in the world with its cannon-balls—the giant toys of our ancestors.

Polya's impressions of Moscow fell upon grateful soil prepared by the stories of Pavel Chernetsov. It was in his presence, twenty odd years ago, that the winged formula was first uttered at the Eighth Congress of Soviets, describing communism as the sum of Soviet power and electrification, which is the technical basis of modern large-scale production. He had sat so close, had the

Yenga delegate Chernetsov, that he could hear the swish of the papers in Lenin's hand as he hacked the air, saying it. Around the family table in the evenings, he loved to recollect again and again how the great city had looked at that hour of dawn, a city, which already then had earned the delighted gratitude of the poor, which is the proof of an idea's impact, and the envious hatred of the rich, which has always been the measure of the enemy's grudging respect. According to Chernetsov, Moscow had looked plain in those days, although the Soviet people, who had already embarked on a path of almost volcanic eruption of values, could have dressed her up in a matter of five years far more smartly than her younger northern sister, whom the whole empire had been making such a fuss of in the course of two centuries. As a matter of fact, it was with the intention of devoting herself wholly to beautifying her country's capital that Polya had come here.

She was put out, as latecomers usually are when they miss the beginning of something big. All the space right up to the horizon was built over, and not a spot remained for her own creations, conceived in heated disputes with her school friends or in the pages of her maiden diary. The city, it seemed, was already ripe for ordinary imperishable fame and what it now needed was only extraordinary deeds, for which Polya was quite unfitted. She felt more insignificant than those children down there, who were so diligently fulfilling their duties. When her eyes travelled in their direction again, she saw Varya at last; she was fighting her way through the blockade of the toddlers, who had surrounded her.

Polya dashed downstairs. The lift was no longer working on account of the dinner-hour. The friends met on the landing of the second floor, and with their arms around each other, walked up to their flat.

"I'm sorry, but I knew you are a clever girl and would find your way here by yourself!" Varya said, looking her friend over with motherly affection. "They've elected me Secretary of the organisation, you know, and I simply haven't got a minute for myself. It's been such a crazy day."

"Why, anything wrong?" Polya asked anxiously.

"On the contrary, everything's grand. I'm feeling on top of the world, it makes me quite dizzy! I tore home in the heat in such a hurry I'm all in a lather. And those little citizens are a

nuisance, too, I can't get rid of them. All the kids of the neighbourhood consider me their best friend," she added with a chuckle,
evidently highly pleased at the circumstance.

2

Indeed, Varya made friends with the children quite effortlessly,
so full was she always of kindly human warmth. Her people
chaffed her that when she married she would have a family of
thirty-eight souls, all suitably clothed, washed and fed; a more
moderate idea of domestic bliss somehow did not fit in with
either her extravagant large-heartedness or her very appearance.
Varya was on the hefty side and the big strong body asked for
a suitable load. No doubt she would have found love and happiness long ago had she been a bit better looking—her face was
rather flat with a thin line of the mouth, and her eyes were set too
far apart. She would have looked more natural somewhere on the
sun-baked slopes of the Tien Shan, astride a shaggy horse, and
headed into the noonday wind with a *kamcha** in her hand and a
string of beads on her browned neck rather than at a desk in
the pedagogical institute. Soberly conscious of her own limitations, Varya made no attempt to improve on Nature. She wore
her hair brushed back smoothly from her forehead without a
parting, and even the white, always stiffly starched collar on the
dark simple dress looked like a pitiful attempt to somehow tone
down the unfairness of Nature.

Varya bombarded her friend with a thousand questions about
Loshkarev, about her folks and the neighbours, about their beloved
outlying forest, about who was now bossing the show in the Komsomol, and whether Marfa Yegorovna, the school-teacher, had
aged—that same Marfa Yegorovna whom the Loshkarevians, in
the absence of a tower clock, set their watches by—and even
about how the dog Balui, the constant companion of all Pavel
Chernetsov's hunting expeditions, was getting on—in short, about
everything and everyone, desirably in the minutest possible detail,
such as no letter, however detailed, could possibly convey. Polya
started off like a babbling brook. Chernetsov was peddling his
bike all over the district as busily as ever, although it looked as
if he still had not got over the death of his wife, Varya's stepmother,

---

Kamcha—a native horse whip.—*Tr.*

and Zoya Petrovna, the neighbour, who had been living in the house across the yard this fourth year, had sent Varya a jar of Yenga honey for old time's sake together with some home-dried mushrooms, so that her darling would not go spending too much money in the capital, and Marfa Yegorovna was still trudging to school through the autumn mud in men's galoshes, but her watch was beginning to go a minute or two slow, and the dog Balui was getting seedy, he didn't chase the chickens any more, but kept sneezing and hugged the chimney corner.

"And Mummy, too, has gone off a bit," Polya continued, as she laid out the fairings from her suitcase. "To look at she's much the same as she used to be, except that she's gone still more serious, but when she was seeing me off she took me aside round by the warehouse and shed a tear on the quiet. You'd think— what's there to cry about now? She looked so small all of a sudden, and began to talk soft too—a thing she had never done before."

"The old are growing older, Polya, and the young are gradually stepping to the fore. That's how it has always been."

For the rest, except in small things, everything was going well. Last winter they had finished cutting down that part of Oblog which had been left standing opposite the Gorinka, so that now, from Shabanov Hill overlooking the jetty, you could see the tall smoke-pipe of the new electric station at Vasilyev Pogost. "It looks sort of roomier without the forest, and one gets a view of industry now, but, you know, darling, it seems to have taken something out of you." And such strong up-river winds attacked the town now, that a recent storm tore the spire from the watch-tower, although it was no longer needed now, and Honoured Physician of the Republic Gavrilov had had his famous black hat blown off his head and whirled away right into the middle of the Yenga where it was swallowed up in the angry foamy wave before everybody's eyes. What's more, there'd been a ghastly howling in the chimneys at night ever since, and the old women, who were not very well up in their meteorology, whispered in the queues that this was the Gorinka and the Sklan grieving for the poor pines which the spring floods had carried off to Kazakhstan or some such place. Incidentally, the rafts had suddenly run aground that year without reaching the Volga, and had had to be refloated, which was quite a job.

"So Pustosha has come down too?" Varya said, distressed.

No, except for just the margin, Pustosha was still standing in

25

all its lusty tawny beauty. They all seemed to have gone crazy in the surrounding kolkhozes—building, marrying, singing songs. In Loshkarev itself a temporary cinema had been opened in the former refectory of the Premilovsky Monastery ... but they had been too lazy to distemper the old plaster, and just before Polya's departure the local crones had been gossiping about some saintly old boys showing through the screen and getting mixed up with the actors every time they had a show on, so that the manager even got a wigging for it from the regional authorities. Oh, yes, she had nearly forgotten—everyone sent Varya their regards of course— blind old Praskovya Andreyevna, and Petya Chmokin the cinema operator and the most gentlemanly dancer in the town of Loshkarev, who was being called up this year, and the Yermakovs, all eleven of them, and Gvidonenko, the director of the Museum of Local Lore, who had discovered two teeth and the vertebra of some fossilised monster all on his own, and Nina Tsiplenkova, who had sent her a note because she had been taken to the maternity hospital the day before ... in a word, everyone remembered darling Varya except the one whom Varya most desired to be remembered by.

"Although they send you their regards, they're sore with you because you write so little, and they're waiting for you to come back with your degree to take over from Marfa Yegorovna who's getting old, poor dear," Polya wound up, admiring the array of presents, then suddenly her face changed and she made a dash for the package in the grey paper, which she had forgotten in the excitement.

Although Varya was dearer to her than a sister, it was not without fear of eliciting a smile, albeit an inoffensive one, that she unwrapped her present. But Varya understood at once, and gratefully pressed her friend's modest personal gift to her bosom. It was a bunch of simple wild flowers, tied together with a sweet box ribbon. There was a bit of everything in it—wild geraniums, the earliest of all flowers to wilt, and meadow myrtle with pink limp petals, and simple clover, which usually reaches Moscow only in the form of pressed hay, and rough grudging St. John's wort, and yellow rattle with almost ripened seeds, and common bedstraw, and dozens of other such charming pale creations of the Russian countryside, gathered in single stalks or two from cherished meadows which they had walked together. It was like a sweet gentle benediction of the Motherland, a pledge of her true and lifelong love.

"It would be good to put them in water now, although I kept them in the kettle all the way. They must be parched, poor things. I just didn't know what to bring you, Varya."

Her face buried in the flowers, Varya smiled at her with those Mongoloid eyes of hers, which, at that moment, were feminine and attractive. There was still some life in those fading flowers; the honey drop had not dried yet in the golden cups of the hemp nettle, the catchfly still stuck to the fingers, and the cotton grass had not lost its silken warmth.

"*Eriophorum vaginatum*," Varya murmured, and never, perhaps, had the Latin of Linnaeus sounded so thrilling; suddenly she recollected that the cotton grass grew only on the water-mead across the river. She stood aghast at the magnitude of the deed. "You mad girl, you crossed the Yenga for this?"

"Oh, it didn't take me long in a boat!" said Polya, radiant with the reflected joy of her friend. "They're still alive, you know—they only want putting in water."

"You're a darling," Varya said, biting her lip. She turned away towards the window and gazed out into the depths of her native land with swimming eyes, seeing there a tiny spot barely marked on the map.

Meanwhile, Polya with a businesslike eye, ran over the room in which she was going to live.

Strictly speaking Varya had no window; in its place was a glass balcony door, but no balcony. The tenants had moved in before the house was quite finished, and the space between the balcony girders opened over an abyss with the long sunlit street at the bottom. Its yellowish afternoon glow was dimly reflected on the ceiling; the room faced West. It was much smaller than the other one, so that the extra bed, still without a pillow, which had been borrowed from a neighbour the day before, occupied all the rest of Varya's floor space. But where, with Natalya Zolotinskaya, every little object bore upon itself the stamp of rooted and immovable complexity, here one could read with ease the life of a Soviet student girl, who had set herself a clear and simple aim. And this is what she travelled with: a *passe-partout* photograph on the wall, showing the two leaders when they met in Gorki, and under it a slightly smaller one of her favourite, Darwin, with boyish eyes, then a small wardrobe in the corner, a stack of books on a little table, and a what-not with articles of simple household use, but no mirror.

"Now tell me about yourself," Varya commanded when she had tucked the bouquet away into a jar. "I couldn't make out from your letters what college you had decided to join."

"Then I'll begin at the very beginning, shall I?"

"You must always begin at the beginning . . . and the shorter the clearer." Varya always tried to be precise and clear, as if she were dictating a test lesson in the class-room. "Only bear in mind that I have to go out again on urgent business in half an hour."

It appeared that Loshkarev's leading citizens had had a hand in the choosing of Polya's profession, but most of their advice had had to be rejected on account of its extremely contradictory nature. Dr. Gavrilov, for instance, had insisted on physics, nay, even astrophysics, which was the one and only science capable, in the next half a century to come, of supplying the answers to all the questions of human existence, which, he claimed, philosophy had been mumbling about to the muddlement of the ordinary man since the days of bumbling Thales.

"On the whole, I agree with that opinion, Varya. Look at the time and energy those philosophers have spent in the last three thousand years, without having arrived at a common view even on such a question as . . . well, as to whether you exist outside me, or you are just the sum of my perceptions . . . like those mock suns, which according to the theory of relativity, form on the parhelic circle," Polya explained, using her fingers to show how she thought it happened. Varya could barely suppress a smile. She could hear the familiar accents of Loshkarev voices in Polya's speech, loudest among them the judicial bass of the chief thinker among Polya's coevals—Rodion Tikhodumov. "Please don't smile, darling. I may be a silly girl, but I also have a right to know *who* I am, and *whence* I come, and *why* . . . otherwise one will die a stupid stick!"

"How is Rodion getting on?" Varya enquired.

"He's all right, growing thinner than ever. Just before I left we had a terrific row, and now I'm through with him," Polya came back.

On the other hand, Comrade Valtasar, the Head of the District Health Department, had urged Polya to go in for medicine, and thus help accelerate the process of eliminating the ailments which we had inherited from the old world. Powerful arguments had also been advanced in favour of chemistry, stock-breeding, and even railway transport. Polya herself had first inclined towards literature, specifically in order to describe the customs of the hillmen and the ancient traditions of that proud race, but she had been dissuaded from that as well as from becoming an artist in order to create sweeping canvasses of the country's leading plants and biggest power stations, as it was not quite the thing to paint ordinary landscapes in these epochal days. Incidentally, Rodion had sarcastically remarked that artistic works on technology subjects only lived as long as the paint kept dry on the canvas, and with the development of socialist production and our advance towards communism they would, dialectically, become a mere travesty of the epic grandeur of our epoch. "It's a case of alternating function, you get me?" Polya hinted significantly. "Such works will have to be touched up a bit every year to keep them from growing obsolete."

She believed, moreover, that the demand for paintings would fall off in the future, because with the high-speed production of works of art there would not be enough museums and galleries in the world soon to hold them, and these completed treasures would have to be stacked in the open; as for private use. . . . She related the case of Chernetsov, who, when presented on his sixtieth birthday with a portrait of the Magnitogorsk iron and steel plant in a lot of colours with a mass of smoke-stacks, had promptly re-presented it to the textile workers' club, leaving on his own wall the same old *Gypsy Girl*. "Just imagine—a thick-lipped gypsy maid in necklaces with a tambourine—and he such an advanced man, you'd think!" Never mind, it would all turn out for the best, Polya reassured her friend. That's when society would throw its army of artists over to beautifying socialist life— dwellings, clothes, utensils, all the ordinary things, which, no less than books, cultivate the taste, and, consequently, the aesthetic exactingness of the toilers towards their own work and behaviour.

"I am absolutely convinced, Varya, that communism will abolish pain, evil, untruth, that is, all that's ugly, misshapen, and mean, that's to say, communism, apart from everything else, stands for perfect beauty everywhere," Polya meandered on less coherently, Rodion not being there to help her, while Varya listened with anxiety not unmixed with pleasure to those strengthening voices from the morrow. "Mark my word, Varya— the simplest articles, in addition to the trade mark, will bear the stamp of their maker, and reviews will be written about them, like those written about books and shows. That's the reason why a well wrought capital adorning a public building is more useful than a dozen mediocre paintings, the content of which could often

29

be expressed more cheaply and sensibly in printer's type. Did we get it hot for these extreme views—Rodion and I! Now it's your turn to scold—go ahead!"

"Oh, I can't judge offhand," Varya answered, consulting her watch. "You talk as if communism had already been built, and there are still mean people about who would rob you of your right to the future. I understand what you're driving at—you protest against the artistic fabric being overloaded with utilitarian tasks, but there's no need to be angry if an artist is invited first to work on a social idea before he tackles material things. It's pleasanter, of course, to work with a paint brush than with a spade, but a spade, nevertheless, is easier to handle than a rifle, isn't it?" Her speech was always punctuated with pauses as if to give her little listeners a chance to follow her.

The argument deepened. Polya stood her ground. When all was said and done, it was only by profound treatment and super-lative execution, and not by the mere superficial expounding of an idea that the art of the past succeeded in glorifying its epoch. She rattled off names, styles, and various works, and one could gather therefrom how versatile that Rodion of hers was for all that he was a keen mathematician. Harmony was temporarily restored by the girls agreeing that the more considerable the burden of art was, the higher its quality had to be.

"But what are you going in for, how long are you going to keep me guessing?"

"Architecture—why?" Polya said with a cocked eye and a lick at her dry lips.

Varya, with a thoughtful air, smoothed out a corner of the oilcloth on the table. She did not want to discourage her friend. She simply intimated that in demanding skill of an artist she should not forget the triple responsibility of the architect, whose stone creations, unfortunately, often outlived all the other monuments of the age. One could avoid reading poorly written books, going to bad shows or exhibitions of mediocre paintings, but one's fellow-citizens could not go about a town built over with bad buildings with their eyes closed.

"Still, Polya, if you feel it's your vocation and that you can tackle it. ... Have you brought any of your drawings with you? Show me."

Polya rummaged among her dresses and undies and fished out from the bottom of her suitcase some drawings done on cardboard folders and the thick paper covers of old magazines.

"You won't laugh at me, will you?" she said, awaiting the verdict with dread.

"H'm, this is not bad at all. I daresay you'll make good." Polya passed up a second and third drawing, but Varya was still holding the first—it happened to be on top. "I say, I'd like to keep this one—may I?"

"Oh, darling, I'll do a much better one than that for you!" Polya cried, delighted at having successfully passed her first test.

"No, it's this one I want," Varya said, a tinge of unwonted weakness colouring her cheeks. "It's so much like him. His breathing likeness, if it wasn't for the closed eyes. It's Nikolai Bobrinin, isn't it?"

"Oh, no!" Polya cried, horrified. "Why, it's Antinous!"

"A-ah!" Varya breathed with relief. "That accounts for the blind look—it gave me quite a turn, like a dead man's. All the same, I'm going to keep this in memory of . . . of the first steps of an architectural celebrity."

Without waiting for the author's consent, she slipped the thing into her table drawer, and feeling her friend's interrogative glance upon her, asked something about Rodion in a tone of utter unconcern. The trick worked splendidly. Polya, childlike, completely forgot the trivial incident. Oh, Rodion . . . why, Varya had no idea how much he had grown up this last year! The teachers in Loshkarev simply avoided asking him his lessons, because he always went so deep into the subject that they were unable to check him, and he asked questions himself which chased them up a tree. By the way, he had half-solved a tricky equation which the brainiest mathematicians of the last century had been racking their brains over without getting anywhere. As a matter of fact, two days before her departure Rodion went to Kazan to enter the Physics and Mathematics Faculty.

"You needn't squint at me, Varya. Just imagine, that lanky kid had the nerve to tell me to my face. . . ."

"You'll tell me the story of your quarrel afterwards, my dear," Varya said, rising. "What's your programme for today? Would you care to go to the Biological Station with me?"

"I have some shopping to do," Polya answered evasively.

"Good. Then we'll have dinner together at six. Don't be late, please, and don't get lost. Anyway, I'll wait for you with dinner."

The conversation ended just in time: the electric kettle was already boiling on the table, and the water was beginning to trickle over the top of the bath.

31

Polya had mapped out her programme of activities while still in the train. It included visits to theatres and art galleries, seeing the architectural monuments, first and foremost the Lenin Mausoleum, that title-leaf of the great book in which she was to inscribe her own name. But her list was planned for the long free period until the studies began, and before starting upon her round of the capital she wanted to indulge certain childish whims of hers, which during the last six months had grown into an action-shaping need.

In Rodion's attic—the dove-cot of which commanded a splendid view of the Yenga—where Rodion secretly read his verses to Polya, among the dusty junk and stacks of pre-revolutionary weeklies, she had come across the recurring advertisement of a professional astrologer. Being intimate with other-world spheres, that gentleman, for the modest sum of one ruble ninety-five kopeks in postage stamps foretold the future, augmented his clients' income at will, grew abundant hair on bald heads, banished all body aches, insomnia, harmful insects, and juvenile vices, and performed many other things which only a hungry rogue with a none too lively imagination could invent. Judging by the inset picture of a fairly youngish turbanned individual with lightning flashes of clairvoyance emanating from his brow, he could not be more than sixty now, and might still be in circulation today unless he had engaged in less harmless activities during the years of the revolution. Polya had kept the yellowed address with the intention, when opportunity offered, of gratifying the legitimate interest of a sinless and enquiring mind in the biology and mode of life of a former day. Precisely because she had missed all those obsolete professions of tsar and banker, water-carrier and matchmaker in her country, and because that fakir was the only piece of flotsam still available for inspection, she wanted to take this last chance of knocking at his door on some plausible pretext and peering into the frowzy eyes of the mysterious *old* past with the same feeling of reverential awe with which she had gazed at the paleontological fossils in Gvidonenko's museum.

A second enterprise of a similar kind was a planned visit to her father. Polya did not have even a photo-acquaintance with him; and her mother, apparently not wishing to rake up the past, had refrained from passing any judgement on her former husband in her daughter's presence. To judge by the rare but uniformly unkind articles in the forestry press, however, he was a gloomy crosspatch with old-fashioned views who failed to grasp the problems of modern forest management. And would that the sins of omission and commission described there were unintentional on his part! Probably it was that, combined with a quarrelsome disposition, which had been the cause of their home being broken up. Polya had not wanted to probe into that mysterious affair and had sided unreservedly with her mother, a feldsher* at the little inter-district hospital, a hard-working, unobtrusive woman who was widely respected. Apart from the printed reports, Polya's preconceived notions of her father rested on one memory of early childhood, brief as a flash of lightning.

Whenever, amid the silence of a close summer night, she heard the dying wail of a railway engine, Polya always conjured up a vision of bottles of bitter medicines, the hard gleam of convex spectacles in massive gold rims, and behind them, the faded remote glance of a man bending over her cot. Polya had caught the measles just before her mother ran away to the Yenga. No one in Loshkarev had such glasses; they really belonged to the doctor, and had been wrongly imputed to Vikhrov. Curiously, it was the very metal of which their frame was made, metal discredited in the eyes of a Komsomol girl by virtue of her education and the course of political events, that determined the unflattering conception which she formed of her father. Gradually prejudice against him had grown into a burning need to avenge her mother, to tell him straight to his face what honest Komsomol opinion thought of him and his likes. Often at home, with a thrill of excitement, she had pictured herself moving through a sumptuous suite of carpeted rooms, past housemaids in starched caps, and entering the sombre half-light of the professorial sanctum with its old-regime immovable furniture, its plush curtains reeking with the profligate odour of cigars, its massive inkstand under the spread wings of a bronze double eagle. Straight from the threshold, without a greeting, without sitting down, she would thank the elderly paunchy gentleman, who had half-risen to his feet behind the desk, for having sent the money for her sustenance in the course of thirteen years without legal reminders. And now she had come, his own grown-up daughter, standing before him as large as life, to tell him that there was no question of Mamma having taken his money under false pretences, as if his

---

* Feldsher—a physician's assistant.—*Tr.*

child were dead, say, although he could have found an opportunity in thirteen years to make sure whether it did exist or not! And now, relieved at last of all his onerous paternal obligations, he could do as he damn well pleased! And then she would go, vanish for ever, leaving him to draw his dismal diagrams of the asp's annual growth. The thing was to face it out and not start blubbering like a cry-baby!

But now, within sight of her object, all Polya's being revolted at the thought of the reprisal which she had planned. It was not cowardice or a fastidious fear of soiling herself by a fleeting contact with what was bad. It was something else, something she could not find words for, perhaps a dread of stumbling upon something unforseen and disappointing. So when descending the stairs an hour later, after her bath, Polya was in no particular hurry. At the back of her mind lurked a fugitive hope that, circumstances being favourable, she would have no time left for that interview. The dance of the poplar fluff was still in progress in Blagoveshchensky Alley, and the spirit of revelry still held sway over the city when she came out into the main thoroughfare. Polya turned left, then left again, and was caught up in the crossroads traffic, with all observable landmarks suddenly obliterated, and it dawned on her that she had lost her way in the vast maze of that wonderland which she had so often dreamed of back in Loshkarev.

There is nothing more entrancing in all the world than walking about a strange city at eighteen, unchaperoned, without fear of being late for school, and with the added joy of life in the shape of fifty rubles given by your Mamma for the gratification of your wildest desires. As it happened, the street of Polya's choice teemed with all kinds of temptations; in one shop window was an alluring display of new books in colourful recumbency, the mere contemplation of which seemed to raise the cultural level of the passers-by; in another, sixteen superlative masters of their craft, with the aid of scientific techniques, were waving the hair of sixteen no less superlative beauties, and in a third there was such a marvellous assortment of shining aluminium kitchen-ware that it set one wondering how the human race had managed before the discovery of this inestimable material boon. For some reason there were no more flowers in the streets, they had all been sold, and enamelled little trolleys with bottled beverages now adorned the street corners, and all kinds of top-level executives were standing about gravely sipping coloured fluids out of goblets, each according to his vein and humour. Polya was drawn irresistibly towards them, for the summer day was still at its blazing height, but while she was hunting in her bag for a suitable coin, two water-carts of a celestial hue sprayed the prickly petrol-reeking heat with a low rain, and so Polya was able to save Mamma's money for more substantial spendings.

She manfully tried to pass temptations by, but they waylaid her and pounced on her in the shape of an ice-cream on a stick, early cherries, candied nuts...and again, because of her new dress, no doubt, she always fell in with nice people. Thus, the scale in the sweet shop pointed to two-hundred and ten grams, although she had only paid for two-hundred at the cash-desk, and the salesgirl had let her get away with it without argument. And when Polya went in to send off two absolutely necessary telegrams with identical texts "Wishing you a happy start", one to a strictly secret address in Kazan, the other to herself in Varya's alley to give that extraordinary occasion a really festive touch, she was given change in delightfully crackly brand-new notes. And again Polya found herself battling with a host of small disintegrating packages, and a melancholy chemist, no doubt an undone alchemist, had himself offered to wrap up all her purchases for her in a single parcel. And so Polya went along, and life seemed to her like that magic staircase out of the fairy-tale: she had but to step on it at the bottom to find herself, after an appropriate number of years, and before she could draw her breath, right at the top. Indeed, her country had everything you needed for happiness—all kinds of palms, and apatites, and responsive human hearts; the people she met as she walked along were all blithe of heart and gay of dress—it was just that kind of a street—and now Polya herself was smiling at everyone, even at the tipsy knife-grinder with his wooden machine slung on his shoulder; she went along, abandoning herself to the spirit of elan that reigned all round her, a spirit born, no doubt, of the awareness of the immensity of space that lay ahead, and the fascinating newness of everything in the world, everything, that is, except her old "rusty-fusties" or "raggeties", as she fondly called her worn-down shoes, which had stood her in such good stead for quite a long time now. And no sooner had she thought of them, when lo! a wizard appeared in the niche of a magnificent house, a black mighty wizard built, as it were, out of brushes, who restored to boots their pristine youth.

"You is one big shine. I see, you is going to marry, beautiful comrade?"

"Oh, better than that, a thousand times better!" laughed Polya, watching the cracked old leather coming out in mirror-like brilliance through the wizardry of flitting hands.

She had lost count of time, and suddenly it struck her that she had been going the pace too hard. True, she had done some mental arithmetic, which told her that three hours of uninterrupted bliss had cost her only twenty-four kopeks per minute, but she would now have to slow down a bit in order to meet the next, perhaps chief temptation lurking round the corner, armed cap-a-pie. The Metro station was obligingly near at hand, so Polya ran from one platform to another, taking a ride along all operative routes, because the Metro was down in her list of sights to be viewed and gaped at. Glittering trains rushed her through dark tunnels, and in their passage, as in a dream, blue and pale pink marble halls kept appearing and disappearing. Here Polya might have been able to observe how her idea concerning the artist's part in handling the decorative scheme of public buildings was being put into effect, but just then, for some reason, she saw nothing before her but a massive desk like a meat counter with the ugly bronze inkstand, and across it, cold and ready for the duel, the man whom *fate* had ordained to be her father. Polya wanted nothing so much as to get away from him, to the other end of the city if possible, but when she asked the whereabouts of the Forestry Institute, on whose grounds Vikhrov had his apartment, her neighbour in the train told her that she had to get out at the next stop. The passengers immediately made way for her to the door and the austere truth. It was the last station on the line and there was no escalator there. The human torrent carried her out.

Only then did she notice what a depressing sweltering day it was—although you could hardly have called it cloudy. The suburban reek of hot asphalt and summer dust assailed her. The city here was advancing upon the plain, which looked like a pitted area after an artillery preparation. Growling tractor rollers were carpeting a smoking lavastream of roadway between dusty potato fields to where a cluster of stately buildings rose up from the soil in reddish blocks. One of the workers of this industrial offensive, wiping the black perspiration from his face, showed Polya the way. It was a twenty minute walk along a paved road between experimental plots and hothouses to the building of her father's Institute, which was housed in the suburban palace of a former Moscow nobleman. A student with a sunburn that matched Polya's was bending over a plant bed, and Polya asked him where the professors lived. The man directed her to two four-storey brick buildings across the way, the living quarters of the teaching staff. A little apart stood a third structure, a wood-built one of a poorer appearance with a porch, covered with blossoming creepers from end to end; in the front garden much patched old underwear was drying on a clothes line. Some odd intuition told Polya that this was the place she was seeking. Twice she passed a leaking water post at which some small boys were having a glorious time, kneading the lovely yellow mud with their feet. The surroundings did not seem to fit in with Polya's ideas of her father's luxurious mode of life; the hostile feeling had not worn off, but it was becoming covered up with the cracks of childish doubts. There was still time to turn back ... but suddenly, from the depths of a little copse through which ran the circuit railway, there came the challenging cockerel cry of a shunting engine.

Then, swept along by the irresistible force of her river, Polya crossed the little street with the intensely green grass pushing up through the cobblestones, walked up to the first floor, and unerringly, in defiance of all logic, rang at the most uninviting door bearing no brass plate on it with the Vikhrov academic initials, a door from which hung shreds of felt padding that had been nailed to it for warmth eighteen years ago when she, Polya, was born.

She also banged on the door with her fist. A bolt was drawn within, and in the dim hall lit by a lantern hanging from the ceiling, she saw the slight, youngish looking, or rather ageless, figure of the professor's servant with an unnaturally low-set head and a dark kerchief falling over her shoulders the way all the elderly peasant women on the Yenga used to wear it until recently. That confused impression was quickly dispelled, however, and once more in a way that ran counter to Polya's expectations.

"Oh, you *are* a comely lass. I suppose you want to see Professor Vikhrov about your examination work?" the hunchbacked little woman said in a kindly tone as she wiped the soap suds from her hands. "Tut, tut, and that professor of ours has gone off to the Tula forest with his students the other day! Now isn't that a shame!" She caressed the girl with her eyes, furtively admiring the freshness of her—or was it the shyness? "I don't seem to remember you, lass—you must be one of the new ones?"

It were better so for Polya—to have come and gratified her curiosity, and to go away unrecognized. Of her original plan not a vestige now remained.

"I am," Polya nodded, forcing a smile into her face.

"I thought so, seeing the way your hands are trembling. You don't have to tremble, my dear, our professor is not a wild beast. Why, goodness me, the students think the world of him! Some of 'em get together here of a Saturday like it was a club." The woman communicated all this with such ingenuous folky kindliness that it would have been shameless not to believe her every word. "Take your hat off, dear, put your parcel down, nobody will steal your things here. He promised to be back afore nightfall. There's nothing worse than going in for an examination for the second time, from what I have seen of it. Come along, dear, I'll give you a snug little place to sit in till you get used to us," she added, bolting the door.

She let Polya pass ahead and did not allow her to peep into the kitchen. "Other people's washing is nothing to look at," she said, ushering her straight into the study and seating her in the shabby favourite armchair; as it happened, the kitchen was just opposite, so that Polya every other minute could hear the measured knocking of the trough against the sink and the splash of the water being poured off. She had only to turn her head to be able, without rising from her seat, to study the arrangements and appointments of the two rooms that made up the Vikhrov flat.

The most difficult thing of all was getting used to the idea that every inch of that creaky, ochre-painted floor had once been crawled over by her own baby knees. Without a doubt, the nursery of the young Vikhrovs in the old days could only have been next door, in the smallest but sunniest and brightest of all the rooms. All kinds of works, taken to pieces, lay heaped in a corner like swept-out rubbish, and one could see a little automatic turning lathe on a bench. Other things there were a man's suit, covered with a dust sheet, hanging on the wall, and an iron bedstead under a woollen blanket, from under which peeped a pair of neatly folded top-boots, obviously not her father's, for she had already noticed that Vikhrov's bed stood in the study behind one of the bookcases. This meant there was a third person here, and for the first time a jealous desire was born in Polya to have a single peep at the person who had taken her place in her father's house.

"Don't you feel bored sitting there all alone, lassie?" the old woman kept asking from the kitchen from time to time.

"No, I'm quite all right," Polya would answer, trying to fall in with her tone.

Polya felt baffled and defeated. The flat was so violently at odds with her preconceived ideas of it that it struck her almost as beggarly, although there was everything here that a man needed for life and work, with the latter obviously ascendant over the former, however. There were no plush curtains there—indeed they were hardly necessary in a dwelling whose inmates followed the forest custom of getting up and going to bed with the sun; there was no sign of gold anywhere, not even of the old gilded volumes, which hostile imagination had so picturesquely painted —those Olympian tomes, gazing down upon the bustling futilities of mortals from behind their plate-glass eminence. None but a real scientist could need just such worker-books with torn covers and scribbled slips between the pages, books that one could make notes in, stuff into one's knapsack when going on an expedition, or even use in barricade fighting, the more so that all the books for which no room was found on the sagging shelves were piled up on the window-sills and stacked to the very ceiling, bound together in tight solid blocks. As usual, the subtle logic of prejudice retreated reluctantly before the clear logic of life. And it was revealed to Polya, although she would not have been able to put it into so many words, that life was always wiser and more convincing than the fictions by which people, for different reasons, try to enhance the beauty of truth or magnify the ugliness of evil.

The furnishings of this tidy well-lit room in which Polya was sitting gave one some indications as to the character of its occupant. Probably he was a self-exacting man, not very expert at arranging his own life. A man who begrudged time and had little use for books that did not help him in his own specialised quest for the truth, a quest which, judging by the subject matter of the books in the nearest bookcase, had led him far afield. That he had wandered a good deal about the country was borne out by a score or so of wooden articles, which no money could buy in the capital—the carved back of a Northern distaff, a little poem in wood; a birch-bark pot of Vologda workmanship with a ver-milion horseman on the bark, a cluster of Tambov painted wooden spoons the colour of old honey, bowls hollowed out of birch and walnut burl, a carved wooden casket paid for by the carver's blindness, a pair of dainty bast sandals off the feet of some rustic Cinderella, and other simple treasures of the Russian forests wrought by the genius of the muzhik. Nothing here pointed to any personal whim of the owner, except perhaps.... Here Polya rose slightly in her chair to examine, behind a pile of manuscripts, the only thing here that looked like gold, the only thing that would have tempted a thief. It was an expensive frame of chased bronze, the size of a postcard, obviously a setting for someone very dear, and Polya could not resist this opportunity of finding out something about Vikhrov's present attachments.

"So you're a new girl—I thought as much. I know all the older ones," the old woman in the kitchen kept repeating as she rattled the washing trough against the wall. "Don't you let life scare you, though. Nothing's going to happen to you except what's been ordained. Bless your heart—you'll pass your exams, you'll go away to work, you'll have babies, and you'll become a baked little apple like me, and laugh at all your old sorrows. What are you taking your examination in—sylviculture or valuation survey?"

"No, valuation survey," Polya said, mechanically repeating the unfamiliar words.

To while away the time the old woman asked some more questions, and Polya answered her at random, her eyes held by the golden gleam on the desk. Any movement on her part would have aroused suspicion in the kitchen. But then the river is always stronger than the tiny leaf. Polya contrived to reach her father's desk without making a noise. The frame was a heavy one of cast bronze, and under the glass was an excellent specimen of amateur photography in the shape of a snap of a really charming young woman. In a wet clinging sarafan that had evidently just been under a summer downpour, she sat on a gigantic tree stump, which resembled the throne of a forest monarch, the splinter serving her as a high Gothic back, and was laughing gaily with her head thrown back, the way one laughs only among friends, after some gay adventure in the heyday of carefree youth. Somebody else, someone who had no place in that document and had been snipped off obliquely by Vikhrov, was holding out a spray of blossoming guelder-rose; dappled sunshine splashed with rain fell upon the woman's bare feet, from which one heavy shoe had slipped off, and upon her protruding collar-bones—because she was leaning back on her hands. Polya recognised first the place—only on the Yenga could one meet with such sylvan giants; then, with a tremor of delight, she recognised her mother. The picture had been taken before Yelena Ivanovna's marriage, when she was called simply Lenochka. And because Polya had never seen her mother in such a mood of light, almost carefree gayety, she was seized by an irresistible desire to extract the photograph from the frame and take it away with her.

And so she would have done but for a creaking of the floor-boards, which made her turn round. Standing in the doorway cheek in hand, peasant-wise, and smiling at her with her eyes screwed up, was the old woman.

"Polya, why didn't you tell me right away, darling?" she said in a tone of gentle rebuke so as not to startle her. "Didn't you know me? I am Taisa, Ivan's sister. Taisa, don't you remember?" She repeated her name more distinctly in the hope that the sound of it would awaken in Polya childish memories of her first nurse, but Polya's face registered nothing but embarrassment and dismay, and the old woman did not dare to embrace her niece with wet hands. "Why, have a good look at me, lassie! What is that you've found there?"

"I've found my Mamma here," Polya answered, realising now that she had misjudged Taisa's age. Her face *was* like an apple, but an apple that had been plucked before its time, and which had wilted and dried up a little in the wind; her glance, however, still retained something that was girlish and unspent.

"But how could you remember me, it's so many years!" she continued, her face crinkling around her sunken eyes. "And then we didn't even say goodbye to each other. Ivan happened to be away on field work when Lenochka took you away with her. It all happened overnight, our world turned for us just like milk." Suddenly she bestirred herself, threw up her hands, and began clearing the table to make some tea for the guest.

As was the custom among simple Russian women, Taisa would have liked nothing so well as to have a little cry and sit till night with their arms about each other, going over the events of the long-vanished years. But Polya, after all she had discovered about her father that day, felt like running away from here without a backward look. She tried not to think what this find on her father's desk could mean; even without that, every minute spent here seemed to her treachery towards her mother.

"I'm not hungry, really, I don't want anything. I just happened to be passing by, so I dropped in," Polya stumbled on, saying the first things that came to her mind.

"But you won't ruin us, my sweet, we're well off. And you don't have to apologise for dropping in on your own father. Hark, there's somebody coming up the stairs—I shouldn't be surprised if that isn't Ivan. You'll have dinner together. Come, give me your hat, I'll hang it up!" she said, and even stamped her foot, the way she used to do when little Polya was naughty. But Polya did not respond, and the old woman desisted, wilting. "Where are you living, lassie—not with strange people, surely?"

"No, I'm staying with an old friend of mine," Polya said, looking down to avoid the other's eyes.

Taisa took the frame from her and carefully put it back in its place.

"You could stay with your father. Look at this flat—big enough to drive a herd of horses in, and only three people living in it! In the mornings we hail each other like in the woods."

"I have everything I need, thank you," Polya doggedly repeated. "So don't be angry with me, Taisa ... er ... Taisa...."

She faltered and fell silent.

"Taisa Matveyevna, if you must use my patronymic," the old woman prompted coldly. "Your father's called Ivan Matveyevich, you know, and I happen to be his elder sister. You're right, though—what's so good about staying here? We live right out of the way—and if you want to go to a theatre, say, you've got to take a tram ride that'll cost you all of a ruble fifty. Then again, the old folks these days are such a dull lot, and they live much too long, they do."

She wiped her lips dry with the back of her hand in an old-womanish way, and stepped away from the door as if letting the bird go free, but glancing up at her darling's face, she forgave her the callous ungratefulness, so understandable considering her youth and the distance of time.

"If you don't want to eat your father's food, lassie, then let me sit round you a bit just as I am."

Not to hurt Taisa's simple homely feelings a second time Polya accepted the necessity of giving a whole hour of her time to her old aunt, for whom she was, besides everything else, a piece of news from home. Taisa was from the Yenga, too—from Krasno-vershya, just above Loshkarev, and she had lived in domestic service in Shikhanov Yam and later with her brother at the Pashutino forestry. So Polya had to describe all the changes she knew of that had taken place in the district during all these years. She sat down submissively by the window, which looked out on the Institute's plantation; the young pines, so unlike their free sisters of the Yenga, stood drawn up in a line there, as if subdued by the fear of being dismissed for negligence.

For all Polya's hurry, the conversation dragged out. Every trivial detail started Taisa off on a train of reminiscences, and in the end she couldn't help dropping three chary tears at the fact that there was no bringing back the old days, sad though they were. Listening to her was interesting and a bit frightening because at any moment that simple honest soul was likely to let slip some revealing important word, lift the veil over the Vikhrovs' family secret, and at this Polya revolted jealously with all her being.

To lead the conversation to safer ground, Polya offered the conjecture that those young pines outside had not been there before, in *those* days. The plantation, she learned, had been laid down when the Institute was founded, but four hectares on the right wing had indeed been cut down for firewood during the civil war, and Ivan had underplanted it himself soon after he took up his job in Moscow.

"They were there in those days too. They were your height, lassie. When I took you out for walks you used to shake hands with them, and call them pricklies. But how can you remember, it was such a long time ago!"

But Polya did remember them, not with her eyes, though, but with the surface of her pricked fingers, perhaps. And because Taisa began telling her how much life Vikhrov had put into that tiny grove, she asked her aunt pointblank about what had been preying on her mind all the time: why, then, if that's the kind of man he is, did they abuse her father?

"That's just it!" the old woman said with a bitter laugh. "That's what they abuse him for, because he protects the forest."

"Protects it from whom? From the people?" Polya said, instantly on her guard, and her voice, like a plucked string, rang with the natural perpetual shame which she felt before those lucky girls and boys whose fathers were never abused.

"Not from the people, lassie, but from the axe. The axe has no eyes," Taisa took her up quickly. "It's made of iron and sits on a helve."

"H'm, I wonder how he protects it, the forest. Does he walk round it with a gun, or what?"

"It's much too big for walking around! So he writes books about our forests getting less and less. You said yourself they'd

43

started on Pustosha. It isn't as if your father nagged about it in an underhand way—all his books are checked and approved by the authorities."

"Wait a minute," Polya interrupted, incorruptibly avoiding the proferred hand. "I want to ask—who, if not the people, is master of the forest? And then, is the professor aware of the building that is going on in our country, and what it's being cut down for ... that forest?"

With slender unpeasant-like fingers Taisa was pulling a bit of cloth to threads.

"Well you see, Polya, he's a woodman, your father is. It's his job, seeing he's been put there to look after the forest. Supposing you fall ill, say, and it made Lenochka sad to see you that way. Well then, some doctors wouldn't think anything about telling a lie just to please the mother, and making out that you was well. They should worry—you're a stranger to them! But for a lie like that they deserve to get it in the neck, if not be put away in a prison-house with forty barred windows on it—isn't that so? So there you are, he doesn't want to deceive his people."

It was the best she could do. Indeed, it would have taken Vikhrov himself too long a time to answer Polya's question, much more time, unfortunately, than Polya, and, to judge by all appearances, her country, disposed of. Taisa smiled forlornly and hung her head with a guilty air. She could not recognise her Polya in this angry creature, who had suddenly become so implacable, although Polya herself could not help feeling that the dark accusations levelled at Vikhrov were a bit rash.

"Of course, it's difficult for me to judge all this offhand," she excused herself, her face blotchy with confusion. "I've never even seen him."

"Come then, I'll show you your father," Taisa said quietly.

She took Polya's hand and led her up to the wall, where in a hand-made fretwork frame, hung a large group photograph of some sixty young forestry graduates, taken long ago. The heroes of the day were banked in rows, like a choir about to perform a jubilee cantata, except that the basses, grave-looking men of more generous amplitude, sat comfortably on chairs in the front, while one of them, obviously the precentor with a bristling moustache, had an armchair to himself; the rest were arranged in an ascending scale of density, those at the very top being jammed together, one shoulder forward. The overflow of post-graduates and employees reclined in the foreground with an independent air, while

Vikhrov already had a chair to himself—true, it was on the extreme right so far, and he was leaning on the knee of the man next to him so as not to be crowded out of the picture. There was not more than a thumbnail of photographic space to every face, but Polya made out her father clearly. It even seemed to her, though she could not be positive about it, that she had met him once, and not so long ago either, and even talked to him, but she could not remember the exact circumstances.

He was a spare man of short stature, with a little beard cultivated in deference to Forestry Department traditions, and big bushy eyebrows sharply uplifted as if in a flash of sudden inspiration; a side parting with a straggling tuft over the forehead gave him the appearance of a craftsman of some semi-intellectual trade. He did not bear the slightest resemblance to *that other one*, to that hateful Vikhrov fat with opulence.

"He's fallen off in looks now, my Ivan, a bit out at elbows, if you know what I mean. The years are going that way, my dear, not this way!"

Polya was silent.

"Tell me, did he ever wear glasses, gold-rimmed glasses?"

"Never. We Vikhrovs all have good eyes. Why do you ask?"

"Oh, I just remembered something. Did he make that frame himself?" Polya asked, turning away.

Taisa rightly understood that her question expressed merely the measure of her confusion. No, Ivan's son, Sergei, had made that frame. He had come into their family soon after Lenochka went away. A fine lad, he was, too. The same age as Polya. It was he who now occupied the corner room, which used to be the Vikhrovs' nursery.

The same thing happens in a water-mead in the spring, when the floodtide runs off and familiar islets crop up in half-dried patches. Gradually, by some kind of elusive signs, Polya began to recognise her father's flat. One of the shelves was occupied from top to bottom by a collection of wood slabs of different tree species, their polished surfaces cut against the grain or with the grain, which Polya had first taken for books. As a matter of fact they *were* books, books on the soils and climate belts of the earth, only very voluminous ones which only the learned could read. And like the engine whistle an hour ago, this smell of dry wood led her back to childhood. With sharpened vision she gazed through the canvas chart of the Soviet forests that hung down to the floor and saw beyond it, uncoloured, as in a dream,

45

another room, darker and smaller, and there, on something downier than grass, herself building little castles out of wood blocks. "There should be a door there behind that chart ... may I go in?" Polya said with a sudden catch in her voice.

"So there is, you're a quick-eyed lass!" Taisa exclaimed, overjoyed. "In your time they had their bedroom there, your parents did. Now we've given it up to the gardener Didyakin and his family. He's a nice quiet man, though, doesn't drink. He's like Ivan, easy to get on with." She straightened her shawl with a sweeping gesture and sighed. "Come to think of it, there was nothing to prevent 'em living together for a thousand years, those two, and closing their eyes together. But there, see how things fell out!"

She could expect her aunt now to turn up the last furrow slice of memory and reveal the parental secret, which had the mouldering odour of the long-forbidden. Sick with dread, Polya reached for her hat. In vain did Taisa plead with her to wait for her father, to look at the things Lenochka had left behind and which Taisa had so lovingly taken care of for the lawful heiress. She went downstairs two steps at a time. Taisa breathlessly caught up with her niece in the street to give her the packages she had forgotten.

"Do come and see us again, lassie," she whispered pleadingly for the last time. "It will be such a joy for the old man!"

"I will, I'll drop in as soon as I've fixed up," Polya nodded, determined never to return to that place again.

4

Polya started home on foot in order to walk off the dreadful turmoil of feelings and conjectures that raged within her; midway, she was caught up by the Metro and swept into its current. Then she walked down that same Glad Street, as she had mentally christened it in a yet-to-be-written letter to her mother, but the people she now came across were all middle-aged and worried looking with eyes turned inwards. Polya was so tired that she had neither the desire nor the strength to look up and investigate the fakir.

She did not mention to Varya a word about her voyage into childhood—she had just wanted to indulge in a few last pranks that were still permitted her today, but would be frowned upon tomorrow.

46

After dinner they went through Polya's purchases, and Varya could only shake her head at the whimsies of her younger sister, who had been left to her own devices for only half a day.

"You make me feel like wanting to cry, Polya! Buying mittens in summer! Well, I can understand that, you may not be able to get them in the winter. I can even forgive you those baby saucepans—they're ... they're cute. But what do you want all that soap for? Besides, what are you, a millionairess, to buy the most expensive soaps?"

"I liked their colours, you know!" Polya smiled disarmingly. "Look what a wonderful range of colours they make!"

"I can't make you out And what's this—lily-of-the-valley drops? Are you ill?"

"No, but I thought the name was so lovely!"

"It's time you came to your senses, Polya, really. After all, you're half a student," Varya lectured her. "Can you imagine anyone trusting such a giddy creature with the building of an apartment house! Now tell me, at least, what use you intend to make of an Italian dictionary in your future activities?"

"Oh, that's the limit, really!" Polya flared up in real earnest. "Life is so broad, and no one knows what may come in useful to him in the future. Now take yourself—can you foresee what you will need in six months time? What if they suddenly send me to Florence, say, to study architecture. What will I do there without knowing the language?"

To be sure, all this could have been obtained at home, in the Loshkarev co-op store, but the goods there did not have the stamp of Moscow novelty upon them and they all smelt a bit of raw-hide leather and paraffin oil.

"By the way, hasn't there been a telegram for me?" Polya enquired with affected casualness.

There were in fact six telegrams for her, one of them signed by Chernetsov and all the next-door neighbours with the dog Balui right at the end. Two were from girl friends, and the fourth was from herself; there was a separate one from her mother. The sixth, and most restrained, containing only three words, was from Kazan, and judging by the figures in the top corner, had been handed in at the very hour that Polya had been standing at the telegraph window. All congratulated her on her coming of age, and Polya was thrilled to the marrow. What a fine thing life was when you were not alone. And how funny those scare-stories of Mamma's sounded about the perils of life in the great city.

"He's in the sulks, that silly Rodion. Coughed up three words. I reminded him about my birthday by telegram, just in case he forgot. I don't know about tomorrow, but today *I'm* the boss," and, seizing her friend, Polya whirled her round the room as far as the narrow space between the bed and the table would permit.

It was a never-to-be-repeated evening, every detail of which was afterwards to appear as a scrap of some precious dream. And since one could not do without guests on such a festive occasion, Varya called the woman next door, who, after putting her grand-daughter to bed, came to join the party.

The three of them, without putting on the light, drank tea with jam, cherries, and candied nuts, and when everything had been discussed, from the cut of the latest dresses to the events in Western Europe, they sat on in silence, gazing at Polya's bouquet, which caught the light of the sundown clouds.

Natalya Zolotinskaya left late. Before going to bed Varya in an undertone gave her friend a few scraps of information about their neighbour. The people who lived in the house called her, among themselves, the Queen of Clubs; her grey hair coiled round her head gave a crown-like effect. She and her grand-daughter were the only surviving members of a once numerous family pack. People guessed that she had not paid lightly for the lightness of her former life, but no one ever heard her complain, not even when, a couple of months ago, her daughter, secretary of some forest research institution, had been killed in a street accident; it was rumoured that the grandmother and little Zoya would now be evicted from the house, as it belonged to this institution. Apart from this, Varya knew practically nothing about her.

"She must have been very beautiful in her youth," said Polya, who was now in bed.

"Yes," Varya answered, gazing down into the blue abyss beyond the balcony door. "By the way, someone wrote me that Kolya Bobrinin is married now—is that true?"

"He married last autumn. He's been sweet on Nina Tsiplenkova for ages. It's funny, you know—about two years ago we were playing at wishes, and he wrote me a note that he would like to have a heart of rustless steel, the boaster! And what does he go and do? He drops his studies and the Komsomol and goes through a church wedding with Nina. And he had the cheek to invite Rodion to be his best-man!"

"Well, you see, all kinds of things happen to people," Varya answered with a yawn, and Polya understood that it was a feigned yawn. "Tomorrow's going to be a busy day, let's go to sleep."

They lay awake for a long time, each in the silence of her own thoughts. A warm rain began pattering in the night outside the balcony. The faces and events of the day floated dimly before Polya. The visions broke the moment they appeared, but that of the lad at the railway station lingered longest. Oh, if she had to arrive again, she would know how to teach that sooty-faced young swanker a lesson for his unbidden patronage! She dismissed him from her thoughts, and his place was immediately taken by Rodion. Surreptitiously they went up into the attic, and then he began to recite his new verses to her, written since her departure, in a slightly sing-song voice, pausing to listen whether anyone was coming, because he considered his association with poetry a weakness unworthy of any thinking personality, leave alone a mathematician.

That night the Nazi planes dropped their first bombs on the sleeping Soviet cities.

CHAPTER TWO

1

The professor returned an hour after Polya had gone, and his sister could not bring herself to tell him about his daughter's visit until late in the night. Taisa deemed it the purpose of her luckless life to look after her brother, and shield him from all, as she called it, aggravating worriment. Many years ago she had come to see him after fifteen years' separation, when he was a forest officer at Pashutino, to ask for some timber to mend her tumbledown cottage in Krasnovershya, but had lingered till night sewing buttons on the bachelor's clothes and had stayed for good. As a matter of fact, she was only his stepsister by a different mother, so it was hardly a sense of kinship or of her own homelessness that had made her subsequently tag after her brother when he moved to the capital city.

With her mild good nature, her love of work, and lack of outside attachments, she would have made a go of it anywhere, and as for her deformity, an accident of infancy, she had long ago accepted it, as others accept the accident of wealth and beauty. Besides, she had but a hazy notion of Vikhrov's forest conservation ideas, and had simply pitied him at first, a lame lonely man, then afterwards had come to believe in the sacredness of the cause he espoused, because he did not seek quick fame or personal gain as others did. They got so used to each other, especially after Lenochka's flight, that they understood each other at a word. As a result, constant silence reigned in the house, which was so conducive to the writing of all kinds of scientific works. Usually, at the close of day, Taisa went into her brother's room to make arrangements for tomorrow's dinner and discuss the events of the day, and when such events were happily lacking, they would sit it out in utter silence, the way the Yenga peasants did in the old days, sitting on their doorsteps with dead pipes before turning in. The adoption of Sergei had not changed the established routine, and it was those evenings, rather than anything else, that drew the three of them, all so different, into a close-knit friendly family.

This time Sergei was detained at work, and Taisa went in by herself for the evening session. The night moths were circling round the table lamp, and Vikhrov, already in his shirt-sleeves, was gazing through the window at his planted wood, whence the cool moisture drew as if from a river.

"Well, let's have it," he said presently without turning round.

Taisa had no news of any importance, except that Gratsiansky had dropped in at noon, asking where the master had gone to and why. Always so slippery and sneering in a blood-chilling way, he had struck her this time as looking rather worried and sleepy, and had not shown his usual sting, but, on the contrary, had tried his best to soothe the old woman's misgivings and forebodings. Indeed, there was something unusual about this visit of his. As often happens towards old age, that man had long ceased to be a friend of Vikhrov's, although he was still counted among his old chums. They had entered the Forest Institute together in 1908, and but for Vikhrov's being banished from St. Petersburg in 1911 for two years, as a result of which he did not finish his education until the very end of the first world war, they would have both graduated in the service of Russia's forests in one and the same year. This forced and really slight distinction gave to Gratsiansky a semblance of seniority, which held throughout their relations.

Having taken their degrees in different subjects, there would seem to be no grounds for any possible future rivalry between them, but their practical work was conducted in close, if not actually competition, then in extremely sharp, at times even violent contact, which seemed only natural to those around them in view of the widely divergent views which they held on scientific matters. In that famous controversy Vikhrov maintained a passive attitude, for he had no inclination to engage in a public duel with his formidable opponent; it would be premature, however, to regard Vikhrov's behaviour as a sign of weakness, disdainful disregard, as it were, of an older comrade's opinions, or a tacit admission of his own mistakes.

No one remembered how that feud between Vikhrov and Gratsiansky, of which the public at large knew nothing, had started, but with the years all those concerned in forestry affairs somehow came to expect that every major work of the former would be followed by a no less weighty counterblast of the latter in the form of an article which had the added advantage of irresponsible passion—so much so that usually a review of Vikhrov's latest book did not appear in the forestry press until Gratsiansky himself had taken a shot at it; this, in jocular lobby parlance was called "chopping old Ivan to splinters". To the lovers of belles-lettres unconversant with the dull problems of forest organisation, those articles, so unassailable in their forceful logic and brilliant style, suggested flattering comparisons with the oratory of Jaurès, the lampoons of Marat, and in one case, in some little foreign journal, even with the philippics of Cicero against Mark Antony, after which, to his credit let it be said, Alexander Gratsiansky went about for a whole week glancing about him shamefacedly and looking not only acutely embarrassed but slightly bedraggled as if splashed by some bad-smelling liquid. The old woodmen held their tongues lest they themselves be dragged under the magnifying glass of closer scrutiny, but some averred confidentially that Gratsiansky's little masterpieces of invective, some of them only a page long, contributed nothing of permanent value to real science. Indeed, for reasons of greater readability and, possibly, secrecy, Professor Gratsiansky studiously avoided either figures or constructive proposals of his own in his articles; their disarming modesty in this respect was sometimes rather glaring. However that might be, even if they did have very little to say about the forests as such, and even if they did at times tend to make the confusion that already existed in forestry affairs worse confounded, of which Vikhrov's supporters whispered in corners, thus revealing their intolerance of comprehensive criticism, Gratsiansky made up for this by showing that he possessed an all-round erudition in everything, unfortunately, except forests, a deadly sarcasm, and, in recent years, a magnanimous reticence on the subject of the true cause of Vikhrov's errors. In short, of all Vikhrov's tolerantly moderate critics he was the most formidable, the most active, the best-informed and most successful, so much so that during the last quarter of a century Vikhrov's reputation never for a single day lost any of its tarnish.

These circumstances did not prevent them from meeting, mostly at official conferences, and occasionally running a tilt at each other by right of fellowship on some current little question of forest regulation. In such cases Gratsiansky would show towards his former friend a kind of open-hearted, almost brotherly, tolerance accompanied by ambiguously sad sighs, as much as to say— ah, well, old chap, you and I understand the futility of all this mutual recrimination, but you can't help it—it's the epoch! And Gratsiansky's eyes, for some reason, would angle off, one staring fixedly and steadily at the bridge of his interlocutor's nose, while the other travelled away over his shoulder to some secret hiding-place nobody knew of. And he would keep throwing out hints about their having to get together sometime over a bottle of dry wine, but he never invited Vikhrov to his place, and intended to drop in on him himself in order to settle all the outstanding world problems at one go, and, while they were at it, to remember the good old days when they ate skilly together out of the same pot at a Greek eating-house in Karavanny Street. The fact is worth a passing mention, that, being the son of a well-to-do Professor of the St. Petersburg Ecclesiastical Academy, Gratsiansky never ate in eating-houses, and the Greek he spoke of always served his food up in chinaware; but it sounded nicer that way, more picturesque, while Vikhrov, to his shame, and despite the fierce resentment that burned up in him, never contradicted that romantic rounding off of reality which people in their declining years are prone to resort to.

However that may be, Gratsiansky possessed no mean gifts of oratory coupled with a nimble mind and a firm obstacle-crushing will, although it was not always accordant with an ever youthful restless heart. Of all Vikhrov's old friends, including Cheredilov and Valery Krainov, who, it was true, was often away travelling, it was he, Gratsiansky, who had offered Vikhrov money when he was in such trouble at work in 1936; it was a fairly considerable sum too, and it looked as if the giver did not expect repayment. This incident, which had revealed the man in the light of a solicitous friend in need, had set Vikhrov thinking about the perverse character of his opponent with his neurasthenic scrambles now into the contra-indicated realm of forestry, now into the history of the Russian revolutionary movement, and, to crown all, into political economy, where he got stuck without achieving anything of note beyond the skimpy volume of thumbnail articles penned on a subject so trivial to the scope of his talents as the person of Vikhrov.

In the hope of being able to prove his case when they met, Vikhrov asked his sister to lay in a supply of dry wine, but shortly afterwards Gratsiansky, this time in one of the great dailies, launched one of his most deadly attacks in which he summed up Vikhrov's perennial attempts to restrict socialist construction; once again, love of the truth must have gained the upper hand over personal sympathies, seeing that Gratsiansky had decided to speak plainly. That last blow below the belt dealt with a hand which, despite old friendship, had not faltered in the act (he had made a point of confessing to this friendship between the lines with an old-man's bitterness) had not, for some reason, been followed up by "official action" in regard to Vikhrov, owing to the intervention of the higher Party authorities. This current setback, however, naturally put Vikhrov's supporters on their guard, scared away the vacillating part of his friends and pupils scattered all over the country's forests, and made Vikhrov himself turn the thought over in his mind once more as to whether he had been correct in the choice of his profession. And so a rupture, which had been developing for so many years, was brought to a head, and in this light, the visit of an avowed enemy only a month after his murderous attack, became an outstanding and puzzling event.

The only explainable reason could be that Gratsiansky sought reconciliation—that, too, sometimes happens in old age—but even that fell to pieces on closer examination. At that stage such a move was highly improbable for it would have meant retreat, capitulation, the utter ruin of Gratsiansky at a time when rumours were afloat that he was being nominated for election as corresponding member of the Academy of Sciences. Rather should the reason be sought in Gratsiansky's heightened, almost seismographic sensitivity to all the shifts and changes in the political climate. Vikhrov had always believed that his ideas, born of the patriotic and scientifically grounded dreams of Russia's progressive forestry pioneers, would some day be widely accepted in the country's economic practice. But the great battle for the forest had been raging for a century and a half, and it would be presumptious to suppose that Vikhrov, of all men, would crown it with victory. He became confused in his mind and was silent.

"I was fool enough to think he'd come trotting down to make up with you, that pal o' yours," Taisa proceeded in a puzzled tone of voice. "I ran into the kitchen for a cup, and would you believe it!—there he was prowling around your desk, kind of fiddling about with the papers on it. What business did he have round your desk?"

"He was after the family jewels, I daresay. You wait, I'll get a big iron box made for them," Ivan said, laughing off not so much his own suspicions as his sister's sympathy. And following up his initial train of thought, he asked whether she had bought the wine.

Taisa confessed that she had bought some port. To her peasant mind it was a sheer waste of money to buy that sour stuff which had neither joy nor strength in it.

"Don't you beat about the bush," she expostulated. "I fear that sworn friend o' yours more than I do a wolf."

It should be said that she had no idea of the vast amount of trouble that man was causing her brother.

"He that's afraid of wolves must not go in a wood. In the old days the forest ranger used to wear a military uniform because he was standing guard over the state forest treasury, like a soldier. And a soldier's not supposed to be afraid."

"You'd better listen to me. Give in and go cap in hand to him before it's too late," his sister said with ominous directness. "He'll fell you, like he felled your teacher." She had in mind the early death of the well-known forest scientist Tulyakov, which had marked the beginning of Gratsiansky's brilliant career. "Out of the woods you've come, and back to the woods you should go. The children have grown up, and we don't need much, you and I. They'll take you on as forest ranger, you're still a good walker. They'll give us a cabin at some division, and I'll make cloudberry pies for you on Sundays."

Usually, Vikhrov would get angry. He did not like these tempting reminders which sapped his strength.

"You see, sister, the trees on the edge of the wood receive more light and food, they grow freely, that's why they're hardier. Now nature's put me on the woodside like an oak, a sort of wind-break. How can I leave it? It'll mean hacking away my own roots, don't you see?"

But this time beneath his banter lay a half-formed consent to take a trip in good season to the Yenga, to stay there a while, take a look round, and try his hand again at the rough work from which he had started exactly a quarter of a century ago; it needed but the slightest jolt now to tip the balance of his decision. Besides, he had been longing to ramble about his native parts, and, while his spine could still bend, to bow to the green cradle from which he first saw the light of day.

Then, feeling that she had failed to influence her brother, Taisa herself ruffled up like a woodland bird.

"It's no laughing matter, Ivan! You've been kicking up a dust this many a year, and what good has it done? They've started on your Pustosha now!" she shouted, knowing his weak spot.

Pustosha was the name of a famous pine forest on the Yenga, mentioned in the ukazes of Peter the Great. It was there that the gentle Sklan, the sacred river of Vikhrov's childhood, had its source.

"Has somebody come from there, or did you get a letter? Who told you this nonsense about Pustosha?"

And so it came out, the story of Polya's visit, which Taisa was so anxious to spare her brother. It sounded so joyless in her telling, that Vikhrov's heart sank with a sense of foreboding. He should have asked for more details about his daughter, but he was afraid to do so, because the very tone of Taisa's communication contained the answer.

"Well ... I suppose she's quite grown up?"

"She's such a sweet and tidy little body, with a mind of her own too. Takes after her grandma Agafya by the looks of it," and she shared with her brother the crumbs of knowledge which she had been able to get out of Polya.

"Perhaps she needs something ... did she leave her address?"

"I forgot all about the address, I was in such a dither." Generally she blamed herself for Polya not wanting to pass the tedious time with her until her father returned. "She had a cute little hat on, I don't mind telling you—yellow straw, and a pretty sarafan with strewn peas. Made it up herself, so she said."

She was obviously keeping back something important; so then Ivan sat down next to her, took her hand, and extracted the whole story from her word by word. It occurred to him for the first time that Gratsiansky's exposures of his dubious and even dangerous activities rarely appeared in the general press, but the forestry publications undoubtedly reached the Pashutino range and might have caught his daughter's eye.

"Well, er . . . was she resentful, did she ask about me?"

Try as she would to make excuses for Polya, Taisa was no good at lying or keeping any secrets, and so Vikhrov learned of the genuine childish scorn that had sounded in Polya's only question concerning the essence of her father's ideas. His daughter then had read and condemned, had disavowed him, joining the camp of his ill-wishers.

He went over to the window and stared bleakly into the night.

"Why are you silent, forest soldier? Fight!" Taisa added with angry vehemence behind his back.

He was miserably mute. Only a few people in the country possessed sufficient knowledge to steer their way amid the forestal confusion, which he mistakenly believed to be of a purely departmental nature. Of course, he should have kept to his own direct humble business of forester and not have meddled in the higher politics of forest exploitation. And so it happened that with his very first book he supported the as yet undiscredited scientific trend of what was called sustained yield management, but if need be he would have repeated his error again today, even though knowing what a turn it was likely to take in the eyes of the callow Soviet youth, although it was for their sake that he had taken upon himself the burden and hardships of his calling. He had a feeling that from now on he would not be able to deliver his introductory lecture, hold his opening talk with the first-year students on the Russian forests with the same confidence as before, and without the harrowing fear of a brickbatted reply into which would be packed all the accusations he had merited.

One reservation should be made, though. Vikhrov had long since reconciled himself to the fact that of all the civic vocations obtaining at the time, his own stood at the bottom of the list. All the others—the surgical table, prospecting, the building of water-power stations, the harvesting of bumper crops, the leading of warships into battle, the creation of cunning machines that did the work of multiple hands, the testing of trial planes and thousands of other occupations—were rightly held by the people to be deeds of valour, which called for supreme effort and mettle. All these fields offered also an opportunity for seeking new horizons, accelerating productive processes, making great discoveries of paramount importance to the public welfare and health; precision, craftsmanship, and the amount of labour expended were tested there by a single compact conclusive result that brought general recognition, government awards and the pride of authorship, and these performances could be repeated again and again until the fatal hour of the summing up struck.

All this, in the eyes of Vikhrov, was lacking in the activity of the forester, which envisaged a prodigious span of life and was subject to the laws of the meagre accumulation of vegetative cells. True, it exemplified in a most striking manner the effect of your true socialistic torch-race, showing how the generations worked together in changing the face of the planet. It took two or even three work lives to raise a full-grown timber tree; and if one aimed at rotational cropping, which was the only correct system, it would take centuries. Science had not yet learned how to grow a crop of formed trees under a five-year plan. And so there were no monuments yet to foresters upon this earth!

Even fainter hopes for quick recognition by their contemporaries fell to the lot of the rank-and-file workers of forest management, which represented a system of forest surveying and working plans for drawing up cutting schedules with a view to obtaining the greatest possible productivity of the forest. Moreover, Vikhrov himself, owing to his age and the position he held in science, was spared the arduous duties of trudging through dense forest thickets and writing up reports on millions of wooded acres which nobody ever read. The newspapers of that epoch sounded the tocsin call for labour heroism, but Vikhrov's profession contained none of those possibilities; he often had it pointed out to him that the life expectancy of the forester came only fourth after bee-keepers, clergymen and gardeners, and that his chief ailment was rheumatism, which could hardly be called a fatal disease. That is why, at times, when mentioning the post he occupied, Vikhrov felt acutely embarrassed, as if he were employed as the Custodian of the Great Bear or Guardian of the South Coast Seascape. He found comfort in the letters of his numerous pupils and in the knowledge that he was one of an army of men in a similar position, an army of obscure toilers working in the remotest forest areas, whose only contact with the blessings of modern civilisation was often maintained by means of a crystal receiver.

Bouts of conscience like these could only be cured by an attitude of meticulous honesty towards his job, and, because he no longer planted forests himself, by the most discreet use of his almost sole tool—felling. The country, however, was demanding timber in ever growing quantities, and the continued practising of old estimates and tempos, as well as adherence to the view which regarded the forest as a self-regenerating gift of God, were likely to have the most undesirable and irreparable consequences. And so Vikhrov developed the habit of assessing his activities not by the number of awards, of which he had none, not by the sense of dubious creative satisfaction derived from the publication of yet another abused book, but, above all, by a rough estimate of the effect that his efforts were likely to have upon the well-being of the generations yet to come.

Polya stood nearest to him in that chain of posterity, so that her opinion meant much to Vikhrov. It looked as if he had frittered away over half a century of his life, if after such a long separation he had not even earned a message of love from his own daughter.

"Yes, sister, you are right," he said, drumming his fingers on the table. "I'll go down there one of these days, visit the old home, ramble about my Pustosha, get wet in the rain, talk things over with the birds. Excellent! Go to bed now, you've done your job. I'll figure the rest out for myself," he added bitterly.

Thus began his second heart-searching, a deeper one even than that which had followed the flight of his wife. The thing was to try to grasp what was taking place in that epoch and what his own human function in it was. In his conviction, the October Revolution had been a battle not only for a fair distribution of material values, but perhaps, first and foremost, for the purity of human values. Only under that condition, he was sincerely convinced, was the prolongation of the human race possible. And if progress, besides standing for greater prosperity, also meant raising the standard of moral obligations—for only a perfect person can achieve perfect happiness—then it was essential for everyone to have a perfect biography that one would not be ashamed to read out aloud in the presence of children, at high noon, in the most crowded public places of the world. This point of view, which was Valery Krainov's, made it strikingly clear how much mankind needed cleansing through storm and tempest.

Valery had been a fellow student of Vikhrov's, the senior companion and leader of their once inseparable St. Petersburg foursome. For him there had existed no inextricable knots, not even in that seemingly dead-end period of despair, tsarist provocations, and the break-up of social forces. His was the clear perspicasious mind of the Lenin school, combined with a gift of almost scientific foresight, and Cheredilov, who, like Gratsiansky, belonged to a clerical milieu, jokingly called him at that period the apostle and forefather of socialist man. Instead of carrying on in the forestry line, Valery first embarked upon Party work, then spent many years abroad in the capacity of Soviet ambassador; as often happens among friends in Russia, Vikhrov met him only once in about ten years. Correspondence was a failure; private events were then fused with public events, and it was quicker to read about them in the papers. In an emergency, however, Vikhrov would always consult him mentally, and between them they solved the most intricate equations of life.

So it was now.

"Define your aim as completely and roughly as you can," said Valery.

"I know it. It's in my books."

"Test it by the future."

"I see no other way of helping that future."

"Then go ahead ... and if you have not achieved your goal, then look back at the road by which you have been going to it."

To carve out time in the morning, before lectures, for his private work, Vikhrov usually went to bed early. This was the first night in years he had sat up late, but then the next day was Sunday, June 22nd. He kept pacing up and down the room, fifteen steps diagonally, peering into every chink of his past. Every time he turned round on reaching his desk, his unfinished article on cankerous growth in the scotch pine would catch his eye. This work was completely outside his speciality and was not meant for publication, but old men have moments when they are in a hurry to commit to paper their unexpended experience on a favourite subject. Just now that elaborate treatise on the injurious effect which the proximity of the aspen had upon the given species, struck him as criminal nonsense in comparison with what he was supposed to do and had not succeeded in doing in life.

He stopped and stared at the yellowish pages of the manuscript, and as if through the slack water of autumn, glimpsed there, at the bottom, the fairy-tale of his childhood. The bitter flavour of it told him it was real. Maturity always begins with the collapse of the fairy-tale, and the boy Ivan had learned all too soon what homely scraps went into the making of the folk tale's fabulous patchwork, how fabulous was the boisterous orgy with which the logdrivers celebrated the floating season, how fabulous the justice which the "walkers" from the villages went forth to seek on behalf of the peasants, and how dry-eyed and sparing was the weeping of the women in fabulous Rus. Nevertheless, not counting the meagre food and the poorness of the home roof, to which peasant children are inured, Vikhrov's life could be said to have begun in fabulous wealth, for he possessed toys that were beyond the reach of the wealthiest man.

It is a wonder how all the boundless spaces of his boyish domains, peopled with legendary figures, found room upon this planet. On the flats, over by Gorinka, with an iron ring through its nose, strutted the copper-skinned bull belonging to the tavern-keeper Zolotukhin, and at the manor house, that loomed whitely on the bluff above the bend, the aged master Sapegin took his regular evening potshots at the crows, whose clamour made it difficult for him to bring his mind to bear upon the changing fortunes of Byzantine history; then there was the overgrown patch of the river's old bed, inhabited by water-nymphs, who, on thundery summer evenings, could be seen from the top of Shabanov Hill, with their hair down, lying in wait for God-fearing Christians in order to tickle them to death with nimble silky fingers; and lastly, in the dense wild wood at Oblog there lived a hairy *blazna*, a local variety of the evil spirit, whose whimsical humour it was, among other things, to fell trees in the autumn season. At the stroke of midnight the welkin rang with the whack of the axe upon the resinous trunk, then came the death-rattle of the falling tree, and the dying gasp of the swishing crown, but never had the young explorers discovered there a single wood chip or a stump.

And this was how the topography of that world looked. In the centre, where the Sklan joined the Yenga, Krasnovershya shelved down to the water's edge, and all round, green, blue and azure, the forest broke away in terraces. The little village was separated from the manor by a pinewood of some hundred and fifty acres, known as Zapolosky, meaning "beyond the strips" of peasants' land. Part of Oblog, an immense wooded tract belonging to Sapegin, wedged down into the ravine from the west, and immediately behind it, dark and forbidding, loomed the impregnable mass of the Pustosha state forests. They were forever wrapped in mist and the sky above them was always drizzling, because, according to unverified juvenile rumour, that was the place where the sky joined up with the earth. The thrilling secret of that ancient forest, which Ivan and his bosom friend Demidka Zolotukhin had invented for themselves, was that the deeper it went the taller the trees grew, so that their shaggy crowns were hidden in the clouds, and an ordinary squirrel could run right up into the heavens and crack his nuts there, sitting astride the horn of the new moon. And from there it was but a stone's throw to the awful bottomless pit, in which there was no stream, no grass, no shade of earthy woes, and only hyperborean gloom held dusky sway there, with something else besides, something which not even the bravest human soul could see and live to tell. It was the Edge of the World.

Oblog was the cause of a famous lawsuit which began soon after the abolition of serfdom. The state-owned forests were a long way off, and the woods in the vicinity belonged to the descendants of various historical families, each more influential than the other, so that between them nothing could be done to provide the emancipated peasants with the woodlots they were entitled to. The population on the Yenga, besides logging, had engaged from time immemorial in woodworking, such as the carving of wooden spoons and wheel-making, while the Krasnovershians had always been famous as chest-makers. The dowry outfits of all the well-to-do brides-to-be in the empire were kept in gaily painted chests of Krasnovershya workmanship lathed with coloured foil and furnished with locks which sang a steely little tune when the key was turned. The peasants used the young limes and oak in the Sapegin forests without let or hindrance until the last of the line, Ilya Apollonovich Sapegin, enlightened servant of the emancipative reform and translator of the Byzantine chronicles into the Russian language, entered into possession. The repeated appeals of the authorities, secular and spiritual, that the muzhiks should not do evil unto their neighbour, even though he were a landlord, fell upon deaf ears, and in the end the enlightened translator gave rein to his angry passions and sought the protection of the law against the annual depredations to his property. In the absence of official records, Vikhrov was able to learn the sad anecdote only by word of mouth from the old residents just before the revolution, when the picturesque settings of popular legend had begun to emerge from the bureaucratic fog of legal chaos.

At first fortune seemed to favour the muzhiks. Owing to frequent changes of place occasioned by devastating fires, Krasnovershya dropped out of the provincial Land Records altogether, and as there was no village standing on the spot referred to there could be no one there to damage the forests. It was a peculiar species of official blindness, for the cure of which Sapegin applied a time-tested remedy popular in Russian usage—the rubbing of the affected eyes with treasury notes, whereupon it immediately came to light that Krasnovershya did exist, and that its founder, the Raskolnik Fedos, had set up his house of prayer on that very spot, in the thickest part of the impenetrable pine forest. In the course of time, however, as is generally the case when man happens to be its neighbour, the forest was reduced to ash, smoke and shavings, and the residue was driven down the river by Fedos's descendants, who would thus seem to have received the forest portion due to them. The case nevertheless made no headway for the simple reason that the shrewd Krasnovershians carted up to town twice a year firewood, grouse, homespun linen and sundry other offerings which were a great help at a dead lift to members of the bar burdened with large families.

According to the same peasant legend, after Sapegin's second gift, the provincial authorities established the fact that the local inhabitants in the person of the runaway Fedos had settled on the Sklan without the permission of the government, and such being the case, they were not entitled to any of the gifts of nature. However, they were unable either to abolish the Krasnovershya muzhiks, as the enlightened translator urged them to do, or to make them pay for damage caused to the landlord's property in the course of a century and a half. Thereupon Sapegin had the case transferred to the Senate, but access to the imperial capital was not forbidden to peasant "walkers" either. According to the stories of the old men, feeling was running very high among the muzhiks. At the great moot of Krasnovershya, to which three adjacent villages were invited, it was decided to fight on, to continue with the production of their world-famous chests, and to seek justice.

Matvei Vikhrov was the third walking envoy of Krasnovershya. The other two had returned with nothing to show beyond a few negligible bruises. The choice had fallen upon Matvei, not because he had pushful ways and a glib tongue, both of which had proved useless in the case of the previous delegates, but on the contrary, because of his amazing mildness which went with an extremely imposing appearance. He was of such towering stature, that when he entered, for instance, the office of the volost administration, which he did by ducking his head under the lintel, everyone half rose instinctively to his feet at the sight of so remarkable a work of nature. He was then over fifty. The nobility of the Russian peasantry was revealed in his calm melodious speech, his dignified greying beard, his slow heavy hands made for feats of *bylina* glory. The humble bow of such a giant was bound to effect the most hardened legal soul, and so it was with the help of Matvei that the Krasnovershians hoped to apprise the existing pillars of the imperial state of their humility, which though peaceful was yet danger-fraught. Another reason for sending him of all men was that he had a younger brother, Afanasy, in St. Petersburg, who occupied the post of janitor and wore a number plate—his insignia of office—and consequently was in a position to point out the secret passages to the heart of the law, and provide a temporary asylum.

The event was not within Ivan's memory, and it was not until a mature age that he learned from his sister the details of that time-honoured custom of speeding a peasant delegate on his way: how the whole village clubbed together to equip him for the journey, each bringing what he could afford—one a five-kopek piece, another a loaf of bread or a foot wrap—and then, under the driving autumn rain and wind, escorted him with lamentations to the outskirts of the village as if to the graveyard, and everyone bowed to him—the people, the trees, and even the prickly rust-coloured thistle by the roadside, and from there he would walk off by himself, his bark-bag on his shoulder, a severed limb of the tree, and that limb was his, Ivan's, father. Many were the injunctions given to Matvei at parting, the chief one being that the forest was God's gift to the community, and it would be a sin to have it pass into individual hands that had never known the feel of an axe. "And don't forget to tell 'em," doddering old Zot was said to have shouted after him, coughing and wheezing, "that when a thousand steal from one, it's a question who's the real thief!"

Matvei Vikhrov went forth upon his apostolic errand in the late autumn of 1892. At first nothing was heard of him, and then he sprang into sensational fame in a rather unexpected fashion. Subsequent rumour had it that for six months he had gone practically without food or rest, trying hard but unsuccessfully to bring the peasants' petition to the ears of a certain semi-influential personage, who, if he could not exactly decide the matter himself, could at least lay it before the highest pillars of the state. But Matvei could never catch him. The policemen and tenants of the neighbouring houses all got to know Matvei as he kept his vigil at the front door in cold weather and wet, and even got to love him for his gentleness, while the generals' wives would ask him to beat their carpets for them or chop their wood, and he would do it all with invariable good humour—remembering his mission—and without pay, but after a while he became noticeably dispirited and began to get thin, because he had run through all his money. Then suddenly fortune smiled on the poor muzhik. The audience he had been craving took place one evening, on the same busy street, when the semi-influential personage and his wife were getting into their sleigh, bound upon some urgent errand.

Kneeling down with the paper resting on his bared head, as his fellow-villagers had bidden him, Matvei waited for the high decision. And verily the sight must have been powerfully impressive even to worldly-wise St. Petersburg, which was hardened to such scenes; but the semi-influential personage passed by, and his wife brushed the petition off Matvei's head with the edge of her fur-lined cloak. The rug had been fastened into place and the coachman had slapped the rein of the left bay, when Matvei, in two bounds, reached the sleigh, and according to the findings of the examining magistrate, committed grievous assault and battery upon the semi-influential personage by striking him upon the neck through his beaver collar with such violence that the said person died on the spot. To this should be added that, according to Ivan's mother, his father never touched liquor, stood out the church service to the last nunc dimittis, and shyly adored birds and every breath of life weaker than himself; therefore his grievance must have been rankling in his breast to break out the way it did through his long cannon-weighted arm. In mildness of disposition and tender love of all things living and growing, Ivan took after his father, but in looks he resembled his mother, Agafya, a spare, uncomplaining, comely woman with sensitive unpeasant-like hands. The neighbours were sorry for her and called her Little Bear after her husband.

Matvei returned to the bosom of his family some three years later, when Ivan had turned five. Guards had started to call on the Vikhrovs in the winter, once on the pretext of having come to the wrong house looking for their chief, and again to ask for a drink of water. There was nothing wrong about their having come in the night—men could be thirsty at night, too!—but on both occasions they had sat about on the bench in the dark until daybreak, when a well-fed man in government service should have been asleep. Then things got quiet, until once, in the dead of night, Matvei came in without knocking. How he had smuggled his huge body past so many spying eyes, deceived the dogs, and opened the gate that was locked from inside, there was no knowing—but there he was, sitting by the table, indifferent to his fate, with his back towards the window, when his wife woke up, roused by a shiver of fear rather than by any noise he may have made. She took it all in even before she had seen her husband properly. An immense moon was shining fit to dazzle the eye.

"Well, here I am, good folks," Matvei said, or at least, so Agafya thought he said, while he fingered the flax that lay on the bench beside him and shook his head; she knew herself that she hadn't scutched it enough—there was too much boon in the stuff.

Unlike the usual tramps, he wore clean clothes, black from top to bottom, and in good repair. Maybe he had taken them off somebody's back on the highway down by Shikhanov Yam, although there had been no robberies in the neighbourhood as far as she knew. He looked just like a tradesman who'd come home for a stay, except that he hadn't brought any fairings; so queer, too, silent, and uncanny, the way dead men appear to you in dreams. Without lighting the lamp, Agafya lowered her legs over the side of the bunk and stared at her husband's new top-boots and his white hands dangling between his knees. As if wishing to make sure of something, she asked how things were there in St. Petersburg. He said that things were all right in St. Petersburg, brass bands played there all day, and they burned lamps there all night long. It occurred to her also to ask where he had come from in those clothes, and learned that he had got leave from the "freezing cold country" he worked in, and it didn't take a shrewd woman long to guess that he meant the grave.

"Where did you get those boots, Matvei?" she asked, because she had never seen such boots even on tradesmen.

She had never known him to be in the habit of repeating one's question—he did so now, listening all the time for something outside.

"These boots? Ah, well, it's no use lying—one sin leads to another, you know!" he gave a grim defiant laugh, but quietly so as not to wake the children. "What are you eating here? They're already eating gout-weed down at Surchalovo—I passed the place. Some life! The muzhiks are panicky with hunger. Even the poor horses have lain down, they're that weak."

Plainly, this was a hint that the master should be fed, but Agafya did not dare to offer him anything—you were not supposed to give the food of the living to the dead, unless you wanted them to haunt the place. So then, not for the sake of complaining, but just to play the fox, the woman started to tell how they'd run clean out of food, and how their hunchbacked little girl had already asked to be allowed to go abegging, but how she, Agafya, had not let her, stepmother though she was, but had gone to Zolotukhin to borrow some corn, seeing as how Matvei would give it all back from the first harvest when he got home, but had run up against his daughter-in-law. "And you know what a hell-cat that woman is, she's got a tongue that'll rip you down to the flesh, worse'n a curry-comb. And the things she said to me, Matvei, the whole village heard 'em, I could have died with shame." Luckily, old Zolotukhin himself came out. He shoved the swearing hussy aside, and weighed out some millet for Agafya, and told her to come every Saturday at closing time to wash the floors in the tavern. Matvei hadn't stirred throughout the story, he only asked in a sort of faraway voice whether Zolotukhin's wife was still alive—she'd been having trouble with her legs, he remembered. He ought to know, coming from where he did, that the old woman had been dead this six months! And then Taisa got down from the stove ledge, and her father patted her, and wanted to know whether the hump on her back hurt her, and Taisa answered in a piping little voice that her back was all right, it didn't hurt any more. And then she tried a guess of her own, and asked whether her Daddy had turned footpad by any chance, and Matvei laughed—these kids, they'd always say something!—and made a hopeless deathly sort of gesture. The pendulum clock ticks loud enough at that time of night, God knows, but Agafya couldn't remember hearing it, her mind was like a sieve. But it must have

66

been real, because the next morning it turned out that Taisa had had the same dream.

The boy Ivan made his father's acquaintance exactly a week later. The guards caught Matvei at Oblog, where he was staying with the local bee-keeper; he was half-asleep and had taken it into his head to put up a resistance, the ridiculous man. There was no way of getting him to the prison hospital, as the high water had torn the ferry-boat loose and swept it away, and they couldn't wait for another one to be driven down or have the prisoner rowed across in a boat on account of his condition. Matvei was brought home in the evening, just on the eve of Whitsun. He lay on his back, gripping the sides of the cart with fingers clenched blue to stifle the pain caused by the jolts, and he breathed rapidly, as though hastening to relish the goodly home-like smell of the Russian village, compounded of the savoury smoke of hearth fires, the night-cooled earth, and the after-dust of the home-driven herd; the whole gun charge had been emptied into his stomach. The coffin was knocked together of the same stolen wood from the Sapegin forest, but they were in such a hurry on account of the local police chief wanting the body of the escaped convict to be disposed of as quickly as possible, that they took the wrong measure and Matvei was boxed up with his knees bent. According to ancient custom, the icon borne at the head of the funeral procession was given to Ivan, a still pure, angelic soul. In honour of the occasion, his mother got out of the family chest a new shirt with coloured gussets under the armpits, like those worn by the young men of the village. To the seven-year-old boy his father's funeral was a treasured memory, a gala event of his childhood. For one thing, Zolotukhin thawed to the extent of giving him a ten-kopek piece all for himself, but thought better of it and gave him instead its equivalent in pep-permint cakes, while the less well-to-do went out of their way to show their kindness towards the fatherless child if only by a pat on the head. From that day of stir and bustle, bathed in the fadeless glow of life, Ivan Vikhrov's memory started to work on its own.

There is nothing in the world more delightful than the spacious-ness of that season, when the field flowers all around are weaving their first colourful pattern, untouched by either the scythe edge or the winter frost, when the young leaves are learning the soft mystery of whispered speech and a scented wave of chill air still flows from the edge of the woods, when the ultimate purpose of all this stupefying enchantment is still not clear, but everything has already had its first taste of the honey of life, and the untrodden grass is already warm in the sunlight, and no matter what may lie ahead, you want to race over it barefoot, forever on and on, till the heart stops beating! On that memorable day the weather had been hot since early in the morning, every living thing was panting for rain, and but for the rattle of wheels over the hard bumpy ruts, the world was utterly still. There were no tears, for one does not weep over a severed limb, but all took their leave of Matvei in their own fashion: the passers-by bared their heads and stepped back to the roadsides, a lark trilled briefly in the sky, and on the chinky wooden bridge, where Matvei had once astonished the world by pushing a hay cart out with his shoulder when it got stuck there, every loose plank bade farewell to the dead man.

All went to the graveyard empty-handed except Ivan, who, to the gnawing envy of Demidka Zolotukhin, carried the icon. Demidka kept offering his services to help carry the holy object—just thirty-five paces, he begged; and although Ivan knew that one ought to share one's pleasure with others, he also knew that Demidka would not let him have it back again.

"Isn't it heavy?" Demidka asked at every five steps.

"Oh, middling ... so-so," Ivan said with a slow-witted air of evasion.

The cart with Matvei was drawn by Zolotukhin's docile white mare, who was waving off the pestering gadflies with her tail, while a skinny foal ran alongside, raising its head from time to time to wonder what that black strange man was doing in the master's cart. Thus Demidka, too, through his father's property, was taking part in that outstanding event. When Matvei legged, the boys would treat themselves to peppermint cakes and jointly examine the icon. An ancient little fellow with a black sackcloth on his head that had a white cross on it threatened them mildly with two fingers not to lark about while doing a serious job. The church smelt sadly of faded birch branches. The priest delivered a not very intelligible sermon on the virtue of humility and the vice of disobedience. Matvei was lowered into the hole by ropes and gently deposited on the yellow sand at the bottom. At this juncture the edge of the belated thunderstorm fired two shots in the air with the sound of an old blunderbuss.

"Don't mind the people, my dear woman, have a good cry, easen your heart," the priest said to Agafya, who was numb with grief, as he took off his wet stole, trying to wring relieving tears from the widow's eyes. "He is far better off than we are, he has nothing more to worry about, and maybe he'll be able to get his message through there! All obstacles are behind him now!" he said, pointing to the arrested clouds, now pink-tinted after the thunderstorm, which resembled the wide-open doors of a great hall, whither Matvei, as Ivan then pictured it, directed his steps with the long stride of the wanderer.

Ivan Vikhrov, by the way, never mentioned this episode in his questionnaires so that nobody should think he was trying to use his father's adventures to whitewash his own activities.

3

It was with Ivan sharing his funeral cakes with Demidka that their intimacy started; during the next few years it grew into a fast friendship. Demidka was only two years older, and both had been left to grow up by themselves without a father's care. Old Zolotukhin, who regarded his family as so many unpaid work hands, had not yet put the youngest one to work making money for him because he was so obviously unfitted either for sitting behind a wagon horse or behind a desk. The intimacy between the boys grew from day to day. The long-armed, big-mouthed Demidka admired Ivan for his flair for nature—a wonderful gift, as natural as hazel eyes, say, in other people, or hardness of heart towards one's neighbour, or supernatural fleet-ness of foot. Ivan could sit for hours watching the habits of the woodpecker, or the milling crowds of the ant cities scattered without number throughout Zapolosky. Everywhere he had a nest, a burrow, or a bee hollow which he had spied out, and if the course of his activities demanded it, he would go into the forest and unerringly, as if reaching for something on the shelf at home, find some nestling, or some strange caterpillar—it may even be that they let themselves be caught, knowing that no harm would come to them at his hands. But while Ivan was content with his disinterested knowledge of Nature's secrets, Demidka brought into all their undertakings a touch of mercantilism, albeit of a still childish innocent nature. A growing courage, a training in physical endurance provided by a three-mile walk in any sort of weather to the parish school, and a slakeless thirst for discovery led them into the wider fields of geographical exploration.

Like the human race at their age, they felt cramped, and were seized with an urge to expend their surplus energies on conquering the great unknown. Thus arose the idea of penetrating beyond Oblog, to the Edge of the World.

It was, in point of fact, a challenge to all the dark forces of the forest and the night. For it was on the border of Oblog and Pustosha that there dwelt Kalina Timofeyevich, a fearsome creature of gigantic stature and quaint deviltry of a kind that was particularly hazardous to the merchantry. An old wives' bogy tale to keep children from straying had, in the course of time, worked itself up into an elaborate legend to the effect that old man Fedos, going forth betimes to perform his blessed labours, did discover a goodman lying on the riverslope with a sword gash in his side, and that he turned out to be no other than the right-hand man of Stenka Razin, the famous outlaw, who had fled the tsar's executioner; and that man was Kalina. The more knowledgeable ones would have you believe that try as Fedos would to incline Kalina towards his soul's salvation by means of an exclusive nourishing diet of dew and blueberries, the man refused to relinquish his wicked ways. Indeed, shortly before the revolution mushroomers and hunters in Oblog would find skeletons of nameless representatives of trade and industry who had perished because of their gold on their way to the celebrated Loshkarev fairs; no wonder the grandfathers of Yenga's rich men would go miles out of their way to avoid an encounter with Kalina. Be that as it may, the evenings on the Yenga were long ones, and wood splinters for lighting were plentiful, and besides, old women were talkative when the year had been good for the crops, and the echo of heroic days, however faint, always finds a ready response in childish souls.

By that time both boys were familiar with the four rules of arithmetic and bewildering scraps of information from biblical cosmogony that only teased the imagination. Ivan had long been consumed with a desire to step within those forbidden precincts called the Edge of the World and to feast his eyes on the miscellaneous mysteries of creation, but he was afraid to go there by himself on account of Kalina, and confided to his friend what was already a ripened purpose to visit Pustosha.

"Just to take one peep, and then go back—otherwise you'll get giddy. It'll suck you down in a jiffy."

"Don't be silly! Who's going to suck us down?" Demidka said cockily.

"What about the Bottomless Pit?"

"The what?"

"Well, the Bottomless Pit. You know, the one they sing about in church."

"Oh, that!" Demidka said, balancing himself on one leg to see how long he could keep it up. "That's all right, old chap. I'll hold on to your heels from behind, so you can look as much as you want."

Suddenly he screwed up his left eye and licked his lips, the way he always did at the thought of profit.

"Whatsermatter?" Ivan asked anxiously.

"I was just thinking—what about lugging a sack along."

"What for?"

"In case we find any treasure. I bet you Kalina didn't blow in on Fedos empty-handed, he must have had a pot of money. Stenka was wallowing in the stuff. Why, he even chucked some of it overboard, it's a fact!"

They had both heard, without understanding its meaning, the old song about the ill-fated Persian princess who had been cast into the Volga as the chieftain's prize. Truth to tell, Ivan himself was not averse to accepting a ruble or two out of Stenka's treasures so as not to have Taisa go abegging; he was sorry for her. For a similar reason he thought they ought to take another pal along—Panka Letyagin, the poorest kid in the village for one thing, and the enviable owner of extraordinary physical strength for another, but Demidka was opposed to the idea, for it meant sharing with an extra partner. That saw the first rift in their relations.

They had intended to start out at daybreak so as to get back the same day, but Zolotukhin had warned his son the evening before that the oil bottles had to be washed, and while the boys were washing them by the river with sand and nettles, the dew had dried away. The sun was well up in the sky when they reached Oblog by way of the old Loshkarev highroad. Carts seldom passed that way even in the autumn, when the fairs were held, and now the place was disturbingly deserted. The cobblestone roadway plunged into the green haze of a clearing and was lost in a hollow, whence came the damp stagnant odour of a lurking place. One could understand the passing travellers who started to pray to St. Guri, St. Samon and St. Aviv three stages before they reached the purlieus of Kalina's haunt.

"I say, there isn't a trail in the woods," Demidka whispered, looking around fearfully. "Not even a thread."

Ivan pointed to a birch that stood all by itself. Long ago, and probably not without good reason, someone had hung up a rusty horseshoe there between the forked branches, and it was half-imbedded in the white flesh of the bark. It was here that the great passage to Pustosha began. Their path was barred at the very outset by a rotting stool, the grave of a forest giant, which had become the cradle of a hundred sprouting young firs. It crunched like a coffin and gave way under Demidka, who barely managed to pull his foot free, but then immediately beyond it, under the club-moss and litter, a trail came into view. It led the boys on obligingly, but kept twisting every minute, running in and out between animal holes, and bearing off into snug seductive little sloughs overgrown with meadow-sweet and valerian.

"Playing tricks," Demidka grinned, conscious of his own power. The forest here had a bedraggled appearance, with sodden tree trunks that looked charred at the bases, and a wild tangle of matted moss hanging down to the ground. It was pretending to be a beggar, who had nothing to give; one minute it would tempt you with a glimpse of ripe raspberries in a glade, then try to buy you off with a nest that had overgrown fledglings in it, or else try to frighten you with a tall juniper, which came blundering out from behind the roots of a fallen fir-tree like a dark-hooded monk. It was these simple tricks on the part of the forest that told them they were going right. Ivan walked on ahead with shining eyes, not missing a single sign in the ravelled writing of the forest—the fresh nibble marks of an elk on an alder, the heaped litter of a woodpecker's chiselling, or, all of a sudden, on a slope, a whole family of wood sorrels; and, as is always the case in the history of man, where, hard on the heels of the discoverer of wonderful continents strides the merchant with a calculating eye for gain, so did the masterful and enterprising Demidka, sack in hand, hurry silently after the boy Ivan.

They went along without speaking, until a halt was called, and then a heated argument arose as to the technique of the search. As everyone knows, the enchanted places on the Yenga are recognisable by the pale shoots of the scaly toothwort, and since heaps of them grow in the Yenga country merely as a blind (you have to choose only those that give off a bluish glow in the darkness and break the tops off right away if you do not want the earth to cleave asunder and swallow you up), there arose a natural anxiety as to the means of defence to be used against the evil spirit which kept watch and ward over ancient buried treasures; just in case, they took a mutual oath not to run away or yell at the sight of danger, no matter how ghastly and horned it was. Opinion was divided again on the question of how the money was to be used, Demidka insisting that before spending anything on lollipops and other such luxuries, they should buy a troika apiece, complete with harness and bells under a silver shaft-bow. Let them stand and wait against the time when their masters would grow up.

"What do you want a troika for?" Ivan said doubtfully.

"Why, we'll become coachmen! D'you know how much a merchant will cough up for a good spanking ride? Last summer one drunken fare of Ganka's came across with a diamond ring. He broke the wind of the horse, Ganka did, but Father didn't say a word!"

"And the diamond?"

"What about the diamond? Burns in the dark, you could light a cigarette by it."

"Spit your death!"

"I spit my death, may I drop down dead if I tell a lie! We hide it at night from thieves in a milk jug."

The temptation was very great. Ivan turned it over in his mind.

"Oh, they're a nuisance, horses are! You have to go out night grazing with them."

"We'll put Panka Letyagin on the job. He'd let himself be buried alive for twenty-five kopeks, he would! You don't want to give him too much, it'll spoil him. Anyway, it's better than begging alms under people's windows."

Ivan said nothing, but a sense of grievance for his meek comrade widened the rift in their friendship.

Gradually the green gloom broke and melted. The pine forest grew drier, and cheerful birch glades appeared here and there, bathed in the orange glow of the cooling sun. The peace of evening was descending upon the world. The trail began to dart hither and thither, then deserted the boys at a wide clearing, which shelved down into a dark echoing glen. On the other side, its resinous breath striking hot upon their faces, mysterious Pustosha rose upwards in shining terraces.

The pine forest began abruptly, without any underbrush. Trees of immense girth buttressed the sky there and it was not difficult to guess whose dwelling lay hidden behind that gigantean stockade.

Its master was preparing for sleep; a stricken old tree, visible from afar, blocked the entrance to his domains like a turnpike. The dreaded Kalina must have been warned of the approach of dangerous humans seeing that he had sent forward his flying scout party to intercept them. Every now and then pale-blue dragon-flies flew past, prophetic omens of quiet pools; bees flung themselves headlong into the blaze of fireweed around last-year's wood piles, while lordly-looking bumble-bees in velvet camisoles poked around in a leisurely fashion. A low strumming filled the pollen-drenched honeyed air. And sinister and aloof in tattered raiments of blue, like a witch at holy day, stood a blasted fir-tree; the trunk-length cleft creaked piteously, warning the boys for the last time to keep out of the fell clutches of the terrible Kalina. But retreat was cut off, night was treading upon their heels. They had eaten all their bread and were getting thirsty, but it was a full hour before their treasure-hunting instinct told them that they had reached the spot.

"How are we going to get back?" Demidka said, beginning to funk on the very threshold of success.

"Shut up, he may hear us, you never know."

Little by little the heat gave way to coolness, and the pine needles to leaves gilded by the glow of sundown. The shadows lengthened, the way back was blotted out. But the happy mistake of Columbus was repeated: instead of bags of gold, the boys discovered a new world. They came upon a tidy gully, from afar a quite ordinary-looking place with not a twig or piece of dead wood in it, with not a single flower on its warm cropped-looking grass, with not the twitter of a bird, as if even making a noise in this place were forbidden. Suddenly, a current of cold air fanned their faces, and with the thrill of the seeker the boys realised that they had stumbled upon the most important treasure in the region, perhaps in the whole world. A flat-topped boulder, obviously Kalina's feasting table, to judge by its great size, lay on the floor of the gully under an awning of ancient lime trees. The reflected glow of the distant spinney shone on its rugged lichened surface like splashes of blood from a slaughtered victim devoured there on the eve. Then the voice of running water called the boys below. They went down and stood with bowed heads, like pilgrims at a sacred shrine.

"There it is," Ivan whispered solemnly.

It was just a spring. Spring water gushing from under a stone in a crib no bigger than a child's hand. Every now and then it began to bubble with angry little squirts, as if threatening to run away, and at such times grains of sand could be seen eddying in its steady ceaseless pulsation. One could gaze at it for a hundred years without tiring. It was the source of a stream, and here, where it began, one could divert it with one's hand, but half a hundred paces farther down it sprang into independent gurgling life upon a pebbly bed.

It was the birthplace of the Sklan, the first tributary of the Yenga, which, in its turn, was the eldest daughter of the great Russian river whose waters cut the northern lowlands in two, so that half the country was sprinkled with the Life Water of this gully. Without it no children, no corn or songs are born, and one gulp of it had given our grandfathers strength for deeds of thousand-year glory. No earthworks or fortress walls could be seen anywhere, but all the possessions of the state—its boundless tilths, its vast libraries and mighty industry, its forests and mountains on the borders—served that spring as a bulwark of protection. It was to keep any impious foot from treading these precincts and befouling this pure spring that the people were building their impregnable ramparts of the spirit, and of strength, keeping grim armies upon their frontiers, and putting all that was dearest to them on sleepless vigil. Ivan grasped nothing of this that evening, but never afterwards did he feel so insignificant as he did then in the presence of that seemingly defenceless little spring, nor did he ever experience such a thrill of pure delight.

When the wonder of it was over, the boys drank their fill on their knees, then drank again—drank for a lifetime, because there was naught else they could take away with them from here.

"Just gushing out of the ground—could you beat it!" Demidka said, wiping his mouth with his sleeve. "What would happen if we was to plug it up?"

"It would bust up the whole earth. It's terrible strong!"

Suddenly the silence was broken by the call of a woodpecker. Another winged sentinel answered the cry, then a third. They were warning some invisible master about these rude intruders. Now they were in for it. A faint murmur rippled across the tree-tops. The forest was plunged in sudden darkness; a mist crept up, and the boys shivered with cold, the cold of fear. Weird fancy-bred shapes loomed in the darkness, now a huge hairy nostril, which seemed to have sniffed out the scent of human trespassers, now a half-shut lidded eye staring past you with deceptive guile. Awaiting the dread workings of doom, the boys huddled together so closely under their sack covering that were it not for the more potent events of the years to come no power on earth could have parted them as long as they lived.

Something in the darkness laughed at the boys' unenviable lot. "There, d'you see it?" Ivan whispered, gripping Demidka's knee.

"Where?"

"Leaning against that trunk ... with a horse's head. Look!"

Demidka looked and shuddered.

"Oo, it's coming for us. We're done for. Don't breathe now, for God's sake!"

To begin with, two trees visibly changed places, and the whitish murk hanging on the bushes like drying nets became torn in places, forming gaps. Then a long semi-transparent body came into swaying motion over the stream and approached the boys, assuming, as it did so, ordinary human shape. It was a relief, though, to find that the horse's head was just a white beard. The big boss must have thought it not worth his while to leave his lair for such a trifle, and had sent his assistant out instead. The latter was probably working for him as a sort of steward, like old Averyanich at the Sapegin manor.

The figure came up and bent over the boys.

"What are you doing there, sitting like a couple o' mushrooms in the road?" the under-boss said not at all sternly, scratching himself under his shirt in anything but the manner of an evil spirit.

"We're drinking water, Grandpa," the treasure-hunters answered both together as sweetly and placatingly as they could.

"And I thought, bless my heart, if this isn't two mushrooms for the frypan! Well, I never! Just sitting there like twinlets!" And he touched Ivan's head, which ducked quickly. "What are you shivering for, young 'un?"

"It's the damp," Ivan said miserably. "We feel a bit chilly."

"Come along inside and warm yourselves. I'll fix you up for the night." He waited, then craftily mentioned something about a special jar of honey, than which nothing more flavoursome could be found in all the world, but the boys didn't care to sizzle on Kalina's frypan. "You've lost your tongues, I see?"

"We can't," moaned the doomed souls.

"How's that?"

"We're scared of Kalina—he'll be wild."

"Why should he be? I am Kalina," the under-boss laughed, and the boys realised that resistance was futile.

During the conversation the old man kept stepping back and drawing closer and so the boys got a good view of him. He looked just like a human being, bald and barefoot, in a long shirt girdled with a piece of string; big dew-washed human feet showed whitely in the grass. But then who didn't know that the magic power of the forest lord lay in just this ability to assume any shape at will, from that of a wolf to a shower of rain, and as for making himself small that was easy as easy to him, otherwise you'd never have been able to shout up to him! You couldn't run away now, and even if you could it was dangerous because you might topple into the abyss on the edge of the world; what's more, that mention of honey had roused the boys' interest.

"We may be only kids, but we're baptised Christians," Demidka said pointedly, intending this both as a warning to the evil spirit and a hint that their unripened souls were sourer than wood apples.

"And I'm not a forest chunk, either, thank goodness! Come along, get up there, or you'll drink up all my water," Kalina said, starting off straight through the woods.

He walked in the lead, the starlight glimmering on his bald head with a drowsy effect. The captives trudged along behind, barely dragging their feet, which caught in the tree roots and club-moss. Their recent terrors were completely drowned in an over-powering desire for sleep. In after years, whenever things went hard with him, Vikhrov would recall the wild beauty of that nocturnal pine forest, the slumberous silence filled with the whisperings of the pines, the blind-eyed little hut with a heap of straw on the floor, and a little before that, an iron dipper with spring water in which a star lay floating and rippling, and a hunk of rye bread with a lump of old honey so thick and delicious that even to this day Vikhrov's fingers would feel sticky and his eyelids grow heavy with sleep at the memory of that late supper at Oblog.

They slept the sleep of doughty heroes, and for their awakening Kalina had in store bird songs as blithe as your tinkling bells under the shaft-bow. But when the guests, in the morning, floated out of sleep like swimmers in cold midstream, all the spells of the night before were broken and the ardour of the treasure-hunter dampened. There was no sign of the forest lord in the hut, and all his royal possessions lay there in full view—a linen towel by the door, a sheepskin on a nail, a bee-smoker and a hatchet under the bench, and other household odds and ends with the smell of an old beehive about them. And gleaming there on the table was a glazed earthen bowl of honey over which, in a shaft of sunlight, circled three bees which had in some miraculous way got into the room through the cobwebbed little window. A black cross charcoaled on the door was the first humdrum detail to dim the romantic glory of Kalina in the eyes of the boys.

Keeping the forest hut in sight all the time, they explored the precincts. Itself resembling a beehive, the hut stood in a pretty pine-carpetted glade with fine stately trees all round it. The tallest of them with a girth of two men's armspreads towered over the board roof of Kalina's dwelling. This old monarch must have found Fedos alive when it first came into the world. Weighted with the burden of the centuries and broken up into islets, its crown dominated the whole of Pustosha. There was none of its age in all that vast forest, and obviously it was at its roots, if anywhere, that the buried treasure was to be sought. Kalina's sleek tom-cat, the size of a young lynx, watched all Demidka's stealthy movements. He pretended to be dozing, but yellow noon shone in the slits of his eyes, which were as green as gooseberries.

Demidka lost no time in confiding his suspicions about that cat to Ivan, whereupon it stalked off into the bushes with a pained sort of look and to the boys' astonishment promptly reappeared in the shape of Kalina carrying a bucket of water. The gentle bees snuggled up to him—he was one of themselves and he was sweet. Making out as if nothing had happened, the old man went inside for some honey, cut up bread and onions on the doorstep, and sat down to share his meal with his guests.

"Here comes Maria Yelizarovna hurrying to join us," he remarked as a squirrel shot down the trunk of the tree like a stone out of the cool blue heights. "Sit down, beastie, and behave yourself in human company," he added, tossing it a piece of bread as it squatted on the lower step. "And whereabouts do you come from, my bonny lads?"

"We're from Krasnovershya, Grandpa," Demidka said, staring at the squirrel spellbound.

"Ah! I haven't been in Krasnovershya for many a long day, ever since they killed poor Matvei. He was a good pal o' mine, used to drop in pretty often."

"Why, that was my Dad!" Ivan cried, overjoyed at the direct intimacy thus established with this lord of the forest, who was so kind and slow only because after his thousand years of life he was too mighty to be angry with anyone and had nowhere to hurry to.

"Well, well, isn't it surprising how beginnings and ends meet! He didn't have his match for strength . . . you don't take after him, though. Mother's son, eh?" Kalina chuckled and extracted a drowned bee from the honey bowl. "Yes, I knew Matvei when he was still a forest ranger. He was working for Sapegin at one time, but they fired him because he was too easy with the peasants. Such a quiet chap, he was, too, as mild as they make 'em. They shot him here, at my place," he said, jerking his head towards the sleeping berth on the stove with a heap of sackcloth on it visible through the door. "He must have been pretty homesick out there in Siberia to make him break jail. They got on to his tracks, worse luck. If it hadn't been for the guards' gun, they would never have got him. I got it hot too. Fikin near blew my head off. 'D'you know what I can do to you, damn your bloody eyes!' he yells at me. 'You've been harbouring a criminal, you have—that's to say, giving him shelter.' And he glared at me like he was going to slash me up to bits. Thank God he's quick at cooling down, though. He fetched me a couple o' cracks, of course, it's only natural, but then he quietened down, and started tucking in the honey. May God send him good health!"

Fikin was the local chief of the police, the terror of the Yenga, and next after the Tsar and Kalina in power and importance as far as the boys were concerned.

"Did he hit you hard?" Demidka enquired, revealing a practical interest in the matter.

"Oh, just wiped my whiskers a couple o' times. You can't blame him, he's got a boss over him too, and a mouthful o' teeth for knocking out—not like me! He's not a bad sort though, quite a decent well-spoken gentleman, I should say."

Ivan heard out this confession with a sense of keen disappointment, but consoled himself with the thought that had Kalina been a hundred years or so younger he would have swung that Fikin sky-high and cracked him down to earth badge, buttons and all. But Kalina's legendary thews were sadly weakened, his back, which had been the prop of the Russian state for so many centuries, was bent, and his *bylina*-sung derring-do had petered out into an old man's feeble admonitions. For the first time Ivan felt a stab of pitying surprise at Kalina's unresentful memories.

"And whose boy will you be, son?"

"Me? The Zolotukhins'," Demidka answered absently, the while he stroked Maria Yelizarovna. She was so tame that she was sniffing something out in his sleeve.

"Ah, the son and heir, I see," murmured the old man, who had heard about the moneyed man of Krasnovershya who was on the make. "Carrying a bag around with you, eh? You'll be a tradesman, live a lonely life, you will. Poverty brings people together, wealth keeps them apart! In your old age you'll be wanting to hang an iron padlock on all creation, but it's not the thief who fears locks—he'll gnaw 'em away with his teeth if he's hungry—it's the master. I'll tell you something, and you mark my words. Soon as you've made a pile o' gold, you just go and give it the slip one dark night. It'll start looking for you, but you just hide yourself, sit it out under a bush. It'll kick up a dust, and whimper a bit, then go off in search of some other poor devil who's his own enemy."

"Why should I, money keeps you warm, they say!" snickered Demidka.

"It's warmest of all when someone else's house is burning!" the old man said, shaking his head ruefully. "Ah, well, warm yourself, if the sun isn't enough for you."

Thus was revealed Kalina's utter ordinariness. There was nothing mysterious about him at all. He was just an old tsarist soldier Kalina Glukhov, who, by the grace of Sapegin, made a bare living out of his twenty bee-hives, and sold all his honey in Loshkarev, on the other side of Pustosha. And so the fairy-tale crumbled, and the Edge of the World, if not lost to the boys for good, had retreated farther westward. But while one of them was experiencing the sad pang of a child's first disappointment, the other kicked loose from the restraining traces.

Demidka seemed to have straightened his back that morning, as though he had at last been untied. He was coming home with a prize. Something in his bag struggled and scratched, demanding to be let out, but he would give it a hard masterful shake, and the movement within would cease. Maria Yelizarovna was paying for her guileless trust towards people.

"Show me," Ivan said, and he stood for a long time guiltily examining the blunt whiskered little muzzle with the quick bright eyes looking up at him from the depths of the bag. "When did you manage it?"

It appeared that Demidka had taken her while the old man was showing Ivan over his droning kingdom, and had hidden her in a tree hollow, which he had covered up by leaning a heavy butt log against it.

"That's enough, she'll run away," he said, twisting the bag top with a proprietary air.

"You ought to let her go, it's a shame!" Ivan said, holding on to the bag with a death grip.

"Don't be silly, man, that squirrel's got a price. You're much too soft from what I see. You've got to be tougher for this life," Demidka said, licking the fresh bites on his hand. "Don't worry, the old man'll get himself another one."

"It's a pity, she's a living thing after all!"

Demidka wrenched the bag out of his friend's hands with ease, using his obvious advantage of age and strength for the first time.

"So's a fish, yet you eat it."

"I'm sorry for the fish too."

The boys discovered that they had gone a roundabout way the day before, and that the short cut was only a two hours' walk to Kalina—still less if you ran. Instead of Ivan it was Demidka now who headed the procession home with the booty on his back. Towards the end of the journey a plan of commercial operations had matured in his mind, and when they came within sight of the village backyards he turned off on to the country track leading to the Sapegins' manor. Out of sheer boredom the people there would buy everything that the women and boys from Krasnovershya and other villages brought them, even bunches of wild flowers. Demidka had no doubts that his squirrel, too, would come in useful in that strange household of theirs.

4

The boys found the familiar gap in the white stone garden wall, crossed the avenue of larches with a neglected pond at the bottom of it, and came out through the park on a lawn facing the veranda, which was thickly entwined with honeysuckle. Their coming was obviously ill-timed, as the Sapegins had a visitor— the great Knishev himself, though wherein his greatness lay no one on the Yenga yet knew. By the coach-house, hitched to an iron-wheeled rug-covered droshky, a restive bay stood munching oats and flicking his tail to keep the gadflies off. This time there was no one to shoo the boys away; it was as if everyone in the place—servants, dogs and all—had hidden themselves away from the Sapegins' ferocious guests.

Vikhrov could not remember, it being such a long time ago, whether Pashka Letyagin, whom they had met on the way, had joined them too, or whether it was only Demidka and he who sat waiting there interminably on the bench outside the veranda, whence came the table clatter and snatches of muffled conversation the drift of which they did not understand until much later. The usual bargaining was going on inside, with trickery and guile, feigned exasperation and idle mutual threats, although the parties, exhausted by the heat, were equally anxious to close the deal. "Wait a minute, Sofia Bogdatyevna, let me get a word in," said a hoarse voice that sounded as if it came out of a cellar. "I've had a good look at that wood o'yours. Titka and I spent the whole morning going over it. How much did we make it, Titka?"

"All depends on how you figure it. If you want to oblige a lady, seeing all those children she has and no man about the house, I dare say you could make it just a little under seven thousand dessiatins," came another jarring apathetic voice, obviously belonging to the buyer's steward. "If you asked me, though, I wouldn't handle a timber lot like that if you gave it to me for nothing. But it's not my money, I should worry."

"Oh, but gentlemen," came the distressed voice of an elderly woman, evidently the mistress. "I have official papers for the forest, I hired a working-plan officer to make the survey. There's at least nine thousand dessiatins of pine alone, not counting the lime-tree stands back of Gorinka, which make another two thousand."

"The trouble with your dessiatin, Sofia Bogdatyevna, is that it's such a small 'un. Why, in Europe two thousand dessiatins is a whole kingdom. I don't care for your lime trees, you can keep 'em, I'll only use the bark. As for the papers, why, I could get you a paper like that for a tenner any day, proving you was General Skobelev himself, whiskers and all!" the hoarse voice went on blandly with an appreciative titter from Titka. "Excuse me for speaking plainly, ma'am. See that, Titka, she's filling up our glasses again. She's as cunning as they make 'em. What's the use of arguing, we can pace it out again. Start first thing in the morning, Titka . . . and take the lady along with you, have a stroll together."

"My legs are my own, cost me nothing," agreed the steward, yawning audibly to indicate his utter lack of interest in the whole affair. "We can go over it again."

"Very well, have it your way," the mistress began again, "let it be only eight. But I'm hard up for money, and I'd like to know how much I shall get cash down. Even at seventy cubic metres to the dessiatin, say...."

"For God's sake, how do you make it seventy, Madam?" Titka groaned in a voice of mock pleading. "Why, with God's help, you might be able to scrape together forty at the outmost."

"Oh, please!" Knishev's victim moaned as if under the highwayman's knife. "Have you no conscience at all, gentlemen? How can you do that to a poor widow? You'll make me seek the protection of the law."

"Oh, you'd better let sleeping dogs lie, ma'am. It's not as if we went for you with bludgeons, is it? We'll take ourselves off in peace, my dear, there's no need to wake the law. Are you stuck to the floor, Titka, or what? Get up, you oak stump, and thank the lady for the refreshments. Come along!"

There was a sound of shifting furniture, a shuffling of feet and helpless feminine sighs.

"Please, gentlemen, sit down, I wish you'd try to put yourself in my place. I've told you everything, as if I were at confession! So many payments are falling due, and bank interest, I don't know what to do. On top of it all I have small grandchildren on my hands, and a son-in-law who's off his head—turn away, children, don't listen. A real psychopathic case!" she repeated with such an air of martyrdom that it would have been sheer heartlessness on the part of the merchants not to raise the price. "Let us work it out roughly. Even if we accept your figure ... say, eight thousand dessiatins at forty cubic metres ... let's say even at five rubles ... all right, even four fifty per sagene.* Add it up on a piece of paper, Koko, what does it amount to? And stop pinching Lenochka, you ought to be ashamed of yourself, a grown up man like you!"

There was a pause, and then a faltering childish voice announced that the sum due for payment was one million three hundred and forty thousand, which showed, in turn, that the grown man was none too strong in his arithmetic.

"There," the mistress said in a small voice, and it was clear to the boys outside that she was beaten.

"Such a raft o' money exists only in Yevtushevsky's sums book, my dear lady," the buyer rasped. "Don't count your profits, count

---

* Sagene—equal to 7 feet.—*Tr.*

my losses. Over two thousand dessiatins is nothing but slash—what the devil am I going to do with it—use it for my samovar? We hardly drink any tea as it is!"

"Dangerous stuff, tea—we don't touch it!" guffawed the steward.

"And then the wood's full o' fail places, and clearings, and the trees are set upon by beetles. I don't want a wood to go mushrooming in, my dear woman. I want timber for sleepers so's people can travel over them. If you want to know there isn't any real merchantable stuff there at all."

"You should have seen the oak we cut in Volyn, down at Count Chernyshov's place—now that was timber!" Titka threw in. "When you looked up—why, Jesus Christ, it took your breath away! It was like hacking at the roots of your own father, but here...."

"Shut up, Titka," the buyer cut him short. "You talk about the forest, but have you ever been in there yourself, ma'am? Everything in Russia is called forest where the scythe and sickle have nothing to do. But Russia's forest was measured by a St. Petersburg official sitting in his armchair in a dressing-gown and using a pair of compasses and a map. It's all just burn and swamp, punky wood, windfalls and small pole wood, and even that is sometimes at the back of beyond, you can't get at it. By the time you haul it down to the wood-yard you'll have a beard that long, get me?"

"Oh dear, you're falling upon me from two sides," the mistress cried frantically.

"It's your own fault, you shouldn't have given us that liquor. This forest has been stolen from the local muzhiks anyway—we heard about that suit o' yours. I'm no better than what you are, a thief, buying stolen goods. And may God help us if the red cock starts crowing in Russia*—we'll both swing on the same rope, my dear lady. Licking honey off a razor, that's what we're doing. Here's my offer: after paying the bank loan and brokerage, I'll give you forty thousand cash down, and mind your son-in-law doesn't get at it, or he'll blow it all on the booze. Your job's to grease palms in the gubernia, mine's the axe. The rest of the money, a hundred and fifty thousand, you'll get by the New Year. I give you till tomorrow to think it over, otherwise I'll pull out for the Don."

---

* An expressive Russian saying meaning wilful fire-raising.—*Tr.*

"Aren't you being too free with your money, sir? You'll be losing on the deal!" Titka wormed in.

"Oh, well, never mind—I'm sorry for the kids! God will reward us for our kindness, I daresay. Now fill the glasses, ma'am, and have 'em serve us up an omelette—we're perishing with hunger."

Thus it came about that the famous Oblog on the Yenga was sold to the axe. The sumptuous splendour of the manor, which seemed an enchanted paradise to the boys, had long borne traces of advanced decay. The abolition of serfdom, which deprived the nobility of free labour power, had compelled the late Sapegin to mortgage his estate in order to introduce the latest innovations in agriculture, according to the fashion of the age; they were to have made his fortune, but they did not. When he died everything started rolling downhill. Infectious disease carried off his pedigree stock, the greenhouse with its trellised apricots fastened to the walls collapsed, and the rotting timber began to show through the crumbling plaster in a corner of the drawing-room. The lilac alone flourished, running riot in the spring and spreading a thick heady aroma around; it crowded out the flower-beds and crept out into the paths, smothering the half-ruined nest of the gentry. The old steward Averyanich, the right hand and eye of the late Sapegin, took to drink, and so the management of affairs passed into the hands of the widow, who had come over from Pomerania as a bride during the master's university years. She was a doughy, sickly lady, who could do little else than count the silver spoons and lock the shutters up at night against imaginary evildoers. Her chief wealth consisted of declining timberland which nobody in that region needed. Rumours that a railway was soon going to be run through Loshkarev to Vologda gave her a last chance to get out of her difficulties. Knishev, albeit a drunken Knishev, was a godsend to the unfortunate widow.

It was the proper thing now to wet the bargain, but as there were only women and children at the table, and Titka knew better than to drink while on duty, the guest celebrated by himself for each in turn, and soon reached a point of saturation when it became necessary either for him to be carried out to the hayloft or for the rest of the company to seek the fresh air. And so all the Sapegins trooped out on to the wooden porch steps, the rickety banisters of which were smothered in cascades of blossomless honeysuckle.

The procession was headed by the mountainous old mistress in a lilac lustrine skirt with purple blotches of recent perturbation covering her sallow unhealthy face. She lived her life out at the manor in complete seclusion as it was only during the summer holidays that her daughter with her sons from the ill-starred marriage came to stay with her. They were walking now at their grandmother's side, both short-cropped boys in duck school-jackets with blue circles round their eyes. Ivan saw the elder one pinning a yellow gadfly on a straw out of languid curiosity, while the younger absently chewed a blade of grass. "They're not long for this world," Demidka sneered.

The old lady was annoyed at having strangers there at such a time, even though they were children; she querulously enquired of a passing housemaid whether Averyanich was about, but no, Averyanich had not shown up yet after he had "got plastered" the night before, as the maid expressed it.

"Well, boys, what have you got there?" the mistress asked from afar.

"A squirrel," muttered Demidka, pulling his cap off, and thus immediately disposing the old lady in his favour.

"And what do you want?" she said, turning towards Ivan.

"We're all together," answered Pasha Letyagin, who, having joined them on the way, thus became a party to the sale of Maria Yelizarovna.

The five Sapegins, not counting the housemaid, clustered round the sellers, the fifth one being a girl of about five in a shabby dress that had once been pink, and a face decorated with coloured rings and stripes that puzzled Ivan. One of the boys with the aid of a box of children's paints had made her up to look like a red Indian. Her name was Lenochka. She, too, was eager to have a look at the little forest beast, but all her attempts were in vain until it occurred to her to sandwich herself between the legs of the older schoolboy. She was rewarded with a smart flick on the head between the pigtails, and crawled back uncomplainingly to the croquet lawn—she was accustomed to an inferior position in the house.

"Show me your squirrel," commanded the younger lady with a nose so dismal and long that by the time one's glance got to the tip of it one had to go back again to remember the beginning.

Bravely, albeit flinchingly, Demidka thrust his hand into the bag and pulled Maria Yelizarovna forth by the scruff. She did not struggle, as she did not know that every living thing here was fondled to death, then buried with suitable chantings in a tiny graveyard that contained all the former pets of the Sapegin boys. Demidka held the squirrel securely and squeezed it slightly— not to avenge the bites, but to make the young masters want to relieve it quickly of its sufferings. They all started pleading with Demidka not to hurt the poor creature, and the unequal duel continued until the weaker gave in. The boys' mother permitted them to spend the contents of their money-boxes, adding in German that here was a chance for them to learn how to make trade deals with the peasants.

"How much does it cost?" the younger asked sweetly, gazing affectionately at the furry little red ball with its limp tail.

Thereupon the older boy tossed the gadfly up into the air—it flew away with its load—and pushed his brother aside with a businesslike air.

"I say, is that a good squirrel you have there?" he began, his thumb under the buckle of his belt.

"Top notch, fierce as anything—I had to tear her off the tree. The blood I lost—buckets of it!" Demidka said, and showed his bitten hand to raise the price of his merchandise.

"Oh, it bites?" the younger said, drawing back.

"Nothing o' the sort," Demidka said, looking down at his feet contemptuously. "I hurt myself while I was going after her." The lie was a timely one, as the squirrel's bad temper was likely to scare away the customers. "She's as gentle as anything. Maria Yelizarovna, her name is."

The household went into a huddle as to where the squirrel was to be kept. The grandmother suggested the cage of a recently deceased goldfinch, but the young generation was for keeping Maria Yelizarovna on a thin wire round the neck so that she could run about.

"Can you wash her with soap?" the younger one asked innocently while the others were still arguing.

"With soap?" Demidka said, pondering the question with the air of a connoisseur. "Why, yes. She'll live in a barrel so long as you feed her. Eats anything except cucumbers. Little animals shouldn't be given bones, though, they're liable to choke."

Ivan felt, not exactly disgusted—he had not yet grasped the essence of private commerce—but ill at ease. At first his attention was drawn to Titka who, in a seedy frockcoat, had crept out into the open so as not to foul the manorial chambers with the smoke of *makhorka*.* He was a dried-up old rascal with a squashed in face and such protruding lips that it was a wonder how Nature had managed to achieve such a remarkable effect. He was sauntering up and down the veranda, maliciously picking the flaking paint off with his finger-nail. And suddenly, as though by some force outside himself, Ivan found himself drawn to Lenochka, who, forgotten by all, was seated contentedly on the croquet lawn, playing with a handful of unripe elderberries which she had collected in her lap.

Ivan shook his head judicially.

"You mustn't eat that, people die from it and are laid away in the yellow sand," he said, taking the berries away from her by right of seniority and throwing them into the bushes. "Who did that to your face, poor kid?"

"The boys," the little girl answered meekly.

"Go and wash it off, it isn't nice, people are looking at you," Ivan said, sensing in her a kindred soul.

"What do you like best of all in the world, tell me, I'll get it for you."

"A birdie," the girl smiled, gazing dazzlingly into his very soul.

And for that single blue gaze, for that slight, barely conscious pang of childish sympathy he took that imperturbable drabbletail to his heart with the love of a lifetime, as he had Kalina Glukhov and his forest spring.

"I'll bring you a barn owl, then. I've got my eye on one. But you'll have to feed him with mice. You can catch 'em easy, though. I'll let you have it for nothing," he added in a gruffer tone of masculine dignity. "Can you get away and come to the pond tomorrow at this time? Will you come?"

The owl was an excellent specimen with great claws, quite a frightful bird although still a baby; through the heavy plumage of mottled grey and white one could feel the tiny body of a sparrow. Ivan waited by the pond till nightfall, and trod quite a trail in the grass, but the woman did not keep the date. It was not until seventeen years later that they met again.

From then on Demidka became the royal contractor to the young scions of the manor. He caught birds for them in glens and at drinking places, covering up the brook with faggot-wood and leaving a tiny patch over which he set a scrap of fishing

---

* *Makhorka*—a strong home-grown tobacco.—*Tr.*

net. His captives needed food, and having been taught from childhood to profit by the humility of the disinherited, he scattered ant heaps in the clearings and made the little toilers collect their choice yellowish eggs for him on a piece of spread canvas. He sold sparrows and finches for nightingales, cultivating by experience the art of commercial deceit, which enabled him to charge four times as much as he had spent on the light labour of capture. Before the astounded gaze of the manor boys, he bailed fishes out of the ooze in the Sapegin pond with leeches clinging all over him, and he never sold anything on credit; when the customer was out of pocket, he would accept anything by way of payment from steel nibs to Byzantine coins filched from grandpa's numismatic collection. And although they did not pass current in the taverns of the empire, Zolotukhin senior looked on with approval while his favourite offspring was cutting his first shark's teeth. In this encounter between the two rival classes each side hated the other, but Demidka was the stronger: he met the sneering arrogance of the sickly mollycoddled young masters with the smouldering hatred of the muzhik.

Ivan spent the rest of the summer at Kalina's; his mother got out of the habit of calling him for his supper. Their day started at dawn, when the first jets of sunlight pierced the moist bluish haze of the sombre forest just as the birds began their roll-call. The old man and the boy went over their realm, noiselessly spying out the news—how Mr. Badger was faring in his barrow, or how the little sister of poor Maria Yelizarovna was moving into her new house in four stages, each time with a baby in her teeth—the age-old litter of pine needles muffled all sound of human footfalls. They usually followed the same route, but in the forest, as in a good book, one can always find an unread page. Here, on the trail, Kalina taught his young friend how to forecast the weather by the dew, and the harvest by the roots of the forest herbs, and other secret lore of the forest in which was concentrated the thousand-year-old experience of the people.

The journey terminated at the high buff of the Yenga. There was a point of land there, known to few, overgrown with cat's paw. Far below, where the sandbanks gleamed through the thin sheet of water, a little tugboat was dragging a family of motley buoys away to their winter home, and a kite was hovering overhead with the blood-red glow of sunset on its wingtip. The fairytale was fading away before the march of autumn, and the world gradually grew bare.

The old man had long crossed the line beyond which difference of age becomes obliterated. Theirs was the short-spoken friendship of the old and the young, as free from the fear of separation as it was from all show of affected caress. The one was resignedly taking his leave of all that passed into the hands of the other. Kalina spoke little about himself, but from between the lines one could gather that he had drained his cup of life without flinching, and all would have been well but for a pinch of ground glass among the dregs. From these stories the Kalina of the fairy-tale ceased to be, and there emerged in his stead a lovable man of the flesh twice as dear to the boy.

"So you're not a holy man, Grandpa? So you'll die then?" Ivan said, disappointed.

Kalina would laugh and pass a leave-taking glance over the purpling woods across the Yenga where the leaves were beginning to fall, at the fields with stooked sheaves here and there that had not yet been gathered in, and farther out a fresh sand embankment of as yet unknown designation running out into the distance, with the town of Loshkarev on the horizon gleaming fifteen versts away with its foil-like windows. Kalina readily explained his creed to his young friend, a creed which Ivan Vikhrov eventually made his own. Were his words to be smoothed out to a bookish pattern they would tell us in effect that there was no god on Earth, but only a never cooling zest for life and the joys of a lucid mind, and at the end of it all a deep yellow grave-hole in which they are melted down into a still finer and nobler alloy. The old man, as usual, was weaving a wicker basket, while the boy lay on his back gazing up into the sky where a marshalled flight of cranes was calmly heading south, its leader a mere detached speck at the point of the wedge. It was difficult for a child's mind to grasp the wisdom of Kalina, but Ivan carried the golden glow of it away with him into life, and once he even tried to recapture it in St. Petersburg during an argument about personal immortality.

Kalina showed himself no less well-informed on matters that concerned the evil spirit. During his free and easy life in the capital, of which he had had a long spell, the old man had discovered that two kinds of devils existed, and that it was only the lower ones, those who sat in government offices, who were remarkable for their evil smell and unsightly pimples. The higher ones, those less accessible to the public view, were, on the contrary, often more than presentable in outward appearance and dwelt in brave houses, from which they levied tribute upon god-fearing souls in the shape of rich food, recruits for wars, wenches for dalliance, and wet-nurses for suckling their baby devils. Hence, they were to be recognised not by their tails, nor by the sulphury fumes that issued with their breath, but as a rule by the tribulations which they inflicted upon the common people. It would all come to an end, though, on the day of wrath, when the toiling people would have their wrongs redressed, and the evil spirits would vanish for ever. In reply to Ivan's innocent question as to whether holy water was any good against the Evil One, the old man said that wasn't a bad remedy at all, especially if you held him under long enough by the scruff of his neck.

"I wish I could take a peep at that evil spirit!" Ivan sighed, listening to the faint plash of the river down by the shallows.

"You wait, my lad, you'll see all you'll want of him!"

Indeed, the boy made his acquaintance before the winter was out.

5

The great logging operation at Oblog was launched in grand Knishev style. A month before it started, Titka made the rounds of all the surrounding villages and stood everyone a treat—even the old women got a glass. The railway people hurried the shippers. Sledging started early that autumn, and at foredawn after St. Dimitri's Day a thousand sledges made for Oblog from all over the district. After their spree the night before the peasants rode swaying, with slackened reins, and a buzzing in the ears; each had an axe glinting under his girdle. A fuzzy-looking sun was rising over the forest when the first pine stems began to fall upon the light snow. The lumbermen had not got into their stride yet; many of them stood about smoking and watching their more zealous brethren completing the squat cabins and tackle.

"Why don't you work, damn you! Come on, you woodpeckers, tap away!" Titka shouted himself hoarse alternately swearing and coaxing, driving and pleading; he dashed about so busily that the muzhiks, still suffering from their hangover, saw him in quadruplicate. "The first train will come and bring you heaps of goods. That's when we'll make whoopee, boys! Come on, stir about, my hearties ..." and he tanked his army up again with vodka.

It wanted but a spark to touch the fire off, and this done, things went roaringly. Zolotukhin sold out quickly and kept sending to Loshkarev to replenish his supplies.

"So that's why it wouldn't shoot—the gun wasn't loaded," a peasant would say, picking up his mittens or brushing his beard after downing a glass. "Now then, where's that greybeard of a giant!"

At sunrise a hail of steel attacked Oblog, a root searcher of a thousand thudding axes. A surging tumult shook the air for miles around, and the black bird of carnage rocketed up in clamorous flight over the field of massacre. For two days the forest stood its ground against the assault, as if fresh came up every night to take the places of those who had fallen; towards the end of the third day, when the lumbering gangs had hacked their way into the heart of the forest, Oblog wavered and began to fall back before the advancing axe. The felled trees were converted on the spot into full-squared sleepers or scantlings, or simply firewood, and sledged away into the frost-hazy distance, where before, at this time of the year, the wolf litters were learning to howl, and where now, unless one's ear deceived one, the whistle of a locomotive broke in upon the stillness of the forest. The felling season for pine is up to March, when the sledge road is still hard-packed, and Knishev was in a hurry as he wanted to tackle the lime-trees in May, as soon as the sap started running.

With the love of novelty peculiar to children, Ivan received the news of Oblog's destruction with heightened interest, but without fear for his old friend. Like all things of the forest at that season, the old man was probably fast asleep in his snowed up home, and one couldn't imagine even such a calamity rousing Kalina from his winter sleep. Suddenly at Christmas time a deep yearning drew Ivan into the forest. A cold snap had set in the evening before, and the road, bestrewn with bark and wisps of hay, presented a scene of festive animation. Strings of sledges loaded with timber were to be met on the road, the glassy tracks singing under their runners. Half-way Ivan was given a lift by Pashka's stepfather, who was returning with an empty sledge. The horse was a brisk, mousy little nag, and they reached the spot in no time. Oblog looked like a pencil drawing done heavily on tracing paper. Ivan walked the rest of the way.

A delicious smell of pine smoke and resin came from the felling area, where men were swinging axes, shouting at horses, dancing to keep themselves warm, disengaging tangled logs with crowbars, and burning the slashings in great docile bonfires. The snow-draped forest glowed pink and mysterious in the morning gloom. Shadows came to darting life every time a tree fell with a long gasp. The still figure of a bearded man with unblinking gaze was being carried out amid shouts—Oblog had lashed out at him with the fury of a pain-maddened beast.

The boy turned left, as if prodded in the shoulder, to where a similar gang was noisily operating in another part of the forest. A wide clearing sloping down into a hollow with clumps of underbrush sticking up on it here and there opened before his astonished gaze. This was not the Oblog he knew, and not until he had seen Kalina's hut standing darkly beneath it did he recognise the famous towering pine with its snowy dishevelled locks tossed in the sky. Men were crowding round it. Impelled by a fear of missing something very important, the boy dashed straight through the shambles, and tried to push his way through the human ring, under the elbows of the grown-ups.

"Hey, what's up with you, young scrub?" someone spoke down to him.

"I've come to see Grandpa Kalina," Ivan pleaded, and they let him through.

The lumberers were standing around in a crowd on the dark foot-thawed snow, staring at the old man with sullen suspicion, as if he were some forest wonder; he was sitting on a fresh stump outside his unheated cabin, the door of which stood wide open. His head was uncovered, and he looked kind of trim and young with his short sheepskin coat thrown over his shoulders; the coppery glow of his last sunrise was reflected on his bald head. Apparently a farewell talk was going on, but it was not this alone that had drawn the lumbermen to the spot. Inside the cabin was Knishev, fortifying himself with honey and mushrooms of Kalina's pickling. Knishev had come down to the Yenga in person to put things right. Everyone was keen to have a look at the famous lumber magnate who was said to have cleared half a million dessiatins and stripped the green mantle away from three great Russian rivers.

"So that's how it is, young fellow-me-lads," Kalina was saying in a quiet level voice, as though reading from a book. "What I'm getting at is this—the land will catch a chill without her green coat, and she'll be poorly for ever after. A cow will have to go seven versts after her bit o' grass, where afore she ate her fill off an *arshin*.* And you'll be having your summer without clouds, you will, and sometimes a winter without snow, and folks will curse that sun up there. And you'll be wanting to use a birch switch in the steam bath, but there won't be any to be had. And if you was to tell your grandchildren how there used to be stumps in the old days on which a man could stretch himself out, they won't believe you. And when you've cut down the last tree of Russia's forests, it's to foreign lands you'll be going to for your bread, my dears."

With watering unseeing eyes he looked round at the denuded space in front of him, at the edge of the doomed forest, and the faces of the peasants, Ivan's among them, and he no longer recognised his young friend. The same malevolent power which had robbed him piecemeal of his teeth, his joys, his fair locks, had now come for his soul. And again, to Ivan's great distress, there was neither resentment nor complaint in Kalina's speeches, only pity for those he was leaving behind.

"What's the use o' shaking heads now!" one of the men answered in the same valedictory tone, as though speaking from an opposite bank. "Once the job's started it's got to be finished."

And then Ivan saw Knishev, who had come out of the cabin accompanied by his retinue. He was a fairly tall man in his prime wearing a long pleated coat of blue cloth. His face, though, was puffy, and his slightly bulging eyes had the faded watery appearance which bespoke the avowed enemy of undistilled beverages. He wore a beard neatly trimmed after the fashion of his class, and would have made quite a brave picture but for his big ears, which resembled the grasps welded to an iron rammer for the convenience of handling. He was well in his cups, and heard out the end of Kalina's tale, picking the beeswax off his teeth with his little finger. On one side of him stood the short-legged Titka, his whole body leaning forward and his long arms hanging down his sides; on the other stood Zolotukhin, long-legged and emaciated in a self-devouring sort of way, with a beaked little head on a long neck and the drilling glance of bleary restless eyes. Although well advanced in years, he still had a lot of grey hair that concealed the bald patch. In deference to Knishev's acknowledged power, he stood bare-headed, holding his high-crowned heavy cap slightly away from him in his outstretched hand. He had attached himself and his sons to Knishev,

---

* *Arshin*—equal to 28 inches.—*Tr.*

that past master at prostituting forests for profit, not so much for the sake of making money as for learning the technique by which it was made. Both, Titka and Zolotukhin, ape and hawk, stood ready to spring to their master's orders.

"Oh, stop yammering, old man. Bewailing Russia before the time. And put your cap on, you bald old cuss, you'll catch a cold," Knishev said with a laugh, coming down the steps with a springy gait, and everyone's fears about a time coming when you would not be able to rake together a bath switch from all over Russia were banished. "Sitting there, keening over the dead, may God forgive me. I bet you wouldn't mind living on a bit longer yourself, eh?"

"Ah, children," Kalina confessed artlessly, "I'd count the sand grains by the seashore for you if only I could get a bit of extra time in this world! Mind you, I feel like I'd lived a thousand years, my legs are all wonky, yet I love life more'n honey!"

"Why shouldn't you live?" Zolotukhin put in patronisingly. "Seeing the way you're sitting there all alone and scaring folks into the bargain, you're not as old as all that."

"I'm young enough, the trouble is all those years have dropped on my shoulders."

"Well then, go on living. You've lived a thousand, now uncork the next—aren't I right, boys?" Knishev threw into the crowd, which made way before him amid a hum of approval. "Hi there, Titka, stand him one!"

A flat silver flask materialised in the dexterous hands of the steward. He filled the cup to the brim, and Kalina nodded his head at the sight of the old bosom friend; a sigh of relief went up in the crowd—the master had not denied the old man his share. Having put the ball in motion, Knishev fell silent and left it to his factotums to keep it rolling between them.

"I daresay you've seen a lot in your thousand years, Kalina?"

"Lots and lots, boys. I served in the cuirassiers, you know. Black horses with black saddles, and plumed brass helmets—we had to have a good outfit. Trumpeters always in front. It was a bit of all right, in the cuirassiers, bless your hearts. Then afterwards, a year afore the freeing of the peasants, we were promoted to dragoons.

"Did you do any fighting?"

"Well yes, I had a horse killed under me by a cannon ball in the Crimea. I wasn't half a lively card in my young days. I was the leading singer in the squadron, you know."

"You don't say so! You've got a gashed eyebrow, a sabre cut, I bet. Didn't you get that lame leg in the war, too?"

"Nay, that was later. The horse I was riding stumbled and my foot got stuck in the stirrup—we were clearing a hurdle under the eyes of the Tsar—this one's father, you know. By the way he doesn't look right in those portraits—he runs more to ginger-ish, if you ask me, with moustaches all the way round to the ears." For want of habit Kalina quickly got fuddled, and Ivan's heart bled at his pitiful tipsy garrulity. "Now let me tell you about the forest, children. . . ."

"Never mind the forest!" Titka cut him short. "You tell us something funny. I bet you got off with all the housemaids in St. Petersburg, now didn't you? Those city gals are hot stuff, eh?" he said, playing down to the crowd of poor peasants hired at twenty-five kopeks a day.

"Why dilly-dally with that kind," Zolotukhin answered for Kalina amid the half-hearted mirthless laughter of the men. "You can go the whole hog there all right!"

"I don't remember about that, it was such a long time ago. I had my brothers on my mind more than anything else," Kalina said evasively. "They all died while I was out there in Petersburg, clearing the tsar's hurdles."

"Were they taken ill, or what?"

"They'd been eating thistle during the famine. Crushed it and ate it. Must have overeaten themselves."

"Tut, tut, see what gluttony leads to," Titka was fool enough to blurt out, and the faces around him darkened and the very sun hid itself for shame.

With eyes full of tears Ivan stared down at the snow—this was the end of his fairy-tale. True, a good half of Oblog still stood intact, but with the death of that venerable pine which cast its shadow upon Kalina's roof the forest, as far as the boy was concerned, ceased to be. The tree could not be left standing there in the clearing, as the first snowstorm would knock it over and it would crush Kalina's cabin like a rotten nut.

"Now, then, my lads, make way there," Knishev said in an expressionless voice. "Let's get a warm up!"

To everyone's surprise, he threw off his coat and stood in an embroidered shirt, white as driven snow, girded with a silver-ornamented Caucasian belt. A dozen hands offered him a selection of gap-toothed filed down saws; but he chose an axe instead from the nearest man. He weighed it in his hand, tested the blade approvingly with his finger-nail—it twanged like a string—spat on his hands to keep the handle from slipping, stamped the snow down, stood still for a minute, listening to the murmur among the tree-tops, then leisurely, as if he were officiating on the scaffold, looked his victim over from head to toe. He was more beautiful than ever just then, was this old monarch of Oblog, standing there in all his ancient grace, straight as a ray and without a single flaw; the snow, like a roseate dream, lingered among his drooping branches. Knishev swung the axe back, and with only half his strength, teasingly, as it were, brought it down on the resinous butt where the roots ran up the trunk like veins, and the boy Ivan almost gasped with astonishment to see no blood spurt on the hands that wielded the axe.

"That's the way to do it," Zolotukhin said. "Look and learn!"

At first the axe rebounded from the frozen sap-wood, then suddenly a fury seized the steel, and a shower of wood chips the colour of bone filled the air. A straight narrow slit was cut into the face of the trunk without a single mishit, and now special skill was required to keep the axe from getting jammed in the wood. The axe's ringing blows steadily grew duller as the steel sank deeper into the trunk and resounded through the forest like the tapping of a woodpecker. A hush fell on the crowd. It seemed as though nothing could rouse the old giant from his winter sleep, then suddenly the breath of death stirred his foliage, and glowing snow dust poured down on Knishev's sweating back. Ivan did not dare to look up; out of the corner of a tear-filled eye he saw the silver pendant on Knishev's belt jump and joggle at every blow.

Unlike him all the others kept their eyes fixed on the merchant who brandished the axe, taking some long-needed exercise. Obviously, he could do that well. It was the only thing on earth he could do well. It was quite an ordinary felling job, really, but the loggers could not shake off a guilty feeling of being witnesses to a piece of wanton mischief, all the more enormous in that they were fully aware of the fatal issue it was bound to have. And although Knishev gave himself no respite, everyone understood that he was trying to prolong the pleasure, a thing that simple people could never forgive even a real executioner. To finish off the job, the merchant passed round to the other side: only a couple of strokes were now needed for the end-all. No one heard the last blow. Knishev tossed the axe away and stepped aside; he was steaming as if he had just come out of the bath-house.

Zolotukhin hurried up and threw his coat over his sweating shoulders, while Titka uncorked the unemptiable flask with a loud pop. The pine stood there as before, bathed in an aura of frost. It did not know that it was already dead.

Although nothing had changed yet, the lumberers backed away.

"There it goes," someone whispered over Ivan's head in a deadened voice.

It was clear to everyone that Knishev, too, had once earned his living by means of the axe, and it was interesting now to see what degree of craftsmanship he had attained. In slipping off its stump the falling pine was liable to cannon Kalina's nutshell of a hut out of existence. A barely perceptible stir was born among the branches, something crunched below and set up a quiver in the top. The pine began to heel over, and all sighed with relief; the second undercut was slightly above the first, and the trunk was taking a safe direction, its weight resting on the future "sloven" or hinge. Suddenly a storm whipped through its awakened crown, snapping branches and bringing down a mush of snow. There is nothing in the world slower than the fall of a tree under whose shade the dim dreams of childhood had visited you.

Without waiting for the end, trembling in every limb, Ivan wandered off to the overcut area. He came back when the fit of despair had spent itself. Kalina was nowhere to be seen, all the men had scattered, and some old fellow, out of idle curiosity, was measuring the stricken phenomenon of Nature with a stick for posterity, while Knishev, in an expensive fur-lined coat, stood on the doorstep lighting a cigarette. Even after so many years it was difficult to understand the fit of ungovernable fury that had seized the quiet peasant lad. But one thing must be assumed if we are to understand all that followed: when a man has a mission to fulfil, life leads him in his youth down skilfully chosen paths in order to cultivate in him the ability and the will to work through to his historical end. One can but guess what miracle it was that put Pashka's catapult into Ivan's hands, and who placed a pebble in them in snowy midwinter.

Knishev only had time to blow out his first cloudlet of smoke when Ivan's gratuitous missile landed on his cheek. Amid the ensuing confusion and torrent of profanity, Ivan, on a sudden inspiration, shouted out two abusive words which were afterwards to ring up and down the Yenga—and again it was a mystery as to who could have whispered into his ear the secret of Knishev's horrible disease. Titka rushed at the offender like a hound, and the boy made off towards the woods across the virgin snow. Youth had the advantage of agility, but in one place, while he was jumping over the slashings, Ivan's felt boot slipped off and he cut his foot open on a branch hidden under the snow. No more than ten paces lay between him and his pursuer, and Professor Vikhrov would assuredly have carried a torn ear through life had not a birch-tree leaning at a convenient angle appeared in his path just in the nick of time. The boy took it in his stride, and sat down in the fork as in a saddle, his teeth bared in unchildlike rage, while Titka stumped about below, licking the snow off his hand with a long tongue and threatening him with his finger until Knishev arrived on the scene.

"Come down, you wolf cub," the big one said, breathless with running and suppressed fury.

"Poxy nob!" the little one repeated, as if he knew that for Knishev, who prided himself on both his health and plebeian descent, nothing could be more insulting than this nickname.

"I'll get you if I have to cut the tree down!"

"Go away, poxy nob," the boy said, trembling in every limb.

At this point Titka took matters in hand.

"You keep an eye on him, sir, while I get a pole. We'll knock him off his perch in a minute, the brat."

Knishev looked at the boy narrowly. He took in the flashing eyes under the shabby cap, and the bare bleeding foot, which had turned slightly blue. Something had worked a change in the man's intentions: not that he felt any pity for the ragged little animal up in the tree; rather was it wonder that in the course of his whole depredatory career, this peasant boy had been the only one in Russia to stand up for the Russian forests with his fists.

"Go away, you fool!" Knishev snapped at Titka. "No, wait a minute—find his boot first," and added in a listless tone that left no room for doubt that he meant what he said, "if you lay a finger on that kid I'll kill you."

Never again, since then, did the boy visit Kalina, not only because it is the natural instinct of childhood to shun grief and death, but simply because he feared to look upon the fragments of a priceless shattered toy. The wound healed slowly; at a lecture once in the St. Petersburg Forest Institute, it occurred to him that but for Kalina Glukhov's fate being mixed up in it, he would probably never have given a thought to the destruction of Oblog in later years. Throughout the world primal progress had been making its ascension by way of the forest steps, and while Vikhrov was accumulating forest lore, dozens of such Oblogs had disappeared before his eyes without leaving any offspring on even a tenth of their area. By that time the image of Kalina had grown somewhat dimmed, to shine forth again in immortal grandeur many years later through Vikhrov's first book.

6

Besides Ivan, who had not been taught any local craft owing to the death of his father, there was no bread-winner in the family, nor did any of Knishev's quarter-rubles fall to their share. Hard though she struggled to make both ends meet, Agafya did not go to tavern-keeper Zolotukhin of an evening to wash the floors. Round about Twelfthtide, in midwinter, Taisa set forth on her begging round of the distant villages, where the name of Vikhrov was not known. She did not beg for alms, did not stretch forth a cupped hand, but sang a ballad under the windows, which she had learned from blind beggar-men, telling how a mother sharpened a cruel knife on a stone wetted with her tears for to kill her poor little children and so rid them of their grievous and hungry lot. Much later, towards her old age, Taisa, in a frank-hearted moment, boasted to her brother that a notorious horse-thief had been moved to tipsy tears by her song. Whether through pride, or because she did not want her son to eat the bread of idleness, Agafya did not let Ivan go out begging with his sister. And so they kept themselves alive until the spring on Taisa's pickings, seasoned with chaff and bark, of which the poor can always have a full larder. It was then that Afanasy, who revered his dead brother as he would a father, came to their assistance. Unmarried, morose and religious, he looked more forbidding even than Matvei, and if we are to believe the reports of those who had known him, surpassed him by far in gentleness of disposition. He wrote to his sister-in-law to quit the widowed hearth, leave the girl in the care of a single aunt in Bakhtarma, and bring Ivan to St. Petersburg, where a vacancy was open at the bakery next door. He could promise no wages, but the advantage of the job was that the boy would always be able to eat all the bread he wanted.

All six of them sat on the black, tarred landing-stage at Krasnovershya, waiting impatiently for the *Eupatia*. Besides his aunt, Ivan's chums had come to see them off, and Demidka kept urging him to go and have a look at the terrific forest fire the likes of which had never been seen before in their parts; the pall of acrid smoke had been hanging over the neighbourhood for over a week.

"Ganka was coming back from Loshkarev with a cartload of kerosene. He got away by the skin of his teeth," Demidka was relating excitedly. "Golly, the flames were chasing him like mad, pawing at his horse's belly. Come on, we can make it a dozen times before the whistle goes!"

"Pooh, I bet you the fires in Petersburg beat this one hollow," Letyagin said, and, with a habit acquired from grown-ups, gravely stroked the place designated for moustaches. "He'll get an eyeful of 'em, don't you worry!"

And so they remained fixed in Ivan's memory for ever after: he grew up, studied, wandered about the country, took scientific degrees, and acquired a stoop, but there they still stood, two barefoot urchins in faded old shirts, arguing in a bluish haze on the dull-green riverside of Krasnovershya.

"Sell the ewe lamb if things get bad. And be kind to the poor little orphan, Agapyevna!" the mother shouted through the ship's hoarse whistle as she bowed goodbye over the rail.

"Don't worry, my dear, this little hunchback is a godsend to me. We'll both feed out of the same bowl," Agapyevna screeched in a goosy voice, clutching Taisa's schoulder as if she were a bag of booty she had just run to earth.

Trains were running already from Loshkarev, but it was cheaper to go half the way by boat, then catch the through train to St. Petersburg. The Vikhrovs travelled in the iron-bound lower deck, among bags of salt and barrels of fat. The place reeked with the smell of overheated oil, the damp ragged clothes of the poor herded together like cattle, and worst of all, after twenty versts out, with suffocating pinewood smoke. Clad in the glow of forest fires, Russia was entering the twentieth century.

After two months of unprecedented drought sky-high pillars of shadowy blue smoke marched across the land, stepping over the rivers. All the coastal timberlands of Archangel lay wrapped in fiery gloom, and the Vistula in its lower sluggish reaches flowed under a film of ashes. Vast areas of the Siberian taiga were smouldering, the great burn of Smolensk joined in places with the blaze of Poshekhonia, and something was smoking even on Chatyr-Dagh in the Crimea. Peat bogs, hay ricks, sawn goods on *t*he wharves were blazing, and no one knew exactly what was burning, where it was burning, and why. The newspapers carried stories now about a tramp in Vladimir who had been seen cooking soup on the skirts of the forest, now about a fox-breeder smoking a vixen out of her kennel; in Saratov one of the local gentry had been shooting quail over a fire, which served him as a lure, and near Chernigov a forest officer had started the calamitous fire to cover up his sins. All through the summer only one court case had been reported in which two Tambov peasants were charged with setting fire to the landowner's wood by way of revenge for his having forbidden them to collect caulking moss. All these served Ivan as object lessons in his study of Russia's forests, and it should be said that Nature spared no pains in narrating to the youngster the sad tale of man's criminal negligence.

Awe-inspiring in the spring, when in spate, the Yenga usually ran low towards the end of summer, but never before had it dwindled to such a sorry state. The little steamer groped her way down the empty river through a dense pall of milky smoke, her running lights burning day and night; soundings were taken all round the clock. "By the mark five, and a half four!" the leadsman kept calling out from the bows, and whenever things got close to the four mark the captain yelled down the brass tube in a satanic voice, "Ease off!" The paddles would smack the water more slowly and the sand would crunch under the *Eupatia's* belly. Here and there from under the rust-coloured turf the peaty subsoil sent up wisps of grey-blue smoke. When the channel brought the old tub close to the bank, the crew worked like fiends, pouring buckets of water over her blistering sides and upper deck and cursing the master for all they were worth for having given sailing orders at such a time. The boat crawled past almost flush with an abandoned catamaran that was now a floating bonfire, and a fox with a burnt tail could be seen swimming across the river. It would have been a bad business to have run aground in such a hellish heat, as they had the night before at Nogatino, where a mendicant pilgrim had been killed outright by the fiery lunge of a blazing tree on the riverside. Worked up to a pitch of wild excitement by the flames, he had made himself a nuisance to the passengers, to whom he had tried to explain that the whitish wreaths which they beheld before their eyes were naught but smoke and the red flashes interspersed therein flames from the very fires of Gehenna, and that sinners would find it still hotter in hell. This had been uttered with the gloating malice of a righteous man directed against those abandoned wretches who had incurred the wrath of the Lord. And now that silenced expert in affairs postmundane was travelling aft, covered up with bast matting from under which he glared at Ivan with a half-open eye. The sight of the dead man was terrifying. The boy edged away, and with his chin resting on the rail, gazed steadfastly at the left bank, which was enveloped in flames.

The forest seemed to be living the way it always lived. Here a puff of wind tore a handful of gilded leaves off an asp, there a startled little flock of red thrushes took wing, followed immediately by a flame-coloured squirrel leaping from one burning branch to another. Already at that time Ivan was struck by the odd resignation to the calamity on the part of those whom it most concerned. True, memory had preserved a naive picture that caught his eye on the outskirts of a squalid forest village somewhat resembling Krasnovershya; a straggling group of old women stood there with icons, while youngsters of his own age, more as a lark than in self-defence, were beating out the creeping flames with fir branches. Judging by the presence of the parish clergy, prayers were being held there and everyone was wailing, and all was drowned out by the ominous rustle coming from the nearby woods, where the fire, as if hobbled and still docile, was browsing peacefully. The little priest stepped forward valiantly and sprinkled holy water at it from a distance with a crosswise gesture and a defiant air, as much as to say—you wait, red one, we shall get the better of you yet, the Virgin and I! One of his drops would seem to have reached the brute, because it suddenly broke cover in a violent outburst of fury amid a crash of falling trunks and a squeal of escaping gas. It came on wall-like, devouring the underbrush, mirrored in the riverside water, and as in every Russian hand-to-hand fight, the "assault wall" was preceded by the screaming young cockerels, the mischievous imps of fire, who tumbled over the dry tussocks and the heather. And there, in the upward rush of hot air, spun a charred bird, unable to drop. With a rustle of release a tall fir by the water's edge clothed itself in purple and joined the majority.

After that there was nothing. The *Eupatia* rounded a point of land. The cruel spectacle was summed up in a remark, uttered by someone over the saddened drooping head of Ivan in a tone of awed delight:

"Whew, what a blaze! I can see the juicy bilberries they'll be having round here next summer!"

It should be said, though, that all these happenings, which took place at the turn of the century, had got a bit out of focus. Memory had smoothed over the details, bringing some out sharply into the foreground, and blurring others; that night Ivan Vikhrov had had to resort to the art of the archeologist in order to decipher the writing once written in blood upon the potsherds of the past.

At noon he learned from the radio about the events of the previous night.

CHAPTER THREE

1

Unlike the enemy, Moscow accepted the war without any boastful threats or street demonstrations. The meetings held at the factories had been businesslike and brief, as if this was just another job of current history, albeit more formidable than those handled before; everyone understood, however, that much more than the fate of the capital city depended on how that job was done. Regret at the interrupted construction was outvoiced by contempt towards the enemy, both this immediate one, and that chief secretive one, who had taken fright at the idea of peaceful competition between the two systems. The war was still far off, and for three whole weeks none but the most negligible changes had affected the order of life in Blagoveshchensky Alley.

Before the term started Varya showed her friend round Moscow. In their spare time, when they were not digging bomb shelters or practising air defence, they made a round of the city's districts from a list which Polya had drawn up. True, the central squares, in their camouflage coat of dull colours, and the more famous buildings with shop windows banked up to the top with sand bags, looked rather unusual. Alongside the playbills were appeals for donors, for volunteers of the home guard, and for women to take their husbands' places in the factories, while in the art galleries, those which had not yet been bodily removed, the first thing that struck the eye were the notices giving directions to the nearest bomb shelters. But the sun was shining as gloriously as ever in a sky of almost unbearable blue, only no one wanted it now, it was too poignant a reminder of vanished days ineffably dear. Here soldiers with rolled greatcoats, there squads of young people with spades on their shoulders, or the first evacuee parties of subdued children, passed through the streets in the heat. The little ones were leaving the city without the usual jollity and singing, but also without tears, their backs unnaturally erect under the weight of their rucksacks; mothers supported their burdens from behind.

At dusk all this was swallowed up in the railway stations, and then, along the highroad, just beyond the plantations of the Forestry Institute, the tanks would begin their all-night movement. The machines swung out west wave upon wave, and Nature shuddered from the clang and chilling touch of all that metal. On such evenings all eyes without exception were turned in one and the same direction—towards the fading streak of sundown in which all saw the fiery glow of oncoming war.

It did not reach Moscow until a month later, when one day, at dawn, a black cloud spread like an ink blot in the sky on Moscow's outskirts. The pasteboard factory at Fili was burning after the first air raid. Before long the enemy struck again, and again outwardly everything remained as before in Moscow, except that a new, grim, compelling meaning was now to be read in her ancient stones. It was in those days that the consciousness of unity ripened in the Muscovites together with a sense of historic superiority over the enemy. That, and a silent anger, mounting in people's breasts and dulling the edge of pain and regret, an anger from which the flame of heroism is kindled. The country already needed it. Strong in the inexpectancy of their attack, the German troops, in the middle of July, broke through to Yartsev by way of Demidov and Dukhov, skirting Smolensk in the north; as in previous wars, it took time to stir the inland vastnesses of Russia. Now the airway to Moscow was thrice shorter, and henceforth every night witnessed a fierce duel between the ack-ack guns and the Nazi bombers on the approaches to Moscow.

At nightfall a flock of silver barrage balloons filled the sky, and the instruments of air-raid warning, never assimilated by the human ear, broke into the noise-melody of the city. They silenced everything, even the murmur of leaves and the infant's cry, as though all living things dreaded to betray their presence, and the streets became so long that it seemed as if one would never reach the end of them, hard though he ran. To Polya, who was used to the stillness of the Yenga, these hours were full of a harrowing expectation of something worse than a direct hit.

With the onset of evening, especially when there was a clear sky, she was afflicted with a malady more acute than anything she had experienced in childhood; she became painfully air conscious, so much so that her speech became jerky and she could not put her hand to anything. She made no complaint, but Varya, on her own initiative, decided to offer her the only medicine there was for this benumbing fear.

Varya brought up the subject one night after she had come in from a spell of roof duty. The raiders had come over early that evening, but had been beaten off and did not show up again owing to the sky clouding. Polya was already at home, busy with the housework, which she regarded as some sort of justification for her presence in the city at such a time. Madam Zolotinskaya came in half an hour later—Varya had invited her to tea on her way in.

"They won't be coming over again tonight, I've put my granddaughter to bed," she said confidently, with the sole aim of setting Polya's fears at rest. The girl looked so pale and scared. "I think it's raining, you didn't get wet, Varya, did you?"

"Oh, that's nothing. I tore my sleeve on a nail in the attic, though. It's a pity you didn't come up, it was a lovely sight, Polya— summer rain over Moscow." She thanked Polya with a nod for the needle and cotton that instantly appeared at her elbow. "I love to look at the wet roofs of Moscow when they shine all along the horizon!"

"Are you sure it ... it's going to be a good rain?" Polya asked, and it wasn't so much the salutary rain and how long it would last that interested her, as it was to hear from the tone of Varya's reply whether her friend despised her for sitting about in the bomb shelter all the time. "I used to love the summer rain, too, on the Yenga ... but here it's much nicer, of course ... more needful."

"It isn't a question of being nice. As a matter of fact Moscow's roofs are anything but attractive—all patchy, with rusty spouts. Looking at it from up there makes you realise the country had more important things to think of all these years than its dwellings. By the way, as a coming architect you would do well to ask yourself why we decorate our cities only from the façade, although we have long since passed to the three-dimensional plane. But from up there Moscow is so familiar, so warm, and homely. You feel like wanting to put your own strength into her, small though it is, for the smaller I am, the more there are of us, isn't that so?" Varya paused to let this sink in. "While I was waiting for the planes—they didn't come, by the way—it occurred to me that those who hadn't shared in the people's sorrow were bound to feel outsiders when the time came for celebrating."

"You are always so strict, Comrade Chernetsova, that I sometimes feel as if I'm sitting behind a school desk in your presence," put in Zolotinskaya, taking pity on Polya. "Things will sort themselves out in time. Leave the child alone."

"I only wanted to ask her ... I want to ask you, Polya, don't you feel you'd like to go up with me there? Let's go tomorrow? You can put cotton wool in your ears if the noise frightens you."

"Not yet, not now!" Polya said, shaking her head vigorously with such genuine terror that both burst out laughing.

"You'll never make a field marshal, I can see," Varya said without reproach or scorn in her voice. "D'you think I'm less afraid of death than you are?"

"Oh, no! It's not that at all."

"Then what is it?"

"I don't know yet."

"In that case hadn't you better go back to the Yenga? And when it's all over. . . ."

"You needn't be so nasty about it, Varya! I feel the meanest person in the country as it is, without you rubbing it in. But I can't, I tell you I can't just now ..." Polya said, and began to cry with mortification. "I just can't understand. . . ."

"What is there to understand, darling? It's war."

"I don't mean that, I mean—I haven't done them any harm, why should they want to kill me?"

The question was put with such frank nakedness that Varya was at a loss for an answer, although in her future capacity as school-teacher she would be expected to know all the answers.

And so everything remained as before. As usual, when the alert was sounded, Varya and the other fire-watchers took up their stations on the roof, armed with gauntlets and long hellish tongs, while Polya would run down into the basement, where a real light was burning and boxes of sand stood in the corners, looking cool and reassuring. It was hushful there, dampish, and really quite nice, as if you were in the ground, except that at the beginning, owing to the lack of other stone-built structures in their alley, crowds of people used to come there from all over the street. Most of them were middle-aged people and mothers with children who had stayed behind in the capital for various reasons. All was silent, and then, into this stillness threaded with the busy breathing of the sleeping children, there trickled the belching sounds of bomb explosions. Polya shut her eyes, and sank into the familiar stupor of childhood, when, falling asleep in the gathering gloom, she would see a clammy frog-skinned giant groping about, muttering to himself, and pretending that he couldn't find what he wanted, and that made it more frightening than ever. She flattened herself against the wall, and had but a single desire—to become as small as a pea and roll away into a hole, if not to disappear altogether.

Gradually, as she became accustomed to war life, Polya recovered the faculty of speech and sight. Thus, in the first-aid nurse who sat dozing by the door, she identified Madam Zolotinskaya, and later came to recognise the lean old man of haughty professorial mien with the bared head and the expensive lap robe, which he wore with the pattern inside in order, apparently, not to be too conspicuous a figure among the other inhabitants of Blagoveshchensky Alley. The professor would sit out the alert in one and the same corner, under a lamp, with a book in his hand, making occasional notes in the margin, but, judging by the time he spent on each line and the frequency with which he turned back to perused pages, he too was not very successful in keeping his mind off the clamouring realities behind the iron door of the shelter. Polya felt drawn to him immediately; he seemed to be the only person there who could help her to solve some of the problems of everyday life that perplexed her mind.

Finding herself beside him one day, she put those problems to him in the order of their rising importance. To begin with, she had long been assailed by doubts as to whether it was permissible to have slit trenches twenty centimetres wider than the regulations prescribed, because that was what always happened when she dug them in the yard owing to the crumbly nature of the earth, and, another thing, did foodstuffs have to be wrapped up in cellophane during an air raid as the A. D. instructions laid down? Her neighbour remarked with an indulgent smile that at the present stage of military operations cellophane could be dispensed with, but that any departure from the engineering requirements was undesirable.

Polya thanked him earnestly for his comprehensive answer, which was appreciated not so much for the invaluable information it contained as for the fact that association with a man of experience released her from the torture of loneliness.

"The reason I troubled you," she gratefully confessed, "was because I can't get any of that blessed cellophane anywhere!"

"For the time being you have every reason to er ... save yourself the trouble of the search," her neighbour said with slow suave reassurance, and touching her tremulous hand, added something about his being ever ready to give helpful advice, to "our mentally alert and ambitious youth," as he expressed it, enunciating his words with visible relish. Then, pushing up his glasses, he manfully tackled the next page.

The air duel outside Moscow was still going on, and although the explosions were now inaudible, the same enforced silence hung over the city. It was hard to believe that desperate tank battles were raging somewhere, and that the new homes of the collective farmers were blazing from end to end, while yesterday's clerks, templaters, and masters of science were crawling forward into the firing line in sweat-stained tunics, Rodion among them! But it was utterly inconceivable that the whole Soviet land west of the Moscow meridian, new-modelled by dint of sheer heroism, was to be gutted with fire, that the steel of armoured wreckage was to pass through the furnaces again and again, and that men were to crawl for thousands of miles, their shirts rotting off their backs from sweat, and today's teenagers were to grow up into soldiers before all this ended.

On such evenings Polya had an opportunity of observing the blind terror of the dogs, who cowered under the shelter seats at the first scream of the sirens, and a flush of shame would stain her cheeks at the thought of what would happen to her if the war dragged on for a whole month more. Finding herself sitting next to the same man again, Polya began to talk in a wild passionate whisper about the meanness of the capitalist rulers who wrung profits out of human anguish. She loved to loiter in childish fancy upon the purlieus of communism, and all the more bitter was her return to that chimerical Dantean circle where everyone tormented everyone else without joy, without gratification, without sense. It was with the possible duration of this hell that Polya's third and principal question was concerned.

"Pardon me, but I didn't catch you," said her learned neighbour, extracting a plug of cotton wool from his ear, an expedient by which some people in those days protected themselves against the too painful impacts of reality.

"I hate to interrupt you, but I wanted to ask—how long will this horror last—a month and a half, three months? Surely not more than six?"

Before gratifying the curiosity of this modest deferential young girl sitting beside him shoulder to shoulder, the professor studied the long nail of his little finger for quite a time.

"Your question has caught me unawares, my dear child," he began judicially, twiddling his pencil. "For us old people the most difficult questions are those which roseate unsophisticated youth put to us. Unfortunately, I can offer you nothing but generalities, voiced thoughts, which er ... you are free to reject should you find them too strongly tinged with my own personal experiences, that sad store of knowledge of an aged, almost worn-out man. Possibly, some of them er ... may strike you as being rather remote from our shining reality, an illogical, to a certain extent perhaps philistine reasoning, with even a reprehensible soupson of pessimism, but all opinion is necessarily a source of contradiction, and apart from everything else, bears the stamp of the place where it has been expressed. In this case, we are sitting in a none too comfortable cave, waiting miserably for the moment when er ... let us face the truth ... when eight floors, not counting the attic and the roof, will tumble about our ears. Lofty thoughts seldom visit a person in such a situation. It is only afterwards that the stately chronicler comes along and packs away into a dozen calligraphic lines years of deprivations, countless miles of conflagrations and thousands of simultaneous gangrenes, but meanwhile.... I am expressing myself rather sketchily, but I hope you are able to follow me?"

"I ... I am trying to," Polya said, quailing before such an exhaustive preamble.

"In the first place, my dear child," her companion proceeded in a weighty well-lubricated voice, "warfare till now has been a means by which the stronger establishes his domination over the weaker and subdues them to his will. Naturally, advantages gained in such a manner cannot be considered enduring. This applies to everything that is gained by threat or violence. No peace treaty clauses are binding upon the grandchildren unless the er ... operation involved the complete extermination of the conquered. This is borne out by the collapse of empires that immediately followed the death of their founders, as in the case of Darious and Xerxes, Alexander and Sargon, Timur and Napoleon, not to mention, of course, this blustering corporal Schicklgruber. Succeeding generations always find the clothes of their forefathers too tight—they usually er ... have them altered. When a bent bar straightens out it springs out into space that does not belong to it ... and so war breeds war. Some people, not without good reason, regard humanity's path of progress as a stand-up altercation—to put it mildly—sometimes with fairly long lulls in between to work up the necessary fat and funds for the next bout. It would be more logical therefore to speak about the duration of these lulls rather than those of the wars. What marks did you get for that ... what's it called ... political ABC?"

"Good marks," Polya answered. She was beginning to tire of his too smooth ambiguous speech, which wanted but a small audience to swell into a widespread lecture.

"Oh, that's quite enough for an understanding of the mechanics of capitalist existence. At this point, though, my child, I am afraid I must disclose a sad fact to you. I fear that with the growth of industrial facilities and the corresponding complication of relations, these pauses will become shorter until such time as mankind has come to its senses or else turned into a gaseous nebula of local importance, when the destructive potential will have utterly suppressed the constructive. 'Here dwelt somewhat reckless quick-tempered gods,' some professor of astronomy from a neighbouring stellar system will say of our planet. I would ask you to take particular note of the fact that er ... all great discoveries are diffused in the air of the epoch and are absorbed by the opponents almost simultaneously. In short, I am relentlessly reminded of a vibrating bar gripped in the vice er ... so to speak, of historical necessity. The thing could be solved simply by an equation, where the elements are the length of the bar, the resilience of the material, the resistance of the surrounding medium, and the initial force applied, but unfortunately, the process we are here dealing with is somewhat more complicated. The thing is, my dear child, the facts of history are built up on a far greater number of coordinates than the human mind is capable of grasping, and the historian's deduction depends entirely on which of these coordinates he chooses to accept as the principal ones. Each age has its own views as to the causality of historical events, and it is not beyond the bounds of probability that er ... the most astonishing discoveries will be made in the future about, say, the Peloponnesian War! Of course, there would be nothing easier than to say that the duration of war depends on the relative strength of reserves, the quality of armaments, the economic power of the rivals, or that, given an equal balance of forces, the scale will be tipped by the level of education of the generals, the fury of the armies, the spiritual equipment of the nation. But I am not sure this equation does not contain other quantities to interpret which we so far lack the necessary instruments, seeing that nothing, I repeat, nothing could avert the destruction of the outstanding civilisations of the past. Give me these masses and quantities, and like Laplace, I undertake to predict their position at any period of time. But you are silent, my young comrade, and I am at a loss to answer your question as to how long this scientifically organised sanguinary disorder, in common parlance called war, is going to last."

Polya was beginning to nod drowsily, but even in that comatose state her whole being unconsciously revolted against this muddle of profundity, where, although all seemed well on the surface, a subtle venom of doubt occasionally bubbled up. She could not but agree, of course, that there was no finality about anything in the world, because the river of life was renewing itself every second. But there was an elusive hint of ill-will lurking in the professor's insinuations, with which, inexperienced as she was in dispute and without Rodion there to help her, she was at a loss to deal with.

"So you think the war will drag on for some time?" Polya sighed.

"Long enough to give you and me many more opportunities for such er ... spontaneous talks." At this point he looked closely at Madam Zolotinskaya, who was leaning towards them with an apathetic air, then added with a touch of envy, obviously not for Polya's benefit, that the young people had everything before them, and could look forward to reaching the foothills of communism. It now remained for him to seal the acquaintance. "By the way, I did not quite get your name?"

"Call me just Polya," she said, raising trustful eyes to his. "And yours?"

Thus he was placed under the pleasant necessity of giving his name. It was Alexander Yakovlevich, and his surname was Gratsiansky. It was a sheer stroke of luck to thus have an expeditious fate bring her together with this eminent forest expert, her father's chief judge, who was able to throw light upon the story of Vikhrov's doubtful repute.

Fortunately, Gratsiansky's attention was distracted for a moment, and Polya had time to recover from the momentary shock.

On the next occasion she took careful stock of her new acquaintance with the lap robe. As before, he sat in profile towards her, but that had its advantages, as his spectacles, and the book, which served him as a screen, did not obscure her view of him. He had a lean ascetic face of lofty grandeur with a touch of hauteur about it, a dull ivory skin, and a short beard streaked with grey; his hair, as if ruffled by the wind of inspiration, was fairly long, and in the hollows under his high forehead lay faint flickering shadows. All this gave him the prize-model appearance of a staunch champion of some eminently noble cause, and that, in its turn, attracted irresistibly. Some attitudes reminded Polya of a Greek Church missionary from the Kuril Islands whose picture she had once seen in *Niva*, an old pre-revolutionary magazine, others of a prophet of old, condemned to the martyr's stake, but for an odd and disconcerting trick of the eyes. Every once in a while, in the impassively lidded depths of his eyes, the pupils would dart about, as if seized with a nervous tic, in a manner that was most unbecoming in a man who preached the word of God or even less uplifting truths. It was as though some haunting memory pursued the man, so that every quarter of an hour or so he had to reassure himself that there was no cause for worry. The river of life must have treated him pretty roughly over the rapids before it swept him out into the estuary of deserved public recognition, and Polya, who had been taught to respect the generation of fathers, correctly interpreted these oddities as the result of some traumatic experience during his activities in the revolutionary underground.

The next minute, though, this interpretation struck her as being bookish. A simpler explanation could be found in the very circumstances of that night. Polya herself was oppressed by that calamity-laden silence as well as by a sense of guilt at sitting there in the shelter like a deserter while others were standing guard on the roofs or marching erect into the attack—as Rodion was doing!—and last but not least by that shuddering eight-storey mass of stone, which made its weight felt more than ever in this low vaulted cellar. It is the way of children to interpret the conduct of their elders by their own limited experience.

Suddenly Polya realised that Gratsiansky had noticed her intent scrutiny out of the tail of his eye; he still kept the little volume in front of him, but he was looking over the top of the page.

"It's folly to come here in such a thin blouse. This is a new building, the plaster hasn't dried yet," he said, removing his spectacles. "Do you want my rug?"

"Thanks, I'm strong. I used to swim across the river late in the autumn and beat all the boys at it."

"Excellent. It's the mad follies of youth that often serve as training practice for the heroic deeds of adulthood," he said, and with a swift impetuous movement surprising in one of his years, he turned his face to Polya. "Come, now, how do you know me, confess!"

She twisted out of it. She hated lies, but at that moment she would have banished all scruples to learn the truth about her father.

"Oh, I read your articles about that ... what's his name?... that scientist who wants to keep the Russian forest locked away from the people."

It was a quotation from one of his own articles, except that the original had hinted maliciously at surprisingly long-living old women, who, since nineteen seventeen, had been hoarding semolina and sugar in the family chests against pressing, and it was to be hoped not too prolonged, political emergencies, after which there would be a return to the "normal", so to speak, life of the good old days.

"Oh, you mean my old controversy with Vikhrov," he smiled, flattered. "Where did you get hold of my er ... hasty handiwork?"

She told him truthfully enough that she had read his articles when she lived with her mother at the forestry division, where it had been a tradition of many years to subscribe to all the forestry periodicals.

"There are not many books at the library there, and I read everything from cover to cover. I've been living in this world for so long and never thought there could be such noisy doings in such a quiet sphere as the forest."

"Pardon me, what division does your mother live in?" he asked quickly.

Polya for precaution's sake named the neighbouring forestry range across the river Gorinka.

"Svyatkovsk, on the Yenga. A godforsaken place, awfully dull!"

"On the contrary, it's a fine place. I visited your parts in my youth—the Pashutino division, to be exact. I was a guest of that very same Vikhrov," Gratsiansky said, savouring the memory with an odd sidling glance somewhere over and beyond Polya's

114

head. "And, tell me, what sort of appraisal did my articles receive in that bright pretty head of yours?"

"I should say they were ... very powerful articles. One thing I can't make out, though, is how men like that come to be in our country and at such a time, too, when all our people are devoting themselves heart and soul to creative labour," she reeled off, as though quoting from a leading article. "And they have the nerve to eat Soviet bread too!"

Gratsiansky received the artless outburst with great sympathy.

"The thing is, my charming child, that we are living in a wonderful age of change and transformation, when the class struggle sometimes assumes extremely fanciful forms, er ... until it ultimately takes the shape of an open clash between the two sides. We must not forget that our enemies, having no chance to do direct damage—a senseless act in any case, considering our tremendous dynamic drive—sometimes resort to more cunning and subtle means, not the least among which are the so-called innocent mistakes, which are usually passed off as scientific points of view. This Vikhrov has an extraordinary propensity for so-called independent thinking. And the greater the scope of the people's activity, the more damaging is the slightest deviation of ideas, be it only by half a degree—don't you think so, my friend?"

Her last slender hope of reprieve for her father was dashed by this verdict, pronounced in a sorrowful tone of belated regret.

"You think ..." Polya began falteringly, biting her lip and making three attempts before she finally got it out. "You think that Vikhrov is sowing these phoney ideas of his on purpose?"

It was not until half a year later, when comparing certain facts, that she recollected that at this point Madam Zolotinskaya opened her eyes and stared hard at Gratsiansky before dozing off again.

"I understand what you are hinting at, but no, I can't believe it," Polya's companion drawled with a sour hesitant mien. "The resistance of that type of person has long since been broken. I should say it has been buried in the concrete of socialist construction. Of course, in poor novels we still come across lurking figures of mystery with shaded lanterns, who have the stolen plans of the city's sewerage system hidden in a tooth filling—it would be difficult these days to work up a clumsy and didactic plot without them—but, judging by the critical reviews, this trick is becoming recognised as a gimmick even in literature.

Besides, the forest is not a military works, you don't need a pass to go there. No, other springs of action are at work here, the rusty springs of an effete society—the brooding resentment of a mediocrity, the wounded vanity of a misfit, and sometimes the sneaking hope of picking up a ruble on the side to make up for what the Soviets had underpaid him." He made a brief natural pause of loyal indignation. "With Vikhrov, of course, it's a different case. There's no denying that he has a certain measure of talent. The trouble is, we are apt to neglect subtle psychological analysis in the too generalised judgements that we make. That is why, in the long run, we never know when and where any public figure of this class, no matter how flawless his record, had drunk of the Death Water, which has been tearing at his vitals ever since. Truth to tell, your version never occurred to me, but . . . no, I can't believe it," he repeated with still greater emphasis and mechanically snapped his book shut just as Polya absent-mindedly glanced into it. "Vikhrov's scientific vagaries are symptoms of a disease rather than of consciously directed will."

He sounded so sincere that Polya was ashamed of her recent dislike, even downright animosity towards her companion, a feeling, by the way, that sprang from a sharpened and often unerring instinct of youth.

"How well you talk, please go on!" she pleaded in a low voice.

"I have known Vikhrov since we were students," Gratsiansky continued, chewing the cud of memories, "and in my eyes he has always been a fairly decent comrade, somewhat obsessed, perhaps, by a persecution mania—forest persecution, I should say, but an honest man withal. Not that I am trying to defend him because we used to eat skilly together once at a humble eating-house on the Karavannaya and were both hounded by the tsarist regime. If anything, I should respect him for the persistence with which he has been trying to put over his economic quasi-theories, had they not er . . . run counter to certain interests of socialist progress. And quasi-theories they are! Look at the map of the Siberian forests and you will realise that no matter what your rate of cutting is, there is not the slightest danger of this literally inexhaustible green ocean ever being depleted."

Polya touched his sleeve.

"Tell me," she entreated, "didn't you try to persuade him—not by scolding, but just as friend to friend, as a big man? Perhaps you would have succeeded in bringing him round to our way of thinking, that is if this Vikhrov is worth the effort of such a man as you!"

Gratsiansky shook his head hopelessly.

"He is a first-rate scholar with a still lucid mind, and ... it is only in youth that we are capable of a complete reappraisal of values. Take Saul, for instance—how old was he on his road to Damascus, or Belinsky when he renounced the Hegelian conciliation? But who would believe in the repentance of a seventy-year-old Galileo? Nevertheless, I reject your quite natural suspicion of malicious intent, although sometimes I am inclined to speculate along those lines myself, only in quite a different way. The thing is, my child, that needy men are apt to have a retentive and grateful memory for any kindness that is shown them."

"What kindness?" Polya asked quietly.

"Any kindness," Gratsiansky let fall meaningly. "There are certain things in Vikhrov's life history which could bear looking into—not by a legal examiner, but by a social psychologist." With the same mistiness of eye which Polya found so distasteful, he hinted that personally he had no doubts such an office would become necessary in the society of tomorrow for the purpose of exploring certain circumstances which eluded the official statistician, "provided, of course, that official statistics aimed not only at corroborating office-room truths, but at discovering new knowledge that would enrich mankind."

And since long sitting in bomb shelters made for a high, if only temporary, degree of intimacy, Gratsiansky delicately revealed to Polya the secret of another man's life. Thus, with a mixed feeling of pain and aversion, she learned from her companion that during all the three years they had been in the Forestry Institute together, Vikhrov had been receiving, "well, not a stipend exactly, but a regular monthly allowance of twenty-five rubles from some unknown private person." The postal orders were signed with an obviously fictitious name, and it was highly improbable, in view of the impoverished state of the working class at that time, that the sender was, say, a turner at the Putilov Works, a sort of incognito lover and patron of the forests. Vikhrov had received those remittances right up to the time of his arrest, but there is reason to believe that they were continued on his return from his two-year exile until he took his degree, which, incidentally, he did with honours. To give him credit, Vikhrov always shared these windfalls with his poorer chums, and afterwards sent a considerable part of the money to his friend Valery Krainov, who was serving his term of exile somewhere beyond the Yenisei. So Vikhrov did not conceal the fact that he received this money, but when his friends asked him about its source he pleaded ignorance.

"Anyway, after the hard school of life I have been through, I personally do not believe very much in philanthropic altruism," Gratsiansky concluded, "and I am inclined to believe that Vikhrov's benefactor had far-seeing plans and counted on the beneficiary's continued gratitude er ... in the future."

The puzzling question was how Vikhrov could accept money from such a mysterious source, but according to Gratsiansky, one could not expect a hungry ragged man to be overscrupulous in such matters, the more so as these gifts had no strings attached to them. "You do not stop to ask whose water you are drinking in the desert; all that matters is that it's cool, clear and capable of quenching thirst."

"I understand, so that was the Death Water he drank of," Polya said, her heart going cold within her. "Tell me, what kind of a person was this Krainov?"

"Oh, he was a splendid comrade, our common friend. He was a student too, only a senior student. Already at that time he had become a professional revolutionary. All three of us—Cheredilov, Vikhrov and I, are greatly indebted to him for our political education. As a matter of fact it was he who drew me into the revolution...." Incidentally, Polya learned that this was the well-known Krainov, who had been serving for twenty years as a Soviet diplomat, which, in turn, pointed to outstanding qualities of mind, tact and Party reputation.

"But in accepting assistance from his comrade Krainov must have known his financial position," Polya said, groping her way out of the dark. "He must have known, then, that this was *clean* money once he accepted it!"

Gratsiansky beamed approval.

"You would make a good criminal investigator," he complimented her intelligence. "That's all very well, except for an accessory circumstance—I should not say an aggravating one, but certainly a suspicious one. I remember a conversation that was started at a farewell party of graduates concerning certain puzzling aspects of this selfsame social psychology, and Vikhrov, of his own accord, told us how, in a drunken moment, a big timber-merchant—a man whose name was on everyone's tongue in Russia in those days, had given him twenty-five rubles. It was the merchant who was drunk, not Vikhrov, although I would have preferred it the other way round. The relationship thus established could have continued further, now couldn't it? I must say, though, that this was in the early hours of the morning and we had all been going it pretty strong, with that deafening Cheredilov—Big Kostroma we called him—strumming a guitar, so that I didn't quite catch how Vikhrov came to be attending that St. Petersburg millionaire's orgy, and what made him blurt out such an unsavoury secret."

"Had you been . . . going it pretty strong, too?" Polya put in for the first time in a brittle little voice.

Alcoholic indulgence, it seemed, had been forbidden Gratsiansky since his youth on account of his delicate health. The name of his ailment, coming from his lips, sounded so refined and mysterious that one could infer that it was bestowed only upon the elect as a reward for the excessive exertion of their intellectual powers. Polya felt greatly tempted to say how good it was for those who did not drink a lot—they could just sit around and keep their ears open. In fact she would have done so had not two deafening explosions occurred one after the other at that very moment somewhere close at hand. The light flickered, the walls shook, and the children woke up and began to scream. Madam Zolotinskaya rushed out. The bombs had fallen in Blagoveshchensky Alley, and someone there might need her medical aid. That evening Polya was hardly aware of the bombing for thinking about her father. As for Gratsiansky, he presented a very instructive picture of a man half-paralysed with fear.

The conversation was not resumed, and presently the All-Clear signal was given on the radio.

3

Polya staggered up to her room. Her legs always felt leaden after coming out of the bomb shelter, and for some reason her back ached. For the first time there was no hot tea on the table for Varya when she returned from roof duty. She found her friend at the open balcony door; leaning her head against the jamb in the dark, Polya was gazing at the silhouetted buildings of the blacked-out city. She did not answer Varya's call, and had to be almost dragged away from the luring dizzy depths. They lowered the blue paper blind and sat down at the table; Polya's tea went cold. She answered all Varya's questions absent-mind-edly, or with an ingratiating smile so poorly simulated that the usually imperturbable Varya was seized with a sense of fore-boding.

"Are you ill?"

"No, I'm all right . . . thanks."

"But what's the matter?"

Polya sat as if deafened—apathetic and mute.

Varya forced her to drink some raspberry tea, put her to bed, and sat stroking the cold palms of her hand—all in silence.

"You'd better not touch me, don't dirty yourself," Polya said, shrinking away. She pulled the blanket up to her neck and stretched her hidden hands down the sides of her body.

"What do you mean?"

"A dreadful secret lies upon me."

Varya made a conscientious effort not to laugh.

"I say, that does sound serious! Luckily, I know all your secrets. Own up, you wicked woman—you've eaten a pastry on the quiet—am I right?"

Polya was shivering with cold. She did not dare to look up.

"You won't kick me out, will you?" she said, and promptly corrected herself so as not to offend Varya. "I mean in general—they won't all kick me out, will they?"

"Who? Kick you out from where?"

"Well, you know, everybody, out of the country."

"I don't like your thoughts, Polya. Who ever heard of a young Soviet girl being deprived of her country!" Suddenly a light struck her. "You don't think we'll be beaten, do you? Why, do you realise how strong we are and how many . . . how much we have of the stuff that makes for victory, and how much more of it we can turn out if we have to? Why, they'd have to kill us off one by one to destroy all we have piled up all these years. And the people won't give you up, you're like a grain in its hand. Now go to sleep!"

The last words were the only ones that seemed to have regis-tered. Polya sat up, and burst forth in feverish haste, her red-dened swollen eyes staring out before her.

"Whatever happens, don't worry about me, Varya, don't be afraid. I won't cast any shadow on you, I won't get you into trouble. Now what else did I want to tell you? I've lost the thread. . . ." Her eyes wandered round the room. "Oh, yes, don't worry—I'll go away by myself if I have to, I'll find my own place. I won't complain, not even to Mamma. I'm sure she's not in the least to blame either. Oh, but I'm talking nonsense, darling! I'm not going anywhere, because I'll try to live it down!" Tears came copiously to her relief and rolled down her cheeks. "D'you know what—I'll do the hardest things of all; something everyone else has given up. I'll just go and do it. I'll work for both of us. What do you say, will I have the strength of two, eh?"

She meant her father, but Varya misunderstood and frowned.

"This is hysterics, stop it, I don't like it. Tell me straight—has anything happened to Rodion?" Then followed crisp curt commands: "Stop it, I tell you! You got a letter from there, from the front, I saw it on the table. Give it to me at once."

Polya's feverish state, not to mention her confused, incoherent speech, prepared Varya to hear the worst, something more terrible even than Rodion's being taken prisoner or having been mortally wounded.

"Oh, no, it's not that at all," Polya said with a shudder, and turning away towards the wall, held out a crumpled cocked-hat note, obviously read and re-read many times, which she had drawn from under her pillow.

Afterwards Varya was ashamed of her first thoughts; but it was a rare troop-train that did not stop in Moscow, the railway stations were close by, and Rodion knew Polya's address. Of course, a commanding officer might not give a soldier leave of absence to go to Blagoveshchensky Alley, but at least he could drop his sweetheart a postcard on his way out to join the army in the field. Anyway, this was his first letter from the front and it was over two weeks old. At least one would know now with what thoughts he had gone to the war. Varya unfolded the sheet impatiently—it was full of pencil holes, and had apparently been written on the knee. She was obliged to go up to the lamp in order to make out the faint pencilled lines.

She stumbled on the chief place right away.

"Probably the only reason I have been silent all this time, my dear, is that I couldn't find a place to sit down in," Rodion came straight to the point with unexpected bluntness. "We are still retreating, retreating day and night to occupy more advantageous defensive lines, as they say in the communiques. On top of it, I was very ill and haven't quite recovered yet—my illness is worse than shell-shock. What makes it so bitter is that I am perfectly well, unscathed, without a single scratch so far. Burn this letter, you're the only person in the world I can tell this to." Varya turned the sheet over. "The thing happened in a Russian village through which our troops were retreating. I was marching last in our company, last in the whole army for all I know. A girl was standing in the roadway, a local girl of about nine, quite a child, and apparently brought up from her first days at school to love the Red Army. She couldn't have known much about the strategical situation, of course. She ran up to us with a bunch of field flowers and I happened to be the one who got it. She had such searching questioning eyes— looking at the noonday sun would have been a thousand times easier. But I forced myself to take the little bunch, because I am not a coward—I swear to you, darling, that I am not a coward. I winced and took it from her, she whom we were leaving to the mercy of the enemy. I have been keeping that dried bunch of flowers ever since, keeping it on my body, as if carrying fire in my bosom, and I'll have it laid on me in the grave, if that is to be. I thought I'd have to go through ordeals of blood before I became a man, but it appears you go through it dry, this font of maturity!" The next two lines were illegible. "And I don't know, darling, whether a lifetime of mine will suffice to repay that gift."

"Yes, your Rodion has grown up, you are right," Varya said deeply moved, refolding the letter. No soldier with such an attitude of mind could ever do anything dishonourable.

Polya's only answer to the ensuing flood of questions was to shake her head and bite her lip. Varya then locked the balcony door, as it turned cool towards daybreak, and spent the rest of the night wide awake in her bed, straining her ears to catch every movement of Polya's. In the morning things were no clearer. Twice Varya attempted to sound Madam Zolotinskaya as to what had happened in the bomb shelter, but in vain; on both occasions Varya had the impression that the Queen of Clubs was being evasive. During the day Polya disappeared, and Varya rushed off in search of her; she did not find her until late in the afternoon. Polya was in the courtyard of the house next door, digging a bomb shelter for strange people. No one had called her there, she had just seen the people working and had picked up a spade that happened to be lying about.

"I was just passing by and spotted a familiar dress. You've come out to take a bit of exercise, I see?" Varya probed skilfully without betraying any anxiety. "Have you had your dinner?"

"I ate what was left over from yesterday. I was tired of sitting there all alone," Polya answered in the same casual manner. "You go along, I'll be home soon."

She did not return until nightfall, when it started to drizzle; she returned with downcast eyes and a drawn face, as though something was burning within her. They read the Informbureau communiqué out over their tea, and Varya, as usual, punctuated the fighting episodes with pauses the clearer to be able to envisage it all. No place names or other indications of the approaching tide of war were mentioned in the communiqué; one guessed the things that had been left unsaid by the way one's heart twinged during the reading. Polya sat with the air of a not very welcome guest. From time to time she glanced at something in her hand held clenched under the table, then gazed absently through the balcony doorway. Perhaps it was because all distracting ornamental details and the evening lights were blacked out, but it seemed to her as if that patch of doorway held a much bigger piece of Moscow's panorama, and the eye more easily embraced the architectural wholeness of the city. Something in its nocturnal profile reminded one of a great battleship swinging out of harbour broadside on to the sea, bound on some long grim cruise; this impression was heightened by the gleaming expanses of the squares which looked like wet decks, and the steel constructions of the new building sites.

With their arms round each other the girls sat listening to the murmur of the rain and the muffled hoots of the motor-cars. They discussed the events of the day—the exhibition of captured planes in one of the central squares, an unfilled crater in "Glad Street", as they had now got into the habit of calling it, Gastello,* whose heroic feat was then a country-wide sensation—everything except Polya's grief.

"It's all wrong somehow," Varya said with a sigh. "Here are we, drinking tea with raspberry jam, while at this very moment, maybe, our boys are running through an unreaped field with bayonets atilt, shouting and dropping."

"That's true," Polya said with dismay, pushing her saucer away from her. "We ought to give it away."

"But who to?"

---

* Gastello—Hero of the Soviet Union, killed in World War II. Plunged his burning plane into a column of German tanks, lorries and petrol tanks.—*Tr.*

"There's a military hospital close by. I saw them being brought in yesterday, so many of them. Not one gave a groan! We'll take it down together tomorrow, shall we?" The resolution made them both feel a bit better for a short while.

The next day Varya announced that she was going away to help build defensive lines; Polya would be left to fend for herself, a whole fortnight. Childlike distress clouded her face and set Varya wondering whether their elders, in giving the youth a sheltered life all these years, had prepared them sufficiently for shouldering a burden as heavy as they themselves had borne at their age? As though reading her thoughts, Polya asked whether she could join Varya's group, and took another furtive peep at her hand.

"All right, I'll talk it over at the Institute," Varya nodded. "By the way, what are you hiding there in your fist?"

"Nothing," Polya said, flushing.

"Show me."

Polya held out her empty hands, palms downward, with bitten finger nails and resin stains from the unpeeled spade handle; it was only in the night, when Varya examined her unclenched hands by the light of a match, that she made out the dark torn blisters on them. Apparently this little pain helped Vikhrov's daughter to bear that greater one, the nature of which Varya, so far, knew nothing.

4

The sirens screamed again just when the girl returned from the theatre. The moonlit night promised a thorough-going raid. Polya went up on the roof of her own accord. Varya recognised her the moment she appeared out of the dormer window in her leather jacket with a gas-mask slung at her side. With a teacher's intuition she expressed neither surprise nor approval. She piloted Polya to the nearest chimney and told her briefly what a grown-up unarmed person had to do when gigantic flying machines attacked his dwelling.

"D'you know, Polya, I waited ever so patiently for your pride to ripen in you." Little did she guess what part Polya's fear of finding herself again in Gratsiansky's company had played in this matter. "Arm yourself—here's a shovel and tongs. Come on, take them, surely you're not going to throw the thing down with your bare hands when it drops on you out of the blue. The others will do the rest. You're not afraid of the height, are you?"

"Just a wee bit," Polya confessed, and couldn't help asking: "What if the thing drops straight on me?"

"In that case . . . just the same, the others will do the rest!" Varya laughed, and without a word of encouragement she went back to her station.

The city was wrapped in a haze of shifting light and shadow, with the moon dodging in and out through a foam of cloud. Everyone who was doing duty that night on Moscow's roofs felt like shooting at her, as one would at a signalling spy bent on villainy, all the more dire that she looked so young and innocent, with the fluffy yellowness of a chick. When she plunged into the clouds the city below resembled a primordial rock-strewn chaos with the canyons of its streets and the black craters of its squares; but when the shadow passed, it became beautiful beyond words once more, like the setting of some heroic spectacle a minute before the main dramatic forces come into play. The air was not exactly cold, it was quiveringly alive with the expectation of a raw and painful contact. Polya's shovel got caught in a wire aerial; it slithered noisily across the iron roof and went hurtling down; it took so long hitting the ground that Polya had time to wipe her clammy brow before the faint clatter of its fall reached her ears. It broke the stillness and served as the signal for the start.

The moon dived into a cloudlet again, and all at once the flashes of defensive gunfire came into short-lived life along the whole southern skyline; a minute later came the faint growling sounds of explosions. Polya suddenly realised that the mass of cliffs all round was full of people, ready to take the enemy's blow upon their own bodies. Then it seemed as if all the floodgates of light and thunder had suddenly been opened; a blast gave Polya a slight push in the back and flung her long broken shadow, together with the silhouettes of the chimneys and roof structures, upon the adjoining buildings. Simultaneously, the ack-ack guns opened up on a nearby roof; now a deathly pale façade, now the crown of an unrecognisable tree leapt out of the darkness. The searchlight beams reeled across the sky, dropping and criss-crossing. They groped about in the folds of the sky with unhurried fingers, searching for something that was making that hideous inescapable sound, like the rattle of stones in a tin can. They kept picking out the wrong things—here a heap of cotton wool, there the body of a fish with motionless fins ... then suddenly something silvery, like the flash of a bird on its wing tips, appeared in the disk of light over Polya's head. A blinded enemy plane was spinning round on one spot.

Polya's imagination painted for her the picture of a tiny creature in it with a ferocious face in goggles pushed up on its forehead, as clammy as Polya's own. It was trying to catch her in its sights—the defenceless Moscow girl who stood there below clinging to the brickwork, and therein, perhaps, was the crux of the all-European duel. Already the shell bursts were blazing around the pilot, but he still tarried in executing the vow he had given to his führer, a vow to reduce to rubble this particular unfinished building of the Forestry Service, together with Polya Vikhrova and the little trunk of hers that had Mamma's photograph in the lid and her new voile dress in it and Rodion's poems at the bottom. For the fraction of a moment Polya experienced that shuddering thrill of more than human fearlessness which attends every noble transformation of the spirit. And that was how Varya remembered her when next the ack-ack guns blazed forth—standing with raised fists, as though threatening to be even with him when the time came.

The others did the rest. The tiny plane began to smoke; pressed earthwards by the pursuing beams it flew west. The Nazi's face faded out. It was not given Polya to see how he died. Another squall struck the darkened city, and when Polya opened her eyes amid a tinkle of shattered glass, a multitude of what looked like torches were flaming and shooting off sparks on the roof all round her. One was burning in the gutter at her very feet, arrested by a spike, and Polya was surprised to find how easy it was to toss that bit of blazing fury over the edge into the darkness. Thousands rained that night, the attack lasting almost until daylight; Polya was physically tired out from the incessant movement—running, slipping and fighting them before they started a serious fire.

Day was dawning, and a rosy streak shone under the blue blind of clouds in the east. It was all over, like a bad dream. Matinal Moscow lay quiet and virginally beautiful. Except for a pall of smoke over Zamoskvorechye, not a vestige remained of the night's fierce fray. A light dew lay upon the deserted roofs like a film of sweat that follows emotional stress.

"I see you are in perfect shape, that's fine," said Varya, herself a past mistress at dealing with incendiary bombs. "The worst thing in these rowdy-dows is our own flak damage. You haven't been hit?"

"I didn't even notice the flak.... To tell you the truth I was wishing so hard it was all over. How much longer d'you think it's going to last—a year? Two years?"

Varya grasped at once what she meant.

"It'll hardly be over by the New Year. You mean the war?" she said.

"No, I mean all this in general."

Varya became thoughtful; she was not quite sure whether her friend had grown up sufficiently to know the truth.

"Well, you see, Polya, the fascists are only an episode in a great historical contest." She paused, then went on, deciding she could risk it. "Just think, if it took thirty years to settle some petty hereditary squabbles between the Red and White roses, how long is it going to take to thrash out the great issue between the red and white halves of mankind? A century wouldn't be too much. You can count about twenty per cent of the job done, though."

Flushed with the excitement of that night, Polya had no difficulty in imagining what she would be like if she had sat out that period in the basement together with Gratsiansky. She would have crawled out into the sun at the end of it an old woman, who had preserved her life merely in order to despise it.

"You don't know how grateful I am to you for having dragged me out of there, Varya."

"For one thing, nobody dragged you out, you crawled up on to the roof yourself. It was bound to happen, anyway. What did you feel? At first you thought they were after you alone, didn't you? Then you saw millions of others like you all around, isn't that so?" She made Polya sit down next to her. "Don't be ashamed, silly. It's only natural for people to fear an attack out of the darkness."

"It wasn't quite like that," Polya said, searching for the Kremlin in the morning twilight. "You know, at first I almost felt I was going to faint, the way one feels when taking a plunge into ice-cold water, and then I saw the enemy overhead, and fear was stripped from me as if together with my skin, and something started turning inside me—the whole body of my soul, if you know what I mean!" The tremor of recent excitement returned to her hands. "Did you see him running away with a hole in his side, did you? He didn't have the guts to ram his machine down. Talk about Icarus...he's not a patch on our Gastello!"

Varya nodded approval, like a teacher listening to a pupil's answers; then, to make sure of her friend's first success, she delivered some school-reader axioms of her own invention, such as, "The big victory does not come until one has gained the small victory over oneself," or "in war cruelty to oneself is as important as hatred towards the enemy," or "a heroic deed, like talent, shortens the path to one's goal." According to her, to overcome the primitive instinct of self-preservation one had to shake off the mystic spell of war, that primordial soul-chilling terror of the unknown, which, as in the case of pre-historic man confronted with the mammoth, an earthquake, or a thunderstorm, paralyses the human will.

"We can draw from this the valuable conclusion," Varya enunciated, as if dictating, and all she wanted for complete resemblance to Marfa Yegorovna of the Loshkarev secondary school were the spectacles—"that the most important thing in the struggle is to see the enemy as large as life, to realise that he is mortal. That is why, at the front, it is of course a hundred times more dangerous than at home, but less frightening, I think, than in the basement of Blagoveshchensky Alley. In the same way people used to call the cholera and the plague the curse of God, until they examined them through the convex glass of the microscope and drove them into a test-tube—that is, they passed from terror to action. Capitalism is no more terrifying than the cholera, my dear, it's only more cunning, more tenacious of life, because it nests in the mind and not in the body. But look at it with the eyes of science, and you will see how unsubstantial it is, how frightened even of you, a slight defenceless girl, and not so much of your factories and mines, as of the shining light of youth in your eyes! Youth will never put up with evil—it will throw itself into the ice-hole, dash into a blazing building. That is why those people are killing children, and want to kill you, too, Polya." She finished and all but ordered Polya to repeat it.

"Varya, you're wonderful!" Polya said half a minute later, her eyes moist and nose comically wrinkled up. "If you get such splendid ideas at twenty-two, what will you be doing at fifty?"

"Don't be silly!" Varya snapped, colouring. "The best thing you can do in your present condition is to shut up."

They sat on the roof till the sun rose, listening to the strident whistle of the martins. Melting into the morning sunbeams, the barrage balloons sank into the industrial haze of the suburbs. The spires, towers and cupolas glowed under the golden fingers of sunrise. The river of life began to roar, and it seemed as if the crane on the nearby building site would start moving at any moment. As Polya's elation cooled, however, the burns on her wrist caused by flying thermite sparks grew more painful. She had not noticed them in the excitement.

"I respect you awfully, Varya," she kept reverting to her thoughts again and again. "There's nothing in the world you don't know—how much rainfall the Turgai steppe gets, and what tributaries the Amazon has—everything! Honestly, don't you think we're wonderful? It isn't conceitedness, it's not that just you and I are wonderful, but you and I along with everyone else, even if we are last and least! You see, we want to do what nobody's been able to do—to make the world a better place, where everything will be fair and wisely arranged, if we have to sort it out grain by grain to do it. No one dared before—they crawled, and cried, and gnawed the earth, but they didn't dare—and we did."

"My dear girl, we only tackle what is practicable. Man isn't called a man because he wears a cap in winter and goes to the cinema on Sundays."

Polya spoke without a stop—the intoxicating draught of the first victory had gone to her head. She candidly confessed that only the day before she had wanted to cut down all the flowers on earth, so that nothing should blossom or rejoice, because at a time when the finest people were dying it was like an insult. She knew now that that had been a childish weakness; one had to protect the flowers with one's body, not destroy them, protect the tender petals of life against the tanks, against alien boots, and mortars. Suddenly she broke off—a little wave of fragrance had assailed her nostrils. Wonderingly, she eagerly sniffed the keen sweet air of averted danger.

"What is that—how lovely?"

"It's the lime trees," Varya said. "You talk about flowers and you don't see them. You think that if there's a war on everything's got to stop? On the contrary, life goes on, Polya. And now, let's go to bed."

"Wait a minute, Varya, let me say 'how do you do' to it."

With head raised and arms lowered, she gazed gratefully at the rising sun. It was very peaceful, but draped lightly with crêpe, as it were.

These, however, were merely deceptive signs of convalescence. Polya was awakened in the morning by a burning sensation in her wrist, which had swelled noticeably; the stabbing pain went up her arm to the very shoulder, but it was not sharp enough to smother that other greater pain. Polya heard the voice of Madam Zolo-tinskaya out in the passage, and by a chain of transmissive links the uneasy doubts about her father came crowding back upon her. She began to see things with painful clarity, and read a new meaning into circumstances which only the day before had seemed reassuring to her—the plain furniture of the Vikhrov's home, and the hearty welcome of that—what was her name?—Taisa, which sounded so unnatural after so long a separation. Evil did not walk about unmasked these days, and if in the past that man could sell his conscience for twenty-five rubles a month, there could not be much he was incapable of doing now, under cover of the war, when the nation's attention was diverted in another direction?

Despite the early hour, Varya was not at home. The gas was burning very low, but Polya did not feel like eating, and could not put her mind to studying for her entrance examinations. She tied her hand up with a handkerchief and went out. She had no aim, and could not do any work with the spade. As a medicine, she chose the same route she had gone along on the day of her arrival, but the stroll down her favourite street brought no relief. They were not selling any more of those jolly tempting things. In one place a dull pain in the teeth roused her from her stupe-faction to find that she had been absently contemplating an array of nickel-plated surgical instruments in a shop window. She winced at the thought of Rodion. She walked on without raising her head, and remembered nothing all the way except a deep hole near the curb, which was filled in when she went back.

Moscow was following its habitual morning routine. Warm loaves were being unloaded from bread vans, and the women janitors were sweeping the streets. At the same time a lorry was carrying away the wreckage of a plane that had been shot down, and slender girls were hauling a long greenish balloon, which looked like a centipede. In search of something she could do to be useful, Polya looked into a number of yards. In one, they were extracting a bomb from a manhole, in another, house-wives were practising shoulder dressings on a little old fellow, a volunteer, who wore his cap at a jaunty angle and was obviously ticklish. Occasionally she stopped to read old street advertisements, and was surprised to find that only a short time ago she could have taken an 11-day trip down the Volga, whereas now after all she had learned about her father, she had to think of ways of justifying her existence. The very word *kinship* acquired a guilty meaning and seemed to make her an accessory. It was not trouble or punishment she feared, it was the shame and loneliness. Suddenly she pictured to herself a soldier with the face of Rodion, standing next to her. He was looking at her hand with amusement, ready to interpret even that unintentional and very painful burn as a deliberate mask to conceal her guilt.

"You don't believe me either?" she says to him with a pitiful smile.

"I don't know. I am far away, I have no time. We are crawling out to the firing line. I can see them already, and one of them is running towards me. I am nearer to him than to you. One of us is going to die in a minute."

Indeed, he looked worried, and what with sunburn and leanness, more grown-up. The grey current of the river flowed through him.

A militiaman came up and told her you were not allowed to stand on the bridge so long. He pretended to be looking at her papers, but actually he was examining her face. Thank goodness, he knew nothing yet about Vikhrov's activities! Yielding to an unconscious urge, she went up to St. Basil in his nine Asiatic caps and passed along the Kremlin wall. The Mausoleum was closed. Polya passed it twice, as once was not enough to tell all her story to the great man, the friend of everything young upon earth. Her full confession, including the story of her life and school graduating marks, took just one and a half ways. Lenin said it wasn't right to waste time on one's personal sorrows when the army had abandoned Smolensk and Kiev. He also said that the way a Soviet person felt depended not only on people's attitude towards him, even though they were big people, but on the knowledge of his own contribution to the deathless cause of socialism. And as she was walking away towards the river, he added by afterthought that he trusted her, and, if she hadn't heard amiss, called her *daughter*. The whole river of life lay becalmed, both her heart and the fire in her hand, while he was talking to her. This had taken her all day. Blue clouds had crept over the city by the time she dragged herself back to Blagoveshchensky Alley.

Noisier than jackdaws before a rain, the children in the yard chanted their song of the loaf. The eight floors seemed eighteen to Polya—the lift-woman, from patriotic motives, had gone to work at a factory. The sky darkened, and after a fortnight's heat there was a feeling of slackening tension in the air. Varya came running in a minute before the storm broke.

Polya learned that the surrender of Vereya to the enemy had hastened her friend's departure for the front-line area by two whole days. "If you really feel like it, Polya, you can come with us. I don't think it will be for long. You'll have a whole week before the exams begin." There was a soundless flash on the horizon, and a blue chill of silence hovered over the city. The wind billowed Varya's dress as she leaned over the balcony to cool off after her rush home. O for the Yenga now, pulling an oar, with the water tippled with foamy crests! With her lusty health and brawny build—much too strong for town use—she looked better and comelier in rough weather, and more in her own element. Polya thought with a pang how much cleverer, cleaner, and more needful to people this plain girl was compared to herself.

It had not started yet. A low rumble rolled sullenly across the darkened sky. The children were shouting again, helping the storm to burst.

"The darlings, look how hard they're trying!" remarked Varya, listening to the children's cries below as if they were music. "It's as if they're trying to scare the war away. My God, how happy people could have been!" she added, shaking her head.

With trembling hands Polya laid the table. Suddenly Varya's favourite cup slipped out of her bandaged hand. It was a family treasure, a present from the porcelain craftsmen of Dulevo to Pavel Chernetsov in memory of their partisan days together during the civil war. It had no great ornamental value—just an austere inscription on virginal white porcelain about war to the palaces and peace to the huts. Turning at the crash, Varya saw dazzling fragments on the floor in a flood of lightning, and the almost black flush of fright on Polya's cheeks. All the pent-up forces of the last few days burst forth. The downpour broke simultaneously all over Moscow. It swirled in waves over the roofs and poured into the room in a cloud of mist and spray, so that even Polya's pillow got wet. Varya tried in vain to comfort her friend. The raincloud stood right over Blagoveshchensky Alley. It was a wonder that so much despair could fit into so small a space. And barely had the shower washed the stale stuffy atmosphere in two mighty sweeps, when an exhilarating mountain freshness flowed over the city.

Tearfully, step by step, Polya revealed her secret, while Varya bandadged her hand and shook her head, wondering which of the two wounds was the more dangerous to life. It was a doleful story of how Polya little by little had lost her father, from the first evening in the lumber-room at Pashutino when she had sat grief-stricken with Gratsiansky's article in her hand, up to the time when she had formed that defensive habit of writing her name, which was also her father's, as illegibly as possible even on her exercise books and when calling her name, of trying to make it sound different by a shift of accent. It would have been easier to accept the idea that her father was a nonentity or that she did not have a father at all than to bear these vague, never fully formulated political insinuations of Gratsiansky's, which looked more sinister than ever in the light of the reports which came from the front.

"A man told me I would make a good criminal investigator. It's true, now I know everything. You just listen, Varya!"

The conversation in the basement had filled up many gaps in the system of Polya's suspicions. Gratsiansky obviously knew much more about Vikhrov than he had told her that time when he had been impelled by an old man's desire simply to show off his knowledge to impress a stranger, a mere slip of a girl. Without a doubt her mother also knew something about her husband's past, seeing the haste with which she had seen fit to remove her daughter to the Yenga to avoid a possible scandal of exposure. Always punctiliously honest in her dealings with the people around her, she must have taken a long time to make up her mind to conceal from them some piece of damning evidence that had accidentally come to her knowledge. If Gratsiansky himself had always been at pains to whitewash a former friend a little because he was afraid his own reputation might suffer, all the more understandable was the faint-hearted logic of a woman who was trying to keep her child happily ignorant. The mystery deepened at every step, until now, at last, her mother too had been dragged into the vortex!

Owing to her ignorance of forest affairs, Polya was unable to gauge the full weight of her father's guilt; obviously, he did not set fire to pinewoods or blow up Soviet sawmills, for that would have been detected at once as something too glaring to be overlooked, but he must have been a consummate artist in that field to have kept his professorial post after all those years of shady activities. Polya believed that the affair called for the most urgent public interference.

"Can't you see, Varya, I'm going to the bottom with a stone round my neck," she mumbled between sobs. "There's only one way out—I must go to our local Komsomol branch, but I have no proofs, and I don't know anyone there. Let's go together right away, we've wasted so many days as it is."

"You're running a temperature, Polya. It must be the burns. You ought to see a doctor. We can go to the Komsomol tomorrow."

Varya was trying to sidetrack the issue, and Polya defined her attitude towards this with an expressive gesture.

"It's all right for you—you're Chernetsova! But put yourself in my place as a Vikhrov. Just imagine us sitting here, then in comes a soldier in a greatcoat riddled with bullets. He does nothing to me, nothing spiteful or painful, but just looks at me with narrowed eyes—at me, not you ... and then where should I be?" Polya said, and looked her flustered doubting friend with a burning glance.

"But I only said we could go there tomorrow," Varya answered, and never had she looked so worried. "But what can you tell them there? You having nothing to go on, and life is much more complicated than any conjectures. For instance, I came back here, knowing beforehand exactly how I'd find things at home, but I could never guess this cup would break. I am not saying anything against that acquaintance of yours in the basement, but what if he deliberately slandered Vikhrov through spite or envy, and just made it look like anxious friendship for safety's sake—what then? There *is* such a familiar type of slander. It's uttered with an air of angelic innocence, as much as to say—this comrade would be a very kind modest fellow if not for that regrettable habit of teaching schoolchildren nasty things. Then he goes home, takes some sausage for supper, and goes to bed feeling fine, as if he had planted a young tree on someone's grave, where it will grow and spread and bear rich fruit. As for your parents' separation, there may be other reasons for it. As far as I remember, your father comes from a peasant family, but your mother—wasn't she from the nobility?"

"Only distantly," Polya put in lamely, floundering still deeper in an attempt to preserve at least her mother.

"That's immaterial. Brought up in different surroundings, they may have held different views on certain aspects of present-day life. So there is your second structure built on sand, my fine architect! It remains to find out how unprejudiced was the criticism of your basement friend—I keep forgetting his name. On the other hand, every piece of work we do is tested by the opinion of the collective body, because in exchange for that work we get bread or boots made by others. Hence the sharpness of public appraisal is commensurate with the work's shortcomings. You've got to look into it closer. Did you read your fathere's books yourself?"

"I tried to, but nothing came of it." Suddenly hope lit up Polya's eyes. "Why, Varya, you're a geographer, and he writes about forests—who could get to the bottom of this better than you. Besides, you're the most patient person in the world. Read his books, please do, and afterwards you'll tell me the plain truth. Will you?" And she swore there and then that she would never ask her for anything else as long as she lived.

"I don't mind," Varya reluctantly agreed. "But where are we going to get those books?"

"Oh, d'you think I'd make you run around the libraries! I have them all here, or nearly all."

And giving her friend no time to back out, she dragged her suitcase forth from under her bed. Thus, among other things, was explained the mystery of her weighty luggage. The books were spread under a layer of clothes, at least a dozen of them in cloth bindings and all extremely bulky. Between them were squeezed pamphlets or simply magazine articles pasted on strips of wallpaper. She was in such a hurry to rid herself of the painful burden that she threw all those kilograms of forest lore straight on to the floor at her friend's feet, with an occasional upward glance to see how she took it. "Well, why don't you say something?" she said guiltily, still on her knees.

"I promised you, and I'll read them for certain . . . in time." Varya did not sound so sure of herself. "He's a prolific writer, I must say. How many are there?"

"Only two books are missing. I tell you what, you start reading, and I'll get the missing volumes for you. I'd advise you to start with the thin ones to get into your stride, you'll find it easier going then. I know by experience."

Things were working out splendidly. Polya beamed with joy, a joy born of implicit faith in the incorruptibility of the judge.

Vikhrov's whole life lay strewn on the floor before them, his dreams and his errors, the evidences of his love and his wrath, and above all, the self-imposed and unrewarded labour undertaken in fulfilment of a boyish vow to Kalina. These were introductions to forest craft, basic principles, the assays of a pupil directed towards an understanding of the forest as a geographical entity, a commodity, a living organism, a climatic factor, a source of raw material for the national economy; Vikhrov evidently believed that his main works were still to come. The top one bore the title *The Fate of the Russian Forest*. Varya picked it up and glanced at the last page—there were seven hundred odd pages in it. The bulk of the book contained columns of decimals printed in small type, tables and maps of Russia dating back almost to the days of Prince Oleg. To read such a work required enthusiasm or hatred besides special knowledge and unwearying patience.

Varya hesitated; she had begun to realise that to pass a well-considered opinion on the subject she would also have to study the views of Vikhrov's opponents as well as official forestry practice in Russia at different periods of history, and that would take at least half a year.

"I'd read all this with pleasure, darling, but I'm not sure I'll manage it before my departure." Suddenly she looked amused, seeing herself in the role of arbiter on forest affairs. "I tell you what, put them all back... tomorrow I'll try to find out the truth in some other way."

"But it's wartime, maybe at this very minute..." Polya insisted disappointedly.

"Never mind about that. The responsibility is mine. In the morning you'll go and see a doctor. Then you'll tackle your algebra, while you still have time. Don't wait for me with dinner tomorrow." She raised her friend's distressed face by her chin and made her smile.

The outlines of the city melted in the warm mist after the rain, and Polya's distress, too, melted under Varya's motherly caress. The night passed undisturbed, and the morning, thank goodness, was cloudy. The doctor chided Polya for being so careless with the incendiary bombs. The beneficent emptiness of semi-recovery lasted all day. Varya returned at dinner-time, cheerful, mysterious and hungry.

"You're looking me over so closely, I'm a bit scared," Polya said with forced humour.

"You have reason to be. Beware! I could gobble you up at one go. Did you cook anything, wretch?"

"I made dinner for two, just in case," she said, still not daring to enquire about the results of Varya's reconnaissance. "Shame on you, wanting to eat me up, and I loving you so."

"One doesn't exclude the other. I once heard Madam Zolotinskaya telling her granddaughter a bedtime story about a giant who was so fond of little children that he always used to put a couple of them away in his belly for the night."

"I don't think it's right to put such ideas into children's heads, it isn't pedagogical," Polya said, still steering clear of the main question. "What's the news in the world?"

Varya drew two pink tickets out of her bag.

"Here, we are celebrating today. Rumours are afloat that some Sonderführer or other has started a revolt in Berlin against his Führer. These are cinema tickets. They're not very good ones, but then we shall be sitting in the stalls among the distinguished representatives of our youth eating gorgeous ice-cream on a stick. Why, this is real millet porridge? Polya, you are acquiring extravagant habits."

"I'm sorry, there's no butter to go with it."

"Anyone can see you haven't had a higher culinary education. What a funny girl you are—whoever eats porridge with butter!"

She smelt the hot steam rising from the plate with relish and mentally approved of Polya's self-control.

After dinner she came forth with the information as to what steps she had taken in her search for the truth about Vikhrov. It had occurred to her the day before that in order to correctly diagnose a patient's condition it was desirable to hear what he had to say for himself first. And so she had gone to the Forestry Institute, where she had waited heroically in the recreation room for about two hours in order to see Polya's father. There had been a scene of animation around the building usual for that time of the year, when the students began to arrive. An office cleaner told Varya that a general Party meeting was in progress in the main auditorium upstairs at which Professor Ivan Vikhrov's application for admission to the Party was being considered. The old woman had called him simply Matveyich. "So there, Polya, I congratulate you on the happy outcome—the flowers will be forthcoming as soon as I get my stipend!" After a while Varya had made his personal acquaintance. He was coming down the stairs, limping and waving his hand as if counting the steps. She started the conversation by telling him that she had a cousin who wanted to study at the Institute, but before doing so she'd like to know what she was letting herself in for, or, as she expressed it in her haste, take a whiff of forest science.

"But I'm going in for architecture! Varya, you told a lie, aren't you ashamed of yourself!"

"For one thing, at your age the choice of a profession is never definite, and what's more, aren't you as good as a cousin to me?"

"All right . . . what did he say?"

The professor had expressed displeasure at the future student not having come herself. "The job of a forester of our type," he had said, "is to be able to count figures in his head, to remember things, to compare, and above all, to walk and walk without sparing his legs." He ironically enquired of Varya what it was exactly that appealed to her protégé in the forest—was it flowers, mushrooms, lilies of the valley, or the firewood itself; he uttered this last word rather testily. Varya accounted for her cousin's choice by hereditary attraction, as the girl's father had been a forest officer all his life.

"As you see, I tried to keep close to the truth."

"Go on, what did he say?"

"He pointed out reasonably enough that a forest worker who failed to inspire his daughter with a greater respect for his job was anything but a genius."

"Fancy saying that about himself! Well, and what did you say?"

"I expressed the hope that the daughter would make up for her parent's oversight."

"Oh, Varya, my head's spinning! And what did he say to that?"

"He laughed and invited you to come and hear his introductory lecture in three weeks' time, even if it meant bringing you down in a pram—those were his very words. By that time we'll just about be back from trench digging." They told Varya in the office that Vikhrov delivered his own course of lectures only to students of the third year and upwards, but it was a tradition of many years standing that the introductory speech was made by him. She learned that even the professors of the other departments came to listen to that defender of the forests in his star part. "I suppose this first talk of his with the freshmen is conducted in simple language, and it's a much better idea to sit there for an hour or two than to try and wade through seven thousand pages of close type."

Polya kept biting her already gnawed finger-nails without concealment until Varya pulled her hand away.

"Tell me, Varya—is he a well-spoken man, at least?"

"You shouldn't judge people by such a criterion, my dear. It may lead you into serious error."

"At least, did he look ... happy at being admitted to the Party at such a time?"

"I didn't notice anything."

All that Varya remembered were his black bushy eyebrows, his sallow complexion, the trimmed Tatar-looking moustaches over his large mouth, made, it would seem, for none too pleasant utterances. The limping gait, the awkward manners, and the wisp of hair lying across his forehead completed the picture of a not very sociable master craftsman in reduced circumstances. Unfortunately, all this had struck Varya as being merely a mask. . . .

"What did you say?" Polya interrupted, startled.

"I said a mask concealing great kindness, I should even say softness of heart."

"But why 'unfortunately'?"

"Not that I like ill-natured people, but I don't like the too soft ones. Too much kindness and mildness give you mutual forbearance, and what we need are proud demanding people who can give as much as they demand from others. That's why I liked him better at first than I did towards the end. Anyway, the lecture will show to what extent you owe him an apology for your too hasty suspicions." She glanced at the clearing sky, which augured a speedy air raid. "Oh, the weather is breaking, I'm afraid our tickets will be wasted."

That was exactly what happened. They did not go to the cinema. The air-raid warning came very early, and never since the beginning of military operations had such a large number of enemy bombers got through into the city. Moscow should have been a heap of ashes by the enemy's reckoning—so much fire had been dropped upon it; but still it was not enough to burn through the thin film of the people's resistance. The girls, nevertheless, were kept very busy that evening, and Polya passed her second test of courage with flying colours.

They happened to be standing side by side on that occasion.

"It's good to be alive, Varya!" Polya shouted during the lulls, as she knocked the sparks off her smouldering mittens. She drew a smile from the fire-fighters as she had in that trolley-bus on the day of her arrival in Moscow. "And to think that I was stupid enough to be sorry I had ever been born."

Varya went about her business in silence, and the more Polya expressed the joy of her complete recovery, the more troubled was Varya by a sense of guilt. Of course, in those days of grave danger and resultant political unity, many honest people joined the Party in order to share with it the burden and responsibility of defending the country. But the same excessive sensitiveness which had yesterday caused Polya to exaggerate her suspicions today made her attach undue significance to her father's action. Varya, in her haste, had somehow forgotten to tell Polya that Professor Gratsiansky had also been admitted to the Party at the same meeting in the Institute.

CHAPTER FOUR

1

Certain inaccuracies in Gratsiansky's account of various lamentable circumstances connected with Vikhrov's youth need to be rectified before we proceed any further. It is true, Vikhrov's biography was somewhat marred by an adventitious circumstance, namely, the acceptance by him of twenty-five rubles from a well-known capitalist; although no receipt was given, the money changed hands in front of witnesses, who, it is true, were long since dead. On the other hand, it was rather unfortunate that not one of Vikhrov's numerous colleagues had courage enough, if not to teach the story-teller a well-deserved corporal lesson, then at least to remonstrate with him for irresponsibly connecting this incident with the whole subsequent faultless activity of his colleague. Gratsiansky, had he wanted to, could have extracted further items of information from the secret hiding-places of his memory, which would have been just as instructive to an inexperienced Soviet girl. For one thing, she would have learned from a reliable source what it meant for a poor person to struggle towards the light of knowledge in those days compared with what it was today; incidentally, the date of the occurrence would have come to light too.

It happened in the late summer of 1899, on the evening the Vikhrovs arrived in St. Petersburg. By the way, both mother and son were put off the train at Mga, two stops from the capital city, for travelling without a ticket, and it was only because they had light bast boots and lighter still luggage, that they were able to complete the journey the same day. For a long time mother and son wandered along the city's endless prospekts, which lost themselves in the whitish gloom of calamity that had then overtaken the whole of Russia. The setting sun, copper-hued through the smoke, gave an eerie aspect to the cathedrals and palaces, the carriages and uniforms. Terrifying objects suddenly loomed out of the mist and assumed the shape of bronze tsars on stone stools, gilded griffins on the bridges and other bewildering things that confounded the mind of a peasant overawed by all the splendour around him. Nothing should be overlooked in considering the state of mind of an eleven-year-old boy, accused by Gratsiansky of reprehensible conduct.

Every piece of evidence should always be examined under a magnifying glass, even though the time spent on it were not justified by the value of the information thus gleaned. By the time his country relations arrived Afanasy Vikhrov had risen to the important post of boots at the Daryal rooming-house. Uncle Vikhrov's living quarters was a small but fairly warm cubbyhole under the staircase. It was large enough, though, to contain, besides a cot and a rickety table, an old armchair propped up with a billet and a Persian carpet rolled up and waiting to be cleaned. Crowded though the room was, the occupants fitted themselves into it comfortably, and accommodated themselves to the sloping boarded ceiling. The bottom corner was assigned to Ivan, while the highest-ceilinged position at the door was occupied by Uncle Afanasy. A cosier place for a family reunion was hardly to be found in all St. Petersburg; the only drawback was the constant running up and down the stairs as a result of which all kinds of rubbish kept dropping from the ceiling on to Afanasy's delectable refreshments.

The only things he had found room for on the table were the salmon and the grouse in congealed gravy. The dish with the jellied suckling pig, for instance, reposed on Agafya's lap, while the teapot, being a thing of third-rate importance, had to be deposited on the floor at their feet. As for the cake with the wonderful fancy work in cream on it, this was placed entirely in Ivan's keeping. Considering the excellence of the fare and the scant wages of a hotel servant coupled with his exceedingly dour looks, one would be inclined to suspect a quite recent robbery of one of the guests. But not even the ultra-vigilant Gratsiansky could have entertained such a suspicion. The whole spread had a somewhat pecked messed-up appearance, but not so bad as to make it unfit for eating. All you had to do was to pull out the fag-ends that were stuck into it, and cut away the nibbled parts. The explanation was that a big moneyed man had been junketting in the Daryal for the last six days and nights running. He had been favouring this place on account of its proximity to the public baths with their excellent steaming facilities, and because of the quietness of the neighbourhood, not to mention the fact that nowhere else in the Russian empire could one be served with such delightful sauerkraut, the reveller's favourite remedy for a hangover. For the first half of the carouse the guest usually hired the eating-room on the ground floor, and two or three days later retired to a private room with a select company of the hardiest survivors, to initiate the wildest part of the revelries. And so Afanasy had not slept for three nights, and while talking with his relations he had twice been obliged to run to the buffet on urgent errands for the roistering merchant.

Returning after the second summons he looked obviously relieved. The spree was tailing off. Before getting into his apartment. he drew forth an opened bottle of sherry from the pocket of his shabby velveteen trousers; he did not drink sherry himself, and had taken it only so that his sister-in-law could have a pick-up after her tiring journey and a taste of high life. Afanasy was a giant of a man, quite as big as Matvei, in a blue dotted shirt worn over his trousers under a waistcoat, with a heavy brooding look and such a huge pitch-black beard that Ivan wondered all his life whether it was by any chance his uncle who had served the famous painter as a model for the rebel *starshina* in *The Execution of the Streltsi*.

"Still on the spree?" Agafya said, blowing on the saucer of tea which she held on the tips of her fingers.

"He's letting up. Asked for some ice. We'll start tidying up in the morning, I daresay."

"Must be a rich man, the way he's going it."

"He has so much money he doesn't know what to do with it. Last time he brought a fortune-teller down with him, now it's a prophet of doom. He's a terrible scolder. makes your flesh creep to hear him curse."

"What's he want a prophet for, Uncle Afanasy?" Ivan asked respectfully. Already then he displayed a grave, unchildlike curiosity.

"To keep his head from getting addled. The fellow's curses do him good, he keeps him around like you do horse-radish to sniff at. You see, the merchant promised to give him money for a monastery, so the old chap is trying his hardest to earn it."

"What's he trade in, that merchant o' yours?" Agafya asked in the same impersonal tone.

"Just nothing. He cuts down forests. They say he's stripped three rivers, and is going to send a fourth one begging."

Afanasy understood very well that it was a wicked thing to denude one's native land. He had even dreamt of telling the Tsar about it when he got the chance, as it was about time the latter started putting things in order in his kingdom. As a waiter, however, he could not help admiring the savage zest and scope of the man's orgies, his demon-like urge for destruction. In this he differed appreciably from his dead brother Matvei.

Afanasy repeated to his subdued kinsfolk what he had heard about the beginning of that remarkable career from the merchant's drunken factotum. Ten years later, in the same accidental way, undergraduate Ivan Vikhrov was to witness its inglorious end. The son of a barge hauler, this future despoiler of forests first worked with his father in a gang of workmen who refloated grounded rafts, felled the protective forests of landowners which still survived here and there in Russia, and worked as a foreman in timber-yards. In short, he slaved hard to earn the hateful horse-radish and kvass that was the woodman's regular diet. One spring poverty drove him to the lower reaches of the Volga, where he was said to have been the pioneer in a dangerous but profitable trade known as "monkeying". At flood-water the timber-floats broke up against the bank and riverside snags, and as often as not, by the end of their journey nothing remained of them but loose drift logs of unidentifiable ownership. The poor riverside "monkeys" fished them out by means of sack booms and resold them to the owners of the logging licences. Crafty rogue that he was, this man crushed all the small fry under foot and in the course of three years climbed out to sharkhood of all-Russian eminence on their crooked rheumatic backs. Bribery of the raftsmen to ensure the use of flimsy lock-downs in rafting doubled his profits. Then, suddenly, he dropped the river. The growth of industry and the increasing demand for forest produce sent him rushing like mad, axe in hand, through the timber lands of the impoverished gentry. Unlike his notorious contemporary, the timber-merchant Sukin, who broke the canopy from Olonets to Pskov, or Afanasyev, who deforested the central provinces, Knishev circled over the whole of Russia like a vulture, looking out for the "plums"; only the death gasp of falling trees could quench his monstrous lust. The cold fire roared all the more swiftly through the Russian forest since the beggared peasantry rose eagerly to the bait of winter earnings. The muzhiks harnessed themselves alongside their half-starved nags and helped the merchant strip the green mantle from their native earth. There was something symbolic in the figure of that patient peasant's hack trembling like a string on a frosty day, steaming and straining at his shabby collar and rope harness as if he would jump out of his very skin, then dropping under the whip, poor devil, to be dragged off to the master's kennels at a ruble per head. And so, when the felling was over, the peasants would often find themselves with no bread, no forests and no horses, and then in a disorganised crowd, they would fall upon those who had cheated them with whatever came handy. After the swish of air-cleaving stakes would come the scratching of judicial pens, the clank of convicts' chains, and the wailing of women, but all these sounds were submerged in the ring of the jubilant axe.

Ivan listened to his uncle with half an ear; only the mention of the hired prophet had imprinted itself on his mind. The curriculums of the parish schools in those days included biblical legends about daring men such as these, whose mission it was to expose the misdeeds of the earthly rulers; for doing this, some had been burnt alive or sawn in halves, while the luckier ones had ascended, safe and sound, straight to heaven. But the boy was not thinking of such entertaining spectacles as these. His was a very modest desire—to take a peep at a professional prophet through a hole made by the smallest of nails. And as soon as his uncle was called away to the revellers a third time, Ivan was blown out of the cubbyhole as if by a wind.

He crept along the crimson strip of carpet, which seemed glued to the floor, until through a half-open door, he heard a rasping contemptuous voice reeling off a string of deadly threats in a singsong voice, as though he were chanting the scriptures. The boy was in luck—he had come upon the prophet of doom in the very ecstasy of denunciation.

"You think, evil-living sinner, that because you got a medal from the Shah of Persia you can get away with anything? No fear, merchant! No fear, you doomed hairy soul you! In the apocalypse there is an un-Russian word *Abaddon*, marked with an asterisk, and the footnote to it gives but a single word: destroyer. Even then John the Divine was hinting at you."

"Stop jabbering, you old driveller! Who would know me in that apocalypse of yours? My business is timber," the denounced one snapped back not unreasonably in a hoarse voice. "You're worse than useless, preacher, you just can't get under my skin. You won't get a kopek out o' me today, I can tell you!"

"You'll be laughing on the wrong side of your face soon, beggarly king. It is written on your brow that your end, your terrible end is nigh. Verily, you are all black within, a soul lined with dogskin. Answer me, whose accurst coffin do I see reflected in those bleared orbs of yours?" the prophet of doom proceeded with a sudden resurge of energy, and not even a titter of provocative feminine laughter could silence him. "Both the dove and the lion have but one mate, but you, O filth-annointed fornicator, why have you dragged hither this goddess of the nether world, this white bone-rattling female! Haste not, you will have all eternity to enjoy her in the grave."

This varied collection of threats was quite an experience to the peasant boy. He put his eye to the keyhole to peep at the prophet before the denounced reprobate could silence him, but there was a key in it. So he poked his head in through the door, at which it noiselessly swung open, and some gay fellow passing down the corridor kicked him from behind. The boy flew through the doorway between the hangings, tripped over a crease in the carpet, and, in fulfilment of his wishes, alighted plump in the middle of the revellers, sitting on the floor and nursing a bruised shoulder.

"Ach, poor young man, he has come a bit late," a feminine voice cooed over him with a slightly Teutonic accent.

Apparently the carousal was at its ebb. Besides Afanasy and a hotel boy standing by the door, only four guests remained in the fairly spacious room with its red plush furniture and walls done in blue imitation marble, like a bar of streaky Kazan soap. A curly-headed fat-bottomed man in a short Hungarian jacket trimmed with black cord lay sleeping on a settee in his socks with his face to the wall; his smart tasseled high-boots stood nearby. A tall skinny female with bloodless cheeks and fathomless hollows under pencilled eyebrows, stood powdering herself by a mirror a little to one side. She was wearing a black dress of breath-taking beauty and an enormous hat with drooping feathers. Ivan had the impression that all these things on her were false and laid on, even the lovely yellow curls, and all that was needed to complete her resemblance to the Pale One the prophet had so ferociously hinted at was a steel scythe on a long snath. The smoke of her long cigarette trickled out of the window, bypassing the prophet, as it were. The latter was a red-haired schismatic Bible-reader—from the Vetluga for all we know—in a long-skirted, close-fitting, greasy kaftan with a belted rosary in the form of leather leaves, which a fascinated kitten was touching gingerly with its paw. In the fourth occupant of the room the boy immediately recognised Knishev.

No, he could not be mistaken—it was he, the man who had demolished Kalina's home. Time, however, had played sad havoc with the timber-merchant since that memorable day when they had met on the Yenga. He had a yellow flabby look about him after his drunken bout, as if he were stuffed with straw, and his eyes bulged worse than ever. No one in Russia yet guessed that the decline of Knishev had already begun. True, he was still capable of working mischief, and worked it to the best of his ability, but more and more often he was outdone by his more enterprising and better educated rivals, who outmatched his un-disciplined profligate talent with their more ruthless and efficient methods of enrichment. Like all strong men who run to seed, Knishev had become kinder to those whom yesterday he would have simply stepped over if they had crossed his path. It was left for him to seek comfort in the thought of life's hollow vani-ties; and everything around him, even the beautiful city outside that lay wrapped in smoky dusk, struck him at the moment more forcibly perhaps than it did the Vetluga prophet as being futile, a passing bubble of emptiness.

He looked at the boy with a curious intensity that was un-fathomable to anyone who had never worn the bast sandals of the lowly peasant. Listlessly he beckoned to him to come closer. Afanasy pushed his nephew forward, as if to receive a blessing, and Knishev drew the resisting boy towards him with an iron hand and locked him between his knees.

"He's just come up from the country, he still feels a bit strange. Ivan, his name is. He's a moody lad, grew up in the woods, you know," his uncle muttered quickly. "We're forest folks, my brother even lost his life through forest affairs. Strong fellow Vasily was—even I was scared of him! And now there are two mouths left—how are you going to feed 'em without a father? I'm trying to fix the lad up at Yegorov's bakery."

"Good," Knishev said benevolently. "It's only the first money that comes hard, but when it does come it stays and makes more money for you. Well, Ivan, say something, amuse me, now that you're here. Maybe you know a song? Sing me something nice. I'd give you the price of a new pair of boots for a sweet song, I would."

"I don't want anything," Ivan said with a vigorous shake of the head. Knishev's wine-laden breath made him gasp.

"Come, come, ducky," Knishev said in a mild indulgent tone. "You won't be getting any wages for God knows how long. Petersburg isn't the village for you—who's going to take you on without boots? Why, Yegorov's got the royal eagle on his signboard, he's a contractor to His Majesty the Tsar. Imagine the Metropolitan coming to your place for a hot *kalach*, and you pop up in front of him like a scarecrow in bast sandals?" Deploring the folly of that young forest wildling, he stroked his head, on which the hair had been clipped in doorsteps by an unskilful hand.

Ivan jerked his head away.

"If you touch me I'll bite you," he threatened in a most convincing manner.

"Would you? Aren't you afraid, little wolf-cub?" Knishev said, and his voice had a sound of grating pebbles in it.

"When was I ever afraid?" the boy answered fearlessly. "Don't you remember the day I took a shy at you in Oblog?"

At this point the prophet stole a look at the youngster that was not without envy, while the hatted Death emitted a fluttery titter. But for Uncle Afanasy, who hastened to the rescue, this would have been the end of Knishev's lucid interval. By listing all the woes, real and imaginary, that had visited the Vikhrov family, he succeeded somehow in averting disaster.

"I remember you now," Knishev said in a frigid voice. "I saved you from Titka. Fangy devil he was. He'd have got his teeth into me too if a falling log hadn't got him last summer. What got your rag out that time, was it because you felt sorry for the forest?"

"That was one reason," Ivan nodded.

Knishev looked up at him with new interest. He saw himself in that fledgling, a boy in a faded old shirt with one glass button at the throat. In his present chastened mood, he caught himself thinking wistfully that he would give up everything, his wealth, his disreputable fame, and the venal love of women, for one never-to-be-recaptured night of childhood spent in a haystack under stars which still believed in him, loved him, danced around him in a twinkling ring.

"Why be sorry for it, Ivan—the forest, I mean. It isn't as if it was yours," Knishev said softly, as though trying to justify himself. "You think others won't strip her clean without me—Russia I mean? Everyone's grabbing what he can. They're reaching out for it from across the seas, so why should a Russian miss his chance when he's right on the spot?" Suddenly his darkened face lit up. "Don't pity her, Ivan. Give her hell, hack her down. She'll be all the better for it!" His voice trailed off, and his knees relaxed their grip—straw does not burn long. "All right, run along, you little fool."

It was here that the incident Gratsiansky referred to took place. The merchant, at parting, pressed a twenty-five ruble note into the boy's hand, but to the surprise of all those present, Ivan refused to accept it. It were as if he sensed something dishonourable in that gift. Knishev then tried to thrust it into the boy's shirt, but failed again. The thing was ridiculous. It was easier, apparently, to hack one's country down than to thrust alms upon a beggar. Opposition always threw Knishev into a towering rage, and who knows how that amusing scene would have ended had not Afanasy intervened a second time. He simply gripped Ivan's hand together with the gift in his own huge fist and led him out of the room. Possibly, if Gratsiansky had been there at the time, a single reproachful look of his would have hardened the boy's resolution, but by a regrettable concatenation of circumstances Vikhrov's austere judge was occupied at the moment in examining a wonderful microscope which his father had given him for his birthday.

Gratsiansky could hardly be blamed however. He got only the bare bones of the story shorn of all the artistic trimmings. Otherwise he would have passed over the reported trivialities and enquired directly into the mysterious allowances of Vikhrov's student days. Knishev's money enabled Ivan to make a number of valuable purchases such as a brand-new cap with a lustrous peak, not to mention a good-as-new jacket of an amplitude that guaranteed to keep its wearer supplied with patches until he came of age. Most important of all was the purchase of an outstanding pair of high-boots, the first in Ivan's life, so squeaky that even the policemen in the street looked round with respect.

The touters at Apraxin Market assured the buyer that such a turn-out would get anyone a job at the Winter Palace.

This proved to be a gross exaggeration, though. Ivan got nothing better than a job at a wood-yard, and in the capacity of apprentice at that; this meant he would receive no wages. But then Agafya found work right away as under-cook at the handsome house with the stone Herculeses over its doorway where Afanasy had formerly worked as janitor.

2

But for his encounter with Knishev being made public in some roundabout way two years after the event Ivan would have had to face a life of perpetual errand running youth. The incident at Oblog, as described in a magazine article, was magnified by its author into a heroic duel between a peasant boy and a notorious despoiler of the forest. For the greater shame of the country's fathers, the names of the actors and of the scene of action were given in full. In those days progressive-minded people had been making great but vain efforts to stem the tide of destruction caused by the axe, and Agafya's employer was that very same Tulyakov of subsequent scandalous fame, who was a lecturer on forestry at the St. Petersburg Forest Institute.

He had expressed a desire to meet this young defender of the Russian forest, but must have been not very insistent about it, since the meeting did not take place until another six months after the appearance of the article, during one of Ivan's regular visits to his mother. That young man was brought forth from behind the cotton curtains, where his mother was surreptitiously feeding him with the family leftovers, and ushered straight into a luxurious but cheerless room resembling the office of a department head rather than the study of a forest scientist. Tulyakov scanned some manuscripts on his huge desk the while he listened absently to the tale of the Yenga's desolation. He knew deeds of Knishev's more heinous than this, and the peasant boy himself had grown since then—he was about fifteen, so that the event had lost its edge by that time. But Ivan's simple tale touched on the circumstances of Matvei's death, on his friendship with Kalina, and on how two boys had knelt in awe by the forest spring. Ivan's voice shook with emotion and for the first time the voice of the future knight errant of forests awoke in him. Suddenly the whole of ravaged Oblog seemed to have crowded into these apartments of the forest potentate—a huge blind mendicant in green rags, mumbling his doleful plaint; Ivan was merely his guide.

Never before had Tulyakov been brought into such close contact with forest woes, the existence of which the bigwigs who dwelt in the capital had always been apt to forget amid the weighty affairs of state. He looked closely, and at first with some annoyance, at his thin little visitor, who had so rudely awakened him from his prosperous complacency to the existence of that greater outdoor Russia. To the professor's credit let it be said that he was so perturbed by Ivan's tale that he failed to notice the marks that his broken-down boots were leaving on the expensive carpet. There ensued a brief conversation, which was to determine Vikhrov's future.

"Well, young man, have you ever thought of devoting yourself . . . well, if not exactly to scientific, then general forest work?" Tulyakov asked in a brisk businesslike tone.

He had to explain his meaning with great patience before he could get a sensible reply out of the lad. Fortunately, the professor was a shrewd man who understood that in the long run we never know whom we are giving a penny to for lollipops.

"It wouldn't be a bad thing, sir, but we can't afford it," the peasant child answered the professor, imitating the solid manner of his uncle.

The professor had no trouble in placing the boy in the well-known forest boarding-school in Lisino, and when he had graduated there, in having him sent on an expedition with a forest survey party. It was Ivan Vikhrov's first broad acquaintance with the forest situation in Russia. He had no opportunity in those days of visiting any areas beyond the two north-western provinces, but that was enough to tell him what was going on in the rest of the empire. Wherever streams still flowed through wooded lands the blows of the axe became as much a part of the silence as the evening church bells, cockcrow, or the tinkle of a sleigh bell on the country road. It was as if the owners of the forests, scared by the first revolution, were in a hurry to get rid of these cumbersome and ill-earned possessions before their rightful master came into his own. The minor tragedy of the Yenga was a mirror of what was taking place all over Russia. Young Vikhrov lacked the knowledge that would have enabled him to foresee what these forest depredations would inevitably lead to, but ever more and more often there arose in his mind angry questionings which were scarcely safe for personal comfort in those days of tsarist vengeance and reaction. As far as he was concerned, those five years were uneventful ones, but on his return to the capital he learned in a single day of the death of his mother and the sinister disappearance of Uncle Afanasy, who, with other Russian simple souls, had taken it into his head to have a heart-to-heart talk with His Tsarist Majesty on that ill-starred Sunday of January the Ninth.* In the dark hall of the Tulyakovs' flat Ivan received his mother's inheritance in the shape of a sheepskin coat and a pair of almost unworn bootees; the professor's fur-lined coat, by the way, was hanging on the hallstand, but he himself did not even deign to come out to look at the cook's grown-up son, apparently considering his account with his conscience settled. There had been no news from Taisa since they had parted, and except for the forest, which could not help him, and the people, who did not suspect his existence yet, Vikhrov was all alone in the world now.

The money he had earned melted away while he was preparing for his school-leaving examinations. What is more, the Forest Institute was closed for six months following the students' disturbances of 1907; he could not count on a scholarship, and the unemployment that existed in those days excluded any hope of regular earnings. He owed the rent for his garret in Ligovka, and the landlady, a corpulent lonely female, became pressing in her invitations to the hungry lodger to come down from his dove-cot to her own snug nest, where he could more fully enjoy her hospitality. He was reduced to a state of dire poverty, and it is doubtful whether even Gratsiansky, for all his ingenuity, would have been able to extricate himself from such an embarrassing situation. It was then that the postman brought Vikhrov that providential remittance of twenty-five rubles with a scribbled message from the sender in a disguised illiterate hand, wishing him success in his good work on behalf of the Russian forest.

A second remittance came a year and a half later, when Vikhrov, now a student of the Forest Institute, began to develop qualities that distinguished Vikhrov the scientist; his desire to protect the spring from Knishev's trampling boot, and his tough plebeian tenacity of purpose already at that early stage deter-

* January 9—known as Bloody Sunday. A peaceful procession of workers led by Father Gapon to present a petition to the Tsar at the Winter Palace was shot down by order of the Tsar on January 9, 1905. Over a thousand were killed and more than five thousand wounded that day.—Tr.

mined the scope, direction, and consequently, the political content of his future work. Whereas the dial of Ivan's childhood clock had known only three divisions—the cowherd's morning pipe, the midday meal, and the home-coming of the herd—now it was covered with dozens of new marks; the smallest division was assigned to sleep, but, as Big Kostroma jokingly remarked, Vikhrov got up even in the middle of the night to cram up on the herbarium. When he had amassed enough information to make his own initial conclusions about the fate of the Russian forest, he set about seeking corroborative truths in the precincts of his chosen science. That left him no time for coaching, drawing illuminated plans, or sitting in for rich lazybones. Indeed, with the rude peasant health that Vikhrov enjoyed, a diet of a pound of rye bread and a fairly plump herring would have been more than enough to keep him happy, but it was not every day that he got even half of that. He had no one to turn to; as for Tulyakov, he simply did not recognise him at the lectures. This period witnessed several most timely remittances from the anonymous benefactor, which arrived at monthly intervals.

They were all for twenty-five rubles, but now there was something profoundly humiliating about these donations, given without a word of explanation. The reiterative similarity of the sum pointed to Knishev, but travelling constantly about the country as he did, he could hardly be expected to follow the career of his one-time assailant for eight years, always discovering, in the nick of time, when he had his starvation spells. Grisha Cheredilov, who was Vikhrov's intimate crony, saw in it the hand of the scheming widow, who was trying, from a distance, to melt the icy heart of her runaway lodger. Valery Krainov, on the other hand—he too was called in for consultation—turned down the widow theory, and, on social grounds, doubted that Knishev was capable of any noble impulses of the soul; in his opinion these gifts could only come from Alexander Gratsiansky, who was well informed about his comrade's poverty and was flush of pocket money. When Vikhrov, left alone with Alexander in the dendrology room, tried one day to thank him and implanted a hasty brotherly kiss on some spot near his ear, Alexander looked embarrassed, but did not deny the implication as he should have done there and then if he were not the giver; instead he mumbled something about all that being a mere trifle between friends and hastily withdrew; the incident left a painful feeling of awkwardness in both of them. The Knishev version seemed the likeliest, and judging by the post-mark on the postal order his benefactor was in St. Petersburg. So one frosty morning in January second-year student Ivan Vikhrov, on the spur of a sudden impulse, decided to clear up his relations with the Russian bourgeoisie. In no very sweet frame of mind because of an empty stomach, he went down into the street in a light summer overcoat, which had served its purpose in toughening his will and constitution, and set off at a brisk walk—he did not limp then—for the Address Bureau in Ligovka. The street seemed interminable in that freezing temperature. His intention was to find out where the merchant put up and to return the money to him with a request that he should in future be spared the honour of receiving unearned benefits. He was prepared to find Knishev in an exasperatingly rich tasselled dressing-gown drinking seltzer; meanwhile a cutting wind from the Neva blew in his face, and within an hour he had to be at the Institute at the other end of the town. All this helped to give a sharper edge to his rehearsed little speech of gratitude; there is hardly any need to quote it, even briefly. He had already passed Volkov Cemetery, near which he was then living, and was approaching Chubarov Street with its doss-houses, night taverns, pot-houses and similar haunts of the city's riff-raff, when Fate suddenly decided to spare the health and time of the young man. Outside a *kazyonka*, as the wine-shops were then called in the empire, he saw a drunkard sitting on the pavement against a filthy wall covered with disgusting stains and red blotches caused by the necks of wax-stoppered bottles smashed against it. His bald head was wrapped in a shawl for warmth, and he had a wooden peg in place of a leg. He had a ragged cap between his knees in which were some coppers and a sweet wrapped in paper, dropped into it apparently by some tender-hearted schoolgirl as she passed by on her blithe way. It was Knishev. He must have been run over by a train or had his leg frozen while lying about drunk in the frost. He was not begging, he was extorting alms by his very appearance. His one bleary eye was staring up at the cold sun without apparently recognising it; indeed, in the state he was in he would hardly have recognised his own mother, his native Volga, or his own country, upon which he had inflicted so much irreparable and wanton damage. His whole left side was immobile, but his right hand had not lost its old habit of making jerky movements, as though he were trying to whip life up in an unappeasable craving to see what there was over there, at the end of it.

"Give her hell, wallop her!" he muttered, but no one now would know what he was mumbling about. "Throttle her, roast her, damn her bloody eyes!"

All the misery that was Russia was to be read in his gaze, but Vikhrov, without regret, stepped over the wooden stump of his leg as if it were a barrier lying across the pavement.

It was clear that Knishev, in his present plight, was beyond caring for the needs of penniless students. Obviously, the source of Vikhrov's wonderful windfalls was to be sought elsewhere, but certainly not at the Baltic Works, and at the height of the Stolypin reprisals at that, when the magistrates were swamped with demands for eviction orders against working-class families who were unable to pay the rents for their squalid hovels. All this gave a certain amount of colour to Gratsiansky's hints about Vikhrov's suspicious connections.

For that matter, if Gratsiansky really wanted to cast a slur on his opponent he could have dragged out a more convincing skeleton from Vikhrov's private cupboard long before its owner had dared to come out with his criticism of modern forest working. We have in mind Vikhrov's marriage into a class which, considering his own humble peasant origin, he should have shunned. And then there was the matter of his adopting the grandson of a Yenga kulak, and his demonstrative attendance at the funeral of that dubious teacher of his. Gratsiansky certainly knew much more about Vikhrov than he cared to disclose in the course of their famous controversy! Most significant of all, however, was the fact that if Vikhrov were given a chance to mend his ways that incorrigible backslider would not have hesitated to repeat all his errors over again.

All this, however, is preceded by a long chain of explanatory circumstances.

3

It was during that St. Petersburg period that the private student fraternity at the Forestry Institute came into being. The members of this fraternity, besides Vikhrov, were Grisha Cheredilov and Valery Krainov, of whom mention has already been made. All three, so unlike each other in all things, supplemented each other, as it were; they shared everything down to an undershirt, and ingenuity could devise no obstacles that would prevent any one of them, at any time of the day or night, from rushing to his comrade's assistance. Already at that time the pattern of their future lives, with the exception perhaps of Cheredilov, began to shape itself. The son of a sottish Kostroma sexton and himself on friendly terms with the bottle, Cheredilov had intended to go in for the doctoring of his fellow-men, but, according to his own confession, he had been picked up, drunk, at the railway station and delivered to the Forestry Institute, where he had handed in his papers; he never came to withdraw them, seeing in this error on the part of the cabman the pointing finger of fate; generally he was nothing loth to amuse his friends with the vagaries of his career. Krainov, the oldest of them all, belonged to the class of "eternal students," but not until later did it become clear why he never had time to concentrate on his studies. He was one of the few in that period of despondency and revolutionary recession to preserve a clear mind and faith in rank-and-file Russia; he had the gift of being able to read the signs of the coming social upsurge in almost imperceptible things, and thus served as a source of hope and cheer to the others; it was through him that Vikhrov came to realise that the salvation of Russia's forests lay not in a self-imposed restraint on the part of the landowners, but in a decisive popular uprising.

The friends were known in the Institute as the Musketeers, until they were joined by a fourth, Gratsiansky, the youngest of them all, and somehow that title passed to him, being used in the singular in an indefinably slighting way. It was not until twenty years later that he was found to have cold eyes, a flair for practical things, and bulldog tenacity, but in those early days he wore his hair long, sported a dandyish jacket, knew no end of verses by heart and wrote bad ones himself; young ladies of good family found his eyes awfully attractive. His versatile gifts and constant obsession with impracticable ideas earned him the sincere affection of the three others, who at the same time disapproved of his weakness for all kinds of fashionable heresies, the number of which in those days served as a measure of social decadence.

This twilight of Soviet pre-history was marked by an ominous quiet. Palace Square in St. Petersburg had been cleared at last of all petitioners, rebels, and the armed populace, and the angel atop of Alexander's column looked down with an awesome gaze, his face turned away from the subdued vastnesses of Russia. Official apathy and drumhead justice had become the way of life in that unfortunate country. The victors scoured the land in search of the vanquished, but there were none. The crushed revolution was not dead or feigning death—it had melted, as it were, for a time in the cloudless wind-scorched sky. The adult defenders of Russian freedom who had not succeeded in hiding themselves underground deeper than the common grave, were dragging themselves in chains and typhus to the convict prisons and exile places of Siberia. There remained the children and the teenagers, those whose mothers had been shot down on Bloody Sunday, and those who had carried cartridges to the barricade fighters of Presnya, crawling on their bellies, or hid their fathers' proclamations under their shirts; there had to be a pause until the succeeding generation had mastered their fathers' experience of insurrection. And when the living had quitted the field of great battle, spectres came to the fore in a gruesome dance of corruption, treachery, and all the unnatural vices to which the weak resort to make up for a natural impotence of body and mind. Its participants were misfits, androgynes, and beast gods worshipping at the shrines of Nietzsche, Judas, and Caesar Borgia; pallid vampires in cadet uniforms; sectarian fanatics with flaming lips; twelve queens dancing naked before dazed spectators; retired Hanoverian princes; an apocalyptic monk parading Nevsky Prospekt in penance chains with a forty-pound altar bread on his chest; mysterious baronesses in masks or in nothing at all; Menshies* who appealed to the intelligentsia to fraternise with the bourgeoisie, police-sanctioned anarchists and many others who had lost all vestiges of honour, nationality, and even sex. All these creatures of the night vanished with the coming of day, leaving no trace or shadow on the face of their country, through which Famine was stalking for the second time since the beginning of the century.

"A kingdom of the dead," Vikhrov had once remarked to his friend Valery Krainov while doing some work on phenology. "I'd give anything, old chap, to take a stroll round that untilled field, to sit round the smoky camp-fire with the lumbermen, to rub shoulders with the old men at the country fairs and get to know what Russia is thinking underneath. We've been caught in a terrible winter, old chap."

The conversation took place in the Institute's plantation, next to a Pennsylvanian pin cherry; the reddish satiny bark glowed

---

* Menshies—meaning Mensheviks.—*Tr.*

through the peel, which fluttered in the stir of an icy wind. Spring was backward that year; snowstorms kept nipping the bloom of Nature.

"Don't let this lull scare you, Ivan. It only means that society is storing up energy. Touch its poles and the difference of potentials will kill you outright. Don't look at the snow-drifts, look here," said Valery, cutting open a swollen but still tightly closed bud, and showing among the green pulp, if not the actual flower, then that dash of already discernible colour that was the harbinger of speedy blossoming. "It was the same that *last* spring, six years ago ... d'you remember? Imagine what's going to happen if all this gets watered twice, at short intervals, by a warm rain."

There was something prophetic about his simile, and Gratsiansky, who happened to be present, was to remember it some seven months later when the first strikes broke out one after another at the Nevsky shipbuilding yard and the Voznesensk Mills.

In addition to a remarkable memory, that gifted young man was endowed with an exploring mind, and like Vikhrov, whose thirst for knowledge knew no bounds, he, too, to a certain extent, sought the truth in all the wells he came across. Given such a wide range of interests, both political and spiritual, Alexander Gratsiansky, while still at the gymnasium, managed to skilfully combine the reading of Marx and Bernstein with a profound interest in Nietzsche, Max Stirner, and even Ramacharaka, with the result that in later years not only was he able to breathe through one nostril on the system of the yogis, but himself invented various methods of arranging the welfare of humanity, thus making sure that the latter, in its hurry, did not overlook Alexander Gratsiansky by any chance. His present austere role of forest judge, which had raised him so high in the estimation of contemporaries, was achieved only by dint of painful quest. After taking his degree, he tried his powers alternately as economist, litterateur and historian. At the close of the civil war he assiduously studied those archives of the St. Petersburg Okhranka—the secret political police—which had survived the debâcle, but no imperishable book on the revolutionary currents among the youth at that period of history was penned by him as a result of these efforts. The very fact that he entered the Forestry Institute of all schools, was rather odd, since this was one of the most democratic schools, which was attended either by the children of men in the forest service through hereditary inclination or by passionate lovers of the hunt and native wild life. Alexander's choice of a career was assignable to a congenital weakness of the chest and the insistence of his mother, a masterful lady, who wanted her son's working life to be spent in quiet sanatorium-like surroundings.

Alexander's Mamma was a dark, haughty, singularly taciturn little woman, who disguised a slight squint with the aid of a mother-of-pearl lorgnette. On Fridays, when the young people, usually without Krainov, gathered at the Gratsiansky's home in fashionable Sergiyevskaya Street, Cheredilov enjoyed being impertinent to her in a mild way and with an air of engaging Russian candour that took the sting out of his words. Once he innocently asked her for her lorgnette in order, as he said, to survey this contemptible world around them through her eyes. A mischievous rogue, he didn't care much for that cosy respectable flat with its shaded lamps casting a subdued greenish light on the carpets, but leaving faces and thoughts in the shadow, with the decadent water-plant patterns on the velvet portières and potted palms standing about everywhere, and buxom housemaids weaving their noiseless way among them like darting goldfish. As a matter of fact, it was a rather stingy house, and the fare, though served up very daintily, was somewhat frugal. Alexander had been trying for a long time to get Krainov to come to these gatherings. It was a case of vanity with him rather than respect, for, with the intuition of a spoilt richling, he sensed beneath Krainov's outward air of nonchalance, a burning truth of the people that was hostile to him. By a happy coincidence, Krainov's visit fell on Alexander's birthday, when one of the guests, in the heat of some trivial argument, made an unguarded reference to the existence of an illegal inter-party organisation among the school youth headed by Alexander and bearing the obviously imitative name of Young Russia.

The principals in that verbal engagement had been introduced to one another a week before by Gratsiansky himself at the aeronautical display held at the beginning of September 1910. St. Petersburg's bored aristocracy filled the grandstands of the Kolomyagi racecourse, looking forward to a thrill in the shape of some spectacular accident, while about ten thousand outside spectators sat about on the grass or on the seats of cabs the quicker to be able to make a dash for safety if any aviators started falling. The programme went fairly smoothly at first, and the public was enjoying the spectacle of an elderly lawyer, who having decided to subdue the elements in a Russian montgolfier of Mr. Drevitsky's system, realised too late the folly of his venture, and started to shout and struggle wildly in the basket. After this the capital's most celebrated fliers began to perform dangerous aerial evolutions over the heads of the crowd at a dizzy height which sometimes reached a thousand feet. Later in the afternoon, Captain Matsievich, a former naval architect and one of the most prominent aviators of his day, was to demonstrate his airmanship. During an interval the trio of Musketeers went to have a look at that latest amazing product of human inventiveness—the aeroplane, consisting of two canvas planes joined together by struts and bracing wires with an iron engine in the middle on sturdy wheels of the bicycle type. Here they were joined by Gratsiansky who was in the company of Natasha Zolotinskaya, a slim girl in a straw hat, who did not take adoring eyes off his face. A minute later another of Alexander's friends came up to them—Sleznyov, a young man with a square head set low on his neck and the sullen look of a man displeased with creation or perhaps with the pimply harvest on his own face. He introduced himself as a student of the Psychoneurological Institute. The man seemed familiar to Krainov, but it was not until several days later that he recalled the circumstances of their first meeting. That was when Vikhrov had run to get ice-cream for the whole company.

Presently the young men were pressed back to make way for a bald-headed colonel, who was attended by a court general and an imperial guard of Ingush Highlanders. Leaning on his scabbard, the Grand Duke questioned the aviator whether a man was likely to catch a cold up in the air, what parts of the rigging Steward of the Household Stolypin had held on to when he went on a flight with Matsievich two days before, and what force it was that lifted such a thumping bit of iron-mongery, weighing several poods, not counting its daredevil crew. He, too, apparently, was strongly tempted to admire the view of St. Petersburg from the air, but was deterred somewhat by the thought of plunging Russia into mourning, since every safely accomplished flight in those days was so much additional evidence of the existence of a divine providence. Krainov listened to the conversation with amusement, while Sleznyov in his turn, watched him from under lowered eyelashes with grudging respect.

"What are you staring at me for? Studying me as one of your psychomedical subjects?" Krainov said gaily, half-turning towards him.

"No, I like open Russian faces that have nothing to conceal," the other answered with an insolent smile, picking a speck of something from his ice-cream wafer with the well-groomed nail of his little finger.

The roar of the ovation immediately subsided as the flying machine ran, bouncing, over the grass, and a few minutes later the spectators, including those outside the enclosure, saw the intrepid captain racing through the blue evening sky at the rate of not less than seventy versts an hour. He had been up for over five minutes and seemed to have forgotten the earth; it was getting dark and the signal gun had been fired, announcing the end of the events, but the aviator kept climbing into the darkening heights after the altitude prize, as everyone guessed at once. At first no one realised what had happened when a black speck detached itself from the aeroplane and began to drop, steadily increasing in size. Then, from the stands and through the gaps in the wall hundreds of people rushed to the scene of the accident, our students amongst them. By the time they squeezed through the police cordon the body of Matsievich had been carried into the waiting ambulance; only a long dent in the ground and a torn off shoulder strap marked the spot where the captain had crashed. In the ensuing silence one could hear the screams of the widow and the womanish sobs of the bearded field manager. Krainov pulled his cap off, and the others followed suit.

The young men turned away in silence. There was an autumn-like chill in the air, and Gratsiansky put his jacket over Natasha's shivering shoulders. An early frost was expected by nightfall.

"What a sky, what a sky over Russia," Vikhrov said quietly as he walked along at Valery's side. "The tragedies it has seen, and yet, just look at it, you'd think nothing had happened!"

Valery looked up. Indeed, the sky looked utterly serene with a sort of ruthless beauty; it was of a soft gentle hue, except along the skyline, where, in Gratsiansky's picturesque simile, it flamed and glowed like a gypsy shawl by a camp-fire.

"It is a fine sky," Valery concurred in the same quiet tone. "Add to it just laws, and universal literacy, and a little more money for science, so that our bravest souls would not have to throw their lives away, and some good roads, and less vodka, with less manhandling of our women—you wouldn't find a better sky in all the world!"

"You've missed the main thing, Krainov, without which all the rest is unthinkable," Sleznyov said in a tone of noble indignation. "Don't forget those who, for a whole century, have been killing the finest people in Russia. Look at them, all seated on the steps of the tsar's throne. They ought to be hoisted on the end of a pitchfork, the swine!" he cried, all but foaming at the mouth as he jabbed an accusing finger at the dispersing crowd, snatching out at random now the swaggering figure of cavalry general Sukhomlinov, now the lean officer of the horse guards Wrangel, now the Japanese guest, Prince Tokugawa, who had come to the display straight from the railway station.

"God, how careless you are, Victor!" Gratsiansky interrupted. "We're not alone here."

Valery said nothing. Sunk deep in his own thoughts, he may not have heard this outburst of Sleznyov's, which had been meant specially for him. Down the vista of the years he could vividly see the staircase of Russia's winged glory, every step stained with the blood of a hero; if only those brave men could obtain one glimpse of the vanquished sky of the future into which they had flung their reconnoitring "crates" of death! Sleznyov apparently regretted his indiscretion; going from one extreme to the other, he suggested that they should all go and dine at the Villa Rodet, by Stroganov Bridge, or, better still, at the Belle Vue, where they had a splendid skittle-alley. "The evening is spoilt anyway," he added with brutal callousness. The proposal was obviously intended for Valery, but he still kept silent, and Sleznyov's disconcerted gaze shifted to Vikhrov. The latter drily pointed out the impropriety of his tone in view of the tragic death of the Russian aviator, and declined the invitation in both their names on the plea that they had neither the time nor the money.

"As for the second item, that's easily remedied. How much do you want?" laughed Sleznyov, making as if he were reaching for his wallet.

"I don't know how you get your money, but I have to work for mine," said Vikhrov.

"More's the pity. If I were you I'd learn to play macao. With a little practice, hee-hee, you can make a good bit that way."

Natasha's hands went up in a gesture of dismay as Vikhrov, his lips white, bore down menacingly on the psychoneurologist. But for the intervention of Cheredilov another grave item of local news would have been reported that day. He caught Vikhrov's sleeve and informed Sleznyov plainly that Vikhrov's father had killed a man and it was rather risky to awaken that hereditary streak in his son.

They parted company without saying goodbye.

4

Within about a week, at the next of the Gratsiansky's "Fridays" there was another row, but for a different reason, and again in the presence of Krainov, who had yielded to Alexander's insistent invitations. Although he had promised that there would not be any strangers there, Alexander, presumably with the idea of bringing about a reconciliation, had invited Sleznyov as well. Besides the usual company there were two skinny girl-students who looked as if they had been pickled in very strong brine. Both were called Nyusha, one was blonde, the other red-haired. There was also a very portentous looking fat young man of about seventeen in a high school uniform of expensive cloth, who somewhat resembled a chocolate bottle trying to look like a dynamite bomb, and, among others, the well-known St. Petersburg God-seeker Akvilonov, conspicuous for his size, who played a good knife and fork all the evening on the smoked salmon. The table was laid with extra care, although the fare was lenten; fast days were so strictly observed in that house that even the head of the family, who had descended from his eminence for the first time to mingle with the young crowd, himself resembled a big stunned fish in a frock coat. With the memory of the event fresh in everyone's mind, the company talked about the funeral of Matsievich, which had taken the form of a great two-hundred-thousand strong street demonstration, and from the immortal glory of the deceased hero the discussion switched over to the immortality of the soul.

Gratsiansky senior, the professor of canon law, set forth his views on the subject at such length and cited so many texts from Origen and Augustine that the guests began to eye each other anxiously, until Alexander's mother gave her husband a hint that others might have something to say on the subject too.

As Vikhrov was sitting next to the host, the ball was offered to him first.

"As a biologist I have no use for such hypotheses as the alleged after-life of the individual, even if they did raise the human being still higher in our eyes," Vikhrov began shyly. "I believe that, left to himself, man would achieve his due share of greatness by his own heroic efforts. At all events, my own science teaches me that all living organisms die for good. Nature is too jealous and grudging a mistress to let her lovers go to a world where she is not and where her laws have no force. Moreover, coming as I do from crude peasant stock, I lack the imagination to conceive of a piece of abstract space going by the name, say, of land-surveyor Ivanov. If he does not occupy any space, then what is he?" At this point Vikhrov suddenly thought of Kalina, of the serene smile with which he faced the inevitable, of his readiness to go through any melting pot, seeing in this the justice of Nature, where everything had to be everything. The absurd claims to life beyond the grave, he said, were peculiar to those who had failed to impress themselves upon the memory of the living in any other way, either by some heroic or at least useful deed, which was the only real immortality. "No, I don't believe it! Never again will any glimmer of consciousness awaken even in the rustle of the cemetery grass. And it's a good thing too, otherwise the memory of past failures and disappointments imparted to the soul would curb the impulses and performances of youth. Matter is forgetful, and nothing on earth remembers what it was before. And that, too, is a good thing, because it gives men a sense of responsibility for the gifts of mind and will bestowed upon them. Therefore, the more complete the dissolution, the dearer every grain of life is. You just mentioned, Professor, the sin of unbelief," Vikhrov said, turning to the host. "To my mind there is no deadlier sin than wasting a single drop of life in such a desert ... in such a desert, I say, as ours. Just so!"

The silence was one of approval. Akvilonov glanced ruefully at the empty dish which had contained the late salmon.

"Long ago, when I was your blissful age, I professed similar convictions. Ah, well, you know your Horace, *Dulce est decipere in loco*!" the learned theologian said with a sympathetic sigh, and ignoring those who sat between, addressed himself directly to Krainov. "Your opinion would be a very welcome contribution, Mr ... er ... !"

"Krayevsky," his wife prompted in a scandalised whisper. "What's the matter with you, Yakov!"

Apparently the parents had heard a good deal about this enigmatic guest from their son, and everyone was now eager to put Alexander's rapturous appraisals to the test. The guest, however, sat smoothing a fold of the tablecloth in silence, whereat Alexander Gratsiansky stepped into the gap with a pet theory of his to the effect that a man at his birth does not differ in any way from a beast, but by daily exercise in prayer, creative effort, or frequent contemplation of the divine, he cultivates and increases the body of his soul, and hence the posthumous longevity of an individual was in direct ratio to the amount of moral work he had performed upon himself. Consequently, already at that time, Alexander confined the pantheon of the blessed to a select circle who had the necessary income for pursuing such an occupation. Akvilonov livened up noticeably, while the two Nyushas, both of plebeian origin, rose up in arms against their leader's indiscretion, all the more tactless for being committed in the presence of the servants.

"Look here, old chap, hadn't you better tell us about that piano you've invented . . . for colour symphonies or something," Cheredilov interposed mockingly. "I just love to watch the workings of that restless insatiable mind of yours, especially when there's suitable grub to go with it."

"Oh no, let's push the piano to the bottom of the agenda, while we clear up one or two points about immortality," Sleznyov said in his grating voice, looking up from an album of family photographs which he had been ostentatiously thumbing through. "We should like to hear what you have to say, Krainov, that is, if the discussion of such a subject"—he smiled a greasy fawning smile—"is not incompatible with your Marxist dignity."

All were silent. The Nyushas' necks lengthened by at least ten centimetres. The fat college boy hawked by way of making known his presence.

"I am no authority on affairs of the after-life," said Krainov, "I intend to devote myself to the forest, the sadly neglected Russian forest. Ah well, people talk about all sorts of queer things during the plague!" This was more than an abstract hint at the prevailing sentiment in the empire; there had actually been some outbreaks of cholera and plague in the capital that month, but everyone rightly understood the reference both to the plague and the Russian forest in its broader meaning. "My friend has already explained that the essential conditions of life are movement, development, and change, that is to say, inevitable death, to which we are all subject, including the death of our personal memory. Strictly speaking, you have my whole answer there, because the belief in immortality is nothing but the desire of the weak to preserve the personal memory from dissolution. And personal memory, by your leave, is the archive of my mind, that is, my ego. On the other hand, the de-individualised state after death is subject to the general laws of the conservation of energy. Isn't that so?" Akvilonov, to whom the question was addressed started in the act of helping himself from the replenished dish of salmon. "That being so, then the subject under discussion—

memory, like everything else in a class society, is tinctured by its social derivation. With the rich, the craving for immortality is expressed in a desire to prolong their recollections of a comfortable house, a lucrative, although sometimes useless post, or even smoked salmon to go with, say ..."—he leisurely consulted the label on the bottle that stood before him—"to go with excellent red wine of Saint-Emilion vintage. The unlimited leisure enjoyed by the dead makes it possible to repeat the whole programme again and again without any extra expense. With the poor, the same idea is expressed in the more modest hope that their grievous earthly experiences will be repeated, if they have to be, in a slightly revised edition. I think you will all agree it would be too cruel to force on them a repeat performance of their earthly experiences. At the same time, one can understand the striving of the poor to prolong themselves in the world to come: ghosts are not afraid of policemen, they are not dependent on exploiters, they have no need for bread, clothes and dwellings. Among Eastern peoples, kept down by the colonial knout and a thousand years of poverty, this belief has found expression in religions of absolute non-existence. They have nothing at all to remember: memory is a curse for them. Imagine if you can"— Valery said, glancing round at his hushed audience—"what hell a man must have gone through to want to escape from life into nothingness. Oddly enough, the most powerful preachers could not think of any assortment of heavenly joys that were not accessible to men upon earth. That's why it is the duty of all educated and honest people to make the toilers see that it is not worth their while undergoing such painful transformations for the sake of improving their material condition when all the joys of life are right at hand ... they only have to reach out for them more resolutely! In short, ladies and gentlemen, you'd do well to agree with me, because belief in personal immortality implies a belief in God, and it would not be becoming for people in your walk of life to admit in the face of the most unmistakable indications that God is lazy, indifferent and wicked. Isn't that so?"

At this point Valery smiled at the hostess, who was nervously tapping the edge of the table with her lorgnette.

"Excuse me, but what are those disagreable impressions of life among the needy classes which you er ... so strongly object to, Mr. Krayevsky," the professor of canon law enquired in a tone of unmitigated sorrow.

"Chiefly those," Valery answered coolly, "which would make Volga peasants die a second time from famine, or bring bullet-riddled children tumbling down from the trees, as happened with us in St. Petersburg on January 9th, or have the hangman, say, put the noose a second time on Alexander Ulyanov. Such things would inevitably lead to a revolt among the ghosts even in the other world. So let us arrange things more sensibly in this world, gentlemen."

The silence of rapt attention suddenly gave place to a silence of dismay. Such an opening promised anything but quiet domestic joys, and Alexander's mother even proposed to the guests a game of lotto. She was insistent but gentle, remembering that it was with these people that her son would have to live and work in the future. Her appeal met with no response, and first Akvilonov slipped away unobserved, the unfinished salmon neglected, and then Alexander's parents withdrew on the plausible excuse of not wishing to be in the way of "our charming and inquisitive youth." It was then that Sleznyov pushed his chair back noisily and demanded a hearing.

He began by expressing his dissatisfaction with Krainov's flippant speech, which, he said, lacked political point. The Russians, he said, had wasted enough time arguing about the benefits of literacy and the harmfulness of bedbugs, and it was high time, therefore, to pass to decisive action, that is, to the direct seizure of power in Russia. Like Cato the Elder he never tired of repeating one and the same phrase about imperial Carthage.

"Naturally, one's point of view depends upon temperament, Mr. Krainov ... and I can't say I liked the way you sneered that time at the air display when I made that remark—you remember? —though I admit it was rather indiscreet. What surprises me is that *you*, as a party, assume the exclusive right of looking after the people's welfare as if all the rest of us wished them ill."

"We do not deny it, gallant youth," Cheredilov spoke up in his usual mock-pulpiteering manner. "We do not deny that others desire their weal too, wish to see parish schools everywhere, waxworks, theatres, anatomical and others. They, too, desire that everyone should have it good, but that they themselves, God willing, should have it better for being so very noble."

"I don't want to vie with you in clownery, Mr. Big Kostroma, or whatever it is they call you—but that doesn't matter," Sleznyov continued with a kind of crunching challenge. "For that matter, Mr. Krainov, your speech struck me as being rather offensive and insinuating against the head of this house, the house we are now sitting in, consuming excellent and delicate food. As an old friend of Alexander's I ask you most insistently, sir, to either apologise here and now or explain your attitude towards his father."

"Oh, do let's have a game of lotto," pleaded young Gratsiansky, his face aflame.

"Be quiet, Alexander, it's a matter of common decency," Sleznyov protested vehemently. "Incidentally, I would have you know, Mr. Krainov, that an illegal organisation of youth has been meeting within these hospitable walls for over a year now, and at this very moment you are privileged to see its central committee!" He uttered the name of the organisation in a loud crisp tone, a name, which thirty-one years later was to emerge from the dim shadows of history. "Unlike other parties, which are just marking time and even have their representatives in the tsarist Duma, we aim at overthrowing the autocracy immediately. Let it begin with the killing off of the dynasty! We're for an honest Russian executioner's block, but we count on your discretion and silence, Krainov. I have finished, I pass the ball on to you!"

He started to light a cigarette in such a violent state of emotion that not one out of ten matches he struck caught alight.

The failure of the revolution of 1905 started a process of disintegration and demoralisation among the fellow-travellers of the revolution. It was clear to Valery that an organisation of so naive a type was merely the dross and scum of social despair. The ebb of a violent storm always leaves some living thing squirming on the shore. By all signs the Sleznyov-Gratsiansky underground society consisted of a dozen or so schoolboy conspirators with the flotsam of wrecked unstable parties, but without the participation of the working-class youth. Its speedy and inglorious end was easily predictable.

"Are there many of you?" Valery asked without looking up.

"That's not the point!" the red-haired Nyusha leapt forward as if she were at the barricades. "One ideaed soldier is worth a company of police thugs."

"Oh, then it's quite serious?" Valery continued in the same tone of frank sadness. "I suppose you have provided yourselves with a pound or two of dynamite, a few handfuls of printer's type, and no doubt a yard-long poisoned dagger?"

"You needn't laught at us, Krainov. We may not have your experience, but at least we're not scared of convict's chains or the Fortress of Peter and Paul. You'll hear about us yet!" Natalya

Zolotinskaya said with flashing eyes, as though taking a vow. "There is a weapon more terrible than dynamite."

Thereupon the high-school boy got up. With brows elevated, he examined the simple iron ring on his little finger, as if to stress the fact that it was anything but selfish interest which had made him plunge into the abyss of the revolution.

"My name is Kazachikhin, and I, too, am authorised, on behalf of ... on behalf. ..." He had intended to express some soaring thoughts and had pulled down his tunic and ruffled his hair by way of preliminaries, but suddenly his voice failed him. He coughed with an odd squeak, as if all the air had escaped from the uncorked chocolate bottle, blushed crimson, then tossed off the glass of wine which Akvilonov had left unfinished, and sat down.

Nevertheless, they were all gazing at Valery with shamefaced childlike rapture, evoked not so much by respect for his obvious seniority or the aura of mystery, exaggerated by Alexander's garrulity, which surrounded him, as by that ungrudging admiration with which youth always recognises a forthright, honest, and genial force. And they waited, waited impatiently for his higher judgement, for some sign of approval, however slight, if not for his call. But Valery said nothing, as if this did not concern him.

"Well then," Sleznyov cried defiantly, as, dull-eyed, he pushed the dishes back on the table, "now that we have openly revealed our aims and even the place of our secret meetings and you have accepted our confidences without going away in good time, but, on the contrary, have deemed it necessary to ask further questions —now we have the right to ask you, what have you done for the revolution, and who are you—a Maximalist, a Bolshevik, or maybe an anarchist, by any chance? Put your cards on the table, Krainov." Then all of a sudden he wilted under the mocking glance of his opponent.

Everyone was puzzled by Valery's ambiguous reply. He was unable, he said, to gratify Sleznyov's imperious curiosity, since he knew of no deed of his worthy of even casual mention or police punishment, or for that matter, public exposure. While feeling sorry for those doomed youngsters, he wanted Alexander Gratsiansky to tell him more explicitly how that organisation had come into being. Valery continued in this half-bantering desultory manner, while his mind was groping among memories. And then it burst upon him in a flash—that secret May-day meeting in the woods outside the town in 1909. After Krainov's brief opening speech about the ways and means for liberating the

Russian working class, a rabid anarchist had taken the floor against him and accused the Bolsheviks of lacking political temperament in exactly the same words as Sleznyov had just used; incidentally, he had spoken so loudly that one would think he was determined to advertise his tirade, if not to the world at large, at least to some police spy who was prowling about in the vicinity. But that secret meeting had been held at night, the speaker had worn pince-nez, and his hair had been somewhat thicker; the tone of voice alone was not enough to go by. But the clearer these details stood out the more did Sleznyov himself seem to shrink before one's eyes, and would probably have shrunk away to nothing had he not adroitly turned the conversation to Alexander's wonderful colour-piano. Whether out of vanity or a desire to help out his comrade, Alexander readily explained how the piano keys were connected with coloured searchlight lanterns which were projected upon a screen formed by any snow hill, around which the select audience could be seated.

The forest Musketeers shrugged their shoulders enigmatically and presently left in a body. Out in the street, in the pouring rain, Sleznyov popped up suddenly from behind a corner and joined Valery just after he had taken leave of his comrades.

"Just a minute, can you spare me just one minute," he mumbled pleadingly, anxious to explain his attitude. "I'm afraid you misunderstood my recent indiscreet challenge, and I must dispel your suspicions, which, being unuttered, are more insulting than if you spat in my face. . . ."

"Go away," Valery mutterd without turning his head. "Go away, or I'll hurt you."

He crossed the road, with Sleznyov following him at a safe distance.

"Maybe I don't count for much just now, being a newcomer to the revolution, and I'd be telling a lie if I said I loved you to distraction, because we hold different views on tactics, but that should not prevent us at least from having mutual respect for each other in face of a common enemy. I am not trying to force a reply out of you, I only ask you to spare me just one minute."

Valery was curious to hear what Sleznyov knew about him. He stopped and began to light a cigarette, and Sleznyov immediately interpreted this as permission to go on.

"I am speaking to you as if at confession! There are rumours that you belonged to the Forest Brethren in Motovilikha as far back as nineteen five," Sleznyov plunged on. "You made it hot for them, I must say! And another version says you were also involved in that clash with the Cossacks on Vasilyevsky Island, you remember, at the Schiff factory? That scar on your temple— you must have got it in a hand-to-hand fight! But no material body can be in two places at the same time, can it? Mind you, I'm not asking how you managed it, but it's simply a stroke of genius, and I just wanted to express my ... well, just humble admiration for a man, who...."

"You'd better go away, Sleznyov," Valery repeated threateningly, staring down at the greenish bubbles of rain that hissed underfoot. The conversation took place outside a chemist's shop window in which stood some coloured glass globes lighted from behind.

"Believe me, that misunderstanding at the Gratsianskys' was not due to any desire to worm out your secrets, but just sheer childishness. We just wanted to assert our equality and independence, so's you shouldn't think ... well, that we're little ones and are afraid of you. It wasn't meant to be an insult. On the contrary, I'm ready to shake hands with you at any moment, because...."

Encouraged by his companion's silence, he touched the sleeve of his coat. This was more than Valery could stand. He put his original threat into execution and crossed the road again.

5

Unless he was deliberately putting on an act, both of Sleznyov's surmises as to Valery's whereabouts during the revolution were wrong. Valery had an air-tight alibi. Working as a propagandist, however, he was a frequent visitor in the working-class districts, and this gave police observers grounds for suspecting him of being a Left wing member of the Russian Social-Democratic Labour Party. From Sleznyov's words it appeared that they suspected him of offences chargeable under Clause One, Article One Hundred and Two, which provided for the trial by a military tribunal of anyone who attempted to overthrow the tsarist regime.

At that period the Bolsheviks were working to preserve and strengthen the illegal Party organisations. Every day explanatory work was conducted wherever the word of truth was capable of being blazoned abroad—from the platform of the Taurida Palace to the study circles and the mutual aid clubs. Valery's interest in Gratsiansky's Young Russia was not due to any desire to lay hands on it, as Sleznyov, still smarting from the slap in the face, shouted from the housetops. Nor was he interested in it merely because he was sorry for Kazachikhin and Natasha, who were heading, if not for the gallows, then straight into the arms of a new Azef* from the Psychoneurological Institute; Valery by the way, never knew that while Sleznyov acted as the technical organiser, Alexander Gratsiansky was the master mind and ideologist of the group. What he did learn was that Sleznyov had been trying to worm himself into the workers' Marxist organisations. In a conversation held several days after the row at Sergiyevskaya, Alexander Gratsiansky confirmed that Sleznyov had been canvassing young printers employed in the government stationery department, and Valery took preventive measures to paralyse enemy influence on the working-class youth.

Gratsiansky, by the way, had borne himself in the grand manner at that conversation, which had taken place in the absence of Cheredilov. Vikhrov, however, had succeeded in drawing Alexander out and the latter, in an outburst of rebellious candour, had told him about the existence of what he described as a formidable political weapon of which he was the proud inventor. It went by the name of "mimetism"; the idea was that you went to work in government offices and even police institutions in order to carry enemy methods to absurd extremities and thus to blow them up from within. Alexander had let slip the remark that great aims were worth their sacrifices, including human ones.

Vikhrov stared at that elegant green-eyed boy and general favourite as if he had started growing horns on his head.

"Oh, but won't you fellows, the make-believers, have to betray someone to them to make them trust you?" he said blandly.

"It can't be helped. Unfortunately, we haven't the civic patience which some people have. We can't stand by looking on abominable doings and waiting for the thing to be brought about by peaceful means," Gratsiansky answered coldly. "Every sacred cause is sealed with the blood of martyrs."

"But aren't you supposed to get the consent of the martyrs first," Vikhrov said, smiling wryly. "If that's the case, then who nominates the candidates—you, Mr. Gratsiansky, or Sleznyov himself?"

Alexander was silent, but he was already fumbling around for a hole that would offer a way of escape. Vikhrov expressed him-

---

* Azef—a notorious agent provocateur before the revolution.—*Tr.*

self strongly on the subject, saying that this satanic device was the lowest depth of depravity, that such things were never forgotten even posthumously, and that none but a blind puppy could let himself be caught in such a simple trap. And although he expressed the full measure of his loathing in no uncertain terms, he still regarded Alexander as a victim rather than a culprit.

"And how far has this thing gone?" Valery, who had been silent all the time, asked very quietly. "Have you established contact?"

"Contact? With whom?" Alexander said airily, his eyes sidling away uneasily.

"The secret police, of course, who else! What practical steps have you taken?"

"Good God, what are you talking about!" Gratsiansky cried, dropping his haughty manner. His face had gone bleak with terror under Valery's chilling gaze. "It's only an idea, so far, only an idea. . . ."

First of all Valery warned the Párty organisations of the capital against Sleznyov, but Young Russia went to pieces very quickly without his intervention. Nothing more was ever heard of its members in the revolutionary movement of the St. Petersburg youth. It should be noted, however, that Gratsiansky disbanded his fledglings of his own accord by way of voluntarily severing all contact with student organisations. He tried his best to make amends, and though he never offered himself for social assignments he used his connections with artistic circles to help organise concerts for the benefit of the poor, and saw to it that Valery indirectly got to know of these activities of his; it was not until the second revolution that Gratsiansky's sins of youth were more or less forgotten in the rush of greater events.

About a year later it became known that Gratsiansky was to deliver a lecture on Pushkin at the People's House of Countess Panina near Ligovka, where, by the way, prominent leaders of the proletarian movement had addressed audiences on various occasions, this being regarded as another opportunity of legally scattering the seed of political thinking among the people. The Musketeers went to hear Gratsiansky speak before a working-class audience, but the lecturer had not been able to come owing to illness. Everyone had good reason to remember that evening of September 1, 1911, because towards the end of it news was received that an attempt had been made on the life of Stolypin in Kiev. The subsequent death of that chief suppressor of the Russian revolution gave rise to police repressions, which affected the majority of the persons referred to. Valery was exiled for life to a remote part of the empire and deprived of all civil rights; the Okhranka found Vikhrov's continued sojourn in the capital undesirable. Cheredilov happily escaped the common lot by leaving for the Kostroma Gubernia, where he had been called out to his dying father. As to Gratsiansky, a search of his house failed to produce any material evidence of his seditionary activities, and according to rumours, he got off with nothing more serious than forty-eight hours detention in the well-known St. Petersburg prison situated on the Mitninskaya Embankment.

Valery was deported to his place of exile in midwinter, just when Vikhrov hit one of his recurrent bad patches; an extremely well-timed sixth remittance from his unknown benefactor, which arrived at that moment was handed over in full to his comrade at the moment of his departure for the frozen wastes of the Arctic region. This time they parted for sixteen years. Friends and comrades, most of them workers of the capital, gathered beforehand outside the gates of the railway station to see him off. It was night, a blizzard was raging, and all were a bit snowed up by the time the party of deportees arrived. First came a metallic clank of something that may have been kettles, then the drawn swords of the escort gleamed in the light of the torches. The convicts walked in pairs but not in step, each occupied with his own thoughts. Together with the political prisoners there were tramps, and sectarians, and two mutineers off the famous *Potemkin*, who had been brought to book, and sedate peasants suffering for the village community like the late Matvei, and a cheerful old man, who had sheltered his son, an escaped convict, and an ill-fated wife, who was being transported to her husband and her own certain doom—in all there were about three hundred of them, slow lead-weighted figures, somehow indefinably alike. "There they are," thought Vikhrov, "the printer's type from which the secret annals of the people's life are set up."

It was a late hour, and the soldiers, too, were sleepy; but all kept moving doggedly, as if performing a most important, albeit compulsory, state duty. Suddenly an old woman standing next to Vikhrov started something that sounded like "there he goes, poor lad, brave dear heart. . . ." As she spoke she pressed a corner of her woollen shawl to her mouth; six men who were with her, all strangers to Vikhrov, began to stir and mutter, too, and pulled their caps off. To those who knew Krainov as an orphan student with only an aunt living somewhere in the Urals, it was surprising to see how many kinsfolk he was leaving behind him in St. Petersburg. He was manacled to a tall skinny lad, who looked glassy with cold, and had such a hacking cough that it became the chief sound of that night. Vikhrov attached himself to the procession when the rear escort stopped to drive on the stragglers.

"Here's some money, everyone sends you their regards take care of yourself," Vikhrov reeled off without expression or commas, handing his comrade a small loaf. "Where are they sending you?"

"For the time being to Motovilikha under police surveillance, and then to some safer place. I'm afraid I can't invite you down," he said with a smile, awkwardly thrusting the loaf into his right inside pocket with his free left hand. "By the way, you can simply call me Stepan now—they've found me out...."

"Who gave you away?"

"I don't know ... but tell Gratsiansky to beware of Sleznyov." He raised his free hand and waved to the workers who stood there bareheaded. "What about Big Kostroma?"

"He's gone home to bury his father. Have you got warm clothes on?"

"Never mind, hatred will keep me warm. Besides, spring is not far off."

Until the soldier came up and thrust them apart, they walked the last three steps of the eleven in silence; it filled the limited time of their meeting better than any words could have done. They parted without a handshake, for Valery's companion on the right suddenly slumped down into the snow; it was as if the earth irresistibly drew to itself his wasted body.

Vikhrov was taken two hours later, on his return home.

6

He spent his two years of exile roaming the Far North of Russia with a party of forest organisers. His knowledge of geodesy and experience in timber survey, like his earlier toughening in the school of poverty, stood the young working-plan officer in good stead. Keen observation of the green ocean out there determined the ultimate course of Vikhrov's career in forest science. Tulyakov had repeatedly emphasised in his lectures that proper forest management meant roads, roads and again roads, without which the forest is just primordial gloom, where everything strains towards the light, struggles, ripens and dies with the sole purpose of one day becoming a thin layer of coal; by roads, however, the professor meant all the necessary engineering resources enabling one to enter the pine thickets, take what one needed, and remove it without difficulty. And now it appeared that roads by themselves would not bring prosperity to this branch of the national economy unless there was a drastic change in the thoughtless attitude towards the forest on the part of the owners, who treated it as an unloved and unprotesting stepchild. All evidence showed that there was not a point in the integral organism of nature where the efforts of long interference did not make themselves felt in the most remote spheres. Centuries of clear cutting followed by wind damage to the unstable firewood species turned the boundless northern plain, levelled down by the glacier, into swampland. As soon as the forest giants, nature's mighty pumps, disappeared, the inevaporable subsoil waters began to accumulate; the water-logged soil became covered with mosses and the tree seeds did not have the strength to push up through the sleazy blanket of tiny moisture-loving plants. It needed wild fires and glacial incursions to harrow down these derelict areas of tundra. It spread ever wider, drained the northern rivers, upset the conditions of water flow in the country, and brought its blood sister, the desert, creeping up from the south-east. Thus, little by little, did the forest engineering which Vikhrov had chosen as his vocation, give place to a broader philosophy of the forest.

Trudging through swamps, sometimes following only the faintest trails blazed by hunters, fighting his way through clouds of mosquitoes and smoking rank makhorka to keep them off, he crossed and recrossed this small patch of his homeland between zero and the 10th meridian in all directions. He took angle measurements, estimated the average run of logs per stocked dessiatin, and in between business, fell in love with the leisurely but not inactive tenor of northern life, which was devoid of all ennervating luxuriousness, and that most tranquil of summers, which lasted just long enough to give every living thing a chance to smile at the sun. He also visited the romantic isle of Kon at the mouth of the Onega, and saw for himself there that their cows ate fish, that their girls bore themselves like proud Unsmiling Princesses, and roguery was unknown. Thence he went upstream to see the dirty work of the foreign concessionaires on the

Onega, who cut down by selective felling the finest high-standing timber in the world, the White-Sea pine, leaving behind them a cluttered and rifled storehouse of Russian timber. On another occasion he crossed the Arctic Circle at the mouth of the Kovda, and sat on a day-warmed builder with the Karelian Anani, a masterhand at fashioning wooden creations, from cinnabar-painted bark pots to the swift fore-and-aft rigged *shnyaks*, which were as steady as a church in the roughest sea.

Orange-tinted evening invaded the sky, and it seemed to him as if there could be no greater bliss than just to sit there, at Knyazhy Bay, with the lapping water murmuring at his feet, to gaze at the glowing sky, which resembled an ancient sea fight amid a welter of blood and flaming sails, to breathe the salty tang of the breeze flavoured with the odours of rotting wood and drying nets, and to listen to the creak of the log boom and Anani's singsong voice.

"You say you hail from a forest country, but I bet you've forgotten your father's trade, eh?" Anani said jocularly, putting the young forester through his catechism. "Now tell me, what kind o' hoops are there?"

"Oak hoops or maple ones."

"What about those with knots in 'em?"

"I'm not buying any...." laughed Vikhrov.

"Bird-cherry hoops aren't bad either," Anani said slyly.

"You can't steam bird-cherry hoops."

Anani seemed very pleased.

"Sensible answer, son, good. Now tell me, what do you know about sledge bindings?"

"Down our way, on the Yenga, they use hemp."

"Quite right: tow's the proper thing to use for frosty weather," Anani said. And each time, for some reason, he added his pet word "panorama".

A passing loon cried in the stillness, the rowlocks of a fishing boat creaked behind the headland, and the sawmill of the merchant Rusanov could be heard pounding on a long strip of island out in the bay. Anani told his companion that the shores of that island, where seagoing ships now moored, had been built up out of sawdust, laths and slabs, which had been thrown into the water as waste.

"Didn't you know—the whole port of Archangel stands on wood. No end of good stuff from heaven and earth has been pitched into the blue sea." By heaven Anani meant the sun, which was practically an object of worship in the Arctic. "Look how much of our gold lies strewn about the forests and roads. We're wasteful livers, son. We don't treat Mother Nature right—we take a bite at the good things she gives us and throw the rest away. We can't complain, we live rich all right, what with cod and ling, and merry dancing lights in the sky, and the cloudberries in the woods—panorama! But look at those hot lands where folks haven't got a hut or a stool, for that matter. In my grandson's ABC book it says they sit on the bare ground or in skin tents. It's a damn shame! And here our young fellows go into the woods, cut down a whopper, chop its green head off, and drive it off by water or rail, and then everyone has a go at it, peeling and sawing, planing and whittling, wasting the only wealth we have, and that poor log melts away like a block of ice on flood-water, and by the time it gets to those hot lands it's no bigger than a spindle. And what's a spindle worth? Mind you, if they didn't chase the timber about like that from place to place, but made huts and stools out of it right here on the spot, our womenfolk would have an extra blouse to make themselves pretty. And if we didn't burn what was left over or let it rot in the sea, but made sensible use of it, we'd be in pocket again. And with the few coppers we made out of it we could bring an apple down to Kovdo for the kiddies, even if it was only a little green one. And why not? Aren't they as good as youngsters anywhere else, and don't they make fine soldiers?" He raised limpid childlike eyes to his spellbound companion. "And there might be enough kopeks left to buy the old folks a handful o' dried raisins, too. I heard say as there was a fruit by the name o' grapes in this world, if it's true. They say they're sweet as sweet. Did you ever eat 'em?"

There was something about Anani that attracted irresistibly and made him akin to Kalina. In the course of time other voices would be added to these two, the voices of his native land, which Vikhrov had overheard in his wanderings. Later, in the famous Vikhrov lectures, it was these voices that spoke through the professor's lips, saying that love for one's country, which was the pen and ink of the nation's history, implied care for Nature's gifts, which were granted for the use not of one, but of a thousand happy and rational generations. And the words with which he wound up one of his lectures belonged to the Karelian from Kovdo rather than to Professor Ivan Vikhrov: "Bend down, do not spare your back, Soviet man, and pick up that handy million that is lying about under your feet." Unfortunately, Vikhrov rashly quoted Anani's parable about the green apple to stress the urgency of the problem of running northern timber production on more profitable lines, and Gratsiansky took advantage of this to qualify it in a private conversation as sentimental demagogy and even a thrust against the friendship of the Soviet peoples.

The conversation took place many years later in the dean's office at the Forestry Institute half an hour before a very memorable conference called to discuss Vikhrov's activities. That day, many people saw them sitting together engaged in friendly converse, for both believed that scientific strife should not affect their personal relations, which dated back to the days of tsarist persecution.

"You're not looking too good, old man. . . . Mind you don't crack up," Gratsiansky cheered his victim with a word of comradely sympathy. "Still on the war path, I see. Frankly, I didn't like that Anani's apple of yours—it's wormy. You are just asking for trouble. Why don't you take it easy, lie fallow for a year or two, er . . . if not three? No one understands better than me, with my weak lungs, what an inestimable blessing good health is."

"With your weak lungs, Gratsiansky, you've lived to nearly fifty and still aren't tired of making a dirty mess on my worktable," Vikhrov said rudely in a sudden bitter outburst, natural in a man who was soon to face a storm of criticism.

"You will have your joke, Ivan, but it's no laughing matter. What's your haemoglobin count? You don't know? It's time you should at your age. You ought to take care of yourself at least for our sakes, your admirers, and er . . . satellites. Just think, what will I have to write about if you . . . well, say, fall ill?" There was open menace in that knife-edged dialogue. "The forest be damned, if it comes to that—a man's health is more important than a log, even if it was of boxwood."

"If you gave me a second life I'd use it to prove the same truths."

A shadow of chronic exasperation crossed the face of Gratsiansky.

"At least you and I know there's no such thing as the truth, my dear man. All we can speak of is man's passionate movement towards it, which constitutes the subject of history. In this case the forest should be regarded as a medium which gave you a chance to express your own individuality, to steel yourself in hardships, and to see the country. By the way, I hear you even visited the Yenisei recently? When did you manage it?"

"Yes, I've been keeping a wood there under observation for fifteen years. I rambled about a good deal in my young days, you know, until I got lame."

"There, why don't you share your impressions? That reminds me, it's a long time since we last cracked a bottle together, tête-à-tête ... in fact, ever since the Okhranka swept us up together with Valery. By the way, how did you manage to get out of exile?" Gratsiansky said, staring suspiciously at the bridge of Vikhrov's nose over the top of his glasses.

Gratsiansky was perfectly well aware that Vikhrov had been released from exile under the amnesty of 1913, and afterwards had wandered about the country for over a year. Indeed, instead of resuming his interrupted studies or zealous public activities as Gratsiansky had done just before the first world war, Vikhrov had gone on a six months' journey through the gubernias of European Russia with even a call at Siberia. By Gratsiansky's calculations, the money that Vikhrov earned in the North could not have kept him going for more than seven weeks, and, like a curious child, he was dying to know whether the gifts of his unknown patron were resumed after his exile or not.

It did look rather mysterious, that vagabondage whim of an apparently sober-minded man, who, although starved of all the good things of life after his term of exile had nevertheless resisted the temptations which life in the capital had to offer him. To go on a thousand-mile ramble, most of the way on foot, and hungry, in order to hear the simple tale of bast-shoed Russia, to get off at the most desolate wayside stations and trudge aimlessly until he struck some highroad, a branchline, or a barely navigable river, then to plod along with pilgrims to some remote cloister, to jog along ticketless in a railway truck, to work his passage up the Kama in a tugboat, and then suddenly disappear again on some other no less dubious enterprise, such as studying tar-separation under the guidance of a one-eyed centenarian somewhere on the Pripyat, or listening to the Astrakhan riverside porters singing the song about their Volga hero in twangy voices hoarse with the tsar's monopoly vodka—the Volga loved to have songs about Stenka Razin sung upon her. And all the way he peered at the lovable wrinkles on the face of his motherland with tenderness and that touch of sadness without which there can be no great love, nor, for that matter, mental health. Himself a peasant, he marvelled at the untapped wealth of her immense spaces, the endurance of her men, and the proud bearing of her women, and he tried, in the pages of the past, to read the future of his tribe, nurtured on black bread and skimmed milk.

Vikhrov's long-cherished dream, to rest his cheek once more upon the withered breast that had nursed him, was coming true. With boots slung over his shoulder, and shirt drenched with salt under the armpits, he trudged the country roads and dried up stream beds from dawn till dusk, and always the same scenes, like reflections in a mirror, were presented to his gaze. As in a waking dream, he walked through joyless weddings or, by contrast, uproarious wakes for the dead, through country fairs with their whirling merry-go-rounds, and Russian fires that left behind them a river of tears and a handful of ashes, through high day feasts, and village gatherings with their boisterous gaiety and tears, their fighting and dancing. He saw subdued fearful children, the bodies of drowned women with daisies clinging to them and horse-thieves trampled to death; lobster-eyed tipsy village policemen dashing off in a droshky to inspect the corpse, blind old men with their bumbled legends of Svyatoslav days, chain-gang sufferers for the cause of the village community—all Russia seemed to have come out to meet Vikhrov in her tear-stained beauty. And then for a week the vast silence of the fields, unbroken even by the creak of the grasshopper, would engulf him once again. The grey flame of the hot dust-laden winds seared the skin on his forehead and his open throat; how gladly he would have rested beneath the pinewood canopy of his richly forested land, but change his direction as he would, no relieving copse loomed upon the murky horizon.

His eyes tired more quickly than his legs. Sitting down by a cool bog with stunted willow-shrubs growing around it, he would gaze into a window of darkling water, where all this hapless life of ours had once originated, and where even now, perhaps, some intrepid microscopic ancestor was swimming across three feet of fearsome ocean. Or, worn out by the heat, he would fling himself down on an unmown watermead and watch the flight of a hawk in the blue or the stir of insect life in the grass jungles. Ants with indrawn bellies scurried up and down their trails, bumble-bees droned among the wild scabious, and digger wasps dragged food to their burrows. And Ivan Vikhrov, the student, would ask them what, in all that ominous silence, had become of the true masters of Russia?

The steady creak of wheels brought him to his feet. A train of some fifteen carts was riding by; men, or rather the shadows of human beings, trudged along by the roadside, some of them leading cows, others travelling light, with just a whip in their hands. Levelled by misfortune, they all looked the same age, as if they had come out of the same nest. They were peasants migrating to richer, and, at a distance, more alluring regions. They walked, as ghosts should, without raising any dust, uncomplainingly and unhurriedly, for they had all the time in the world with more to spare. The procession began and ended with those ancient trundling carts which seemed to be coming out of the dim depths of the ages. Alongside the horse trudged a tall peasant with black rings round his eyes, and immediately behind him his heaven-sent wife to have sons by, the help scratch the earth with the wooden plough and curse all creation; noon to them was darker than night. Swaying on a heap of junk in one of the carts sat an old man, yellowed by life, with a sleeping grandson on his knees. The blazing sun struck full upon the child's throat. And perhaps because ghosts take no heed of the living, none turned a head towards Vikhrov as he stood by the roadside, not even the children.

He was drawn into the current and found himself stepping out alongside the cart. He learned that all these people were victims of a fire from a village near Kadom and were moving out to a new spacious home in the Altai, that this woman had already buried her mother on the way—thank God she was released from life's misery at last—and that they didn't have very far to go now, and by-and-by, God willing, they'd be t' other side of the Ural mountains, and from there it was only a stone's throw. "And when you get to Krestovoye Village," the woman recited like a lesson learnt by heart, while she stared out before her as in a trance, "you will come to a wonderful valley smothered in flowers, but do not go there, keep left all the time towards China. By and by you will come to unmown meadows, and unfelled forests, and brimming rivers full of fish, and lots of ducks in the pools, and as for clover ..." a fellow-villager of theirs had written in a letter, "good Lor', you don't know where to start cutting it!"

"It's a long way, Grandpa, will you make it?"

"Well, we'll see," the old man said, livening up at the chance to talk with a human. "I'm still in the runnin'. To be sure, I'm no good any more at yoking a horse or bending a sled runner, cause I'm a well-digger, you see. Why, bless your heart, man, you'd be surprised the number o' wells I've sunk in my lifetime! I've got a secret key to water, I don't mind telling you. Lead me out by the arm to the wildest desert or the snowiest land, and I'll tell you the exact spot in the snow where to sink your spade. You'll be drenched afore you can jump clear. There was Zveropontov, now, the landowner—maybe you've heard of him?—well, would you believe it, he once came down for me in a troika in the middle o' the night. 'Grandpa Yefrem,' he says, 'I want you to find real gushing water for me.' I knew the Zveropontov estate like my own hand—it's all stony ground there."

"I suppose you set pans out at night and read the signs by the dew," said Vikhrov.

"Not me, I know a better trick than that."

"Oh, shut up for God's sake, you bloody chatterbox!" the owner of the cart cut him short roughly.

"Keeps swearing at me all the time, but I don't mind, I'm deaf, I don't hear him," the old man resumed after a minute's silence, winking at Vikhrov. "He's wild because I don't let him in on the secret of that key, and where should I be without that little key o' mine, a lonely old man like me? Mind you, he's no son o' mine, not even an in-law, yet he's taking me along in his cart. Bless your heart, he'd never part with me, not if he was drowning, he wouldn't. You'd better leave me alone or I'll go and die on you!" he said, wagging a gnarled earthy finger at the man.

Then the vision grew blurred and ran together into a dusty cloudlet, and Vikhrov was left standing in the road alone with his thoughts. Presently the welcome green, so far only treetops, appeared over the hillcrest. Vikhrov had come at the last minute. A stand of birches over a gully, which had survived by some miracle amid the bleak desolation around it, was being cut down for firewood, so that the logs could be removed at the first sledding, bone-dry and resonant. It happened to be the lunch-hour. but the woodcutters were just sitting about on the logs in relaxed attitudes, enjoying the thought of a good square meal and the grateful coolness of the fading foliage. Only one restless fellow with a twitching eyelid and a jaw tied up with a rag, went on working despite the heat, and it was curious to see the furious gusto with which he was destroying this last remaining vestige of his woodland wealth. Among the full-grown birches was a sprinkling of quite young trees fit only for brooms; he chopped them down at a single stroke by bending the slender stems down to the golden litter like so many necks of sacrificed goslings. In heated imagination, perhaps, he saw this innocent young coppice growth as something personalised. Incidentally, the cutters had been felling high above ground level, either through laziness, or because they had in mind stool layering, or perhaps with the intention of coming back for the stumps when the cold weather set in.

"What was the name of the departed?" Vikhrov said for a start, sitting down on a log.

"What's that?" the busy toiler said gruffly, his axe poised in mid air. But there must have been something about that unkempt, barefooted student that gave him the right to command an answer, because the man went on: "Ah, you mean this bit o' wood? Honey Grove, we called it, sacred wood."

The name suggested the presence of lime trees in bygone days, but look as close as he would, Vikhrov could find no trace of them in the sun-spangled copse. Men strolled up, curious to know who the wayfarer was, and the funnier the honorifics Vikhrov gave himself by way of introduction the quicker was good companionship established. The conversation started with a joke, someone suggesting a whiff of "his lordship's 'baccy," and when Vikhrov produced an empty pouch, it was a signal to share their own tobacco with him.

"That wood must have been in the way. You'll have more room now."

"Nay, it stood where it belonged, all right," one of the peasants answered. "Some merchant just took a fancy to it."

"Aren't you sorry to lose it?"

"The old women cried for a week. They used to come down here at Whitsun when they were girls to make garlands. Ah well, it isn't a planted wood, it's God's property."

"If it was ours, as if we had planted it with our own hands, it would be a different story," said a man right at the back. "When it comes to that, what is ours in Russia barring the graveyard? There's only one highroad, and even that you're allowed to use as a favour!"

"But this is the peasants' farm woodlot, isn't it? It isn't just anybody's," Vikhrov insisted. "No, brothers, you don't love the forest, that's what it is. Why should you, when you've always got it handy."

The peasants were silent, and all eyes prodded the restless toiler with the bandaged cheek to give the stranger a clinching answer. He started quietly, but there was a wheezy noise in his lungs and the word was introduced by a whistle.

"He rolls his words off smooth, he does, just like a goldfinch!" he opened his attack upon Vikhrov, addressing the company at large, and his body twitching as if in a fit. "He cracks a joke at us muzhiks and doesn't even laugh. It's all right for him, he's all on his own, by the looks of it. He thinks we eat honey-cakes here, but it's chaff we eat! Take me now. I've got seven mouths at home, seven gun muzzles pointed at me every evening, asking to be loaded up! And not a crumb o' bread in the house. Now let me give you an example. . . ."

"You watch Nefed, now. He says it with bite and punch, he does!" those nearest to him began to egg the speaker on.

"Well then, I have a daughter, for example, a lass of twelve, a juicy apple of a girl," whistled Nefed. "But to save the rest o' the family, that is, my sons and bread-winners, I decide, say, to part with her. So I puts a halter round her neck and takes her down to the fair, and some kind-hearted merchant will buy my apple for a pood o' white flour. Now I ask you, my learned man, who's more to blame for this? Not me, surely? And you think my account with that merchant is settled? No bloody fear! The whole bottom has fallen out o' my life. I'm a desperate man!"

"Not everything in this world is meant to be bought, you've got to have a heart," the others broke out like a forest murmuring in the wind.

Prompted by an honest desire to share with the people the knowledge he had acquired, Vikhrov began to explain the role of the forest in the country's general economy. He spoke about the harm caused by soil erosion, the deforesting of river sources and the march of the desert, and all the time he was painfully aware that Valery would have conducted this talk in a different way entirely. But he did not know this other correct approach. He was listened to politely, and an occasional yawn was covered up with a hand so as not to hurt the feelings of that kindly disposed young man with the torn boots, who was willing to share his all with them, little though it was.

"But some day all this will become *yours*, sooner perhaps than anyone dare imagine, just as soon as the people gather their wits and strength," Vikhrov plunged on desperately. "And we shall have to plant the forests again then, all over again."

"Why not, if you have the means," Nefed said. "Planting is done by the hand, and the muzhik always has his hands on him. As for the rivers getting shallow, you're right there. A raft with salt ran aground at the carrying-place here, and would you believe it, it lasted the peasants two years! Regular godsend, it was." He reached for his axe. "Well, lads, that'll do jabbering, let's get on with the job. With God's help we'll be through with it by nightfall."

Vikhrov went away, painfully embarrassed, feeling that he was an outsider there. He could feel with his back the amused grins of these peasants as well as of Valery Krainov from the faraway Lena. Valery walked beside him, almost tangible, and the following imaginary conversation took place between them.

"Well, Ivan, a complete fiasco, eh?"

"The worst of it is I couldn't find a common language with them, muzhik though I am myself. No, Valery, people don't love the forest in Russia. The ancient memory of the backbreaking toil that went into the clearing of boundless woodlands for crops is still alive to this day. I'd starve our captains of education to death for having failed in two hundred years to implant in our people if not a sense of gratitude, then at least a sense of fair play towards our mute green friend."

"Keep your hair on," laughed Valery in the rustle of the starveling rye. "You think the remedy lies in the study circles, in self-education?"

"It's a question of culture, directed, of course, towards the emancipation and happiness of the people. There you have both the aim and the path to it."

"Culture, old chap, is not a box of old books, however admirable they are, but movement, action, the ability to think *forward*. Seek a base, dig till you strike firm ground, Ivan. Otherwise your forest will come tumbling down on your own head."

"I understand, Valery, you're asking me to join you on the big trail. It's the right way, but what will become of my forest by the time we get there by way of the greater Lena?"

They parted for a time to meet again and continue the argument all through the night in a haystack to the accompaniment of the corncrake's harsh cry. It is worthy of note that towards the end of his journey Vikhrov found himself more and more often agreeing with the compelling logic of his friend.

The heat continued unabated, and the last juices of the fields were drained away upwards. The earth cried out for at least a stir of air but there was nothing, not a puff of wind remained in all the Russian land! Before the pinch of earth, which he had taken in memory of Honey Grove, had had time to dry upon his palm, Vikhrov's ear caught a low droning sound, like that of a funeral dirge. Drawn towards the sound he presently came upon a prematurely yellow cornfield. It stood upon a rise, which looked like the bulge of a heaving breast breathing its last. A group of people in their Sunday clothes, among them ancient women on their knees, huddled around an icon, which resembled the dark door of a peasant barn, except that it was decorated with tarnished silver-plated brass, embroidered cloths and bunches of bindweeds. The grim faces of saints and of angels with spears gazed from the gonfalons into the shameless, darkly fathomless sky. At that same time the dynasty was celebrating its three-hundredth anniversary, and kings went avisiting each other, but here, in the heart of the country, the village priest, just another of your muzhiks in gilded sackcloth, was busy sprinkling holy water over the drooping oats, smothered in the flowers of famine, and upon the parched purplish clayey soil beneath it, which was to yield the wherewithal for tsarist rents and taxes and cathedral splendour, for the upkeep of the armed host and the support of the country's world-famed arts, for the embellishment of the royal capital, and just a little grain to keep the wolf from the door until the spring brought relief in the shape of nettles, gout-weeds, and sorrel.

Taking pity, as it were, on the despair of the country's bread-winners, a tiny cloud the size of a baby's fist appeared on the horizon, then scurried forth and began to spread. It shot out puffs of real lighting, released a thirty-seconds' downpour, then ran off with a ripped side to visit other supplicants. It grew dark quickly, and all went away happily contented with the success of their prayers.

"There, we've prayed out a little rain," an old woman remarked meekly to Vikhrov, as she drank in the smell of rain-washed weeds. "And people say there's no God!"

"It wasn't much of a rain, though, Grandma."

"Well, there was only one little cloud for the lot of us. You've got to share and share alike. If we all went for it together there'd be so much rain we'd be drawned!"

Looking back upon it, Vikhrov often thought that this was but a step removed from the realisation of that power which lies in the joined hands of the people.

Student Vikhrov plucked a sprig of wormwood growing underfoot or an empty corn ear smeared with tar on a field balk, and tried to guess from them what this land would come to within the next half a century unless some thunderous tocsin roused Russia from her heavy noonday slumber.

8

The summer lasted just long enough for a hasty round of the green south-east. Vikhrov made his acquaintance with the West a year later, wearing the grey. He had not managed to make the visit he had planned to the thinning relict groves of yews and box on the other side of the Caucasian range or to touch the vanishing specimens of Georgian Zelkova in the valley of the Rion, or the strawberry tree on the Black Sea coast. But then he visited the last surviving islets of the southern woodlands, beginning with the Buzuluk oasis on the borderline of the Orenburg and Trans-Volga steppes, where, owing to the nearness of the desert, it was a rare pine-tree that reached the age of forty. He went deep into the heart of Ship Wood to listen to the evening conversation of the oaks, but even there, in the depths of that sanctuary, the rasp of the saw pursued him; veterans and the direct kin of the Petrine fleet were being hacked down for beer and wine cask staves. He admired also at autumn sunset the coppery boles of the Khrenovsky pine forest on the Bityug, than which there was no greater delight for a forester, and paid his tribute of wonder to the great human feat of Kamennaya Steppe. On his way back by snow trail he passed through the denuded ravished Tula Abatis, and saw that the fate of the state-owned forests was little better than that of the privately-owned ones. The ceaseless din of destruction sounded throughout the country—the landowners felt revolution in the air.

It was the year 1913, a year filled with uneasy presentiments. Discontent was growing among the people, strikes were spreading, and once more, as a kind of try out, forests caught alight to reach full blaze within the next two summers. Perhaps because the people were husbanding their fury for the decisive forward leap, a listless emptiness filled the wastes of the land, but the poets of the doomed class perceived therein a vision of countless hordes, preparing to storm the tottering walls of the old order. They were terrified to look into the darkened face of Russia at that eleventh hour before the misery of a nation flowed from the heart into clenched fists and became a revolution. The same ominous hush hung over the rest of Europe; Vikhrov wrote to Valery on the Lena that this quiet could only end in spontaneous ignition.

The year before the war Vikhrov spent at the Forestry Institute outside St. Petersburg and at the ebb of day he seemed to hear a long-drawn-out song of unhuman burden weaving itself into the voices of spring. Few could make out the words of that song, which was a call to march forth towards an already visible goal. Sometimes the wind would drop for a week, then suddenly begin to blow with such violence that none but those whose roots went deep could hope to stand their ground upon the Russian plain. Then, one summer day, a stoutish bowlered gentleman with a reeking mouth under a slobbery moustache fell upon Vikhrov's neck as he was passing down the street and began to kiss him ravenously, mostly on the eyebrow, on the occasion of the first world war being declared. Vikhrov was called up a month after it broke out; in those days, however, wars were dangerous only within the radius of a three-inch gun. After a hectic life of sleepless studies and tutoring, Vikhrov did very well on army rations—he managed to put on weight during a single summer. Towards the autumn, however, he found himself at Soldau with Samsonov's Second Army, which was defeated not by the enemy but by treachery. It was one of those military debacles which involve, by choice, the loss of either life or honour, unless both are retained at the cost of at least a temporary loss of reason. Only this could account for the fact that after wandering about for three months in the forest he remembered neither the age nor the type of stands of the well-cared-for Augustov woods. A summer night at Byelostok in 1915, when two dirigibles with the chilling name of Zeppelin attacked the town, proved conclusively to Vikhrov that it was impossible for people to exist under the old conditions. Women ran for shelter with crying infants, hurling curses at the flying German sausage, from which men shot at them with revolvers and threw all kinds of lethal objects at them, including those diabolic novelties of war—metallic darts, which, when they struck the crown of a gaping victim, got stuck in the very middle of him. A blinding flash accompanied by a roar broke the thread of Vikhrov's reflections on the precarious state of capitalist civilisation; he came to in a hospital bed with an excruciating pain in the knee, around which all the rest of the world was arranged radially.

Three months later he was discharged from hospital, no longer fit for running in skirmish line or going through any of the various motions required of a private of the 108th Saratov Infantry Regiment of the 27th Division; but then his injury enabled him to complete his work for taking his degree, so that within another year he took up his post as forest officer in his native district, some fifteen versts from Krasnovershya.

"Well, that's that," he said to himself aloud, trying to sum up the meaning of this first completed cycle of his life. "Very interesting. Just so!"

On his first Sunday morning he rode out to Krasnovershya to visit his home. The hills looked lower, the roads shorter and straighter. The Zapolosky Ride brought the young forester out into a horseshoe clearing of squat little buildings with derelict gaps of desolation, like missing teeth. He greeted the old scene of his childhood. Rank nettles grew round the boarded up log hut of the Vikhrovs and pushed their way up through the mouldering floor-boards of the steps. After filling his eyes with the sight, he knocked at the house next door, and a little girl brought him out a bucket of water with a dipper of local workmanship floating in it; he drank until the water ran down his neck. He discovered, among other things, that Taisa was living in domestic service at the Zolotukhin house in Shikhanov Yam, whither the latter had moved after the last big fire at Krasnovershya. According to his informer, the old man had "cracked up" after all his sons had been killed in the war, all, that is, except Demidka, who had been reported missing. Hearing voices, a dark-coloured puppy came out on to the doorstep. Vikhrov teased him with a twig to get a bark out of him, but it was no use; the pup walked away with a disapproving backward look at the too sportive stranger.

Gadflies were pestering his horse, and, besides, Vikhrov could no longer put off the meeting for the sake of which he had undertaken that trip.

"Did you live here?" the girl asked him at parting, screwing up her eyes against the sun. "I don't seem to remember you."

"You're too little to remember me," Vikhrov laughed. "There used to be a great big forest round here with squirrels jumping about on the roofs." He caught himself thinking that Oblog, too, some time in the future, would make an excellent theme for a folk legend.

"You're kidding! I've been living here for years and there's never been anything here but fields."

"Then I mustn't have been either," Vikhrov said rather oddly, and limping, he led his horse towards the forest.

Nature had managed to tidy up the stumps and comb the grass in expectation of her dear guest. He had to hobble about over the hummocks to locate the approximate site of Kalina's cabin. The clearing and the spring were overgrown with hazel and the whole place had a half-familiar look, except for Pustosha which loomed mysteriously in the distance. The Shikhanov road ran through here, the road he and Demidka had taken in their search for buried treasure twelve years ago. He felt tempted to hail Kalina aloud: a hundred pages of poetic experiences preceded his intention. But something checked that naive impulse to re-enter the same river, perhaps the noise of a herd crashing through the underbrush.

The way to Shikhanov Yam lay through the Sapegin forest holding. The same brown coniferous giants towered on all sides, some of them at the age-limit of tree life. Some leaned on one another for support like old couples, others bowed to the ground, forming arches of lodged trunks, but most of them performed their Atlantean service well, and upheld the heavens with their mighty shoulders. Everything at their bases looked dwarfed. Delicately woven carpets of barberries and ripening cowberries caught the eye here and there, with occasionally a clump of eagle fern, which the awed and delighted imagination of childhood used to people with the harmless denizens of the woods. Now, for the forester, all these things had become merely the outward signs by which one could determine the nature of the soil and the economic value of the vegetable cover that had settled upon it. This, then, was a full-grown, neglected pine stand abounding in deadwood, something in the nature of a museum rarity amid the mass slaughter of the trees that was going on in Russia. The state of the property bespoke a niggardly and improvident owner, and Vikhrov decided in his mind to look up that model monstrosity in his manor at the first opportunity. The drowsy lassitude of noon crept upon him, overtook him, pulled him off his horse. For two hours waves of cool green flowed over the new forester until the chill touch of evening awakened him.

He ended his tour of the division with a visit to Shikhanov Yam. That village of ill-fame stood within the semicircle of the state-owned Pustosha forest on the banks of the Gorinka, a river which made up for what it lacked in fish by a splendid view of the meadow reaches beyond. All those prosperous two-storied iron-roofed houses were accounted for by the proximity of a high-road which, for about two-hundred years, had carried dashing post-troikas, merchandise, and the roistering gentry. Zolotukhin's tavern now stood on the edge of the village; two crooked bird-cherry trees wreathed in the tow of knawel stood like lost souls at the covered doorsteps that led up into the keeper's apartments. Hens were pecking spilled oats around the horse post, and a soldier with a wooden leg was sitting on the step, twining a horse-hair lash on a cowherd's whip, a lash so stinging as if he would put into it all the rankling resentment which he kept hidden from the world. Vikhrov went into the empty tavern, but he did not cross into the inner room reserved for the better class of customers. He sat down at a table covered with oilcloth near the door. He was given a handful of biscuits, two baked eggs, and a glass of muddy tea *with war*, as they told him, instead of sugar. The hoped-for meeting with his sister did not take place—she had been sent off to Loshkarev with a horse and cart for paraffin oil.

It was the summer of nineteen sixteen, the time—about seven o'clock. As often happens in calamitous times, a gloomy silence reigned over the place—no children laughed, no dogs barked. Behind a desk by the open window sat a leathery old man—Zolotukhin, the master. With his beard grasped in his fist, he was gazing at the endless ribbon of the road, which dipped in the folds of the landscape to reappear, running westward, a third of its width. It looked bleak and desolate, without even a cloud of dust or a jingling horse bell along its whole length. Bathed in the glow of sunset that made it look like a cake with icing on it, the world was waiting for something—the fields for rain, the tavern-keeper for his lost sons, Vikhrov for something new, anything that would break the old bonds. The new age, however, was seventeen years late in coming. It was during that year, the halcyon year preceding the storm, that certain events of great significance to Vikhrov occurred.

CHAPTER FIVE

1

The initial successes of the German invasion arising from a number of unfortunate political circumstances, in the summer of 1941, while not deciding the outcome of the war, nevertheless enabled the aggressors to drive a deep wedge into Soviet spaces. There was something suicidal in the grim determination with which the enemy took that plunge from the height of his all-European might. Like the Napoleonic army, which invaded Russia on an early June morning, the Germans moved towards their destruction along the same tried highroad via Smolensk. Easy military successes in the West had dulled in the Germans of those days the edge of their characteristic curiosity in regard to the world round them, including their Eastern neighbour, her history, her national character, and the nature of the political changes that had taken place in her manner of life.

The Nazi losses mounted as their front extended and their end drew near. The vehemence of the enemy onslaught confronted the Soviet command with the immediate task of stemming the offensive at all cost. From the bitterness of defeat and a sense of historical peril was born a partisan fury, and henceforth Russian villages girt in flames were sold to the conqueror at a price which, in the West, he had sometimes paid for fortresses. Thus began the holy patriotic war, in which the Soviet people, besides fighting for their land, defended values that belonged to the remotest generations.

The spearhead of the enemy's fury was levelled at the capital. It appeared to him the final step towards world supremacy, as if its mere possession could have influenced the trend of greater history. He had to have Moscow, be it even a dead and devastated Moscow; the bloodier the spoils, the dearer they are to the savage. And although it was a rare night when the enemy bombing squadrons did not attack the blacked-out city, Moscow remained practically unscathed in spite of everything. True, she had turned slightly grey, powdered by the ashes of war, like a dwelling that gathers dust when its master goes away for a long time. In all other respects the capital lived its life with the same fulness of sensation, except that the shows were often interrupted by air-alert intervals and that the participants of chess tournaments and their fans gathered with gas-masks strapped to their hips. As autumn approached the recent disarray gave place everywhere to smooth teamwork. Millions of hands came to the help of vast industry; railway depots were building armoured trains as an unscheduled side-line, mineral water factories were manufacturing formidable mortars, soldiers' wives were punching cases for anti-tank mines.

And so Moscow settled down to the routine of war life, and night duty became a permanent feature of the working day. As soon as twilight gathered, Polya, of her own accord, went up on the roof with Varya. Both of them had learned the knack of throwing off the incendiary bombs without their mittens before the stabiliser had had time to get hot. From the height of their eight storeys the girls were better able to see the roads of suburban Moscow in the flush of converging war. Somewhere out there, probably, Pavel Chernetsov was trudging east with a staff and a knapsack, while Polya's mother, in a cart containing the hospital paraphernalia, brought up the rear of the straggling refugee column. But the days passed, and no father of Varya's or mother of Polya's turned up at Blagoveshchensky Alley to embrace their daughters. It was not fear for their near ones, least of all anxiety for their own safety that gripped Varya and Polya during the hours of night that preceded the raid, but a sense of the inadequacy of their own miserable efforts in face of the overwhelming calamity that threatened their country. Every day one read reports in the papers describing the heroic deeds of soldiers and printing their pictures. Most of them were young men, of the same age as the girls, and like them, members of the Komsomol. Every time they read the communiqués the girls fell silent and did not raise their eyes. The very act of morning tea-drinking, sugarless though it was, seemed to them now a crime so unnatural and heinous that it was not even mentioned in the list of war "don'ts". Voluntary non-staff work at the factory nurseries of the neighbourhood brought no relief.

The thing started before the actual bombing, when Moscow noticeably emptied, unloading from both ends at once. At one end, detachments of the home guard went straight into action, like a hundred and thirty years ago, and young people went out to build defensive works, while from the railway stations at the other end, trainloads of factory machinery and Moscow's children were moving out to the Ural wilds, where they would be safe from the hazards of the half-besieged capital. The children, subdued like sparrows in a rain, were now being moved out in crowded buses, and the city watched them go with a long narrowed glance. All understood that this was the least irreparable of separations, because the tons of soldiers' cocked-hat letters had not yet passed from the postmen's bags into the hands of their addressees. They knew that the greater pain was still to come. In the very realisation of the magnitude of the troubles and labours to come there was something that helped people to count off the days that remained until victory.

Only down below, under the windows of house No. 8a, children's voices could still be heard, stirring a hope that things at the front had changed for the better and that the dicision of the State Committee of Defence ordering the evacuation of the children would be out of date by the time it reached Blagoveshchensky Alley. But one day, early in August, after a turbulent night, Varya woke up with a startled sense of sudden change. Just as she was, in her night-dress, she looked out, but saw nothing there that threatened life or limb. She had been awakened by the absence of the customary birdlike prattle of the children, which used to fill her for the whole day with an exhilarating sense of buoyancy and confidence, a sense of something multitudinous and plentiful.

And the moment she was left alone with her thoughts and the empty sky, she recalled a woodlet on the Yenga, or rather a woodland nook draped in club-moss, which she alone had known, because the youth of Loshkarev had preferred to take their strolls on the nearby cliff where the pines hung over the river. And when her girl friends drifted away with the boys for whispered confidences or lovering, their chilled fingers entwined, and Bobrinin, too, led away his girl, a new one every time—but never Varya!— she would steal away unobserved to a glade, hidden amid the pines, and fling herself down on her back with arms spread wide, and lie there all alone, big and ungainly, like Ilya the buoy-keeper's boat with its tossed oars, gazing up at the sky until it began to rock her gently on its motherly wave. She vividly imagined another lying there now on the same spot, still warm and identifiable, his eyes open and yet so dead that an ant was crawling over his face and on to his dimmed eyeball without him caring. Varya swayed and knocked something off the windowsill. Polya saw her slumped down on the floor with her face in her knees.

"Varya, what's the matter?"

"Leave me alone. I'll be all right in a moment. I looked down and it made me dizzy."

Polya tried in vain to pull her hands away from her face.

"Have some water. I thought they were coming over again. What's the time?"

"My watch has stopped. Put the water away. It's early yet, it's Sunday today . . . go to sleep."

Keeping her eyes on her friend all the time, Polya went over to the balcony, but there was nothing there, neither the wood on the Yenga, nor the body of Bobrinin—nothing but an immensity of sky, airy, blue and brazen. And so clear was the night-becalmed air, laden with the autumn-like scent of fennel, that the clatter of hooves of the patrol squad could be heard right up here, on the eighth floor. The break of summer could be felt everywhere, but most of all, perhaps, in the worn dusty leaves of the poplars. Then it dawned on Polya that the children's play-ground down below was empty, and that boisterous song of the loaf, which used to wake her in the mornings, now seemed the most inspired symphonic creation of life to her.

"Things are very bad, you know," Polya said, taking the dress which she had washed the evening before off the line.

"What is?"

"At the front. I can imagine what's happening on the railways with all those children, and all that iron-mongery of war going opposite ways. It looks like it's going to be a long story, otherwise they wouldn't start evacuating them."

Meanwhile Varya had recovered from her fright.

"Naturally, it isn't for half a year, and it isn't for ever either," she said.

They dressed, but were no longer in a hurry to go anywhere; they had got so used to each other during the last six weeks that the same thoughts often occurred to them at the same time. Both of them were now thinking sadly that with the departure of the nurseries they could sleep till dinner-time if they wished. When a child's laugh reached them through the wall, they both rushed out together, snatching up the last remaining sweet to pay for the joy.

They were mistaken. Madam Zolotinskaya was preparing a farewell breakfast for her granddaughter, who was almost fitted out already for the journey. Never had the child looked so happy. A few days before this they had been to the Zoo, and the best thing of all there was the lion, who had snapped at a fly. All the neighbours knew the story of her grandmother's old debt, which had been held up because there were so many torn stockings which Moscow's ladies wanted mended. Sitting up in her cot with a little mirror, the girl was playing the sunbeam on grandma's mouth, and voiced her delight whenever she succeeded in doing so. And what a lark it was when grandma, like that lion at the Zoo, tried to catch the mischievous imp of a beam, which would wriggle out and go dancing about all over her face.

"You'll go for a ride on a lovely river in a pretty ship," Grandma Natalya was saying, picking the last grains of red caviar out of the dish. "Every night you'll sleep in a new place until you come to a pretty white house on a high green hill. You will have a thousand little girl friends and you will be taught the nicest songs in the world." The child asked a question, but it was indistinct because she was sitting with her back to the door. Her grandmother answered with a calmness that was remarkable at such a moment—no, only sick ships slept in the garage at night, but the healthy ones, like people in the war, worked in the open day and night. "Aren't you coming in, girls, is it anything urgent?" she called out, annoyed by the repeated rustlings outside the door, which was slightly ajar.

Never had the girls found Zolotinskaya's room so disorderly. Winter clothes were lying about on the floor, and the potted geranium, unwatered the evening before, stood forlorn and drooping on the windowsill as if it knew it was going to part with its little mistress. Varya plausibly explained their intrusion by saying they wanted to say goodbye before leaving for their trench-digging job. The woman relented and invited them to sit down. Polya perched on the arm of the chair next to Varya. By force of habit, she glanced at herself in the oval mirror with the crack running down it from corner to corner, and again two identical girls looked out at her; they were slightly thinner ones this time, but every inch Muscovites, and Polya was glad that the silly shine of provincial newness was rubbed off her at last.

"Are you going together with Zoya?" Varya asked their neighbour.

"No, I'm staying in Moscow."

"I'm asking because ... there's really no need now for you to lay yourself open to risks, when you can so easily avoid them."

"Oh, I've seen so much in the past, Comrade Chernetsova, that anything the future may hold for me is a mere trifle," smiled Madam Zolotinskaya. "Surely, in such a big job as war is, there must be something even an old woman could do? Leave me that at least! Besides, I have no near ones at the front, and that makes me feel bad." She forthwith offered to look after the girls' room during their absence, especially as she had accepted similar commissions from at least a dozen other tenants who had gone to the front; some of them had even given her money to pay the rent and other bills—against her receipt, of course, she hastened to add in a crisp tone. "In short, my granddaughter and I held a family council and decided to part company for a time."

"But Zoya will miss her grandma," Polya said, admiring the soft irradiated curls on the child's neck.

"Oh, I doubt it. She will be happier there without me." Madam Zolotinskaya held that the cloying affection of the old was bound to become a burden to those they loved. Besides, her sight had become so poor in the last six months that she would have been obliged to turn customers away had they not fallen off by themselves; and separation would spare the child the distressing spectacle of human dilapidation, and eventually other bitter and irksome duties. "I see you don't agree with me again, my dear Comrade Chernetsova?"

Their frequent abstract disputes usually began that way. There were many things that Varya liked about this rather austere taciturn woman of another age and alien environment, but for some odd reason her every thought roused in Varya a spirit of contradiction.

"Yes, I think you are wrong," she took her up. "The way you put it, parents must not count on their children's bread in their old age ... is that it? But in life we have to pay for everything, and children should be taught certain duties when they are still little." She even quoted the example of posterity, who would come into possession of an unsullied world free from evil not just by way of legal inheritance, but under a strict obligation to protect and increase the colossal labour of their fathers. "It's wrong, and even bad for the children themselves. So don't repudiate your sacred rights, Natalya Sergeyevna—those rights are safeguarded by specially created stern laws!"

Nodding and smiling at the eager girl, so young and just, but childless, Madam Zolotinskaya packed her granddaughter's trousseau in a tight canvas rucksack with a dog embroidered on the flap, and she allowed the fluffy little things to linger in her hands, as though she were trying to memorise them by touch. She answered Varya that the highest laws were those that were implied, written in the heart, and the more society had of them the higher would its moral standard be. Hence it was Comrade Chernetsova's duty as a future school-teacher not only to instil in her pupils the cardinal civil virtues, but to make them an unconscious need—virtues such as love of country, respect for the old, and thrifty care of socialist property.

"Of course, it's all a matter of personal beliefs, Varya, but I doubt whether I shall ever need the protection of the Soviet court. I don't think I would ever be able to swallow a piece of bread that had been bought with the proceeds from the auction sale of my Zoya's property," she said, glancing anxiously at the clock.

Varya was silenced.

"Is it time for you to be going?" she said, getting up and looking at the old woman with respect.

"No, don't go yet. We still have seven whole minutes at our disposal. Zoya and I will have plenty of time to say goodbye to each other at the landing-stage." And without waiting for Varya to brace herself for further argument, she turned to her friend: "Have you seen your father yet, at least to verify your opinion of him?"

"I went there but he wasn't in," Polya confessed, blushing.

"Be sure to catch him in." The presence of Zoya seemed to encourage her to candid talk. "In spite of what I know of him, your father strikes me as being a worthy man and a conscientious scientist."

"Did you read his books?" Polya burst out.

"No, but ... as I told you last time, I often had occasion to meet that ... well, his opponent. Besides, I heard snatches of your conversation with him in the bomb shelter by accident. Unfortunately, I haven't the time to go into details, but your father's opponent belongs to that class of biased judges who see things not as they really are but rather as they stand reflected in their own suspicious and ... not always kindly nature. Such people are incapable of keeping an open mind, and in their old age they pay heavily for their errors and indiscretions. But then you have an enviably straight road before you, Polya. You will not have to grope about in the darkness for life's goal, and consequently stumble and fall like ... well, like some of us have had to" She kept glancing at the door while saying this, and apparently wishing to cover up her mysterious hint, she advised Polya not to judge her father too hastily, as this was liable to lead her to rash acts and darken her faith in people.

"You're quite right. It all depends on how you fall, you might hurt yourself for a lifetime," Polya timidly concurred, noticing for the second time that Madam Zolotinskaya was trying simultaneously to whitewash that man in her own eyes and punish him for some old unpardoned offence, while Varya, for her part, also noted that it had something to do with the way Madam Zolotinskaya kept looking towards the door, as though she were expecting someone who was not coming and fell ever lower in her estimation with every minute.

"That's all now. Come along, Zoya, we must be going," her grandmother said, and began to adjust the rucksack with the enamelled cup tied to the side of it on the child's back.

The girls went to see off that last party of Moscow's children, but it all ended early, and that hot idle August day was engraved forever in Polya's memory. They did not feel like returning to the empty house after leave-taking. They roamed the town, visited the principal squares, and called on Pushkin, taking up a position where he would be looking at them; they grieved over the Bolshoi Theatre, uglified by the camouflage, and a pink-faced artilleryman from the anti-aircraft battery stationed in the adjacent square joined in their argument about the flying steeds on the pediment; they smiled to the Kremlin stars and heard out the farewell chimes of the tower clock with a pang of sadness. It was still only noon, and the train did not leave for Bryansk until midnight. Army trucks lumbered past, and from above the clouds came the almost continuous snarl of climbing aircraft; everyone was rushing about, bound on some momentous errand of state— everyone except these two, who were doomed to inactivity. Varya assayed the opinion that under communism the highest punishment for the lowest deeds would be suspension from work.

They went down to the river and walked along the deserted embankment in the hope of somehow squandering their hateful wealth. That was when Polya got the idea of going into a cinema; she wanted to get the feel of the war, even if it were only through the latest issue of the news reel, and to catch a glimpse perhaps of a Loshkarev lad, who had not been sending those cocked-hat letters now for such a long time. Indeed, no sooner had the field engineers gone off the screen after repairing a bridge at a river crossing, and the Tula gunsmith hung a padlock on his door and left for the forward lines with his two grown-up daughters, than the meager audience were shown a front-line performance by artists. It was here among the soldiers, on the fringe of a badly scarred wood, that Polya, with a chill sense of the supernatural, discovered Rodion; he was listening to the singer with lowered head, stroking the rifle that lay across his knees. Although he was sitting with his back to her, she would have recognised him even in the dark, by touch, among thousands of his kind, by the wisp of unkempt hair that ran down the youthful hollow of his nape.

That half-minute screen vision, like a gentle rain at twilight, filled Polya with a long-lingering sense of refreshing joy. It was with her all the time when, quietly elated, she went up the darkened staircase with Varya for her things, and when, from the door of the box-car, she gazed at the receding city with the barrage balloons in its fading sky . . . and even later, when, exhausted by her struggle with the wobbly ill-adjusted handle of her spade, she sat down on the edge of the trench to recover her breath, and when, dropping with fatigue, she spooned up the soldier's porridge cooked in a real field kitchen. Rodion was alive, alive! And childlike, she believed that he would return to her, to their secluded dove-cot in Loshkarev, as soon as he had done listening to that front-line concert.

If only she could take a peep like that at Mummy somewhere, even in a dream!

2

At the beginning, while they were all poking around, barely managing from dawn till dusk to shovel up their quota of two cubic metres of earth, they differed from one another in a way, but afterwards, when their dresses got shabby, and the clay dust ate into their skin through the sunburn, a dust so thick that no comb could tear the hair apart, all these Moscow girls, strung out for miles under the blazing sky, began to look like sisters, acquiring that sacred family likeness which is achieved through the self-abnegatory and equal labours of war. Each had her own individual sorrows, but they were all submerged in the dogged, conquering multitude and distributed equally among all to be drained away in sweat and dried up in the hot suns. Within a week, as soon as Polya had become used to the hardships which had fallen to the lot of her generation, her old malady returned to her with redoubled force.

With the front steadily drawing nearer, the work was carried on in shifts all round the clock. The furious clang of spades could now be heard at night-time as well, mingling with the creak of carts and the lowing of herds that were being driven inland; the highroad passed within half a mile of the working site. Varya and Polya slept at the back slope of the now completed anti-tank ditch; the clayey earth, heated during the day, was scorching hot through the groundsheet. Straight in front of them, a creditable imitation of Swan Lake, there glimmered in the moonlight an enchanted little pond with an oozy bed and black poplars growing round it; in the absence of a wood in the vicinity, the girls dived into this pond to escape the air thug, who had got into the habit of hedge-hopping over the site two or three times in the course of an evening to scare the working women. Probably a skittle-alley habitue from somewhere near Zwickau, he was so constant in this sordid licentious passion of his, that before long everybody was able to identify his yellow-bellied dirty machine by the round oil stain behind the white cross, and by the deep spluttering laugh of his machine-gun. He did not come over at night, as he could not see what hits he had made in the dark, and was therefore unable to write home to his old mother boasting of his feats in this safe and fascinating hunt.

That night the two girls lay numb with fatigue, listening to the stealthy sounds of the approaching war, punctuated by the cries of a baby from the kolkhoz evacuees bivouacked under the roadside embankment.

"Why don't you sleep? We're moving to a new site tomorrow morning."

"It's so stuffy. My God, how lovely it is on the Yenga now! Would I like to dive into the river from the steep! You can't imagine how dirty I am, Varya."

"But then look how terribly self-dependent you've become! You do look funny, though all streaky," Varya said, having in mind the coloured trickles from Polya's beret, which had dyed her neck and shoulders after the morning rain. "What are you thinking about now?"

Polya said she believed Madam Zolotinskaya had a reason for letting her granddaughter be evacuated without her. She had nothing left to live for, really, and it was brutal to die in front of someone you loved. Without a doubt, she had had a presentiment of something that last time, and, of course, after her separation from Zoya, she had stopped going down into the bomb-shelter at night, and maybe ... at that very minute a big black drop, with its stabiliser glinting in the moonlight, was passing through the floors of house No. 8a in Blagoveshchensky Alley.

"I've thought it all out, Varya—people must die by themselves. The animals understand that better than we do. In that respect they have more delicacy than people."

Varya raised herself on her elbow and looked anxiously at her friend, who was lying on her back with her arms under her head. She would have scolded her but for that silvery track running from Polya's eyes down her cheek.

"Darling, I like neither the drift of your thoughts nor the tone in which you express them," Varya said sternly. "On the contrary, I am perfectly sure that the very next day found that old woman on her granddaughter's trail. You can't imagine what grandmothers with her social background are capable of. Besides, you have thousands of people left in Moscow who are much nearer to you than Zolotinskaya ... it makes your blood run cold to think what may happen to them. What makes you think of her of all people?"

She managed nevertheless to gradually unravel Polya's little skein. Judging by Zolotinskaya's behaviour the morning they had parted, she knew much more about Gratsiansky than she had let out that time in an attempt to avert some dark evil hanging over Polya. And shameful though it was to employ such arguments for purely personal reasons, in the event of Zolotinskaya's death Polya would lose the last opportunity of solving the riddle of that man and throwing off the burden of her father's secret.

"Look here, I emphatically demand that you stop this digging up of the dead," Varya said with disgust. "Take my word, if there was an ounce of credibility in that story, the special investigator would have looked into it long ago. And I thought that I had cured you, fool that I am, by my going to the Forestry Institute. Who has broken your spirit, darling? You're innocent of another man's past, and can look anyone in this country in the face without flinching."

"Anyone?" Polya queried with narrowed eyes. "Ha, you say anyone?"

"Yes," Varya answered less confidently. She was put out by the mocking gleam in her eyes. "I think Rodion is a sensible enough boy. It's not as if he were receiving from your father a million-ruble dowry of ill-gotten money."

"I don't want it!" Polya said with angry vehemence. "I tell you—I don't want to have to look anyone pleadingly in the face in order to be forgiven for something I don't know anything about. You needn't worry, I'll get over it myself somehow, without an investigator. Don't forget, it's not a question of my father this time. I've been thinking a lot and I've come to the conclusion that in a long war it's not only at the front that people get killed."

"I don't understand. Lately you often talk as if you were in a fever, just a lot of gibberish. Translate it into human language for me, will you please," Varya entreated.

But Polya herself had nothing but conjecture to go on so far; like a child at play, she shuffled the alphabetical blocks of known adventitious circumstances, making them up in to all possible combinations in the hope of forming some understandable word. She stumbled on it sometimes, but to check herself she had to get back quickly to Blagoveshchensky Alley before the demolition bomb hit it—she believed at that time that the bomb for their building had not only been made but had been raised aloft.

The conversation was interrupted by the distant grumbling of the long-range guns.

"Hear that?" Varya said in a flat voice.

"It looks like our trenches will be needed soon. We're wasting too much time on idle chatter. Tomorrow I'll propose raising the quota at least up to two and a half cubic metres."

The two girls resumed their discussion of Polya's thoughts a fortnight later, when they returned home.

Whether it was from embarrassment at being discovered in the girls' room or because she repented the frankness of her last talk at parting, but Madam Zolotinskaya met Polya with a chilliness that ruled out any possibility of irrelevant questioning. She gave the girls the key and the paid rent bill, and apologised for having tidied up the room without their permission; there had been so much dust about lately, and the windows had never been closed to prevent the panes from being blown in by the blast. "Oh, that's all right, don't mention it!" the girls answered both together embarrassedly and guiltily, because both of them had been wrong in their conjectures about their neighbour. She had not run away after her granddaughter, and was unhurt, like all the rest of Moscow.

Contrary to their misgivings, a cursory examination revealed that the capital city stood intact. The Kremlin clock still conducted its time-study of history, Pushkin was thinking out his verses on the heroism of his descendents, and the bronze horses on the theatre were careening along, eager to see the exhibition of enemy planes which had been shot down on the outskirts of Moscow and were now gathered on the square below. Thanks to the obliging lieutenant, who turned up again, the girls were able to peep into the cockpit of one of these planes, look at the charred seat, and touch the levers and buttons by aid of which killing is performed. Polya even went round to the other side but the familiar oil stain on the fuselage was not there. It meant that that other one was still flying, still hugging the idea of making bullet holes in Polya Vikhrova to the glory of his führer. And all of a sudden, as though the knowledge of it had entered her soul in a most material manner, Polya realised that soon, albeit not tomorrow, she would meet her murderer face to face, just the two of them, not counting Death, who would sit waiting patiently on a stool a little way off.

Polya only had to shut her eyes to see this meeting with the old world in all its details, a dread but fascinating meeting at which she would be taking her examination for the rank of a human. It was not given her to know what force would snatch her from the safety of Moscow and fling her to the edge of a frontline village, only just occupied by a German unit—probably the same whirlwind that was driving trainloads of iron and people from end to end of the land, that chilled one's face when one opened out the newspaper, and at times lifted one off the ground, as it were—and would push her into a cottage, an ordinary peasant's cottage with patchwork carpet strips on the floor, looking so gay in the sunshine, and plants in broken pots standing in the windows, the traditional plants of the Russian countryside, the common four o'clock, say, or begonias, with leaves wilting from the heat; the pathetic image of the drooping geranium in the neighbour's room on the day of her granddaughter's departure haunted her. Polya, of course, would be pushed in roughly, so that she would pitch forward on her face, and while she was lying there at the feet of the chief executioner, she would work out her plan of escape with lightning-like resolution, as always happens in such cases. She would have to ask permission in a stupid little voice to water those poor green things, and, of course, the Nazis and their grinning friend on the stool would fall for the bait in the belief that this Soviet kid would then reveal to them the innermost designs of the Red Army and its generals. With their permission she would go over to the window, and then all she had to do was to push the glass out with her body, make a dash of fifty paces to the cliff, and plunge over it into her Yenga, gloriously, like Yermak or Chapayev. And if she couldn't do that, she would have managed in their preliminary conversation to tell that dude with the swastika on his sleeve all that the girls of the Soviet land thought of him and his ilk.

It was the kind of naive day-dreaming about heroism that is familiar in various versions to many young people, and like flying in one's dreams, is a sign of approaching maturity. This reminded her of a precious evening on the Yenga. Once, shortly after the school-leaving examinations, Polya and Rodion were sitting on the famous Lovers' Headland over the river sweep, and being her mother all over, she had felt a bit shivery. Rodion had had to cover her shoulders with an old postman's cloak, a relic of his father's preserved in the family chest. It had been so wonderful all round that Polya had even allowed Rodion to hold the cloak in place on her shoulder with a terribly hot hand in case some wind tore it off. This had not prevented them from discussing certain pressing world problems, among them the natural urge of youth to test itself on something big and frightening, the way Maxim Gorky and other outstanding personalities of human progress had done. The two young people agreed without argument that an intelligent person could only learn his worth through the amount of work or the degree of selflessness he was capable of. But the moment they touched upon that impulse of the spirit, which makes the hero swoop down to his exploit like a bird from the heights, Rodion advanced the silly argument that not everyone was capable of such a thing, that only a person who had worked hard on himself could do it, because to be able to take such a plunge from what he called the "fiery-winded" heights, one had to scale them first. Such a reservation obviously imposed a restriction on the mass character of such a desirable thing as heroism, and Polya was so offended for her generation that she pushed Rodion's hand off her shoulder and called him the sorriest figure of our age ... surely not for the mere sake of now acknowledging that he might have been right?

Polya had already discovered that the war offered many tempting opportunities for noble deeds such as seldom occur in peacetime, but always something had checked her. It was not due to a lack of conviction or any doubts as to her preparedness for an act of heroism, that is to say, a lack of contempt for pain, but something quite different. She thought, among other things, that death was the highest rostrum, and that it ill became a Soviet citizen to depart this life without having his last condemnatory word to say against those who killed every living thing that they touched with so much as their breath. She did not know yet what never-to-be-repeated words she would fling into the face of her murderer; those words, apparently, had not ripened yet.

"You're upset again, sister, aren't you?"

"Yes . . . but now it's quite different," Polya said, hiding her eyes and hands from Varya lest she guessed what a wretched bungling soul she was.

3

It was getting near enrolment time in the universities, but instead of making drawings of plaster-casts or going over her school course in preparation for the examinations, Polya strolled all day along the embankments, trying to choose the words with which she would square her account with the old world—not in order to keep them against an emergency, but just as a matter of self-respect; she couldn't very well go to the Komsomol local to have a decent death speech typed out for her. Polya's eloquence immediately failed her after the first school phrase about the significance of the proletarian revolution for the universal happiness of the working people, and she glanced round in bewilderment, trapped in a maze of subordinate clauses bristling with punctuation marks like so many nails. Something prevented her from rising to those "fiery-winded" heights of Rodion's, which, translated into Polya's tongue, meant human purity. Exhausted by the struggle, she looked down at her feet—she was held back still by the leaden weight of her father's unravelled secret.

At the pupils' meetings Polya had always been good at making speeches about the value of criticism as a means of social education. For the first time she reflected on the possible motives and uses of that method, and at once floundered in a sea of childish questions. Why had those terrible books of Vikhrov's been printed if they created such confusion in the minds of the young generation as Gratsiansky claimed? Why hadn't his fellow scientists helped him to quash his opponent, and why, on the other hand, were they silenced the moment they dared to come out in Vikhrov's defence? And why, if he at all valued his honest name as a Soviet citizen, did not Vikhrov kick the bark off his slanderer's shins for his nasty supercilious insinuations, even at the risk of getting hauled up for a "breach of the peace"! Polya guessed that behind this inextricable knot lay something dark, something that was usually kept from children. In her search for the truth,

206

and, consequently, her own purity, it remained for Polya to look up the living witnesses of the past, all, that is, except Gratsiansky, of another meeting with whom she could not think now without a shudder. But Madam Zolotinskaya was always in a hurry and so kindly unapproachable whenever they met that one would think she knew beforehand all the thousand and one tactless perplexities Polya yearned to bombard her with. It was then, with rekindled hope, that Polya decided to go and see Taisa once more, and try, in a heart-to-heart talk, to glean at least a grain of the forbidden knowledge, even if it meant injuring her mother's reputation. As there was no telephone at her father's flat, she tried the Institute, only to learn that the professor was out of town, visiting a sanctuary somewhere in the Urals.

No Russian woman could pretend like that—no. Taisa gave no sob at seeing her niece in the doorway, she did not start to hug and kiss her, as Polya had feared all the way coming down. Her face lit up and she became all atremble as she drew her niece inside lest she lose her again for another eternity.

"We'll go into the kitchen, it's cosier in there," Taisa muttered, and her agitation communicated itself to Polya. "Sergei said he'd be late today, and if there is an air-raid warning he'll spend the night at the depot, so we've got the place all to ourselves. It's nice and clean in the kitchen, and we'll have a good long look at each other."

She tucked her visitor into a corner between a small plywood cupboard and a table covered with an oilcloth, which, though worn threadbare, had no cuts in it, and began to split a billet of wood to light a fire in the stove with—somehow Polya was terribly pleased to think of a forest professor sitting without firewood!—but then she got a splinter in her hand, and decided, on a sudden extravagant impulse, to put the kettle on the electric stove.

"Your father will be ever so upset when he hears you've been here again without him. You must excuse him, darling, he can't help it, what with that forest job of his."

"Never mind, better luck next time," Polya brushed the matter aside, anxious to avoid useless and tiresome explanations. "You shouldn't use up electricity for my sake, though."

"The kettle's only half full, just three cups. Besides, we don't burn the midnight oil, you know. Last month's electric bill was down by seven rubles. Try the honey, it's from Bashkiria. One of Ivan's pupils sent him a little keg." She found it impossible to decline her aunt's pressing invitations. "I'm not asking anything about yourself, seeing as you're sitting there alive and well. What does Lena write?"

"There was only one letter from mother waiting for me when I got back, an old one. I know it almost by heart. She writes that she caught a slight cold, but then got over it."

"She ought to be scolded for sitting about in draughts, she ought to know better at her age." Taisa tried to imagine what was happening on the Yenga, which was occupied by the Germans. She wilted, then straightened the kerchief on her head with an habitual gesture, and glanced at Polya. "Did you go on a far journey, little one? Was it after food, or just a trip?"

"No, we went to dig trenches. There was a lot of us Moscow girls there, several thousand."

"I see. I thought you looked browned. Just like the skin on baked milk. It's a good thing to do your bit in a sacred cause," Taisa said, shaking her head ruefully at the sight of Polya's blistered hands. "Thank you for the labour, our little defender."

"Oh, nonsense!" Polya said, flushing. "Here I'm sitting with you, eating honey, and all the while our girls are having such a hard time, you can't imagine. One maybe is dragging a wounded soldier from the battlefield, while another, all beaten up and bleeding, is standing in front of a Nazi interrogator. And there are strangers all round, and she has no chance of jumping out of the window."

The unmerited praise made her feel ashamed and at the same time she was a bit pleased that her first steps in life could gladden someone else besides her mother. She wanted to share her impressions with Taisa, to tell her how the mouldering blue clay smelt at a depth, and how a traitor had made them dig the ditch with the rampart on the wrong side so that the German tanks could easily take it on the run, and how afterwards he had been led away, his face buried in his hands, amid a general silence of loathing, while Polya was appointed team leader at the breakdown section, not just for fun, but in order that she should gain experience on a practical job, so that afterwards she kept a check of the amount of earthwork herself and gave the air warning whenever that flying cur came over on a strafing raid. But this was nothing compared to the story about old Paramonich.

He had come down one day to see what the Moscow girls were doing, and introduced himself as the perennial chief of the pig farm that one could see just across the pond, back of the trampled rye—a post which he had held since the beginning of kolkhoz life. He walked without a stick, a sturdy upstanding specimen of the Slav race, with the stature of a guardsman and a venerable show-piece of a beard rarely to be found outside grand opera. He came fairly often after that to unburden his heart to the "young 'uns", and work went with a livelier swing with them, too, under his encouraging remarks: "Come on, my hearties, keep it up, you busy little bees, help the soldier boys. Won't they cuddle you when they come home from the war!" "Mind you don't spoil us, Grandpa. What about self-criticism?" the girls answered in a chorus. "Oh, no," he answered gravely, spreading his hands. "You'll only spoil a good horse with the whip—he'll be afeard o' you. The Russian wants knowing. With a little encouragement he'll move heaven and earth, he will."

Although he put on a brave front, he obviously grieved for his ruined farm, of which only a prize hog remained on his hands. It was supposed to be too delicate for transportation. When the Nazi airmen took that hog's life by a lucky hit, Paramonich handed the carcass over to the commissariat for the girls' mess. The raider, by the way, was in the habit of popping up suddenly from behind the hill and skimming along the trench so low that one could almost reach him with a spade.

The pond was none too safe as a shelter either. Polya had nearly been drowned once by the wave which the blast had raised on the water. Nevertheless, every living thing, flushed by the roar of the engine, rushed there for safety. Paramonich was the only exception. Whether it was because he was afraid to wet his famous beard or because it ill became him, with all those medals and St. George's crosses pinned on his shirt, to bend before a German whelp, it was difficult to say. "A young goat, by the looks of it. There he goes, frisking about, full o' mischief. I wouldn't do it if I were him, no I wouldn't. Shouldn't be surprised if he has grown-up sisters too. They're going to suffer plenty for their brother's doings," Paramonich muttered, and shook a finger at the yellow-bellied one until one day a spatter of lead slashed the old man from temple to groin.

Taisa heard the story out with a sad illumined smile.

"It only goes to show how proud our people are in the face of the enemy. You must all have had a good cry over that poor old man?" she said in a calm sedate manner, and Polya thought she drew herself up and even became better-looking.

"You bet. We buried him right there. I helped to dig the grave," Polya said. Taisa took her hand and Polya did not withdraw it. "That's about all that happened there, I believe."

They were silent for the conventional graveside minute, and strange to say, Polya all of a sudden became keenly aware of her blood ties with this woman, not yet through Vikhrov, but through this shot old man Paramonich. It was quite easy now to pass on to the main object of her visit. She enquired of Taisa in a casual tone, whether she had ever come across a man by the name of Gratsiansky in her life.

"Who doesn't know that shifty one?" Taisa said apprehensively after a slight pause. "Ivan's deadly friend.... He lives with his mother just two stops from the railway station square. A quicksilvery old woman, as thrifty as they make 'em."

"So you've been there, Auntie Taisa?"

"Yes, I went there once," Taisa said in that sneering tone of cold animosity which old people use when speaking of very bad eggs. "Ivan sent me there once with a present for him—a book, and she kept me outside in the passage. But you know what a sharp-eyed lot we Vikhrovs are. I peeped in through the glass door, and bless us all!—there they were airing rice on the floor with all the windows open, like a regular threshing-barn!"

"But what were they airing it for?" Polya asked incredulously.

"Well, there are all kinds of reasons. For one thing it may go mouldy if you're not careful, or some weevil or other may get at it, and then your whole hoard's lost! They're keeping it for a rainy day, until private trade comes back."

"How interesting," Polya whispered, and again she couldn't help wondering at this man, who accused a comrade of all the deadly sins while he and his mother aired a rice hoard on the sly. "But what rainy days are they afraid of? D you mean, in case anything happens to the Soviet power?"

"There are all kinds o' days, my dear. Some of 'em are sunny, some of 'em rainy," Taisa said evasively, then asked what Polya wanted with that man.

A strange stupefaction came over Polya. Her hands grew numb and her throat dry. Taisa's hint seemed to lend colour to the latest and most terrible variant of her suspicions. But first she had to make sure that no woman, no mother of hers, had been the cause of this old-standing conflict between Vikhrov and Gratsiansky, and Polya nerved herself for a direct question, although the mere unuttered thought of it seemed blasphemous to her.

"Tell me, Auntie Taisa... did Mamma ever meet that man?"

"Why, sure. After the revolution, in twenty-one or twenty-two—I'm not sure which—he spent a fortnight with Ivan at Pashutino, and Lena was there too. It wasn't until after they moved to Moscow that they fell out with each other. Would you believe it, that Alexander didn't show his nose for five years, then all of a sudden up he pops—to call on an old friend, as he put it. He always dropped on you like that, without warning. He'd brush the rime off his moustache, embrace Ivan in a brotherly way, then turn the knife in the wound and betake himself off. That time when Lena left us, and Ivan lay dead drunk, for the first time in his life, I thought I heard someone knocking. I looked out, and there if you please was Alexander, as large as life. What a nose that man has for smelling out a dead body! He was just dying to come in and gloat over Ivan, but I wouldn't let him in."

Judging by the bare outline of events that swam into ken from the dim unknown, the cruellest cause for a quarrel would seem to have been ruled out. Obviously, the villain would not have dragged himself down there if he was in any way to blame for the break-up of the Vikhrov family. Appropriately, just when the kettle began to boil, the light was switched off in the whole district and the ensuing darkness brought the two women closer together and made mutual candour more easy.

"Just a minute, let me get this straight," Polya interrupted, deeply agitated. "Did you ever hear Father ... or anyone else reproach Mamma because she was one of the gentry?"

The other threw up her hands.

"Gentry indeed! Bless you, the Tatars, the old-clothes men who went round the houses in Russia with their sacks, crying *shurum-burum*, were also called *princes*. She grew up in a manor, that's all. It's no use trying to explain to a fool that some people who begged for their bread lived freer than she did. Why, I received her in my arms half-dead, Ivan took her straight out of the noose, you might say."

4

The sad tale was somewhat confused in Taisa's telling owing to the remoteness of the events, but she had heard it from reliable lips that three-year-old Lena was brought down at Christmas, and, after the bell had been rung, was left on the landing of the Sapegins' town flat. Everything had been taken into consideration in this act of parental despair—from the holiday mood of the prosperous half-German family to the well-contrived gilt paper crown on the child's head; this was the only evidence, if evidence it was, of her non-humble origin. Her name and age were given in an accompanying note tacked on her back with black thread. Fortune itself was knocking at the Sapegin door. Indeed, one could not look without tender emotion upon that tiny fairy, that *Christ Kind* to see how she slid across the parquet, toddling round the lit up fir-tree, falling and not hurting herself, how happy she was, and how meekly she bore the caresses and curiosity of the boys of the house. Sapegin's widow had recently lost her aged companion and reader, and this decided the fate of the foundling. Lena was carried off to the Yenga, where she was to complete the whole circle of life of the hanger-on, become the plaything of the rich, an errand girl, sport for the young bachelor masters, a nurse to her paralysed benefactress, the chief keener, and then the watchdog in the hall, where she looked after the fur coats of the heirs while they were junketing at the funeral feast.

The girl occupied fourth place in the manor after the old woman, the fan palm, which the late Ilya Sapegin had grown from a pip, and a blue vicious lap-dog who was forever shivering like the soul of a dastard. Lower down in the scale came the comparatively few menials, the local suppliants, and all manner of caterers of the good things of life, of whom passing mention should be made of that humblest of woodsmen, Kalina Glukhov, who supplied wild honey of remarkable curative properties. At the manorial table the girl quickly picked up good manners and fluent German, while during the summer holidays an overgrown student, who acted as constant escort to his unhappily married young mistress in the capacity of her children's tutor, shared with her his meagre knowledge. In the dresses which she received as gifts Lena looked a real young lady. She could, on occasion, entertain an important guest, and did not mar the charming landscape round her. The peasant women who came to sell their wares simply did not seem to notice her, but the girl soon became aware of their unfriendly examining glances, softened by the humility of the poor. On the other hand, Lena never achieved the servility of her predecessor, who would enquire of her decrepit mistress every morning: "I hope you slept well, Ma'am, I hope the fleas didn't bother you"—and never learned to listen at keyholes what the servants and the grandchildren were whispering about the old lady's approaching end, or to hear out her nightly homilies when she was unable to fall asleep. They usually took the form of an account of the misadventures of an abstract street girl, who was punished for her ingratitude towards her benefactress and her trustfulness towards the first swaggering officer who came her way. Not until she had the fifteen-year-old girl reduced to a state of whimpering misery would the old woman forgive her her imaginary offence and promise to take her with her when the Lord let her go home at last to Pomerania; it was there that she had made the acquaintance of the late Sapegin, who was graduating the local university. Having eaten Russian salt for half a century, she constantly complained about the injurious effects of that country's imperfections upon her health.

Meanwhile, the estate was going to the dogs; tired of waiting, the grandchildren were trying to get their hands on the inheritance while their grandmother was still alive, and there was no prospect of anyone buying the remaining part of Oblog. During the winter, life barely lingered in the surviving wing of the house where the draughts from under the floor-boards were not so fierce and the corners not so freezing. To cut down expenses the old woman gradually narrowed down the circle of servants, combined the job of stableman with that of coachman, of butler with clerk; the thing was to tide over the time until fair weather set in with the end of the Russo-German war. But instead of the expected peace, sinister rumours reached the Yenga. Although nothing had happened yet to the badly shaken tsarist regime, the occupants of the stately ancestral homes began to experience that depressing precariousness of existence which is familiar to the besieged garrisons of outlying fortresses. In Sapegin's own household people were already talking openly about what the soldiers would do with the gentry when they came back from the trenches, and the things Lena heard about her people from the old woman made her blanch at the thought of ever having to meet them face to face. Her dependent position, always teetering between grace and disgrace, when she would be banished for weeks to the servants' hall, had taught Lena at an early age to compare the elegant idleness of her life with the grim pattern of life around her. She always tingled with shame, for instance, when she had to help her guardian down from her carriage at the church-door—she was so glaringly massive. "Lady-ox" the peasants called her. But now Lena invented any excuse to avoid being seen with Madam Sapegina outside the gates so as not to irritate that patient, remembering judge, who saw so well for all that his eyes were lowered to the ground. Day and night he stared through the walls of the manor, saw and remembered everything, and nothing, neither Lena's orphanage nor her legs bitten in childhood by the pet dog, neither the bitter bread of the slave-girl nor the offensive attentions of the young masters, could justify in his eyes the fact that she belonged to the condemned feudal system. While other girls of her age lived in a land of roseate dreams, Lena lived in a land of nocturnal terrors, and Vikhrov could do nothing, generous though his motives were, to extinguish in her those first half-conscious gleams of responsibility towards the people.

According to Taisa, Polya's parents became acquainted soon after the new forester arrived to take up his duties. While still in hospital after receiving his wound, he had planned a big work directed against the landowners' maltreatment of the forests, and it would have been unreasonable in his position to miss the opportunity of thumbing through the papers in the well-known case of the Krasnovershya peasants' suit over Oblog, which were right there at hand. And so early in the summer we find him visiting the manor house in order to burrow in Sapegin's archives, with the permission of his widow, of course. When he left his house, neither his doubtful gift of persuasion nor the remoteness of that disgraceful affair inspired in him any hopes of success, but in the afternoon a gracious summer shower had swept over the crimson clover, leaving it steaming after the heat; Nature's benevolent mood, he felt, could not but raise kindly feelings in the landowners as well. As he passed the pond and turned into the larch drive of the ancient Sapegin park, Vikhrov's droshky immediately drew level with a girl, who struck him not by her beauty, but, on the contrary, by a sort of meek domestic ordinariness. Judging by her uncovered head and short city-style frock, she belonged to the place, although she was obviously not one of the young ladies, since she was barefoot and wore a coloured comb in her wet hair—one of those combs that are sold at country fairs. She was going the same way, in the direction of the house, which loomed whitely among the trees, and was shovelling the air back comically with an arm bent at the elbow as though anxious to get away from the rustle of the overtaking wheels. Possibly the girl felt embarrassed before a strange official because of her wet dress, which clung to her back and breasts.

Vikhrov said something disparaging about the rain in which both of them had been caught; she stood up for it warmly, as though it were a friend of hers. "Every one has his work to do." Asked whether she was visiting the Sapegins, the girl answered that since the beginning of the war and with the estate having run to seed, even the heirs had stopped visiting that godforsaken place. "Speaking for myself, I've been a-visiting here this seventeenth year now, worse luck!" she said, and Vikhrov noticed that she used rustic turns of speech. He felt a bit awkward, too, riding in the droshky while she was walking, but he could not bring himself to step down and thus reveal his lameness. For no other reason than to keep the conversation going, the forester revealed the aim of his visit. The girl laughed at his simplicity. Nothing in the world could interrupt the old woman's afternoon nap; besides, last year Feklusha had been lugging all kinds of crackly papers from the late master's room and burning them in the kitchen stove all through the winter.

"And I thought you'd come to buy our wood. We've been waiting ever so long for buyers."

"I've got enough of my own," Vikhrov said.

As a matter of fact he was not received that day, but two days later he drove up again to the lawn facing the veranda where Demidka had once sold the captive squirrel. He must have had weighty reasons for appearing as he did in such hot weather in full dress uniform with a turn-down velvet collar. Madam Sapegina reclined in an armchair, befrilled, beflounced and becushioned, gazing at the portrait of her husband, which hung on the wall between girandoles under muslin covers grey with dust. Her dropsical tallowy face gradually assumed a lugubrious expression as Vikhrov set forth his forestry ideas, which, he claimed, could leave no decent person living in Russia unmoved and when, to clinch the argument, he added that his book would run into at least a thousand pages, she stole a startled glance at her visitor out of the tail of her eye. Probably she expected this top-booted, bearded, countrified official to pull a batch of close-written sheets out of his pocket and start reading her into fits, as her late husband often used to do. Indeed, there was something almost indecent about the way Vikhrov, with the shamelessness of youth, was robbing the old lady of those last precious minutes that remained to her before her departure to Pomerania. Suddenly, however, the mistress livened up, and a tearful gleam flickered under her paralysed eyelid.

"Very agreeable... educated man... a gentleman...." she quavered, drowning her words in short gasps. "You see yourself .. the dilemma I'm in ... ought to help me out ... such a charming young man."

"By all means ... I'd be only too pleased..." the forester made haste to assure her, infected by her jerky manner of speech. To show how willing he was he laid his unfinished cigarette down on the plush table-cloth behind a bark-basket lined with maple leaves containing strawberries.

"Time I went home ... bones ... but where's the money to come from? Mortgage deeds at the bank ... haven't a penny ... stripped me clean ... first that crank ... then loving grandchildren.... I wish you'd help.... You can clean it all out afterwards for all I care!"

Things had taken an unexpected turn, and in practical affairs Vikhrov was as simple-hearted as a child. Apparently it was a question of money, and he began to cast about in his mind when his next pay was due.

"I'd be only too glad, if you don't mind waiting a little ... at the moment I'm out of pocket, what with having to set up in a new home."

"Oh, your money's of no use," groaned the lady of the manor, annoyed at his plebeian dullness. "I have another eight thousand at Oblog. You probably know all those timber crooks there ... couldn't you send round some rascal of a dealer ... all the same the scamps will send it down the drain. I'll make it worth your while...." Her head fell back, exhausted, and only her fingers moved, running up and down her knee to illustrate the tip which the go-between would get.

For the moment the forester did not seem to grasp what he was being hired for; he was a bit surprised at the extent to which long consumption of Russian food had helped that foolish old woman to master the native speech. Then suddenly a vision of his father lying bent-kneed under the holy images, and next to him tipsy Kalina on a stump, rose vividly to his mind, and a mist swam before his eyes. His hatred of this class, always somewhat bookish because he had left the village at an early age, suddenly rose in a jet of muzhik blood, and while he was searching for a word to splash into the eyes of the arrogant gentry, all kinds of complaisant figures began to appear in answer to the mistress's bell: a little girl with fiery red hair bearing home-made currant wine, an inebrious old man of flunkeyish appearance wearing something pongee from off the master's shoulders, and lastly the larch avenue girl, the one Vikhrov had been tremulously waiting for all that hour. The first two looked at the old woman's hands and vanished immediately at a sign which they alone could interpret.

Sapegina uttered a half-interrogatory sound.

"It's me," the third, remaining one said.

"I don't see ... you have a name," the old woman said in a sharp crackly voice.

"Well, it's me, Helen," the girl answered submissively, but her lips puckered as if from a lemon.

"She's got out of hand ... completely! There, just look at her, putting the wasps on to me."

For a minute the girl looked down, her lip caught in her teeth.

"You asked for the jam yourself three days ago and haven't eaten it. That's why the wasps are flying about!" Something rang in her voice, then faded away. "Very well, I'll take it away."

"Why didn't you finish it, then, if it's been standing for three days. Good heavens, now there's a smell of burning. She'll burn me alive, that girl."

It was the table-cloth smouldering under Vikhrov's cigarette. He furtively put it out and hid it in his pocket. And again the girl was silent just long enough to draw the breath she had been holding in.

"Shall we lay the table here or on the veranda?"

"There, out there. Show him the box with the papers ... not that one ... the other. Give him a snack or something to go with the vodka ... this gentleman here in the top-boots," the old woman said with a barely perceptible nod towards the forester, who, now forgotten, was watching these domestic proceedings with lively interest. "Well, don't stand there staring ... haven't you ever seen a man before!"

Inured to it all, the girl did not answer, and only the tips of her fingers stirred slightly and her cocked eyebrow twitched.

Something prevented Vikhrov from leaving the manor at once. It was not the common man's dogged determination to have his own way, but rather a need to somehow make up to the girl for having been a reluctant witness to the humiliating scene with her mistress. On leaving the drawing-room he tried awkwardly to squeeze her hand, but Lena recoiled, mistaking his intention, and gave him a haughty look; he had time to notice the premature wrinkles round her eyes.

"And what do they pay you for such insults?" he said quietly.

"What's that to you? You don't want to hire me, do you?"

"I just asked out of interest and sympathy."

"Why should they pay me, I'm not a servant here," she said, and changed the subject. "Will you start on the vodka first or look through the box?"

"I prefer to start with the box," Vikhrov answered with an ironic bow.

"Then we'll have to go through the yard."

Passing a roofless coach-house overgrown with rank weeds, then through a darkened study, in which a Kurd yataghan crossed with a halberd gleamed over an old-fashioned bureau in a sunbeam which filtered through a crack in the closed shutters, the girl led the visitor up a spiral staircase, and while he was climbing it, she unlocked the door to the sanctum of the late historian and translator. The rather low-ceilinged room with its half-empty bookshelves smelt of mice and straw; the floor was littered with nibbled scraps of paper. Coloured twilight filtered through the Byzantine marble screen of the casement.

"Here's all that's left after Feklusha," said Vikhrov's guide, and, turning away, she sat down on the cobwebbed window-sill.

It was with a sense of awed dismay that the Pashutino forester surveyed the litter of scattered books and priceless manuscripts worthy of a national museum, the fruit of someone's inspired exploit, stolen perhaps from the flames of fanatics to eventually make their long journey from the scavenger's bag in Asia Minor to the antiquarian's counter in Paris, bought by a Russian nobleman, paid for by the serf labour of Vikhrov's grandfathers, and now doomed to decay through proprietary ignorance. He picked up a handsome book that lay in his line of vision—an iconography of the Venetian doges—and wiped the narrow earthy imprint of Feklusha's bare foot from the copperplate of Niccoló Contarini with his sleeve. Then, picking up at random a sheet of paper written over in a scrawly hand, he read with a smile Sapegin's dissertation on the inescapable despotism of Byzantium in the Russian body politic. No, one would hardly find here so much as a line of reference to an obscure Yenga muzhik shot down in an unequal struggle; it would also have been useless to look for it in that half-devastated iron coffer where, apparently, the most sacred treasures had been kept. Judging by the blurred inscription on the covers, on top lay a fragment of an ancient Greek Gospel; brown blotches of rain had washed off the cinnabar and gold of thousand-year beauty, and Vikhrov tried to figure out how much Russian flax and timber had gone into the purchase of the warped mouldering parchment which he held in his hand.

"The roof wants mending, my dear sirs!" he said angrily, and tossed the book back among the litter.

The next minute he felt sorry for his companion, who sat silent and apathetic on the window-sill. To soften the recent indignity wrought upon her by her mistress, he said that insults from the sick and the aged did not count really, although, of course, all repressed unuttered resentment only tended to increase the extent of one's slavery. He was constrained to ask whether she had heard him.

"Why, of course! You talk about the roofs, but they're leaking everywhere. The old woman doesn't want to have any repairs done to the house. We're saving up money to go away." With a slight show of interest, she suddenly asked whereabouts the land of Pomerania lay.

"So you've decided to leave Russia with the old woman?"

"I daresay she'll deceive me, but I wouldn't mind going, though. I'm scared to remain here all by myself."

"Scared of what?"

"They'll kill me."

He frowned.

"Who will?"

"The muzhiks," she answered, as, with trembling fingers, she arranged all the dead butterflies on the window-sill in a ring with their antennae towards the centre. How they had got in there in the course of a quarter of a century was nothing short of a miracle. "You can't imagine how they hate us! I even dream of them coming in through those gates of an evening to make short work of us." She pointed to the gateway looming whitely through the window amid the dark foliage of the park. "Eleven men, all in black, as if coming from mass ... after prayers, that is. With Zolotukhin, the tavern-keeper, in front."

"Do they come with axes, or simply with stakes?" Vikhrov asked with intense curiosity. Often had he thought about that inescapable eventuality which arises on the borderline of patience and

in defence of the downtrodden—in short, about sanitation cuttings, to use an idiom of his profession.

"You can't tell . . . they have their hands behind their backs.
It seems as if the house has caught fire at the back porch, and
smoke creeps along the ground. I hide among the lilac, holding
back my breath; mind you, they don't try to catch me, they just
watch me with half an eye to see which way I'll run."

"What nonsense. Who has frightened you like this—the old
woman?"

"I don't know, really. Maybe it's her. She's become so fretful,
keeps talking to the portrait all the time. Or else she wakes
me up in the middle of the night and makes me listen for the
sound of the murderers. 'I've got one foot in the grave, so it's
all the same to me,' she says, 'but you're a young girl, God
knows what they'll do to you.' " She said this clear-eyed, as
though not understanding the import of the words she uttered,
and Vikhrov realised the origin of those premature wrinkles
round her eyes. "God, I wish I grew old quickly so that it
shouldn't matter to me either."

That painful sigh, that passionate resignation to her fate, had
shocked Vikhrov. As every honest man would have done in his
place, he began to speak warmly about his people, the most fair-
minded and generous of all peoples, because it had no equal in
strength of spirit and the sweeping grandeur of its history; he
spoke about its fellow feeling and sympathy for other people's
misfortunes, about the slow sad measure of its songs, with special
tender mention of *Nochenka—Sweet Night*—about its faith in
pure proud man, which it had borne like a candle through its
long stormy night; he left out nothing that could rid this girl,
who had caught his fancy, of her harrowing visions, and mentioned first and foremost selfless work, which alone could win
the recognition of the people, because nothing escaped its notice,
not a single secret grain whether of good or evil perpetrated in
this world.

She nodded patiently at his attempts to help a stranger in distress by means of such clever decorative words.

"You speak very well. I daresay you are right about a song
being the reverse side of a prayer. Ah, well, thank you for
that. . . ."

"You have nothing to thank me for yet, my dear lady," he
said embarrassedly. "Haven't you ever tried to get closer to
these people, these very good people, I repeat?"

"What do you mean? Worm myself into their favour?"

"No, I mean to speak openly with the people, because they're your own people ... or have you locked yourself up in the castle?"

"Well, yes, I tried," the girl admitted coldly, flashing a row of splendid teeth. "Only the other day, for instance, *their* girls danced and sang in a ring at Zapolosky, as they always do before the haymaking. I wanted so much to sing with them I could hardly keep myself back. I went up as close as I could, hoping they'd call me. But as soon as they saw me they all stopped at once and ran off down the field bound. One of them looked back, and pointed at me, and laughed. ..."

"And you got offended?"

"Why should I be offended with them. I can't even bind a sheaf. They make me feel cheap. All I've been taught is to sew and darn and do the old woman's washing for her ... she won't let strangers do it. True, I'm good at pickling cherries too—we have a larder full of 'em and no one to sample them. I'll fill up a bowl for you, they'll go well with the vodka." Then suddenly she wiped it all off with the remark: "Never mind, the fire will eat it all up!"

Pity and a strange stirring of sudden doubt as to her sincerity fought within him. He searched her eyes. "Do you really believe it ... the fire, I mean, or are you just playing about with words?"

Resentment snaked across her lips.

"Why should I?"

"That's just what I'm trying to get at."

"You can make fun of me, if you like, but I can even show you the place where it will start. It's not as if I'm complaining, I don't even know who you are," she said, withdrawn, and got up, sweeping the fly cemetery off the window-sill. "Are you going to rummage about in this old junk, or will you be going home? I have lots of chores there waiting to be done."

Locking the book sanctuary against Feklusha's devastating raids, the girl waited patiently upstairs while he clumped down in the dark. The young people made for the droshky which was hitched to a century-old lime tree at the left wing of the house where Knishev's had once stood. At Vikhrov's earnest request, however, they went there by a roundabout way, skirting the pond, for he was keen to revisit the old places of his childhood adventures with Demidka, and in particular, to see whether the grass had straightened up where he had trampled it down in his long

221

hopeless pacing with the barn-owl under his shirt. On the way he asked his companion casually whether Helen was her real name, and she told him, without a hint of bitterness or resentment, that they used to call her Lena and Lenochka, but just before the war, when at the whim of the young masters, they had reupholstered the furniture with English stuff, pruned the park, and introduced saddle-horses and hounds, they had, while they were about it, renamed her too in keeping with the manor's new style.

And once more Vikhrov caught a hint of intentional design in this frank belittlement of herself. It was not humility, but an unaddressed challenge to no one in particular to come and rid her of her fears and daily humiliations. He accepted the reproach.

"In that case, if you don't mind, I'll call you Lenochka, in the old way. Helen sounds so outlandish here in the Russian countryside," he said, adding in an old man's tone, as if no other relations except those of friendship and sympathy were conceivable between them, "take my advice and run away from here. Run away at once, without a backward look, just as you are, without anything."

"Where can I go to?" she laughed mirthlessly, her hands clasped behind her neck. "I might marry, but all our young men are lying in the earth these days. One man did ask me to marry him, though—young Zolotukhin, if you know him. But he did it through his father. It's a long story, makes me sick to think of it. I'd have married him, anything's better than the axe! They changed their minds, I don't know why. It isn't as if I was a bold piece or suffered from fits or anything like that. I was younger then and better looking than I am now. And then the old woman doesn't let anyone come near me. She's afraid I'll leave her. The heirs are having a good time in St. Petersburg—who's going to look after her? She only let me go with you because you're so ... well er ... unsuitable." This frank half-hint of how innocuous her lame and awkward companion was in this respect was meant to dispel any secret unworthy suspicions he was likely to entertain as to her hidden intentions. "Well, I can't stand here chatting all day. I must go and feed the old woman, otherwise she'll nag me to death again and complain to the portrait about me all the evening."

At this point Polya asked why the Zolotukhins had not taken advantage of the desperate position her mother was in, and Taisa explained that from the very beginning the Sapegins' half-lady had not suited the book of the Shikhanov tavern-keeper; presently the war started, and Demidka was taken prisoner by the Germans. The matchmaking was simply a trick on Zolotukhin's part to get round the old lady with whom he was haggling over the purchase of Zapolosky. Since Polya had no idea what life was like in those days Taisa had to touch on certain trivial details without which Polya would not have been able to understand what was to come.

5

The origin of the Zolotukhin fortune was known to Polya's companion only from the stories of the Yenga's old inhabitants. Rumour had it that Zolotukhin spent his youth travelling about the region as a rag-and-bone merchant, who bartered sugar candy and cheap haberdashery for flax waste, iron scrap, and the horns and hoofs of slaughtered cattle. He slept in his cart, too, so that during church services and holidays he had to stand apart, because even through the smell of the incense he reeked of carrion and the warm stench of dire human poverty. A little later, Taisa had a distinct remembrance of herself outside his house, the most conspicuous house in Krasnovershya with heart-shaped little openings cut out in the shutters and a boarded roof—not because they could not afford an iron one (the iron for it had been lying in the barn for a long time!)—but simply to keep off the evil eye of envious neighbours. It was the only window at which she was given a shiny copper coin instead of the usual crust of bread. At the beginning of the century, when his elder sons and his daughters had married, Zolotukhin started a sideline in groceries and went in for jobbing at the fairs, but his main business was the carting of goods and passengers. His drunken fares never arrived frost-bitten, and not so much as a nail was ever missing from the loads entrusted to him. But for Knishev's famous raid upon the Yenga forests, he would have resigned himself to the inferior dignity of local harpy. Ever since he had watched that hustler of a St. Petersburg merchant playing the skin game and giving him an object lesson in money-making, Zolotukhin had lost all peace of mind; and by the time he had completed that gratuitous course of training by feeding barrels of rotting fish slightly sprinkled with wine to the lumberjacks, the money itch had got so bad that he all but went on the highway with a bludgeon.

First of all he took a closer look at himself and hated the petty vanities of his life, when he picked scattered oat grains out of the muck with his fingers and carried them furtively in his cupped hand to the farmyard cock so that the latter would not be diverted from his direct responsibilities; he hated the paltry parochial respect which he enjoyed, and the prosperity which he had achieved, a prosperity which made him a watchdog in his own yard; he hated the squealing of the pigs in the sty, the glimmer of the icon-lamps, the old family chests with clothes that had been paid for with his youth and had never been worn; even his sons-in-law, those meek uncomplaining unpaid labourers, he hated for the horsey contentment with life that shone in their faces. Round about that time the Zolotukhins stopped giving coppers to Taisa, because from now on the family often went to bed hungry themselves; he had even driven some of the extra fat off his pet, Demidka. The latter had fully justified the parental hopes at first, but as he grew older he began to show a dislike for trade; he started to go in for reading books, despite his father's corporal admonitions, and fell a victim to that form of mental ailment, which, in the idiom of the countryside, goes by the name of "heavy thinking". His early death spared the old man the bitter taste of utter disappointment.

The elder Zolotukhin was then over fifty; his youth had passed, but to him it seemed that he had merely come a bit late for the looting of Russia, which had started long before. He was haunted by dreams, each wilder than the other, of discovering oil, if not virgin gold, in his back yard, of being elected to the State Duma where, according to popular rumour, they paid a hundred rubles a head for each sitting, and to dash out on the platform of the Taurida Palace and yell at all those sleek business men in cuffs and rings and with well-groomed beards—*me too!*"—and have them make way for him and share their profits. Having heard a good deal about the new currents that were stirring from the local priest, the Reverend Trinitatov—a lover of horseflesh, a radical, and a subscriber to illustrated St. Petersburg magazines— Zolotukhin, who regarded his peasant origin as a hereditary asset, was looking forward on the quiet to the revolution. If he had made a bit under the Tsar, then how he would let himself go in fleecing his fellow Christians without the Tsar, when they started settling the hash of the accursed gentry. The thing was to husband his strength so as to be there with his bludgeon when the grand Russian share-out started. Inspired by Knishev's object lesson to try his hand at the forest, he decided, as a first step, to tackle Sapegin's Zapolosky adjoining the manor on the Krasnovershya side.

It was a well-stocked fifteen-hundred-acre grove of full-grown pines of the kind that yield a log run of three clean twenty-one foot lengths without flaws, knots or frost cracks; overhanging the riverside meadows, it just asked to be floated downstream. It was not too big—just big enough for a start. The tavern-keeper was not out for profit, although he had it all figured out to a kopek; what he wanted was to get the knack of it. Confident of success, he went to see the lady of the manor with the deposit money in his pocket, but came away disappointed, although he had not actually been refused. Sapegin's widow was willing to sell any part of her estate except Zapolosky, which served as a natural screen against the winter winds and the wails of the railway engines, which had a very depressing effect upon her. After a second visit Zolotukhin became offended with Madam Sapegina in real earnest: she had whacked up such a chunk for a stranger like Knishev, and wouldn't spare a grain for a neighbour. In the course of time it became a habit with the old man to visit the manor on Sundays after the church service, and he would sit there sighing over the wasted wealth, sipping bitter coffee from a saucer with the repugnance of an ascetic Old Believer, and nagging, nagging, steadily wearing down the obstinacy of the old woman by flattery, mild threats, and casual mention of all kinds of horrific examples. He would enquire whether the property was insured against fire, or finger the shutter hinges and shake his head ruefully. Ungratified, this thing became a mental obsession with Zolotukhin, and caused him considerable loss; he even postponed his removal to Shikhanov Yam, where he had found a house suitable for a tavern with an inn; he could not take a step now until he had crossed the enchanted line of Zapolosky.

In appearance he was gaunt, tall and wiry, with a deeply furrowed face and a scrappy beard resembling dry rootlets; there was a look of hungry longing in his reddish-lashed eyes, which blinked rapidly and piteously. Masterful with others, Madam Sapegina quailed in his presence, and tried to avoid his eyes from a sense of self-preservation; she did not dismiss him, though, for fear of making a powerful enemy, as well as from a morbid temptation to get first-hand information from him about the temper of what she considered her chief enemy. Her sojourn in Russia had convinced her that there was no other country in the world so dangerous to the owners of property, and no one there could guard himself against the future. This sense of precariousness on the part of this foreign, although Russianised, lady was Zolotukhin's trump card in the game he was playing.

The servants let him in without hindrance for the judicious reason that their mistress would betake herself off to Pomerania whereas Zolotukhin would stay with them for ever. He patiently stood out his cap-in-hand minute by the veranda until he heard the permissive creak of either the armchair or its occupant, who by that time would be reclining under a canvas sunshade in a lace cap through which could be seen her yellow skin.

"It's me, Zolotukhin from Krasnovershya. May I come in?" he would say, ascending the steps, and always taking care to tread on the loose board, the end of which tipped up and made the old woman start. "Well, have you made up your mind yet about that timber lot?"

"I have other things to think of, Timofeyich. I'm ill and worried."

"We're all ill and worried," Zolotukhin grunted comfortingly, bearing down on her like inevitable calamity. "Every little bird has its troubles. Don't make a wry face, my dear. I can go away if I've come at the wrong time."

"That's all right, sit down, I'm always glad to see you, Timofeyich," she said, motioning as if by mistake to a low bench next to her, although a sister to the armchair she was sitting in stood nearby. "Well, how is life outside?"

"Life is just what the Evangelist John said it would be. It's as if they're doing embroidery on his pattern. They say a secret paper has been picked up at the tannery. The writing on it says the earth's gone dry and needs sprinkling a bit with red rain. D'you get what they're driving at? Another thing—they've gone and bumped off the huntsman at Polushubovo. They found his body in the aspen wood near the road, just as you come out beyond Skopna. Hit him smack in the dial with a shot gun ... looks like nobody."

"Who could have done it?"

"Why, our good brother-Christians, of course—who else? Looks like they'd been after the master—you know, the one who'd gone to law with the muzhiks over the flood-meadow. It seems the master had given him his checked jacket as a present for his faithful service, and that faithful fool goes and puts it on to go out in the woods of all places."

The widow stared bleakly at the clumps of lilac, which stirred in the wind, and a deathly chill flowed into her swollen legs despite the thick home-knitted stockings she was wearing.

"Why do you try to frighten me, Timofeyich? It isn't good-neighbourly, really."

"I can't help it, that's how it is. If they keep on like this they'll soon kill off all the authorities in the world, believe me. Lifting their hand against the government—it's terrible to think of! I'm not trying to frighten you, my dear woman. You needn't fear me. The ones you have to fear are those who fear you." And after waving this knife about under her nose, he sheathed it in a soft chuckle. "Thinking of you, my dear, made me feel sorry. I bet you must be scared to death in the autumn nights? If anything happens, God forbid, it's a pretty long step to the telegraph office to ask for helpin' troops to be sent out. I shouldn't trust the servants, if I were you. They'll be the first to cut your throat. I'm telling you this not as a theorist, but as a practical man who knows the peasants. You'd better keep on the right side of us rude ignorant muzhiks. That was a foolish thing you did with Oblog, but it's too late now, you have fallen just the same, so I'd advise you to hire some old woman who looks like you and send her out in your shawl once in a while to take a stroll in the park. Somebody's sure to take a pot-shot at her, and that's where we grab the blighters and put the kibosh on them, eh? Better still if you moved to Loshkarev out o' harm's way. I'd give you the horses to move over, seeing that they're standing idle just now."

Giving her no time to collect her wits he dashed off bright-hued pictures of town life. He would find her an apartment with a view of the shipping or any other artistic scenery, and it would be right next to a church, so she would not have to drag herself a mile through the mud. The rest of the time she would be eating porridge with sour cream from his Simmental, or reading about the calamities of the days to come in the Good Book, and listening to the big feet of the policeman as he tramped up and down outside the window in full fighting trim. "Christ Almighty, for a fiver a month I'll get you a whopping grenadier on a chain." As for the estate, he would find her a real buyer, not one of your jiggery-pokery fellow-me-lads who'd only think how to get round her. "Why, if the price was reasonable I wouldn't mind taking it for myself." And so he unburdened his heart to her, tried to enmesh her like a spider a fly, which Providence itself had destined for his sustenance, but which, for some immoral reasons, was evading his toils. Madam Sapegina always had some excuse —the depreciation of money in wartime, or her unwillingness to strip the manor grounds, and finally her intention to keep Zapolosky as a wedding gift for her ward, if an eligible man could be found some ten years from now. It was this last consideration that induced Zolotukhin to come matchmaking for his son. So be it, then, he would take the wood with Lenochka thrown in.

Like Polya, who got the story from Taisa, Vikhrov got it from Lenochka when he called at the manor again a few days later. This time he sent Feklusha to call her out, and in the mysterious grin of that red-haired girl, who was insolently chewing the honey-cake she had been bribed with, in the very absurdity of the pretext which he had invented for calling, Lenochka read the avowal of the Pashutino forester. She came running out smartened up, with an inept flower in her hair, and new shoes on her bare feet. A bit out of breath, too, for fear that he would tire of waiting and go away. And then they walked through the park in the afternoon shadows, and all was clear to both of them, Vikhrov this time exaggerating his physical defect rather than trying to conceal it, so that she should know it, and get accustomed to it, and have no illusions about him.

He walked along at her side, limping heavily, and patting the heads of the tall ferns as he listened to the continuation of the sad story of a girl's life in bondage, and began to perceive the origin of Lenochka's terrors.

"Did he try to get round the old woman—the elder Zolotukhin! One day he'd bring her some herbs to cure boils, which he got from a quack-doctor thirty miles away, the next he'd promise to send his daughters-in-law down to weed the strawberries. He ended up with an offer to take the burden off her hands—meaning me!" Lenochka concluded her frank confession, as though she wanted Vikhrov to know everything beforehand and not to blame her afterwards for having concealed her true motives. "But my old woman wouldn't budge. 'What if she doesn't fancy him,' she says. 'He's nothing but a muzhik, that Demidka of yours.' He just laughed. 'Why shouldn't she? Of course, you've got to give her a hint.' He chuckled and patted the top of his boot threateningly, as if he was getting a whip out. I was standing behind the door, as my kind always does, and saw it all through the keyhole." Lenochka stopped, frowning at her companion's long silence. Then suddenly she caught his sleeve. "Oh, how interesting, show me, what is it?"

She shook her head as she examined the button on his cuff, which was sewn on with thin bell wire.

"A soldier's habit. It's quicker and stronger. Just so."

"Doesn't it prick?"

"No, I bend the ends in with pliers," Vikhrov calmly explained. "This is an old job, though. I now have someone to sew buttons on for me."

She let go of his sleeve at once.

"Is that so? Have you been married long?"

"No, my sister is living with me," he hastened to undeceive her.

"Oh, that's good," she laughed, catching her breath. "I suppose you never had a proper cooked meal before."

"I'm living like a king now."

The droshky came into view ahead of them. It was hitched to the archway, which had birch shoots growing from it. The forester began to take his leave of Lenochka. He understood that the flower in her hair was specially for him, yet he could not quite make up his mind whether that gave him a right to take the girl's hand or not. Actually, he could have walked away with this most precious purchase of his life there and then; what held him back was her eagerness to throw herself away on the first person she met, so long as she could flee the fears that pursued her. Already then he loved her too well to take advantage of her misfortune. To prove to her how serious his feelings were he jocularly reminded Lenochka that they had known each other years ago, when he first experienced the inconstency of a woman's heart.

She became animated, and her eyes danced.

"How old could I have been? I don't remember it at all, neither the squirrel, nor your chum.... Oh, of course"—she seemed to have seen something through a mist—"that *was* Demid Zolotukhin, wasn't it? Who was to know! I say, you seem to be sniffing at me—what's the matter?"

"I thought you smelt of lime-blossom."

"So I do. I've been picking and drying it all the morning. The old woman wants it in case of a cold. Mind you, my fingers still smell."

"It can't be, let me see," Vikhrov said incredulously, raising them to his face to prove to himself the odour's remarkable stability.

Lenochka drew her hand away with an effort.

"I wish I had a photograph of myself at that age. I must have looked funny in that pink frock with my face painted like a Red Indian's."

"You were shy and quiet, but I like you better the way you are now," the forester murmured, his eyes adding that she would grow dearer still as time went on.

She received the confession in silence, and Vikhrov at that time did not notice the troubled look that was to come into her eyes whenever he spoke to her about his feelings; she had nothing to repay them with.

"Well, I must be going, Feklusha must be looking for me. Will I get it through you! You'd better go."

Three days later the forester came riding down at sunset, flustered and incoherent over a missing cigarette-case with which cherished memories were supposed to be associated. Lenochka found him rummaging about in the bushes as she was returning from the dairy, and the oddest part about it was that they had not come this way at all on his last visit. They had to go all round the park again, trying to follow the previous route, and no matter what Lenochka started to talk about the forester always lead the conversation back to the lost cigarette-case. The thing must have been very dear to him, because his face looked drawn and thinner than when she last saw him.

"Was it a gold one, or what?"

"No, just plain metal, but it was from a comrade of mine in Siberian exile."

"Goodness, you do take on about it! You'll find your snuff-box all right!"

Her tone told him that she had long since guessed the state of his mind; fortunately, they had reached the gates. Vikhrov stood twisting his cap in his hands, a uniform cap with a cockade of oak leaves on the green band.

"You've been crying again today," he reproached her in a low voice. "Still waiting for the fire?"

Her eyes flashed angrily in the twilight.

"I wish it came quickly!"

"Then do something about it. Fight or run away, but don't stand doing nothing." He was suggesting a way out of the situation of which she was to avail herself a year later. "At any rate, you have nothing to be afraid of: you're not an heiress, or a relative, you're just a housekeeper here ... an imprisoned squirrel in a black sack, that's what you are!"

He dived into his pocket for a cigarette and in his haste pulled out the missing cigarette-case. Incidentally, it looked like a soldier's soap-box. His face went crimson; he whipped the horse, and was nearly thrown out into the ditch as the droshky tore downhill, bouncing over the pot-holes.

After a brief absence, however, Vikhrov once more became a regular visitor at the manor, so that the servants all got to know him, and Feklusha would announce him unceremoniously as the Pashutino wood-goblin who had popped up again in his droshky. Silently and clandestinely, like conspirators, they slipped through the gates and walked along the edge of darkening Zapolosky, and the more lonely it was, the farther apart they kept. In the pink flush of sunset the field looked like clover in bloom; their length-ened shadows travelled ahead of them across the dry stubble. In those days Lenochka showed an eager curiosity about roads. "Where does it go?" she would ask. She wanted to know where they would take a runaway from the Yenga, and respect for the girl made him interpret her questions as a resolve to follow that trail with him all her life long, through nights, and troubles, and mountains, for as long as she had the strength to walk, to see and touch, to breathe, wonder and learn. He belonged to that type of men—shy, unskilled in the science of the heart—who, not being sure of their own personal charm, try to show themselves to those they love in the element where they ruled supreme, whether it was the boundless waters or the bowels of the earth, the nocturnal sky or the atom, which, too, had its endless ladder into the mysterious and unfathomable depths; he had himself one day expressed the thought that only maturity was capable of creating great books, but the most enchanting of them were written by lovers. Vikhrov led his beloved across the whole world by the familiar paths of his botanical landscapes. There he did not limp. From the Russian forests, through Pustosha, he dragged his victim, tired before half the journey was over, straight off to the Trans-Caspian steppes, across the Himalayas, past Darjeeling, which had always lured him, making a call at Sumatra, that primordial experimental workshop of Nature, and farther on to the uttermost limits of his dreams, to the ocean.... And, in pass-ing, he showed the girl with an air of proprietory pride what can be created out of sunlight, humus, and moisture—the entire vegetable spectre, from the wonderful unassuming woodsorrels of the North to that repulsive and regal marvel, the Rafflesia of the tropics. After going all round the world they came back to where they were.

One day, startled by the tinkle of horse bells on the road, she interrupted him in the middle of his speech.

"Look, there comes Zolotukhin again! That's his shaft-bow shining. Quick, let's hide in the gully before he sees us." After running twenty paces, she looked back impatiently before sliding down into the gully over the smooth waxed-looking grass. "Don't stand there like a stump! Goodness, how clumsy you are!"

Vikhrov stood by the roadside, looking down at the ground. He was lame, and couldn't go any faster. He did not say a word until he drove away. He was seen no more at the manor, although never had Lenochka needed his support more than she did throughout that autumn and at the close of the winter, when it became clear that Russia was in for a period of great upheavals.

Very often now Lenochka could be seen walking down the familiar woodside all by herself, startling the sleek well-fed rooks. The rustle of the fallen leaves underfoot supplanted the conversation with her friend. "And we, we too were part of the world," they whispered to her, dragging themselves over the ground in a weary race. "We have had our pleasure, and are now departing without regret, contented and for ever. . . ." It was that season when the forest smells in turns of mushrooms, incense, and finally the sharp tang of hard-frozen snow.

That autumn prison seemed to her a blessing by comparison—at least people came out of it sooner or later. A tomtit—always the same one—called her onward to peace and quiet with its tiny bell. Taisa often saw Sapegin's ward at the deserted landing-stage. Leaning on the mooring post, she would stand there for a long time staring at the lisping water, already leaden and ice-crusted, as it lapped the tarred sides. No one led Lenochka away from the dangerous spectacle. Was it not because every person, when maturing, has to find out for himself how leaden and hopeless it is down there as well, in the depths.

CHAPTER SIX

1

The Pashutino forester was very busy that autumn. He had taken over his division in a sadly neglected state owing to the effects of the first world war. As a matter of fact, no one had gone in for science there before the war either, although there was an excellent forestry library, and reclamation work, too, was suspended owing to the cuts in appropriations. At the same time the Loshkarev branchline became an important factor in front-line shipments; uncontrolled fuel-wood fellings for the railway and the adjacent capitals threatened the timber forests of the Yenga with destruction. It required no little effort, without men or means, to carry out even partial forest regeneration in the cutover areas. The war had put a stop to the local industries, rural building, and even to range repairs. Life on the Yenga came to a standstill.

The disastrous state of the country, engulfed in economic and military ruin, demanded that the national destinies be put into the hands of the people themselves. After the February revolution everything that had survived the greed of yesterday's masters—the earth's green wealth included—became dearer than ever to the lawful heirs of Russia. This, in turn, helped to call attention to those who were engaged in the business of preserving and perpetuating the forest, which still remained the chief source of the country's revival. And so the Yenga community considered itself in duty bound to celebrate the seventieth birthday of Minei Lisagonov, the wood ranger of the 9th Division and Vikhrov's indefatigable assistant, with a frugal dinner to which twenty-five of his comrades were invited. In those early months following the overthrow of the autocracy it had not become a custom yet to take notice of the small cogs in the state machine. Neither the Deputy Conservator of Loshkarev, who was a local bigwig, nor the clergyman the Rev. Trinitatov, with whom the Pashutino forester was on bad terms, cared a rap for the hoary forest veteran, who had been guarding Pustosha for half a century. Nevertheless, despite the bogged down April roads, the afore-mentioned personages invited themselves down in order to queue up at this likely door into Russia's tomorrow. They came with gifts, too—the Deputy Conservator with a compass for determining all the four directions of the globe, while his Reverence, amid the applause of the assembled company, drew forth from under his cassock a sizeable bottle of that soothing home-distilled beverage locally known as Teneriffe, which he compounded in proper season with the aid of honey and certain secret herbs. Taisa, who had taken up permanent residence with her brother by that time, was able to recount all the circum-stances of that memorable feast in minute detail.

The first toast, capped with horse-radish, paid appropriate tribute to the forests as a national boon. In his speech Ivan Vikhrov propounded the idea, which was later to become the main thesis of his first book, that the forests should be granted the same rights of citizenship as the other sources of public welfare. The guest from Loshkarev soberly observed that the forest, unlike other resources, was not threatened with depletion, as it was continually renewing itself, whereupon Yegor Sevastyanich, the worthy feldsher at the local little hospital, pointed out very appropriately, the while he stroked his huge grizzled moustaches, that all the world's important timberlands were known and numbered, whereas new mines and pits were being opened every year. This was followed by a conciliatory toast to "the land we live in", and although the glasses clinked more merrily than ever, and deep inroads were made in Taisa's mushroom dishes, it was clear even then that everyone read his own meaning into that noble phrase. And when, after the salt-fish pie, the Deputy Conservator proposed the health of the gallant band of foresters, young Vikhrov perkily enquired whether His Excellency had in mind the handful of yes-men on top, who had failed to keep even the protection forests of Russia from being plundered, or the Little Man, whose name was legion, the rank-and-file of the forest toilers, who watched the work of destruction with impotent fury. All at once the air became tense.

"What were we to do then, in your opinion, Mr. Vikhrov?" the forest general said drily.

"Shout about what is happening in your own official sphere, fight and even die, dammit, if that is necessary in the performance of your duty."

"As a high forest officer you are probably aware that privately-owned forests do not come within the jurisdiction of our department?"

"Then the people will have to fill in that gap in forest legislation by force!" It was this phrase that was subsequently interpreted as proof of Vikhrov's Bolshevist views and caused his dismissal just a week before the October rising.

The dispute switched over into the labyrinths of forest statistics. Most of the guests were out of their depths here, but the general sympathy was with Vikhrov. Some had been friends of his father, others had met him at Kalina's as a barefooted lad. Accustomed as they were to going to bed with the birds, the foresters listened sleepily to the raging argument, while at the lower end of the table the rangers burst into raucous song; they had managed to get hold of some of that pernicious stuff which passed locally as cognac of the sinister "Three Bones" brand. With a view to restoring peace and good fellowship, the Reverend Trinitatov boasted of having raced in a Bashkir *baiga* near Ufa in the golden days of his youth, and having even won a foal as a prize. This introduced the subject of horses, and Yegor Sevastyanich, who was well in his cups by now, boasted of having recently bought an admirable mare for his medical rounds. According to him, she had been in the service of some important bishop before the revolution, and even had a letter of commendation from him or something of that kind. At this, everyone who was in a position to do so, went outside to have a look at the new acquisition.

It was a very rough night. Spring was breaking the fetters of winter with loud crunchings, and the air was full of gurgling noises. The sleepy shivering stable-boy led the beauty out of her stall, and everyone was lavish of praise. Deep-chested and tall, dapple-grey as the sky that night, she twitched her ears, and pawed the ground, trying to stand before the wind, which had strengthened so much towards midnight that it almost blew out the wick in the chinky hurricane lamp; it was the middle of April. Father Trinitatov alone was vinegary in his comments, for which the mare's owner classed him among that execrable species of connoisseurs, who were ready to find fault with the sun itself so as to keep their reputation in the eyes of the public, and even called him a Nematoda, an insult which the priest greatly resented. Leading the mare by the halter to the screening wood-stack where it was a bit quieter and exposing the rest of the company to the lingering torture of a biting wind and the wet misery of an oozing sky, Father Trinitatov proceeded to a more elaborate examination. He pulled his victim's lips apart, lifted each leg in turn by the fetlock, tapped the skull over the eye, blew into the horse's nostril, and then laid his ear to its belly in an endeavour to discover what effects all this had upon the animal's vitals, while the mare made ineffectual attempts at retaliation by trying to catch her examiner's sleeve and certain other parts of him between her teeth. Then, coughing and sneezing, all trooped back to continue the discussion on horses in cosier surroundings, Vikhrov, in the capacity of host, bringing up the rear of the procession. It was here that the at first inexplicable glow above the dark rim of the Pashutino nursery was accounted for.

"I wonder what it can be burning so long and brightly in our district?" Father Trinitatov, who was walking in front, asked the feldsher.

"It's dying down now, Father, but a couple of hours ago it was blazing like anything," the stable-boy answered for his master excitedly, and a cold shiver went through Vikhrov. "It must be the muzhiks at Sapegino setting fire to the place."

There were two other villages in the direction of the fire, but in the mind of everyone Sapegino stood first in the waiting list for burning down, and a better night for smoking the accursed Lady-Ox out of her lair could hardly have been chosen.

Vikhrov's first thought was for Lenochka. It took him a minute to snatch his sheepskin coat off the nail and order the sledge to catch up with him on the road to Krasnovershya; the shorter way was through Maximkovo, but he was not sure about the little bridge across the Sklan—it was washed away every year during the spate. The tattered sky scudded overhead, breaking into crimson foam over the fire glow, which gradually faded and presently died out altogether. In its place, while Vikhrov was fighting his way through the storm to the big forest, a lopsided luminosity, grotesque and blurred—obviously the moon—floated out of the grey milky mist. Gaunt headless trunks loomed ghostlike through the shadowy murk on both sides of the squelching road. He kept sinking knee-deep into the soggy snow at the roadsides. Never had the spring been in such a hurry. The many-voiced hum of multitudinous efforts flowed through the forest, distinct among them the sighs of the settling snow-crust, alternating with the hiss of awakening water, and all drowned in the boom of the blustering wind, which was helping the river to shift off the ice.

Vikhrov could not make out where he was, and not until he came to an unfamiliar-looking hollow and saw two crossed pines rubbing against each other did he realise that he was heading straight for Maximkovo. He was about to force his way through the fir underbrush into the adjacent clearing and paused to take his bearings, when a moving human figure appeared ahead of him in the darkness. It was so incredible that anybody should be in such a place and in such foul weather that he thought it was his imagination playing tricks with him. But the figure was actually advancing towards him, and like him, stumbling every minute over the pot-holes in the road; this meant, by the way, that the bridge over the Sklan was intact; the shadowy figure staggered along bareheaded, drenched to the skin, and like that time in the larch drive, one arm was stretched forward from the elbow; by this characteristic gesture Vikhrov recognised the person who was dearest to him in the world. Indeed, it was Lenochka.

Many years later, during one of Vikhrov's "roastings" at the Forestry Institute, Gratsiansky reminded the audience of the unseemly conduct of a state employee towards a dependent of the landed gentry, apparently leaving him no alternative between hiding from her behind a tree and demanding gruffly at the point of a gun what she was doing at night in a state-owned forest. And it occurred to no one at the time what his own opinion was of those with whom he wished to curry favour as a guardian of the civic virtues. Even if Vikhrov could have foreseen what trouble that girl was going to cause him, he would not have acted in any other way. What he did, trembling from head to foot, was to knead her chilled hands in an attempt to restore to her the power of speech and pour some of his own living warmth into her; and, as if she already belonged to him, to rub her shoulders, which were wet and ice-cold under her flimsy jacket, most particularly that already benumbed hollow between the shoulder-blades through which spring death, according to his calculations, was to enter her, and to gaze and gaze into the wet face, now only half-familiar with its twitching mouth and sunken eye-sockets shaded off to the very cheek-bones.

"Steady, my love, it's quite near. . . . They've been heating the bath-house for the timber-squarers here. . . . Can't you run? Just try, we must get there quickly!" he muttered, wrapping his sheepskin about her fumblingly, and afraid to think what she had on her feet, which sank in the snowy slush, while he looked round for the hundredth time, but there was no sign of the sledge.

Lenochka did not recognise him in the feldsher's shaggy cap which he had snatched up at random out of the heap of clothes; nor did she recognise anyone for three weeks afterwards; she kept stammering a clumsy lie about having gone out for a walk to get the stove fumes out of her head and having lost her way. She talked now without a stop, and certain links in her speech were lost in the chatter of her teeth. In a sudden burst of confidence she told a disjointed tale of how Zolotukhin and his gang of kulaks had attacked the manor at nightfall . . . of how they had spared nothing there, not even the lilac bush by the veranda, because even the lilac in that place was accurst... and how one of them had raised his hand at the screaming Feklusha, but had not dared to hit the poor orphan... no, he hadn't dared, because he must have realised that an orphan's wrongs were punished hardest by God. As for the old woman....

"...She'd been promising to take me with her to Pomerania, but she never did. What a shame.... And I've gone and lost my comb too." Lenochka was going to push a wisp of clinging wet hair back from her forehead, but she forgot, and looked at her raised hand in wonder. "Oh, what a pity about that comb.... Now she won't take me to Pomerania with her. I went out for a walk with a headache, but the ice-drift started on the river." So the house of the Pashutino forester, to her mind, was the only safe place in the world.

"Come on, damn it all!" Vikhrov yelled, trying to reach her clouded mind through the din of spring.

Lenochka was saved by the Russian bath, by Taisa's devotion to her brother, and by her own blind will to live, which had carried her eight miles through the stormy night. Her night lasted a whole month, her recovery began one morning. When she first opened her eyes a pink-clad Siberian apple-tree was gazing through the wide-open window, and a handful of blossoms, blown in by the wind, lay upon the quilt. The world looked wonderfully new and shiny when Lenochka, grown thin, descended the doorsteps unassisted and set foot upon the grass, which was dotted with the first dandelions. She felt slightly dizzy from the heady smell of mouldering sawdust warmed by the hot noon-day sun, and still more, perhaps, from the immense sweep of sky through which the clouds sped, clouds so huge yet so noiseless. A sense of unpardoned guilt made the girl avoid a busy bumble-bee on a flower—he was at home here, and working, while she was a newcomer from burnt-down Sapegino, a sponger, whom kind people had given shelter to out of pity. Near the well she met a local young woman with a yoke on her shoulder who responded affably but somewhat coldly to Lenochka's timid bow. A husband at the front, legitimate children, and the weight of two full buckets gave her a right to that somewhat haughty dignity. No one pestered Lenochka with either pity or curiosity, but everyone knew all there was to know. Besides, when all was said and done, someone had to take down the readings of the weather-vane at the Pashutino meteo-station and the amount of precipitation deposited in the course of the day. There was a

hope, though only a slender one so far, that yesterday was forgotten and done with; the ghastly night had passed for Lenochka
without leaving a trace beyond the fact that it had chilled her
for the rest of her life, as it were. Moreover, she formed the
habit, as soon as dusk fell, of crouching in a distant corner somewhere near the stove, but Taisa always found an excuse for
leading her up to the window and showing her the empty country road to Krasnovershya, so bumpy that it would shake your
soul loose in the autumn, so deserted as only such roads can be
after the end of a sanguinary war.

To Lenochka's sorrow there had not been a drop of rain for
two months running, so there was nothing really for her to write
down, and forced inactivity gave her a guilty feeling of eating
the unearned bread of idleness. Nor did the situation change much
when, thanks to her broad hints to Taisa, she was given the extra
job of selecting coniferous seeds and testing them for germina-
tion. The work was easy enough for a schoolgirl, but lack of
knowledge prevented Lenochka from giving herself up to it sufficiently to be able to sit down unashamed at the table with all
the others. Vikhrov must have understood her state of mind if
he suggested, of his own accord, that she should be sent away
to study; besides, he wanted her to see life and other men before
accepting the proposal of a lame and dull forester. The idea
appealed to Lenochka. Only a change of scene could cure her
of the harrowing fear that she would one day be run down to
earth here as well. Yegor Sevastyanich had connections at the
Loshkarev Training Courses for Hospital Nurses, and it took
Taisa only a week to prepare the necessary outfit for her, from
coarse linen underwear to an old-fashioned all-weather overcoat
with puff sleeves, which she had bought with her meagre earnings
as a farm-hand two years before she moved over to her brother.

"Thank you. I'll work it off, as true as I live I will!" Lenochka whispered hotly at parting, as she stood dressed and ready
to go.

With a fatherly hand Vikhrov smoothed the coat down on her
back—it kept bunching, although it had been altered—and gave
her behind closed doors part of the salary he had just drawn
with a promise to share with her in future too.

"Take it, come...! My tastes are simple, and it's a bit too
early for me to start saving up for old age. It isn't a present,
it's just a passing sum, which I also used to get from strangers
when I was your age. Later on you can pass it on to someone

else in need, this little debt. Now everything depends upon you. Knowledge will help you to become more useful to people. Love life, help to make it cleaner, and when you come back you will take care of my old-man ailments free of charge. There, just so."

"Why, you're not old at all, sir," Lenochka said none too confidently, and Vikhrov was thinking what efforts would be needed in future to weed out those servile inflections which had crept into her speech during those years of complete dependence. "Not as much as a grey hair!"

"That's because I brush my hair with the boot brush so as not to waste any of the polish. Now, off you go to the cart. Yegor Sevastyanich is cross, the flies are pestering his beauty."

The Pashutino forester was then barely thirty, but to Lenochka he was, if not actually an old man, then the youngest looking of humanity's tutors; she made a fumbling attempt to kiss his hand. Vikhrov shouted something at her about getting rid of her other slavish habits besides her ridiculous fear of life, slammed the door, and did not even come out on the doorstep to wave a handkerchief to her as she rode away.

2

The work that he had started on his book and the trips to the capital's libraries which it involved helped the forester to tide over his two-years' separation from Lenochka almost without corresponding. His messages to Loshkarev, consisting of wordly counsels, fitted into the message margins of his postal orders, but the very thought of their future meeting made his work easier; if it is true that every outstanding work, in addition to its main thematic purpose, is dictated by an ulterior motive concealed from the reader in the author's own creative life, then for Vikhrov this consisted in introducing the girl to the forest by means of his book, as he would introduce her to his family, and let her help him as best she could in his fight for her new friends. To do this he had to strain a lake of historical data and statistical proofs, as well as of his own observations and thoughts on life, through the slow trickle of ink that ran from his pen to the paper. It remained for him now to copy out fair a sizeable pile of sheets covered with scrawly handwriting, when it suddenly became clear that his broad generalisations were not sufficiently documented, that the profusion of poetic images detracted from the scientific value of the book, and that instead of the research which he had planned the result was a poem on the grievous fate of the forest.

So one morning, crossing out all that he had done, he put a clean sheet in front of him, and got into a muddle right away, the moment he tried to define the forest as an object of science. There was no lack of current definitions at that time, all of them mutually irreconcilable, because each reflected its author's individual view as to what place the forest occupied in the economics of the age, and, consequently, the political as well as scientific trend to which he belonged. Disputes raged to as lively an accompaniment of axes, so that the laymen began to wonder uneasily whether the object of this controversial war would survive by the time the truth was hammered out. Realising the importance of this struggle, dogmatic though it sometimes was, Vikhrov decided to make a closer approach to common sense, that is, to bring things in line with the interests of the national economy and communist posterity. And so the book was to start with a critical review of historical conceptions of the forest with parallel reports showing its depletion in Russia; in the course of this work it became necessary to trace the origin of that vulgar formula which interpreted the forest and the tree as factory and worker producing timber. The quotation was given in one of Tulyakov's books, and the pupil wrote a letter to his teacher asking to be allowed to see the original source whenever convenient.

The meeting took place during one of the young forester's visits to St. Petersburg, some year and a half after the revolution, in the same gloomy study with its heavy curtains close-drawn against life, which was, in fact, rather noisy that winter. Nothing had changed there since Vikhrov's student days, except that in place of the box of cigars, a phalanx of drug phials stood deployed for decisive battle on the Palace-Square expanse of desk top, while the flank of the desk, which used to be littered with furiously scribbled manuscripts, was now tenanted by a neat stack of those consolatory books, which find their way into such homes through the back door shortly before the undertaker —the Bible, books on medicinal herbs, and something astro-charlatanic, headed by an encyclopedia of Tibetan witch doctory. Tulyakov had crossed the age threshold when all life's flaming sensations are gently ousted by the contemplation of the process of physical dissolution that has started within. The dimmed eyes of the old man, who was sitting at the desk in his fur coat with a raised collar, told a more circumstantial tale about the changes that had taken place there. There was a smell of smouldering wick from the icon lamp, which had been discreetly extinguished by some member of the household while Vikhrov was in the hall.

The professor chided the young man for making such a risky trip to the capital, seemingly on foot, for the sake of such an obvious trifle.

"You shouldn't have taken your coat off, colleague," his former teacher bumbled. "It's cold in here, and there's no sense in looking for more trouble than history has doled out to us."

"I don't cut a big enough figure yet to take so much care of myself," said the ex-pupil. "Incidentally, I had an excellent journey, and, besides, it's nice and thawy outside."

The conversation then shifted to slippery ground—the causes of Russia's calamities. This, and especially the false tone in which the professor expressed his astonishment on hearing that traffic had been restored on the railways, made Vikhrov curtail his visit and pass abruptly to the direct object for which he had made it. The old man gave no sign that he had recognised his student, but Vikhrov saw at once that he remembered him even as a woodyard boy. The book was on the top shelf under the dusty ceiling, which looked pretty grimy from the smoking iron stove.

"Take it down, it's the third on the right, I believe, leather-bound," Tulyakov said, nodding towards the step-ladder. "I must warn you, though, the book is written in some outlandish tongue. I don't remember whether it was translated into Russian or not."

"That's all right, I have a smattering of double Dutch," Vikhrov said from the top step with an unforced laugh.

It was Puthon's forgotten work *Traité de l'économie forestière*, and one could well imagine the dismay of that aristocratic forest scientist, could he but see this cook's son hastily thumbing through this volume of scientific lore in a foreign language without any difficulty.

"Do you want some paper?" Tulyakov said, making himself companionable.

Vikhrov nodded gratefully without tearing himself away from the page.

"Thank you, I have brought some with me," he said, then glanced at the date of publication. "Damn it, how tragically little people knew only yesterday!"

"But in those days men's ignorance was more than compensated by the excellent condition of the forests," the professor observed wryly. "It looks as if the basic truths about the forest will be discovered when it will have disappeared completely off the face of the earth, and that, I believe, is quite within the bounds of human possibility. What do you want that information for, my young colleague?"

Tersely but clearly Vikhrov informed his host of the subject he had chosen for his work and the difficulties he met with. The professor commented with ironic respect on the intention of the Pashutino forester to espouse the sacred cause of forest defence, a job, which, in the past, had proved too much for Russia's most distinguished foresters; he also muttered something about the harmfulness of self-confidence in public as well as in private life.

"I'll send you my book if it's ever published," Vikhrov said imperturbably, continuing to make notes.

Tulyakov got some bone-dry tobacco out of a drawer and pushed it across the desk towards his visitor without inviting him to smoke.

"I don't seem to remember you, but I gathered from your letter that you attended my lectures and were even familiar with my later harmful works?"

"Yes, and what's more I had frequent occasion to convince myself of your kindness towards the young," Vikhrov drew a bow at a venture.

"It's very flattering to hear something pleasant about oneself for a change. Would you care to dine with me? I have boiled oil-cake for dinner today. Ever ate it?"

"Yes, when I was a child, but thanks, I've had my dinner today," Vikhrov nodded absently without accepting the challenge. He was smiling at a particularly naive page of Puthon's.

"May I be allowed, then, to ask to what extent you share my opinions about the forest?" Tulyakov asked tentatively, not without concealed agitation.

His visitor's demeanour seemed to show that Tulyakov's recent booklet opposing the nationalisation of the forests had not yet reached the backwoods of the Yenga. Hooted off the boards a year later, this booklet was meantime greeted with an ominous silence among the author's contemporaries and closest pupils.

"I'm inclined to share them," Vikhrov said, "if you mean sustained-yield forestry and not your last unfortunate essay." He had in mind that system of forestry practice under which the annual cut is limited to the volume of the annual growth in order

to preserve the timber resources. "Your recent booklet disappointed me though luckily it's the shortest thing you've written. I'm
not apologising for being so blunt. We are entering a stormy
period of life, a period of uncertain duration, when the success
of a great cause will depend upon how strict contemporaries and
the generations to come will be towards each other. I think that
article of yours is a gross mistake. But then dangerous inaccuracies have cropped up in your previous books as well, Professor."

"Will you kindly explain yourself ... more fully," the latter
said falteringly, moving the phials about on the desk like so
many chess figures.

"Well, as far as I can judge, I always felt that your comparison of the forests and the raw material extracted from them
with capital and rent was narrow-minded. The forest is a sum of
productive and not production forces. You could only call it
Capital if it became a means for exploiting people."

Tulyakov all but lunged towards him across his desk.

"To my mind your formula, as it stands, is meaningless. The
productive forces are productive because they manifest themselves
in production. Your objection is much too deep for me." He got
mixed up and grew angry. "And let me remind you, my none
too young or polite visitor, that I have been quoting Marx in
the very first volume of my *Forest Management*, long before you
appeared in my kitchen, and even received a neck reward for
my pains from the authorities concerned."

"You sound as though you had discovered Marx for the Russian forest scientists," Vikhrov said, trying to restrain a challenging ardour. "I still remember your kindness, and have no
wish to hurt your feelings by seeming suspicious, but I can
hardly believe that Tulyakov is capable of demanding approval
of his obvious errors by way of repaying the debt of gratitude
for the remittances which he regularly sent me in my student
days." He reeled this off on a sudden inspiration, and his host
did not even attempt to deny it. "I only wanted to warn you,
Professor, that careless handling of higher economic mathematics
may lead you into pretty cheerless labyrinths."

"Is that a threat?"

"No, a desire to save one of Russia's most eminent forest
scientists from a second fall. Just so."

Tulyakov's grey unshaven cheeks flushed.

"So you did read that really awful booklet of mine?"

"Yes," Vikhrov said drily, putting his notes away. "It made

me feel sad, after having seen you in your full lustre, to read all that bravado, which nothing but inexplicable bitterness can account for. At first I intended to write you an open letter, but decided that my future book would be a better reply. Don't be angry with me, I am your friend. I have always considered your books to be forestry classics, and my unseemly tone is not so much due to bad manners as to concern about what is going to happen to them now. If I were you I would go round all the book stalls in Russia and spend my last kopek buying up that unfortunate production, and feed it to that iron greedy-guts there"—with a nod towards the stove—"buy it up before the young generation has grown. What has scared you in the revolution— you, the son of a peasant, if my information is correct, who has forgotten his ignorant Vologda kinsfolk? Walk through the country, in a peasant's *armyak* if need be, listen to the hum of awakening in the Russian forest, and try to take an airing in that bracing icy draught. Yes, you are very ill, Professor." He got up, thinking he had said enough to be promptly evicted, but he was not, and that encouraged him. "Look here, I could take you along with me to the Yenga right now! What about it?"

"Well, I do declare! No one yet has ever tried to doctor me with such cauteries," Tulyakov muttered, too disconcerted to be angry.

"Did you ever ask yourself, Professor, why others abstained from prescribing that medicine?"

Vikhrov seemed to be hinting at the over-refined delicacy peculiar to people of that intellectual set, which would not allow them to mar the last minutes of old age in a century when it was the fashion not to spare them. It meant that others had resigned themselves to Tulyakov's inglorious end, while the cook's son was the first to use fire for his resurrection. Both felt touched; the old man suddenly complimented his visitor on his noble understanding of mutual civic responsibility, which Vikhrov had expressed through the simile of the rope by which people are tied together when scaling the heights of an otherwise inaccessible glacier, so that one cannot fall or swerve aside without upsetting the order of ascension. Their eyes met. Tulyakov shuffled sadly over to the window, whence there came a sudden burst of rifle fire.

"I could explain how it happened," he said bleakly, staring at something through the ice-filmed window, "but I'm afraid that until the new order has settled down no one is going to listen to a long and tedious apologia from Professor Tulyakov, and after that ... after that it will be too late in any case."

"Come away from the window, Professor," Vikhrov said after a second burst of machine-gun fire.

"You are right, young man, people knew tragically little. Those of yesterday will always have known tragically little. It's painful for the living, but it would be worse for progress if the realities made us arrive at an opposite conclusion," he continued thinking aloud. "You are right, I have become so old and unfair towards life that I am no longer sure I have a moral right to my slice of bread from future harvests, and that, naturally, makes a man bitter. But your words are true, and yours is the most merciless truth on earth, the truth of honest and uncompromising youth. The doubts of dusk always look naive in the morning. At any rate, I wouldn't wish you at my age to have to listen to such things from the most able of your pupils, things about age, *armyaks* and bravado. By the way, have you got it on you ... my booklet, I mean?"

"No, I left it at home, at the forest range."

It was then that Tulyakov hit upon a singular form of repaying the pleasure which Vikhrov had given him. He offered to buy off Vikhrov's copy of the condemned article, and in order to whet the seller's appetite, he started unloading from his desk tied-up batches of files containing the accumulated archive miscellany of decades; more recent papers were simply pushed under the strings with which they were tied together. In Vikhrov's eyes all that paper junk was priceless, especially as one of the sheafs was found to contain several notebooks of Tulyakov's teacher—a cursory forest chronicle enabling one to trace the rolling up of the green carpet in European Russia. In hoarding that material Tulyakov, apparently, had intended to tackle the same subject as Vikhrov, but had kept putting it off, like a death-hour shrift, and was now parting with his treasure without regret, like a silviculturist passing on to his successor his favourite grove, which had not attained maturity yet. He even threw in an old suitcase to get it down to the railway station in.

They sat on till nightfall, talking about the forest. The old man solemnly lighted a bit of candle, the last one in the land, he believed; candles were no longer sold, they had to be *got*. Vikhrov went away when only ten minutes of stearine were left.

"Take that bundle of chatwood with you," Tulyakov said at parting, pointing to the suitcase. "No one has come out of the forest yet with empty hands. Love the forest, young man. And mind the handle of the suitcase doesn't break off."

"That's all right, I happen to have some string with me," answered Vikhrov.

He was too young to understand either the appeal to the judges' mercy or the suicidal anguish which that gift contained; he was not even curious to know why Tulyakov had not used the material himself, the mere publication of which with a commentary would have repaired his reputation in the eyes of his contemporaries of the thirties.

It was a rare collection of documentary evidence against the plunderers of the Russian forest. Together with such gems as workers' pay-rolls, notarial forward contracts, bank claims against ruined forest owners, and even copies of Senate acts concerning sensational forest lawsuits of the nineteenth century, there were no less valuable domestic documents pertaining to the private lives of the timber-industry bourgeoisie—their felling and logging licences, their intimate correspondence, scandalous press cuttings about their night revels in the capital's restaurants, torn menus and fabulous dinner bills, and, among others, the pearl of the collection—a batch of illiterate letters from Germaine, a migratory *café chantant* canary, to the notorious Knishev, ransomed probably from the drunkard for half a stoff of vodka. It was these fallen leaves of the epoch, which, as a rule, moulder away to nothing by the time the historian gets to it, that enabled Vikhrov eventually to draw fairly expressive pictures showing how the national wealth was split up among the pockets of the parasites, and to give to the documentation of his accusatory chapters the force of material evidence. All this taken together predetermined the success of *The Fate of the Russian Forest*; the civic indignation roused by these glaring crimes gave to his book the quality of a keen-edged sword against the overthrown class, a weapon which the young order, not yet steady on its feet, so badly needed. In his subsequent attack upon the book, Gratsiansky, naturally, took advantage of the fact that the author, in his preface, mentioned the tarnished name of Tulyakov, to whom he owed that generous gift.

3

The manuscript was sent to the publishers in the autumn of the next year. Hearing nothing for six months, Vikhrov began to think of going to Moscow himself for a reply, when one evening, towards the end of winter, a wide country sledge drew up at the forester's house on the last sleighing. At first Vikhrov felt only the cold draught from wide-opened doors, then he saw his sister through the curtained window with a travelling basket in her hands. A woman with a half-familiar face and a kind of guilty air was taking her sheepskin coat off on the doorstep and pushing off Vikhrov's setter by the name of Bubbles, who was trying to lick her face. Vikhrov recognised Lenochka by the sleeve puffs of her now frayed coat and by the dark wisp of hair that escaped from under her shawl; eager though he was to have a look at that dear face, he did not go out to greet the newcomer until he had found an easy old man's grumbling tone suitable for the occasion. It appeared that the medical courses in Loshkarev had closed down in view of their reorganisation into a medical college to be located in the regional centre, and Lenochka had not been included in the new enrolment; for the sake of brevity she made no mention of the fact that she had failed to appear before the selection committee of the District Health Department for fear of questions about her social origin. Later, over the evening samovar, the neighbours gathered at the forester's to hear what the new arrival had to say about herself, what she had heard about the overthrow of world capital, and what the price of butter was on the market, while she huddled by the heated stove and gave a shy answer to all questions that everything was fine. Yegor Sevastyanich dropped in too. He jocularly expressed the fear that Lenochka would now steal all his patients, but it was clear to those present that the only way out for her now was to marry. Even Bubbles stretched himself at her feet as if he had divined with the intuition of a dependent soul that she was going to be his mistress.

Within a week after her arrival, Lenochka's illness, which seemed to have abated in the course of those years, struck at her again. To her former fears and morbid sense of dependency were added a knowledge of her unpardonable guilt, somewhat exaggerated but not entirely groundless. News had reached Pashutino in a roundabout way that the young Sapegins had been killed on the Denikin front—not on the Soviet side, of course. No one in the village had ever hinted at anything in Lenochka's presence, but the seed of overheard rumour instantly took root in the prepared soil. Lenochka thought that it was upon her, the sole survivor of that shipwrecked family, that the punishment for all the crimes of the overthrown regime was bound to fall. It was not only the evening road she was afraid of now—any trifle, the wry glance of a passer-by, a caller in military uniform, a letter with the capital's post-mark likely to contain some intimation that her very existence was objectionable to the rest of humanity—all this assumed a special significance, which she alone knew of. Furtively, she ran down to the river and dropped her gold brooch into the ice-hole—the brooch which the old woman had given her in one of her tender moments—destroying that last piece of incriminating evidence of her association with world capitalism. She had chosen the ice-hole instead of the well because someone might accidentally scoop it out with a pail. Now she could go and work with Yegor Sevastyanich with a clean conscience. She threw herself into her job with a will, but her illness proved to be so strong that not even by working twice round the clock could she attain that blessed degree of fatigue which brought forgetfulness. There was none in that little hospital quieter than her, more hardworking. Nevertheless, she was to receive her first blow here; it was dealt her by Semyonikha.

Vetrova, known as Semyonikha, was a tall gaunt old woman from the neighbouring village of Polushubovo, the mother of five sons, who were famous on the Yenga. The two elder ones, lance-corporals in the army, had been killed in the first world war, the next two were serving in the navy, one of them, according to rumour, having risen to all-Russian eminence in St. Petersburg within a month of the revolution, while the other, within that same month, had died the death of a hero at the hands of Yudenich's troops near Narva. Mark, the fifth and youngest, had also run away to become a sailor when still a boy, but had never reached the sea and served aboard river boats of the Kama flotilla, which was fighting the advancing Kolchak at that moment. Maternal pride and grief had given her that slow stern air which is often to be found in placards depicting the motherland, and not everyone could sustain the piercing glance of her sorrow-clouded eyes. Yegor Sevastyanich, who had frequent and illegitimate recourse to the hospital's supply of absolute alcohol, always felt uneasy in her presence despite his popularity with the local inhabitants, and as for Lenochka, she simply avoided her. They met by accident in the dressing room, and since Lenochka's state of mind was outwardly expressed in an ingratiating moistness of eye and a humble obligingness of manner, it was only natural that Semyonikha, who knew all about the misadventures of the Sapegins' protégée, should doubt her sincerity. She said to Lenochka: "I say, Miss, what makes you so sugar sweet? Are you trying to live something down?" in such a calm, ominously kind tone that Lenochka all but lost the use of her legs.

Not even marriage could save her now, for it would not rid her of close public scrutiny. Besides, Vikhrov did nothing; her silent malady baffled him; he understood her dependent position, and did not even dare to submit to her high judgement the thousand odd pages which he had written for her own sake. New themes clamoured for his pen, but he hardly ever sat down at his desk, and roamed about the thawed bogs most of the time with a gun or greeted the dawn in a secluded shack in Pustosha. Spring was coming in with a rush, and though the forest stood blue and unawakened, the ice-crust on the Pashutino ponds had already turned green, and the rooks had started house repairs on the old nests. Lenochka was wasting away with a shy smile; the quicker she melted away with the snows the more sympathy and kindness was she surrounded with. At times, however, a hidden untamed force deep within her flashed into life from under her lowered eyelashes, desperate like a sudden yearning for escape. Although Yegor Sevastyanich's knowledge of the human body did not extend beyond the symptoms of dropsy and hernia, he nevertheless strongly advised Taisa not to leave the girl alone, especially after dark.

Thereupon Taisa decided to speed things up.

"I want to talk to you, Ivan," she told her brother. "The poor child is just pining away."

"She must have caught a cold. Brew her some raspberry tea and have the bath-house heated up."

"Ah me, you'd do better to build your nest instead of shooting innocent beasts and wearing your boots out in the brake. This is the midsummer of your life, Ivan."

"You want to dandle your nephews, I see?" her brother laughed it off. "All right, I don't mind, find me some lonely widow with a wooden leg to make up a pair."

She persisted, the while she picked invisible motes off the sleeve of his regulation jacket.

"Oh, stop boasting about your failings! At least, you're insured now against all woes. Bless me, a husband like you in wartime is worth his weight in gold! The whole district is waiting for your wedding. What are you both torturing yourselves for? Just look at her, she's eating her heart out."

"Be careful sister, you may drive her into a mudhole. Let go of my arm, and don't be silly. Just so!" And he betook himself off again to the outlying divisions of his domains, where the heath-cocks' duels rang lustier with every dawn, and the bleating of the snipe sounded so tantalising at dusk.

His resistance made Taisa try to hasten the course of events by tackling the other end. She put it into Lenochka's head to ask her brother what the aims of his profession were, particularly, what it was he loved the forest for so much; and that was as good as asking him about the meaning of his life. It would take Vikhrov all day to answer a question like that, and during that time, according to Taisa's cunning calculations, they would have it out between them. In fact Lenochka had often asked herself why Vikhrov had not chosen something nice for the subject of his book, something like an apple-tree or a gooseberry bush instead of just ordinary trees, which grew by themselves without anyone tending them. The most convenient place for answering such basic questions of existence was the forest, where the visual aids were at hand. Vikhrov arranged the excursion for an early hour the next morning so as to complete Lenochka's initiation into forest craft before nightfall. They set out from Pashutino with the bless-ings of the whole village, bestowed from behind drawn curtains, and, as everyone noticed, unaccompanied by Bubbles. A fairly large field with a country track running through the middle of it adjoined the forestry division from the east; no one came away from the window until the lecturer and his audience had disap-peared in the undergrowth.

It was a raw sunless early morning in May filled with an expect-ant hush, as if before the beginning of a concert, when all are assembled and are only waiting for the tarrying conductor, and invisible birds are practising snatches of tomorrow's melodies on toy clarinets, and then the woodpecker in his black-and-yellow tail-coat raps for attention, and suddenly the most powerful of life's laws is set in motion, and under the surge of the awakened juices the winter sleep is broken, and the forest clads itself in the murmurous robes of summer. But all that is of tomorrow; meantime there is nothing to gladden the eye except a timid greening of the woodland glades in the open places, which look as if touched with a tyro's brush, and the fussy rooks pecking the thawed earth in last year's furrow.

Upon entering the forest Vikhrov plucked a bud from a hare-nibbled bird-cherry tree and held it out to his companion in the palm of his hand with the solemn air of one offering a present to one's bride on the threshold of their new home.

"What's it for?" Lenochka asked.

"They're my friends; my family humbly begs you to accept this gift for lack of richer ones," the forester said with deep feeling. "Don't spurn it, take it. Just so!"

Rubbed between the fingers, the bud smelt of bitter almonds, and gave a festive touch to the misty-grey brooding scene around them.

"Oh, how lovely it smells!" Lenochka said, surprised.

"I'll show you dozens of little revelations hidden from intruding eyes!" the forester said gravely. "We shall have to turn off the path, though. You are not feeling cold yet, are you?"

"No. Aunt Taisa made me dress warm." Suddenly it dawned on her that the most important and welcome event in her life was going to take place that day. It made her feel at once sad, frightened, and happy.

The place best suited for the purpose was the upper reaches of the Sklan, where the very age and noble maturity of the sylvan giants inspired respect for the profession of the forester, but Vikhrov, for some reason, led his lady love in the direction of Shikhanov Yam, first along the drainage ditches, left unfinished since the autumn and now covered with an ice-film at the edges, and then straight across country into the swampiest thickets of what had once been Oblog, which looked desolate even in the summertime. Evidently, the forester intended to start at the bottom of the scale in order, at the close of the day, to astonish Lenochka with the spectacle of the stars caught in the canopied nets of the pines. Clay-coloured water oozed from under the tussocky mounds the moment one stepped on them, and Lenochka gradually began to realise what she had let herself in for. And as if aware how much its fate depended upon that girl, the forest made obeisance to her, now saluting her from afar with the nodding lungwort flower, now, in the sunny places, spreading a golden carpet of lesser celandine for her to tread upon, and in the colder and wetter places beguiling the eye with the pale-green clusters of the saxifrage, or, smiling at her from time to time with the blue eyes of the budding hepatica whose eyelashes fluttered almost perceptibly.

"Well, do you find it interesting here?" Vikhrov asked with the jealous courtesy of a host.

"Very," Lenochka nodded. "I've never been in the woods at such a time."

The country kept getting lower and the forest more and more sombre and desolate; the vernal water squelched under the spongy sod of brown moss. It was a mixed stand of poorly stocked coppice wood, plagued by all the forestial scourges, waterlogged in places, and of the same indeterminate age as people who had fallen on evil days; nevertheless, a stand-up fight of the species was being waged here. The dark elder-trees, shaggy with dry clinging hops, crept up from the stream and attacked the crooked consumptive birches, which seemed to have risen on tiptoes over the unwholesome quaggy swamp, but almost everywhere the spear-topped fir-trees had broken through the leafy canopy and were advancing in an irresistible onslaught. But it was a dear-bought victory. Some of them stood leafless, others with slimy clusters of honey agaric sitting at their roots. Guided by this sign, the forester without an effort broke off a piece of bark on a nearby tree, and without going into explanations for the time being, solemnly showed Lenochka the underside which was tun-nelled by the bark beetle. Thus began the funniest declaration of love ever known.

"And so we enter the forest," Vikhrov said in jerky agitated tones, "or, as some armchair pundits call it, 'bio-geo-phyto-coenose', which, translated into ordinary foresters' language, means a complex association of living, predominantly vegetable organisms, which have the quality of self-perpetuation and are in constant interaction with the soil, climate and the landscape. As you see, nothing has been omitted in this definition of the forest, except, perhaps, a 'zoocoenose' in the shape of a bird of passage, which leaves a certain amount of nitrous accumulation in its summer residence." He laughed with the harsh sound of a tree rubbing against another. "Nothing has been omitted, I say, except the human activity in it, and those essential conditions which enable the forest to fulfil its principal tasks on life's main front. Of course, in the fenced off reserves and the trackless taiga of Siberia, we shall still find ancient groves and thickets, but just look what the ordinary forest of today is like, the forest whose existence we only remember with an axe in our hand. You are not finding it difficult to follow me, are you?"

"Oh, no, not at all!" Lenochka said submissively. One could put up with more than this for the sake of that other bigger thing.

After this forestial introduction she expected him to utter those beautiful words that are usually said on such occasions, something about his love and something nice about herself that would endear him to her for a lifetime. Instead, Vikhrov settled down to a good long monologue about the hydrographic chart of the locality, about geological scars from an ancient glacier, about hardpan or something forming a deadly stony barrier to the roots at that spot, as if he could see fifty feet below the surface, and even about the origin of the peasant belief, confirmed by Vitruvius, that to get the best wood a tree had to be cut down under a waning moon, and about the popular belief that birch seeds could not bear the touch of a human hand. He spoke also about the imperative needs and ancient wrongs of the forest, and since quite a few of them had piled up in the course of Russian history, by the time Vikhrov got to Grigory Kotoshikhin the bell started ringing for dinner at the range. Considering the frail constitution of the girl, who was standing ankle-deep in the icy water, he skipped half a dozen tsars for brevity's sake, and was appalled at the length of what still remained, but it was only in the language of the forest that he could tell Lenochka about the joint cares and worries that lay in store for them, and which at times were out of all proportion to the small joys of the forester.

Never afterwards did he speak so convincingly and feelingly on his favourite subject; many a classic page of his future books was cast in the rough at that moment of passionate inspiration. None the less clearly, through all that bewildering mass of deductions, formulas and botanical Latin, did Lenochka catch the hidden love call, an appeal almost, dressed in inflated words—all those ardent intonations that reach a woman from afar, through all barriers of prohibition, dreams, and virgin ignorance. And if Vikhrov's declaration of love had been only a little simpler, like that of the majority of men, she would have married him willingly in order honestly to darn his clothes, bring up his children, and share the sorrows of Gratsiansky's doing, but he cast too much at her feet, piling one thing on top of another—his thoughts, the plans for his as yet unwritten books, and his very life, and again Lenochka found that she could never repay his overwhelming generosity in equal measure. The forest crowded around them, cold, choking in water and disheartened, listening to the mutterings of its defender with the wary look of a deaf-mute.

"Are you sure I'm not boring you?" Vikhrov enquired rather uncertainly from time to time.

"Oh, no, on the contrary!" Lenochka smiled, trying to forget the damp chill that trickled to the soles of her feet through her worn-out boots. "I never thought one could talk about this so interestingly and ... so much. Please go on." She waited patiently. Now at last, she thought, he would tell her that life without her was inconceivable, and she would consent right away before he had had time to finish what he was going to say, and then they might even manage to get back in time for tea, and she would be able to put on Taisa's snug old *valenky*,* and would have her first night without dreams woven of pursuits, stealthy stirrings behind her back, and cross-examinations.

"It will soon be over now," Vikhrov said encouragingly. "Now, where were we? Ah, yes, a word in passing on the sad tale of our northern forests. ..."

All that was wanting, perhaps, for a complete introduction to the science of forestry was a passing mention of the different types of stands, the methods of lumbering, and the systems of forest management, but before these concluding remarks he had to mention, if only briefly, the names of those who, in the past, had had a good word to say for the forest. It was the very genealogy of his ideas, and it would have been impossible to pass over the opinions of Marx and Engels, still less those of Lenin, on primitive methods of forest working; after that there sprang to his lips, of their own accord, the royal curses of Peter hurled at the heads of those who had despoiled the country's oaks, and the lamentations of Prince Vasilchikov, who bewailed the ruin of Russia's greenwoods, and the forest instructions of the Code Napoleon, and, finally, the closing chord—a eulogy to the forest by a certain Bernard de Clairvaux.

"Bernard what?" Lenochka contributed, merely to show that she was not missing anything.

Checked in the headlong course of his fervent sermon, Vikhrov glanced at her with annoyance. Possible because of the dim light, he noticed neither her blue lips nor the air of entreaty with which she was shifting her weight from one foot to the other.

"There was a Frenchman by that name in the twelfth century ... why?"

"Did he have anything to do with forests, too?"

"Unfortunately he was only an abbot and a preacher, but ... why should it matter to you?"

She did not know herself; it was simply that in a conversation

---

* *Valenky*—high felt boots for winter wear.—*Tr.*

about Russian pines and birches the foreign name had caught her ear. The enlisting of this unfortunate Bernard as a protector of the Russian forest was to cause Vikhrov no end of trouble in the future, so much so that only an editorial in the central press saved his maiden attempt from utter annihilation.

Vikhrov took no heed of the warning signs, however, and the next minute Lenochka pressed her face against a birch and began to sob so violently that the tree-top quivered overhead. The lecture had nothing to do with it, of course; it was simply that she had tried to figure out how much more she would have to go through until her unknown guilt was finally forgotten.

"Don't mind me ... it's just that I'm not used to it, it'll soon pass," Lenochka sobbed, wiping away her tears and leaving white streaks on her cheeks from the birch bark. "Now I've gone and spoiled the walk for you!"

"No, it's me who should beg your pardon, my dear. I can imagine the kind of lecturer I am going to make, judging by this start. Come, calm yourself, please do," Vikhrov muttered, not daring to look up at her.

"That's all right, it's passing already. After this rain things will be coming along grandly," she said, attempting a joke, but her shoulders still shook. "I just saw myself standing like that all my life, a stupid clot ... like in a hole. And then my boot is leaking a bit. Never mind now, it's all over."

Meanwhile the wind had blown the mist away. Hot steaming rays pierced the gloom of the fir-grove; somewhere in the depths beyond it, bathed in sunshine, gleamed the almost sheer slope of a gully that led up from the hollow. Turning her head, Lenochka stood listening to the gutteral babble that came from there.

"What's that?"

"It's the water," Vikhrov said miserably. "Let's come out in the sun and dry ourselves."

Here, in this narrow gully, the warmth had come a week earlier; the coltsfoot was blossoming in profusion on the drying clay among the purplish shadows of the still bare branches. The stream weaved its way between the stones; they served as convenient steps by which one could ascend, holding on to the red willow twigs with last-year's faded leafage clinging to them. Immediately round the bend a deep pool with a real waterfall about a hand and a half high came into view. The young people, of one accord, sat down on the natural bench of a landslip; the forester helped Lenochka to take off her wet overshoes, which soon began to steam in the sunshine.

"It's not bad here either. Just so," Vikhrov said, glancing around him. "Don't be angry with me, please. I miscalculated the length of my ... lecture, but I've been waiting so long for a chance to talk to you ... about the most important thing of all."

"Please don't," Lenochka checked him pleadingly. "Let us listen to the water. What is it murmuring about?"

"Probably prattling to its friends, who are doomed to stand on one spot, about all that it has seen in its wanderings."

For about a minute they both gazed at the clean-washed pebbles at the bottom of the pool, where the current eddied in taut limpid jets.

"It does look like a wanderer," Lenochka agreed. "Why doesn't it take a rest. There's nothing so gabby as water...."

"Not counting myself," Vikhrov added ruefully.

"That's not true. You spoke very well about the forest. I'm uneducated, of course, and didn't understand much of it, but I felt sorry for it."

"Then I spoke badly," laughed Vikhrov. "What the forest needs is fair play, not pity ... like all living things in the world."

The conversation grew simpler and things seemed to be going smoothly.

"I never knew what it was to have a mother," Lenochka said suddenly, perhaps trying to force herself to get used to this man. "You must have had a kind one ... did you love her? Tell me something about her."

Before Vikhrov could answer her a thrush suddenly burst into song. He sang very little, just a try-out before the cold sundown, but so feelingly as no one else had sung yet since the winter.

"I don't know," Vikhrov mused aloud, trying to hit a spinning leaf in the water with a pebble. "It's not a thing one can talk about offhand. Peasant children in Russia were never demonstrative—there you have the toughening effect of a thousand years soldiering experience of the nation. Besides, I parted with my mother at an early age. I don't remember whether I ever said a loving word to her. A peasant mother is a part of Nature, the most intimate one, and perhaps that is why I still feel her narrowed, slightly saddened gaze upon myself, like that bestowed on a son who is leaving home for ever. And you can no more get away from it than you can from the sky above you. That's why the need for constant intercourse with their native land is so strong among the Russians, and that's why a Russian never feels at home in a foreign land. Valery of course is right about national ties among our common people being stronger than personal, or even kindred ties. In short, when my eyes first opened upon the world I found the forest bending over me. There you have the roots and reason for my devotion to it. Just so."

He stopped and listened; mingling with the murmur of approaching voices, the bark of a dog rang through the woods.

"Who is Valery?" Lenochka asked softly.

"My Institute friends were much nearer to me than kinsfolk," Vikhrov proceeded, deaf to her question. "Our trio was held up as an example of friendship till the war scattered us all ... not counting other events, of course. Some day this selfless solidarity among like-minded people will become the only form of human kinship. It's like a pair of spare wings ... and if you weaken in the grand flight they will keep you up and save you from crashing. Well then, in this troika Valery was the wheel-horse."

He spoke with his elbows on his knees, gazing at the outer brim of the pool, where the slow current was combing green strands of alga clinging to a twig. The gleaming ripples flowed across his cheek, and there was something in that man that was becoming dear to Lenochka; she might have uttered certain decisive words herself at that moment but for the sudden loud crackle of dead branchwood overhead followed immediately by Bubbles, who came tumbling down with a rush and began to lick her face. In response to his eager welcoming bark, a man's voice quite close at hand called the forester twice by his name.

"They're looking for us. You stay here, I'll find out what it's all about," Vikhrov said with annoyance, rising to his feet.

He went away, and his footfalls were not heard for a long time. A yellow butterfly came to see who was sitting there. The air got cooler, the sun hid itself, but there was still no sign of Vikhrov. It began to drizzle, and the water in the gully puckered. Lenochka pulled on her boots, which were still damp, and moved away under the awning of a fir-tree higher up. Two strangers appeared among the trees in the company of the forester, who was explaining something to them in an agitated manner. One of them was wearing a long cavalryman's greatcoat with a map-case slung from the belt. Bubbles began to show signs of excitement. Everything became clear to Lenochka; she stood up, drew a deep breath, and pulling her coat down, began to pick bits of clinging grass off it with benumbed fingers.

"I was just telling her about you," Vikhrov was saying to his companions with obvious embarrassment. "Let me introduce you— Lenochka. These are my very same good friends from St. Petersburg. Talk of the devil. . . ."

4

The taller one with the cavernous eye-sockets, who was wearing the long-skirted army coat—it had a distinctive hospital smell about it—muttered ironically, "I see, I see" and gave his name as Cheredilov. The other, in a short calfskin coat, with a short beard like Vikhrov's raised a battered old hat, revealing the high forehead and long hair of a dreamer.

"We've come unexpectedly, and I'm afraid we've frightened you, but we are Ivan's trusty bosom friends," he said, searching Lenochka's face, which was still pale, and humorously expressing the hope that the good news which they had brought would make up to some extent for the commotion they had caused.

"On the contrary, I guessed at once who you were from the description," the girl answered, somewhat recovering her composure "Vikhrov often talks about your inseparable St. Petersburg trio— he was talking about it only today—and how you went into exile ... and all the rest of it. You're that third one, the chief one—Valery Krainov, aren't you?"

"Oh no, I happen to be the fourth, a sort of supernumerary. And my name is Gratsiansky," the newcomer said, and when that name brought only a look of perplexity on Lenochka's face he offered the sarcastic conjecture that Vikhrov must have pared him down in his stories so as not to stuff such a pretty head with all kinds of trifles. "De nihilo—nihil ... not a bad gag, that, don't you think so?" he turned to Vikhrov, blandly serene.

The joy of reunion was marred by other trivial incidents, which would not be worth mentioning had they not been the first intimations of a rift in that celebrated fraternity. It started on the way home, as soon as Lenochka had gone on ahead with Bubbles to help Taisa about the house. To the drizzle was added a cutting wind, but the friends were in no hurry to get to the table; they wanted to restore the lost feeling of intimacy and get properly chilled before the nip of vodka. Vikhrov asked eager questions about the news in the capital, about affairs in the Far East, where the last of the interventionists were being smoked out with the aid of gunpowder, and, lastly, about friends and acquaintances. He learned that Tulyakov had resumed his chair at the Institute, Sleznyov had disappeared without a trace, and Valery had gone through the whole civil war in the capacity of member of the military council of the different fronts—that is where Cheredilov had met him!—after which he was said to have gone abroad to attend a trade-union conference.

"That Valery of yours is making a big noise in the world, climbing to the top," Cheredilov wound up on a note of grudging admiration.

"I'm glad our people are making the grade," Vikhrov said earnestly. "I wanted to write to him, but I felt awkward about reminding anyone of my existence at such a hectic time."

"You were quite right," Gratsiansky remarked gravely. "The gods of Olympus do not like to be reminded of the past, when they touched friends for three rubles and moved across the earth on foot."

"That's why I'd like to be a Brazilian king, say, for two or three years, just for the sake of the experience," Cheredilov said with a wink to Gratsiansky. "And you two would pay me a visit for old times sake. I wonder whether I, too, would receive you through my aide-de-camp in full regalia, or treat you just like old pals? The air must be different in those mountainous heights." Cheredilov was clearly hinting at some circumstances of his last meeting with Valery Krainov, circumstances which were known to Gratsiansky and were offensive to the memory of their old friendship.

It was not so much the disgruntled comment on an absent comrade that stung Vikhrov at the time as the comparison of his revolutionary posts with the office of a king. In reply to Vikhrov's guarded question as to what had happened, Cheredilov laughed bitterly; according to him, the biblical youth in the den of lions did not feel half as uncomfortable as he did in Comrade Krainov's official railway carriage, where he was hauled over the coals alleged-ly for someone else's exaggerated blunders. "We're flowing, growing, becoming a State" Cheredilov croaked with unconcealed hostility, adding that only the military hospital saved him from Krainov's wrath and the official penalties accruing therefrom. And then Vikhrov, whose conscience had been wincing all the way from the carbolic emanations of Cheredilov's hard-worn army coat, suddenly expressed a naive and noble envy towards all those people, who, during those sacred years, had been smashing a gateway into the new world with a rifle and a revolutionary song on their lips, as he expressed it in the heat of the moment.

The newcomers merely looked at each other on hearing these "home-front" raptures, while Cheredilov even coughed meaningly for Gratsiansky's benefit; no, it was not the glowing reflection of great struggles, but the apathy of utter weariness that Vikhrov read in his ashy face. It was difficult to trace the former wag, the fun-loving darling of fortune, in this gaunt lanky soldier, many of whose like were to be met those days at the railway evacuation centres and the hungry markets of the civil war.

"You must have been badly hit, Grisha, if they put you in the hospital," Vikhrov remarked with respect.

"You wouldn't see me coming down to this convalescent home of yours otherwise," laughed Cheredilov. "I thought of going to my father's place at first, but then decided that foresters were better off for food these days than church sextons."

"Then your old man is still alive?" Vikhrov indiscreetly showed his surprise, remembering the reason for Cheredilov's disappearance from St. Petersburg ten years before.

"Alive and kicking, the old cuss!" Cheredilov waved the question aside, then suddenly darted a resentful look at Vikhrov's flushed face. "Well, and what have you been smashing here, hee-hee ... during these sacred years?"

The question sounded so rude that Gratsiansky glanced askance at his companion.

"Nothing much to boast about, I'm afraid, old chap," Vikhrov candidly confessed after a slight pause. Timidly conscious of his own inadequacy, he did not mention either his work on forest reclamation or his participation in the activities of the local Committees of Poor Peasants. "I'm fit enough for yelling 'hurrah', but as for running in a bayonet charge.... You see, after that wound my leg is a bit stiff at the knee. Just so."

"That lamentable circumstance, I see, does not prevent you from plucking the flowers of pleasure. We didn't er ... scare you off by chance, did we?" Cheredilov said with a leering wink, nudging Vikhrov with his elbow. "Don't be angry, old chap, it was your sister who showed us the way to the forest, to the scene of the crime."

Vikhrov merely grunted. He could not find it in him to take offence at a front-liner, who had somewhat neglected his table manners during trench life. To fill the embarrassing pause and give his friend a chance to extricate himself, he hastily switched the subject over to the history of the Yenga forests during the last forty-seven years, when suddenly Cheredilov enquired whether Vikhrov was married.

"Don't be funny, Big Kostroma! What girl will marry a lame scarecrow like me!"

"Then who was that er ... ripe peach you had with you?"

"She lives at the forestry range," Vikhrov said evasively, and to avoid idle conjectures, he briefly related to his friends how she came to be at Pashutino. "Why do you ask?"

"Oh, just like that. She's not a bad looker, eyelashes like barley, damn it. You're fixed up here like a lord of the manor. Bet you have a cow, too, eh?"

"I don't see the connection, perhaps you'll explain," Vikhrov said, frowning. "We here in the provinces are a bit behind in the social graces."

"I mean—tremble, old boy! First I'm going to ruin you on the milk, and then I may make a start on something else."

This time Vikhrov's feelings overcame even his respect for Cheredilov's carbolic.

"Well, my dear chap," he intoned without raising his voice, "the duty of a host compels me to put up even with coarseness on the part of a dear guest, provided, of course, that it is not repeated. Better let us keep silent, at least until feeding time. Just so."

Vikhrov was showing a new side of himself which his visitors had never suspected. Back in St. Petersburg he was held to be one of those mild and convenient simpletons who are looked upon as fair game by practical jokers; it is from men like him, notwithstanding their obvious poverty, that the more insolent borrow money for drinks without any intention of giving it back. Gratsiansky, who was silent all the way, measured Vikhrov with a cold scrutiny. As for Cheredilov, he simply couldn't understand what had provoked the rebuff. Fortunately, the house was no more than a hundred paces away; Taisa was already on the doorstep, inviting them to the table, where, amidst a variety of glazed earthenware bowls and pots stood a jug of baked milk with a browned skin on it. Without taking his things off, Cheredilov poked his finger through the skin and drained the jug in one breath, while Yegor Sevastyanich, who happened to be present, remarked aloud that the visitor had an iron constitution for the stuff, and Gratsiansky answered for his friend that he scorned enemy slander, after which all laughed in a friendly way and sent round the loving-cup with the homebrew, and pricked vanities were soothed with the savoury steam of the rich *shchi*, which was so balsamic after a long walk.

Towards nightfall, after a sweltering bath, when all were gathered over the birch-lip tea, the guests, somewhat restrainedly so as not to give him a swelled head, congratulated Vikhrov on his Moscow success, which, considering that he was just a rank-and-file woodsman, was unexampled. True, neither of them had had a chance even to thumb through the fresh copy of his book in Moscow, "since, improvident fools that they were, they had neglected to have their names put down in the waiting list", but Gratsiansky, who was doing the book section in the *Forestry Herald*, had heard from reliable sources that a certain personage of great consequence had commented favourably on Vikhrov, whom he was said to have called a "Soviet" Tulyakov. Vikhrov received this pleasant news in a rather absent-minded way. He was thinking all the time where and on what pretext he could send Lenochka away from Pashutino during the visitors' stay there so as to avoid further gossip.

For the next three evenings, the bad weather preventing him from showing off his domains to his friends, he read out to them passages from his book, and Gratsiansky sat out all three evenings in utter silence with a sad pained expression. Cheredilov, on the other hand, could not quite recover from the initial shock of it, as though he could not by any stretch of imagination believe that this book, this lusty masterful shout and wrathful irony aimed at the squanderers of Russia's green wealth, could come from so puny a human agency. Vikhrov, unfortunately, was a poor politician, and he made no attempt out of courtesy at least to find out what his listeners thought about it, and Gratsiansky was constrained to enquire sarcastically whether he cared to hear the opinions of people who were not quite laymen as far as that subject was concerned. He first let Cheredilov have his say, though, and the latter was forced to admit that Ivan had turned out a book that would have a powerful impact.

"On the whole, you write forcibly, although it could have been toned down a bit so's not to clash with some opinions," he hinted delicately.

"Thank you," Vikhrov nodded ironically. "You have to talk to the axe in its own ruthless language."

Then came Gratsiansky's turn.

"Well, I'm afraid I can't be very comforting, Ivan," he began, wiping his pince-nez to collect his thoughts. "To a certain extent

Grigory is right, perhaps ... forgive me this uninvited candour, which is always the measure of a man's respect towards his interlocutor. I like your provincial enthusiasm, I admit, although it does have an unpleasant touch of rigourism about it, and the work itself strikes me as a sizeable job, er ... not only because of the amount of paper that was used up, far from it! But the trouble with you, Ivan, is that in coming to the defence of the Green Friend, as you have none too happily called your protégé, you have embarked on a dangerous voyage. It's not even a question of your going all soft over the object of your affection, which, inevitably, tends to belittle it, by the way ... what is more, your blunder is not that you liken the forest to a living being, although, I repeat, that kind of idyllic anthropomorphism in our day will hardly bring you the quiet joys of creative work ... no, Ivan, your trouble is that you forget the fundamental role of the forest, which in the course of centuries has served not only as a means of the nation's livelihood, but also as an unprotesting buffer-spring to the state economics of Russia. In bewailing the fate of the forests of yesterday you are thrusting a pattern of conduct on the morrow, when we shall be needing more timber than ever, er ... mostly from the stocks of European territories, as it happens. But that's how it has always been and will always be, my dear Ivan, until, a hundred years hence, we, that is, liberated mankind, will have gathered sufficient strength to rectify the barbarous blunders of the past on a planetary scale. Be comforted, old chap—progress will not cease. With the depletion of the local forests it will simply shift its ground to other untouched districts. If it comes to that the capital city could be shifted eastward a bit, too, somewhere out in the Urals. But," he wagged a threatening little finger, and the pince-nez in his hand shot forth a long rapier-like gleam, "is it worth your while, you naive slyboots you, to get in the way of the lumberjack, who is armed with an axe and inflamed by a great idea? Just think, my friend."

While he was dragging all this out of himself peevishly word by word, Vikhrov sat chafing. He realised that his uncompromising defence of the forest was likely to provoke a no less passionate opposition, but what stung particularly was this threatening tone and the flippant accusation of such a deadly sin as cunning, when he had always suffered in life from his lack of it.

"Drop it, Alexander. The man hasn't found his feet yet, and here you are trying to hamstring him with a penknife," Cheredilov stood up for him, while at the same time squeezing the author's hand by way of encouragement. "Don't you worry, Ivan, can't you see he's just teasing you?"

"Then tell him to cut it out!" Vikhrov said, simmering. "I'll hit it off with the lumberjack, all right. We're citizens of one country, after all."

"But don't think you are going to keep me out of this conversation, er ... as easily as you threw me out of our St. Petersburg trio," Gratsiansky said with an ironical smile, dropping his pince-nez into a chamois leather case with a conciliatory gesture. "At any rate, your book is one of those that have to be printed. Every unprinted book increases the force of the historical accusation contained in it ... but I claim first right to make a detailed reply. Anyway, I'm your friend, so let us drink ... not to your book, no, but to your getting away with it."

Taisa was genuinely distressed at this passage of arms between the young men, for she could foresee the practical scope which their future dissensions would assume; she took a saner view of the underlying springs of conduct in this initial quarrel than her brother did. In time to come she would shake her head ruefully at her brother's angry surmises concerning Gratsiansky, who, he believed simply had no love for the forest, nor his country either, for that matter. It wasn't that at all, she thought. Besides, at that time Gratsiansky may have loved Russia, but without the joyous glow, the tacit willingness to lay down his life for her, which is the way of all people who create everyday values and their country's glory. Gratsiansky loved her as a fascinating glamorous theme conceived during the disintegrative years of his majority—with her dashing troikas, later glorified on the cigarette boxes for foreign tourists, with her picturesque cloisters on riverside bluffs—although he had known Russian monks only from fiction—with the blood-curdling whistle of robbers at hushed darksome dawns, as pictured from his luxurious apartment in Sergiyevskaya Street, with the chain-gang in song-glorified Vladimirka,* of which he stood in deathly terror, with all those fanciful patterns on the curtains behind which the ordinary citizens of the empire lived and suffered, with the ordinary tsarist shootings of unarmed crowds, with the ordinary *moortsovka*** on the worker's table, with the

---

* Vladimirka—popular name of the route by which convicts were deported to Siberia in old Russia. They walked in chained gangs under military escort.—*Tr.*

** *Moortsovka*—a cold soup of kvass, rye bread and onions.—*Tr.*

ordinary famines, cholera and squalor. In the skimpy reviews, which he occasionally wrote in those days for the *Forest Herald*, Gratsiansky loved to call the Soviet epoch "days of creation", whose chief romantic attraction for him was that one never knew what quaint surprises they had in store at the very end. Unconsciously he even desired the prolongation of that tragic atmosphere of chaos and ferment, because it helped to stave off inevitable and suicidal disillusionment. Not that he was already in touch with fugitive types in homely garb, greasy frock-coats, and gendarmes' uniforms—he despised them!—but he was beginning to feel irritated by contact with the growing popular Truth, since it showed up his own social and moral fibre by contrast. As a matter of fact Vikhrov's book had been a revelation to him; only a lawful, though naive, heir of the national wealth could dare so boldly to set before the community, even though prematurely, the problems of Soviet forest management while Gratsiansky himself was gazing back yearningly at the retreating shore; it also showed how far he had lagged behind his friend. It had not entered his head yet at that time that it was easier to ride into the future on the back of the man in front.

Another no less startling revelation followed close upon the heels of the first, when one warm sunny day Vikhrov showed his guests over his domains. The need of somehow vindicating himself in the eyes of Cheredilov for having sat the war out at home, for this blessed peace and quiet of the Yenga and for Taisa's pancakes, had been torturing him all the week. Little by little the flippant ironical mood of his guests gave place to a respectful silence. They had discovered that the Pashutino forest range was a model of good management without stumps or burns, astonishingly free from birch timberlings in the extensive and disorderly wartime cuttings, but with a multitude of little sanctuaries of all kinds. The young growth in the plots was arranged in steps, according to age, like children in a classroom, nourished by human hands over and above what the northern climate and the meagre Yenga podsol could give them. They were beginning to fall into line with the green ranks of their elders along the light and tidy cut-throughs. True, there were unavoidable patches of wasteful aspen here and there, and an obvious lack of run-off ditches in the waterlogged places, but then the forester's first day of creation lasts for decades!

"The place is chockful of good stuff, like the home of a kulak!" It was a subdued Gratsiansky who paid his friend this compliment; even he, who had already lost touch with his science, was struck by what, under wartime conditions, was nothing short of a feat. "I say, what's that queer duck doing here—it's a Crimean pine, isn't it?"

"No, the needles here are longer and denser. It's just a whim of mine," Vikhrov said, apologetically. "I'm trying out the cedar on the Yenga. A new raw material for the trades, no bugs will get into the woodwork, and our grandchildren will have nuts to crack."

"I don't seem to recognise this cedar of yours," Cheredilov boomed, put on his dignity; and when they came to a nursery of oaklings, the first attempt in that part of the country to raise frost-hardy fast-growing oaks, frank admiration gained the upper hand in him over jealous envy towards a comrade who had beat him to it. "You win, old chap! Marvellous, simply marvellous! And take my word for it, Ivan, it's the chief wood-goblin in Russia you are going to be. Here, let's give you a kiss, father forester, for these jolly green children of yours!"

It was a deeply moved Vikhrov he took to his bosom with widespread arms in the old-fashioned way, while Gratsiansky joined them from the side, the whole Pashutino forest thus acting as witness to their immoderate raptures, which should be borne in mind for the sake of comparison with their later appraisals of Vikhrov's activities. An involuntary exclamation was wrung from Cheredilov as to where the lame devil got all that energy from. In response to this the host, after a slight hesitation, conducted them through the whole forest to that secret nook, where, at the dawn of life, he had first met Kalina. He did this with a sense of shame and uneasiness; after all, they were grow-up bearded fellows, and Vikhrov's fancy might set them laughing unless they were prepared for it in advance. Trust towards his friends swept away all misgivings. It was a long way to go, and Gratsiansky had time to break off a stick of nut-tree and cover it with an elaborate design with the aid a mother-of-pearl penknife housed in another chamois leather case; the bark peeled off with astonishing ease.

It should be noted, however, that with the passage of time the bright image of Kalina had grown somewhat blurred and misty in Vikhrov's mind, while at the same time acquiring certain new traits of awesome grandeur and immortality apart from those which childish fancy had long since endowed him with. In short, there was not a spot on earth more sacred to Ivan Vikhrov than this woodland nook on the south-eastern edge of Pustosha. After the pillage of Oblog, the common pasture lands of Polushubovo came close up to the spring, and only a rickety fence and Vikhrov's hedges now protected the gully against the invasion of the peasant herd. The slopes were so thickly overgrown with hazel that one had to force one's way through the tangle of branches, and this, taken together with Vikhrov's mysterious silence, piqued the curiosity of his companions. All three descended the slope, and then their guide knelt down, and carefully drew aside a branch of meadow-sweet growing over the spring.

There was no cry of a woodpecker, for Vikhrov himself was now the guardian of the sanctuary. A brocaded cloth of lichen, torn in places, hung in shreds from Kalina's stone table. Nothing else had changed during the quarter of a century; the same ever-lasting jet pulsated in its crib, slowly stirring the sand grains. And though a shaft of sunlight breaking through the young leafage flooded the gully with a diffused radiance, one had to bend down in order to make out the secret birthplace of the river.

"There," Vikhrov said, stepping aside and looking round with the air of a man showing his mother's amulet or his sweetheart's photograph to a stranger.

"Well, well, this *is* interesting. Water, the primary element, so to speak," Cheredilov muttered vaguely, nudging Gratsiansky. "Maybe *you* know what this parable means, Alexander, seeing that you're our lambent flame of intellect?"

Although he repeated the question Gratsiansky did not hear him. His pale face reflected a wild tumult of soul, as if the thing pulsing there before him was a human heart stripped of all its coverings. Leaning on his stick, he stared spellbound through his corded pince-nez into the narrow neck of the spring where the defenceless sandy little bosom rose and fell in wilful rhythm.

"Spry little thing," Gratsiansky murmured, baring his teeth for some incomprehensible reason, then, with a sudden fencing thrust, he plunged his stick into the spring and fiercely twisted it round twice in the dark little cavern of its throat.

What followed merged in a single sound—Cheredilov's grunt of annoyance, Vikhrov's shout "I'll kill you!", and the snap of the stick, which was torn in two, rather than broken, in his hands, while Gratsiansky watched the flight of the fragments with an odd fascinated look. Then, after the thunderclap, all three stood there panting exhaustedly, shocked by what had happened, until a clear vein of water broke through the rust-coloured mud of the spring.

"Well, I think we've had enough lyrics for today," Gratsiansky said with an effort, his face still pale. "Never mind your water ... it'll heal. Take us back for dinner, you've walked us off our legs today."

Silently they started home, and Cheredilov on the way made a lame attempt to excuse his friend's conduct; he asked Vikhrov half-jokingly whether he didn't mind their poking around the woods with such scant respect.

"You ought to know that when the earth is stamped down hard under men's soles it does not do the trees any good," Vikhrov answered drily. "But I shall try to make up to the forest for any damage which my old friends may do it."

What had made Gratsiansky act the disgusting way he did remained a mystery, and Cheredilov, who liked on occasion to hold forth about the cause of the famous forestry controversy, was inclined at first to put it down to a seizure of hypnotic terror with a touch of momentary madness, but later, when he became thick with Gratsiansky, he even justified his behaviour on the grounds of scientific curiosity towards natural phenomena, placing his friend on a level almost with Humboldt. To Cheredilov's credit let it be said, this staunch friendship of his with Gratsiansky did not begin until after an ineffectual and rather clumsy attempt on his part to make friends with Vikhrov. It happened after a lapse of time, during which all three pretended hard that they had completely forgotten the incident at the spring. As Gratsiansky contemplated writing an article on Yenga antiquity, in which he intended, among other things, to expose certain reactionary mystic elements in peasant folklore, and particularly Kalina Glukhov— exactly on what grounds, he had not decided yet—Vikhrov gave up his own room to him. As for Cheredilov, he put him up in his small study, where an iron bedstead was dragged down from the garret to make company for the leather sofa.

5

The warm weather set in early on the Yenga that year.

The air at bedtime was stifling, and through the open window the rain could be heard pattering half-heartedly on the roof. Every now and again a flash of summer lightning would light up the timbered walls with Vikhrov's shotgun hanging under the portrait of Tulyakov's teacher Tursky, the uncleared table, and Cheredilov's gnarly feet protruding through the bars of the bedstead. Vikhrov, on the sofa, had started to doze off when Cheredilov took it into his head to make his crazy confession; the desire to make a clean breast of it was so strong and sincere that he dropped his churchy affectations of speech, which were designed to hide the banality of his thoughts.

It started with the guest turning his pillow over on the cool side all the time, thus preventing his host from falling asleep.

"I'm sorry, Ivan, forgive me everything, will you," he began with such a gusty sigh that the springs quivered and twanged under him.

"That's all right, go to sleep," Vikhrov answered sleepily and turned his face to the wall.

"I'm sorry I put my foot in it that time about the girl. Your sister didn't tell us she was your fiancée."

"She isn't yet. Never mind, let's go to sleep. Just so."

"You've become so secretive, Ivan. But I noticed you get all adither in her presence. And then, what made you pack her off to the feldsher's, as if you don't trust us. What is she—a book-keeper?"

"No. I told you already. She hasn't quite finished the medical courses."

"Ah, a sick-nurse then. Good idea that—medical aid always on the spot, but. . . ." He had intended to say something else, but had not been able to—perhaps because of the suffocating atmosphere preceding the storm, perhaps because he was too lazy to waste a mental effort on trifles. "I'm not trying to dissuade you, of course. . . ."

"And I haven't asked your advice, Grigory. I tell you what, you'd better go and lie down in the hayloft, you'll fall asleep quicker. You'll find a tarpaulin sheet there."

The storm couldn't get under way, somehow; thunder rolled over the Yenga and a slanting spatter of rain struck the window-panes, then all was quiet again. Cheredilov lowered his feet down the side of the bed, which jangled with all its springs, and lighted a cigarette.

"And altogether you made me feel thoroughly ashamed of myself, Ivan. I understand why you arranged that stupid walk and the demonstration of your forestry jobs. You wanted to show off before a soldier, as much as to say—we haven't been sleeping either! You knocked me flat, Ivan, it's a fact. And to crown it all, that fellow—you know, the one in charge of the sawing team—went and dragged me off to his place yesterday."

"Ah, Yefim Stepanich," Vikhrov said, and swearing inwardly, reached out also for the tobacco.

"That's the one. He treated me to a regular posh meal, seeing as I was a soldier who'd been fighting the holy war of the workers and peasants. Wanted me to tell him about things and about the world's future arrangement. And I just blinked and munched his Sunday patties—they might have been filled with broken glass instead of cloudberries for all I knew."

"That's a profound and valuable observation on your part. He is a nuisance, that old man. He can pester a fellow to death with his questions, especially if he gets hold of a new one. Just so."

"That's not the point, don't interrupt me. I feel rotten as it is, a sort of dryness at the heart, as if I had robbed the two of you. All that about the hospital, you know—why, I wasn't wounded at all; when I was at army headquarters, I just went out one evening in a country sleigh to see a girl friend of mine, a school-teacher, in one of the nearby villages, and the two of us, me and the driver, fell asleep at a level crossing. When I woke up I was all by myself in a hospital cot, like Lazarus in his shroud. I was flung out from under the train by a miracle. A gypsy told my fortune once; she said I'd live two hundred and forty happy years over and above the natural span. It's coming true, you see." The joke was probably meant to tone down the unpleasant effect of his penitential outburst.

He was restless; judging by the creak of the floor-boards and the shifting glow of his cigarette in the darkness, he was pacing from corner to corner. It was still stuffy, and only once in a while a faint breeze billowed the curtains. Obviously there was no stopping Cheredilov now until the storm broke.

"What can I tell you?" Vikhrov began, the light of his match showing him a strange tall figure in hospital underwear that was too short for him; he was clutching his head. "It's a good thing you have that, well ... the conscience of the epoch, I think they call it. Never mind, it's not so bad. You'll have plenty of time to make it up to Yefim's children if not to Yefim, seeing that you have another two-hundred and forty years to do it in. You'd better go to sleep, old chap. Just so."

"That's just what I wanted to talk to you about—how to make it up," Cheredilov said, and after groping about in the dark, sat down on the edge of Vikhrov's sofa. "Maybe you won't understand me. You're like a child of eight, without contradictions or doubts, without a harmful curiosity towards the seamy side of certain sacred things. You're a moderate drinker, too. Altogether, you're a saint, and sitting in your presence gives me a sort of guilt complex. And a saintly soul combined with sobriety and the obstinacy of a buffalo can be a monstrous, resistless force. Such people don't rust in the rain and leave plenty of chips behind them, and they shut the door behind them very correctly when they leave the world, grateful, as it were, for the good time they had had."

"These are not your words, Grigory. They're none too profound, but they're not yours all the same. Pardon me for saying so, but you would never have thought of them. I should listen less to Gratsiansky, if I were you. He's a sharp, but dangerous man, one who can lead a simple fellow into a bog and leave him there. Now take a piece of brotherly advice—dab your temples with water out of the carafe and go to sleep."

The welcome rain seemed to have started; it scratched at the roof for a minute or two, then trickled down the spout into the barrel under the window with a faint tinkle.

"It's all very well for you to joke," Cheredilov said with a mirthless smile. "You're a man with an obsession, an aim, for which you'd lay down your life without thinking twice about it, and with talent besides, that is, an ability to see and find the gold that lies underfoot. And if I'm not Galileo, if I haven't got that gift—so what then?"

"Talent is, in the first place, a purposeful will to action," Vikhrov said meekly. "No, you're just a sceptic, Grigory, and sceptics are having a thin time of it these days. You have to go straight for your bear now, and God help the man who hasn't an honest truth to believe in. In short, choose your plough according to your strength and taste, harness yourself to it and pull."

"That's just what I'm asking you to advise me about—what plough I should choose. My thoughts are pretty meagre, of course, so you can wipe the floor with me, or, as the old saying goes, chastise me with whips and scorpions, but understand me." This fit of verbosity and sudden transition to a church vocabulary showed how ashamed he was at having to unmask before Vikhrov. "I can't help it, Ivan, for the life of me I just can't work up any enthusiasm for the forest. All right, you plant a million seedlings, say, but then along comes this Yelizar Stepanich of yours with a gang. . . ."

"Yefim Stepanich," Vikhrov corrected him dismally.

"It makes no difference—Yefim, then ... comes along and hacks them down, and there's nothing left of you! You can't very well pledge your descendants to preserve this cherished offspring of your heart's blood. Well then, thinks I, I'll have to choose something more rock-like, if you know what I mean. Don't laugh at me, please, Ivan, I'm confiding this to you as I would to a brother." Cheredilov was silent, and try as Vikhrov would to peer into the darkness, he could make nothing out beyond a pale longish patch. "And then it was revealed to me betimes, as it says in the Holy Writ, that I could gird up my loins and venture upon a general description of our whole native flora, or even that of the whole world, damn it! I could start with the pioneers of the soil, the mosses and lichens, and in five years or so pass on to the Kochia and Salicornia. It's a long story, and meanwhile the salary dribbles into your pocket. But I glanced around me, old chap, and stood aghast. Everything that counts had already been described, and classified, and put away in herbariums. The old scientists had it much easier—they struck treasure wherever they dug."

"But that isn't true, stupid," Vikhrov said with annoyance. "Theophrastus knew only five hundred plants, Pliny as much as a thousand, while Linnaeus increased this number tenfold, and today it runs into all of a hundred and fifty thousand. True, after Linnaeus, most of the discoveries were in the cryptogamia series, but the most unexpected treasures are those which you can only see under a magnifying glass, the magnifying glass of brain and will."

"I agree," the other said, "I agree with you, old chap, that if I rummaged about hard enough I might be able to scrape together some of the leavings in the bag of Nature. Possibly, towards the end of my allotted two hundred and forty years, I may manage to add half a dozen Cladonia and a couple of paltry fungusses to the grand total to the joy of all connoisseurs. Of course, they won't put up a bronze statue to me for it, but they may confer some scholarly rank, and I'll become what Gratsiansky calls *Sitzfleisch*, or something like a liveried door-keeper at the portals of science. But in the end you'll die all the same, won't you? Then why all this sweat, tears, and worn out trouser-seats, where's the sense?"

"What the devil do you want a monument for, you Big Kostroma, you?" Vikhrov said, trying hard to keep his temper. "You don't need a monument, Grigory—you won't look any too good in bronze." Ruffled though he was, he felt in duty bound as a friend to try to explain to Cheredilov the feat of those obscure scientists, whose collective effort it was that built up the atoll islands of knowledge, until a genius defined their form and place on the map of science. The other expressed his doubts, and Vikhrov clenched his teeth. "Anyone would think you're Prometheus, judging by the torments you're suffering, Grigory. At least you could try to tell me more coherently what bird it is gnawing at your liver."

"Very well, O, wise one, I'll tell you!" Cheredilov snapped. "It's this; what is life for?"

The silence lasted a full minute.

"Well, of all the—" Vikhrov said, angry now in real earnest. "When a man is given the sun it's bad taste for him to ask of what use it is." Then, not to upset himself still more, he disengaged his benumbed leg from under his comrade and went off to the hayloft himself with his blanket under his arm.

Naturally, Cheredilov had not believed that Vikhrov could cure his perennial sterility and futile heart-searchings at a single stroke, but he had been hoping secretly that his friend, besides sympathising with his sufferings, would himself confess some of his own secrets in order to ease for Cheredilov the burden of his lonely barrenness. He felt cruelly insulted at Vikhrov's going away, and from then on he did his best to pay him back in full measure for the humiliating experience.

By dawn a storm worthy of the Yenga broke at last, and in the morning an agent arrived in Pashutino from the gubernia town to take stock of the landowners' forests. Vikhrov spent the next month riding about with him, and when he came home he found his Moscow guests gone; they had taken leave of him by a note containing a word of thanks for his hospitality, a word of kindly greeting, and an ominous invitation to visit them and taste the pleasures of the capital. Apparently, they had already had a forewarning of the imminent changes in the life of the Pashutino forest officer, because a month later an official notice arrived transferring Vikhrov to Moscow, to the chair of the Forestry Institute as Tulyakov's assistant.

6

All the villagers turned out to see off that kindly soul, Ivan Vikhrov, whom they had taken to their hearts. The last-minute instructions had been given to the officer who remained in charge,

274

the "stirrup dram" had been drunk, and the last embrace exchanged with Yegor Sevastyanich, who whispered to the departing forester that he needn't worry about Lenochka, he would take her into his own home as a daughter; already the cart was standing at the door, and Taisa, black as a thundercloud, was putting the last bundles of books away in the back, her face turned away from Bubbles, who was whimpering at her feet; already the peasants had doffed their caps—those who had them—and the women were getting ready to shed a tear at parting, when suddenly Vikhrov sprang down from the cart and went to the back of the house he was leaving.

There, bending over the beds behind the currant bushes, Lenochka was weeding the cucumbers, which were in their fifth leaf, and was doing it so thoroughly that one would think she was bent on winning the approval of the future masters of the forestry division.

"I say ... I was so busy that I didn't have time to tell you the main thing, Yelena Ivanovna," Vikhrov began, giving her her full name and patronymic for the first time, as he wanted this most important act of his life to be performed with due solemnity. "It's too long to explain, but ... my book and all my successes here are mostly due to you. You were in every line I wrote, and every tree I planted. You stood at my elbow, listening to me, watching my spade or my pen, and approving. I believe I could do ten times as much for people if you became my wife. But if you ever went out of my life it would hit me harder than I care to imagine. Now say something ... just so."

"What do you see in me?" she said without looking up. "You are sure to find someone younger and better looking in Moscow now."

"Never mind that," said Vikhrov. "But we must go at once, we have to catch the train."

She straightened up, still hesitating, and wiped the clayey earth off her fingers, then glanced at Vikhrov with flooded grateful eyes.

"You will never regret it, Ivan Matveyevich," she said, nodding her head under stress of grateful emotion. "Believe me, I'll be a good wife to you. Whatever happens you will never hear a bad word from me."

"Thank you, that's very good," said Vikhrov. "Now go and get your things."

"What things have I got! I must get a wash, though, before the journey."

"All right, I'll wait," he said, respectfully kissing first her hollow cheek, then her hand with the now dried bits of earth clinging to it.

He had not finished his cigarette yet when Lenochka came out towards him through the back door with a bundle wrapped up in a newspaper and a shawl thrown over her shoulders. The forester offered her his arm, and in full view of the village, led his bride to the cart. Limping, he took his time, although there was a train to catch. Everyone around smiled their farewell, while Yefim's quick-witted wife dashed off to the family chest and came back with a length of homespun linen which she presented to the bride. Lenochka burst into tears of gratitude, and everyone liked her still better for it. The people of Pashutino stood about for a long time, discussing the successful termination of the prolonged love affair; in their simplicity they took the beginning of life's story for its end.

Polya sat through all the three hours in the same corner of the kitchen, not daring to interrupt Taisa with a question or an exclamation, not even when her heart cried out. The substation did not switch on the light all the time Polya was there. It was as if Taisa were thumbing through a book by memory in the darkness, recounting the best-remembered pages of it in a rustling papery voice. There were many things which she did not know. Her brother did not take her into his confidence in personal matters; only inexpert conjectures based on later investigations helped Polya to piece together that period of her father's life. Apparently, while they had been talking, there had been an air-raid warning, but they only heard the All-Clear signal.

Towards the very end of Taisa's story someone quietly opened the front door, and groping his way along the wall in the darkness, passed into the bathroom. One could hear the sound of the soap cake falling into the sink as it slipped from the user's hands, and after a waiting pause the water ran softly.

"It's all right, make all the noise you want—we're not sleeping, your father's not at home," Taisa called out. "I've left some soup on the table. It's warm."

276

"Thanks, I've had a bite in the train." The young voice from behind the partition sounded familiar to Polya.

"Eating cold food again, I daresay," his aunt said in a tone of mild reproof. "That's Sergei come home from work. I'll call him if you like. We've been lucky with him, he's a good lad, Sergei is. He's a brother of yours, in a manner o' speaking."

Polya flatly refused to meet him or accept her aunt's invitation to stay for the night. She had decided beforehand that the story of this boy's birth had a direct bearing on the break-up of the family, and it was more than she could endure at the moment to receive another secret. Besides. . . .

"Do you know what date it is tomorrow?" she asked in a whisper.

"Well, just figure it out. Today's the thirty-first of August, my dear."

"I'm sorry, Aunt Taisa, I just can't do it. I've got to get up early tomorrow. I must go home."

The hour being late, Taisa went to see her niece off to the Metro station. They were enveloped immediately in the hot breath of an autumn breeze and the chill uncertainty of the blacked-out suburb. All the way they talked about the trivial things of life, and suddenly a quiet question, now the most important question of all, broke through the swarm of Polya's thoughts.

"Auntie Taisa, tell me, was she beautiful? Better than Mamma?"

"Who are you talking about, my dear?" her aunt said.

"Well, the other woman, Sergei's mother. Is she still living?"

"You silly child! Now fancy saying such a thing! When Lenochka left us, he didn't as much as look at anyone, our Ivan didn't. Never mind, I don't blame you. The things a person will think of in the dark!"

To dispel Polya's jealous suspicions Taisa was prepared to continue her story right there and then, out in the street, but there was little time to spare before the curfew. They began to meet night patrols at the street corners, and women and children crowded round the Metro doors, waiting to be let in for the night.

"You'll tell me next time. Come and see me now. Not tomorrow, though, I've got very important business to see to first thing in the morning," Polya said, giving her address at parting.

They kissed as though they had never parted during the last thirteen years.

The next morning the weather in Moscow was fair, with a mild south-westerly breeze; Polya had cold shivers of excitement, although she was wearing the blue jumper her mother had knitted for her before her departure. She came to her father's lecture with a full hour to spare, and strolled for a long time about the walks of the Institute's plantation until she was drawn into the stream of young people, all as immature and excited as she was. No one demanded a pass or a student's card. Polya ascended to the second floor by the worn stairs, which had water barrels standing on the landing; she passed down a barrack-like corridor, which had a rather ill-kept look because of the numerous notices posted up on its walls, and entered the lecture-hall together with the others. It was a dingy room with black benches arranged amphitheatrically, but the bright foliage outside the window, irradiated by a low sun, was reflected in the old parquet and the heavy low-hanging ceiling, and the effect tended to dispel one's first impression of academic frigidity and gloom. Although it was wartime, the place was packed; the introductory address was intended for the freshmen of all the faculties. From what she overheard around her Polya also gathered that the undergraduates of the senior courses and even the teachers of the related subjects came there on that day; Polya ascribed this interest to the lecturer's notoriety.

She found a seat right at the top, near the ceiling, which was scribbled over with pencilled notes, and her sunburnt neighbour, a girl student just back from her summer practice, promptly shared with her rapturous reminiscences of a similar lecture the year before, when the walls of the building, as she put it, were pushed aside, and the audience had such a real feel of a dense bilberry-carpeted pine forest that it seemed as if in another minute or two the birds would start singing in defiance of the established rules and decorum of the lecture-hall. Polya thawed somewhat in the consolatory warmth of those words: gratefully she noted that after Varya this was decidedly the most sensitive and educated girl in the world.

Polya began to take stock of her surroundings. Way below, facing her, stood a shabby ink-stained table with a thick glass and a water-bottle on it, green in the reflected light of the window; the wall behind it was crowded with portraits of bearded patriarchs of Russian forest lore, and by the door, leaning against a physical map of the country, stood a specimen tree with cuts made on its trunk at regular intervals. And nothing more, except a sand-box and an imposing young man in an asbestos helmet who was pacing up and down in front of it. The helmet was respectfully snatched off, however, when the hum of voices died down and a short brisk old man with grizzled temples and a rumpled little beard appeared at the table. His old lustrine coat had a greenish shine on the side that was turned towards the window. Polya found it hard to get used to the idea that this was her father. He started off in a somewhat old-fashioned manner, using figurative turns of speech that sounded quaint in such an official place, but without the false fervour Polya had so feared; for one thing, he avoided figures, since these were likely to tax the untrained attention of the new students. Evidently, the war, too, had something to do with the professor's avoidance of his usual landscape digressions. Now and then he would pause over some inaccordant phrase, his fists resting on the table while he peered at his audience as if searching for a possible opponent in the hushed rows before him, but a kind of close-drawing sincerity grew as he warmed to his subject, and imperceptibly, the lecture turned into a heart-to-heart talk between an old forester and his future associates.

It may have been because facing him sat tomorrow's soldiers that Vikhrov's opening words sounded hesitant; in addition, the lecturer's voice proved to be a low and rather husky one, so that Polya missed the opening.

"What did he say?" she asked the neighbour on her right, a prim elderly woman, who presented a disagreeable contrast to the excited young generation.

"You're interrupting my work, Comrade!" the stenographer snapped, shaking Polya's hand off her sleeve and dashing off strange unintelligible symbols in her writing pad.

People began hissing at them, and Polya froze into silence, her face aflame, as though afraid someone might read in it her secret fears.

2

"Only four days ago," Vikhrov was saying, "our army abandoned yet another Soviet town, Dnepropetrovsk, before the onslaught of a stubborn and—in the light of greater history—

279

thoughtless enemy. Our minds are far removed from the subject which has brought us together here beneath the turbulent sky of our capital. But the whole thorny path of development of matter, from the amoeba to proud thinking man, inspires us with confidence that there will be yet another victory of light over darkness, of reason over brutality, and that the day is not far off when the knowledge you will have accumulated will be needed more than ever by the people who have sent you here. Let your work be guided by love for your country and gratitude to those brothers and sons of ours who are now bearing the brunt of history's ordeal on the battle-fronts.

"I am fully aware of the responsibility of my task, which is to engage your attention with a talk on such a specific, though important subject as the Russian forest amid the thunder of the greatest war in history. The most cherished and urgent affairs are thrust into the background in face of the danger that is threatening the Soviet people and the very springs of its existence, the forest included. Yet you have not come here to listen to a lecture on field surgery or the tactics of in-fighting, you have come to hear a brief sketch about the role of the tree in Russian life, about the intelligent activity demanded of the patriot in this most neglected branch of our economy, which never enjoyed the public attention it deserves, and about certain questions of forestcraft, which are still debatable and whose solution is a problem of the greatest urgency if we are not to endanger the welfare of future generations. In this building you will learn to grow new forests and tame wild uncurbed stands in order to harness them effectively into the chariot of socialist economics; you will study in practice both the relation of the forest to climate, soils and environment, and the mighty changes which this interplay produces, an exceedingly intensive interplay measured by centuries; here you will come to appreciate how important organisation and strict control are in this seemingly inexhaustible storehouse of Nature, from which men have always drawn as much as they could take away. The forest is the only source of wealth, open to everybody, upon which Nature, through kindness or craft, has not hung her weighty padlock. She entrusted this treasure, as it were, to man's good sense, in order that he shall carry into effect here that fair-planned system which she herself is unable to carry out. In short, within the next five years you will acquire skills and knowledge justifying the terrible, deadly power of the axe. But in order to be of the greatest use to your country, good intentions or a cursory acquaintance with the theory of forest management are not enough. Unless you study the past you cannot map out the highroad into the morrow, for human experience feeds on the memory of errors committed.

"You all know how vast time seems to us in childhood, when the day lasts an eternity, and no matter how much of it you spend on marvellous voyages and discoveries there is always ten times as much left. A boundless space, as it were, lies spread before the child, and it seems as if no wings can possibly carry you to the edge of it. So it was at the dawn of the Russians, when after being encamped for five centuries in the Carpathians, the hitherto united Slav tribe spread from there to all four points of the earth; our people chose the East. One day all was silenced—the creak of carts, the wail of infants, the bellowing of the oxen—and our ancestors for the last time gazed down from the eagle heights upon the immense space that spread before them, lost in the morning mist. A beautiful untrodden valley lay between the three mountain ridges, and rivers trimmed with green furs flowed through it in slow-paced majesty. Only the song of the *bayans** and the foresight of the old men could foreglimpse through the blue mists of the horizons and the unborn centuries that train of majestic events which was to be the making of Russia. Probably it happened in the morning and early in the summer, when our country looks its best. On the right, alternating with leafy woods, stretched the steppe, its lush luxuriant grass rippling in the wind, while on the left towered a vast pine forest, almost a taiga, which ran down from the Alaun Heights in several arms; the widest of them, the Dnieper arm, reached the shores of the Cimmerian, now the Black, Sea. Thousands of smiling little lakes, noticeably increasing in number towards the north, gleamed in the sun, for the earth still bore the traces of the comparatively recent (in point of geological time) glacial spring. Then the forefather of Svyatoslav** gave the sign, and the tribe, like a flame, leapt down and flooded the deserted foothills. Thus the first line of our history was recorded with thousands of ponderous iron-bound wheels. That morning may have lasted a century, but everything that concerns the unknown is believable.

"Notice how the economic conditions of life will work with

---

* *Bayan*—an ancient Russian minstrel.—*Tr.*
** Svyatoslav—Prince of Kiev, ruled in 945-972 A.D. A distinguished military leader.—*Tr.*

Nature in modelling the appearance of these people. No one pampered them from childhood. Nature relaxed her rigours for only three months in the year. Never were they to know the carefree joys of life which had been bestowed upon the West-European nations from their cradle by the proximity of the sea, the warm currents, and the mountain ranges, that reliable defence against barbarian invasions and the caprices of climate. Our people were to be scorched by the Asiatic sun, and chilled by the Arctic frosts, and this was to tell in the extremes of the national character. The sharp fluctuations in the continental temperature were to develop in them a tremendous capacity for performing cyclopean deeds in the briefest space of time; their thousand-year struggle for national identity was to cultivate in them a silent heroic fortitude capable of enduring any suffering, while the country's economics was to urge them to seek a seaway commensurate with their strength and natural gifts. Similarly, the almost unchanging face of Nature throughout all the twenty parallels, and the absence of any natural barriers were to determine their striving towards unity, which was the only true guarantee of all-Slav independence. The remoteness of an alien disintegrating civilisation was to make them create their own—a brilliant and inimitable civilisation. The crafts and shifting cultivation were to lead them by river ways to all parts of the mainland. In fierce skirmishes with the steppe dwellers they were to defend their young State, and steel their valour and their no less celebrated self-discipline in the process. That is how we began.

"It would be ungrateful not to mention the forest among the educators and all-too-few patrons of our people. As the steppe cultivated in our ancestors a love of freedom and the heroic sport of single combat, so did the forest teach them caution, keenness of observation, diligence, and that heavy stubborn tread with which Russians have always moved towards the goal they had set themselves. The forest was our home, and perhaps no other element of Nature has set so strong a stamp upon the morals and manners of our ancestors. The tree is raw material fit for immediate use, and any piece of sharpened iron set on a handle converted it into a valuable item of primitive existence. A better way of expressing its role is to say that the forest greeted the Russian at his birth and attended him through all the stages of his life— with the cradle of the infant and the first booting, with the nut and the wild strawberry, with the peg-top, the steam-bath switch and the balalaika, the splinter that did service for a lamp in the peasant's hut, and the painted shaft-bows at weddings, with the wild honey and the beaver, the fisherman's boat or the naval bark, the mushroom and incense, the staff of the wanderer, the coffin hollowed out of a log, and, lastly, the wooden cross on the grave decorated with fir branches. And here is a list of the earliest Russian wares, the other side of that civilisation's medal: bast and boards, beams and chutes, wheel rims and bark, charcoal and bass, pitch and potash. But the same forest yielded a flow of richer gifts: fragrant Valdai bast matting, gay Ryazan sleds and Kholmogori chests lined with sealskin, honey and wax, sables and black fox for the dandies of Byzantium.

"With the growth of human needs the forest opened up its coffers with increasing generosity, and no wonder that our timber industry today employs more hands than any other respectable branch of Soviet economy. Could it be because we have been living too long on full forestial board and lodging that this Russia of ours has remained wooden for so long?

"It is to that remote period that we owe the birth of our contradictory attitude towards the forest—a mixture of exaggerated maudlin affection and indifference, if not neglect, and sometimes sheer hostility towards it, a feeling which we have inherited from our woodmen ancestors. When we do get down one day with a vengeance to the great business of forest regeneration we shall first have to teach our left hand to respect the work of the right one, and cultivate in our children habits of thrift and care for the forest, that gift of Nature, which is unable to fly away from its offender to the safety of the skies, or, like the exasperated gold fish of the fairy-tale, to plunge into the watery chasm, or, at the worst, to write frantic reports to those in authority. Let us hope, that, planted by our own hand, it will become dearer to us than an inheritance. Apparently, too great an abundance of forestlands became an obstacle to the development and settlement of a propagative and active nation; on the other hand, its shift towards the north diminished the importance of overseas commerce and enhanced the role of agriculture, which was hampered again by the forest. The axe was powerless to fight the thickets, which came creeping up from all sides, and so the first woodcutter in ancient Russia was the fire. The peasant burned the felled summer-dried trees in the clearing, thus fertilising the virgin soil with ash, and ploughed the reclaimed land to barley; on the Volga it was turnips, and in my native parts flax; he harvested two or three crops, then gave the cut-over area a rest, let it lie fallow, leaving it to the sun and rain to heal the wounds he had inflicted.

"And so the forest fed, clothed, and warmed us, Russians. In the course of time, when the molten human lava from the mother volcano of Asia will have descended upon ancient Rus together with the hot dry winds and the locusts, the forest was to be the first obstacle in its path. There was no barrier against the wicked shedders of blood, as the chronicler expressed it, other than the people's will for defence and the impenetrable thickets, which served as a trap for the foe. There, on the margin of the forest-steppe, those earliest fortification works of ancient Russia were to arise—terraces built of rough-hewn timbers and packed with earth, from behind which it was so convenient to shoot at a frenzied target curvetting on a horse, tarred parapets behind ditches, snug stockades and citadels, which, from the fourteenth century, were to be called kremlins, and finally the abattises, which survive to this day: a chain of magnificent leafy forests stretching for hundreds of miles with trees laid flat in front of them like a formidable breakwater to check the advancing cavalry.

"The hordes and scorching winds that sprang up on the plateaux of Mongolia and Tibet moved clockwise with the centre somewhere across the Volga, while the Russians moved eastward in the same direction with the slow steady thrust of a battering ram, settling for all time on the high bluffs of the Siberian rivers, to which they were anchored by their fathers' graveyards and man's natural attachment to the place where he first saw the light of day or shed his blood in hand-to-hand battle. Two centuries later, prime Voronezh oak, larch, and the northern pine, converted into the ship's frames and stern-posts of the Russian fleet, were to carry our pennants across all the seas, so that if old Father Urals today receives nation-wide tribute for his socialist machines of peace and war, it would only be fair to grant the Russian forest a share, however slight, in the thunderous glory that was Hankoudd and Corfu, Sinop and Çeşma.

"There is not a tribe on earth that did not in childhood possess a poetic little mirror of its own in which its world was fancifully reflected. And so life's earliest impressions shaped themselves into epos, a priceless manual of the national biography as well as of the survivals of material culture. Alerted to danger, our forefather, like a child in the dark, saw everywhere motionless faces turned towards him, now grim and murderous, now kindly and maternally gentle. Thus were born the pagan gods, creations of terror or gratitude, awkward attempts to interpret realities by the limited means of an imperfect philosophic vocabulary. In due course those naive images of the gods were to step down from the rude material on which they had been traced with the help of flint or arrowhead; they were to demand for themselves numerous servants, marble dwellings, honours, even bloody sacrifices, until one day the magic mirror broke, and man, left face to face with Nature, took upon himself full responsibility for keeping order in the world as far as it was in his power to do so.

"Among the elements, which our ancestors worshipped for their power, goodness or beauty, were sylvic giants like those oaks, which only recently towered on Hortitsa, or the pines on lake Seliger, sung by Ivan Shishkin,* that splendid champion of the Russian forest. They were deeply revered, and at their feet justice was administered and wrong redressed, and the *bayans* composed ballads about the deeds and prowess of the tribe. Poetic superstition jealously guarded our southern sacred groves dedicated to the thunder god Perun, until that carved debunked log with the golden whiskers floated away down the Dnieper, propelled by a new faith and queen. Since then the scanty Russian Olympus dwindled, and our only remaining dubious bogy is now the *lesovik, leshi,* or wood-goblin.

"He is certainly not the erlking of the popular German ballad, that crafty monarch of the woods; ours is simpler and kindlier. Ours is just an ex-god, a most unassuming deity in sack-cloth, who discharges the duties of a caretaker in the woods and dwells under an old tree stool. Popular rumour claims that the *leshis* are also patriots of the forests to which they are attached, and at times of civil strife are said to wallop one another with century-old trees. Neither are they free from human weaknesses. Thus, the intensive deforestation of eighteen forty-three in the Vetluga and Varnavino districts, which led to the mass migration of the squirrel population to the north, was reflected in a peasant tale which claimed that the local *leshi* had lost his forest denizens to his Volodga neighbour in a game of cards. All in all, the Russian *leshi* is quite a harmless individual, although he does like to put the wind up a belated traveller now and again, not so much for his own amusement as to give his victim

---

* The famous Russian landscape painter.—*Tr.*

285

something to tell his grandchildren about on a blizzardy winter night on the eve of the New Year. When the ascetic urge to flee worldly temptations was to drive the Russian hermit to the seclusion of his woodland hut—*duplina*, as it was called in old-church language—the hunter and the bee-keeper, the man-at-arms and the merchant would make their way into these untrodden woody fastnesses hot upon his heels; for the first time then the forest jungle was to waver and have the light let into it all the way from the Volga to Beloye Ozero, and Christian legend was to endow the Russian *leshi* with horns and enter him in the list of commonplace devils, who played all kinds of scurvy tricks on Christian souls whom he caught napping. From now on he was easily to be quelled, and fooled, and browbeaten by means of the cross, the printed word, or simply a firebrand. From that time the forest's sole protection was to be our good sense and conscience.

"In this way the idea of the forest as a living creature extremely well disposed to and active in the interests of our people came to take shape. It nursed no grudge against Russians, not even when they forced it rather unceremoniously to make way. It is high time that we sang praise to his merits, this dear old man, the genial companion of our childhood, the lion-hearted warrior who stood to the death, the unfailing supplier of raw material, the feeder of rivers, and the guardian of crops. Yet we have no such song about the forest as we have, say, about the steppe or the Volga, which gave us no sables for export, fed us with no honey-cakes, nor served us as permanent provisioners from the cradle to the five-year plans of today. True, we are still prone to lift our bashful basses at parties in praise of the willow and the birch, the guelder rose and the rowan of which we speak always with compassionate love, but these songs, always about the secondary species and always with the axe playing a conspicuous part, are tinctured with horrified admiration at their unhappy fate rather than with appreciation of the age-old loyalty and might of the Russian forest, the greatest forest in the world, whose commercial fame, already in the previous century, had reached as far as the Cape of Good Hope.

"A possible explanation might be found in the national memory of the broken ploughshares and gruelling toil involved in clearing and breaking up the forestland, in the eternal striving to break the benumbing spell woven by the monotonous splash of the branches, in the perpetual wariness inspired by the proxi-

mity of bear dens, dens of robbers, and haunted places, in the
need to shake off the century-old guardianship of the forest,
since freedom and sunlight were always dearer to us than a
well-fed and inaudible existence. Historical reasons made us
endeavour to push apart the forested falls as far as we could.
Even so nothing changed in our attitude towards the forest, when
it was depleted to such an extent that all was clear field from
the Black Sea to Vologda. We should speak more often about
the proven errors of the past, a repetition of which may griev-
ously affect the well-being of posterity. We may as well admit
at the start—the forests were not spared in the rest of Europe
either, with this fatal difference in the consequences, though, that
the western rivers spring from a bounteous glacial store, whereas
ours arise from frail woodland springs, and it is much easier with
us to upset the finely adjusted balance of Nature by careless
treatment of the forest.

"There is scarcely another nation which has entered history
with such a rich coniferous mantle upon its shoulders. To the
distinguished foreign emissaries who travelled through our
country to see the magic mysteries of the East, ancient Russia was
a dense thicket with occasional gaps in it formed by human
settlements. Hence arose our dangerous reputation as a forest
country, which cheapened our green merchandise in the eyes of
the foreign consumer and created a harmful millionaire psychology among the indigenous population. There was to come a day
when Peter would punish the ravishers of protective groves by
having their nostrils torn and condemning the offenders to chain-
gangs. Meanwhile, Russia had so many forests that clearance
was awarded with exemption from taxation for a period of fifteen
years, and slightly towards the north, for all of forty years. The
forest rose in such an impenetrable wall and was so fabulously
stocked that the *bylinas* of ancient Russian epic made the breaking of forest roads a task for only national heroes. In the tenth
and twelfth centuries all the vast lands of Kiev were covered with
woods, and some rivers, now denuded, were clad in murmurous
emerald silks all the way down to the sea; even now untold
black oak lies idle and unused in the Dnieper bed near Kherson.
If that's the case, then why sing about it! You could roam about
for a thousand days in any direction, and everywhere the forest
would trail at your heels like a faithful shaggy dog. It is here
that we should seek the roots of our neglectful treatment of
the forest. We simply took no notice of it, because it was our

own, a permanent homely fixture, always handy, like air and water, like the bag strapped to one's back, where one could grope about even with a sleepy hand and be sure to find whatever one needed for body and soul. We accepted its services and bounties without ever giving a thought to its needs and troubles. The Russian ascetic, who retired into the trackless pine forest, was called a *pustinnik*—dweller in a waste. The dense-wooded country of my childhood was called *pustosha*—wasteland. That is why the forest has not received its full due either in the national legends or songs.

"*Russkaya Pravda*,* the Novgorod Acts of the fourteenth century, as well as the Code of Tsar Alexei Mikhailovich only mention the forest in connection with the necessity of protecting private bee-keeping. Ivan III was to forbid the felling of trees in the vicinity of the Troitsky Monastery, but this, too, did not signify any attempt to regulate felling or establish property rights on timberland, that is, an attempt to find a place for it in civil legislation; it was merely a desire to protect the 'praying brethren' from mundane molestation. Russia was still 'rivery, fishy and woody'. Under the same Ivan elk and aurochs roamed the woods of Uglich together with the bear and the chamois. But Moscow laid about her ever more vigorously with the axe until Alexei forbade felling within a radius of thirty versts round the capital city—again merely to preserve the royal hunting grounds. The unfelled forests all round murmured and swayed as of old— the forests of Kolomna and Murom, of Suzdal and Bryansk, the inaccessible forests of Kurma and Vladimir—a bottomless well of sylvan wealth, which nothing, it seemed, could drain in a thousand years.

"It is not a question of pity—if man doesn't do the felling, time will do it, and then there is no forest-slaughterer more ruthless. It was indeed a 'dark' forest, where new lives were piled up on lives which had not completed their destined circle, and where the dead lay mouldering at the feet of their successors. All is silent in such a forest, save on the woodside, where the grouse, with drunken eyes, can be heard sounding his mating call in the spring. Periodic disasters, such as hurricanes, the invasions of wood borers, or the rise of ground-water level, checked this silent, headlong drive towards the sunlight, the everlasting race of the

---

* *Russkaya Pravda*—a code of feudal laws and regulations in eleventh-twelfth century Russia based on the common law.—*Tr.*

earth's living juices. Sometimes it was the fire, which swept away the reigning coniferous dynasty to enthrone another—the deciduous —in its stead. But life was stronger than any interference. The black or yellow isles of death skinned over with leafy young coppices, which, in turn, were killed by the heavy canopy of fir. Human interference had not yet threatened the Russian forest, but the time was not far off when the joint fury of the axes would begin to overcome the slow accumulation of vegetable cells.

"Everyone was now helping himself, and there was still enough to go round. At the beginning of the seventeenth century high-standing timber and crude distillation products from the Northern Dvina were shipped to the London market for the first time. There was still plenty of forest wealth in Russia, but it was being ladled out fast with a ladle that kept growing in size. With the danger of nomad invasions from the South removed, even the sacred abatis woods were put to the axe for government needs. Meanwhile the steppe was on its triumphant march northwards, and suddenly the alarmed voice of Pososhkov, the first conservationist concerned as yet with only the Orenburg and other forests across the Volga, rang through the land. It was the voice of the national conscience of the age, and it touched all aspects of civic life. As a matter of fact, Pososhkov's advice about planting small woods around the denuded Russian villages between whiles has lost none of its significance to this day. But even without the intervention of this patriot, the exigencies of defence would have compelled the country in any case to adopt drastic measures of forest conservation.

"When the building of the fleet at Azov began to make serious inroads into the ancient oak forests along the river Voronezh and the marginal lands the oak came under the personal protection of Peter, who declared it the inviolable fund of the admiralty. Following the oak, the ash-tree and the maple, the elm and the larch, and later high-standing pine, were proclaimed protective species. The wanton use of oak for axles and runners, wheels and rims, was punishable with penal servitude, be the offender a lord or his steward, while fellings were fined at the rate of ten rubles, two out of every three rubles going to the forester—an attempt to paralyse the almighty bribe. Previously logging was done with the aid of the axe and wedges, so that the proverbial splinters* flew about all the way from Archangel to Astrakhan; now timber users,

---

* From the Russian proverb "When a forest is felled splinters fly" (cf. "You cannot make an omelet without breaking eggs").—Tr.

for the sake of economy, were obliged to do at least a tenth of their lumbering with the saw; apparently they had not learnt tooth setting, because half a century later the muzhik's axe was still going strong. In the Petrine period unlicensed felling was first superceded in this country by an appearance of regulated felling; although it was still a long way off to any real scientific under-standing of the protective role of the forest on water-flow and climate, tree-felling within thirty-two versts of a river, and the building of camp-fires closer than within two sagenes of a tree were severely punished already at that time. In the mining areas orders were given to take care of torse-fibred birch that went for gun-stocks, and the use of building timber for fuel was forbidden; the extravagant old-time burials in 'stump' coffins hollowed out of oak were paid for at quadrupled rates, and damage to growing plants in the towns was rewarded with penal servitude and whip-ping. Nevertheless, the admirals' reports about unlicensed fellings, as a result of which the woods were becoming understocked, grew more frequent, and we see protective banks, three sagenes high, thrown up along the margin of the crown forests on the Neva and the Gulf of Finland, with gallows on them five versts apart.

"At first glance forest policy remained unchanged even after the stick had dropped from Peter's dead hand: for instance, his daughter repeated her father's waldmeister instructions concerning the planting and cultivation of high forests from the vicinity of which the local inhabitants were to be removed (1754). Both Catherines deplored the irreparable losses caused by the firing of the woods around the capital to fertilise the land; they forbade free felling, and offered maternal advice to the effect that the forest should be protected from grazing cattle and thieves of the night, that tar should be distilled from stumps and roots, and that only blown trees and breakage should be used for firewood. One can imagine how the dependent peasants must have laughed through their tears! The Second, solicitous of Russia's welfare—for were not Diderot and Voltaire in Europe watching the queen, mistress of fifteen million serf barbarians!—even commanded Potemkin to 'strew' plenty of acorns over the ground around Odessa, so that our grandchildren should not have to bring oak down from the north to repair the ships of the Russian fleet. But in spite of all the floggings administered for kindling camp-fires, of all the hangings done for poaching and trespassing, the oak and high-standing pine were wiped clean off the descriptive landskarten from the upper Volga to Nizhni-Novgorod. By restricting the peasants' firebote and granting chartered liberties to the nobility for the purpose of upholding her dubious right as a foreigner to the Russian throne, the Empress graciously placed the Russian forests in the keeping of the persons upon whose lands they were standing, and freed them of all obligations connected with their protection and care (1782). From now on the all-powerful Admiralty itself did not dare to take any timber without the concent of and payment to its owner.

"The heart of woman is frail; although the ladies who sat upon the Russian throne favoured the forest because of its excellent amenities, they showed a far more tender affection for the first estate and its individual and younger members. The forest became a casket of souvenirs for awarding favourites, and naturally, the properties thus bestowed happened to be in the most populous regions of the country, for the royal gift was worthless without serf peasants to go with it. Anne presented Biron with the Baltic forests, among other Kurland latifundia, for his unspecified 'special qualities and praiseworthy deeds', as stated in the imperial ukase, while Elisabeth gave her Shuvalov monopoly rights on timber exports from the north of Russia. Thus the forest areas were gradually split up, and the number of forest owners was augmented, all obsessed with a mania for showing off their nobility at home and especially abroad. The honest Russian pine was shipped out there in exchange for petit-maitre rags, botanical 'curios', stout, tobacco and other frivolous items listed by Chelishchev. The forests of Russia were still standing, but they were noticeably fewer than before; thus, when Elisabeth travelled to Kiev, the idea of building palaces at the stations had to be abandoned owing to the shortage of timber in the Ukraine, and taverns were erected instead (1743).

"Now let us follow the thread of that little whim of the lady mentioned above and see where it leads us to. His Lordship Shuvalov sold his monopoly to the foreign shipbuilder Gomm, and that worthy gentleman attacked the virgin forests of the Onega with might and main. The said Pyotr Chelishchev, an honest major in the service of Catherine and Radishchev's friend, who was suspected of co-authorship with him in the writing of *A Journey from St. Petersburg to Moscow* describes with pain and much gnashing of teeth the fifteen-year activities of Gomm, that villainous vagabond, as he calls him; himself a contemporary and living witness, Chelishchev saw the trail of destruction that he left behind him. Owing to Gomm's alleged sudden ruin immense stacks of high-grade timber a thousand feet wide and eighteen feet high, stretching without gaps for nearly a mile along the shores of the Onega, timber cut by the Russian axe with money borrowed from the Russian public purse, were left to rot and go waste. It took this timber twenty years to rot away. Curiously, already at that time, our patriot saw behind Gomm's actions a deliberate design on the part of his government to work mischief to our country through deforestation. Chelishchev mentions another man—a merchant by standing, a Swede by birth, and a despoiler by trade. So let us give them their due, all those enlightened foreign seafarers, who gave us an object lesson in western capitalism. By deception and bribery they acquired the privilege of cutting down our finest pines nine inches in diameter at the top-end; it wasn't until later, when the quality of the standing crop sharply declined owing to the depletion of the accessible timberlands, that this standard was reduced to seven and a half inches. Only the butt log, marked twice with the importer's brand—once at the stump end, and again three axe-handle lengths higher up—was exportable; the rest was left to rot where it was, and contaminate the healthy forest, which sickened as a result of the wasteful practice of 'picking the plums.' This system of selective felling, by the way, was practised right up to 1930, until the concession was obliged to betake itself off, leaving no memory of itself in the way of roads, workers' townships, or a good name. Every loss is a fourfold one unless you draw a proper lesson from it.

"In those remote days the first blast-furnaces were fired up in Russia. Hi there, you forests, make way! Demidov has taken the axe! Russia's young metallurgy began to mow down the primeval forests of the middle Urals; the iron of Kargopol and Ustyug, followed by that of Tula, devoured the surrounding woods at the rate of two tons of charcoal, that is, eighteen cubic metres of firewood, to every ton of cast iron. At the same time grain exports were unable to refill the depleted imperial treasury. Potash, tar and timber came to the rescue—at a quarter of a ruble per full-size century-old log. And so the forests of high-standing timber around Archangel were mown down, the larch disappeared from the Dvina, and ships were allowed to use pine planking down to the water-line. Acutest of all was the shortage of fine wood: already under Elisabeth our principal greenwoods—those of Kazan and Tambov—were pock-marked with clearings. In those days the old men of the Volga still recalled, with a tear of delight in their eye, trees on whose cut stumps a man could sleep stretched out.

In Dokuchayev's day there were still oak stumps in the steppes seven and a half metres in circumference, but now these were unknown. Strictly speaking, special conservation measures should have been taken at the time in regard to those last surviving forest monarchs, the living witnesses of our past, whom the local authorities were accustomed to look upon as so much reserve 'firewood.'

"Paul tried to reimpose the stringencies of Peter, and once more the state was confronted with the urgent problem of forest regulation. Meanwhile naval officers were scouring the country in search of mature woods. It was the failure of this search that accounted for such an extraordinary measure as the suspension of timber exports. Alexander, however, was to remove this ban in order to revive the languishing treasury. The forests were placed in charge of the Minister of Finance, and that was as good as giving a cow into the care of a tiger to be milked and tended with affection. The forest now became the ruble of the old folk-tale which could never be changed; as at the beginning of the century, it was used to stop up the holes in the state budget, and towards the end, when the landowner economy lost its trusty hacks—the slaving serfs—the forest would be used to patch up the uniforms of the nobility. Almighty Graft quickly settled the contradictions that arose between the available forests and conscience, between the plunderer and the law. We would add that the department was run by important Germans, who spoke poor Russian, while the forest cabins were tenanted by half-starved down-and-outs hired for the sake of cheapness from among the invalids: naturally, they looked upon their office as a means of helping out their incomes and providing for their old age. Here are two figures for comparison: in the year when Pushkin perished the total income from forestlands was six hundred thousand rubles, whereas wood pilfering in the Kazan Gubernia alone amounted to as much as fifteen millions. The Court Report for 1838 describes the grievous condition of our green stocks in thirteen provinces, and its titled author demands that the forest guards should be reinforced by well-armed soldiers; he doesn't mention the artillery, though, thank goodness for that! Thus Nicholas's decision took shape to form a special corps of forest officers with a military set-up and army ranks in order to tighten up the disintegrating forest economy with a hoop of iron. The privately-owned woods, however, were still free from government control, a circumstance which was to have very grave consequences, as we shall see.

"We now come to the saddest page of our brief tale of Russia's deforestation. It begins with the fall of serfdom, and for decades afterwards the whole of Russia was swept, as it were, by a cold forest fire. By the eighties it had become an assault upon the forests on a hitherto unprecedented scale; only Russia's bad roads and the tremendous amount of labour required for felling century-old trees by the rough and ready methods of our grandfathers curbed that wanton slaughter of our Green Friend. And if such examples of profligacy were left by the muzhik's dented old axe, one can easily imagine what records of forest depredation can be achieved by the arbitrary rule of modern techniques. It was fortunate for Russia that our up-and-coming young commerce did not possess the modern electric saw, which would have played havoc with our great pine forests of the north and scalped the land all the way to Pechora and Murmansk, thus hastening the southward march of the tundra. Two potent factors were responsible for the slaughter of the forests in the nineteenth century: the downfall of Russian feudalism, followed by the impoverishment of the nobility, who were unable to run their estates efficiently with voluntary hired labour, and the rapid development of our industry. If wood had blazed before in the furnaces of the sugar refineries, breweries, and distilleries, now its principal consumer was the metal industry. In the Urals it was already starved for fuel and was lagging appreciably behind the South, where immense deposits of cheap underground coal had been most opportunely discovered. The building of railways gave a new impetus to forest devastation. All over the world, however, the introduction of the locomotive led to over-felling, that is, consumption of timber at a rate exceeding the annual increment. It was a compulsory loan out of the rations of the unborn generations, the silence of the creditor in such cases usually being taken for unqualified consent. Meanwhile the birth of the cellulose industry was drawing near: like the coal mines, it would attack the fine-zoned Vologda spruce, which could even be used for musical instruments. The demand rose, the rate of felling increased, prices doubled. Sawmills sang their clattering song even in the steppe . . . and so, towards the end of the last century, wood consumption reached the figure of two-hundred and seventy million cubic metres. Members of all the wealthy classes took the most active part in that haphazard pillage known as capitalist progress. Russia resounded with the crash of falling forest giants, which drowned the noise of the shooting in the Crimean campaign, which had just ended.

"Progress arm in arm with profit invaded the coniferous

thickets, leaving behind a trail of battle-scarred chaos, a melancholy aftermath, and a disproportionately small number of petty industrial enterprises. Such a mad lust for wealth had previously been seen only during the gold rushes. At the head of that witch-struck whirligig, illumined by that novelty of engineering, the magic electric lamps, and generously primed with champagne to make it go round more merrily, strutted the well-favoured grinning 'whistler-robbers' with stars and medals on their chests, followed by others with bowlers at a rakish angle and a hungry insolent gleam in their eyes. The rich crop of corpses, if only those of forestial origin, and the warm odour of decay lured the night bird and the midges from the dens of Europe, all kinds of fairies in clouds of lace and respectable-looking bank speculators with travelling-bags. And once more the bearded Russian forest, by courtesy of the government, bows down to the ground to foreign scalawags. Everyone now is felling, picking out the choicest pieces—the newborn kulak class, ready to hack down the trees in the cemetery at the head of its own mother's grave; the monastic brethren on the claustral estates, who thank the Lord for His merciful bounty and leave to Him the thankless task of forest regeneration; the conscript fathers, like those of Kherson town, who razed their famous acacias when they were having the telephone laid; a motley mob of travelling agents from the western provinces, never before seen in the Russian forest, who buy up from the nobles at a reasonable price their property rights, and from the peasants their allotments through the medium of the volost elders who, taking a leaf out of their master's book, also started felling, not because there was any need to do so or because they wanted to lay in a stock for a prospective buyer, but simply because of an intense itching of the hands. And so, little by little, that sturdy branch on which we had been sitting since the days of Gostomysl,* begins to wear thin. More and more often, as in an oppressive dream, the thought of the profligate exploitation of the Russian forest preys on the minds of Russian patriots. We find Aksakov now weeping over Vasilchikov's forest article, and although everyone realises that improvidence will have its inevitable reward, the society of the day acts according to the tested hypocritical rule: just one more sin, another go, and then repentance! The magnitude of the forest destruction can be judged from the figures of rail

---

* Gostomysl—a burgomaster of ancient Novgorod.—*Tr.*

and water-way traffic quoted by Lenin in *The Development of Capitalism in Russia.*

"The newspapers of the day regarded all this as an unavoidable phase in the development of the national economy. The sordid story of a merchant murdered in a rooming-house was greater news value than the wholesale slaughter of the forests. Only from an occasional item in the forestry magazines could one judge of the ruthless efficiency with which the green mantle was being stripped from the Russian plain. The first to go was the oak, the stands of which had been thinned out to such a degree that felling was started on individuals which had been overlooked; but the specimens which had survived until quite recently in Merzlyakov's song *Amid the Valleys Smooth,* all covered with burls and gnarls, were only fit to act as windbreaks on the skirts and had no timber value. The Black Sea Admiralty cleared the last of the Kiev, Poltava, Kherson and Kazan greenwoods, where islands of some ten thousand giants had managed to survive. In sight of all, the green glory of the Kuban—the leafy forest near Maikop—was wiped out for railway sleepers, and Cossack hearts were sorely grieved. The woods around Saratov, mentioned in the document of 1763, under cover of which Pugachev had crept up to that town unobserved, fell to the axe of the settlers. Round about 1877 the forest chronicles mourn the despoiled stands on the Vitegra, as before that they had mourned the pillared pine forest of Pelageyevka in the Izyum District—who remembers it now? And who knows that not so very long ago foxes were hunted with hounds and partridges caught with nets in former Novomoskovsk, where now there is the bleak desolation of sand dunes. Although we may well believe that some two hundred years ago the whole region between the Volga and the Don was densely wooded, who would believe that as late as the sixties the Dnieper, from Ekaterinoslav to Alexandrov, was buried in oak thickets? Contemporaries deplored the fact that the full-grown merchantable lime-trees survived only along the river Belaya, but even here drunken forest Death was to come lurching in with green wine and brick-tea. He was to stagger through the dense primeval *urmans* of Bashkiria with axe and accordion, hack down all the mature trees, and debark all the regrowth, poisoning the Ufimka and the Tanap with the stench of soaking bast, and end up, perhaps, by starting a fire to spite the governor-general for his belated official vigilance.

"No less sad and instructive is the fate of the forests between

Yelatma and Murom around which many a folk-tale has been woven; the hundred thousand acres presented to the Viksun millowner eventually passed into the hands of Englishmen, who effectively applied their colonial practices there. The concessionaire in those days was a power to be reckoned with in our country. That debonair foreigner M. Letelier worked against time, cutting down the immense-girthed walnut logs of Namangan and Andizhan and sparing neither coppice growth nor mother-trees, while another one, familiarly known as Emerik Gavrilovich, cleared the age-old jungles of black poplar on the Middle Volga. No little wealth was to trickle away in the outlying regions during the years of intervention, when the whiteguards in the North and the Mensheviks in the South were to let the White Sea pine and the box-tree respectively go in exchange for weapons for their hopeless cause. No less deplorable, taken all round, was the fate of many Georgian forests, and this told on the character of the Caucasian rivers. The forests of Chambar near Telav came down, and towards the close of the century those south of Gori, on the feudal estates of Satarkhno, Satsitsiano, and Sajavakho shared the same fate. The dead lay strewn over the slopes with green faded manes, and there were not enough buffaloes to haul them down. Only those survived over which the eagles' aeries stood guard. Heavy downpours of rain washed the soil away to the bare rocks. The old Georgian elm was depleted in the accessible gorges, and the zelkova moved its home from the Rion Valley into the legends of the bards, where their blood brothers, the oaks from Khortitsa, had long since found a refuge. We find the local inhabitants complaining more and more about the hot wind burning the maize in Imeretia, Guria, and Mingrelia, while the bareheaded Kura and Aragva went mad in the spring; so does the hand of a clock race round when its regulator, the pendulum, has been removed.

"At the turn of the century the high forests of Vasilsursk containing oaks that remembered Grozny fall to the axe, and the dried-up springs there are silenced for ever. The Mali Zhiguli hills are denuded, and the Khmelevsk sandbanks fling themselves across the Volga channel like a death noose. The sands begin to crop up on the Desna at Novgorod-Seversky, and somewhat later the appearance of those flying scouts of the desert are reported from Byelorussia. When Tursky, my teacher's teacher, explored the upper reaches of the Oka in the eighties, he discovered a mutitude of villages with forest names but no forest beyond a few small spinneys, which the old men cherished as they would a father's benediction. Things are no happier in Siberia, where, near Kansk for example, the feather-grass steppe spreads in a blue waste where living people remember the taiga to have stood. At the same time cries of alarm at forest ruin arise from the remote hinterland of the Baikal and from the Amur, cries which never reach the ears of the powers that be. On Sakhalin, the green barriers sheltering the Dui valley are cut down, and closer to our time the watersheds of the Upper Lena and South Yenisei are to be stripped of their forest cover. Who knows whether that impenetrable Varnachya Gorge near Irkutsk with its gushing springs, at which the vagabond of the famous Russian song rested, still exists? It is raging unabated to this day, that death-dealing white fire; already in our day the Valdai watershed from which flow six great Russian rivers, not counting the Dnieper, which starts in the vicinity, has been stripped bare. The age-old pine forest Devil's Nook near Kazan, the gardens on lake Kaban, as well as the splendid Derzhavin garden are gradually disappearing, and a good start has been made on Dubki, where not so long ago the proletarians of Kazan held their illegal Mayday rallies. True, people coming from the Yenisei report that the pine pillars there still support the glowing sky at sunset, but only because they cannot be towed out on account of the rapids.

"Naturally, with the growth of towns and population and the development of trade and industry, the forest was to be drawn into the country's economic turnover on an increasing scale. However, it was the duty of the tsarist government to glance more often at the spreading yellow patches on the country's green map, and take care that abundance today did not lead to a dearth tomorrow. Another thing to speculate on was why a hundred odd million registered dessiatins of Russian forests yielded only a million and a half rubles in 1861 whereas a million dessiatins of French forests yielded ten millions in the same currency. The remedy lay in switching the bulk of lumbering operations to the mature overstocked swamp forests of the near North· and gradually developing the declining Siberian taiga. The capitalist, however, was not able to invest money in building settlements, roads, railways and new wharves. True, shortly before the revolution the Murmansk Railway opened the way South to Olonets timber, but the railway itself came into being not through timber requirements, but for the transportation of imported military equipment, the lack of which threatened the empire with defeat. What is more, the southern forestowner reduced the price for his timber and tried to secure for himself a favourable freight tariff in order to provide against a possible northern competitor. We find some scoundrelly firewood traders trying to secure a ban on coal. The arrogance of the plunderer went to the extent of insolently demanding that 'no restrictions be temporarily placed on intensive felling' since deforestation was the 'child of necessity'. We do not know what this pathetic expression was supposed to mean, but we do know that a hundred and thirty tons of truffles alone were imported from France in 1869 to the value of two million rubles at wholesale prices; this dainty dish was hardly intended for the palate of the muzhik.

"Not counting the woodmen, who rarely wielded a facile pen, few people in Russia wrote about the effects that this wanton license of the proprietor was to have upon the climate, agriculture, and landscape of the beloved homeland. The law encouraged crime. Cut-over areas, being considered unfit for farming, were taxed lower, and, besides, they did not involve guarding expenses. In the pledging of estates with the mortgage banks, which had sprung up like mushrooms to give a helping hand to the impoverished nobility, stumps were valued higher than standing timber with its comparatively low rental. Convenient theories were born, claiming that forests desiccated the soil. Engelhardt was followed in 1876 by a Mr. Zalmanov who wrote an article about the harmfulness of the forest in Russia; altogether, fools caused no less harm to the forest than the plunderers. Observation of the winds, among other things, revealed that the forests of Ryazan, for instance, provided moisture to the fields of Turkey, which benefit, considering that country's unfriendly attitude towards Russia, was quite uncalled for. Finally, in connection with a scheme to buy up privately-owned forests, rumours were spread that they were to be appropriated without compensation, with the result that in Roslavl forest holdings went for sixty rubles a dessiatin, a forester's cockaded cap costing twelve. In short, it was hack away for all you're worth, it'll grow all the better for it! Besides, it was safer to keep money than woods, what with the increase in unlicensed felling, by means of which the Russian peasantry readjusted the unfair balance of wealth. The government retaliated by instituting justices of the peace, who dispensed summary corporal justice to the offenders; bloody clashes between the landowners' guards and the population grew more frequent. The number of forest-offence cases mushroomed from eleven thousand in 1866 to a hundred and seventeen thousand a year towards the end of the century.

"In most provinces the peasants received no wood lots at all, and those who did usually sold them to profiteers to meet their arrears and feed their families during crop failures. For a broom and an armful of twigs one had to go cap in hand to the landowner who was none too kindly disposed towards the peasants; and the peasant was hardly to blame if he was a bit lax in observing the rules of scientific felling during his nightly visits to the master's grove. The laws which prevent the poor man from giving his child food and warmth were never secure. Incidentally, even in those days the by no means underpaid thinkers of the State could have invented some simple machine for converting our vast rich peatbogs into 'firewood'—may you never know a word more vile and senseless than that one, my young foresters! During the years of your study you will learn that, in putting a log into the fire you are burning miraculous materials, the list of which chemistry will ever hardly exhaust, leave alone such imponderable treasures as green shade, or the song of the nightingale, which dies without smoke or ash. Timber is a bounty which we shall appreciate in proportion as it disappears from the face of the earth. Up till now we have been taking from it only the cellulose, and running the priceless lignin and gum into the river to the destruction of our own fish. Thank God we *have* learnt to produce from it spirits, binders and tanning extracts, for which the bark of the fifteen-year-old oaklings was formerly used. For a whole century industry and transport had been burning timber recklessly in their furnaces; it was not until 1892 that petroleum and coal took half this grievous burden off the shoulders of the forest. Nevertheless, the next year a hundred and fifty million cubic metres of timber went for 'firewood production'. An immeasurably greater quantity of timber was burnt in forest fires; in 1915 millions of square miles were burned over, and the smoke pall held up the ripening of the crops in some places for over a fortnight. In short, under an imperfect social system it is the fact that something survives at all rather than the magnitude of the loss that causes surprise.

"Among the various timber-consuming items mention should be made of the peasant industries, which were the mainstay of lower-class Russia; here are the figures of former wastage and improvidence. Wood in all its forms had long been a commodity of Russian export. Wood burning for potash consumed a thousand cubic metres of willow, elm, and linden to the ton. Tar and pitch were distilled, and the most precious by-products simply went up into the air, with birch bark going at fifteen kopeks per pood.* Eight hundred and fifty thousand poods of bast were sold at the Nizhni-Novgorod Fair in 1855. This does not include bast-sandals —the traditional footwear of the pre-revolutionary peasant—for every pair of which three saplings, or twelve seven-foot lengths of fibre were used and the serviceable life of which seldom exceeded two weeks. The Vyatka Gubernia alone produced thirteen and a half million pairs of bast-sandals in 1877, and the lime-tree has been practically wiped out in that region. Five years ago I visited my home town on the Yenga, and standing on the Loshkarev bluff I thought sadly of the days of my childhood, when caravans and dozens of huge timber floats, barges, and catamarans, each consisting of three hundred logs, floated down it. In the nineteenth century ten thousand such timber cargoes were taken out yearly to the poorly wooded regions of the country. With the introduction of iron vessels the consumption of ship-timber dropped only to find a new consumer in the railways. What is more, the wood crafts were run barbarously—the kulak bosses who held the village craftsmen in bondage, did not care a hoot for forest woes. For the sake of the bark or the seeds—at five kopeks a *chetverik*!** —full-grown birches and pines were cut down, just as today, judging from newspaper reports, gigantic, sky-buttressing cedars are being felled in Siberia during nut-gathering.

"Naturally, when there is too much of anything it inevitably trickles through the fingers, but already in those days it was trickling through them faster than sand. And then, all of a sudden, the millers, as one man, noticed a drop in the low watermark, and old-timers noted in their diaries that the suslik was now hopping about where the bear used to prowl. From Nizhni-Novgorod you could now see straight through to Kostroma, and from Voronezh to Saratov; sand-storms were knocking at the gates of Ryazan like a mob of yellow ghosts from the past, while the salt marshes, the wormwood, and all kinds of prickly demon-growth, above what the Mongolian cavalry had brought hither on

---

* Pood—equal to 16 kg.—*Tr.*
** *Chetverik*—equal to 2.98 pk.—*Tr.*

its hooves and in its manes, crept forth from beyond the Caspian bent on conquest. Over three and a half million hectares of land have been blanketed by shifting sands in the Astrakhan Region during the last century. The Don and the Dnieper were becoming steppe rivers, and hitherto gentle brooks were bursting dams in the spring, while at the height of the summer they became timidly torpid and buried themselves in the sand like the Asiatic lizard at the sight of a man. The shallows were spreading along stream courses; their valleys were widening and their strength ebbing, and finally their beds began to show through. More and more often passengers were asked to take a stroll ashore while their old tub of a boat crawled across the shoals on her belly. The daughters of the Volga were no longer able to feed their mother, and only the eldest of them from the land of unfelled trees, the Kama, still maintained her pristine glory. Unless man did something to protect the rivers, they would protect themselves by checking his one-sided destructive activities; they would not let his steamers go upstream, they would parch his ploughlands, and spoil the floating season—and three quarters of our timber harvest is transported by water. Things like that have happened in our day, too, the water level dropping so sharply as a result of riverside felling that rafts of the same season got stranded in the shallows on the upper reaches of the Kama, the Vichegda, the Northern Dvina and the Belaya; the bed of the Kama, by the way, is paved with a six-metre layer of deadheads—sunken logs.

"And so the balance of Nature is seriously disturbed, with disastrous results. Springs dry up, lakes become peaty, slack waters become covered with arrowheads and bulrushes. The earth languishes without its grassy cover; one day people were to learn by bitter experience what it costs to replace the sod that has been wantonly torn from it and to make the acorn strike root in the salt marsh. When the forest goes it goes for good. There is nothing now to prevent the soil from being washed away by run-off. Gullies and ravines form in growing numbers, working as gigantic draining ditches, black-earth dredgers. In the South, where we have eighty thousand collective farms, the bulk of the melting snows run off rapidly and uselessly before the frozen soil can catch the moisture, and they sweep away the fertile surface soil. In the summer months, when the crops are ripening, the rivers suck away what remains of the scant ground waters. And so we are letting a monster into our Soviet house, deliverance from whom will require a far greater effort than the one we expended in banishing the forest.

"According to popular belief, the woods draw water to themselves to then let it go on its further travels in the form of a cloud. That is to say, the forest makes every drop of water do double and triple work. The more forests there are the more often will those constant two-hundred millimetres of precipitation which we receive on the average every year from the ocean touch the earth in the form of rain. Moreover, we omit from our calculations the extra moisture which the trees themselves pump out of the depths with their roots, those imposing automatic pumps of high efficiency. The forest brings the sea closer, and is itself like a sea with its cloud-ships moored for the night at its green havens ... but the axe falls to work, and the aerial transports of moisture sail straight across the land without putting in at the ruined way-stops. On the other hand, imagine the appalling future of the northern plain with its excess of moisture and inadequate drainage when it has been denuded of forest and becomes still more water-logged, thus quickening the march of the permafrost, since the sun cannot warm the earth under its tundra coat of moss. I would have you know, by the way, that a theory exists, asserting that the northern forests are the rearguard of a new glacial period.

"The disturbed conditions of water-flow have long been telling on the well-being of the nation. Crop failures hit the country hard every decade—1891—1901—1911. Nor is peasant life all honey in between. Rinderpest kills off the cattle, and fodder is scarce—not even the bitter mouldy straw off the roofs, which always served our farmers as a reserve for a rainy day, is any help. Dismal God-invoking processions with cross and icons move across the scorched fields to the sound of prayers and the steady rasp of the nearby saw. Migrants trudge endlessly in search of places untouched by native capitalism—unmowed meadows, unmuddied waters, and uncut woodlands—for is our country not vast and boundless! Mothers knead chaff mixed with nettles and gout-weed for their children, the while they gaze anxiously at the wan-blue glassy sky. Wonder of wonders!—axes are knocking along the Sura and the Irgiz, but echo answers back with children's cries from across the Volga. And so we have Dokuchayev comparing Russian farming with a gamble, and in 1893 the agronomist Izmailsky prophecies the speedy transformation of the steppes into desert, and this is followed in the press by a still more ominous prophecy: 'Years shall pass, and the *aryks** will come to Ryazan. It is only a lucky traveller who will find a well with brakish water at Kharkov.' This is the calamity from which socialism is called upon to save our peasantry.

"In the ancient struggle between forest and steppe man has been taking an active part on the side of the latter. It would be presumptuous to ascribe climatic damage only to human agency, but still more dangerous would it be to underestimate this damage under the conditions of modern technique. Do not let your anxieties be allayed by the not very comforting thought that this tiresome dispute about the forests has been raging since the days of Reaumur and Buffon; Democritus accounted for the presence of salt by the evaporation of the seas, and Kant deplored the water that our planet was losing, and our historian Solovyov warned us that the deserts were on the march ... but look, mankind still exists, despite the zealous use of firearms! All the worse for mankind. People have always had to pay cruelly for ignoring the so-called 'banal' truths. There is indeed scientific evidence pointing to the desiccation of south-western Russia owing to the rise of the continent and the withdrawal of the glacier to the north, and of the former Sea of Sarmatia into the Caspian depression. It would seem that it's all the fault of the earth's cosmic old age which is supposed to be drying up the vast water floor—the place of our present habitation; that's how the landmarks have been set on the climatic dial, and the forests have nothing to do with it. On the other hand, the same multi-faced science tells us that we happen to be living in a period of humidification of our planet, since the level of some lakes has risen so considerably within the last five thousand years that the lake villages of our neolithic ancestors are now submerged, and therefore the forests do not come into the picture yet. A third opinion holds that climate is subject to fluctuations of thirty-five-year periods, with drought periods alternating with cold damp weather, and that what we are now having is one of these inauspicious spells—we've just got to wait until it blows over. Some opinions claim that the encroachment of the steppe started almost as far back as the Paleocene, and the process is such a slow one that the Russians have all the carefree time in the world before them. One can easily imagine what havoc the axe will work while the gentlemen of science are getting at the truth.

---

* Irrigation ditches of the arid East.—*Tr.*

304

initial waste after barking amounts to almost half of the whole mass of organic matter. If we put inevitable loss in transportation and floating only at ten per cent, figure out what part the industrial enterprises get from every felled tree—mind you, it's still a long way to the consumer. The log finds its way to the sawmill, and there the 'splinters fly' still harder in the shape of slabs and lathends and sawdust, which, in the manufacture of dressed boards and plywood, amount to half the timber used; in the making of furniture another third goes to waste. Snow does not melt half as fast in transit as timber does; sometimes only a tenth of it remains at the end of its journey. This makes no allowance for the customary waste at the cutting areas themselves, as a result of damage caused in logging, firing of the branches, careless bucking, and incomplete removal of felled stands. Visit the remote sawmills, where even today everything that is too thick to go into the saw frame is treated as waste. One can easily envisage the sad fate of a grain farm manager, who would dare to permit such a reckless waste of a crop that had been maturing in the field for a hundred years!

"Naturally, the revision of our attitude to the forest is not going to be an easy job, but was it not stern necessity which made man invent the lever and the wheel, new forms of driving power and machines, the socialist revolution and other beneficent ways of bettering life, without which the human race would have run wild and degenerated. True, all the economies in the world are to blame for this wanton waste of the forests, but then ours is a socialist economy!

"Probably no forest fires have caused so much damage to our timberlands as this hypnotic spell cast by Russia's former woodland wealth. The extent of Russia's forests was always measured with approximate accuracy. The official data of two related Soviet institutions concerning the country's forests in 1930 differ to the extent of all the forests of Sweden, which is one of Europe's three timber exporters. Four years later our wooded area shrank mysteriously by 117 million hectares to increase again the next year by 62 million. More mysterious still is the behaviour of the watershed protection forests; despite intensive felling their area shows an increase of three million hectares between 1936 and 1938, and as much as twenty million in 1940. Moreover, it turns out that the forest area of this famous 'third' includes all the lands, which, after the demarcation, were found to be unfit for agriculture, such as cuttings and wastelands, burnt-over areas and swamps, brush and even quarries and sand pits. The Soviet kopek likes to be taken care of, and the forest, like fish or fur animals, is an unguarded part of the State Bank. For that reason, the smooth-tongued whisperings of the consolers about the supposedly thriving condition of our forests should be tested by the only true and proven touchstone—that is, how will our deeds and words affect the welfare of posterity.

"The consolers will also reassure us that we are cutting *below* the annual increment. Don't you believe them. They estimate the increment by the total forestlands, including the wilds of Siberia, where the standing timber, even to this day, is rotting on the stump. We have always boasted about our forests on the Yenisei and the Ob, but did our lumbering at Tula and Ryazan. It's time we took a look round now to see how much of that 'magic ruble' we have left, and examine what remains of it through the magnifying glass of scientific forest management, which, by the way, has not been taught with us for fifteen years. Of course, even today it is still difficult to imagine our country without the blue margin on its horizon, and I even anticipate protests from laymen and city dwellers who rent cottages in the country in the summer that I am painting the picture of the Russian forest with an over-anxious brush. 'Why, only the other day,' I am sure to be told, 'Mrs. so-and-so went mushrooming in the aspen grove and came back with a full basket!' In the past, too, malicious attempts were made to misinterpret our appeal for thrifty and careful treatment of the forest as a demand to ban all felling. I am ready to concede that there is a prime in the life of every man, when he stores up life's impressions with hungry zest, but afterwards, no matter how young he may remain till the end of his days, he will merely be diluting his stock of accumulated experience with the observations of novelty. My personal experience was formed in the years of intensive and profligate exploitation of the forests. However, it was not to alarm you with the magnitude of the job facing you that I was obliged to touch on certain sad obvious facts, but simply out of desire to share with you an impatient creative concern, without which we, foresters, become mere armchair sitters and recorders of forestial woes.

"Today already full-fledged masters of your country, in a few years' time you will stand at its helm. Some of you will become scientists and planners, others captains of industry, law-makers and members of parliament. In your swift stride forwards, just figure out from the heights of grand strategy whether it is right to take only the timber that is 'handy', whether we should, for instance, work the town outskirts for firewood, cut the ribbon forests of Altai or the massifs of the Upper Ob which screen the Kulundinsk Steppe—the granary of Siberia—from the hot Mongolian winds, as well as the woods around the socialist works and building sites. Just think, would it not be more correct, in place of this hurried semi-nomad method of lumbering, to set up a settled and highly progressive type of lumbering enterprise with a permanent force of workers, that is, to bring the processing closer to the raw material, and save the pood-weight crumbs from falling off our extravagant table. Would it not be more profitable to make the cutting area the primary production unit of a diversified lumbering enterprise, which is to provide itself with a stable and continuous crop, extracting all that can be extracted from the timber on the spot without giving the railways extra work to do in carrying eighty per cent of sawdust, chips and moisture ? This would make our timber exploitation a progressive branch of agriculture, it would enhance the merchantable value of the felled tree, make for greater prosperity in the Russian northern region, which does not grow even an apple of its own, and would provide the means for immediate reafforestation within the bounds of every timber enterprise. Just check up—is it necessary to tush the timber without first lopping the branchwood and thus ripping away the soil cover together with the regrowth, or to continue tapping for resin in the exhausted regions of the Ukraine and Byelorussia instead of the Olonets forests, as directed by Soviet law, or to leave fuel wood in the cutting area, exposing it to windfall and turning the area into a refuse dump. Is it not time we started taking care of the doomed groves by making it compulsory for all timber designed for outdoor construction to be properly impregnated and treated, by reducing the amount of chip waste and firewood, and by re-working up paper utility refuse. Big money and ominous happenings are usually made up of dropped kopeks and overlooked trifles.

"Some of you will become forest teachers, workers of inestimable value, because more important even than growing forests is to create the makers and protectors of forests. No ABC book is complete that does not contain a brief introduction explaining the significance and beauty of our countryside, the forest included; and it is a bad teacher who has failed to teach his flock this most useful and noblest of sciences. Explain to the children patiently that the forest stands for one's native land, that patriotism is measured by the amount of work one has put into her; vagabonds and parasites have always been strangers to this feeling of Country. Learn to make use of the boundless time and energy of your charges, which are as good for creation as they are for destruction, and there will be less ruined trees, maltreated gardens, rifled nests and ant-heaps, which children often regard as proofs of their derring-do. There are things no budget or official department can cope with half as well as a nation-wide purposeful impulse. I believe it is the Komsomol youth and the schoolchildren, the future masters of the transformed land, who should take the lead in this crusade for our Green Friend.

"The time has come to repay our debt to this taciturn comrade. At the festival of forest revival let industry greet him with machines no less powerful than those it had used to draw its strength from him from the moment it was born. Only by glancing at the truthful forest map of the country will you realise the magnitude of that debt and the urgency of its repayment. Although, according to Timiryazev, the forester and the farmer have the same aims, both of them trying to obtain the greatest possible yield from the plant, the former gathers in his harvest yearly, whereas the forester is almost a stranger to the creative satisfaction which should reward every long effort. Your crop will take a long time to ripen, my young friends, and few of you will live to see the harvest. But one day, bareheaded and with deep emotion, you will pass through the murmurous, almost palatial halls of the Kamennaya Steppe with its malachite walls of trees and roof of dazzling clouds born of them. That inspired chaftsman of the woods, Vasili Dokuchayev, and his hard-working apprentices, saw them only in imagination. To the builder of human happiness a dream is as effective an instrument as knowledge or ideas, and a silviculturist without dreams is just nothing. Of course, there are no second-rate professions in our country, but it seems to me that in our job of the forester the socialist succession of the generations is more clearly expressed than in any other. And who knows, when you come grey of head to stand beneath the closed crowns of your nurselings, whether you will not feel ten times more proud than the creators of hasty books, half-finished buildings, or machines that age so quickly.

"Any work you may do for the good of the forest will be made so much easier by the support of the people. When, after the famine of 1891, the Forest Department sent an authoritative committee out to investigate the causes of periodic droughts, it made a round of the forest-steppe, travelling light, in a droshky, and consisted of a single man—Dokuchayev. True, the year after that the number of committee members was doubled in view of the complexity of the tasks that were set it. So don't be afraid of loneliness—the whole people is with you, a people who has come to realise the power of its joined hands! And so, you are coming to the aid of the forest just in time; as the centuries go, the gratuitous gifts of this world are becoming less and less, and if we are to avoid future sorrow we must spend wisely and sometimes repay every kopek of the trust money we have taken from Nature. In short, what I have been trying to explain to you here is the meaning of Marx's words to the effect that the whole community, the nation and even all contemporaneous societies taken together are not the owners of the Earth; they merely use it, and, like good fathers of families, should leave it improved for the generations to come.

"In no other country is a man given a chance to be not a shameless exploiter of Nature, nor a helpless little leaf in its torrent, but a great directing force of the universe. To do that he must spy out the mysterious interplay of forces that unite all phenomena into a living organic whole, in order to lighten and speed up the work of Nature in her striving towards perfection, which she is trying to achieve blindly, wastefully, by a myriad of trials and cruel errors. In this lies the purpose and meaning of human reason; socialism is the most honest and economical form of its activity. We are moving along our path with unprecedented strides, but evil, potent though doomed, will continue to place obstacles in our path. Today it has loosed on us another of its hounds, who, in his bestial ignorance, believes that he is acting on his own volition. But we have all the prior experience of history to tell us that the bright thousand-named hero of folk legend always conquered the monster who lay guarding the source of human happiness.

"Glory to our people and our army! Welcome, young foresters!"

The lecturer concluded with a gesture that invited his listeners, as it were, to pass under the imaginary green arch behind him, then he reached for the water bottle ... and suddenly everything was drowned in a crash of applause.

Polya threw herself back relieved. She felt somewhat dizzy, like a person coming out for the first time into the fresh air after an illness. Everyone was leaning forward, as if jerked into that position by a sudden stop. Only now was she able to distinguish the members of the anti-Vikhrov party; true, they were in a considerable minority. Some chuckled and whispered at the number of times the speaker had used the word "which", and two others yawned openly with the air of disgusted connoisseurs of the fine arts, who had been saddled with an unpleasant duty. Jealous anxiety for her father told Polya that there was more to come. In fact, the professor had hardly announced, according to the usual custom, that he was ready to answer questions, when a young man of impeccable appearance got up in the first row— a last-year undergraduate and favourite pupil of Gratsiansky, as Polya's well-informed neighbour immediately told her. True, he already had a bald oily spot on his head, the touch of youthfulness being provided by a neatly trimmed moustache, while the impression of impeccability was due in equal proportions to a suede sport jacket of excellent quality and that air of respectful and slightly languid dignity which serves cutthroats and experienced knifers as a scabbard to hide the blade of vengeance.

"By your leave, I have two questions at once, Professor," he said with a bow, pushing the slide fastener on his chest up and then down again. "As far as I know, the collective farms are cutting their woods too. It would be highly desirable if you could touch more fully on the scope and character of the *actual* fellings in modern, Soviet, times."

A slight stir and hum of disapproval ran through the room; to the freshmen this was merely an indication that the Institute was clearly the scene of a fierce struggle, but the others understood the provocative point of the question.

"I have only the same information that you have," Vikhrov answered, drinking the water in leisurely gulps. "You know the state plan and the extent of collective farm consumption—multiply this by the coefficient of clearance of the felling area. It's your own fault if you haven't learnt to handle statistical data after all the years you have been in Professor Gratsiansky's department. Your next question?"

Accustomed to all the vagaries of these self-igniting discussions, Vikhrov's opponent smiled.

"Thank you," he said, studying the moulding on the dusty ceiling over the professor's head. "My second question is quite a trivial one. We all liked your comparison of er ... the tribe with the torrent. It's so very novel and fresh, *merci*. But a minute before that you spoke with such engaging warmth about your brothers and sons, as you called them, who ... pardon me," he added, consulting a suede pocket diary, "who bore the brunt of history's ordeal. Would the professor kindly point out exactly which of his relatives he had in mind here?"

One had to know the professor's family very well indeed to be able to deal such a telling blow. Her face crimson with shame, mainly on account of herself, Polya looked round eagerly, seeking support and intercession, but the audience maintained an expectant silence. So did the lecturer, who took a painfully long time putting his empty glass back into its place.

"Your question has no bearing on the subject, but I shall answer it," Vikhrov began quietly, and everyone half-rose in his seat the better to be able to hear his reply. As for Polya, she shut her eyes, dreading what she believed to be inevitable disaster. "I employed that turn of phrase to denote the more-than-kindred ties of common citizenship which binds a nation in the face of a great crisis. Thus, should you not succeed in avoiding the army when your time comes to be called up I shall have to include you, too, in that category. Unfortunately, though, I have no near relatives—as you understand the word—at the front, and I'm too old myself, and, as you will have noticed, lame. Just so."

There was some scattered applause, which was hissed into silence by the majority, but no more questions were forthcoming. The next moment the lecture-hall was filled with the hum of a disturbed beehive, and when Polya pulled her hands away from her flaming face, because it was about her they had been speaking, the professor was not there, and his place behind the desk down there was taken by that young man who in his excitement had forgotten to take his cap off during the lecture. He waved his red-topped Cossack cap to command silence, and his scowling face boded no good. When the noise died down, he expressed in a boyish bass his regret at having been a bit late in taking the size of that slick citizen with the mean questions and had thereby let him insult the old gentleman who had met them all so hospitably on the edge of the Russian forest. When someone in the audience remarked that there was no reason for him to go off the deep end like that, the lad answered scornfully that another thing he hated was fascism, and he had come to hate it long before yesterday when he became personally involved, and therefore he would try his best to reduce it, as he expressed it with restraint, to little less than nothing.

"I think we ought to condemn the behaviour of such sneaks who try to cash in on wartime troubles to stick fire-brands under people's roofs. I hate it all—fascism in any shape or form, double-dealing, and foul play," the lad wound up, and jamming his cap down up to his eyebrows to free his hands for a possible emergency, he passed his eye slowly over the audience.

This time the prolonged applause swelled into an ovation, a tribute to his pluck, his spirit of young irreconcilability to all that was mean. With all the others, Polya ran down to shake the hand of that unknown lad from the Kuban, and almost succeeded in breaking through the close ring to wait for her turn, when a sudden suspicion quenched the impulse. It struck her all of a sudden that he might be that mysterious Sergei whom she had refused to be introduced to the day before. It was only natural to assume that, having been brought up in the home of a forester, he, too, should choose the forest road as his path in life, and that was why he now stood up for his guardian. The doubt had to be cleared up at once. She hurried down the steps to discover the truth.

The young man left with a group of boys, all as grimly aggressive as he, and Polya followed them until they melted away. Left alone, he looked round sternly when Polya hailed him in the long dusty lane. He was wearing a cheap semi-cotton coat, a cloth shirt with a mass of small buttons like the stops on an accordion, and heavy boots with footballed toes; he made up for the modesty of his attire by an exotic kubanka with a bit of flame in lieu of a top, the creation of some upcountry genius in a one-man hatmaking establishment. No, this lad was altogether different from Taisa's darling, whose image in Polya's jealous and prejudiced mind was anything but attractive. This one was more like Rodion; he, too, had a noble heart beating beneath a rough exterior.

"You spoke so well for Vikhrov, it just took my breath away," she gratefully confessed, forgetting the innocent wiles by which she had planned to worm the necessary information out of him.

"Oh, nonsense," he said. "Where the devil do they come from? No matter how hard you try to wash 'em off they keep crawling over you. You going in for forestry too?"

"I don't know yet," she said evasively, and gave her name in case they met again in this life.

"And mine's Kasyan. Fancy giving a boy such a name!" he said with a laugh, kicking a loose stone in the pavement backwards and forwards. "Unless it's at the lectures, we'll hardly meet very soon. I don't think I'll stick it out here very long, though. I'll go to the front soon. I feel all sore inside, like a scratched place. He got my dander up, that bald dude in the foreign leather. Those pests have to be burnt out of their holes, if you ask me." With narrowed eyes he looked away over the roofs, as though he had heard a call from there. "Well, I've got to go—goodbye."

A strange weakness of convalescence swept over Polya. She sank on a bench outside a gate, and stared blankly at a limpid little stone in the roadway, as if trying, like that stone did, to saturate herself with a winter-long supply of light from the diffused autumn sunshine.

Polya never remembered either the hour of the day or the street where this happened. On the spur of a sudden inexplicable impulse she picked the stone up from the roadway.

CHAPTER EIGHT

1

The simplest thing would have been to take the trolley-bus on the Outer Ring route, past the railway stations, but she walked instead through the centre to prolong that feeling of thoughtless exhilarating buoyancy verging on physical weightlessness, which she had already experienced on the first day of her arrival from the Yenga. The Moscow that lay before her was not that old Moscow with its costless wonders; a variety of wartime changes struck the eye, from the damaged buildings with the torn-off plaster and plywood shields in the windows to the deep weal in the roadway made by the sharp swerve of a tank. And no longer did she look to her country's capital for her own tiny share of happiness; rather did she feel like spreading herself over it in a protective cloudlet, if only she had corporeal material enough.

Moscow looked rather empty—not because there was less life in it, but because the war had swept from it all that was inessential, that prevented it from concentrating on the main job. For the rest little had changed—the traffic stream flowed as before, motor-cars with the clay of front-line country tracks on their bodies swished by, and the pedestrians were no less than usual at the end of the day. And all this, in the long run, was moving westward, with the single exception of Polya, who was mooning about on her own inconsequential business. She could not rid herself of a feeling of being a tiny leaf spinning round in an enchanted backwater, unable to break away and join the beckoning stretch of river. She climbed the stairs to her flat on the eighth floor with a sense of guilt induced by her misplaced festive mood. The question about Vikhrov's relatives at the front was gradually beginning to distil its poison.

Varya was ironing a steaming tunic when Polya came in, flung herself upon the bed and stretched herself ecstatically with closed eyes.

"They've kept you a long time for the first round. But why did you run off so early without a cup of tea?" Varya said, dexterously piloting the iron round the brass buttons on the cuff. "Warm the soup up in the kitchen, you builder of great edifices. How was the lecture?"

"I never thought a person could be knocked up with happiness, Varya. Give me a drink, my mouth is parched." And disjointedly, branching off every now and then into unimportant details, she began to tell the story of the most difficult examination that Vikhrov had ever had to pass in his life.

Varya asked her friend whether she liked her father's lecture, but Polya could not sort out her impressions. So far she felt neither dismay at the unworthy suspicions which she had entertained of her father, nor a legitimate dislike for his mysterious opponent. Varya understood her state of mind—the fatigue of victory and the triumph of purity, perhaps the most important of all human liberties. Nothing was to prevent Polya now from taking any path in life that she wished without the risk of being rudely pulled up or shouted at.

"But tell me, what struck you most in his lecture?" Varya asked.

"I don't know, and I don't remember anything, Varya, but from now on I'll probably take greater care even if I only walk in the forest. For two hours running I was like on hot coals, racking my brains to try to recollect where I had seen that man. Then he happened to mention his visit to Loshkarev five years ago, and the mist cleared at once. I remembered him sitting at our table one day, and your father Pavel Arefyich, questioning me in an unnatural sort of way about my inclinations and plans in life, while *he* sat silent, twisting a button on his sleeve. The reason I remember him is because he stumbled over the mat as he was going out—he's lame, you know, my father is. So that *was* Vikhrov!"

"That's not surprising at all," Varya said, folding the ironed tunic on the bed. "He simply came to have a look at his daughter."

"Then why didn't he say so?"

Varya apparently was too preoccupied with her own thoughts to pay proper attention to someone else's.

"Oh, darling, these old people are much too subtle and crotchety for us to understand. Just read *their* books, the way they sometimes complicate what you'd think to be the most natural relations between people. A different social pattern, different habits," Varya said with a little sneer of superiority as she began to pack a suitcase that stood opened on the table. "And generally, when you thumb through your school notes on history, it all sounds so smooth, and logical, and grand, but when you look at the dried blood between the lines, it only makes your heart twitch, if it's a softish one. Just look back, you unawakened soul, you, at the so-called highroad of humanity, and what will you not find there: crusades of maniacs, bonfires of books and bonfires under old women, ships with deadly shot-holes, cities in flames— sometimes it strikes you as a sort of mixture of overpowering inspiration and the writhes, a caravan of the blind, yet it always moves onward, forever onward, to the glacial heights. That's what you've got to love people for, Polya!"

"You know, just before Rodion went to Kazan he wrote quite a nice little poem for *me*, just a few lines, about that very thing—it's engraved on my mind," Polya caught her up eagerly. "It's about living matter, that verse, how it first came into being somewhere in a lagoon with blue-green algae and then turned into human beings, and how they slowly mounted to cloud-ridden heights, and how painful and terrifying it was to breathe the rarefied atmosphere of the mountains. And it ended up like this:

> *But from those summits lordly*
> *No soul has yet come down*
> *Back to the home primordial—*
> *The silt so soft and brown.*

She sat up, leaning on her elbow, waiting for Varya's stern verdict.

"Not bad for a boy of his age," Varya said, stretching the point somewhat. "And he has correctly noted, so to speak, the continuity of the biological process without recessions."

"He's rather a gifted young chap, on the whole," Polya murmured blushingly in a casual way, and suddenly became aware of the suitcase with the missing lock, and the things scattered about, and the inevitable litter that invariably accompanies hasty preparations for a journey. "You're not going anywhere, Varya, are you?"

Varya proceeded with the packing, her back turned to her friend.

"Well, you see, they're sending me on an assignment . . . it isn't a difficult one, but rather troublesome," she explained hesitatingly. "It won't be very soon, but they told me to be ready at any moment. Don't ask me any questions please, I can't tell you anything."

"And what about me?" Polya said, with a catch in her voice.

"You'll stay in Moscow, study at the Institute, and look after this big, good, slightly unfinished building. In short, run the house and be a good girl. I'm glad that your childish, but quite dreadful suspicions about your father have been dispelled at last."

Polya stepped round the table, raised her friend's head by the chin and looked into her eyes.

"Varya, you have betrayed me. You swore to share everything with me, everything in the world. You must have made up your mind about *this* a long time ago, but you didn't say anything. You kept it from me, you have deceived me. I know where you are going."

"On the contrary, Polya. They're sending me far behind the lines."

"Oh, you always speak the truth, you do! But you omit to mention whose lines. Anyway, we're going together."

Varya bit her lip as people do when they are angry with themselves for having given away a secret.

"Don't you realise how silly it is, Polya. Now let's drop this talk please. There are things which a person ought to understand without being told."

"Every person has a right to be different from another in some way. Accept the fact that in my case this difference is due to a low I.Q." She gripped her shoulders with both hands. "But how could you ever think for a moment that I wouldn't have it in me to do the same thing ... you know what I mean!"

This was followed by a tumultuous eruption of despair, with all the little clouds that had been gathering in the course of the day bursting in a rain of tears from Polya's eyes; none but children weep such big tears. Varya waited patiently, with occasional glances at the clock, for the outburst to spend itself, and made no attempt to check it; at last Polya glanced at her nervously through her wet laced fingers.

"I am waiting patiently until you've finished, Polya," Varya said with sobering calmness. "Now judge for yourself, what are you good for the way you are now? What they need *there* is iron, and not just any kind of iron either, and here you are taking on because they won't let you play about with death. Maybe you think real life's a contest in recklessness, a game at dangerous exploit, a race to the common grave, and the one who gets there first is a hero, is that it? The qualities required of you are quite different, above all—a realisation of the importance of the place assigned to you, a clear understanding of the mission, however small, imposed on you by history. You have a Komsomol card under your pillow—think of it more often, it will teach you to perform big deeds." She threw a pretty checked shawl over her shoulders—the best thing she had, which was worn only on festive days of special good humour. "So listen to me, then, Polya. I am leaving this evening, and I've got to go away now for an hour or so. So's you don't sit blubbering here all by yourself till you get used to it, hadn't you better go and sit with Madam Zolotinskaya while I'm away? Come on, I'll take you in to her. Or perhaps you'll manage it alone, what do you say?"

The woman next door had been abed this third day, and Polya knew it; Varya's humiliating intention of leaving her under the care of her elders was accepted by her as a merited punishment.

"It won't happen again, Varya. You can go away with an easy mind, don't worry. Yes, I'll manage," she said with downcast head.

"Now that's better. Smile now, no, with your eyes as well. Wash your hands and have your dinner. As a reward for good conduct I'm giving you my favourite book—*The Beagle*. I've inscribed it already. You'll read it afterwards. It's my route, too, but one that never took place." She handed Polya an illustrated edition of Darwin's *Journal of a Naturalist*, which was full of Varya's marginal notes. "There's a letter for you under your pillow."

325

"From Mamma?" Polya said quickly.

"No, from the front again."

For the sake of cultivating will-power and self-discipline Polya did not open Rodion's letter until after she had visited the sick woman next door. She brought some water up for Madam Zolotinskaya from a lower floor, helped her to wash and began to tidy up the room, which had been sadly neglected since the departure of the woman's granddaughter. Although she longed to, Polya asked no leading questions about Gratsiansky that evening, so that it should not appear as if she were expecting a reward for her services. A cheerless orange-hued sunset crept along the wall towards the child's cot, and the loudspeaker rattled in the corridor.

"You shouldn't have taken all this trouble," the woman said to Polya, who was collecting the reels and skeins from the overturned work basket on the floor. "I remember perfectly well where everything lies in this *big box*. Altogether, despite the inevitable ills of age, I am not living at all badly!"

"Then let's have it just a tiny bit better—you don't mind, do you?" Polya joked, involuntarily imitating Varya's tone of seniority. "I can imagine how dull it must be to lie alone all day like this. What's wrong with you?"

"Nothing at all. I'm just taking a little rest from a long spell of doing nothing," Zolotinskaya said in a perfectly natural tone of voice. "No, thanks, I don't want anything to eat. Comrade Chernetsova brought me some tea this morning. Very nice of her, I'm sure. Is she going away for long?"

"Oh, no, she'll be back in a couple of weeks or so." Then suddenly out it came. "If you like I'll go and fetch your acquaintance from the ground floor? I don't suppose he knows you're ill."

Zolotinskaya smiled faintly.

"You are persistent, Polya ... but, really, there's nothing more I can tell you about Gratsiansky. We met long ago, and we have been complete strangers since. Really, I could have tidied up myself, all the more that I intended to get up tomorrow. After all, I'm a member of the Sanitary Defence, and that's a very great honour for me. Besides, you never know what may happen through my being absent." She spoke with unconcealed satisfaction of the position which she had achieved in the world, then lay for half a minute listening to the radio story coming from the corridor about the resourceful manager of a butter factory in the front-line area, who had organised his own staff to repulse a tank attack. "What's that thing you've got tied on your head in such warm weather?"

Polya had nothing on her head, and the question only showed how much Zolotinskaya's sight had deteriorated during the last month.

"I put Varya's shawl on to keep the dust off my hair," Polya invented on the spur of the moment.

"Funny, why is it so green?"

"Varya likes green."

"Why should you tell me an untruth, Polya?" the woman said slowly. "It's yellow."

"It's a bit on the greenish side, I should say."

Polya waited anxiously for Zolotinskaya to express a desire to see the thing at closer range, but the latter understood, because, looking now at the halo round Polya's head it seemed to take on all the colours of the rainbow. She began to talk about her granddaughter in a level voice, as if nothing had happened.

The girl, together with the other children, had been fixed up splendidly on the Kama in the palace of a former shipowner; the chairman of the district administration brought presents for the little refugees and sung the Moscow Loaf Song with them in a Tatar accent. The same woman, who had gone out to join her child, wrote in her letter that Zoya had got quite used to the collective and had completely forgotten the sad circumstances of her parting with her grandmother. At this point the old woman observed with a sigh that the Christians had written libraries of books in luxurious bindings in defence of the children, but only the Bolsheviks had undertaken *at all cost* to safeguard their future against the consequences of the world's imperfections.

"I don't mean only the evacuation, that's the easiest thing of all," she said in answer to Polya's remark that it was dangerous to leave the little ones in a half-besieged city. "It's rather painful to have to discover such truths in your declining years, when you've really got nothing more to give to people."

"I can't believe that living people should have nothing to give to other living people."

"You are right, Polya, and that's one reason why I must hurry. Thank you, go and get some sleep. This too-clear evening promises a bad night. I'll try to get some sleep too."

It was nightfall when Polya unfolded Rodion's cocked-hat letter. Judging by the handwriting, it had been written in three stages. This time it merely contained snatches of a soldier's thoughts and the front-line facts that begot them; the comparatively calm tone of the letter was a sign of the author's mental good health, which, under conditions of ruthless warfare, is inseparable from the physical. "We are all riding towards the sun across the Russian land. I'm afraid we shall soon meet, though our meeting will be none too joyous," Rodion wrote allegorically. "We snap back occasionally, then go rolling on again along the Radishchev route,* but not in a carriage, not with jingling Valdai bells, but aboard a jolty iron box, so that I get a good view of everything around me."

"You ask, what is the most striking thing in the war? I don't know, dearest, but I do know that it's not the dead—they are more frightful, but also more understandable than anything else. I have seen blazing children's cots in village nurseries, I have seen a frog hopping across a mine-field, and a bird in the grass with its head torn off—you see all kinds of things when you crawl on your belly—and it all sets you thinking. I saw an elderly fellow in a state farm busily crushing eggs with his boots in crates prepared for shipment—so that the enemy should not get them. There were no people left in the neighbourhood, everything was crackling in a smoky gloom. 'Well, I think that's about all,' he said, looking round with a businesslike air before splashing the last of the paraffin oil into the flames. I noticed a gold star on his chest. I saw also prisoners of war and spoke to them. It's strange, you'd think this was a different age with a different sky above us, but they still live the old way, according to the law of the fang. But best of all I remember a horse left behind in a village, an old horse—they'd forgotten it. It didn't go anywhere even after I had let it loose and used a twig to make it go, but it looked at me in such a way that I started off at a run to catch up with my iron carriage. No, darling, the heaviest thing in the war is not metal, nor guns, but a soldier's thoughts.

"And so, little by little, the heart produced that special hormone, which has to be added to the gunpowder to ensure victory. You would not know me now, Polya. I've grown older, bitterer, better, and I don't want happiness with you on any other land except my own, a land cloudless and liberated ... and how I want to keep myself safe from the miseries that I see here

---

* A reference to Radishchev's book *A Journey from St. Petersburg to Moscow.*—Tr.

every day! It was only at the beginning that I retreated with an air of enticing the enemy into the heart of the country after the Parthian manner, but when I fought down this excessive fear of the enemy as well as my own childish eagerness, I came to realise that in war it's give and take with a smile. No, darling, the war hasn't started yet, the Russian war is yet to come. I still find time to chat with you. I am sitting side by side with you even now, holding your warm hand with its bitten nails in my own. Do you feel how rough it has become?"

"What a darling you are!" Polya murmured with quivering lips, and kissed the edge of the letter.

The gathering darkness obliterated the rest of Rodion's letter, and that was a good thing, because it left something for tomorrow. Varya found her friend at the open balcony door when she got back. With hands clasped behind her head, she was gazing at the silvery starlight reflected on the barrage balloons.

"Oh, you've packed up my things ... good. We have a whole whopper of a minute to spare, then. My comrades are waiting for me downstairs." She changed quickly, and put her arm round Polya's shoulders, noticing as she did so the piece of paper in her hand. "What does Rodion write?"

"He's well. Promises to win the war."

"There, you see how nice everything is working out. I'm sure you'll be getting good news about Mamma in a day or two. Well, what were you thinking about, sisterkin, you might as well confess now at parting?" Varya said in a tone that cut to the heart.

"I was thinking how good this world could be to live in. Why then must people bear this, all this unnecessary anguish, which can so easily be avoided, anguish that makes you want to put the stars out and crawl back into the primeval mud?"

"What can you do about it? The old won't give in without a fight, and the quest for more perfect forms of life always costs people dear," Varya uttered slowly, as if she were simultaneously writing it in chalk on a blackboard. "The progressive development of thinking matter involves renunciation of all that is habitual and outmoded, and that is by no means painless."

"But you and I are getting old, too, and development will never cease. The pain is everlasting, then?"

Varya laughed.

"Everyone knows that all the academies in the world could not gratify the curiosity of a single child. I can comfort you though—under communism this discrepancy between the old and new will be overcome without the present pain—so I think. Does that reply satisfy you?"

Polya had no time for further questions. A searchlight beam wavering on the jagged skyline returned them to reality.

"Yes," Polya answered, and removed Varya's hand from her shoulder herself. "They'll be coming over soon, and you have to get to the station. Come along, I'll see you down."

"That's all right, we have a car, it won't take long. We have a night pass, and the streets are quite empty." Varya became thoughtfully silent, and as usual at partings, forgot to say the main thing. "Keep that drawing whatever happens—the one you gave me, you remember? If I were you I'd certainly make friends with your father. You owe him more than an apology. Well, be a good child, love life, and look after Moscow. The nights are getting cooler, please put on something warm when you go up on the roof. Don't see me off, I don't like it."

For several moments, as she leaned over the banister, Polya expected her friend to come up again and embrace her for the last time, but within the minute the running footsteps were silenced, then sprang to life again to melt in the alien rustling noises of the staircase.

Polya managed to run back to the balcony and caught the throb of the started engine. Softly she uttered Varya's name, and thought she saw a handkerchief waved twice in response down below. True to the promise she had given, she fought back the numb feeling of loneliness, then gropingly, without sitting down, she ate something out of a plate, and made ready to go on duty. She did not part with Varya all night: mentally she accompanied her through the dim railway station, and with her arm around her sat beside her for a long time at the open door of the box car, watching the starry glint on the racing rails. Just before daybreak, when she returned from the roof, Polya fell asleep without undressing, and in that brief space Varya left her for good on the westbound road.

2

Unable to resist the sudden impulse Polya ran out into the street first thing in the morning with the intention of returning home no more. After long hesitation between the Enlistment Office and the Komsomol local she chose the latter, because she had made the personal acquaintance of the Secretary there when she had gone to register on her arrival in Moscow. In response to her knock a youthful voice behind the door bade her enter. Polya was in luck—despite the early hour the chief was in his little office, breakfasting out of a paper. He was a very young man in a khaki tunic, not the one she knew, the tall brown-eyed one with a brow on which sat the shadow of state preoccupation, but another, temporarily in charge, smaller in stature and unassuming in manner, with the same dark circles of sleepless nights under the eyes as Polya had, and who answered to the homely name of Sapozhkov.

"Pardon me, but a comrade sat here ..." Polya began disappointedly, ready to beat a retreat.

He cast a quick keen glance at the visitor, then buried himself again in the report, typed out on tissue paper.

"That shows what a rare visitor you are at your local. I've been here for over a week now. I'll just finish reading this report, sit down," he said, and without looking up he handed her the second sandwich across the desk—it had some kind of smoked food in it, judging by the savoury smell. "Go on, eat it while you're waiting, I've already had a bite this morning. But be careful, that fish is awkwardly constructed, it has hooks in it," he went on. "I see what it is. The girl is fed up with sitting at home, she's dying for a real big job—am I right?"

"Uhu," Polya confirmed, astonished at his perspicacity and glad to think that things were not going at all badly for a start.

Polya took a bite at the sandwich and found it much too small; she would rather it were not so tasty.

"Charming, charming," the Secretary said, buried in the report. "Well, how are things down at your place? Had a troublesome night, I daresay? They sure dropped some fire—regular Pompeii."

"Oh, we hardly got any of it this time," Polya said, stealing a glance at the glass of cold tea that stood on the desk.

"That's all right, have it," Sapozhkov read her thoughts with marvellous ease. He moved the tea up to her with his disengaged hand.

Still without looking up, and making energetic notes in the margin of the report, he questioned the visitor as to when and where she was born, who her parents were, and, above all, by exactly what means and resources at her disposal she hoped to squelch Nazi Germany in the shortest possible time. There was no trace of irony or superiority in his voice; on the contrary, it sounded dully matter-of-fact, because dozens of girls called on him every day on the same errand. He complimented her, though, on her knowledge of German and the Morse code with a tapping speed of up to forty signs a minute. In this connection he even asked Polya, in an offhand way, whether she happened to be a mountain-climber, but unfortunately, owing to the absence of any sizeable mountains on the Yenga, a sad gap in Polya's education was revealed.

"You don't have to make excuses, the absence of mountains is not your fault," the Secretary nodded sympathetically as he locked the report away in a drawer. "Well, Vikhrova, your intentions are very praiseworthy. So you are not afraid of death, not the least little bit, eh?"

"The only thing I'm afraid of is an *ignoble* death," Polya said, emphasising the word. More than anything else she feared to cut a silly figure, the way she had done with Varya.

"A very interesting thought, that," the Secretary acquiesced, slightly puckering his brow, "but no doubt you wanted to say that what one should fear most is an ignoble life. It's a bit too early for you and me to be thinking about death. Don't you agree with me?"

"Well, yes. But death too . . ." said Polya.

"I'm very glad that I understood you rightly."

Here Secretary Sapozhkov stepped from behind his desk as if to stretch his legs, but Polya realised only too well that he merely wanted to take a better look at her before making his final decision. Although she tried to hide her feet under the chair, he made a particular note of her shoes, which were much the worse for wear by this time. And suddenly it dawned on her that her dream was dashed, that it had been an unforgivable error on her part to accept refreshments from Sapozhkov, who had been trying to soften the blow of his flat refusal.

"What are you staring at me for?" Polya said hastily, blushing, and glanced despairingly at the glass now drained beyond recall. "You don't read the papers by the looks of it. Come on, shoo me out! They keep coming on and on, they're getting ready to enter the Kremlin, while all we can do is to wave people off. You think I'm a chick who's come to defend the country with its baby wing, but I'm like a mine now, an explosive mine, if you want to know. Do you understand?" This and a good deal more tumbled from her lips in a rush of wasted vehemence.

He had the patience to hear her out.

"If that's how you feel, Vikhrova, I can imagine what an opinion you must have of me. He's fixed himself up with a cushy job in the rear, shuffling papers about for show, and chewing smoked fish while he's at it. But, as you see, I'm doing it without a twinge of conscience. As for the Kremlin, I doubt it—*they*'d have to step over all Russia to do it, and that's much too big a thing for them." He sat down in the armchair facing her, knee to knee. "Well, tell me about yourself now. What have you come to study for?"

"For architect," Polya said miserably with trembling lips.

"There, you see. Can you imagine how much of everything we shall have to build when this war is over? Why, our appetite will be ten times as big then. And we'll have to build beautifully, dash it. People are fed up with these black boxes with unfinished courtyards and rusty stains on the façades. You've got to build so that your work stands for ages, and not just one and a half bricks thick. You fellows had better look out."

"That's what I'm doing," Polya nodded, deciding to get *something* out of Sapozhkov at least. "Maybe you'll fix me up at some munitions factory?"

"What for? We can find you a job all right, if it comes to that, but you've come here to study, haven't you? Don't worry, our summons will find you when you're wanted. In what year are you?"

"It's my first year," Polya said rather uncertainly.

"Fine, so you've got all before you. Isn't it grand to know there are still wastelands in this world that haven't been built over, rivers that haven't been harnessed, steppes that still need planting, and all kinds of hidden treasures waiting to be discovered? I think highly of your profession, although personally I intend to go in for hydraulic engineering—I love the water. I like to tame it, the fat lazy thing, get it worked up to a white frenzy. You don't expect me to sit at this desk for ever. And I must be a poor kind of Secretary if every kid can come and yell at me for being a monster of cruelty because I won't let her go to the front, if you please. Ah, you girls, what a troublesome lot you are!" he said, wagging his head in a manner so rueful and amusing for one of his years that Polya was quite unaware that he had taken her hand in his in a boyish friendly way, just like Rodion. "You know, I think there is nothing in the world more wonderful than the desert. It's got to be absolutely bare, with nothing in it. And I come along with an army of braves, like you, and fill it up chockful, so that it becomes crowded with towns, and trees, and obedient noiseless machines carrying out the orders of life ... my orders, what? It makes you dizzy with joy to think what a tremendous power you've got to pump into Mother Nature, the frowzy slummocky old thing, to make her bring out all her golden keys to you on a platter. 'Come on there, let's have 'em all, what are you hiding there behind your back?' Well, doesn't it make your head go round?"

"It does a bit," Polya said in a fascinated whisper, and all of a sudden she felt so light and easy with this subduer of the untamed elements that she decided to try and worm out of him what she had not had time to get out of Varya. "Well, and what next?"

"What do you mean what next?" the Secretary said with a flick of his eyes.

"I mean, what shall we do next, in a hundred years, when everything has been built, the enemies beaten, and the old world left behind?"

Another girl peeped in at the door, and the Secretary, with a sigh, rose from his chair.

"I'm sorry, Vikhrova, but for the time being I can't reveal that secret of history to you—so far it's one of the great mysteries. Pop in and see me in a hundred years time, then we'll sit down with you and discuss plans for the future at our leisure—I can tell by your eyes that you have no time to spare now. You'll be late for your lecture." He checked her in the doorway, though, with a question as to whether she had any other requests and wishes within the limits of his modest capacities, and his glance slipped down once more to her worn shoes. "Come on, no strangers here."

Polya's heart leapt with sudden hope.

"If I've got to stay here in Moscow I'd very much like to get a place in Red Square for the October parade."

Secretary Sapozhkov glanced at her quickly, and saw such a long-cherished provincial dream shining in her eyes that he did not have the heart to refuse her a second time.

"It's very difficult, getting a ticket for the October parade. I can't promise you anything, Vikhrova," he said, thoughtfully scratching an inkstain on the desk. "I'm not such a powerful wizard as all that, but ... I promise to put a word in for you when I meet the comrades it depends upon. And now, so long."

Following his advice, Polya went in for her studies in good earnest, but academic life at the Institute was at a lowish ebb. The students were busy camouflaging the squares against air attacks, and the teachers, one after the other, joined the home guards. There was talk about the Architectural Institute itself being evacuated. What's more, the Fire-Fighting Service had its headquarters on the ground floor, and these constant reminders of the war distracted the attention of the students from the subjects the professors lectured on none too confidently. The war reports hinted vaguely at the approach of the front, and in this light the absence of letters from her mother could easily be accounted for by the German occupation of the Yenga. Her accumulated anxieties clamoured for an outlet, and while Sapozhkov at the Komsomol local was trying to think up some duties for Polya, Zolotinskaya, who knew everything that was going on at house No. 8a, gave her various errands to perform, such as sending off a soldier's parcel, or standing in the bread queue for the house portress, who had fallen ill. Fatigue saved Polya from herself for a time, but did not give that sense of reassurance and serenity which relief from years of anxious suspicion about her father might have been expected to bring.

When there was no work to do, Polya took up her textbook, but it dropped from her hand, and her eyes closed with fatigue after her all-night duty; suddenly there came that intermediate stage between sleep and wakefulness, when the brain still works, but is no longer controlled by realities or logic. One day she dreamt it was winter with snowflakes spinning about in the air, and she had climbed to the top of a nearby belfry and was looking at her house in Blagoveshchensky Alley, to which she dare not return under pain of death. She was afraid to go there because of the soldiers, who crouched against the wall outside the entrance as if they were not there, and she could not fathom their designs, try as she might. Indeed, no one in the world could read their intentions, because their faces were hidden under deep iron helmets, all except the officer's who wore a winged fascist cap and who had to kill a certain person there. Probably the man the fascist had to kill was that one in the staircase window, who was coming down without a thought, and she couldn't warn him of the danger because she had no voice to shout with, no strength to tear her feet away from the stone they seemed frozen to, no time to run out into the street. She would not have made it in time, anyhow, because the man was coming out of the doorway already, and she saw that it was Gratsiansky, and wanted very much to save him because he was a prominent Soviet professor in spite of all the sorrow he had caused her, but the soldiers were surrounding him, loading their rifles, and in another minute he would be shot, but he didn't care in the least, did Gratsiansky. He even seemed to wink at Polya, as much as to say, you just watch me, you little goose. He winked to the soldiers and showed them something that was hidden in the palm of his hand, and all of a sudden the guard fell back and the officer saluted Gratsiansky, who went about his business. But Polya was curious to know what that business was, and she crept after him from street to street, and suddenly someone hailed her from behind, and she realised that this had been a ruse to get her out of the belfry, and now they were all standing round her, Gratsiansky as well, and this was the end of her.

Polya woke up with a headache, in a clammy perspiration. The bed stood right in the sunshine, and the low autumn sun poured the residue of the day's heat upon her through the balcony opening, while Taisa, loaded with gifts, looked in through the door, panting from the difficult stairs. She deposited her shopping bag by the door and sat down beside Polya, who continued to stare through her aunt into the baffling eyes of Gratsiansky, trying to read in them her doom.

"I thought I'd never get here, you do live high up. It's only when you climb eight flights of stairs that you get to know what a load of sins you carry about with you," Taisa was saying while she was recovering her wind. "Ivan wanted to come with me, but they sent a car for him from the tiptop forest administration," she went on, stroking and caressing her niece. "You're hot, you haven't caught a chill, I hope? What are you keeping your eyes down for, looking away from me? Maybe I've come at the wrong time, old nuisance that I am?"

"Oh, no, Aunt Taisa, I'm so glad," Polya said, feeling quite limp after her interrupted dream.

"You don't look it," Taisa said reprovingly. "At least you might give your aunt a kiss."

"On the contrary, you've come just in time, Aunt Taisa, it's as if you've pulled me away from a well," Polya explained obscurely and gave her a hug. She was grateful to her for having prevented her from making some frightful discovery about Gratsiansky. "Have a rest, get your breath. I'll make the bed myself afterwards."

Unsteadily she crossed over to the table to drink some luke-warm water—it had been standing in the sun too.

"I was so upset that time for Ivan's sake. Fancy saying such a thing about Ivan and Sergei!" Taisa was saying. "We adopted Sergei, but for goodness sake don't let the cat out of the bag, you'll ruin everything. He doesn't remember his home any more or his real name—it's just Sergei Vikhrov, Sergei Vikhrov all the time. Maybe it isn't right by today's measure, but in the old days it was kind o' sinful to drive even a blind pup out o' the house—it's a living creature. In the old days people used to say, you never know who may knock at your door with an infant hand. He may go away, for all you know, and carry your luck away with him in his beggar's bag. That's just it, my dear."

Taisa kept up this patter the while she took her gifts out of the shopping bag and set them out in their proper places, so that they would keep longer without getting spoilt. Everything about her just then had a restful effect on Polya—the musical lilt of her speech, the steady equable light in her eyes, like that of a sunless noonday, even the homely, wormwoody smell of unused clothes kept until needed under lock and key. Behind her caution, however, behind the evasive tones in which she spoke about Sergei's birth, Polya felt the presence of another iron door with another secret behind it. And then, trembling with fear lest she touch something forbidden, Polya followed her aunt down into the dank dark cellar of an old man's life story—for so does it appear to the serene soul of a child, although that man were her own father.

What she heard frightened Polya, because the direct logic of it made her shift to her mother what she had thought to be her father's blame for the break-up of the family.

3

Taisa had so few personal reminiscences of her own that she filled all the vacant spaces in her memory with events from other people's lives. Her story began with the young Vikhrovs leaving the forestry division for the capital, a journey which was marked by the loss of all their luggage, so that they had to provide themselves anew with everything except books. Unexpectedly, Vikhrov's successful book brought money too, fabulous money for those days, if measured by the number of naughts.

Because all the cares of the new household had fallen upon her shoulders, Taisa remembered exactly how long it had taken them to get new linen, and how she had painted the hospital-type bedsteads which they had bought on the cheap, and how much they had paid the cabinet-maker's widow for an unfinished sideboard with fancy carvings, which, by the way, had a habit of throwing open its doors in the middle of the night with such a ghostly and mournful sigh that Lenochka would wake up with a thumping heart and wait for something to happen. All the five years they had been living together the Vikhrovs had been intending to call a man in to mend it, because it was a pity to spoil a good thing by tinkering with it yourself, but after Lenochka had run away there wasn't any need for it, as the other members of the family were exceptionally sound sleepers. That perhaps was the only detail of the past which the mother had told the daughter in a light-hearted minute.

At the beginning it did Taisa's heart good to see how zealously her sister-in-law was building their nest. She put all the experience of her housekeeping with the Sapegins into the furnishing of the two rooms in the old wing of the Institute; they received the third room after the child was born. Lenochka was much more cheerful in the new place, away from the hateful Yenga. She simply had no time to brood, because no matter how busy you were kept there was always some nook or cranny in the nest where you could stick another feather. She wanted to lay in a store of firewood and food, to lock herself in and not have to leave the house, to have money to last a long time; Ivan even approved these domestic habits of the home-bird and a thrift verging on stinginess, never suspecting their origin; actually, they were preparations for a long siege. Every time he came home from work he found some cosy novelty that added to the family sense of well-being in the shape of chintz curtains or a bunch of maple leaves in an earthenware jug mixed with flowering dogwood, and Lenochka's humming little song, an elusive melody without words, just like a forest bird's. He was at his creative best at that period. The rough copy of his new book lay on the kitchen table, which served as his writing desk. And if they did not go to the cinema in the evening or go and have Russian pie with a colleague, Ivan would do some carpentry job or, more willingly, read out loud some of the time-tested classics of the duller kind, the more calorific, as he expressed it, punctuated with intervals for expressing delight or making explanatory comments. Thus was erected that solid rock-built domestic base—an object of perhaps premature derision—whence many a former scholar of Vikhrov's type rose to the heights of their science without fear of their feet sinking in the slough of life's petty cares. In a word, all the events of a rather humdrum professorial life could easily be envisaged forty years ahead. We see balsamines blossoming on the window-sills, the youngest daughter babbling in the sunlight on the floor, and Vikhrov calling his wife now dovey, now mother for the sake of upholding the dignity of the domestic establishment. And so it would go on until the time when a numerous and moderately sobbing offspring would bury the toilers side by side in a Moscow cemetery.

In Moscow too Lenochka was the same shy timorous creature of the Yenga; and like many of his contemporaries, Vikhrov had every opportunity of preserving her in that primitive state, so convenient for housekeeping purposes, till the end of her days, her education confined to a wartime provincial course in medical-nurse training. However, Vikhrov spent all the leisure hours of their first years in broadening her horizon, particularly awakening in her a sense of human dignity. And even if he had foreseen the risk he was exposing their precarious domestic happiness to, he would still not have been able to suppress the innate pedagogical feeling of being a debtor towards everyone who knew less about the surrounding world than he did. He even contrived to make the entertainments of city life—none too frequent on account of their living so far away from the theatres and museums—auxiliary institutions of his domestic university. Lenochka, of course, never scaled the gleaming summits of culture, but from the heights which she did attain, the world's pattern, which looked so confused at close quarters, became noticeably simpler and more intelligible. Deep down in a gorge, through a mist of centuries, as it were, there glimmered the hard-trodden road of humanity, all in loops of errors and delusions; like the pillar of fire in the biblical wilderness, it was lured on by the dream of perfect justice and bliss, without which it would long since have been reduced to a swarm of wretched ruthless insects. While he was at it, Vikhrov tried to instil in his pupil the idea of life's sacredness and the means by which people's devious wanderings in search of food and joys could be reduced; he emphasised also that the sorrows of the individual were as nothing compared to the happiness of the many, and its good was sacriligious outside the good of the overwhelming majority. Truth to tell, Vikhrov did much better at forestry lectures. It was rather fortunate that Gratsiansky never attended any of his readings. He would certainly have ridiculed his historical views mercilessly, especially his provincial awe at the toll which human progress took in suffering.

As soon as the ladies began to yawn, Vikhrov would whip up their flagging interest with historical pictures, such as the death of the beautiful Hypatia, torn limb from limb by the Alexandrian monks, or the hundred and fifty thousand blinded Bulgarians who trudged home from their Byzantine captivity, or the Mongol *batyr* Jamugu, who directed his own slow execution in the presence of Genghiz Khan,* often adding such lurid details of his own invention that Taisa's knitting would drop from her hands and the pupils of Lenochka's eyes would darken; the more peaceful a person is the more is he given to the reading of sensational reports. The next morning most of this faded out of the untrained memory of Vikhrov's wife, but the work of the mind and heart, once performed, is never lost. Thanks to those evening sessions Lenochka developed such a taste for reading that but for Taisa the housekeeping would have been sadly neglected. She was seized with an insatiable thirst for knowledge, which was only natural after so long a blindness. Whereas at first books merely helped her to beguile the time, by the end of the second year she had learned to appreciate them for the mental work which had to be done on them in order to get at the honey they contained. Incident-ally, the classics, richly represented in Vikhrov's library, were so unlike the translated novels in Sapegin's manor—works "on the life of flies", as she once called them, and her husband was pleased to note her development and enlightenment. Now, when reading books, Lenochka experienced the envious curiosity of a beggar girl peeping in at strange people through a brightly lit window from the inclement gloom. The thoughts of the characters were always beyond her, but the mere sound of their speeches was mysteriously attuned to the voices that sounded within her. Suddenly it was revealed to her that all the good books spoke about the same thing, about the fellow-travellers on the great road of life, she herself among them. Nay more, there was not a book but contained some reference to her own private thoughts and even-growing doubts. Probably schoolchildren felt the same way when they discovered the dot of their own home village on the outspread map of the world.

---

* The ghastly procedure is described by Rashid-ad-din.—*Tr.*

It appeared that long before Lenochka's birth people had known the clinics of her mental ailment, which consisted of an inexorable need to love, to rejoice, to act. More, the authors of the books she had read knew every detail of her intimate life with the man who had become her saviour, her tutor, and ultimately her husband in consideration of the trouble he had gone to. They saw right through her pathetic awkward wiles, which bade fair to become a perpetual lie from which not even death could deliver her, not if she were laid together with Vikhrov under the same stone; and, of course, they all guessed that she had not loved him from the start. This constant element of suspicious restraint in his wife's character, which worried Vikhrov so much, was aggravated by an inexplicably painful susceptibility to each and every fact of life, even of the most innocuous kind. Every contact left a searing lingering mark upon her. Her disease entered upon a new phase, and that at a time when Taisa believed that all that was lacking for complete happiness were some runners to be knitted for the what-not and some long-haired composers or grown-over ponds in autumn parks to be fitted into the cheap ready-made frames which had been bought long ago.

"At first she seemed a bit better, then it came over her again. She ate her heart out, did nothing about the house. Wandered about the place, all adaze with reading, and thin as a flower stalk. She never went out, just peeped through the curtains once in a while. Ivan would ask her, tell me what you want, I'll get it for you from across the seas, but she just patted his cheek and shook her head with a guilty sort o' smile. He took her all the way down to the Caucasus to take her out of herself, but it wasn't any good. He's had in no end o' doctors; one of 'em he'd be helping on with his coat while another would be knocking at the door. Some of 'em were pretty sniffy, I might tell you. One says, 'in the old days the rich used to take such as she to Egypt for a hot sand cure'—would you believe it! 'But seeing as we're now having happiness for all,' he says, 'maybe your wife'll come round with a few days in bed.' And Ivan's lips would tremble, the while he fussed about and bowed 'em out. And then I began to notice that Lenochka was getting more shivery than ever...." Taisa omitted to mention in her reminiscences that all this coincided with the last months of her sister-in-law's pregnancy.

Lenochka spent the next year in a mute standstill flight from her own numb anguish, and all the time there glimmered dimly in her mind a single avenue of escape, a tiny eyehole through which she would never be able to thread herself without drawing blood. Peering through this slit she saw a road running out into the distance with gay beautiful people upon it, and she was walking among them, light, erect, free from humiliating anxieties, from the constant expectation of moral exposure, from her own self. She would wake up in the middle of the night, not daring to move her shoulder lest she awaken her husband who slept at her side, and listen to the disturbing whistles of the locomotives from the circuit railway nearby, which seemed to be luring her away. It was no longer a nervous consciousness of having concealed the fact that she belonged to the overthrown regime that tormented her now, but a harrowing conviction that everyone around guessed what a terrible price she was paying for her bread, for her peace, for her more than modest clothes, for her security from imaginary ghosts. A naturally sensitive skin and impressionable mind tended to heighten in her that sense of constant chilling nakedness. An intent look would throw her off her balance, even if it was from her daughter on her lap; her daughter made her feel more ashamed than anyone else! To crown all Taisa happened to mention the popular belief that children born out of a loveless marriage were unhappy. The sad end was drawing near.

During the last few years preceding the catastrophe the Vikhrovs had practically no visitors except for a few students, who were in love with their teacher because of his versatile knowledge and the inextinguishable ardour of his soul, which made them forget the difference in their ages. The Russian forest, allegiance to which they had all sworn as to a part of their homeland, was an inexhaustible subject of discussion, and judging by the grateful appreciation expressed by former students in their letters to their teacher, which continued to come in from all over in the course of the next quarter of a century, many of their books, which subsequently won public recognition, were conceived at these little forestry assemblies. Almost like Kalina's honey had been for Vikhrov, the frugal Vikhrovs' tea, often without sugar, remained a sweet unforgettable memory for those young people. It was served by Taisa in prodigious quantities—none of this young undergraduates' set was acquainted with the professor's wife. Judging by the photograph on the host's desk she was a jolly sort and a good looker, too, a fact, which, contrasted with her husband's lameness and plain looks, called forth some playful though harmless comment.

4

Only one man, a last-year student and Vikhrov's favourite pupil, Pavel Osminov, knew about his unhappy domestic life. A native of the rugged Vaga, he bore the stamp of his origin upon him; he was a lean, sociable man with a peculiar northern accent and the keen black eyes of a hunter. He was one of those gifted men who go in for science not so much to acquire knowledge, as to get more specific information on what they had seemingly known since the day they were born. He had a flair for grasping things quickly, and could not only pass a shrewd opinion on quantum mechanics, which was then the vogue, or the forestry heresies of Tulyakov, but also revealed an intimate knowledge of the secret workings of the feminine heart. Vikhrov liked him for his devotion to the forest, and a no less attractive quality of never, throughout his ascent of the social ladder, forgetting his word-bound kinsfolk of the Shenkursk forest country. He was an honest and, apparently, a courageous man, for he was the only one who had had the pluck to dedicate his first thin book to appear in print to Vikhrov at a time when the latter's persecution by Gratsiansky was at its remorseless height. He was a more frequent visitor at the Vikhrovs than any of the others, and often came in the host's absence; it is worthy of note that he was the only person to whom Lenochka could bring herself to confide her most secret doubts. True, she did this in a half-humorous way, pretending to be speaking for a non-existent girl friend, yet during their talks her whole perturbed inner self stood so patently revealed that his attitude towards Vikhrov's wife was somewhat warmer and more friendly than was permissible in an intimate and favourite pupil. Possibly he had something to do with the catastrophe that followed, but the very fact that both the sister and brother blamed him alone for all their troubles at first, goes to show how far they were from understanding the true origin of Lenochka's malady.

Returning home earlier than usual one day, Vikhrov let himself in with his latch key, and, seeing Osminov's coat on the hall stand, he lingered in the passage for some reason without taking his things off. Sounds of lively conversation, not the first of its kind, judging by its character, issued from his little study. It was not Vikhrov's way to eavesdrop outside the door, but he suddenly felt a tingling curiosity about the too obviously imaginary girl friend they were talking about in there. His sister was out, and though the talk was carried on in undertones, he was able by cupping his hand to his ear, standing up on tiptoes and slightly craning his neck, to catch everything they were saying.

"I've tried to tell her time and again, but it's no use," Lenochka said, replying to a tactical remark of Osminov's about it being her direct duty to help her friend out. "But how, how can you save a person in her position? Besides, there are aggravating circumstances in her case in the shape of a child."

"She cannot be hinting at Polya, surely ... and to a stranger too?" Vikhrov wondered, and leaning forward still more, he absently straightened the turned up corner of the rug with his lame foot.

"No, I just cannot approve the suicidal thoughts of your friend. Only a completely frustrated personality can contemplate such a thing," Osminov boomed, and began to knock his pipe out—against the edge of the desk, to judge by the sound. "I can't believe that a young interesting woman can have nothing left in her soul but ashes."

"Oh, but my friend admits that she's a shallow person," Lenochka broke in as if inviting a vehement refutal. "The thing is, a flute plays to everyone who puts his lips to it, Osminov. And altogether you're a credulous inexperienced child for all that frightful forest beard of yours. No, something else is needed here, something strong ... I don't know myself yet what."

H'm, they're getting along like a house on fire. She never talks to *me* about death. Kind of hinting he should go ahead and save her and not be shy about it, for he'd get his reward. Things have gone rather far, I see—Vikhrov, with flaming ears, was thinking. The fact that in spite of their obvious spiritual intimacy they addressed each other formally was somewhat comforting though.

"It's very difficult for me to prescribe a remedy for your absent friend," Osminov began in a roundabout way, "but I had formed a different opinion of her. I gather from what you said that she is good, kind-hearted, and fairly intelligent, if she is able to read the author's motives behind the deeds of book characters. I believe she has the makings of a good citizen, because if she hadn't she would not feel the need to be honester and cleaner. She is also strong, if, as you say, she is not afraid of hard work and poor living. And, lastly, she is young, consequently, she has time in which to rectify her mistakes," the words escaped him with perhaps too strong an emphasis, a fact that was immediately construed by Vikhrov as the trick of an experienced lady-killer.

"But advise her when next you see her to learn to quench her thirst from the original springs of life and not from books; in my opinion even the best of them express only a private point of view and deal only with a limited area of life. There hasn't been a mirror yet that fully reflected the whole world." He started to relight his pipe, which stubbornly resisted his efforts, judging by the number of matches he used. "Does your friend's husband know that she is unhappy with him?"

"I don't think so," Lenochka said doubtfully, shaking her head. "He is a very strong man, obsessed by his work ... and everything in the world is just food for his mind, merely material to support his idea. It simply doesn't occur to him that such"—a note of irony had crept into her voice—"such a round-the-clock care of a person, of his wife, may embarrass her."

"You mean," Osminov said, playing up to her a bit crudely, "that the cat does not ask the mouse he has swallowed whether it feels happy now, so safe, snug and warm inside him? Do I understand you correctly?"

"Go on, kick him out, the lame devil, pry him loose!" Vikhrov thought with a twisted smile, making an involuntary gesture as if to help him with it.

"It's very funny, but ... it isn't true," Lenochka stood up for her husband, but her voice again sounded unfamiliar to him, a stranger's voice. "On the contrary, my friend told me she had never met a fairer, more generous-hearted man. But he has shouldered such a heavy stone that other people's lighter burdens are simply unworthy of his attention."

"In that case allow me to speak my mind more fully, because, from what you have told me, I have been able to form a vivid idea of the man," Osminov said, throwing off all pretence. "I think him a distinguished specimen of that noble human brand whose fine qualities come out only gradually, and whose attractions grow with the years, and since you have admitted from the outset...."

Vikhrov listened to all this as he toyed with the objects on the pier-table, which had lost for him all shape, weight and purpose. He was not insulted, he was frightened by the note of respectful animosity in Lenochka's voice and the fact that she had let it escape her while discussing him with a stranger, most important of all with a man more attractive than he was; he would have liked to think that she was expressing her revulsion at their unfortunate marriage rather than hatred of himself. After all, he had tried to anticipate her every wish. Naturally, owing to the despotic haste with which he had tried to pass on to her the weightless wealth of knowledge amassed by dint of hard work, her individuality to some extent had become submerged in his— that was a fact, and so this, on her part, was a legitimate revolt. Ah, well, under her outer covering of apathy and reserve, he had always felt in Lenochka the taut wound-up spring that was ever ready to uncoil, and when that happened it was bound to hurt the person who was holding it.

Most opportunely, Vikhrov glanced at himself in the flecked tarnished mirror and realised that it would not do to appear before the young people the way he was. On the one hand, he had no grounds for bursting in upon them, say, with a kitchen knife, on the other he was not obliged to listen to himself being discussed by a man he had been imprudent enough to warm at the domestic hearth. Therefore, noiselessly, Vikhrov went back into the street to take an airing and put his face and feelings in order. The weather was just right—a dense March twilight with the year's last snow-drift swirling around the fences in furious eddies.

It was only a question of time now when the inevitable storm would break. So far, apparently, Lenochka had neither plans nor the will to take the decisive step. It took two events, following one upon the other, to help her make up her mind. Early in April, when there was a touch of spring in the air, Vikhrov took his wife to an organ recital at the Conservatoire—an outstanding event even in the brilliant workaday life of musical Moscow. The celebrity from Germany proved to be a thickset stoop-shouldered old man with a leonine mane, a man built specially, it seemed, to command that machine of sounds. At last, Lenochka was to hear in action that mysterious conglomeration of singing wood and silvery pipes which occupied the whole wall. During the first part of the recital the organist played the C-Minor Fugue, the G-Major Fantasia and four Choral Preludes by Bach.

She did not know, and did not care who had composed those long-drawn compelling meditations on things so remote from the aspirations of the present age; the enduring power of music lies precisely in the fact that everyone, within the bounds of his own experience, reads his own meaning into the musical line. Lenochka's attention was suddenly drawn to a reed which began to sing over the water, and through the deep modulated drone, one could see what a multitude of reeds there was out there.

Then a soft murmurous wind passed overhead, making them bow to it, and children began to sing with them, and moved by an overmastering impulse, the surrounding walls, the famous oval portraits, and she herself, every tingling drop of blood in her, joined in the hymn. It was as if someone big and sorrowing had passed by her in quest of the most important thing of all, but had not found it, and spread his hands in a stately gesture of grief, then glanced up at the swollen blue above him, but there, too, it was nowhere to be found. And then everything—the children, the wind—raced across the meadow, while a cloud, upreared with curiosity in the blue heights, followed them towards a placid round little lake in which shone a reflection of someone whose presence inspired delight and awe, and then rings appeared from the first drops, and puckered the mirror-like surface. Presently the sky poured down, and the children and the wind stood subdued in the sheets of rain, not understanding yet what all this meant. And the flowers were already blossoming all round, and the first long-toothed beast, not quite finished yet, passed slightly to one side, but did not touch anybody, because he did not know yet either what he was for. Then a slanting hazy beam of light stabbed the thickened, intolerably stuffy air and fell upon Lenochka's face, leaving in her a particle of grateful coolness.

She leaned back in her seat, her face glowing, her eyes closed. What she had just heard was about her too.

"Want a sweet?" Vikhrov asked at her side. "I have some peppermints, they're refreshing."

"No, thanks. I feel so good. . . ."

"Did you notice that lovely passage in the lower scale? By the way, do you know that some organists take their boots off when they play? It's supposed to give them a better feel of the pedal."

He fell silent, and Lenochka was beginning to hope that he would leave her alone now. However, taking advantage of his wife's temporary good humour, Vikhrov addressed himself to her ear, into which he whispered scraps of information about the composer and the social significance of the works that were being performed, and what the classics of Marxism thought about music, without which knowledge, he was sincerely convinced, no cultured person could derive true enjoyment from art. As usual, he had done some reading up for the occasion, and gave a brief outline of Bach's birth and parentage and the main points of his biography, enlarging somewhat on the details of his Dresden tournament with the organist Marchand, who ran away, terrified by his formidable opponent.

"Another thing—notice what powerful means of seduction the church disposed of only quite recently. Imagine the gloomy pointed arches and vaulting of Early Gothic, and you will feel this medieval choral sinking into your soul, striking roots and becoming an everlasting part of it. That's why I contend that you cannot oust the survivals of the past with today's marching songs—you can only do it with works of genuine art, don't you see? Hence. . . ."

"Please, Ivan, stop it," Lenochka said.

"But this is something that every thinking person should know, my dear."

"For God's sake, you'll make me scream!" his wife said in a sibilant whisper, and her husband shrank, crushed by that tone of deep-seated irritation.

During the latter part of the recital, however, something prevented her from giving herself up to the music. It may have been the absence of a support at the back of her head, or the overpowering smell of perfume coming from the dyed blonde in front of her. The odd feeling of uneasiness did not leave her throughout the performance of the F-Major Italian Concerto; only snatches of it reached her through a growing sense of almost physical discomfort. She sat up with annoyance and looked round—a man in the guests' box on her left was staring at her. With an unconscious gesture she patted her hair and the turn-down collar of her dress, but he was still staring; apparently, he knew something about her. He did not look more than forty-five, but his head was almost white; she remembered no other details except a quizzical gleam in his slightly narrowed eyes and a scar on his temple which was clearly discernible at the twenty paces that separated them. He looked a scholar, like her husband, only of some other all-transcending human science, and his scrutiny was disconcerting—it was as if he knew how, that very morning, almost the moment she awoke, she had tried to lull her husband's possible suspicions by a deceptive show of meekness. She felt altogether ill at ease when the man smiled faintly and pointed to Vikhrov with a rather familiar motion of his head.

"Take me down to the bar, Ivan," she said, feeling the strength ebbing out of her. "I want a drink. I don't feel well."

"Hadn't we better wait until the interval?"

But already she was running down the aisle, followed by hissing protests, when, to her horror, she saw out of the corner of her eye that the man in the box had got up, too. He came into the bar half a minute after they did, and sat down at a distant table. While she was powdering her face, dabbing the puff just any-where, she saw him in her little mirror, sipping his Narzan behind her back, his head lowered with an air of patient ironic expec-tation. Thereupon, pleading dizziness, Lenochka started home in a hurry, but her pursuer followed them down into the vestibule, and suddenly, going close up to Vikhrov, he asked him in a tone of reproach whether he was not ashamed of himself, giving him-self such airs in front of old friends.

"I've been trailing after you all through the interval, waving greetings to your wife, and you never gave me a glance, not even out of mere jealousy, you old image! Come on, introduce me to your wife!"

"Valery!" Vikhrov cried out in a boyish falsetto, throwing him-self upon his neck. Lenochka, limp and weak from the sudden release, saw tears in her husband's eyes.

It was a reunion of old friends, in the true Russian style, and the cloak-room attendants, who had been idly wagging tongues, were treated to the entertaining spectacle of two top-level com-rades slapping each other's backs, stepping aside to look at each other, and then starting all over again to rumple each other's new expensive jackets.

"Why the dickens didn't you let me know you were in Mos-cow?" Vikhrov kept rebuking him after he had introduced him to Lenochka.

"I thought you were still ensconced at the forest range, writ-ing those challenging books of yours ... none too successfully, I hear. I read Alexander's attempts to bring you to your senses, yes I did," Valery said, searching his friend's face.

"Did you run through the book yourself, at least?"

Valery took his time answering.

"It's too thick, old chap, I didn't have time to finish it."

Vikhrov chewed his moustaches. What could he expect of others when even Valery spoke about his work with such restraint.

"Yes, I must have made a bloomer," he said evasively, hesitat-ing to tell his friend there and then about the forest struggle, which had been raging for so long. "I'm afraid I over-reached myself, wrong-headed zeal, you know. Anyway, what are you doing now, have you come for long?"

"No, you tell me about yourself first, I'm the elder," Valery insisted half-jokingly.

Since the events of so many years could not be squeezed into as many words, and Vikhrov lived too far out in the suburbs to go there at that hour, Valery insisted on their going to his hotel, all the more that he was expecting an important phone call that night. His car was waiting outside the Conservatoire. And although Lenochka could barely stand on her feet, she accepted the invitation in order to prolong the thoughtless joy of at least temporary release from her misery.

"Excuse me, Ivan, but I don't think you were right to leave Alexander's vicious attack go unanswered," Valery said in the car. "There's a good deal of baited demagogy in his leftism, especially in that idea of his about retarding the process of crystallisation in the molten torrent of the revolution, whose business is to flow and burn—remember? I've even memorised one particularly dubious phrase of his: 'When the lava cools, its crevices become a breeding place not only for beautiful flowers, fruit trees, and useful insects, but also for the microbes of ancient passions, which have often destroyed the greatest civilisations.' You can't build a cottage, or gather a harvest on flaming lava, though. I don't trust those men who claim a monopoly of speaking in the name of the people by right of strong vocal chords. Our people, like all other peoples, want peace and quiet above all. In a word, Alexander's criticism struck me as being slippery and not impartial, but you were silent, and the ordinary reader got the impression that you were trying to dodge the issue and keep out of the big fight."

"But that's a job for the police, to protect the work-place of law-abiding citizens against troublesome characters," Ivan said sharply. "I'm too busy, I've got my hands full."

"I got your book after I read his article. You were right to raise the subject, and chose your time well too. As for that rather unusual digression at the beginning of the third chapter concerning the winter forest, it just asks to go into a school-reader. I was sitting under an awning at the time in a fairly hot country, and it was like a sudden handful of Russian snow sent from home. I kept it in my heart for a long time, Ivan."

"Until it melted?" Ivan said with a wry smile. "Don't be sore, I'm just letting off steam. The trouble is, Gratsiansky's regular massage has raised a rather painful blister on the neck. So there was something in the book you did like?"

350

"It's a useful book, and I read it through at a single sitting," Valery said, this time in a grave tone. "I don't agree with Gratsiansky, although, I must admit, your ideas are pitched a bit too high."

Vikhrov got excited.

"I'm only a woodsman, in this case just the hand of a manometer on a locomotive boiler, but I daren't lie, because the engine-driver looks at me when he's taking an incline or picking up speed. But you can easily chuck that dreary instrument into the ditch and put another in its place, a bright nickel-plated one with its hand permanently riveted at the degree of optimism, like Gratsiansky."

"All right, don't jump down my throat," laughed Valery. "Do you see much of him?"

"He calls once in a while, but he doesn't invite me to his place. His mother is not exactly an agreeable person. You ought to remember her from St. Petersburg days—a black old woman with a lorgnette."

"Why, of course. Is he married?"

"I don't think there's anyone in Moscow who knows such details."

Lenochka said nothing all the way; she had heard a good deal about Valery from her husband, but had never seen men of his calibre at close quarters. With a dry click at the floors, the lift raised them to the top of an austere unlived-in looking building with a military janitor at the door. The official appointments of the place, from the silk curtains and bevel-edged mirrors between the windows to the trolley with the cold and tasteless food on it did not harmonise somehow either with Valery's engaging simplicity or a passing ironic remark of his concerning the blessings of a diplomatic life. The things around him, some of them even gilt, were to him the inevitable stock-in-trade of his profession, like a scalpel or a trowel to someone else, and Lenochka thought that a peasant's hut with its poor utensils could be a similar tool for doing big things. This thought, during the last few days, had been occupying her mind to the exclusion of all else.

"Why, isn't your family here," Lenochka murmured, looking round the lit-up suite of spotless rooms with its furniture upholstered in damask.

"My family lives in Leningrad, I have my flat there. I'm just staying here between one foreign trip and another. You can't very well drag your children about with you all over the world.

If I settle down somewhere more securely, then it'll be different," he hinted as he poured wine out in the glasses, and threw a glance at the telephone. "I only have a son, though, and an old aunt, almost like you. Don't you remember meeting her once, Ivan, as we were coming out of the Institute, seventeen years ago, and she called me by my real name—surely you haven't forgotten?"

"Is he a big boy?" Lenochka inserted, feeling sorry for him.

"He just turned eight today." Valery fell silent as he poured the wine out, and the dark trickle from the bottle stopped for a moment while he mentally bade good night to his son. "If I have time, I'll drop in to see them on my way back. I'm living a life of luxury, as you see, Ivan—banquets, apartments, bowing and scraping ... the most likely-looking sharks in tailcoats and elderly sirens naked to the waist."

"That'll do for me, I hardly drink anything," Vikhrov said, arresting his hand in the act of filling his glass. Lenochka was listening with rapt attention. "Now, tell me more about the kind of people you meet—I bet you have met kings too, eh? How are they getting on there, what are they doing?"

They drank to sons and descendants and wished them a happier life in a cleaner world.

"I've not met any kings yet. It's not a question of kings these days," Valery said musingly as he set his glass down, then abruptly changed the subject. "What's your own opinion about that comrade?"

"Who do you mean?"

"Your critic, Alexander Gratsiansky. Tell me, is he an honest man?"

"Rather an unhappy man, I should say. I'm afraid that although he's a rising star, he's a hopelessly barren one. You remember Pharaoh's dream about the seven lean cows?"

Valery let the remark drift past his ears.

"From what I read in the newspapers you were not the only one he attacked."

"His first act was to bring down Tulyakov. That was how he made a name for himself. If you've been following our affairs, you will have noticed that he has never made any constructive suggestions in any way useful to forest interests. One thing is certain, that citizen will never go to the scaffold for his convictions!"

"A fluid that takes the form of any vessel it's poured into—is that it?"

"Well, yes ... but I would add that that fluid is the hydro-fluoric acid of so-called scepsis, which corrodes the very glass that contains it. It will eat it away and leak out to the last drop. You see, their own sterility has always served failures as a magnifying glass through which they examine the successes of their contemporaries. Alexander would have done the same thing in any field, he would slake the thirst of perpetual negation. I think that's the reason why that book of his about the pre-revolutionary youth was a flop. Mind you, he spent a whole year in the archives."

"I never heard of that. I suppose he wanted to make up for that ridiculous Young Russia adventure of his, you remember?" Valery said with a fresh note of interest in his voice. "I missed that book. When did it come out?"

"It was never printed. Our historian switched over to forest statistics," Vikhrov said, then suddenly wilted. "I'm sorry, Valery, I believe I've begun to settle personal scores with him. At any rate, he's an interesting speaker, and one who wields a sharp pen at that ... a gifted and modest man. The other day he refused a rather flattering post."

"Perhaps he was afraid of the too close public attention which it involved?" Valery said, giving Vikhrov time to digest this, but the latter said nothing. "Let me explain the reasons for my curiosity. Just now you asked me about the meetings I had had with people abroad, and that reminded me of one very odd one." And he told Ivan about a quite ordinary little adventure such as frequently occurred in the lives of the Soviet personnel abroad.

The scene was the sea front of a quiet little Italian town where Valery was spending a three-day recess in the work of a current international conference. He was beguiling the time until lunch in a deck-chair—as it happened, with Vikhrov's book in his lap—watching the gay figures on the dazzling noonday beach in the distance. The shouts of the children, the boom of the surf, the rustling of the palms overhead, and all the other sounds customary to a seaside resort, swam in upon the fatigue of prolix and useless debates. Somewhere behind his back the shingles crunched and there appeared before Valery a dried-up little old man of highly respectable appearance in a light suit, which, but for the frayed sleeves, was as neat as if it had just come straight from the cleaners. He was not selling anything, he did not ask for money or sympathy, as one might have expected, but looked with that long reminding look that invites identification. Valery made a gesture of impatience and annoyance. At that the old gentleman touched the rim of his straw hat with two fingers in military fashion, and amiably enquired whether it was not Mr. Krainov that he had the honour of addressing; obviously, the prominent Russian Bolshevik had already attracted notice in the town. The question had been put in French, without any accent, so that Valery, at the moment, had no helpful signs other than the exasperatingly familiar and compelling gaze; the old man seemed to be putting eyes and will into the very brain of his paralysed victim. He expressed his satisfaction at the fine weather and was pleased to note that the perturbations of youth had in no visible way affected Mr. Krainov's health and blooming looks. "Will you please convey my compliments and best wishes to Mr. Gratsiansky, should you chance to meet him. A very versatile ... though somewhat sportive young man. Yes, unfortunately it's me, that very same one ..." he ruefully admitted, this time in Russian, to his dumbfounded companion. *"Tout passe, tout casse, tout lasse,"* he added, and with a frivolous gesture, he walked away with the shaky gait that bespoke both the infirmity of age and the disappointments of the émigré years.

"And who do you think it was? You'll never guess—Chandvetsky!"

There was such a crushing force in the name, that although Vikhrov continued to look at his friend, he saw something quite different through him. There rose to his mind the image of a lieutenant-colonel of the gendarmes, already then a man of no youthful age—rumoured to be a favourite of Stolypin, and, after him, the cleverest man in the camp of reaction. Vikhrov could see him, rheumatic fingers interlocked on the large bare desk, drawling something in a listless jaded voice about the biological inequality of the individuals, and consequently, the immutability of the established laws of human society—about the abyss into which Russia was being drawn by the too ardent youth, who needed strict fatherly guidance, and something more in the same vein, which roused a furious opposition in one's soul. "You want to make life sterile-clean, Mr. Vikhrov, but absolutely pure elements exist only in the retorts of the chemists and often cost society a price that makes them prohibitive for general consumption. Aren't you afraid of the high cost?" he murmured with the air of a bored tempter, and once again, at the height of the interrogation, Vikhrov broke imaginary pencils out of the bronze holder in front of him.

"What a memory!" he said with surprise and loathing. "And so many of us fellows passed through his hands! Just a minute, though, wasn't he a thickset sturdily built man?"

"He must have shrunk in his old age, but that's not the point, old chap. I remember you writing me on the Yenisei that the same officer who had examined you also examined Andrei Teplov and..."—he named a man known to all the country, who now worked in the Far East. "That means he had a tremendous choice. Then what made him remember Alexander Gratsiansky of all men, the one who got off lightest of all for his criminal connection with me?"

"You're wrong, Valery," Vikhrov said, standing up stoutly for his enemy. "If there were the least grounds for thinking the awful thing you've just hinted at, what sense was there in Chandvetsky giving his own people away? The gendarme simply recognised you, it stirred up the dregs again, and he just couldn't resist the temptation of throwing a handful of sand into our sliding pistons, which he hates so much. He could have done the same thing by writing an anonymous letter to you or me, calculating that it would be read in the proper quarters before it reached its addressee. He could have just dropped a hint, damn it, or a mere sideways glance would have done the trick just as well ... and any simple-minded investigator would finish the job for him. To make it look plausible he chose the most vulnerable of our Musketeers. If you ask me it was sheer impotent malice, which, luckily, only burns out the spot on which it burns itself."

"You may be right," Valery said after some hesitation and resumed the duties of hospitable host.

Lenochka knew too little about Gratsiansky to take part in the conversation, but after the manner of people with a troubled conscience, who immediately try on the cap of other people's judgements and opinions, she was appalled at the thought of so old an offence being able to rouse suspicions after the lapse of so many years. Even when the conversation touched on Valery's meetings with Western intellectuals, she managed to find something that directly applied to her.

"I have an impression," Valery said, "that many people in Europe are beginning to realise the inevitability of social changes —naturally, this realisation will be strengthened in the course of time under the influence of facts. These include some of the people who, without having ever directly belonged to the bourgeoisie, have to a certain extent been making their living out of the calamities of war, out of the humility of human want, out of the ignorance of their neighbours, their tragic disunity, if you like. There are lots of herbs on the human meadow, which do not clutch and throttle their victims the way the big parasites do, but touch the roots of a neighbour lightly with their suckers. What's that thing called ... I'm beginning to forget my botany?"

"*Melampyrum nemorosum*—cow-wheat," Vikhrov prompted, very pleased that his friend was still thinking in terms of their common science, although he had left the forest. "The same thing is done by the whole family of *Rhinantus apterus*, the fig-wort."

"That's it, the fig-wort," Valery said, pouncing on the word as if it were a lucky find. "The trouble is that the real thinking people often get to the truth on foot or on ancient bicycles, although we have long had high-speed transport into the morrow. You're not bored, are you?" he suddenly turned to Lenochka.

"On the contrary, I'm trying not to miss a word," she said, and blushed at being caught out in her thoughts.

"One noted physicist, for instance, let me into the secret of his home-made discovery that social relations in human society were bound to change with its numerical growth, which demanded a more complex economic structure. He even acceded that only under communism would his science get the opportunity for unlimited research, but he wanted that to happen later, when he wouldn't be here. They're held by fear of losing their imaginary liberties. It's like parting with an old family sofa—you hate doing it even though it is prickly and has unpleasant tenants in the cracks, for, after all, you have been lolling on it for half a century. Yes, Ivan, capitalism is becoming a public sewer. As a matter of fact there's only one thing you can do—I told him so at the time—and that's to go to meet your fears."

"What did you say?" Lenochka queried, leaning forward, her face aflame.

"Go to meet your fears, I told him ... that is, overcome this base, purely bodily fear of social changes, of often imaginary hardships, of the black bread of revolution, of the common people's joys of living, until the decent mansion fit for refined natures has been erected. There can be no victory without this, and woe to the chick that doesn't dare to break its narrow shell. If I were them I'd take the plunge into my future without thinking." Valery shook his head with a sigh of regret. "Enough of that. Better tell me about yourself, take me through your forest primeval, give me a treat."

"There are not many such forests left anywhere near," Vikhrov took up the thread of the conversation. It may have been because he felt upon himself all the time his wife's gliding comparing glance, but for the rest of that evening he was on top of his form when he spoke about his plans for the next ten years to come.

5

Soon after the telephone call, which came through exactly at midnight, the host drove his guests home himself; Vikhrov was going away for two days on business the next morning. The catastrophe occurred towards the close of the second day, when Taisa went across the road to borrow some yeast from a neighbour. There had not been a shadow of impending disaster; on the contrary, according to Taisa's evidence, that afternoon, after an interval of three years, the sound of Lenochka's hesitant song had reached her twice in the kitchen, and she was not singing to Polya, she was singing to herself, in fits and starts, and Taisa, in her simplicity, decided that Lenochka was on the mend. But when she came back from the neighbour Lenochka was gone. The flat was empty and the door had been left half open so that they should not have to break the lock. Everything was in its place, including Lenochka's favourite knickknacks, and one might think the young woman had gone out with Polya for a breath of the crisp night air, were it not for the sinister absence of the child's things.

Horrified, Taisa rushed out in pursuit of the runaways; Vikhrov would be back at any moment. She ran through all the streets of the neighbourhood, desperately aware of the futility of her search and unable to think of anything to tell her brother in self-justification. She crept back into the flat towards midnight; Vikhrov was already at home. He lay on the floor of his little study, his arms flung wide, but he was not dead, as one might have been led to suppose at first, he was merely drunk, so drunk that he did not recognise his sister. An empty vodka bottle stood on his desk—the one that had been kept for the heart-to-heart talk with Gratsiansky. His face was convulsed, but that may have been the effect of the shifting gleams coming from the burning stove.

Vikhrov was in a state of semi-consciousness; unused to alcoholic drinks, he did not achieve insensibility straight away. Inarticulate words bubbled at his lips as if he had taken poison, and it was not difficult to guess that he was talking to his successful rival.

"Oh, it's clear enough, one might have made out by listening carefully. "She'll be happier with you, but you ... you have robbed me, Osminov! You win, you're the better man. I'm lame, just a forester ... a sorrowing one, but you are cruel, clever, and young. Gratsiansky says that when a nation irradiates too much of itself it gets stingy, egoistic. But I'm cast in a different mould, yes sir! I wouldn't dip into my teacher's jacket hanging on a chair while he left the room to get some refreshments for you, no ... just so! —" and similar incoherent and inconsequential confessions uttered in a queer voice that seemed to come out of a damp barrel.

Lest her brother be discovered by strangers in that condition, his sister dragged him on to the bed behind the screen where she intended to doctor him with warm milk left over from Polya; Vikhrov had a lecture in the morning, and he was always careful not to miss his duties at the Institute if he could help it. On second thoughts, however, Taisa decided that it would do him no harm to remain in that condition a little longer. It was then that Gratsiansky turned up to gloat over the dead body, and Taisa was put to extraordinary shifts to get rid of him. She spent the rest of the night trying to decipher the crooked lurching lines on the scrap of paper which she had picked up from the floor. Poured out as it were scalding hot, without commas, Lenochka's letter occupied several sheets, but rummage about as she would on the desk Taisa could find neither the beginning nor the end.

"...and all because I did not love you, Ivan, and never did, not even *that* time, you remember? You should have understood it at the outset, you're so understanding, everyone thinks highly of you, and the students adore you. Osminov says you didn't ask me anything because you didn't want to make me lie to you. Even the people around us understand, but I'm not angry with you, and please don't scold him, he thinks the world of you. It's not that I didn't love you because there was nothing to love you for, any woman would think it an honour to be your wife, but simply because I couldn't think of love just then. Besides, what happiness could I give you. I'd have sat like that in one place all my life, tied up in a knot. As if I had got through to some party with a forged ticket, and was afraid the ticket-collector would suddenly come up and make me show it—where would I be then? Maybe he wouldn't turn me out, but just to see the look in his eyes would make me wish I were dead. Maybe I'd have got used to it, but I did so want to make good, Ivan. At bottom I am not bad really, I was only dodging ever since a child after that cad Zolotukhin frightened me for life. I can't, I just can't go on with it, Ivan, do you understand? Give my regards to your friend Valery Krainov. It was he who untied me to go to meet my fears. And when I made up my mind to do it, I felt so happy all at once—the water was sweeter, the sky bluer. Do not look for me anywhere, I shall not come back even if I do not make a go of it at the new place. I realise only too well what this means to you, Ivan, but a drowning person catches at anything, and your hand, your life, were the straw to me. It's not going to be easy for me either, having to look my daughter in the face as long as I live. If you ever meet her, don't tell her everything—how I forced myself on you at Pashutino, worse than a homeless pup. . . ."

This was the end of Taisa's story.

"Thanks be to God, everything went off well, though. We didn't die from it, and people didn't notice anything at first, and then they got used to it," Taisa said in conclusion. "He's made of tough stuff, Ivan is. Ever since a child, if he gashed his foot on a piece of iron, or had a fight with somebody, he'd never drop a tear. It was the same this time, except that he was a bit late for his lecture."

"How old was I then, Auntie Taisa?"

"You were getting on for six already. You walked out on your own little feet, poor darling."

Her version of her brother's domestic tragedy, by the way, sounded much simpler than it really was. It was like a history of the world written for children. It was now without jealousy or indignation, merely with fear for her mother, that Polya awaited the continuation of her aunt's story; the appearance of that boy in the Vikhrov home had become a greater mystery than ever. No one else in the world now remembered Sergei's parentage except Gratsiansky, and he kept the knowledge sheathed in his bosom in order, when the moment was opportune and an influential witness happened to be present, to deal his opponent a death-blow.

After Lenochka's flight everything in Vikhrov's house remained as before, but without that main thing, which had served in a measure to compensate his long separation from the forest, the manifold worries of his profession, and the discomforts of a cold dilapidated house. The neighbours and friends were told that the doctors had sent Mrs. Vikhrov away for a cure at our own Soviet hot sands, which turned out to be twice as salubrious as the Egyptian. As before, in the evenings, the brother and sister met to exchange items of news, or, just as if nothing had happened, to read out loud from some book in the presence of third empty seat. Polya's unfinished knitted jumper lay there, so no one sat in it, as if its owner had absented herself for a minute in the next room. By tacit agreement, however, the names of Lenochka and Osminov were never uttered in the house ever since the event. For all Vikhrov's moral strength, this double loss of his wife and daughter would have had the gravest consequences for him had not his active work completely absorbed both his grief and his leisure. True, in view of the prevailing vagueness of opinion on the subject of forest organisation in the transition period, he had postponed writing his textbook, but made up for it that year with a dozen and a half excellent articles, so that Gratsiansky was kept pretty busy tearing them to pieces.

"Those little things of yours are getting me down, Ivan," he once joked slyly and ambiguously during a visit at Vikhrov's. "Your bigger things are more to my liking, I must say. Your first book, for all its shortcomings, was a profound and courageous essay. It's a forest classic, old chap! But don't expect quick fame from it. A book like that could not be appreciated by contemporaries—you know why, don't you? By the way, is it true what they say about your wife?" he added, his eyes sidling away over his listener's ear.

"I intend to tackle some of the more urgent problems of Northern forest management."

"What a hankering you have for these dangerous themes!" Gratsiansky said with sceptic surprise. "Mind you don't knock yourself up, though. You have family trouble, too, but there you stand as cool as a baobab. Where has your wife gone to?"

"I'm not after fame. The Soviet power considers me as one of themselves, fame or no fame. Just so!"

"What a grouchy fellow you're becoming, Ivan!"

Having heard of the departure of Vikhrov's wife, the students stopped gathering at their professor's place for a time. The first to call, about a month after the event, was Osminov, not, let it be noted, in connection with the work he was writing for his degree, but because, as he had the cheek to say, he missed his teacher. He was quite respectful, slightly withdrawn, and looked a bit thinner, but betrayed neither embarrassment nor remorse, so much so that Taisa could only shake her head at the ruthless self-discipline and poise of these young men nowadays. Vikhrov, too, for his part, found in himself the strength not to mention a word about what had happened. He still counted Osminov among the immediate successors of his forest views, and predicted for him much greater success precisely because he possessed that strong sense of belonging, which so often distinguishes the post-October generation from the older men in the world of science. The common interests were more important to them both than the personal, so that towards the end of the second visit Vikhrov bluntly enquired of the young man whether, at that particular moment, he stood in any need of his financial assistance. Osminov looked hard at his teacher, embraced him impulsively, if none too appropriately, and accepted a small sum pending the fee he was shortly expecting for a review he had written. He became a more frequent visitor after that, and it so happened that tea-drinking was superceded by a tiny decanter of vodka with cucumbers of Taisa's pickling and two slices of black bread. These philosophical collations, at which the abstract problems of existence were discussed, rather resembled duels of intellect and learning, in which Osminov revealed both growing prowess and utter tranquillity of conscience. Some shameful force kept drawing Vikhrov to his imaginary rival, a need, perhaps, to see the man who, only that morning, had looked into the sweet sleepy eyes of his wife.

For nearly six months Vikhrov hesitated whether to send Lenochka's clothes and linen—that part of it, naturally, which had not been used yet—to Osminov with a note, or to ask him, tactfully, to take them away himself. It would save the young people expenses which must have been embarrassing in their position. Finally, the professor decided to do it in a bantering manly way, to which end he started a roundabout conversation about the state of the country's light industry, the shortage of wearing apparel and other such pertinent matters. And just when his teacher nerved himself to take the plunge, the pupil unexpectedly asked him whether he had any information as to where Mrs. Vikhrov was and how she had fixed up in her new place. For some seconds Vikhrov stared dully at the smoke of Osminov's pipe, and his heart leapt with foolish hope, only to be seared the next with panic: better that she had been with Osminov! Lenochka had no one in the world besides these two rivals. Certain mysterious hints in her letters and, before that, in the conversation which he had overheard, now took on ominous shape. For all he knew, while he had been writing his articles, eating his *shchi*, and playing blindman's buff with Osminov, the river may have been dragging his wife's body about under the ice. The thought of his daughter reassured him somewhat, but not enough to relieve him of the torments of uncertainty.

Enquiries in letters to acquaintances yielded no results. It had not occurred either to him or his sister to look for Lenochka on the Yenga, at the old hearth of all her troubles. The mystery was not cleared up until the close of the next spring. Just before going to bed Taisa heard a timid intermittent tap on the front door, and looking through the chained door on to the dim staircase, she saw a tall bearded rustic-looking man of about her own age; in a hollow wheedling tone he asked to see Ivan Vikhrov. Considering the time of night and their suburban situation, it was left for her to slam the door to, which she did without a moment's delay. When she had finished washing up, she decided to have another look on the staircase to set her mind at ease, and this time she saw nothing; only the feeble whimpering of a child broke the silence of the staircase. It so happened that Gratsiansky had come visiting that evening; the wished-for talk had not come off, and the guest was taking his leave, as he was in the habit of going to bed early for the sake of his health. Vikhrov threw the door open himself. The late visitor was sitting on the stairs, his beard between his knees; he stood up as soon as the light fell upon him. As a matter of fact there were two of them there—the other being a boy of seven, who stood swaying with sleepiness, clutching the man's sleeve. He wore high-boots, like his father, and a drenching wet homespun coat. It was raining hard outside, an icy spring downpour. Vikhrov enquired frowningly where they came from and what they wanted.

"From the Yenga, sort of dropped in to see an old friend," the man explained without looking up, while his hand rested on the child's shoulder like that of a blind man. It was difficult to recognise him now, after the lapse of exactly three decades, and so he added in a low ingratiating tone, like the password of an accomplice, whether his host had forgotten that night at the forest spring, when they had been the guests of Kalina Timofeyich.

He did not try to force his way into the flat, and was not importunate; probably he would have gone away at once had he been sent about his business. To no one, not even that woman who had run away, had Vikhrov mentioned such details of his childhood, and there was only one man in the world besides himself who would remember Kalina's patronymic.

"Come in, er ... Demid..." Vikhrov said in a faltering voice, and made way to let his visitors pass into the hall.

"Fellow-countrymen, I see?" Gratsiansky remarked perfunctorily. He was putting on his coat in the hall.

On account of the rain, or possibly out of spite, he took a long time over it, and put on the wrong galoshes; without greeting the newcomers, he joked about the kind of countrymen who gadded about visiting their "forest M.P." at disreputable hours of the night. Being nimble-minded, he put two and two together, and shrewdly guessed at once what it took the Vikhrovs six months to find out. At last Gratsiansky left, promising to finish the tale of his forest criticisms the next time they met—which, by the way, was twelve years later.

When Vikhrov returned to his room Taisa was undressing the boy, who all but dropped out of her hands with fatigue. Within a minute, he was ensconced in the sanctity of Lenochka's high-backed armchair, and fell asleep with flushed cheeks, slightly swollen from the cold and fatigue, which seemed to reflect the patchy glow of a camp-fire.

"Hang them up in front of the fire to dry," Vikhrov said to his sister in an undertone, pointing to the boy's clothes, which had left wet marks on the floor; then he looked up at his visitor. "Don't stand there like a beggar, Demid. You're unused to me, I see ... it's a long time since we've seen each other, old chap. I wonder what you're doing now. Come on, take your things off and warm yourself up with some tea. Just so! The son and heir?"

"Aye, that's him," Zolotukhin laughed into his beard and began to execute the host's commands in the order in which they were given.

He sat down at the table, from which the food had not been cleared away after Gratsiansky, and sampled each dish sparingly; he held the glass of tea in both hands for a long time, as if it were life's greatest blessing. An opened bottle of vodka stood tantalisingly before him on the table; he declined it at first, then poured a little out in his glass, and suddenly becoming emboldened, filled it up to its patterned band, then, upon further reflection, pushed it back into the middle of the table.

"I'd been figuring to call on you for ever so long, Vikhrov, and now it worked out only by chance, as I'm changing trains here. I was a prisoner of war, and when I came home I missed you at the forest range just by a week. It's funny, I braved death so many times during the war, but here, at your door, I funked. Would you believe it, I couldn't get myself to knock even, you'd think I'd lost the use of my arms. Ah well, I thought, I'll take my chance. I mean to say, we might die without having seen each other again."

"Oh, nonsense," Vikhrov said, struggling against a feeling of pity. "Go on, drink, don't be shy!"

A last vision of childhood rose before him: the acrid milk of wood burn, the smoke cap over the southern part of Pustosha, the dirty deck of the *Eupatia*, the huddle of children at the landing-stage on the shores he was leaving behind him. . . . But try as he would to link all these circumstances with the man who sat dejectedly before him, the real Demidka remained there behind, this one was a stranger who rang false, as it were, and was loaded with a burden of sorrows of which Vikhrov knew nothing. The brooding gash-like crease between the eyebrows, the wandering glance, and last, but not least, the restless startled-looking hands— all tended to heighten the effect of vague alarm that emanated from Demid. Whether it was because there was nothing else to talk about really, Ivan asked about Kalina's life after the Vikhrovs' departure from Krasnovershya. It was such a long time ago, however, that Demid could not be expected to remember such trivial details. He did believe, though, that Kalina's cabin had stood for another year, at most, in the clearings, which had become grown over with birch coppice, and then, like its master, had faded away, or rather, at a word from Kalina, had been refused into some other indefinable form of existence.

"As to where and how he departed this life, no one knows. No one has ever seen the grave of the forest beast. Maybe they do bury themselves in the ground when they die. Even a stone drowns itself in the sea." In thought Demid Zolotukhin was already far away from the Yenga. "I'm fed up with it, Ivan, fed up to the teeth, and I decided to pull out to new places. I've torn myself up by the roots. It's a hell of a job, though, booking train tickets. People queue up the night before."

364

"Where's your wife, at the railway station?" Vikhrov asked to gratify an unaccountable curiosity.

"No, I've been a widower these last five years. I thought I'd bring the kid down here so he wouldn't have to knock about in that queue without sleep, I'll pick him up as soon as I get the tickets, and then off we go. He's a good boy, Sergei—that's his christened name. If he wakes up and gives any trouble you just smack him, that's all right. The way I look at it, it's better to teach 'em when they're young than have 'em get it in the neck real hard afterwards."

"That's all right, we'll manage till the morning without quarrelling," Vikhrov reassured him, moving the food up on the table. "And what places are you heading for?"

"Well, seeing as how things are shaping up these days I decided to make for the Amur. My brother-in-law wrote me it was a big country with a mighty lot o' wood beasts and hardly any humans to speak of."

"So you're seeking seclusion, Demid? Why's that?"

"Well, the war has taken it out of me, somehow. Mind you I'm not old and haven't spent my strength—just over forty, I am—but I feel as if I'd ate a bellyful o' toadstools—you remember them, they grew in Oblog? Maybe there'll be more grub on the Amur."

"But where will you find a better place?" Vikhrov said doubtfully. "You always had plenty of everything at home, and I daresay your barns couldn't hold what your father left you. Have you still got those horses?"

"Horses be damned! I was burnt out, razed clean to the ground in a single night."

His words, to Vikhrov, had a sound of inaccurate truth.

"It must have been a big fire?"

"Pretty big ... yes," Zolotukhin confirmed in a toneless voice, and, without looking up, he drained his glass at one gulp, holding it tipped until the last drop had rolled off. "I'm not sorry about the property, not a bit. You're better off travelling light and footloose, criticising things left and right. Our tavern in Shikhanov was burnt down while my wife was still alive, God rest her soul. Some of the neighbours played a joke on us—there are lots of jokers about these days. I don't care about the horses either, they were a bloody nuisance in any case."

The vodka went to his head; it smoothed the crease between his eyebrows, and even started him off boasting how much happier he felt after the fire, because there was nothing dear to him in the world any more. Suddenly a harsh chuckle broke from his lips.

"Something you've remembered, Demid?"

The other stared into the fire for a long time without answering; blue little flames flickered over the smouldering charcoals, and a pungent sourish vapour rose from the sheepskin coat spread on chairs.

"A funny thing happened to my old man. It's all over and done with, so's there's no harm in talking about it now," Demid began. "The muzhiks told me about it afterwards, as I was only a nipper at the time. I daresay you remember that the Zolotukhins had always been in the carter business. At first they delivered game to Moscow, then, when things began to develop, they went in for other lines. Dad had a hell of a job making the grade, money-mad though he was. You know how hard it is, earning your first kopek. I remember Mum telling him just before she died, 'You picked on me because o' my being so small, you figured I'd use less soap.'" And Demid sought his listener's sympathy by enlarging on the torments which the family suffered from the avaricious will of his father. "Once at Shrovetide, just on Shrove Sunday, it was too, Dad was coming back empty from a long run, and well, you know how it is, just murmured a bit at his Maker for setting up in the world all kinds o' mangy tykes, while he never had a chance to make an easy ruble, always pinching and paring, rummaging about in a ton o' muck to fish out a kopek. And just when he was giving the Almighty a piece of his mind, who should he meet coming up the hill at Burn Spinny—you remember the place?—but the merchant Yashchikov from Loshkarev, looking as sorry a sight you'd ever seen. It was like this: he'd got himself a tart in Polushubovo—Stesha, a regular young vixen, she was, and a peach, too—always had a pack after her, until the famous Dontsov, the escaped convict took her up. Playing the highwayman hereabouts with a gang o' runaways, he was. This Yashchikov chap still used to visit her though, for old time's sake. Spent a mint o' money on her, the whole village used to make whoopee. Well, this Dontsov bloke goes and comes home afore his time, and was he mad at that merchant! He didn't do him in, though, didn't touch his money either so's not to dirty Stesha. He just dragged him out on to the road, gave him what for, and told him to hook it and not show his damned nose again. Men in those days were rough and ready you know, and it was a wild country, I daresay you remember. Pretty rotten outlook for him, what with Dontsov and his gang behind, and the real wolves in front, howling his funeral song. It was coming on dark, and them wolves were in heat—they'd have swallowed him whole, buttons and bootlaces. There he stood, did our richling, in the freezing cold dusk-down, drunk and beaten up, with his fur coat thrown open and one of its sleeves missing, abegging my Dad to take him in his sledge. 'No, it ain't handy for me to go back with you, I'm sorry, sir. Besides, I'm carrying kerosene, you'll be stinking with it something awful,' my old man says to him. 'Never mind, give me a lift at least to Kondirev Wood, for Christ's sake,' Yashchikov begged almost in tears. 'I'll make you a rich man, I'll swamp you with orders.' And the fool goes and shows him a fat wallet, full o' hundred ruble notes. My old man, I may tell you, was church-warden, and he'd figured on getting in in time for vespers, but it struck him, why, this was God's own answer to his Christian complaint. He had sent him Yashchikov as the fatted calf. There are caches that lie and caches that walk. It was risky, of course, but then all business was built on blood, and if they found human remains the wolves had been at people would think it was Dontsov's doing. Every decent coachman had a hatchet under the seat in case of an emergency. No one had seen them there, so he took the merchant in and drove off."

Zolotukhin drained a second fuller glass without invitation. His face darkened and he stared at the floor as though he had lost the thread of the story.

"Take a bite of cucumber at least, my dear fellow, otherwise you'll never book that ticket of yours," Vikhrov said, hinting at the late hour.

"Yashchikov felt so snug and warm in the smelly hay that he hugged himself for joy. Here were the church bells ringing in the distance, drifting over the forest, the stars atwinkle in the sky, and all it wanted was angels to complete the lovely picture. 'It was the hand o' God that guided you here,' Yashchikov says to my old man. 'I thought it was all up with me, and just as I remembered Saint Nicholas I heard your sleigh bells coming to the rescue.' 'Well, it looks like our prayers met at the altar of the Lord,' my old man thinks to himself. 'We'll see who has the better of it.' And when they came out to Kalina's gully, where you and I sat—you remember that moss-grown horseshoe on the birch?—my Dad started cursing, making out as if the thongs of the horse's collar had come undone. He told Yashchikov to get out and hold up the shaft, but the man was no fool, he saw at once that if the hame had really come apart the shaft-bow would have sagged. He got out nonetheless ... and Dad went for him with murder in his eye. But the moment he swung the axe, the head flew off as if by God's own intervention and he was left with just the bare helve in his hand, worse luck. That merchant then gave my old boy the works—he socked him in the jaw with his right, then with his left, then with both fists together. After he'd warmed himself up on him in real good style, Yashchikov sprang into his sledge and made off together with the kerosene. Our highwayman barely managed to crawl home by the next morning, no sledge, no horse and half his beard gone. He was laid up for about a week until he came round—damned rotten luck! Yashchikov boasted about it afterwards among his cronies. He was a mighty powerful man, by the way—could tie a poker up into knots, he could. A year afterwards he killed himself with a four-inch nail."

"What?" Vikhrov said, looking up startled.

"He was showing a nail trick to his pot companions when he was drunk, and went and swallowed the blessed thing. By the time they rushed him to the hospital and cut him open, he'd given up the ghost."

Vikhrov's face darkened.

"If you intended to amuse me with your story, then you have a queer idea of fun, Zolotukhin."

"It's a funny story all right, Vikhrov, the trouble is you still can't forgive me for that squirrel, Maria Yelizarovna," the other said with a restrained laugh. "Every story of mine has a meaning, and the moral of this one is this: from what I can see, people everywhere are fighting each other, all out to better themselves, but fate steps in and hands it out to them—to one man a nail down his throat, to another lockjaw, like Dad got it. God likes to have his joke with us fellows, he does! Now I ask you, what's the sense in it?" His eyes travelled over the stacks of books crowding Vikhrov's study, as if seeking an answer there.

Everything about him then—the unamusing story about his father, by which he probably wanted to make up for the free meal and the vodka, and the question itself, which sounded like an invitation to an abstract discussion of things remote from the present-day realities—all suggested the idea that the visitor was trying his hardest to prolong his stay under a dry safe roof.

"Don't beat about the bush, Zolotukhin. What are you out for in life yourself?"

The other took his time in answering. He first listened to the sound of the rain outside the window.

"Are you hinting at my former wealth? No, it's not so simple, Vikhrov. To be sure, what trust can there be these days in such a ... piece of capitalist wreckage as I am, but let me tell you it's not just a barrel of corned beef you're talking to—it has a soul in it, too, dammit. I'm looking for nothing except peace and quiet, and a light feeling here," he said, tapping his bulging breast pocket from which came the sound of a crackling note.

And suddenly, independent of his will, all the bitter memories of his Krasnovershya childhood surged up from the bottom of Vikhrov's soul—the nibbled crusts from Taisa's bag, old Zolotukhin's insistent reminders of an evening to the boy of ten to send his mother down to wash the floors in his tavern.

"Oh, but that's happiness you're wanting, Demid," Vikhrov said with a frigid laugh, "and that's not a thing you can just pick up by the roadside. You have to pay cash down for it, and pay in advance. You say you're over forty, but tell me, how many instalments have you paid? So there you are, you seeker of quiet!"

Their talk ended there. For the sake of the child, who was sleeping peacefully in the armchair, they both tried to round it off without causing mutual offence. Presently the visitor bestirred himself to go to the station, and only a humble gratitude for the hospitality shown him betrayed the tumult of feelings with which he was leaving this place never to return. Not until much later did the Vikhrovs recollect the look of anguish on his face when he touched the heated stove before leaving, as if he would take a handful of the warmth away with him into the inclement weather, or, how he had asked for neither bread nor money for his journey, but furtively, toyingly, had hidden a lump of Vikhrov's sugar in his clenched hand, or how, at parting, he had cast a last glance at his son who clutched a piece of Taisa's honey-cake in his fist. It all showed that Zolotukhin's visit had not been unpremeditated. At parting Vikhrov enquired by what miracle Zolotukhin had been able to find him in the capital. It turned out that none other than Mrs. Vikhrov had given him the address at the Pashutino hospital, to which he had carted down some firewood a month and a half ago. Naturally, his excitement at this discovery overshadowed Vikhrov's thoughts as to the actual reasons for Demid's migration to the Amur. For one thing, it was a joy to learn that Lenochka was alive and well, and apparently contented, for another, it restored to Vikhrov his favourite pupil. The rest of the night the Vikhrovs spent talking about the runaway and wondering at their having forgotten, in the turmoil of the search, to look for her on the Yenga.

The next morning Vikhrov sent his wife his first remittance for the support of his daughter, and a letter to the Pashutino feldsher containing an apology for his long silence and a mass of leading questions together with his second book freshly abused by Gratsiansky. Yegor Sevastyanich's answer contained information that threw some light on the details of Lenochka's flight.

2

Spring came late to the Yenga in 1929. The birches did not turn green until mid-May, but the snows shrank long before, and the sledge runners had been scraping ground since April. Carters gave Lenochka and her daughter a lift from the railway station as far as the ferry turning; sledding across the river had ceased and the snow was spongy, as if riddled with small shot. They had to walk down to the bank, which was lost in the bluish haze rising from the patches of open water. The forest had not awakened yet, but it had already washed itself with thaw water here and there along the slopes. The going was hard in the rut, and the roadside snow afforded no hold for even a child's foot. Before they had gone half the way the little girl began to droop from fatigue, and her mother regretted that in so recklessly making her wild bid for liberty she had not warned Yegor Sevastyanich by letter that she was coming. It was nightfall by the time they dragged themselves, both with wet feet, to the annex of the squat log house in which the Pashutino feldsher dwelt. No one answered the door; in Pashutino people went to bed when darkness fell.

The mother whispered to her daughter that grandpa would wake up in a minute and let them in to the warmth, but there was not a sound to be heard save the faint gurglings of spring all around them, and the lazy, sleepy yap of a mongrel at the other end of the village. Expecting the worst, Yelena Vikhrova gazed at a solitary blue star hanging behind an icicle under the eaves; the drops that slid off it contained a particle of its gentle radiance.

The longer she stood freezing with her daughter under a stranger's window the more forcibly was the inevitability of her return to the Yenga brought home to her. Ever since a child she had felt the falsity of her position in the Sapegins' household, especially on the eve of the revolution, when the class rifts had utterly undermined the seemingly invulnerable monolith of the state. So loud was the shouting about the treachery and crimes of the doomed social order in those closing months of what was virtually a lost war, so virulent the hatred and slander which this evoked among the thinning ranks of the old woman's visitors, so strong the wave of retribution that began to sweep the county from time to time, and so challenging the existence of this lonely and paralysed owner of still numerous landed properties, that Lenochka one day caught herself thinking with horror of the time when, for lack of other defendants, her turn would come to be sued for the past, even for things she knew nothing about. With the sharpened sense of a turncoat she felt upon herself the scowling looks, full of malevolent curiosity, of the common people, but her obligations towards her helpless mistress and guardian and the fear of added distrust from *that* quarter—that is, the same sense of personal dignity—prevented her from deserting the hapless house which the servants had already abandoned. To this day she remembered those agonisingly dreary spring evenings spent alone with the silent old woman, the feverish glances cast through the window at the main drive with the wide-open inviting gates at the end of it, the suspicious rustling noises at the street door, the nocturnal creakings of the shutters, that dreaded suspense in anticipation—not even of death, nor even of pain, albeit a long-drawn pain without surcease—but of a careless touch to her soul, to the sorest spot in it. Thus began her malady of *fear* mingled with a sense of bewildered guilt and inferiority, which Vikhrov had been too busy to cure her of—that ceaseless day-and-night mental flight, seeking escape anywhere, be it to a foreign land or to the grave. In this event, however, she would never have been able to discover where and with whom the truth lay, and consequently, the only thing left for her was to start life at the very place she had run away from into her unhappy marriage.

There was still no sign of movement behind the feldsher's windows, but after the second knock a lighted match swam past inside, and a minute later a familiar lanky figure with a cigarette in its mouth and a raincoat thrown over its night clothes appeared on the doorstep.

"Isn't the day long enough for you that you must run around at night!" the feldsher grumbled with a barking cough. "Is it that urgent, what is it?"

"We've come to you straight from the train, Yegor Sevastya-nich," Yelena said, feeling that she had no right now to use her husband's name. "I'm so sorry, we don't let you get any sleep."

The feldsher, who had just returned from one of his calls, drew his coat closer about him in silence. The tarpaulin stood up stiffly on his back. Very fittingly, Polya began to whimper just then, exactly as Demid's boy was to do on Vikhrov's landing a year later, and a sob escaped her mother, too.

"You needn't cry before you're hurt!" the old man shouted at her. "Bring the child inside and unpack him—we'll examine him in a minute. Wait on the doorstep while I get dressed, I shan't be long."

An old-fashioned oil lamp with a frosted glass shade barely lit up the cheerless cubbyhole papered with newspapers and with a pair of elk's antlers over a book-stand. Blessing the darkness, Yelena made a clean breast of it to the old man, confessing everything down to the last little stain—her very life was at stake. Yegor Sevastyanich shambled about from corner to corner, his bare feet in galoshes; turning up the thickened wick he glanced at the child lying snugly in his bed. Having finished only four classes of the army medical training school, he shied at diagnosing affairs of the heart, in this particular case the behaviour of a young and good-looking woman, who had taken it into her head to exchange the amenities of city life for the doubtful joys of existence in the backwoods. Considering the time of night, her urge to prove to someone her right to her country's air, as she expressed it on the spur of the moment, sounded rather false. As if anyone could take that away from a person. The old man ran over in his mind the various suspicious possibilities that were then current, but the Loshkarev District had neither war plants nor secret industries in it except for a small felt factory twenty kilometres away. In a word, during all his forty years of medical practice he had never had such a rare and, apparently, urgent case to deal with. Besides, the woman was asking so little that it was impossible to refuse her.

"I don't know what to do with you, really, my girl. I suppose you've forgotten all you knew? Maybe you'll ask for some job in Loshkarev?" he muttered uneasily, unable to forget she was a professor's wife.

"The important thing for me now is to stay *here*, Yegor Sevastyanich. I don't care if I start as a nurse."

Thereupon, after feeding his visitor with stale bachelor's fare out of a painted bowl standing on the table, the feldsher threw on his shoulders a shaggy travelling coat, known throughout the district as "the twelve dogs" from the number of canine skins that went to the making of it, and retired for the night to the stableman's lodge.

Although her intentions looked clear enough, Mrs. Vikhrov had gone to the Yenga with a feeling of taking a leap in the dark—to die and be born again. She awoke to the blithe sounds of a Sunday morning. The host's pup, his paws sprawled, was yelping in a beam of sunlight, and from the passage came the splash of water being emptied into a tub; in addition, the sparrows were uproariously jolly outside the twin-framed window, and Yegor Sevastyanich was telling someone off for some sin of omission. Everything had worked out without the anticipated vexations, and her daughter had not even caught a cold during the journey; thus did Lenochka—Yelena Ivanovna as everyone now called her—begin her second life. She managed betimes to rent part of a room in the cottage of a local old maid, bought some millet for porridge and three pots at the market, and made arrangements for starting her duties that very evening. She was a bit terrified at first that she would not find her feet, but somehow she did not feel so chilly any more in the cold wooden building where she now spent the greater part of her time. It was a ramshackle little divisional hospital of Zemstvo origin, the creation of Yegor Sevastyanich, containing a dozen beds and no city-bred fancies; but then it had a little of everything there; an out-patient department with pictures of all kinds of diseases on the walls, a real maternity ward, and even a little pharmacy of its own with a door of frosted glass which creaked so loudly that the minor ailments blenched, as it were, before the actual medicine was taken. The patients lay under thin short blankets, very grateful for everything, and even enjoying being ill childishly, as only peasants can; the care and kindness meant more to them than the naive cure-alls. Perhaps the most lingering and dangerous illness there was the one Yelena Ivanovna was suffering from.

She expended herself as long as she could stand on her legs, and kept no count of the days; so strong was the egoism of her despair, that for the sake of her work she often forgot about her daughter, who was left on the hands of the old maid. The youngest of the three nurses there, she silently tackled whatever job there was going, and soon the atmosphere in that institution became, if not warmer, at least homelier, as it always does when a new hard-working mistress comes into the house. The defensive attitude of the hospital staff gave place to curiosity as to how long she could keep it up. Meanwhile, rumour swiftly spread the news of the return of the Sapegins' ward throughout the neighbourhood; she was called "the Sapegin girl" in common parlance, since few people there knew her by her husband's name. Every minute of the day Yelena Ivanovna felt upon herself the thousand-eyed scrutiny of the people; the Pashutino children, especially, frightened her until she got used to it, by standing up on the earth-mound round the hut and peeping in at her window; truth to tell, only the break-up of the river ice and the imprisoning mire, which cut off all retreat, helped her to get over the hesitancies of the first and most difficult week. Even Father Trinitatov, who was already off-colour by that time, made a point of dropping in to see Yegor Sevastyanich with the object of discussing the medical aspects of the chronically inflamed condition of his sciatic nerve, the while he shook his head long and ruefully at the spectacle of so attractive a wife of a city-dwelling scientist scrubbing the dirtied floors of the entry with such humble zeal. No one ever heard a refusal or a complaint from her, nor, for that matter, a joke. Not infrequently Yelena Ivanovna had occasion to accompany Yegor Sevastyanich on his trips to distant confinement cases or accidents, and everywhere she was met with vague silence, as if she was not there at all, although she had already earned the unofficial reputation of bringing luck. At the end of six months nothing remained of her terrors before these people except a lurking fear of meeting the famous Semyonikha face to face—not because the old woman might hurt her by some unmerited reproach again, but because the mental peace she was trying so hard to achieve depended, in the long run, upon that woman's judgement. The meeting was unavoidable, as the old woman lived in Polushubovo nearby with her unmarried son—the first person on the Yenga, by the way, not counting Yegor Sevastyanich, who showed kindly sympathy towards Yelena Ivanovna.

He was Semyonikha's last and youngest son, Mark, the only surviving one by that time. In stature, too, he came short of his brothers, who were all legendary formidable figures on the Yenga. But then he was the gayest and most spirited of all the Vetrovs, with a mischievous twinkle in his blue eyes—the most enviable swain on the Yenga. Besides his basic duties as village librarian in Polushubovo, he voluntarily shouldered a number of public responsibilities, such as writing paragraphs for the district newspaper, putting through economic measures, explaining the policy of the workers' and peasants' government with compelling logic—in a word, he helped the new Soviet way of life to establish itself there. His reading-hut, to which, for lack of a sufficient education of his own, he had enlisted the services of intellectuals from the surrounding villages, attracted crowds, who came to hear the answers to such stirring and momentous questions as the existence of God and the decay of capitalism, but chiefly to have at least a look at the miracle of science that stood covered up with an embroidered tea-cloth against the time it was used. Before showing his audience the simple plywood box with the speaking crystal embedded in its little cup, Mark always made a little opening speech concerning scientific discoveries and the development of the human intellect under communism, the advent of which he planned for the next year or two, and he did this with such élan and reverence, that had he had an education he would have been one of the most distinguished educators of his day. "Oh, dry up for God's sake, turn that gadget o' yours on," the audience pleaded, and the most fascinating thing about Vetrov's "radivon", as the peasants called it, was that one could daily hear the future speaking to them through it with the voice of Moscow.

Early the next winter Mark dropped in on Yelena Ivanovna "in passing", as he said, but clearly with a purpose. Those were the turbulent days of collectivisation, and although one heard nothing but good reports all round about the new nurse, there was something he wanted to satisfy himself about personally. It was evening, the old maid's spinning-wheel was droning, and Yelena Ivanovna in the light of the oil "blinker" was feeding Polya after twenty-four hours' duty. The visitor took off his leather jacket and cap, pulled down his rather tight-fitting military tunic, and then introduced himself.

"I've come to make your acquaintance ... like the town governor in Gogol's play *Inspector General*," he said, trying to

375

give a half-jocular turn to the forthcoming conversation. "Is there anything you need, have you anything to complain of?"

"Thanks, I'm living all right, same as everyone. Sit down and have a rest, once you've come," Yelena Ivanovna said without expression, and, as Mark noted at the time with satisfaction, she went on with what she was doing without glancing up at him once throughout the evening.

Taking careful stock of his surroundings, he asked her about her work on the Yenga, about Moscow, where he was going in a month's time to attend some courses, and, finally, about her social views and demands—not that he was able to satisfy any of her needs, but because he hoped, through her answers, to probe the seriousness of that newly arrived lady's designs and her political morale. He was to discover that Yelena Ivanovna possessed all the essential attributes for human existence and dignity. He noticed also, among other things, the chinky floors, from which came a smelly chill, and where beadlike shiny objects could be seen rolling back and forth along them.

"What's that under the floor-boards, looks like beads rolling about?"

"Those are rats, my dear man. Would you like a pair for breeding?" the sharp-tongued old maid answered for her lodger. "They're keeping an eye on us, too, in case we mint false money of a night."

"That's very bad and wrong," Mark Vetrov said after a slight pause, a flicker of disapproval in his eyes. "And the little girl can catch a cold, too. What you want here is a few laths driven into the cracks. I'll do it myself one of these days. It's only temporary, my going about like this with a briefcase. I'm just an ordinary carpenter. That accounts for Mark, the bible name. Mind you, all our family are carpenters."

"To be sure, I know you all," Yelena Ivanovna said with a grateful little smile. "I've heard such a lot about the Four Winds during these six months. So you are the fifth then?"

"Oh, no, that's what they call my brothers. I don't come into it! They broke age-old trees across their knees, that's a fact. Yefim, the eldest, he rode in a railway engine with Lenin, his bodyguard. Yes, the Vetrovs flew that high! But I'm no great shakes, just a capful o' wind, you might say."

He also asked why Yelena Ivanovna never visited the reading-hut to raise what he called her socio-cultural level by means of a scientific booklet or to listen to the beautiful radio music

376

from Moscow with the singing of various celebrated artists. The old maid expressed reasonable doubt that an ordinary voice could yell its way to the Yenga over so long a distance, and without wires at that, at which Mark, his elbow accidentally touching Yelena Ivanovna every now and again, began to explain with the aid of pencil and paper how the air waves got caught in the coils and all the rest of it, and once got quite warmed up on his favourite subject about the number of useful, wonderful, undiscovered things that lay about under the fettered feet of chained humanity.

"You must come round for certain. Maybe you feel shy of people? You think they'll look at you?" Mark went on probing. "You have nothing to be afraid of, you can look people honestly in the face."

"You must have enough people there without me, packed like cucumbers in a barrel, I daresay," Yelena Ivanovna hesitated. "By the time my turn comes there'll be nothing left."

"Come in the evening, after I shut up. Bring your daughter along if you like, so's you can be together. If you're scared of the wolves, I'll see you home."

Far more strongly than by her good looks did this woman attract him by her severe independence, the determination with which she worked to get herself accepted in life. He felt suddenly disconcerted by the erratic turn his thoughts had taken, and the mocking glance of the old maid which he caught upon himself. Presently he went away, almost without taking his leave, and left behind him a sensation of space and blue-skied noon. Yelena Ivanovna cudgelled her brains trying to remember who he so poignantly reminded her of. "Why, of course, that hawk, that sparrow-hawk," she said to herself, discovering his likeness in the memory of her trip to the Caucasus with her husband. The same taut creature, assured of its own deathlessness, had sat upon the rock, preening its outspread wing, with one eye watching the woman standing in the window of the railway carriage.

3

In the morning, when the occupants of the room were out, Mark mended all the cracks in the floor, and a couple of days later, on his way to the post-office at Shikhanov Yam, he dropped in on Yelena Ivanovna, this time at the hospital, to see how the

377

lonely woman had fixed up there at the new place. One reason for his visit to the post-office was to find out whether anybody else was helping her from a distance to while away her loneliness. In a week or two she got used to his visits; after all, Mark was only four years younger than she was. Only four, less two months. Yet, though she liked the sincere unspent force of him, she put an end to their meetings. It was not even fear of the all-powerful Semyonikha that checked her midway; she merely punished herself for toying with the idea of attaining happiness and her objective at one stroke without all the intervening stages; strictly speaking, it only meant changing two letters in her name. As it happened, Mark was called out to take a month's training course for activists in Loshkarev, and things broke off naturally. Nevertheless, exactly at midnight on New Year's eve, he woke her by a knock at her window, which was just over her bed, and invited her through the latched door to come and listen to a New Year radio concert which had been announced from Moscow. He added, lowering his voice to a whisper, that he had specially got away for that day, that reception of distant stations was particularly good on such frosty nights, and that they would have the library all to themselves and would be able to listen in to their heart's content. Yelena Ivanovna longed to hear some music, but at first the voice of reason was stronger than her awakened feelings.

"Why don't you open the door, it's hard to talk like this," he said from the other side.

"No, that's quite unnecessary. Besides, it's late," she answered, holding the latch against herself, and knowing beforehand that she would let herself be talked into it. "And it's so far and the weather's so cold."

"We'll take the short cut through the gully, it won't take a minute," Mark answered in a low voice. "Open the door, I'm not a thief, I haven't come with stolen goods."

After a moment's hesitation, she ran to get her quilted jacket, and hastily putting on her shawl she joined the young man on the doorstep. The woods around were wrapped in such friendly darkness, and Polya slept so soundly, and the eyes of Mark shining out at her were so pleadingly submissive that she gave way to the temptation of running down to Polushubovo for an hour.

"Button up your throat, you'll catch cold," Mark said, keeping his hands behind his back. "Or let me do it, where are your buttons?"

"That's all right, I'll do it myself."

Elated, still half-dreaming, Yelena Ivanovna ran on to the crisp, hard-grained, silver-tinged snow, ran softly so as not to waken her landlady, or rather, herself. As awkward with women as that first one of hers had been, Mark talked all the way about Chapayev, who had flown through the steppe like an eagle, and who, like Yermak, had lost his life among the rapids. Yelena Ivanovna had read the book, but in Mark's rendering the familiar episodes looked more vivid and fresh, with an emotional colouring whose origin she guessed at with a woman's unerring instinct. And he was so unlike himself, so unlike that recent menacing figure at the village meeting, when he had fulminated against the kulaks "who stuck together like grass snakes in the autumn" and sabotaged grain deliveries to the state. They had to walk in single file down a narrow trail that was barely trodden among the snow-drifts, which looked mysterious and oddly pink now, as they should do in such a dream. Yelena Ivanovna hurried on and kept running ahead, Mark catching up with her, and the intoxicating air of New Year's night went to her head. At the last moment she looked back with longing and a prayer for forgiveness to the daughter she had left behind, then suddenly screamed in so piercing a voice that the forest re-echoed it twice. The glow of a fire, almost smokeless in the utter calm, rose over Pashutino, and one could not tell, through the fringed skirt of the woods, what was burning there.

When they returned to the village, panting hard with the effort of running, the little hospital was blazing like a pinewood camp-fire. Hot festive tongues of flame, drowning the noise and tumult, leapt out of the windows, into which the patients, lined-up from the well, were pouring toylike pails of water. There was nothing left to save really, but just as a matter of routine someone was hacking the door down with an axe, while others were pulling the dilapidated roof apart with hooks to complete the work of the fire. Crimson-hued spring set in within a radius of a hundred and fifty paces; the snow melted on the surrounding trees, and the near branches burst into glowing blossom. Yegor Sevastyanich stood a little to one side with a steriliser in his hand; a tiny reflected fire flickered in the dull nickel of the box, snatched in time from the flames. The old man stood in his jacket, bareheaded, and the hospital laundress kept trying to throw the Twelve Dogs over his shoulders, but he held her off, drove her away, inexorable, like one standing in a guard of honour at a beloved coffin.

"Who lifted his hand against *you*, Yegor Sevastyanich, eh?" Mark demanded in a voice deep with emotion and repressed fury.

"The same fiends, those drinkers of human blood, that's who!" Yegor Sevastyanich cried in a half-strangled voice, and he let himself be led away only when the roof over the pharmacy fell in.

The disaster was without casualties, and without many consequences either; pending the building of a new and better place, the hospital was transferred to the isolation ward, a separate wooden building in the yard which had survived the fire. The worst of it was that Yegor Sevastyanich began to pour liquid consolation into himself for the loss of his creation, to which he had sacrificed all his thoughts, energies and personal savings. As far as could be judged from the charred remains, the preliminary investigation failed to discover incendiarism, but the fire happened to coincide with the first steps towards the reorganisation of agriculture along socialist lines, and rumour persistently ascribed it to malicious intent. Incidentally, it was discovered that Demid Zolotukhin, one of the shrewdest of the neighbourhood's former rich men, had disappeared from Shikhanov Yam some six weeks before that, in fact soon after the appearance in the press of the well-known policy-making article concerning the peasantry; he had disappeared with his son, no one knew where, and surprisingly enough, without having set fire to his house, which he was leaving behind with all his property when he had every possibility of burning it down. Three others, richer than he, had been able to prove their innocence rather cleverly.

"Never mind, we'll find them, if we have to search beyond the sea to do it!" Mark said ominously at the current meeting of the village poor, and his words winged their way through the district.

It was the Year of Great Change, and the events connected with it held up Mark's departure to Loshkarev. His meetings with Yelena Ivanovna ceased of themselves—that inexplicable fire had risen between them. The reading-hut in Polushubovo closed down, as its master was immersed in work of far greater importance. It was amazing how he managed to be everywhere; today he would attack the kulaks for concealing their unthreshed grain or selling off their horses, as a result of which the wood-carting plan was not being fulfilled, and the next morning he would be appealing to the population twenty kilometres away to plough the land collectively to flax, and frustrate the crafty designs of the Pope at Rome, who, in concert with Cardinal Pompili, was then trying to engineer a crusade against the Soviet Republic; he toured the district all the spring on a finance assignment to "mobilise funds", as the confiscation of unlawful surpluses was then called, and while he was at it, to check up on seed stocks for the spring sowing, set up "tow teams" of young veterans of the revolution such as himself, in other words, he took the lead in the socialist drive on the Yenga. Collectivisation in the district started in the winter of 1930, and immediately afterwards the first shots of kulak resistance rang out.

The regional newspaper frequently mentioned the name of the celebrated Yenga librarian, who was fearlessly promulgating Soviet ideas in the countryside; in the course of six months he was repeatedly called out to Loshkarev to attend conferences, and on his last summer visit the newspaper awarded the Polushubovo library a valve receiving set, which had long been one of Mark's cherished dreams. He was returning late in the afternoon after a rain; everything was wrapped in a haze of mist, and the cows had just been driven in. He should have gone through the village, but he was hungry after his journey and eager to try his new toy, and so he took a short cut by way of the backyards. It was here, right next to his house, that two men with covered faces shot at him from their hiding-place and galloped away in the direction of Duboviki. Alarmed by the shooting, Semyonikha rushed forward to meet her son, but he had the presence of mind to dash into the cottage and deposit his precious burden on the bench.

"That's all right, Ma, I'm alive!" he managed to say, with an air of listening to something, before he slumped down.

An hour later, when the deputy chairman of the Executive Committee Potashnikov and the attorney general, who had been visiting Kondirev Wood in connection with the failure to take the necessary measures against kulak sabotage, came dashing down to Polushubovo, the feldsher was nowhere to be found. He was discovered later and brought down in one of his "consolation" conditions; the militiaman, who had kept ordering the crowd away from the windows helped him to mount the rickety steps of the Vetrovs' porch. All the local authorities, four of them, stood at a table with a small oil lamp on it, motionless and solemn, as men who have just heard a declaration of war. Their shadows, too big for the walls, broke in the middle and overlaid the smoky ceiling. Mark lay unconscious at their feet on the floor, a dark little pool at his side; kneeling at his head, his mother was stroking the hair back from his brow, which was clammy with the touch of death. And there was not a sound, it seemed, throughout the hushed district save the shallow-rapid breathing of the unconscious man, like the gasps of a locomotive when it stops for a moment at a wayside station after a long run.

"Don't tread on him," Potashnikov greeted the newcomer. "You've kept us waiting a long time, your lordship!"

Yegor Sevastyanich knelt down and lifted the end of the heavy sodden towel that had been laid over Mark's shirt, while the chairman of the village Soviet squatted next to him with the lamp, trying to read in the old man's face his verdict and his intentions. One bullet had gone right through at a slight angle without touching the intestine, but the ragged outlet was much more sinister than the tiny hole in the stomach; the other was a trifling flesh wound. The pulse was obliterated at times, and Yegor Sevastyanich shook his head portentously. It was dangerous, he said, to convey the wounded man to the district centre, but on the other hand, he added, urgent surgical intervention was needed. The chiefs looked at one another—they had already noticed the feldsher's unsteady gait and the hands which shook not only from age. True, the roads had dried, but even if they phoned for a doctor immediately he would not reach Polushubovo before daybreak. The conference proceeded in silence, looks being more eloquent than words, but they could think of no other way out.

"Well then," the attorney general broke the deafening silence, "go ahead and do something."

"I can't," said Yegor Sevastyanich. "An abdominal operation is needed. I'm only a feldsher, I have no right by law."

"But we *are* the law, aren't we?" Potashnikov laughed bitterly. "What we decide is law, what more do you want, I'd like to know?" And he glanced with sceptical contempt at Yegor Sevastyanich's long dangling arms. "Anyone would think there'd never been any shooting on the Yenga before."

"Mostly axes and stakes were used here in the old days," Yegor Sevastyanich said with hanging head. "There was a case, though, about forty years ago, when an escaped convict was shot in the same place at Kalina's cabin. He didn't live long."

"I see," snapped Potashnikov, his whole aspect seeming to say: Ah, doctor, doctor, what a silly chap you are! I drink myself, but I keep my head! After that he handed him over to the attorney general with his eyes, thinking with annoyance: "It's our fault. We thought, what a world-famed man o' science we have here in Pashutino, and he's gone to the dogs, hasn't grown an inch in forty years. Everything's got to be changed here, everything, damn it." And that irrevocable diagnosis was the beginning of Yegor Sevastyanich's downfall.

"Tell me, citizen, are you a member of the Party?" the attorney general politely enquired, adjusting the spectacles on his nose.

"No, but I am a Russian. And you needn't sniff at me. I'm not denying anything."

"But don't you realise what issues are at stake in the world today, and who, I repeat, *who* it is lying unconscious at your feet there?"

"Why, yes, that's Mark Vetrov. I should know, I delivered him as a baby ... you ask Semyonikha."

The chiefs were younger than him, they were very honest and hotheaded men. They, too, had often received anonymous threatening letters, but Mark must have been the better man seeing that the enemy's choice had fallen upon him first. Catching the drift of this talk, Yegor Sevastyanich began to explain that it wasn't a question of convictions, but of the training which he had received, that in his field as well there were generals and ensigns, and that in the subordinate position he held the most he was allowed to do was to give an injection of camphor until the doctor arrived, and to dry dress the wound, and he dare not take upon himself any responsibility greater than that.

"You've got too much to say for yourself!" Potashnikov shouted in a whisper through clenched teeth. "What Russian are you if you're afraid for your own skin? Man alive, do something, don't stand there looking at me!"

The chairman of the village Soviet went out immediately to phone for a real doctor—surgeon Vlasov of the district centre hospital, while the others helped Yegor Sevastyanich with his humble job, and then, between them, they carried the groaning librarian to the bunk. They waited until ice was brought from the cellar of a kulak and the telephone brought the good news that Vlasov was leaving in three minutes. Potashnikov and the prosecutor hurried back to Loshkarev. It was a close cloudy night punctuated with flashes of summer lightning. The crowd was still there when the men came out of the cottage.

"So there you are, comrades," Potashnikov said to the subdued peasants. "That's the price people have to pay for your happiness.

They demand a high price, damn 'em. But we can afford to pay them cash down. Take good care of your defenders, my children, you have no one nearer to you in all the world. So there you are." He picked up a twig, paused as if wanting to say something more, but only made a cut at the damp heavy air with it, and went towards the tarantass, which stood looming by the wattle fence with its top raised.

Yegor Sevastyanich then asked Potashnikov whether he was to give up his official duties right away, to which the latter replied that until a suitable candidate was found for the job there was no particular hurry, and that a constant watch was to be set up immediately at the wounded man's bedside on his, Yegor Sevastyanich's responsibility. And that he was to choose an efficient nurse for the job, someone true to the core, to keep the feeble spark alive in the precious man.

"And be quick about it, step lively! After that you can resume your interrupted occupation. Only take it with a snack!" Potashnikov threw out disgustedly, jerking the reins.

There was only one nurse at the Pashutino hospital who met the requirements of those in authority.

4

When she arrived at the Vetrovs' cottage to take up her duties, Yelena Ivanovna saw the back of Semyonikha through the open passage door. The old woman was sitting on a stool beside her son, rocking backwards and forwards, as if she were lulling his last sleep by force of old habit. She did not answer, did not even look round at the newcomer's greeting, if that greeting was ever uttered—Yelena Ivanovna was not sure of it, because she lost her voice completely through fear. A crazed fly was darting about under the ceiling in the stuffy air; it knocked into the stove, then filled the silence again with its irritating buzz. Yelena Ivanovna laid out the simple contents of her rural medical bag on the table, and plucking up courage, asked in an even voice how the patient was feeling.

"He's all right, I think he will pass into God's hands by morning," the old woman breathed. With a stiff unbending hand, she smoothed a fold of the clean shirt that was thrown over the bag of ice, as if she were laying out a corpse. "His dead brothers must be missing him, they were very fond of him when they were

384

alive. They'd always give him a honey-cake or send him cloth for a jacket."

"Oh, you mustn't lose heart, Anna Semyonovna. Men get hit much worse than that in the war, but they get better. The doctor will come and do everything necessary, and then he'll begin to mend, you'll see. Now let me sit there."

She put all of herself into those quiet words of professional comfort, which she had learnt in the past year, and although she was using them for the first time, she apparently achieved her purpose. The old woman looked up at her with a hopeful unrecognising gaze and made way for her.

Heartened by that good sign, Yelena Ivanovna put a flat peasant's pillow without a case under the head of the wounded man, and wanted to open the window, but the rotten frame refused to yield; one of the panes dropped outside with a glassy cry. With a pounding heart, Yelena Ivanovna sat down at the foot of the bed and looked into Mark's face for the first time. This man who lay tossing deliriously in front of her was nothing like the one who had come knocking at her heart that New Year's night. He was a very different and puzzling one, so haggard and helpless that pity for him conquered even that unaccountable, sickening fear of Semyonikha by which she had been racked all the way. Mark kept throwing his hand down as if groping for something that could give him relief. Sometimes he asked for water in a barely audible voice, and his mother would rush for the drinking bowl, but Yelena Ivanovna would not allow it, he was not supposed to drink now. Thus passed the whole of the first night.

"Maybe you can give him some powders at least," his mother said from time to time wringing her hands in anguish. "When Yefim lay adying in the hospital they gave him medicines out o' seven different coloured phials. He'd have pulled through without them, though, if he hadn't got dirtied inside by the explosive bullet."

"No, Anna Semyonovna, he's not supposed to have any medicine now either."

It was the longest and stuffiest of all July nights; it was getting near daybreak when the furious rumble of long-awaited wheels sounded outside and came to rest before the window. Vlasov burst into the room, followed by a sobered Yegor Sevastyanich, who had been waiting for him on the outskirts of the village. They got rid of the old woman by sending her to take a walk to Pashutino and back. Water flowed and instruments clinked when it was still quite dark outside, but by the time the operation came to an end the greyish light of dawn stood reflected in Mark's ashy cheeks, which were turned towards the window. Vlasov lighted a cigarette and blew the smoke out with relish, commenting on the delightful tones of the Russian shepherd's horn, which sounded outside, and complimenting Yelena Ivanovna of her efficient hands; judging by the sequels, he must have repeated this opinion of her in certain quarters. After giving her parting instructions, he glanced at the quenched eyes of Yegor Sevastyanich, who, for quite different reasons this time, could hardly stand on his feet, and offered his colleague to drive him home. The old woman was pursuaded to take a nap, and Yelena Ivanovna was left alone with the man, who, like a ray of light, had flashed upon her life and sped on without having warmed it.

And so after a year's schooling in independence this woman took her first examination—an eight-day fight for another person's life, upon the saving of which depended something bigger than mere personal success. Her reward was the learning of certain things which dashed her modest hopes of happiness and taught her the wise detachment which, with people of her profession, is the hallmark of true knowledge and courage. The first three nights were the hardest. For two of them Yelena Ivanovna did not get a wink of sleep. Curiously, as soon as she was relieved by the senior and more experienced nurse from Pashutino, the wounded man began to fight harder for breath and had more frequent attacks of sickness alternating with insatiable thirst. His burning hot parched lips glistened with a glassy luster, his pulse faded away, and the weight of the ice became so insufferable that it wrung from him a moan. The pain restored him to partial consciousness; he would answer to his name and even open his eyes, but he saw things that were beyond Yelena Ivanovna, and on one occasion he called out in that familiar voice of New Year's eve, but it was not her he was calling.

At times it looked as if peritonitis was setting in; Vlasov, on his second visit, had warned about it with a sigh of medical impotence. Some powerful remedy not yet specified in any pharmacopoeia was needed to snatch this lad, whom the country so badly needed, from the clutches of death, and Yelena Ivanovna gave all of herself to the task, as if she possessed an inexhaustible supply of that most efficacious of medicines. Two thoughts were uppermost in her mind at that time: that Mark deserved a better, younger and freer woman than she was; the other was the haunting thought that Polya might fall ill with dysentery, which was then rife in that neighbourhood. The old maid brought her news about her daughter together with her food. It was only by a tremendous effort of will that she did not drop with fatigue. She would start awake with a sense of guilt to feel a searching probing look upon her; and each time Semyonikha would be nearby, mending her poor clothes with a thick needle, or, using the stove ledge as a table, eating the apparently same two pieces of greenish rusty-looking herring out of a paper, or dozing in a corner with half an eye.

Yelena Ivanovna also had sufficient time to take furtive stock of Semyonikha. She must have been extremely good-looking in her youth, a prim little fir-tree of a maid with branches done up in plaits—need and harsh peasant sorrows had turned them into rough dragging locks. The loss of her sons had merely added to her erectness and mournful dignity; tall, without a single grey hair, she looked sternly from beneath a white, always neat and tight-drawn kerchief, which looked as if it had been starched. In all those eight days she had not said a kind word to Yelena Ivanovna, had not offered to relieve her or to share her meal with her; it was as if she understood how important it was for a person in her position to prove her worth without hindrance.

Mark's temperature began to drop on the sixth day, and towards the end of the eighth, when official visitors came, the sick man asked to be moved to the bench by the window where he could see the stir of life in the village. His request was granted on the responsibility of the D.E.C. chairman, who believed that gratifying the patient's wish at this stage of the illness was the best possible medicine. Through the dim glass only the tops of the street willows were visible, but Mark, wincing as if with sweet pain, gazed hungrily at the martlets as they threaded the fading sky. Presently his mother went out to see Potashnikov and his retinue to the door and to meet the doctors who had just driven up.

"Looks like I've turned the corner," Mark said when he was left alone with Yelena Ivanovna. "I used to think there was nothing more frightful than *that*, but nothing in the world could scare me any more."

"When the worst is over there's nothing but good to look forward to," she answered soberly and impassively as she leaned over for the thermometer. "Now you'll go to the sunny south, to the warm sands. We have very good sands in our country, as good as in Egypt!"

He tried, rather uncertainly, to catch her hand, but she managed effortlessly to avoid his apologetic gratitude, which was such a usual thing with convalescents.

"I must have been lying about like this for quite a time. Has it been hard on you, Yelena Ivanovna? You even look a bit older in the face."

She could hardly take offence at this awkwardly expressed pity.

"It's our duty to nurse the sick. That's why we're never shot at," she turned it off with a joke, finding the mercury column with difficulty in the failing light. Then she went over to the table to write down his evening temperature.

While the doctors were talking to Potashnikov on the doorstep, Mark made another attempt to keep the ball rolling; clearly, he was expecting to be forgiven for something, but Yelena Ivanovna said nothing. Forgiveness would have meant admitting her momentary weakness, which fortunately had gone unpunished. The medical examination confirmed that the crisis in the wounded man's condition has passed. It grew colder towards the night and rained steadily till the morning. For the first time Mark fell into a light, restful and unfeverish sleep. Yelena Ivanovna went out, too, and dropped on to a heap of hay in the dark entry, where it was not so stuffy and there were no pestering flies.

Her legs were numb with fatigue and she could not fall asleep. A smell of farm animals and dampness came from the cow-shed. She lay on her back with open eyes; it was her last night in the Vetrovs' house. She could hear the floor-boards creaking behind the wall, where Semyonikha spent her sleepless time; since her son had shown definite signs of recovery she had become more restless than ever. Then the door opened, and through half-closed eyelids, Yelena Ivanovna saw the figure of the old woman in a ray of yellow light from the oil lamp.

"Are you sleeping, lass? Mind you don't catch cold there," she said softly, not to rouse her in case she was asleep, but Yelena Ivanovna did not answer her. She no longer cared.

A minute later Semyonikha reappeared with a sheepskin coat and gently covered the sleeping woman. She turned away, then came back again, kneeled down and tucked the coat under her outstretched numb legs. Nothing else happened, but to Yelena

Ivanovna this was glad tidings which meant that she had been admitted at last to the great kindly warmth, had been welcomed into a house that was more inaccessible perhaps to an outsider than many a palatial mansion. She had been accepted at a time when she least expected her efforts to be noticed. She had won her right to her country which happier people received as a matter of course together with their mothers' milk. Yelena Ivanovna lay listening for a long time to the pattering rain. Visions of things left far behind drifted past like cloudlets of memory. They were not the visions of childhood, nor the flames of the wrecked manor, which had for ever chilled her blood with the imagined horrors of popular wrath, but some unimportant, barely recognisable details inscribed upon the margins of events.

Mark was still asleep when Yelena Ivanovna came into the hut after having washed herself in the backyard. A wooden bowl of sour milk mixed with curd cheese stood ready for her on the table with slices of rye bread next to it.

"Have a bite, dearie, sit with me a little. I'll be forgetting how to speak soon," Semyonikha said gently, as if nothing had ever happened between them, when Yelena Ivanovna took her seat at the table. "I can't tell you how precious a human word is when you get old! And you must be feeling lonesome, too, I daresay, without your daughter."

Yelena Ivanovna was surprised to discover how easy she suddenly felt in this woman's company.

"That's all right, I'll be going home soon. We'll see plenty of each other," she said, dipping a crust into the white gruel and carrying it to her mouth while she cupped her other hand beneath it, peasant-wise, so as not to lose a crumb.

The old woman opened out at parting and started off on a train of reminiscences about her girlhood, mentioning, among other things, her late husband, a Yenga blacksmith famed for his extraordinary strength, who was such a kindly soul and skilled workman that everyone who had to do with him had the highest opinion of him.

"And if he had an argument with anybody—you never knew what kind o' person a wind would blow into the smithy—my Nikolai would not insult him, would not say a bad word, he'd just unbend some old horseshoe in his great hands in front of the man, give a short laugh and go back to what he was doing. Mark takes after me, though. You'd be surprised what a singer I was! Have some more, dearie, help yourself."

"I've had enough, thank you ever so much for your bread and kindness," Yelena Ivanovna said, rising from the table with a sedate bow, the way hired cowherds, haymakers, and carpenters from distant regions used to do in the old days, with the confident dignity that comes from the knowledge of a useful job well done.

"I'll be frank with you, my dear—in my mind I had buried Mark and shut the stone on my heart. And I was terribly sorry he hadn't married before that, my dear—at least there'd be a grandson to cheer my lonely heart. He's got his eye on a likely lass at Loshkarev—she's the sister-in-law of the chief accountant there, you know, the man who manages all the money.

"That's very good, I wish them a long happy life," Yelena Ivanovna said with a smile as she drew the curtain on the window to keep the sun from waking Mark. "Have they known each other long?"

"They must have got acquainted on his last visit. I don't know what charm she used, the little witch, but he thinks the world of her," Semyonikha boasted as she wiped the table dry. "I hope you'll come and celebrate with us, dearie."

Yelena Ivanovna promised to drop in for an hour if she could spare the time. With work having started on the new building she had twice as much to do now in the hospital. She received the news about Mark as retribution for her cruel treatment of her husband, which she had not fully realised until now. Most propitiously, at this moment, she was called to the telephone. The Party Secretary of the region wanted to speak to her. He asked after the health of the celebrated librarian, and while he was at it, consulted her about sending Comrade Vetrov away for a holiday, not to the hot sands, as she had originally supposed, but to the seaside, to a marble palace amid green cypresses, where none but tsars and their near relatives used to take their holidays. In a level professional voice Yelena Ivanovna answered that the sea air was also very good for patients who had undergone a recent intestinal operation.

Three days later Doctor Vlasov drove down to Polushubovo once more to convey the librarian to the railway station, whence he was to travel to the regional centre to be placed under the care of the biggest physicians. When Yelena Ivanovna bent over him to beat the hay up under his head Mark glided over her with an embarrassed eye, but he read nothing in her face save professional solicitude for his comfort during the jolting ride. And although she felt they would never meet again, she went back into the hut to pack her little suitcase before the Sapegins' tarantass disappeared beyond the edge of the village.

On the whole, she had stood up to the test extremely well, even though the old maid did find her lady lodger looking a bit drawn and washed out. But then Yelena Ivanovna stopped growing older after that, and her appearance settled into a fixed mould—that of a serene imperturbable woman, not noticeably inclined to mirth, but always briskly cheerful and attentive beyond the mere limits of professional duty, and surprisingly not once falling ill for years at a time. At first, on the pretext of coming to boast how well Mark was doing for himself, old Semyonikha used to bring Polya milk or curds wrapped in cheese cloth; the Vikhrovs had no cow of their own at that time. At the opening of the new hospital Potashnikov asked Yelena Ivanovna her opinion about the Pashutino feldsher, and she was able to save the shaken reputation of that unfortunate old man. Shortly afterwards nurse Vikhrova was elected to the managing board of the consumers' cooperative society. This was her first step. Subsequent everyday practice helped her to realise that the joy of giving oneself to people was immeasurably greater than that of taking from them, and that all people without exception fell into just these two categories. Some three years later she simply could not imagine any other pattern of life for herself.

5

These shifts in the life of the older generation coincided with a period when the younger was forming its first impressions of the world. The shady banks of the Sklan, luxuriant with meadow-sweet and valerian, and with pale-blue dragon-flies hovering over slumbrous pools, became Polya's playground, just as the ram-shackle two-storey house next to the plantation of the Forestry Institute became Sergei's home. Almost the same age and with a similar background, they were born into a country where the new established order was completely geared for the service of the young. With the growing strength of Soviet society there grew in the children an unconscious aversion to the former mode of life, whose sting they had both felt. They envisaged the past as a kind of vast burial ground full of mouldering bones and hoarded treasures. Running forward slightly, it should be said that with the years Sergei found the latter oddly disproportionate to the lamentable conditions of life under which they were created, if one was to believe the textbooks; what he overlooked was the hoard's hoary age. Between them were strong points of resemblance: like Polya, who had spent that whole memorable evening wandering about the streets to get the bitter taste of Taisa's story out of her mouth, Sergei as well deliberately avoided asking any questions as to who had brought him out of the rain into the hospitable warmth of the Vikhrovs' home, and why; he always wanted to fall asleep at that thought, to sleep over the memory of that night. Demid Zolotukhin, incidentally, deceived his old friend—he did not come back for his boy either the next day or the year after, when the matter was cleared up, and never wrote to Vikhrov to enquire about his son, no doubt through fear of throwing his shadow upon his benefactor.

Sergei's adoption partly filled the painful void that formed in the family after its break up. Moreover, the presence of a blithe young spirit, who paid for the kindness shown him with warm affection, was a certain comfort to Ivan Vikhrov in his scientific adversities. Everything that was to have been the daughter's was now given to this thin, precocious boy with the inquisitive mind. He knew no hardships, but neither did he indulge in the usual boyish pranks; unedifying fairy-tales were then considered harmful indulgence, and the tiny electric train which ran through all the rooms on rails was the only thing that had escaped the fate of the other toys. The holding of public offices at school had instilled in Sergei a premature need for wielding authority; he allowed himself a considerable freedom of thought and held this to be permissible in a leader of men. It was dinned into him every minute of the day that all those hydroprojects and construction jobs were being done specially for him, but he was relieved of any burden of thought about those young members of the working class, boys of practically his own age, who were working at those building sites. All the world's wisdom came to him ready-made and bottled, and he had no need to work things out for himself. By a system of intensive supplementary studies Vikhrov taught the boy a dangerously daring method of dealing with problems over which he himself had struggled so hard in his student days, forgetting that it was the difficulty of his struggle for a world outlook and the time it had taken him, the constant conflict with alien ideas, which had helped him to discover the truth for himself. The older generation, which had experienced all the ills of social injustice, tried their hardest to rid the rising generation of humiliating want and insure them for all time against any possible diseases of the spirit. Not infrequently, with this end in view, they cultivated in the young a prophylactic contempt for outmoded views, an attitude of indulgent irony towards the imperfections of all previous human thinking, towards the adversities of a world history adapted to the comprehension of a child. The reading of famous works at the evening sessions did not cease in the Vikhrovs' home with the departure of Yelena Ivanovna, and it was an invariable practice of Ivan Vikhrov's to begin with a discussion of the prefaces, which were specially designed to counteract the pernicious influences contained in the books themselves. However, fearing that such an over-asepticised diet might lower his pupil's resistance to spiritual infection, Vikhrov gave him, besides "leading" books, other reading matter "which dragged you down to the bottom", as Sergei ironically put it.

"The trouble is, my dear pater," he suddenly announced one day, "that all these wings which have outlived their usefulness are bound to become weights on the feet of humanity unless they are thrown off in good time. Don't think it's mental laziness, but if I were in the place of the fathers, and bearing in mind the sad fate of Lot's wife, I would not allow the young people to look back at the old world they are leaving behind or to overload themselves with its ancient seductions. The lighter your knapsack the longer the day's march; as for all the rest—back with it, back to the baggage train with it!" And these indubitable signs of growth in Sergei, his first steps towards assimilating the cultural legacy were noted by the pater with a light but painful astonishment.

In short, the boy grew by leaps and bounds, gladdening the hearts of his near ones by his exemplary behaviour and his progress at school, yet more and more often Ivan Vikhrov was pained by his son's hasty opinions about the books he had read. He understood that young men of all epochs had been prone to mock at and even to break off the noses of alien dumb-struck idols on the ruins of an outworn civilisation, and he was least inclined to defend a past that was dead and done with; when he was about the same age, however, he had borne himself more modestly and with slightly greater respect in the pantheons. It had been the fashion then with some people to affect a superficial bookish sociology, which, running up a debt against the future, spared no authorities. Ivan Vikhrov could not help comparing the furious attacks of the "Lefts" at that period with the cheeky élan of the youngsters in yellow jackets during his own student days, when they defied Pushkin over a mug of beer at the tables of St. Petersburg's taverns. True, in Sergei's case it was merely a boyish temptation to flaunt his superficial knowledge; he sincerely believed that the dashing radicalism of his views would appeal to the older people, who had worked so hard to overthrow the old world. He had not been taught yet that a nimble mind without the justification of its own achievements, even though it were backed by the opinion of the age, is the arrogance of a half-scholar. Sergei had to discover this for himself, and the sooner he did so the less chance was there that disillusion would swing him in an opposite and undesirable direction.

Thus, after reading the Bible, Sergei, with a sorrowful air, expressed himself to the effect that for a slave-owning epoch it was pretty hot stuff and not without a social punch, but—"my God, whoever thinks of starting to build a house from the roof?" Sergei deplored the fact that for all his sympathy towards the Galilean fishermen, Christ had not sufficiently studied his milieu and had failed to take into account the experience of Spartacus, removed from him by a space of only seventy years. The boy was ready to grant, by a stretch, that the book had lasted people two thousand years, but then had not Vikhrov himself brought him up in the belief that almost throughout that period it had rested on suppressed reason, and by asserting the primacy of puerile lucidity and poverty, had paved the way for the despotic rule of darkness and money. For such a betrayal Sergei denied Christianity even that subordinate role of epos which is usually granted to superannuated religions. The author of Confessions fared still worse at the hands of Sergei, who called them the biography of a brilliant idler, who, instead of challenging feudalism on the barricades, had started a traffic in dubious secrets. Anticipating Vikhrov's dreary protests, he reminded him of Hume's appraisal of the author, who had read little and seen little, and preferred to use his fertile imagination in his quest for the truth.

His voice shrilling comically off key, Sergei also condemned other classics of philosophy and fiction, which, in the eyes of Ivan Vikhrov, had been the landmarks of entire social formations.

"All those 'novellas' are much of a muchness. Everywhere the events of life are strung on the thread of a love interest. I'd do away with that genre entirely, and introduce instead a documentary chronicle with a useful educative angle. It's about time literature was made to punch in on the common time-clock along with the other builders of the future!"

"But, my dear fellow, who's going to read those protocols of yours?"

"Don't you worry, they'll read them if there's nothing else to read, my dear pater."

Vikhrov frowned.

"Please don't call me 'pater'. Our relationship is nothing to be ashamed of. I really am your father, and that word rightly claims priority in every language. Just so."

"Oh, I didn't mean anything," Sergei said, abashed, and pleaded forgiveness by a touch of the hand. "Believe me, I have nothing against love as a biological necessity, but it's rather offensive to have it paraded as man's basic activity. Mind you, it's taking an unpleasant trend too. At least the previous authors gave their heroes poems to read, lilac to smell, whereas the later ones are always in a hurry to shut the page door on them bashfully."

"That's just what I was saying. It's like this, my boy," Vikhrov began in his best professorial manner, "every living thing blossoms and opens out to its fullest in the season of love, whether it be an apple-tree or a bird. With the angiospermae, their membership of the botanical family is determined also by the flower. The human being stands out all the more nobly in the splendour of his moral character, and so the poetry of love serves as an excellent magnifying glass for examining the hero's moral values."

"Aha," Vikhrov junior took him up quickly, "so work and struggle do not suit your purpose of moral investigation?" He shut the window demonstratively, lest anyone in the street should overhear such expressions of opinion from a man so dear to him, a member of the civil service too.

"Some people hold that Nature's primary purpose is the perpetuation of the species," Vikhrov said defensively. "Thus, as soon as an individual becomes incapable of fulfilling her designs, Nature simply withdraws her gifts from it, including the instrument by which she acts upon the world. Trees, for instance, become twice as fruitful with the approach of death. On the other hand, Abelard, if you remember, lost his poetic powers completely after he. . . ."

"Oh, who cares what happened to trees before us!" the younger one interrupted, glad of a chance to show the old man that he had not wasted his time and energies on his education. "It's much simpler, Father. The hero of yesterday's literature was an aristocrat, a *rentier*, a landowner, sufficiently provided with unearned bread to be able to devote himself completely to the problems of the perpetuation of the species, as you call it. But then you yourself keep repeating on every occasion that it is the job of the human being to bring intelligence into the workings of Nature. Well then"—and his voice rose to an unpleasant meeting-hall pitch—"if the citizens of this world had taken a closer interest in these things before us we wouldn't be obliged now to clear up the mess they have made. There'd be less sorrow, too, and that love of yours would have profited by it as well, so there would have been no need to bury Romeo and Juliet before their time."

"There would not have been a magnificent tragic poem either," the elder backed away, trying not to slip in the process.

"You mean that with the proper organisation of productive relations contradictions will fade away and there will be nothing to write about? Don't be afraid, Grand Old Man, our age will create new tragedies, but they will be tragedies more worthy of the human being."

"I don't see them yet. I wish you'd get me one to read, son!" Vikhrov said, annoyed for demeaning himself by such tactics.

They resumed the argument several days later in one of Moscow's museums, where they went first thing in the morning every Sunday.

"Prepare yourself to see a miracle," Vikhrov said, leading Sergei past the relics of Egypt, Rome and the Italian Renaissance straight towards the Venus of Milo. "Just look at this. What do you say now, fiery youth?"

The famous armless goddess stood in a large hall amid other immortal creations of her age, against the background of a Pergamene frieze depicting a combat of giants. On the left, Laocoön and his sons were being punished by serpents for having insulted the Olympian deity, and on the right, the ferocious brothers were avenging their mother by binding the wife of the tyrant to the horns of the wild Farnese Bull. Bathed in the diffused top light, calm and gentle in her virginal semi-nudity, Venus stood all alone amid this violence, the creation of poetic human reverence towards the productive powers of the earth, as Vikhrov explained it.

All the lords of ancient kingdoms and the nether regions, all those kings and demons, bulls and gods crowded in the adjoining halls seemed to him merely the menials of the great goddess. Of course, she should have stood against blue velvet falling in heavy folds in lieu of the brilliant Aegean sky, but even here, amid this crowded concours of pain and terror, even in this plaster mould mellowed by a warm tint of yellow, one could judge of the perfection of the Parisian original.

Sergei lowered himself on a bench and stared at the statue with an amused glance.

"H'm, pretty expressive, I should say, as far as the perpetuation of the species is concerned. Seeing that this was born in other times and climes, though, I'd dress her up a bit for the time being."

"Why, you're simply a monk, Sergei!" Vikhrov flared up. "Not even Savonarola, but just an Alexandrian monk out of the fifth century. Be careful, don't throw stones ... *this* may take offence and leave the world for a long time. You are looking at the beauty of the world."

"But not of mine," the young man said with a mocking smile, lowering his eyes as if to avoid temptation. "By that word we have been taught to understand a perfect form filled with a no less lofty content. What leading ideas of our day have you found to attract you in this stone? Besides, no work of art exists outside its environment. I ask you, can this thing serve me even as an aid in the study of that remote epoch? The author was stewing in a seething cauldron of events, and yet he did not notice the brutalities of ancient slavery, the horrors of the Peloponnesian War, or the bloody campaigns of Alexander. And, altogether, isn't it a darkish word, Father—Beauty. Too often has it been used as a guise for falsehood and crime. Ruins always appear attractive at sunset, but take a good look at the ancient reptiles that lurk in the cracks. No, that won't do for my Hellenic ideal. Don't you give in yet, Father?"

"You may be right in some ways, but I must say your rightness makes me feel sad, Sergei. Usually people begin to have doubts about the worth of life's blessings after they have thoroughly enjoyed them."

"We have no time, Father, we've got to overfulfil the plan of life," Sergei exulted.

"Well, to a certain extent, I daresay, you have succeeded."

They were sitting in the middle of the lofty echoing hall with its glass ceiling, and on the seat behind them sat a youngish man in a jacket of semi-military cut, whom they had not noticed before. He looked like a school-teacher. Taking a hesitant half-turn about the room, he suddenly accosted the Vikhrovs, apologising for interfering in their argument.

"My name is Morshchikhin. May I be allowed to give you a hand?" he said to Ivan Vikhrov, adjusting his small old-fashioned spectacles, which gave a droll but loveable effect to his lanky figure. "I've been sitting here throughout your dispute, and since I have a certain interest in problems of our cultural legacy I should like to put in a word for this stone lady."

"Who has already suffered, by the way, from some irascible critic," Ivan Vikhrov inserted, hinting at her missing arms.

"I doubt whether it's the result of anyone's conscious act, though. Fanatics have always started with heads. Antique noses in particular aroused in them a fierce itch of activity. This lady must have simply received a shock—Milo is a volcanic island, you know," Morshchikhin said, nodding his thanks for the seat offered him. "And so the young prosecutor is entering into possession of his legacy and starts on art?"

"That goddess of yours is in no danger for the time being," Sergei parried. "I only wanted to say that we would create our own Venus, a new one, when necessary."

Morshchikhin leaned forward, and a tuft of hair hung comically over his eyebrows.

"A praiseworthy intention, I am sure. So it's to be a new one, brand new? And what modern identification marks do you intend to give her? Are you going to put a spanner in her hand or touch her up a bit with mazut to leave no doubt as to what class she belongs to?"

"I understand myself that Venus doesn't need any identity papers," Sergei promptly retorted. "But we are living in a transition period which is equivalent to a millennium. So a document will do no harm. The new will only be born after a second dethronement of Uranus by Cronus."

This was a sprightly attempt to floor his opponent by showing off his knowledge of Greek mythology. Morshchikhin heard him out gravely, but his eyes behind the oval lenses of his glasses twinkled with amusement.

"In what way will she be new, though?"

"I don't know yet ... at any rate, it won't be the marbled mutton of prehistoric times. And philosophically as well, it will be of a more decent material. As a matter of fact the gentler sex didn't fare much better in the biblical legend about Adam's rib either—did they?"

Sergei was hinting at the proverbial sea foam, that academic screen, which concealed from the children the forbidden details of the myth. But try as Sergei would to scintillate on the subject of the goddess's birth, Morshchikhin denied himself the proferred pleasure of acting as his audience.

"Twice you have hinted that you have read Hesiod," he broke in, his face slightly darkening. "I'm afraid the discussion of this goddess's genealogy will lead us away from the subject, all the more that in Homer, for example, she is born in quite a normal way. But since I am so fortunate as to have met such a well-read comrade, I presume you also know Lenin's speech at the Third Congress of the Komsomol?"

"I am a Komsomol member myself," Sergei said, reddening and bracing himself for the snub which his audacity had merited.

"That relieves me of the necessity of quotation. Then you will remember, young man, what Lenin said about our having to build communism with the means and resources left to us by the old society?"

"I do not scorn the cultural legacy. Our conversation does not give you any ground for accusing me of being unwilling to read or learn, does it?" Sergei said defensively.

"Not at all. Lenin, though, warned against that very gap between the book and living practice, against the dogmatists and boasters. I'd like to warn you against harmful presumptions in regard to such unique treasures of the past, which have been built up out of millions of unknown human meditations and workdays. This applies also to our own sacred things, the hearths of national self-consciousness. This statue contains all the clarity of ancient thought, and belief in the beauty of human predestination—you should also bear in mind the brutal conditions of the times in which this mother's amulet, hung upon the breast of posterity, was created. Besides, this is not an aristocrat you are looking at. This woman, armless though she is, has a work record of twenty-two centuries. A 'certain' Gleb Uspensky used to make dates with her as a medicine against the sordidness of life. He said that to kill her would mean robbing the world of its sun. Another crank by the name of Heine wept in front of her on a Louvre bench. Presumably, those two were more tearfully inclined than you are. Wouldn't you like to have a smack at them, too, while you are at it, young man, seeing that the dead offer no resistance? But these two considered themselves the legitimate heirs to all that was best in the amassed gigantean labours of their ancestors; and generally, to appreciate beauty and spiritual values one must view them from a spot where they are best seen. And you would give all this, this ancestral home of ours, over to the cave-men of our day. I daresay the cave-men were more charitable than the present-day monopolists. They gobbled the weaker *au natural*, without making dainty dishes out of human suffering by running it through the complex stills of modern civilisation. So when you throw things out of the window in laudable anger, mind you do not rob yourself, my young and active friend."

In a low voice attuned to the subdued atmosphere of the museum he proceeded to talk about the continuity of the generations, without which every new phase would have to start with the invention of fire and the wheel. "I don't mean the single continuous stream of Fouqué, Draper, or our own Danilevsky, for whom all civilisations had the same stage settings"—here Sergei was made to blush with shame at his own ignorance. The conversation had turned into a condensed lecture on progress in its Marxian interpretation—with the assimilation of the positive achievements of the past and their elevation to the highest plane of perfection—on Lenin's theory of spiral development with similar coils arranging themselves one above the other. Sergei's face was a crimson study of despair; he bit his lip, and winced at every unfamiliar name or concept that was uttered. The Hegelian *aufheben* sounded like the crack of a whip to him. If Morshchikhin's intention was not only to elucidate the truth but to punish the young man for showing off his superficial knowledge he fully achieved his purpose. Characteristically, however, instead of causing resentment or vain obstinacy, the lesson excited in the boy an awed admiration of the older man's mature logic of mind. The latter, for his part, became aware of an attitude of sincere repentance and self-critical impartiality in his companion.

Although Morshchikhin was a busy man, they began to meet regularly from that day, always discovering in each other new attractive qualities. Their warm intimacy, despite an age difference of nearly ten years, developed to such an extent that Sergei passed from Vikhrov's tutelage to the free pupilage of Morshchikhin. All his former associates with loud names and loud scarves imported from Paris were sacrificed to this new friendship.

In those days parents often set extravagant hopes on a sort of abstract friendship, which was supposed to have arrived at last between the generations; to a certain extent they sought justification in it for relaxing their everyday supervision of the growing generation. This was particularly true of some well-to-do families, where misconceived civil obligations towards the future found their sole expression in the care for their own children, although they knew by personal experience that timber raised on meagre soils is more resinous, fine-zoned, and hard. Ivan Vikhrov's mistakes placed him somewhere in the middle; through fear of losing Sergei's friendship he put up with the tone of equality or ironical condescension with which his fosterling received his lectures, those grumbling whimsies of a dear but sometimes tiresome old man. It was not until later, shortly before the war, that Vikhrov began to experience genuine alarm at the thought that Sergei's latitudinarianism in respect of the remote values of the human spirit might switch over to nearer and more positive ones.

Morshchikhin liked to visit that house. Personal friendship in those days stood for the victorious unity of the country; he had no family of his own, and his cheerless bachelor's room, which he humorously called his garage, fully answered that description. He became almost a fixture in the Vikhrovs' household, so much so that Taisa often said she wouldn't mind adopting that bespectacled fellow if only a bit could be knocked off his age and rank.

During one of his visits Vikhrov asked his advice about Sergei, who had just turned eighteen. Himself a man who had risen from the lower classes, Morshchikhin conceded that nothing short of an unsweetened independent work life could remedy the defects of Sergei's upbringing; he held that most young men of the intellectual strata would benefit considerably if made to work a year or so before entering the universities.

In the end things took their own course. Coming home later than usual that evening, Sergei showed the visitor his neat collection of books on art, of which he was very proud; he lived in Polya's room, which he had half turned into a mechanical workshop with heaps of tool parts, old electrical relays and brass oddments littered about the corners. A neat lathe mounted together with a motor on a bench revealed Sergei to Morshchikhin in a new unfamiliar aspect.

"Amusing yourself with your old toys, I see," he said, picking up from the floor a toy electric train that had been partly taken to pieces.

"No, I'm trying to work in some improvements," Sergei said in some confusion. "A spiral advance to a higher level." He confessed confidentially to a long-standing passion for all kinds of machinery aimed at conquering time and space, and, as he then expressed it, lengthening the span of human life.

Asked what he intended to become in future, Sergei declared grandly that he was prepared to become anything from a radioman in a space rocket to a molecule in a sword blade.

"What about something more down-to-earth?" the visitor said wryly, annoyed at his repeated ambitious attempt to impress people by being different. "Speaking of conquering space, by the way, did you ever feel like wanting to take a ride in a real locomotive? I could help you in that line. You seem to have the makings of a fairly decent engine-driver."

The boy flushed with pleasure, and thus it came about that a toy and certain circumstances of Morshchikhin's biography determined the pattern of Sergei's life for several years ahead. Upon graduating from the university Morshchikhin had been sent to work as a propagandist at the district Party Committee on whose territory the Forestry Institute was situated. At the time he made the acquaintance of the Vikhrovs he was completing a correspondence course at the Higher Party School and only had his thesis to write; in addition, he was conducting a seminar on the history of the Party at an important working-class centre of the district—the Deyevsk Central Depot on one of the North-Western railways; Morshchikhin's father had worked there in his day and he himself had spent his childhood there. He had no trouble in fixing Sergei up with a job there. Of the two preferred jobs—that of fitter's apprentice in the hoisting shop and fireman —the young man chose the latter for romantic reasons; a detail like that would look like a lifelong title of honour in the questionnaire of a Soviet young man.

After six months on his new job Sergei somewhat modified his attitude towards the Milo statue; it became something ineluctable, if not actually dear, to the grimy-faced boy off the tender. Towards the end of his half-year term, before taking his examination for the fourth grade qualifying him for the job of engineer's mate, Sergei underwent his first test of courage and will. During a trip, while he was raking the fire at one of the stations, a displaced grate-bar fell into the ash-pan, and the young fireman volunteered to set it back immediately in its place so as not to delay the train. To do this the temperature in the furnace had to be reduced somewhat so that one could squeeze one's body through the fire-door hole up to the waist. "You'd better be careful, Vikhrov, it's hot as hell in there," said the engine-driver. "That's all right, Lazo* had it hotter. I'll be all right," Sergei said cockily, annoyed at still being looked upon as the molly-coddled son of a professor. Dashing water over his clothes, he wrapped some wet sack-cloth round himself and dived into the dark burning-hot hole. The job was done in two stages, and the deed afterwards discussed at the Komsomol meeting. A week later he came with four other youngsters to take his examinations.

In a smoky little room with sooty windows looking out on the turn-table, sat the depot administration and veteran engine-drivers, who had come to have a look at their replacements. None of them so much as touched the wrench which Sergei had made to fit the given nut or his gage blocks, which were so perfectly finished that they stuck when put together. But after the usual questions concerning engine handling and maintenance, one grey-haired instructor by the name of Markelich, who was a notable figure at the Depot, put the novice through his semaphore catechism; apparently, during his own apprenticeship, he had bumped a loaded train into the tail-end of another standing on the line in front or had seen someone else do it, and for fifty years afterwards had always looked upon signalisation as the peak of loco-motive learning. Rather snappy at first, he thawed a bit towards the end and looked at Sergei with a kindlier eye. Sergei was now expecting to be asked about his singed eyebrows and his bandaged hand, which had received burns through the mitten while he was fixing the grate-bar.

Indeed, the old man's eyes suddenly seemed to light up with a look of real interest.

"He's smart, he'll make good all right," Markelich said, holding a match to his pipe. "And now tell me, sonny"—Sergei got ready to describe his deed briefly and drily, as becomes all distinguished heroes—"tell me—you don't touch the demon drink, do you? We old fellows were not to blame, really—the tsarist

---

* Lazo—a hero of the civil war in Siberia and the Far East. Was burnt in a locomotive furnace after being brutally tortured by the Japanese and the Russian whiteguards in 1920.—*Tr.*

regime drove us to it. But you live happier, you don't have to touch the stuff, unless it be a glass o' wine once in a blue moon just to buck you up," he said, brushing his moustache with a swaggering air, and it dawned on Sergei that his feat was but a trifle, a quite ordinary event in that bigger life into which he was being initiated.

The old man did not let him go until he was perfectly satisfied that the novice also knew the engine signals for fire and air-raid alarms—it was the fourth day of the war.

CHAPTER TEN

1

Although there was a war on and all people's thoughts were for the front, Polya could not leave her own private troubles be for the very reason that the times demanded of everyone the greatest moral cleanness. Like her mother, there was no price in the world she would not pay to be able to look her people squarely in the face. Vikhrov, without knowing it, had passed his daughter's test, which was all the more · severe in that children usually pass judgement on evidence that almost eludes the law and do not punish by aught save eternal contempt. The preliminary investigations inclined in his favour, and it now remained to study the history of his scientific feud with Gratsiansky. The reassuring impression created by his September lecture, by the way, was somewhat dimmed in the harsher light of further reflection. Even a child understood that no man, however wicked, would have dared, if only from an instinct of self-preservation, to address young people in any other way than he had done, and that at a time when such fierce battles were raging around Moscow.

At this stage of the investigations Taisa was unable to help her niece; Polya learned something eventually from the young engineer's mate, and a good deal was disclosed by a chance phrase which she overheard one ghastly December night. Meanwhile, morbidly scrupulous like her mother, Polya probed for the truth by ingenious wiles and hard efforts, as a result of which her almost overpowering impulse to rush off to the front in Varya's wake received a temporary check. She had to do this with an absolutely unburdened conscience, otherwise her decision would look like suicidal hysterics. On various pretexts the girl interviewed her father's colleagues. They gave their consultation willingly but shut up at once at the mention of Vikhrov's chief critic; eventually closer familiarity with the state of the forests in European Russia and with the forest disputes of the thirties exercised no little influence on Polya's ultimate choice of a profession. Osminov, whose acquaintance she made at the end of November, was the only one to tell her the facts about the famous controversy and share with her his scant information about her father's opponent. It is noteworthy that even then, in the private talk they had in a remote front-line village, Major Osminov's tone of evasive friendliness all but concealed his actual personal opinion.

Gradually, Alexander Gratsiansky took shape in Polya's mind as a majestic but somewhat enigmatic figure; he appeared to her as a man ascetically reserved, and skilfully armoured against prying curiosity; she was to discover, for instance, that there was not a soul in the world who dared to drop in on him informally without first telephoning him. In the first place, he proved to possess none of the usual human foibles. To be sure, at a time when it was the custom among men in the Soviet land to adorn themselves with nothing but the private virtues, Gratsiansky wore a signet ring with an antique intaglio on his forefinger. It was no ordinary ring, however. According to the mysterious hints dropped by its owner he had received it, in a collateral line of succession, from some confidant of no less a person than Herzen, and he therefore took the liberty of wearing it not because he wished to stand apart from other mortals or even to make up for the suffering he had endured at the hands of the autocracy, but merely, so to speak, as a token of spiritual succession from the world's outstanding champions for the cause of liberation. By virtue of these hereditary rights Gratsiansky held offices simultaneously in at least a dozen committees, editorial staffs, and sundry scientific institutions; at the Forestry Institute he held a chair of a rather vague denomination, namely, "the organisation of the industrial utilisation of forests." Of course, the problems under this heading, such as road construction, fire control, technical equipment, forest protection and housing arrangements for the lumberers, were each studied separately at the three other corresponding faculties, but Professor Gratsiansky embraced them, as it were, with his universal genius and outstanding temperament, so that none of the management attempted to define his functions for fear of making a powerful enemy and raising his own blood pressure. Nevertheless, according to Osminov, Gratsiansky had enriched forestry practices by a number of extremely interesting proposals, which unfortunately were either impracticable or useless; at any rate, they would have done no harm had they been dictated by the interests of the forest and not by a striving of their author to crush his rivals in science by the weight of his infallible intellect, which, if not very deep, was at least amazing in breadth and scope. In a word, in the eyes of simpletons, this man deserved the greatest respect for having selflessly shouldered the burden of general supervision of forest affairs in the country at large, in consequence of which editorial staffs lent him their ear, colleagues fawned upon him, and old forest lecturers of the milder brand felt obliged to quote him, though it hurt them to do so.

Gratsiansky achieved this by sheer personal talent and with the sole aid of his critical articles, the deadly sarcasm of which raised him, as it were, above the crowd of his mediocre and indolent contemporaries. Whispered jokes were cracked that as soon as he had finished off his colleagues marked down for annihilation, he would use the thunderbolts of his passion against certain backward phenomena of Nature in order to bring them to a desirable state of perfection. Apart from this, Gratsiansky occasionally presented the world with short, extremely cautious, but extraordinarily erudite forewords to other men's books; however, he did not thus honour just any current booklets on forests, but only outstanding works of the past, putting his finger on the root of the evil and showing in what manner it was to be cast out therefrom. He wrote no big books of his own for publication, not because he was reluctant to overload the printing trade, not even from a praiseworthy fear of falling into some punishable error, but merely on account of his failing health, particularly, a low haemoglobin count, which barely reached 63.5 per cent. Persistent rumour had been claiming for the whole of fifteen years that Gratsiansky was preparing for the press a fat bible on forestry consisting of three and a half thousand pages of small type, not counting annotations, after the publication of which it would be left for all forest scientists to curl up and die at his pedestal from envy and insignificance. He would certainly have carried out his threat but for the express veto of the doctors. His frail constitution considered, it was clearly no mean feat of Gratsiansky's to have overthrown such a Goliath of an adversary as Tulyakov, whom he had pulled to little pieces for his old-fashioned theories of forest management. And Sergei alone, out of understandable boyish pity for his father, ascribed to Gratsiansky such a degree of robust health that it would be almost an act of common kindness to impair it slightly for the good of the country and forestcraft; Ivan Vikhrov had made the boy promise on his word of honour that he would do no harm to his opponent.

Gratsiansky's brilliant career started in the middle of the twenties when *The Fate of the Russian Forest* was followed by the first edition of Vikhrov's *Introduction to Forestcraft*. It may well be that this book broke no new sensational ground, but it was informed by a feeling of such intense concern for the future which no Soviet scientist worthy of the name could very well dispense with; few people before him had dared to speak out so boldly on behalf of the forest. The author's premises were based on the well-known fact that forest products were articles of primary necessity and therefore the annual demand for them recurred in approximately the same but ever-growing dimensions. Vikhrov deduced therefrom that the object of the forest manager was to maintain the forests in a condition that would ensure the greatest possible yield of excellent timber. For this purpose, felling based on the rate of annual growth and the age of the stands should be made good by proper restocking and carried out in such a way that by the time the last cutting area was cleared the first would have grown a new crop of mature timber. The possible gap between supply and demand which this might lead to was, in the author's opinion, to be filled by developing the virgin forests of the European North, Siberia and the Soviet Far East, by reducing prodigal waste in processing, by a more thrifty attitude on the part of the man in the felling area, by regeneration of the forests through restocking of felled and planting of waste areas, by increasing the annual wood increment through proper care of the forests and reclamation of swampy woods, by fire protection, and lastly by fighting wood rot in timber produce and stands, and substituting metal for wood wherever possible. "Better to shed sweat than tears," Vikhrov concluded one of his chapters. "Unless these simple axioms are understood and accepted, forestry becomes a mere matter of forest utilisation. We can please ourselves about it, of course, if we are willing to set the needs of the future at naught." Ivan Vikhrov thus followed the line of previous Russian foresters with this sad difference that his unfortunate book appeared on the eve of the most intensive exploitation of the forests in the country's history. Naturally, any theory involving a reconstruction of the greatest national industry attracted to itself heightened public attention and was bound to rouse objections. Supported though it was by all kinds of calculations, Vikhrov's uncompromising attitude sometimes alarmed some of his own numerous followers, although his demand only amounted to a plea for the establishment of a stricter system of forest management. In those days Vikhrov acquired quite a few serious critics, of whom Gratsiansky, the most belligerent one, immediately became conspicuous for his brilliancy of wit and punching power. Inspired by his easy victory over Tulyakov and the recent lively controversy around the question of reducing the felling rotation cycle, he opened Vikhrov's honest-hearted book at random, sought out the root of evil therein, probed to its whys and wherefores, weighed the pros and cons, filled in the gaps, which the author was alleged to have deliberately left for obscurity's sake, and presented this rehash to the world with a proper emotional seasoning that made it as hot a dish as ever sent man to the gallows.

In those days many people looked upon praise as corruptive liberalism, while the negation of the good for the sake of the desirable better was regarded as pedagogical wisdom. His success so emboldened the reviewer, who had thus suddenly risen from humble obscurity, that when Vikhrov's next book *The Forest as an Economic Object* appeared he struck out at it still harder, and, truth to tell, below the belt. To the astonishment of the bystanders, his colleague once more took the blow standing. "No, my dear Professor, you can't scare us with forest laws, which the bourgeoisie invented for their own use. It's we who make the laws," Gratsiansky wrote with dubious authority, for all the forest acts of the Soviet Government, beginning with Lenin's famous decree of 1918, restricted felling to the amount of the annual increment. "To spite you we shall cut down everything when the time comes, we shall spare neither the Volga nor the Mezen, which is so dear to your heart, we shall strip the Pechora and the Kama down to the bone, do the same to the Dnieper and the Dvina, the Angara and the Yenisei, and whatever else you have hidden away there in your bosom, damn it!" Another line in this strain and the author would have thrown a fit, it seemed. But neither in this article nor in the whole subsequent series of his printed criticisms did Gratsiansky ever come to real grips with any current forest problem. He did not deign to waste his energies on the trivialities of lumbering practices; just as there were engineers in turbine construction or specialists on the middle ear, Gratsiansky considered himself a specialist on the root of evil, albeit, for the time being, that of forestial origin. All the rest he left to his "boys", the neophytes of science, who had joined him in the expectation of quicker returns in the harvesting of life's joys. They were the Dizzy Doxies, so-called because of an extremely orthodox pliancy towards all four points of the compass.

And so a strange twin star rose above the Russian forest, the blazing heat of the one being tempered by the subduing coolness of the other, and its name was Vikhrov and Gratsiansky, both scientists of standing reputation in that field. Their contemporaries gradually became accustomed to the idea that it was the fate of the former to be constantly supplying something new to be ground in the dreary millstones of the latter. The harder grain, such as the author's references to posterity, were promptly rejected before the eyes of the unsuspecting reader, branded as "Vikhrov's tricks"; and when Vikhrov was behindhand in feeding up his stuff, Gratsiansky goaded him into activity by press comments in which he hinted at his suspiciously long-delayed creative halts. Over a number of years he climbed his hill by using Vikhrov's books as stepping stones, and the importance of each book corresponded mathematically to the height of his ascent. Nevertheless, Gratsiansky found it to his advantage to sustain Vikhrov's reputation as one of the most eminent, if questionable, forest scientists of his age, for in this way he was able to keep their relations on a sustained yield basis, which afforded him, as it were, a guaranteed annual return. Crushing his opponent out of existence would have spelt disaster for himself.

To keep in good striking form during the years of Vikhrov's enforced idleness, Gratsiansky re-examined his former books, which, he alleged, had prematurely taken their place in the gold fund of forest literature. One such critical article published in the mid-thirties dealt with a now half-forgotten book of Vikhrov's *The Fate of the Russian Forest*. The article was written for a change over modified initials, but it was impossible to mistake the accusatory note of Gratsiansky's formulations. The writer started out by relegating the book to the rank of belles-lettres on account of its numerous poetic digressions. This untied his hands. Step by step he ferreted out in it contemplative objectivism and philistine economism, vicious traces of supra-class eclecticism and mechanistic empiricism, and an indisputable tendency towards idealistic nihilism and pseudo-scientific vulgarism, exemplified, first and foremost, by the anthropomorphistic expression—which was not Vikhrov's, by the way—that "the forest ploughs the land", a thing it could not do really because it was not a human being. Incidentally, the writer questioned the extent of the Ukraine's wooded lands in the days of the Gostomysls, which Vikhrov had obviously exaggerated, and bitterly ridiculed his concern over the climatic dangers involved in the wanton felling of the forests, since, according to Heraclitus, the climate changes too, and who knows whether eucalyptuses would not be growing around Vologda in a year or two. Finally, the critic made a virulent attack on the title-page which dedicated the book of all persons, to the Yenga honey-merchant Kalina Glukhov. On the whole, it was a scurrilous nasty sort of article, which made everyone feel a bit uncomfortable, but its closing lines raised the question of safeguarding the youth from Vikhrov's pernicious influence, and that was a thing that could not be entirely overlooked.

2

Vikhrov learned, to his surprise, that the shot had been fired from within the precincts of the Forestry Scientific Committee, to be more exact, by its newly appointed Assistant Director Cheredilov; the Director, Academician Tarakantsev, a classmate of the late V. V. Dokuchayev, was a mild pernickety old fellow. Rumours of the marvellous changes in Cheredilov's career had reached Vikhrov before that. He was said to have achieved advancement through the good offices of his friend Gratsiansky and his own rare gift of deference to those in authority, so much so, that, in the event, say, of his chief, Tarakantsev, leaning his hand upon him as he would upon the arm-rest of his chair, the cranium of the blessed one would instantly assume the shape and curve of the master's hand. This, however, may have been merely slanderous gossip on the part of overlooked enviers; the lucky ones, on the contrary, endowed him with so many hitherto unappreciated qualities as would have more than filled a goodly sized whale of virtues. At any rate, the appearance of that article explained why, living in the same city, Cheredilov had not paid Vikhrov a single friendly call since they had come to Moscow. So Vikhrov, impelled by purely exploratory motives, decided to call on him himself at his new home.

"I may get him to come and have dinner, so have some potatoes baked in their jackets—he used to like them in the days of his youth. As for the bottled stuff, I'll buy some of that on my way back," he instructed Taisa before setting out on his errand.

The Forestry Scientific Committee was situated in a noisy Moscow street, on the third floor of an old building entirely occupied by a mass of subsidiary institutions and offices with mysterious names, which communicated with each other by means of dingy staircases and passages; Vikhrov wandered about there for a long time as if in a real forest. He went down a dismal corridor, where painters on platforms were splashing liquid chalk about, passed the offices of some mysterious institution by the name of Dor-Khim-Vosk, and the local Trade Union Committee of Registry Office Employees, and turning a corner entered a small but exceedingly charming room with a view of a little gilded Moscow cupola dating to no later than the sixteenth century, and with panelled walls skilfully painted in imitation oak. True, there was nothing else in the room that bespoke the forest, but the whole colour scheme was reminiscent of the cool green shadows of a morning copse and had such a restful look about it that one would think it an ideal place for quiet cerebration. Instead, life here under the direction of G. P. Cheredilov was at its busiest.

The reception-room was empty and through the open door of the inner office one could hear the rasping voice of Cheredilov which rose to a slightly whistling falsetto of fury.

"But my dear girl, you have been put there to protect me and my valuable time against unorganised intrusions, and I demand— do you hear me?—I demand that you should be equal to the task imposed upon you," Cheredilov snapped at something subordinate, which emitted an answering squeak. "And should any applicants and cadgers continue to phone and make themselves a nuisance, I want to hammer this into your head once and for all—I have no relatives, no comrades whatever, let alone friends. Even asleep I am always a busy man, a government executive, a pillar, that's what I am. Now run along, Mary Stuart or whatever your name is, and do the duty which history has imposed upon you. Have I made myself clear?"

Vikhrov thought with a touch of grim humour that he had come just at the right time.

A superstitious visitor would have put his visit off for at least a month, but Vikhrov knew only too well how quickly his former chum cooled off. Not to embarrass the secretary, he tactfully withdrew for half an hour to watch the violent activities of the house painters; when he returned, he found a curly-haired female of over medium age at the secretary's desk with spots of lingering colour in her cheeks. She asked his name apprehensively, and although he repeated it and assured her that he would not annoy Comrade Cheredilov, fire a shot gun at him, or borrow money from him, she consented to announce him only after her chief had finished drafting his plan of current measures for the next six months aimed at improving the office routine. Within an hour she went into the sanctum to fulfil her promise, after prudently putting the lid on her typewriter, which had some unfinished work in it. Cheredilov, it appeared, was still busy, so would he please read one of the magazines while her chief was on the trunk-line.

Vikhrov read through his magazine, paced up and down the carpet strip, and looked into the general office, where there was the same smell of leatherette, and arithmometers snarled at him through drifting layers of tobacco smoke. By all signs Cheredilov ruled his scientific domain with a rod of iron and kept his staff up to scratch. This sector of the forest front presented a scene of intense, albeit, to an outsider, rather incomprehensible activities. So much so that the secretary stopped pounding her typewriter in case the visitor, God forbid, should overhear what she was typing about. Occasionally someone would slip noiselessly into the sanctum—now the office-woman with a lunch tray, now the pay-clerk (it was the first of the month), and finally a flat pince-nezed lady whose job it was to record the thoughts, feelings and orders of Comrade Cheredilov in stenographic characters. On these occasions Vikhrov caught a glimpse of the inner sanctum revealing the edge of an immense desk from under which there peeped a familiar sandaled foot of formidable size, a well-planed spruce board placed there to provide a touch of scientific colour, and finally a hygrometer on the wall to warn one when the air reached a degree of dryness that was injurious to the health.

Vikhrov was reminded of a day, a quarter of a century ago, when the Musketeers had all gone swimming in a stream in the country outside St. Petersburg. It was May and the water was rather chilly. Vikhrov and Valery had swum to the other side, but Cheredilov was still standing knee-deep in the water, snorting, dabbing his chest, and hawking like a deacon about to invoke the Lord's blessings; he could not pluck up courage to dip his large body, which was already loose and flabby, into the stinging

412

cold water. As for Gratsiansky, he had basked unashamedly in the sun on the sandy bank without even taking off his coat and the student's cap with the plush band. While Vikhrov was absorbed in his humorous meditations, Cheredilov, through an inner door, had passed into the upper spheres to attend an urgent conference, but this did not become known until an hour later. After waiting fruitlessly until nightfall, Vikhrov betook himself to a Russian bath, which always had the effect of restoring his good humour.

The numerous appreciative comments on his criticised book by forestry colleagues had convinced Vikhrov that he was right; he was simple-minded enough to believe that the failure of his errand was due to a quite ordinary misunderstanding. Like his uncle Afanasy, he cherished until old age the childish belief that he merely had to explain his forest anxieties to his opponents in an atmosphere of easy friendliness for Gratsiansky, and after him Cheredilov, to throw themselves upon his neck with tears of remorse and reconciliation. The next Sunday morning Vikhrov took a train to Cheredilov's summer-place outside Moscow. It was a lovely June day, and the walk through the ancient pine wood, the only surviving one for hundreds of miles around, was in itself a delightful aesthetic experience. Cheredilov's house was concealed from the public view behind a high fence surmounted by a comb of rusty nails, and was an excellent place both for restoring one's health by means of pinewood exhalations and for making certain observations of a social and ethical nature. The surrounding trees were kept in perfect order, the soil at the roots was loosened with loving care, and the dry branches all the way up the trunks were cut off with a garden saw; numerous nesting-boxes, those one-roomed flats for feathered newly-weds, provided further evidence of the care which the master took that everybody within the radius of his personal property should feel happy and contented. The same forethought was lavished on the plants, which were disposed here and there in astonishing diversity and profusion, from ordinary gooseberries to walnut trees, planted in deep shadow to add to the fulness of living rather than in expectation of any crop. In short, it was a well-appointed little paradise, just over an acre in extent, properly legalised through a notary public.

As soon as Vikhrov entered the grounds a shaggy cur of un-investigated breed rushed at him with a triple-keyed sobbing bark; only the chain and the merciful intervention of a chauffeur who was washing his car prevented the beast from tearing the brave intruder to pieces. The visitor gave it a wide berth and passed between rows of blossoming sweet peas towards a two-storeyed wooden building with towers and embrasures in the form of peaceful verandahs barricaded with clustering vines. Coming through the wicket, Vikhrov had noticed a watchful eye following his movements from above through the slightly parted greenery, and now, at closer quarters, he recognised the pyjamaed figure of Cheredilov. He waved his hat to him, and further concealment became senseless.

"Oh, it's you!" Cheredilov spoke down with a marked lack of enthusiasm, yet without resentment at having his peace disturbed. "I was wondering who it could be, paying a visit without notice. Well, well, I didn't expect this honour, but I'm glad to see you. How are you getting on? Still writing, I hear?"

"Yes, old chap, I had a mind to use up all the paper in the world, but the paper-mills are working too fast for me, I can't catch up with them," Vikhrov said, dabbing his hot neck and head with a handkerchief. "Pardon me for having missed seeing you the other day in your temple of science."

"That's all right," Cheredilov said forgivingly, the humour lost upon him. "How is it I didn't hear your car, though. You couldn't have pedalled down from town on a bike, surely?"

For the sake of self-preservation, Vikhrov perhaps should have turned away immediately after this, but being a scientist, he never allowed personal motives to affect his interest in the living phenomena of Nature.

"I came down by train, old chap. An occasional walk is good for you at our age. I was going to call on a sick friend hereabouts, but found that he'd gone away on a business trip," Vikhrov lied frivolously. "So I thought I might as well drop in on my way and thrash things out with you. Pretty close, looks like rain, doesn't it?"

"What d'you mean, thrash what out?" Cheredilov said guardedly, pushing his head through the vine.

"Well, just a talk about life in general," Vikhrov said with a rueful smile, stroking his neck. "You don't know everything in the world, you might hear something new from me."

"Still, I'd like to know beforehand what you're going to talk about," the one on the upper terrace insisted. As a top-level executive, he could not very well allow himself thus unceremoniously to be drawn into some undesirable abyss.

"The same old things, Grigory—about the forest, about my books and your attitude towards them," Vikhrov explained, suddenly overcome by a sickening weakness. He still did not go away, so as not to give the impression that he resented friendly criticism.

"I see," the one above muttered with a thoughtful air. He vanished, then reappeared a minute or two later as if nothing had happened. "Very well, I don't mind, old chap, if you think it may do you good."

Vikhrov had visualised a somewhat warmer meeting than this. He had had no thought of asking any favours of Cheredilov or soliciting his protection against his own impending troubles, he merely wanted to restrain this happy-go-lucky, and at one time fairly decent lazybones from the errors, so prejudicial to the forest, which he had fallen into under the influence of Gratsiansky. It could not be said that Vikhrov had chosen the wrong time either. Cheredilov had Sunday guests. Through the open windows came the smell of Sunday pies, slightly burnt in the baking, and the clatter of plates and dishes mingled with the gay raucous sound of a gramophone playing a rollicking folk tune. What is more, Vikhrov was very thirsty, and all the way from the station he had been picturing to himself a cool misted jug of home-made kvass, but he waited in vain to be invited upstairs into the very Garden of Eden. He simply failed to understand that his visit, following on the heels of that merciless article and with the added prospect of more "slams" to come, could not only mar Cheredilov's relaxation in the bosom of his family and friends, but, in a certain sense, prejudice the position of the good host himself. At the same time Cheredilov felt flattered that this forest brawler, who had been knocked off his perch at last, had come down to see him cap in hand of his own accord. He could not resist the temptation of teaching him a little lesson for that unpardoned night in Pashutino long ago, when Vikhrov had heard out his confession with a yawn and even a touch of lofty tolerance.

"No, Ivan, I have no objection whatever to giving you my views," Cheredilov spoke down in a tone of anxious sympathy. "For one thing, between you and me, I rather like your books—not so much for their contents as for that ... what d'you call it ... that enthusiasm of yours, always burning at white heat, so to speak. Naturally, you can't help burning in such an epoch, we all burn, but can't you do it somehow a bit cooler, old chap. I love Nature as much as you do, and I don't have to tell you

415

that wandering about the woods with a basket is my second ruling passion, but you've been bumbling about that sustained yield utilisation of yours for so many years—pardon me for being so blunt about it—and with so much incantation, too, that people are sick and tired of hearing it. I can't explain it, but that word doesn't take on, somehow, can't you use something else instead—intensive utilisation of forests, say, or even reproduction of the forest, if you can't think of anything better. The thing is to express yourself in a way that will start a pleasant train of thoughts in people instead of giving them the bellyache. Gratsiansky is a different proposition! But then he's a gifted man. Look at the kicks you've been getting from him, yet you still keep at it. Now, tell me, why the dickens, for instance, did you have to go and attend Tulyakov's funeral?"

"He was a great scientist and he was my teacher," Vikhrov said quietly and gravely. "Besides, people followed his coffin who were your chiefs at the time. Just so."

"You can't go by them. Think of Noah's wise sons, and turn away. Don't think I'm trying to teach you good behaviour or toadyism, Ivan. I want you to learn social tact. Now, why did you have to start that dirge on a billet of wood? Damn it all, what if they are cutting down the protection-forests! You should worry! What if the woodland wealth *is* being squandered—you won't be asked to make good the waste, will you? It's not as if you were a salaried officer put in charge of that forest treasury."

"No one can put me in charge of what is my own civil duties," Vikhrov answered drily, shifting from one foot to the other. "You and I have to think of these things, because behind us moves an army of a million unreasoning axes of flawless steel. The purpose of my knowledge, as I understand it, is to keep the forest in good order and let the people know of all changes that have taken place in it. Try to imagine, Grigory, what would happen to a scout who regularly reported agreeable but false information to his superior officer."

"You're flying your kites pretty high, aren't you—a sort of self-appointed public manometer, eh?" Cheredilov said with an air of sad disapproval, depositing himself on something which his wife, solicitous of his Sunday rest, had placed there for him to sit on. "I'm not trying to talk you out of it, but you're not made of stone, after all. You've waved your flag once or twice, now step aside. The engine will crush you, you crazy man. Let others live, and you'll live to a hundred and twenty-one yourself."

It was impossible at this point not to touch upon current forest affairs. Cheredilov, it should be mentioned, did not adhere to any single point of view on the geometrical grounds that only three simultaneous ones could provide a maximum of cohesion to the plane of good living. As he would not have had sufficient time to expound all three of them before dinner, he confined himself to Gratsiansky's old prescription, which recommended taking things easy, lying fallow for a time, and, if the writing itch became too bad, writing something inoffensive, something, say, about the role of the cambium in the vegetable organism with the main accent on combating the survivals of idealism in the minds of contemporaries. Cheredilov expounded all this in a wooden edifying tone, like a radio set, and Vikhrov could hardly believe that the same man had sung his star-song *Nochenka* at the students' parties, and sung it in a way that gripped one's heart and brought a mist of tears to one's eyes.

Vikhrov's spirits drooped sharply, the sky clouded, too, and to cap it all, his neck grew painfully stiff from the long strain of looking up. But the subject concerned the most important thing in his life, and personal discomfort could be disregarded for a time.

"I've got you taped now, Grigory," he took him up in a tone whose acerbity was rather out of place in a man of his position. "In exchange for the good things of life you want me to don fox guise, but I'd like to keep my human aspect, I've got used to it. What I've come to tell you is that you've gone through my unfortunate book none too conscientiously. In face of the whole country you have attributed to me the intention of putting industrialisation on rations, but you do not mention a word about my detailed tables showing where and how much timber can be cropped without ruining our forest wealth. You have accused me of deliberately ignoring the plight of the forest workers under tsarism, although I have three pages describing how a certain Knishev fed the Yenga lumbermen tainted food. I leave it to you to find a name for the person who tries to trump up a charge against his own friend, even though a former one. And lastly, you have come to a secret arrangement with Gratsiansky to—"

"Wait a minute," Cheredilov interrupted him, his face paling slightly, "I'm beginning to forget things in my old age—but what Knishev is that? Wasn't that the fellow who slipped you a little gift to the tune of twenty-five rubles?"

Suddenly the music indoors broke off, and a spatter of rain, together with a gust of wind, swept the iron roof; several drops fell upon the upturned face of Ivan Vikhrov. A man coming awake on the verandah could be heard asking for beer or a cocktail or something cold in a mellow voice, but he was hissed to silence by a dozen voices; all the household together with the guests were now enjoying the free spectacle from the safety of their retreat.

"In our honest country work is honoured above all else, Grigory, and therefore, even if my book was the worst of all books published with the approval of the authorities, you should have treated a friend's work with respect," the man below said in a tone of grave reproval, blinking at the rain that flooded his eye-sockets. "A certain Pliny said there was not a book in the world so bad that an intelligent reader could not derive some benefit from it."

"And what does your St. Bernard of Clairvaux have to say about it?" the upper one lunged forward through the vine in a fit of fury, and hands could be seen reaching out to him from all sides to pull him away from the railings.

"I wouldn't spare the forest when it's a question of breaking through the fiery ring of nation-wide calamity," Vikhrov continued under the now pouring rain, which he swallowed together with the air. "But I think those people who talk about making short work of the forest in peacetime according to the practice of wartime fellings are wicked people. That's why our conversation, too, goes beyond a mere clash of forest management ideas and becomes. . . ."

"Come on, let's know where you stand!" Cheredilov said ominously, leaning out at the risk of injuring health and limb.

"I mean it grows into a political fight."

Something indoors dropped and broke with a crash, then a strained feminine voice called from within: "Grigory, why don't you come to the table, you have guests, after all." The rest was drowned in the noise of the heavy downpour. For some moments Cheredilov glared at the lame, terrifyingly cool man standing there below.

"You've inherited the good breeding of the common herd, I see. Wasn't it your father who worked in St. Petersburg as a bouncer or something?" Cheredilov shouted through the storm.

At that Vikhrov turned away, and with a sense of duty fulfilled, retraced his steps to the garden gate without any more fear of getting wet. It was showering harder than ever, a roistering gambolling rainstorm that set all the grasses and branches dancing. In the forest glades the pink-and-gold spray could be seen bursting into tiny rainbows under the sun, which was already peeping out in the torn swooning heights. There was a last crash of thunder, and then a magic scented languor spread through the washed world. Vikhrov's jacket was steaming by the time he strode into the station, and for some reason the queue at the booking-office let him take his ticket out of turn, and he accepted the honour with the air of a man who had just fought their battle for them. He was not grieved at what had happened, for the profession of a forester always involved the risk of getting caught in bad weather.

3

The day of reckoning came a month later, when, as a result of Cheredilov's article, Vikhrov was asked to make his report to the Scientific Council of the Forestry Institute. A Committee of Enquiry headed by Gratsiansky had made a ten-day study of his teaching activities, and it was whispered that Tarakantsev, after reading the Committee's sixty-three-page report, had sung out in a quavery falsetto to the tune of *Eugene Onegin*, "He's killed...." Everyone understood that Vikhrov's dismissal was a foregone conclusion, and all went to the public meeting for the sole and frustrated purpose of hearing what the shining lights of forestcraft had to say on the subject. The meeting was held in the crowded assembly-hall of the Institute, which had once resounded to the mazurkas of Catherine's grandees. In the back left-hand corner, under the gallery, sat Gratsiansky's Dizzy Doxies in a detached group; conspicuous among them for their aggressive air was the leading triad of the group—comrades Andreichik, Yeichik and simply Chik, the oldest and most dangerous of them all with grey walrus moustaches and spectacles of telescopic device. The public, by the way, judiciously pretended not to notice the comic similarity of their names. As soon as the report began the non-smoking Chik took a seat in the front row, writing pad in hand, with a public-prosecutor air, while the other two adjourned to the corridor, whence, cigarettes in hand, they peeped in at the door and winked at each other while awaiting their turn. Gratsiansky himself was absent owing, as was respectfully whispered in the lobby, to a sharp drop of haemoglobin in his rundown constitution.

Knowing beforehand what was going to happen, Vikhrov made his report in half the time allowed him. He made no mention of his department, and instead of repenting the misdeeds imputed to him, he started straight off by expounding his well-known theories, and did this with such obstinate coolness and clarity as if he were addressing little children, as if he were teasing fate. He chalked figures on the board from memory. No longer relying on his own undermined authority, he often cited the opinions of Russia's outstanding forest personalities and even went to the extent of quoting a mere chemist—Mendeleyev, who was supposed to have said that we ought to leave our descendants no less than we receive ourselves. What grieved his friends still more—they regarded it as criminal pessimism—was his mentioning how many years it would take a stand of planted trees to reach the maturity of a Petrine crop of formed trees with an outturn of five-hundred cubic metres to the hectare. And, finally, he evoked a storm of indignation not only in the enemy camp, but among some of the platform party too, by defiantly announcing that he was prepared to listen to and consider any constructive counter-proposals from the opposing side.

"*In articulo mortis* one could have behaved with more decency," Chik shouted, noising his indignation with the help of his writing pad.

Not to tire the meeting with figures, the co-report of the committee studiously avoided all Vikhrov's statistical tables and calculations, but dealt at length with his objections to clear felling, on the grounds that it allegedly disturbed the so-called balance in the given plant society. According to Vikhrov, the co-report said, Nature acted spontaneously, whereas man acted consciously, because he weakened one thing in her and strengthened others. Consequently, according to Vikhrov, man and Nature were antagonists, and man's work was inimic to Nature. From this the Committee concluded that Vikhrov believed man was incapable of coordinating his activities with Nature and perceiving her processes, and this led directly to the most dangerous kind of agnosticism. The fact that Vikhrov called for a study of the natural laws of the forest as a means of mastering the elements was a minor detail conveniently overlooked in the heat of controversy. It followed from this that Vikhrov was preaching to the students the conflict of man and Nature, mind and matter, and that was something that smacked of reactionary clericalism. Taken together, all this pointed to Vikhrov's adherence to Kantianism, Spencerianism, Machism, Dochmanism and even Vakulianism—an allusion to the Institute's inveterate caretaker Vakula Trepereshchenko, who, in defiance of all educated reasoning, clung obstinately to his belief in the life to come. The ensuing debates followed the pattern of a concert performance.

After the muddled speeches of Osminov and other disconcerted supporters of Vikhrov, after the speech of Tarakantsev, in which he claimed that permanent denudation, though stimulating the metamorphisation of biogeocoenose, *ceterum* is not identified with its degradation—after this one of the Dizzy Doxies was let loose to start the hunt. He began right off the bat by saying that Vikhrov's demand for a greater return of the forest reminded him of the Prussian junkers who tried to obtain a regular return from their latifundia by means of forest management on a sustained yield basis. This concept, long since condemned in the Soviet land, revealed Vikhrov's predilection for alien and downright hostile socio-economic systems. And generally, he proceeded, some of Vikhrov's personal links with the old world, now prematurely forgotten, would bear looking into more closely ... especially those between his wife and a landowner lady from Pomerania, who had stripped the Yenga forests to the bone. This made it abundantly clear that it was Vikhrov and no other who was the chief advocate and apologist of deforestation, who deliberately tried to restrict forest regeneration, that is to say, wanted to rob our socialist descendants. "Out of respect for these walls we say nothing about the political motives that guided Vikhrov's actions, though it is these more than anything else that call for urgent measures to be taken in his case." Immediately after this Chik took the floor without giving the meeting any breathing-space. As he lumbered towards the platform like a heavy siege gun, smiling deprecatingly at the trivial occasion which had necessitated his tearing himself away from grave and important business, the Chair shook under Vikhrov in time with his slow creaking steps.

Chik began by jocosely confessing that he had never been in a Russian forest, although, when he was younger, in his emigrant days, he often went for rambles in the Tyrolese *Dauerwalde*, as they were called—rambles undertaken for love of hiking rather than out of any interest in a survival of antiquity which was as grotesque as a beard on the face of a thinking creature of our advanced epoch. Generally speaking, according to his prognosis, the forest is a slow culture which, in the not distant future, is bound to give way to plants with a lower growth period such as hemp, say, or bocconia. None the less, he, Chik, was highly amused at the lame professor's tearful tirade *in memoriam* of the forests, coniferous and deciduous, uttered in the widowly voice of Yaroslavna and in the ornamental style of Danila Zatochnik.

"I should say that the report we have just listened to is full of absurdities," Chik said in the manner of an idol of the public, "and points to a puerile and enviable vacancy of mind on the part of this spokesman of forest humanism, although I doubt whether in these turbulent times our society can afford to put up with a sentimental attitude towards the forest, which makes an object of worship out of an ordinary log. This reminds me of another learned forester of ours—Graff, who, on leaving the Veliko-Anadol forestry division, embraced every single tree trunk, although he was not under the influence of alcohol. A still more touching comic, if you like, was that colonel of the Forest Officers' Corps and manager of the state property of the Tula Gubernia, who died in 1874 and asked in his will that fir branches should be put in his coffin, and expressed the hope that the trees would forgive him that wanton damage, ha, ha! I had the doubtful pleasure of reading one of the works of our simple-minded colleague before this—the name of the book has slipped my memory at the moment—and what particularly struck me was his fussy zeal and uncritical preference for all kinds of mediocre thinkers, irrespective of their social credo. To be sure, St. Bernard of Clairvaux considered oaks and beeches his teachers, which probably explains the wholesome morality of his teachings, while Thomas à Kempis found solace only in the dense leafy woods. But the least a teacher of our sensitive splendid youth should know is that we have long since rejected the philistine idea of peace and quiet in favour of the permanent liberative tempests. If the author really wants to give his Soviet readers a good laugh I would advise him to include Confucios in his congenial company, seeing that that old gentleman, if I am not mistaken, had made some profound utterances about the usefulness of cypresses. No, my heart-burning colleague, spare us your laments, remove your semi-respectable dead from our highroad, beginning with the aforementioned St. Bernard, one of the fomentors of the first crusade. I daresay we can manage to straighten out our sovereign, if somewhat neglected forest affairs without the help of your six-hundred-year-old mildewed Varangians. Let me remind you, my forest-loving colleague, that thinking man started the day when he climbed down from his tree and left the virgin thickets for the open field. Thus, deforestation, if not quite a progressive thing, is at any rate a perfectly natural process in the development of culture. The countries of the West have long since succeeded in freeing themselves of these trammels to progress. Dud Dudley as far back as 1665 and Colbert four years later prophesied irreparable calamities to their countries as a result of deforestation, yet the absence of forests, to this day, does not prevent them from leading a prosperous life and even scheming against a powerful country, which possesses almost a third of the world's stocks of timber. Vikhrov's comparison of the forest with the mythical Atlas, who is said to have upheld the heavens of world economics for centuries, calls to mind the image of Atlas's brother Prometheus, whose name derives from the Indo-Germanic *prâmathyus* rather than from the Greek, and means 'rubbing wood against wood' in order to produce fire. Consequently, if Prometheus were a supporter of the professor now under discussion, *ipso facto*, the flame of even bourgeois progress would never have been kindled in the world. If this is Mr. Vikhrov's attitude to bourgeois progress we can well imagine what short work he would have made of our own proletarian progress if he had the power. Some of the bourgeois sibyls, by the way, have been repeatedly threatening us with all kinds of dire consequences for our courageous conduct in history, and we shall not allow anyone to blackmail us with talk about a bald planet, all the more that I myself, as you see, have no very luxuriant vegetation cover. On the contrary!" he added, stroking his perfectly bald pate. "Nor does the lack of it inconvenience me very much, except perhaps in the case of the fair sex, who cannot forgive me this lack of poetic locks."

"You ought to be ashamed of yourself, you sordid old man!" Vikhrov said, shaking his head, and everyone was amazed at his fearlessness at such a moment.

Chik poured himself a glass of water as if nothing had happened. "I must do justice, though, to the enthusiasm with which this aggressive zealot of the forest calls us back into the jungle," Chik wound up. "I don't deny that there is a certain attraction and cheapness in primitive life, but I'm afraid I'm a bit too old and heavy to sit for long even on the most comfortable bough. I presume that our little-esteemed colleague will appreciate our sincere striving to relieve him of both the embarrassing bonds of civilisation and his official post. A happy journey back to the forest *in saccula sacculorum*, O bearded child of Nature!"

Never, in all his long practice, had he ever had occasion to return to his seat unapplauded after half an hour's pyrotechnic exhibition of names, quotations and anecdotes, which have here been briefly summarised. Everyone stared down at his knees uncomfortably—all except the Dizzy Doxies, who expressed their warm approval at this auspicious opening of the attack. Even so, a certain confusion was noticeable among them, too, and the cigarette-smokers were no longer spoiling for a fight. The audience cast sympathetic glances at Vikhrov, who seemed indifferent to his fate, and at that very moment Gratsiansky himself came upon the scene of battle, leaning upon the arm of his favourite pupil. To all appearances, nothing short of superb courage and con-sciousness of a public and moral duty to be discharged could have impelled a man in his condition to leave his sick bed. Unshaven, shuffling, his life ebbing away almost at every step, he passed down the hushed rows, chin sunk in a woollen muffler, and with that air of mournful triumph one usually wears at the funeral of a person who has too long denied his contemporaries that slight pleasure. Deficiency of haemoglobin notwithstanding, the light of fiendish inspiration gleamed from under his pallid drooping eyelids as the distance between him and his victim diminished. In view of such obvious ill-health, he went straight up on to the platform before the disconcerted chairman could give him the floor out of turn.

He stood awhile with downcast eyes amid a dead silence, as though submerged in a flood of memories or perhaps trying to pull himself together.

"How do you do, Ivan ... are you there!" he gave utterance at last in a choked voice, turning an unseeing eye upon Vikhrov, who was sitting within five paces of him. His face was the ashiest any living person could have. "How do you do, ex-brother, ex-friend. As you see, I am very ill, but the guilty consciousness of our long association has raised me from my lonely bed, er ... not only in order to publicly repent of that association, but above all to take my leave of you for ever. For many a year have we marched together, if not hand in hand, then step for step, and, believe me, my conscience is clear. Hundreds of times, to the best of my ability, have I tried to keep you away from the brink, which—oh, no, I don't only mean Knishev!—which lured you. Admittedly, I sometimes did it none too delicately, but the public reputation of a friend had always been dearer to me than his personal favour. You know only too well that one doesn't think of a man's hair-do, or his very hair, when trying to save him from drowning. And what beautiful things you could have created to the joy of the assembled, er ... leading forest lights of our beloved country, had you applied the calories and kilowatts of your dangerous and gushing energy to other purposes." Gratsiansky's voice at this point sank to a lingering 'cello-like note of anguish.

"Come to the point, Gratsiansky," Osminov spoke up bravely. He even stood up, but sat down again immediately under his dull chilling glance.

"At this last moment of parting, Ivan, I should like to enumerate once more those grave differences that severed us for ever," Gratsiansky continued in the same tone of one weeping over the grave. "You tried to secure civil rights for the forest while secretly attempting to free it of civil obligations, and that at a time when the cannibals of our day, the Knishevs, who er ... broke your back without an effort, are trying to fell us all to the ground. Yes, we loved you, but could we afford to look after your forest and wait billions of years for it to fall and become anthracite by itself? Then uncover your breast, Ivan, show us brother-like what disease it is gnawing you from within er ... so that we can cut it away for you. Explain to us simple souls from what political platform you called upon us to ponder every stroke of the axe. With your bright intellect and almost indisputable knowledge, you could not help knowing, Ivan, that one minute multiplied by a million Soviet lumbermen makes two years idly wasted. Standing on the brink, confess at last for what diabòlic purpose you tried to limit Soviet fellings to the annual growth, in other words, to leave the foundation pits of our five-year plans gaping holes?"

"Call the police, someone! It's time to stop this farce!" a voice, disguised for safety's sake, shouted from a back seat.

A squall swept through the hall.

"The forest means water," Osminov shouted. "Who's going to drive our turbines, then—the hot dry winds, maybe?"

"Let's have no brawling at a funeral," Chik snarled, half-turning, and at this point Gratsiansky's voice broke like that of a widow at the first knock of the hammer on the coffin lid.

"There, we are calling to you in a thousand voices, Ivan, but you do not answer. We shall leave here with aching hearts to make good by our hard selfless work the harm which your writings have caused. But I cast this handful of earth into your early grave with a feeling of gratitude for all those joys, and unfortunately er ... disappointed hopes, which you gave us. Ivan, in the days of our youth and our joint revolutionary struggle."

Those sitting near him detected even an unshed tear of fairly considerable size and yellowish hue—the latter, no doubt, due to the lights—in Gratsiansky's eye as he descended the platform; the Dizzy Doxies promptly wrapped him up in a fur coat and rushed him home to make up for his lost haemoglobin. Much of his work, however, was undone by the Secretary of the Institute's Party organisation. He was a youngish man, a candidate of the Mechanisation Department, and one of that admirable band of Party intellectuals who had been drafted to leadership straight from the aforementioned foundation pits of the current five-year plan. He had little to do with the prevailing forestry dissensions on account of his speciality and took no sides in the dispute, but being a sensible outspoken man, he disapproved of the turn which the discussion had taken. He had no intention of defending Vikhrov and merely remarked sarcastically that the controversial methods of his opponents were rather unseemly in builders of communism, especially when such vital economic issues were at stake. While having the greatest respect for Professor Gratsiansky's past, the Secretary nevertheless called his speech a fit of bourgeois rhetoric aimed at clouding the truth; figures were best disproved by figures, he said. Finally, he roundly condemned the sneering flippancy of Comrade Chik's speech, who had dared to compare public criticism with hot bricks. Vikhrov refused to make any concluding remarks. Towards night it became known that the higher authorities had asked for the shorthand report of the meeting to be sent to them.

Nevertheless the election meeting at Vikhrov's department was fixed for the next evening and the voting-papers for the ballot were prepared. Rumour had already banished the disgraced professor to the Altai Forest Division and nominated Cheredilov in his stead, although, according to the general opinion, he was hardly fit for the job of reception clerk in an undertaker's office, when, unexpectedly, the former was re-elected by a majority and the announcement was simultaneously made that the latter was expelled from the Scientific Committee. The next morning, among a pile of congratulatory telegrams, Vikhrov found a message from the frightened Gratsiansky signed by all the Dizzy Doxies and listing personal virtues which he had never suspected in himself. That memorable event, which took place in 1936, scarcely affected Vikhrov's health and status, not counting the two years' silence, during which he did not write a single line. It was not until the very eve of the great war that his two-volume *Introduction to Forestcraft* suddenly appeared. Gratsiansky regarded this as a faithless breach of the truce. It was his scathing criticism of this book that gave rise to the sinister and fortunately baseless rumours of Gratsiansky's advancement to the position of corresponding member of the Academy of Sciences, of which earlier mention had been made.

He was in the heyday of his fame; it was considered indecent not to mention Gratsiansky's name in the same line with the celebrities of Soviet agriculture, horticulture and market gardening. Even Vikhrov now bowed the head to him with a sense of guilt, not on account of his theories, but from the knowledge of his own intellectual limitations, which prevented him from appreciating the full stature of that scientist. And although nothing yet pointed to Gratsiansky's decline, an unaccountable sense of frustration suddenly became evident in all his bearing and behaviour. He began to make up to unobtrusive members of the staff who usually lapsed into silence in his presence, often spoke about his intention of taking up pure mathematics again or starting a history career, and followed Vikhrov with an almost pleading look whenever he happened to limp past.

It was at the end of September 1941, at a last meeting to discuss the details of evacuation, that they found themselves together at the same table. Suddenly, without any air-raid warning, the ack-ack guns crashed into action all round, and the Scientific Council moved to the vaulted cellar in which Catherine's grandee used to keep his spirituous stocks.

"Mind you, Ivan, the walls still smell after all those centuries! The breath of Dionysius," Gratsiansky confided in a whisper, his shoulder touching Vikhrov's. "You don't intend to leave Moscow, I see? I've decided to stay, too ... somebody's got to look after the Institute. I hear you've finished another book? Keeping the pot boiling, eh?" Vikhrov said nothing. Gratsiansky then tried a direct question: "Something epoch-making again in three volumes?"

"No, this time simply a guide to the use of timber for defensive purposes," Vikhrov answered drily, although actually he was working on wood for aircraft purposes. "I was interested in the technology of damp wood at one time. Just so."

"You ought to be more careful, old chap. Take me, I write with one hand and cross out at the same time with the other. The other day I came across a verbatim report of your introductory lecture this year. The things you write made me clutch my head. Why do you keep teasing the geese, Ivan? Don't you realise—*they* call *all this* opium for the people, while you—"

"Who are *they*?" Vikhrov said frowning. "They are we."

"Just what I said—we. A war is on, and you go and start that rigmarole to our callow youth about wood-goblins and hermits and things ... in that ancient Russian jargon of yours too."

"That jargon is the language of my grandfathers. What thieves' Latin would you have me use?" Vikhrov flared up. "Besides, I'm in the habit of respecting the common sense of my audience. And now let's keep quiet, we're interrupting the meeting. Just so."

A minute later Gratsiansky resumed his attack.

"We're old men now, Ivan, and we'll lay our bones without having had it out with each other. We ought to, eh? We ought to get together over some heart-warming wine, with the bombs crashing all round while we gaze into each other's eyes. I don't think we'd play the hypocrite under a hail of bombs, would we?"

"We'll talk about that some other time ... when we've won the war," Vikhrov said evasively.

"Yes, we'll win for certain ... although I'm afraid it won't be very soon. We ought to meet before that. You won't turn me away if I knock at your door one of these days in the evening, will you?" Receiving no reply, he added very quietly, so as to be able afterwards to deny he ever said it: "You are a big man, you possess the inexhaustible spring of Life Water, whereas I ... I am very lonely and miserable, Ivan."

"You *are* a nuisance today. Oh, all right, come and see me." For the first time in years Vikhrov glanced curiously at his face; it was bleak and charred-looking, as if consumed by some internal flame. He already knew that Gratsiansky's Dizzy Doxies had begun to desert him on the quiet for a new rising star of as yet undetermined orientation.

Something was eating Gratsiansky. It may have been the sudden fear of the gambler whose quarter of a century's run of good luck had dazzled all his contemporaries. So strong, in spite of everything, was Vikhrov's belief in himself, that he resolved to make this last attempt to convince his crafty opponent who wielded such power in their tiny world.

Before long Gratsiansky was frightened again, this time in real earnest.

The defence of the Soviet capital had reached its most critical stage. In the subsequent course of the war there were no few episodes which overshadowed the greatest battles of history in territorial extent, the numbers of participants involved and the complexity of strategic manoeuvre, but the battle for Moscow surpassed them all in its significance for world history. At the general meeting of the Deyevsk Depot, where the building of an armoured train as a gift to the army was being discussed, Mor-shchikhin called those events "a school of future victory".

Even before the advent of the winter of forty-one, it became clear that the enemy's plan of making short work of the Soviet armies had failed. The boasted six weeks set for the capture of the ancient capital had dragged into six months, with Moscow, for all practical purposes, no nearer than the coasts of America. The crack troops of the Nazi regular army strewed the fields of Byelorussia long before the first wet snow of the year fell. Hastily diluted with second-line replacements, the German machine still rolled eastward, but its rate of advance had dropped from the initial sixty kilometres a day to two kilometres, and even these were gained at a price unheard-of in Europe. The conquerors had been taught at their school desks that a plain confronted them, but they found instead an unassailable mountain range marked on no map—the resistance of a great people. Obstinacy and desperation then prompted the Berlin staff to make another attempt to ram the Soviet defences with soldier bodies. A frantic October drive brought Nazi Germany to the distant approaches to Moscow, where, a month and a half later, a famous battle was to be held, a repetition, almost, of Borodino, but with a different outcome and on an area of a hundred and twenty thousand square kilometres.

Moscow was a day's march from the enemy hordes—a tantalising mirage which had hypnotised former conquerors and a first-class fortress of the new world. In anticipation of rest and warmth, soldier pleasures and booty, fifty enemy divisions stood mounted for the attack with all their military bag and baggage. The light snow-flakes melted on the battle-heated iron and dripped into the vision slots. Wrapped and muffled up in stolen old clothes, breathing on their freezing hands to warm them, the conquerors stared hard into the murk of the Russian snowfall, the harbinger of winter, but saw nothing there to comfort them, neither golden cupolas nor kneeling Soviet boyars with the keys of the city on a plate of precious metal. All they saw were silvered forests standing in all their lustrous gentle beauty, and snow-drifts flowing over the knolly fields. Nazi Germany was to experience here the most bloody disappointment that had ever fallen to the lot of a swaggering reckless army.

The second German attempt to press home their attack ended in failure, but the enemy's proximity placed the capital in a state of siege. In a fit of fury the enemy sent bomber squadrons over in broad daylight, but only a few of them succeeded in breaking through to Moscow's sky. They made up for it by jettisoning their death loads in the evening rush hours, when the streets were crowded with people after the work shifts. Nothing could stop Moscow from breathing and thinking, nothing could stop her machines from working. By morning unseen hands would have repaired the damage to her buildings, statues and pavements. After the short-lived confusion in the middle of October, when the reeking shadow of war had crept into the suburbs of Moscow, complete tranquillity was restored among the inhabitants of the capital. The war and its air raids became a part of life's everyday routine; the chronicler will find no glowing colours in the Moscow of those days. It discarded, as it were, all its ornaments, its ancient gilding, even the autumnal purple of its boulevards in exchange for that peerless beauty which is born from contempt of death. Snow-trimmed rusty "gooseberries" and rail obstacles barred the roads on the outskirts, and cars rushed through the gaps in the anti-tank stoplines, heading for the welter of wintry sunset, which resembled a haemorrhage. All belted with defensive lines, the city was like a sailor of civil-war days bristling with leather harness, and, as in the civil war, the workers' battalions, grim and silent, were leaving for the front. Many probably remember the weeping young girl in a beret and battered shoes, who ran alongside the marching ranks, right in the roadway.

For a whole month Polya stood amid this torrent of west-bound humanity. She thought it sinful, in the highest sense of the word, to desert her Moscow roof at such a time and rush for the safety of Tashkent together with her Institute. She received no letters from anywhere, made no new friends in place of Varya, and Taisa was unwell. Hers was the loneliness of the tiny leaf spinning in the whirlpool. Everything around her cried out for heroic deeds, newspaper reports of burning Russian villages alternated with photographs of bullet-ridden Komsomol cards, with pictures of Gastello's disciples, with solemn oaths to fight for Moscow—the command post of new history—to the last drop of blood. Twinges of conscience were no longer dulled by fatigue caused by night duty on the slippery hoar-frosted roof. It seemed as if the very air and the bread that she ate had been stolen from the heroes, as if all her voluntary duties were merely an excuse not to do her highest duty. At the dispensary, where she got herself a job on the advice of the Komsomol Secretary, Polya was considered an innocent, and no one suspected what it cost her to achieve what others achieved without thought or effort. She could not make out how it happened that she had become one of life's stragglers. From the very outset posters on every street corner had called her to the nurses' training class, to the factory machine, to the steering-wheel of the lorry, to the third stage of the Metro construction, where her youth and health were wanted for the fight with the running ground. But it had seemed at first, as it had to many, that the Soviet troops would beat the enemy hands down in a week or two at the outside, and then.... Meanwhile, the October holidays were approaching.

The day before Polya ran down to the recruiting office again during the lunch hour to ask to be sent to the front. There was a queue in the stuffy corridor, the walls of which were hung with placards. In front of Polya stood a schoolboy with four homing pigeons which he had brought as a gift for the Soviet army. No one smiled at the boy, as it wasn't a question of pigeons; everyone tried to give him plenty of room, for a bird was a small thing and couldn't do without air. In an hour, by studying the placards, Polya had learnt the works of a hand grenade and how to dress a fractured leg. The major from the First Department eyed the girl over narrowly and promised to remember her when making up the next list. Children were not allowed to go to the war yet, he explained. It was a six minute walk to the local branch of the Komsomol. On the desk in the familiar private office, as though waiting for her, stood the undrainable glass of tea, but in place of Sapozhkov there sat a lean girl with the grey face of Destiny, if there can be a destiny twenty-five years old.

"I see, yes," she interrupted Polya straightaway. "I'm taking the place of Sapozhkov. No, not temporarily. If it's about being sent to the front I'd advise you to apply to the car-building plant at Mitishchi, they need workers badly there." Her eyes swept Polya's face as she added, "Unless it's something personal?"

"Not quite, but ... I'd like to see him," Polya timidly insisted, feeling awkward about engaging Destiny in a private talk. "I won't keep him long."

"Unfortunately that's quite impossible," Destiny said, without looking up from her papers. "Comrade Sapozhkov was killed at Narofominsk the day before yesterday."

Polya staggered as if the same splinter had hit her coming through. She went out. It was evening by the time she came home, and she could hardly remember what she had been doing in the interval; all she knew was that Sapozhkov had been walking with her all the time and that he had had the face of Rodion. It was a bad night. Two hundred and fifty planes were trying to get through to Moscow, and dozens of them were brought down by defensive fire. She could not fall asleep after coming down from the roof; the cold in the damp unheated flat grew worse and worse. Zolotinskaya was detained that night at her medical station.

Snow was falling heavily in the grey pre-dawn outside the window; occasionally it was whipped up into a blizzard. So began the November holidays. Usually, on that day, Chernetsov switched on his radio set first thing in the morning, and he and his family sat listening to the vast hum of the Moscow demonstration. By force of habit Polya went out into the corridor and stood under the black disk of the loudspeaker hanging on a nail. The grand parade was hardly to be expected that year. Red Square packed with troops would have been a tempting target for the enemy aircraft. Nevertheless, Polya was waiting for something as she sat rocking herself on the chest belonging to one of the tenants who shared the flat. The radio was silent, but occasionally an odd rustle issued from it like the sound of swept snow or creeping iron. She tried hard all the time to make out the face of Comrade Sapozhkov, who suddenly rose before her in titanic stature. Like all people who have lost someone near to them, she was tormented by regret at having missed telling him something that mattered most of all, something kind and deserving. She must have dozed off, because when she opened her eyes again she saw a courier in a white sheepskin coat standing in front of her. In the light of an electric torch he read out her name on a coloured card and did not hand it to her until he had checked it with her passport and given her face a close scrutiny. It was an invitation card to Red Square. Invitations were not delivered that year, but the parade

was due to begin in less than an hour, and probably hers was
the only exception in the whole capital.

Comrade Sapozhkov had kept his Komsomol promise after
death.

5

Polya ran through the blacked-out empty city, floundering in
the soft snow. Night still lingered, but the snowstorm was over;
every now and then cars sped past without lights and the snow-
swathed figure of a night patrol loomed round a corner. As she
drew near the centre of the city she came across army units on
the march and the figures of people hurrying in the same direction as herself. She passed through the cordon, past heavy military
machines in whitened covers, and entered the square. She had
just enough time to find her place in the darkness, recover her
breath and prepare herself for the historic event of which she
was to be a participant.

Everything pointed to its extraordinary nature—the chill
shuddery hour, too early for a parade, the silence brooding over
the half-filled stands, the large number of uniformed people
among the guests. There was no one in the square younger than
Polya, and she was allowed without question to pass into the front
row. She waited so eagerly for it to begin that she no longer
felt her own body, and together with all the rest kept looking
every minute at the shadowy outlines of the clock dial on the
Spasskaya Tower with both its hands nearing the eight, at the still
empty snow-powdered ledges of Lenin's Mausoleum, and at the
low sleepy-looking clouds, which you could almost reach with
your hand. When she looked up at them the snow granules pricked
her cheeks with a sobering effect.

The girl was about to receive within her the impress of a page
of world history, comparable in significance to a great battle
won. Some of its paragraphs Polya had read or seen before on
pictures, on the screen and in books—the squares of troops in
dull-green helmets, trench caps, and fur caps with ear-flaps
against the fading background of a grey building decorated with
long streamers rippled by a wintry breeze and calling to victory,
the whorled domes of St. Basil, looking ghostlike in the brightening sky, and the Kremlin wall with the snow-drifts of the night's
blizzard, deep as those on the Yenga, clinging around its base.

There was something tormentingly familiar about the people around her, especially one lad there in a workman's cap, but it wasn't because she had met them all individually in the streets of Moscow, it was because an intimate feeling of belonging to the same family made them all resemble one another. She had experienced before, though to a much lesser degree, this excitement of feverish silence, full of wonderful promise, and accentuated by the silence of the great military band in the centre. Mingling together in that hour of military stress, all this caught one by the throat with a poignant sense of newly discovered novelty. Paper and film had never been able to convey the majesty of that deep hush in Red Square, a hush which was ready at any moment to turn into a storm.

Realising that it was this she would always be asked about till the end of her days, Polya stuffed away into the crannies of memory all the scraps of impressions and snatches of talk around her, tinctured by patriotic concern and pride for the eternal city, for this rational mode of life, for the youth laid in the foundation pits of the five-year plans. People spoke in undertones about the traditional meeting held in the Underground the night before, about the furious battles at Yakhroma, where the two sides were fighting for positions for their December duel, about the factories beyond the Urals which were disgorging a lava of tanks day and night, about the mysterious Siberian echelons, which were supposed to be concentrating around Moscow all the time. Gradually the sky cleared in patches, and one could not read without an effort the inscription on the long crimson streamers about the socialist revolution having overthrown the imperialists and proclaimed peace among the nations. In vain did Polya mentally flog the clock hands. She was learning the impassive lesson of history, which allows nothing to happen until that which goes before has taken its proper place; the latecomers had not yet arrived, the chain of guards had not been drawn up in front of the stands, and the cameramen had not yet trained their lenses in all directions so that descendants a century later could see everything that took place.

Every time she looked at the clock tower Polya saw the profile of the boy next to her out of the corner of her eye, and she was ready to swear that she had met him under some far-back and quite different circumstances. Judging by his sidelong glances, he too was trying to place her, but he could not, because the funny straw hat she had worn that time was replaced by an old woollen shawl with a burnt corner. This mutual interest gave Polya courage to confide to the stranger her childish fears as to whether such an immense multitude of details and faces would fit into the narrow film, and whether they hadn't forgotten to set out the microphones—it was important that the front, the country and the world at large should hear the pulse of Red Square at that moment, all its sounds, from the clop of horses' hoofs to the thousand-voiced soldiers' response to the greetings of the commander, who was already riding round the troops.

"This is just the kind of thing our Leningrad boys need, don't you think so?" Polya said, having in view the blockade of the northern capital, which had recently begun. "To me such a broadcast would have been more welcome than bread."

"They're making a magnificent stand," the lad said proudly in the reassuring tone of an elder. "My job sometimes takes me down there, nearabout. They say the theatrical school there is producing *Don Carlos* and lectures on Renaissance architecture are being read at the Academy."

"Really?" Polya queried doubtfully.

She vividly imagined what the level of Leningrad life must be if such ordinary pursuits were placed to the credit of its inhabitants. A hum of applause swept over the stands and drowned her whisper. It was like a wind rushing through the square. Polya stood up on her knees on the balustrade and, over the heads of the agitated multitude, she saw the men who then bore the burden of responsibility for the country and the ideas it stood for. Polya thought their ascension of the Mausoleum by the inner stairs much too leisurely for such an occasion, and although she could only see their backs, she easily identified them all by the silhouette against the morning sky, by a military cap, or by some other sign made familiar to the eye by years of visual practice. Some of the details were filled in for her by more experienced neighbours and her own excited girlish intuition, and the rest she saw a week later in the newsreel. After that the Kremlin chimes rang out in slightly hoarse measured tones. On the last stroke a horseman wearing black unageing moustaches rode out of the gate, and instantly the parade commander galloped towards him from the other end of the square.

"Budyonny," Polya's neighbour informed her. "There he is, receiving the report, now he's going round to greet the troops. Just look at his horse, what a fine animal!" He must have taken the girl in from head to foot, because he added: "I'm afraid you'll take to your bed after this parade. Come on, I've got some paper with me, put some in your shoes before it's too late. They'll keep your feet warm."

Polya glanced down blankly at her battered "rusty-fusties" sunk in the snowy slush, and he was obliged to repeat his advice.

"Oh, it doesn't matter now. Can't you understand!" she brushed him aside, a hot flush of rapture flooding her cheeks.

The cheers of the troops rolled across the square from the opposite side now. The parade commander ascended the Mausoleum. Drawn sabre blades glinted and dozens of officers simultaneously shouted out a command. At that moment probably all was hushed throughout the Soviet land, wherever there was a bit of wire with a membrane at the end of it. The radio carried the reverberating echoes of Red Square over the silenced city, and every whispered sound there immediately became the possession of history. Polya felt neither the press of the crowd around her nor the icy touch of the thawed snow on her feet, she was all tense quivering attention. Her quickened ears caught the slightest sound, from the crunch of snow attending the relief of the guards to the rhythmic swish of a bird's wing cleaving the heights above the square, and all went down through the wide-flung doors of memory. It seemed as if the whole surging populace had flooded the wide expanses around Moscow as in former years of national affliction, when, as now, the primary warmth of a great unity was slowly generated from the cohesive mass, a warmth which invariably rose to white heat in which, in turn, the pain of tragic loss and the bitterness of military defeat were forged into fury and wisdom, those ever faithful companions of victory. That momentary silence, pregnant with the consciousness of national immortality, was for Polya the pulsating climax of the November parade. Immediately after this, through the crashes of the artillery salute, the melody of the proletarian anthem broke upon the air, and never perhaps had its battle-call sounded more convincing since the beginning of modern history.

"I bet your heart's thumping like mad? Drink it in, it happens once in a lifetime," Polya's young mentor whispered hotly behind her. "Can you imagine how many eyes, barrels, and wings are guarding the sky now over you?"

"What do you think," Polya asked without turning round, "is there anybody here from over there, from their camp?"

"Why?"

"I'd like them to see how many there are of us and what we're

436

like. I wish I could have just a peep at it through the crack—the old world, I mean!"

"You'll get more peeps than you want, don't you worry," the lad prophesied with a grin.

He squeezed her hand painfully, but she bore it—if not for him she would have missed so many details. A mine of information, as all boys are, he named the makes of the different cars and the arms of service as they went past. Being an inexperienced pupil, though, she got them all mixed up in the parade evolutions. The march past, as far as she could remember, was started by the infantry in full kit, with cartridge pouches slung from their belts and field spades at their hips; it was not like at an ordinary parade. They were going straight through to the fighting lines. The different units, ranked twenty deep, marched past battalion by battalion—sailors and the home guards, the internal security units with bayonets atilt, trainees of the military schools and of the academies of all arms of the service, political thought included. And among them, armed detachments of Moscow workers bearing the limp velvet of seasoned banners, beneath whose shadow they were to grapple once more with their bitter enemy.

And then the prancing cavalry rode past with sabres drawn for the charge, and after them, like a gust of song from the civil war, dashed the machine-gun carts. Searchlights and sound-rangers, which Polya's neighbour promptly described as the eyes and ears of the front-line nights, drove by slowly, searching the sky above the Mausoleum; ack-ack guns sped by with a rubbery tread, and self-propelled anti-tank guns scratched the granite paving-blocks through the snow with their caterpillar claws. Scarcely had the clank of their descent towards the river died away, when the signalmen took up their position with flags near the Historical Museum. Like fossil monsters of geological ages, machines of the most weighty military argumentation appeared upon the square. The ancient walls of Moscow shuddered as all this ponderous iron-mongery of war flowed past them westward bound to fight the last desperate battle with barbarism before, as Polya fondly believed, vanishing for ever from the face of the earth. Nevertheless, it was not this formidable and obedient machinery of war, enveloping the square with the roar and fumes of its engines that counted, it was the unbendable will of the people who manned it, those who sat in the commanders' cars and at the sights of the siege guns, or those who stood in the turrets of the armoured Juggernauts, or gazed from the motorised infantry lorries at Moscow's sky with a grim determination that made them resemble the heroes of ancient Rus.

Welded into one, they were going from here to give their life-blood to their country, drop by drop, they were going out to settle the hash of the Nazi serpent, which had wound its coils around their capital; they were going away, and were leaving nothing personal behind them except Moscow. Polya, too, was drawn into this mighty crater of movement. The clothes on her became tight, as though the girdle had been drawn taut, and her body swung itself into the rhythm of the march. Because she had no red flower to toss to the tankman, who, she thought, had glanced at her, Polya wanted to see him off as far as the suburbs at least. The parade was over, but she could not get through the cordon to follow in the wake of the tanks, which had made for the embankment; her young mentor, too, had meanwhile been swallowed up in the home-going crowd. Only then did it dawn upon her that he was the boy who had carried her luggage for her at the railway station six months ago. How sweetly the sprayed peonies on the street corners had smelt, and how brightly the sky had shone over Moscow.

She did not feel like going back to the lonely chillness of Blagoveshchensky Alley and to Natalya Zolotinskaya; running to Taisa for sympathy was still more shameful. She started aimlessly up the main street, past the new houses with their boarded and sand-bagged shop windows. Unfortunately, without Varya and Comrade Sapozhkov there was no one to complain to about not being allowed to go to the front, although she was quite capable now of standing up for those ruby stars on the Kremlin spires, for that lanky Ivan* and Pushkin in his cloak trimmed with ermine after the snowstorm, and for jolly old Vasya** facing the Spasskaya Gate in his gay motley and the cap-and-bells of his cupolas, for that slack homely river and the boundless horizons beyond it wreathed in the smoke of industrial Moscow. Her eyes were smarting, no doubt the result of a sleepless night; she turned into a side street at the back of the Moscow Soviet, and leaned against a stand with month-old sodden neswpapers in it. This unfrequented place, carpeted with snow, was the best possible place for a person in her emotional condition. Owing to the snow

---

* Meaning the Kremlin bell-tower Ivan the Great.—*Tr.*

** Vasya—diminutive of Vasily (Basil), refers to the Church of St. Basil in Red Square.—*Tr.*

she did not hear the approach of an elderly man in a sheepskin cap.

Presumably, he took a fairly long time choosing a suitable moment to intervene, and when finally he did so, it was in an amused familiar tone such as doctors use with children.

"Well, young lady, what's it all about?" he said, tugging at her sleeve and peering into her face. "Oh, what a flood. Why, you'll spoil your eyes. Has someone hurt you or ... is it a bad letter you've received from the front?" He paused for a reply, but Polya shook her head with such a vigorous gesture of despair that it was almost a shameful thing now to leave her in such a state. "If there wasn't a bad letter then what are you doing here, disturbing the peace?"

"I'm not disturbing anything, I just stopped to read the newspaper," Polya said, sobbing more openly than ever.

Through the rainbow film that misted her eyes, Polya saw only grey tufts of eyebrows and moustaches on the tired pouchy face of a man who had seen plenty of human suffering. A little later, when her eyelashes had begun to dry, she saw an odd badge on the collar of his military coat in the form of a goblet, like the ones they used to serve ice-cream in the happy old days, with a snake over it.

"But you *are* disturbing the peace," the important-looking old man insisted. "A war is on, a serious war too, and you young people shouldn't be crying at such a time. If you're not careful they'll hand us out such a kaput that we won't dare utter a squeak for half a century. Who's going to fight, then, who's going to make shells, say, or patch up our wounded soldiers? I thought somebody had been killed, really."

"So he has," Polya said, quietening down, while her shoulders still quivered. "Sapozhkov has been killed and I, wretched girl, am still living."

"That's very sad, of course," the old man agreed sympathetically. "I've had someone killed too, but I'm not crying and moaning."

"How can you help crying," Polya said. "The whole country's in danger, the people are straining their hardest to carry out their liberative mission, and I'm the only one to lie snug in its lap. Her ladyship!"

"All the more reason not to cry," her companion judicially remarked. "Your tears at such a time are a sort of waste of fuel, don't you think so? I've been following you all the way from the square, really. I saw the clouds gathering there. Come along, we'll discuss certain pressing world problems over a cup of tea. You needn't be afraid of me. I happen to be that dampish old boy, brigade surgeon Strunnikov, you have been reading about there," he said, pointing to his portrait in the wet newspaper hanging in front of Polya.

While Polya was debating with herself whether it was quite moral to engage in tea-drinking at such a crucial moment in history, immediately after such a parade, Strunnikov took her hand in a fatherly way and piloted her to a handsome five-storey building two streets farther down. He warned Polya to be more cheerful at breakfast and, for reasons of his own, not to mention anything about Sapozhkov having been killed. His gruff kindness invited perfect candour, and what she didn't have time to tell him on the way she finished telling him an hour later over an omelette so utterly delicious that it made her feel almost conscience-smitten to eat it, and in the presence of his wife, a small, young-looking woman with red swollen eyelids. Grief had found a recent home in the large cheerless flat of this old couple. Polya did not withhold from them a single secret, beginning with her recent worries over her father and ending with her half-formed intention to renounce her undeserved happiness with Rodion. She confessed everything except that her feet were wet, and the childish confession was heard out by her two elders without a smile; they merely exchanged glances from time to time, or else lowered their eyes to pick the same bit of bothersome fluff from their knees.

"And so life is just slipping past me," Polya wound up her story.

She was then asked by what means she expected to realise her praiseworthy enmity towards the old world. This time the question did not take her unawares. Her previous blunders at the recruiting office and with Sapozhkov had taught her a lesson and she had somewhat widened her field of possibilities so as to have something to choose from. She had guessed at once that Strunnikov was an influential person. She declared she would have been quite good at laying explosive mines under enemy troop-trains or doing anything else that was dangerous to life and limb; if need be, she could even work in the anti-tank battalion whose job she could guess at from hearsay, anything, so long as she could avenge, as she expressed it, man's desecrated dream.

"I may be little-bitsy, and look a bit shabby, but I've got

everything, and what I haven't I'll get for myself. And what I don't know I'll learn. Why, they even teach bears to walk the rope!"

Strunnikov said that, being a surgeon, all these things were not in his line, and Polya's heart sank at first. As it happened, however, he had organised his military hospital only that month and needed efficient girls with a secondary education. Polya listened to him in an agony of uncertain hope that now, at last, the tiny leaf would be swept out into midstream.

"Are all your people in Moscow?"

"All except my mother, who has been cut off by the front out there, on the Yenga. Mother and I lived apart from Father."

"Did he leave you?"

"No, Mother and I went away ourselves. Not that she had a difficult character, but she's like me, very sensitive about things ... things of the conscience, you know!" she said, sustaining the old man's steady look.

The testimony pointed in Polya's favour; without a doubt, the fact that she had assisted her mother during the summer months had given her some experience in hospital life, and a pass to Red Square on such a morning was as satisfying a reference as any; besides, Strunnikov seldom erred in his diagnoses and he had medicines for all ailments in the world.

"Let's be clear on this—there are two things I will not stand for in my establishment, and that's moping and dirt. I need jolly girls, girls as quick as mercury," he warned her after another long talk at their second meeting. "The chief vitamin in my pharmacy is laughter."

Polya nodded eagerly as she listened.

"Goodness me!" she cried, unable to believe her good luck. "You can't imagine what a jolly person I am! They used to call me a rattlebox at school. If need be, I can dance a jig, without music even. D'you want me to show you?"

The old couple laughed, and the upshot of it was that a week later Polya was issued a tunic and crude high-boots of different sizes; this was easily remedied by the simple use of cardboard. Instead of the long-desired greatcoat she was entitled only to a padded jacket, but then it warmed her soul so much better than her fur coat with the squirrel collar. Drafting for the hospital was nearing completion, and it could be safely predicted that if this run of good luck continued the tiny leaf bade fare soon to catch up with Rodion and Varya. The sense of being useful wrought such a dignified change in Polya's manner and appearance that she no longer felt ashamed to present herself before her father.

She went there on the day before their departure, so that nothing, not even Taisa's tears, could shake the irrevocable decision she had taken.

CHAPTER ELEVEN

1

Round about that time an idea was hit upon at the Deyevsk depot where Sergei Vikhrov was employed, which was subsequently taken up by other railwaymen of the capital. After the parade in Red Square the Deyevsk men, through their Party organisation, applied to the government asking to be given an extra-plan job. Considering that they were now handling a greater volume of work as a result of increased military shipments, they were given the job of making bayonets for the home guards. The patriots felt offended at being given such a trivial job, and put forward a counter-plan on their own initiative to build an armoured train for the front manned by their own workers, the way this used to be done during the civil war.

In the capacity of district Secretary for propaganda Morshchikhin helped the old workers of the Deyevsk depot to put their proposal through the proper channels. Just before that the enemy's half-ring had been drawn still closer on a number of sections, and Moscow, following the example of her ancestors, was preparing for street fighting, and, in the last resort, to blow up her factories, preferring the gigantic work of rehabilitation after victory to the shame of surrender. The general meeting at the depot took place the very same evening after the sappers had gone through the shops to plan the layout of the explosive charges. A delegation of workers went immediately to military district headquarters, but the idea had struck H.Q. at first as being impracticable.

Since the beginning of the war the Deyevsk depot had been making field kitchens and ski-runners for machine-guns, welding tricky reliable tank hindrances and repairing ancient locomotives.

"You can't get at the damned thing," a youngster of the trade-school replacements would say, scratching his head in an old-mannish way as he stared at some ancient relic of an engine, to get at the pistons of which one had to first remove the entire pilot end. "Gee, what an old crock!"

"Get on with the job. The war will put it through the mincer. You kids have got spoilt by new gadgets!" their elders grumbled, remembering the mad heroic runs of nineteen eighteen. "It's thrift that does it."

It wasn't until the fourth day that the long-looked-for chiefs came down at last to ascertain the depot's productive abilities. There were two of them—one a huge brigade commissar of unbelievably peaceful aspect, wearing a fur-lined military coat, the other a steely looking figure with his left moustache sticking up and out from constant twirling.

There had been a brief spell of slushy weather in mid-October. The wet snow fell and melted on the black barren depot ground. Thirty elderly local worthies, sponsors of the armoured train idea and veterans of the city's proletarian guard, stood lined up on the tracks near the water-pump shoulder to shoulder, all tough bristling characters as dependable as the Russian rifle of the 1891 model; the comparison was Morshchikhin's, who met the visitors. The commissar expressed his doubts about the need for lining up in such weather, which he thought premature, but he was told that it was more heart-cheering to a worker that way. Then the chief of the depot reported to the visitors about the number of workers present, not counting those who were out on the line or engaged in building log pillboxes at the city's approaches nearby.

"Greetings to the working class!" the one in the fur-lined khaki began, and everyone was pleased to hear what a strong impressive voice he had, his peaceful appearance, the wet weather, and other discouraging circumstances notwithstanding; apparently he, too, liked the hearty sound of the workers' response which mingled with the shrill cry of an engine that happened to be leaving for the fighting lines.

Escorted by the local chiefs, the visitors walked down the line, the one in the fur-lined coat asking all kinds of questions as befitted such an occasion. Thus, for form's sake, he enquired of the flank-man Grigoryev, the eldest in the ranks, how that noble idea had started with them. The latter showed his two well-scrubbed hands by way of reply, as much as to say that a patriot's conscience was in his hands. Asked what the workers were striving after most of all and what folks thought about the military setbacks, the old man willingly explained that the working people were striving after such a smashing victory for all time as would enable them thereafter to reach the terminal of our epoch at full speed and without hindrance; as for the surrender of Soviet cities, he pointed out that according to the testimony of history books it had always been the habit of our ancestors to lure the enemy into the depths of Russia's forests.

Counter-questions being invited, another veteran engine-driver, Markelich, enquired with dignity what parts the visitor himself came from and who his people were. Not a man in all the country would dare to evade his imperious curiosity.

"My father was a Tula gunsmith. We have seven Communists in the family, of which I am the only one still serving on the home front," the chief one said with a smile. "Does my answer satisfy you, Dad, or does it not?"

"It sounds all right," the old man said. "D'you mind saying also what your military rank is and where you fought for the Soviet power?"

"I'm a member of the War Council, and I served as a private in the Forty-Sixth Infantry Division in nineteen twenty."

"Very glad to hear it," said Grigoryev, stroking his moustaches, although he stood in the ranks. "Then we must've met in Simferopol, we were disarming Makhno that year, if you remember. I was in the Fifteenth Sivash Division. Seeing as we're such old acquaintances I'd like to hope we'll have your assistance in this business."

The brigade commissar was about to suggest a walk through the workshops when his eye passed over the callow youths from the industrial school, who had joined the ranks in the meantime. Chilled to the marrow in their uniform tunics, they were so keen to show their readiness and military bearing that although he was in a hurry to attend an important conference in the Kremlin he stayed to say a few kind words to his young successors, his country's hope and future. The visitors went away, leaving instructions to speed up the erection of the armoured train in view, as they said, of the situation at the front having become more difficult.

The choice fell upon an "OV" type switching engine, an evacuee from the Rzhev depot, which, although built at the beginning of the century, had just come straight from overhaul, a fact which was disclosed by her fresh coat of paint and thick tires. Doubting whether such a feeble piece of motive power, nicknamed *Ovechka* (lamb) by the railwaymen, would be able to haul the 500-ton armoured train, Sergei came out at the meeting with a vehement appeal to choose a more powerful engine, not to be stingy where the sacred cause of defending the socialist motherland was concerned; his speech was regarded as a piece of presumptuous ignorance on the part of a "ham"; it was greeted with indulgent smiles and left unanswered. This, after the incident with Morshchikhin, was the professorial scion's second lesson in modesty for trying to buy public recognition on the cheap; luckily, he was leaving on a run to the Leningrad area the next morning. As he learned later, no other engine, plated with armour, would have been able to get through the depot gates. The OV was the only machine suitable for the purpose, capable of negotiating any bend or curve, an engine as hardy and docile as a peasant horse, with the added convenience of being easier to haul back on to the track if derailed.

Only yesterday, with fussy cries, she had been shunting cars up and down the lines. Now she was led into the stall to get a wash, and the workers swooped upon her like a flock of rooks. Men went down to the next station during a bombing raid to inspect a factory-built armoured train undergoing repairs there; they made measurements, and drew plans, and where drawings were missing on account of the haste the instinctive knack of the worker came to their assistance. Old tires were used to make swivel mounts for the tender's "forty-fiver," as the ack-ack gun had been christened; they fixed brackets for the armour plating evacuated from the west, which they cut out by rule of thumb, like a workman's overalls, so that it should not be too cumbersome in a fight on the one hand, and not make its wearer blush in the company of other first-class machines of Soviet big industry on the other. The din of riveting and the roar of electric welding drowned out the sounds of both the creeping rumours about military setbacks and of the air raids. If tinny mutterings and the scream of diving Junkers did break through the roof, a grim promise of retribution fell from stern-set young lips: "You'll be laughing on the wrong side of your face soon, you tyke!"

Beginning from October the men working on the armoured train lived barrack-fashion in the nearby club. Continuous guidance was now needed, and the Party committee office was turned into combat headquarters with people on duty there day and night; Morshchikhin, the leading spirit of the whole affair, often spent the night there on a wooden sofa with a gas-mask for a pillow. By the time Sergei returned from his trip things had made considerable headway.

They got back to Moscow before nightfall and the crew searched the cityscape with their eyes, looking for changes wrought within the week and a half they had been away. The eternal city stood unscathed in the shadowy perspective of spires, factory chimneys, and something else there along the horizon. Tattered wreaths of trailing smoke hung over the roofs as before, in some places indistinguishable from the gloom that was creeping up from the east; the All-Clear had just been sounded. On the way back from the Leningrad area they had had to pick up some trucks with evacuated factory machinery, and while they were handing these over at the marshalling yard for further shipment, November evening had deepened. Here at the distributing station Sergei saw the glow of a distant fire in the sky in the direction of the Forestry Institute—at least, so it seemed to him.

The engine was in good repair, and the station-master on duty sent it immediately to coal up. By the time they put the engine on the pit by the water-pump to be taken over by the relieving crew, dusk had fallen; the glow in the sky had spread. Sergei did not leave until he had done what he was supposed to do on returning from a run, that is, rake out the fire-box and wipe the connecting-rods for inspection. Anxiety for his near ones did not leave him. A whiff of burning, the acrid smell of human grief rather than of engine smoke, assailed his nostrils from time to time, and then a note of violent weeping could almost be heard in the wintry wind. Sergei ran home without hope of finding his father and Taisa in the old place, but the fire proved to be much nearer, and he breathed again. On a waste plot near the students' hostel a small wooden building was burning down, and the sparks danced prettily in the frosty air. Sergei was then sorry he had not dropped in on Morshchikhin on his way home and taken a shower while he was at it; while he hesitated, gazing at the cold fading streak of sundown in the sky, three men going in the direction of the depot came round a corner towards him.

He knew engine-driver Timofei Titov and his mate Kolya Lavtsov, but the third one, a tall taciturn man in a long greatcoat, who introduced himself as artilleryman Samokhin, was a stranger to him. Sergei went back with them.

"Talk of the devil!" laughed Lavtsov. "Timofei and I were just saying you were the very man. And the moment his name is mentioned up he pops. Looks like the kid's heart has been telling him, doesn't it, gunner?"

"I daresay he'll win the vote," Samokhin boomed down.

Sergei wisely held his peace. During the past year he had got the hang of his job and did his duties satisfactorily, taking care not to stand out in any way from these taciturn rather than sombre men, who were utterly devoted to their work. He had learned by experience, for instance, that driving heavy trains through bomb raids on soft Moscow-mined coal and going down steep gradients during a snowfall were much the same as dragging the whole load on one's own back; he even became inured to the risk of being squashed flat in case of a false step. He had even succeeded in striking up a bantering friendship with some of the depot youngsters, but although he threw himself into his job with zeal and looked more grimy-faced than anyone else, he never fully succeeded in "belonging", in being treated by the workers of the depot as one of themselves. The reason was to be sought in a subtle difference in shades of thinking, conditioned by social origin and education. Sergei felt this most acutely in the presence of engine-driver Titov, a short-spoken retiring man, who was rumoured to have a large family. Sergei had a feeling that Titov never let him out of his field of vision while at the same time not seeming to notice him; he considered Sergei's work at the depot the passing whim of a "young gentleman", whereas for him the railway was not only a means of livelihood but an instrument of his human activity, if not the very meaning of life.

Things were much simpler with Morshchikhin, still more so with Kolya Lavtsov, although it was Lavtsov from wrom he had had most to put up with at first. For one thing, he used to invite Sergei every pay-day to join him in a cocktail bar to "relax in a cultured way", as he called it. Not that he wanted a partner for his epicurean alcoholic whimsies—Lavtsov never drank and had only been there twice before within eighteen months—but for the sheer pleasure of watching Sergei's embarrassed refusal, his fastidious tastes in the matter of amusements, his comic attempts to keep within the bounds of rigid professional precept.

"So what do you say about joining the crowd?" Kolya Lavtsov persisted.

"I don't mind good company," Sergei said, not to disgrace himself in the eyes of Titov, who had never shown any such propensities before. "A pick-me-up is not bad once in a while.

Only I don't think this is quite the right time for it, if you ask me."

"So that's what the professor's child has got on his mind, eh?" Lavtsov said teasingly, knowing how sensitive Sergei was to this nickname. "Bless me if the fellow doesn't think we're inviting him to a glass and a trailer!"

The trailer in this case stood for ordinary beer used to bring about a quicker effect of the basic liquor.

"Oh, come off it, look who's sticking his nose up in the air! How long have you been an engine-man?" Titov interrupted him sedately, and Sergei threw a grateful glance at the engine-driver, whose face glowed in the sudden reflected glare of the fire, which they happened to be passing.

"We'll see what kind o' showing you'll make yourself," Samokhin spoke again from somewhere high up.

For a while they walked on in silence. An icy wind blew at their backs and tore at their caps.

"Just back from a trip, Vikhrov, I see?" Titov began, obviously trying to smooth over Lavtsov's indiscretion. "You've seen how people are living these days, had an eyeful, I daresay?"

"They're living a pretty hungry life, Timofei Stepanovich. True, we got no farther than Ladoga," Sergei began reporting, excited at thus being directly addressed by Titov for the first time. "Owing to the awkward configuration of the shore the freight had to be hauled down to the lake by horse and cart. A wheat barge was sunk there by a bomb just before we arrived. People stripped right there in the snow near the ice hole and dived into the freezing cold water with tubs and buckets. They baled the grain out as much as they could. With all these freights for Leningrad, there hasn't been a handful of anything missing, not even if a sack is torn. There *was* one thief there, though..." he broke off, realising that Titov was so engrossed in his own thoughts that he was hardly listening to him.

"That freight is more precious than gold," the artilleryman spoke down. "Have they opened the road there yet?"

"Not yet, the ice is too thin." The famous Road of Life to Leningrad across Lake Ladoga was not opened until the twenty-sixth of November of that year.

"We heard over the selector that you got it on your back?" Titov queried.

The story of the air attack would have taken a good half hour to tell, but Sergei manfully conquered the temptation to boast of how, at dawn the day before yesterday, a Junkers had snipped off two flats from the tail-end of their train, like an autogenous cutting job, of how, with the rupture of the brake pipe, the train had stopped almost dead in its tracks, and of how, knocked flat by the jolt, they were expecting a second blow, this time to the head, but luckily the enemy airman was returning from a raid and had jettisoned his last bomb.

Instead, Sergei only said, "Can't be helped, Timofei Stepanovich, it's war," and spat on the snow through his teeth with no little skill.

"Fine! So you've had your first taste of a soldier's life?" Lavtsov again said mockingly. "You ought to stand us one for such an occasion."

Again no one supported him and they walked along for half a minute in silence.

"Of course, the Soviet power will find the means to repulse the enemy without us—the Party hasn't let us doze all these years. Still, this is a big thing we've started with the armoured train, Sergei Vikhrov. It's our own workers' job," Titov said, coming to the point without slackening his pace. "It's a world job, in a manner o' speaking, because it won't be all sugar and honey for the other countries if we lose this fight with fascism. But it's our fight more than anybody's. No one has put so much into this land around here as we of the working class have," he said with a sweeping gesture. "Sometimes, when travelling, you look out o' the engine window over your right shoulder, and it makes your head go round to think of it. Why, we sifted every grain of sand through our hands, and our blood marks are left on every one of them. This Soviet land of ours is worth double the price now." He stopped, and they all stood around Sergei, who had deposited his travelling box—"street-organ" in depot parlance—on the snow. "To make a long story short, it's been arranged. I'm going with the armoured train as chief engine-driver, and I'm taking three of you fellows as mates. I've picked two already from among the snappier ones, Lavtsov's one of them. As for the third, I just have to whistle to have a thousand of 'em falling over themselves." He placed a heavy hand on Sergei's shoulder. "Well, son, seeing as you're a hard-working fellow, we've decided to put our trust in you and take you along in our armoured train gang as engine-driver's mate. Get me?"

"The Komsomol is for you too," Lavtsov put in. "Well, shout hurray, say you'll join our crowd, Sergei!"

Sergei caught his breath. It was the very thing he had yearned for—this knighthood of initiation, and what is more, from the hand of that stern unsmiling man, who was identified in his eyes with the working class. But Sergei was oddly silent, though not from the sudden realisation of what grim implications this offer had. Something bigger than that implied in a mere call-up or so natural a proceeding to a Soviet young man as enrolment in the Komsomol was now being demanded of him. To be one of three was so much harder than to be one of a million. If he was dismayed at the moment, it was not by the perils of war, but by the sense of responsibility he would be assuming for the whole order of things in the world, this stunned unhappy world. At this point Samokhin got out a cigarette and Lavtsov reached for one; Titov did not smoke. And so it happened that Sergei's reflections were limited to the brief space of time in which it takes to light a cigarette. Luckily, the matches were blown out in the wind one after another.

"Of course, you and I are inexperienced soldiers, but I don't have to tell you that no one is born a soldier," Titov was saying. "Soldiers are made in the clash of life, so to speak. Samokhin here will help us out with his advice too."

"You just wink and we'll convert you to our faith in no time," the artilleryman said, puffing the smoke over his head. "When you get going real mad there'll be no holding you back, take my word."

"But you needn't feel you have to go, Sergei Vikhrov", the old engine-driver continued, removing the weight of his hand from Sergei's shoulder. "In war everything is possible, bodily injuries too. The chances are you might find yourself with nothing to dance with! Anyway, we're not going tomorrow and we're not asking you for a receipt. Think it over, talk it over with your people."

Sergei could tarry no longer with his reply. He drew a deep breath of the tingling air, seasoned with the sulphurous fumes of the depot. Yes, he took upon himself the defence of life, and with it, the hatred for its countless enemies; yes, he was renouncing something dear and customary, above all the freedom to dispose of his time and his body at his own discretion, in exchange for the friendship and recognition of the vast working-class multitude, for the immense spaces of the future, for the right to look upon all human grief without twinges of conscience. He gave his reply in that last fraction of a minute when the slightest delay would have had ineradicable consequences.

"There's nothing to talk over. I said I don't mind good company," Sergei announced, trying to conceal a note of exultation, although he had not thought this would happen in such an ordinary way, not even at a red-topped table, but on the go, under the searchlighted canopy of Moscow's suburban sky. "I'd like to have a wash, though, after the trip, and get some sleep. I feel kind of stiff all over."

"You've got plenty of time, we'll even have time to drop in at the cocktail bar," Lavtsov joked. This time he sounded quite chummy. "We'll take Timofei Stepanovich along with us to take a course in aristocratic conduct."

And again Sergei expected, at that solemn moment, that engine-driver Titov would at least shake his hand if not hug him by way of sealing their contract of life and death. Apparently this was considered unnecessary among people who had made it their aim to achieve the triumph of life over death.

"Pipe down, young cock, before you get yourself in the soup," the engine-driver interrupted Lavtsov with gruff kindness. "You'd better go and show him our gee-gee."

They were deafened by the clatter of pneumatic hammers and the jarring screach of flues being scaled. Yesterday's meek "lamb" could now be identified only by her geometric outline; clad almost completely in armour plates, including the cab and the steam dome, she stood on the pit at the rear wall of the shop. A shower of electric-welding sparks was reflected in an oily puddle on the earthen floor; something was being welded in the frontal part, on the side of the smoke-box. The black locomotives crouching in the greenish wavering shadows seemed to be envying their sister, who was being enrobed for a deed of valour.

Sergei climbed all over the engine together with Lavtsov, feeling every bolt and rivet; he peeped into the cab as well—from now on it was to be his home, more dear to him than the one in which his father and Taisa were waiting for him so impatiently.

"Well?" Lavtsov shouted through the roar with unconcealed pride. "Do you like this comrade in the iron coat?"

"Won't she be a bit heavy on the move?" Sergei said gravely.

"What, what did you say?" Latsov queried, shouting into his

ear as if they were in the thick of a real battle. "Let's get out of here."

They went out into the washing shop next door where it was quieter and where a tank turret was being smoothly lowered by winch on to an eight-wheeler flat.

"I was saying, wouldn't the springs be a bit too weak for such a casement?"

"Don't you worry!" grinned Lavtsov. "We laid on up to seventeen plates. She'll be a real snorter! Now frankly, Sergei, you have no down on me, have you?"

"Why should I?" Sergei answered, feigning surprise.

"Well, I mean, for ragging you like I did. But it was just fun, I wanted to see what you were like when you were mad. Come on, put it there!" Lavtsov said, proferring his hand for a brotherly handshake.

The few weeks that remained until their departure for the front passed for Sergei as in a hazy dream. Owing to faults which kept cropping up and a shortage of hands, the engine crew of the amoured train never left the depot now at all. Every morning, under the command of artilleryman Samokhin, they went to the sand pits back of the Forestry Institute for grenade-throwing practice or crawled in the snow, aiming at an imaginary enemy. Headquarters were hurrying them on; at the end of November frosty weather set in, and the iron stuck to one's fingers; despite Sergei's struggles, Taisa smeared her darling's chapped hands with ration fat whenever he came home to sleep, and sighed forebodingly. Sergei at that time looked older than his years; a defiant soldierly crease formed between his brows and around his mouth. He fought shy of Taisa's loving cares, and became more and more a stranger, clothing his heart in an armour that was more necessary in war than any outward covering. Like Polya, he kept moving farther and farther away from Taisa towards that "fiery-winded" line, beyond which there lay a sea of time which she could neither fathom nor control.

And so, gradually, the paths of Polya and Sergei converged towards an inevitable crossing. Both were drawn into the blazing fire of the epoch by a subconscious feeling that some day its burns would become the identification marks of mankind's future citizenship. If Polya's visit to her father had happened half an hour earlier, she would have made the acquaintance of Sergei, who came that evening to show himself to the old folks in his new tank outfit. But that premature meeting would not have brought the young people so closely together as would the welding bonds of struggle, of prolonged happiness or sorrow, or the mutual joyous knowledge of averted death.

3

Ivan Vikhrov was discussing an important matter with Morshchikhin when Polya called, and she did not dare to intrude. Besides, her aunt was in a hurry to queue up for bread, and after her recent suspicions, dispelled though they were, she was afraid to find herself tête-à-tête with her father. At the same time, in view of her urgent departure for the front, she had a seemingly trivial but actually very great favour to ask her father which could not be put off until their future meeting. She decided to wait in the kitchen until her aunt came back; Taisa had been detained by an air alert. Chance thus made Polya an involuntary witness to an anything but secret conversation about the misadventures of Vikhrov's companion, which evoked Polya's deep sympathy.

It concerned the delay in the writing of his thesis due to the lack of certain materials, which were kept in the now inaccessible archives of Leningrad. Morshchikhin was telling Vikhrov that he managed to get away for a week that summer to burrow in the archives, but after four days there he had been obliged to return to Moscow on account of the war, and afterwards the blockade had put a complete stop to his work. He had not had time even to copy out some very interesting St. Petersburg documents, which, he thought at the time, had a touch of unsolved mystery about them. There was an engaging note of unappeased curiosity in Morshchikhin's voice, and Polya sympathised with him all the more that she herself was leaving Moscow without having fully solved the riddle of Gratsiansky. Vikhrov's companion added that these documents might come in useful to him on the long journey that he was contemplating.

"I'm glad Sergei is going to the front with you together," said a husky voice, which Polya recognised as her father's. "It's a good thing for my boy."

"Yes, I've been appointed commissar of the armoured train. Don't be sorry for your son. He needs this more than even you and I."

"I've been wanting to tell you that Sergei is not ..." Vikhrov

began hesitatingly, apparently intending to explain his relationship with Sergei, but a heavy thud amid the crackle of the ack-
ack guns in the nearby copse shook the window-panes and the
dishes in the sideboard and changed the drift of the interrupted
conversation.

For about half a minute they sat listening to the receding
tread of the explosions, intermingled with the angry snapping of
the ack-ack guns.

"I wonder whether they're bombing our depot," Morshchikhin
said worriedly. "By the way, is there any shelter round about
here?"

"We have one in the yard, but it has been flooded since the
autumn. We usually stay at home. D'you want to go down?"

"Oh, no, it isn't the thing for us soldiers. I was only thinking
of your safety."

"Oh, then let's continue our talk," Vikhrov said. He paused
long enough to readjust his thoughts. "And so you believe you
will have plenty of leisure at the front to write your thesis?"

"I don't think anything of the sort," laughed Morshchikhin.
"But here I've been busy day and night, and as a rule I didn't
go to sleep until dawn. Out there it'll be different. We figure
that the war will go on for at least another six months, and we
can't be fighting all that time. During the breaks I could at least
use my leisure to solve a puzzling riddle, which historians, for
some reason, have completely overlooked; I could work out a
dozen possible variants, and if I was lucky enough, dash off
something in the rough. Have you ever noticed how clearly and
logically the mind works in moments of danger?"

Vikhrov was thinking that this work would serve Morshchikhin
rather as an extra hoop for his coopering his will, a difficult chess
problem capable of relieving the monotony of war routine. After
a slight pause, he agreed with his visitor. Since the Institute had
been evacuated and the air raids had become more frequent,
Vikhrov hardly ever left his desk, and could not stop wondering
how clearly his mind worked, what a capacity the page had, and
how light his pen was. It seemed as if the dream of life was in
a hurry to commit itself to paper before stray chance shattered
it and buried it beneath its rubble.

"I didn't quite grasp what period approximately your thesis
covers," Vikhrov said.

"Not to spread myself out too much, I have confined it to the
revolutionary movement among the student youth, those of St.

Petersburg to be more exact. In short, it covers the last ten years preceding the February revolution, that is, the period of the Stolypin reaction, the decline and rising tide of the revolutionary movement. I'd like to deal in detail with the Zubatov affair." And if to keep Polya from being bored while she was waiting her turn, he went into a lengthy description of the notorious tsarist secret police officer, who invented police socialism to lead the workers away from revolutionary activities.

"But after nineteen five that trick was fully exposed," Vikhrov said slowly, still listening to the fading sounds of the air raid. "I think tsarism killed the Zubatov game with its own hands on January 9th. By the way, I eventually found out that my late uncle carried an icon of some saint or other in a silver frame in front of that famous procession. The same bullet went through the two of them. You can see for yourself what a giant he was." Polya heard footsteps, and could guess who her father was pointing to on the large reproduction of *The Execution of the Streltsi* that hung on his wall.

Morshchikhin explained the Party and political motives of his task. He thought it would be a good thing for modern youth to look back at this period of Russian history. After its defeat in this war—and Morshchikhin never doubted it—the old set-up would start organising new headquarters while at the same time reverting to the well-tried tactics of seducement by mealy-mouthed liberal ideas and the sham liberties of bourgeois democracy—to the allurements of legalised class collaboration, that is, the tactics of deception, bribery, sops, and fatherly police benevolence. The first to be thus attacked, Morshchikhin predicted, would be the countries which had swung away from capitalism as a result of the war. It was there that the old world would try to recruit traitors from among the simpletons and the waverers, those who were quick to burn up and quick to cool off, in all fields of trade union, sports and religious activities. Thus, the Zubatov venture interested Morshchikhin as a classic police method of taming the malcontents, and obviously, what Morshchikhin's thesis lacked was striking examples of this method's practical application.

"To tell you the truth, Professor, I purposely broached this subject with you, because, having lived in St. Petersburg at the time, you might be able to give me some details about it. From what Sergei has told me, you took part in the revolutionary rallies and secret meetings, and in the organisation of benefits. I therefore thought you might have—"

He did not finish the sentence. A rising snarling bark, prolonged as eternity, broke upon the air, followed by a grunt of bestial gratification, which shook the ramshackle house to its very foundations.

"I thought they had gone, but I see one ruffian has come back to throw a last brickbat, even if only to smash a window," Vikhrov said through his teeth when the tinkle of shattered glass had died away. "What a mean shameful trick. Well, I'm listening to you, Morshchikhin."

"Well then, I wanted to ask whether you have any notes or diaries left over from that time, or perhaps letters from friends who had suffered."

Vikhrov took his time answering; he was picking up the fragments of something that had fallen from the window-sill.

"I'm afraid I never kept any diaries," he said at last, and Polya was sorry that her father was not able to do such a nice man a good turn. "My biography was much too disorderly to allow me to drag such a bag of souvenirs about with me. My participation in the revolution is extremely doubtful too. I belonged for too long a time to that class of scientists, still prevalent in the West, who consider themselves at peace with their conscience if they scrupulously discharge their professional duties. Like God's little bees, they do not stop to think who collects their honey of inspiration, and why other people should enrich themselves at the cost of their sleepless nights, which they resell on the stock exchanges, often to the detriment of the rest of humanity. In addition, they smash their crockery for them from time to time with rattles like these. I came to the revolution by way of my Forest, and to tell you the truth, a pretty deep forest it was, too, judging by the number of beatings I got. My exile, too, was a clear misunderstanding, if anything—I didn't deserve it; I just paid for my intimacy with a big Party man, that's all. You may have heard the name—Krainov? He's your man. With his gigantic memory, he'd do the work of a whole archive for you. If it's not a military secret, when are you leaving for the front?"

"I don't know, but it's going to be soon. Tomorrow we're giving the armoured train a trial run."

"Then you'll hardly have time. Just before the war Krainov wrote to me from the other hemisphere that he hoped to visit

456

Moscow round about Christmas. It's a curious coincidence, by the way. I remember, on the evening that Stolypin was assassinated, he and I went to Countess Panina's People's House—there was such a philanthropical educational establishment in St. Petersburg at that time. We went to hear a lecture by a friend of ours, but it didn't take place as the lecturer failed to turn up. We spent the rest of the evening strolling along the embankment. It was one of our last meetings just before the mass arrests started. Well, this Krainov regarded Menshevism, too, as one of the principal hues in the chromatic spectrum of Zubatovism." All of a sudden Vikhrov clicked his tongue, and Polya realised with relief that a happy thought had struck her father. "I think I've found a loophole, if not an actual way out for you, Morshchikhin. Have you ever come across the word mimetism?"

"I don't remember. Is it some philosophical gimmick of the day?"

"Not quite. Translated from the French it means to imitate. That was the name by which political mimicry for subversive ends went among our youth circles. An agent provocateur in St. Petersburg by name of Sleznyov, who has now been exposed, sponsored an association among the student youth, whose members were urged to get jobs in the government offices, including the Okhranka, in order to blow up the hateful tsarist regime from within by carrying its measures to an absurdity. I could give you the address of a former school-fellow of mine, if you like. He was nearly caught in that vile trap himself. We knew each other at the Forestry Institute."

"Is he a forest scientist too?"

"In a way. We are not on good terms, though. He holds very destructive views on the Russian forest, that man does, and lately I have formed the conviction that he is actuated by careerist motives. He is able to get away with it to some extent because many of us still take radicalism to be a sign of good faith. Well, does it suit you?"

"It's simply a godsend," Morshchikhin said, and there was a hopeful note in his voice. "Hasn't that acquaintance of yours evacuated east?"

"No, he's staying in Moscow, and for the noblest of reasons, too. What's more," Vikhrov said, waxing enthusiastic, "he intended to write something on the same subject himself in his young days and spent over a year rummaging through the archives of the Police Department, in 'His Majesty's Private Bureau', but he lost interest in the job and chucked it in the middle. I'm sure the material he has collected is just lying about unused. If you go and see him before you leave he'll be pleased to let you have them for a few days to copy out. Owing to our sharp dissensions, though, you'd better not tell him I sent you. Simply flatter him—in this case the game is worth the candle. The thing is that for all his outward charm he is a morbidly ambitious man, hence rather erratic, I should even say, casual in his treatment of people. By the way, it was he who was to have read that lecture that did not take place on the first of September 1911, that is, on the evening Stolypin was shot. Like Krainov, I felt terribly ashamed about a comrade of ours having let down a workers' audience—a fairly numerous one on that occasion, by the way—especially as the rank-and-file worker in those days saw a friend in every man who wore a student's uniform."

"Perhaps the lecturer didn't come because he was ill?"

"Possibly," Vikhrov said doubtfully. "At the Institute the next morning he complained of a headache. I only remember the incident because Krainov told him off about it in my presence, and I must tell you, I had seldom seen that calm man in such a temper. So you'd better hurry, Morshchikhin, this is an uncommon piece of good luck." Vikhrov took such a long time rummaging about among his pocket diaries, that although the name of Gratsiansky had not been mentioned yet, Polya could hardly restrain herself from using the open door as a prompt box to tell her father the address he was looking for.

Morshchikhin sat on until the All Clear, and after he had seen him out Vikhrov happened to glance into the kitchen. Polya jumped up from the stool and hastily pulled her tunic down. She waited with a sick feeling for the exclamations, the distressing embraces, even reproaches for having forgotten the common decencies of kinship; but it was not quite like that.

4

It had been Polya's intention, apart from that trifling secret favour, to express to her father her contrite satisfaction at his having won the day in the face of malicious slander, to compliment him on his September lecture, and approve of his having joined the Party, in other words, to cheer the poor old man up in his lonely vale of years. She found, however, a youthful, smiling man with alert keen eyes, who looked anything but a pathetic object of compassion. Her mind was in a turmoil, and the speeches she had been rehearsing were clean forgotten. She fumbled nervously with the buckle of her belt, her self-possession completely gone.

Vikhrov took in the Komsomol badge on her tunic, which was still stiff with newness, the bitten fingernails, the startled grey eyes. He longed to gaze into those eyes, which reminded him of others, now slightly dim in the memory, but he looked away so as not to put her out still more.

"I heard something moving about in the kitchen and I couldn't think what it was. I'm glad to see you at last. Well, how do you do, my girl." And without waiting for a reply he led her into his room by the hand, a numb cold hand just like her mother's had been that time.

"Let me go, that's all right," Polya said, trying to disengage it.

He picked up an ashtray to put it on the desk, but changed his mind and looked round for something else, which he could not find; he gave his tie an angry tug, then jerked a heavy armchair out into the middle of the room for Polya with surprising ease. She realised with dismay that her father was as agitated as she was.

"There, sit down. Just so."

"That's all right, I'll sit here in the corner," Polya said.

"No, sit down here ... you're not a stranger. This is your house, you know. For me you never left it for a minute, but how quietly you behaved all these years. Now we shan't let you go until we've got everything out of you. I wanted to go and see you myself a hundred times, but your aunt forbid it ... in your name. Taisa never tells me a lie. Well, let's get to know each other. I've been waiting for you a long long time. You're a Komsomol girl, so you've got to be absolutely frank—what do you blame me for?"

"Nothing, but it just happened that way. I wanted to see you the moment I arrived, but all kinds of things kept interfering, and then...." She looked towards the kitchen as if seeking escape or help there, but Taisa had not come back yet from the bread queue.

"Wait a minute, how many years is it since I heard your voice? Not since thirty-six, surely? I specially dropped in at Loshkarev when I was in your parts last year to have a look at you—don't you remember? Unfortunately, I couldn't disclose my identity at that time, I dared not. I was in trouble at the Institute." His eyes went over Polya swiftly. "I took a short enforced holiday, and you know how it is in cases of great disappointments, you suddenly feel drawn to the healing springs of childhood. That's how I came to be on the Yenga."

His worst fears seemed to be coming true.

"I know, Papa, I read all about it," Polya nodded.

"And you believed it? Believed what they wrote about me?"

"I couldn't help believing it, Papa."

"Quite right, go on doing that, you must always believe," he said hurriedly, sacrificing himself to life's intrinsic and permanent values. "We often overlook the fact that children are apt to remember some of the erroneous and painful manipulations which are performed on their fathers in their presence. But in this case, my girl, you may believe me too. I did not steal, I did not sell my country, did not cheat, although I must admit to being a none too clever man seeing that I have failed in a lifetime of effort to prove the most obvious and banal things to my people." He lowered his eyes. "Did Mamma read it too?"

"I kept it hidden from her for a long time, but then she found the cuttings under my pillow. We understood then why one of your postal orders came two months late. But you need not have apologised about the money in your letters, we were living quite well ... and still are. Last winter we even bought a radio set!"

Vikhrov stared hard at his outspread hands.

"I wasn't sending you the money only to help you out, but to have the right in my old age to sit with you the way we are doing now, to take your hand and talk about life. Just so. You'll understand that one day all too clearly, although I wish you never felt that need half as strongly as I do." And abruptly, as if rejoicing at something, he changed the subject. "But everything has turned out for the best: you have grown up, you're a Komsomol, and already in the army, I see?"

"I'm going to the war, I've come to say goodbye," Polya said, looking up, and without brushing away the tears of emotion that welled up in her eyes, she smiled into her father's face.

He looked at his hands again, or rather through his fingers at her heavy top-boots, and she, catching the direction of his glance, tucked her legs away under the table to make them look a bit smaller.

"Everybody's coming to say goodbye now ... you're the third today. They're saying goodbye in the neighbouring houses too, in the neighbouring cities and countries. This is a season of great separations and changes all over the world. The meetings will be fewer, I'm afraid." He skipped a speculative thought, which he believed too abstract for an adolescent like Polya. "But that's unavoidable. Don't be ashamed of your boots, my child. Today there is no clothing more smart and honest than yours is. Were you called up, or did you join the army yourself?"

"I went of my own free will."

"Just so. Youth is defending itself. It's curious, by the way. Some poets find a certain rapture in battle. I was able to check up on this in 1915, but my experience did not confirm this point of view. What attracts you there? Is it the rapture, is it a desire to brave danger, to test yourself, is it patriotic conscience, wrath, wounded pride, or maybe just a desire to win your laurels," he prompted, trying to help her choose the correct definition. "Not any of these?"

"No, that's not it," Polya shook her head. "I can't explain it."

"Give me a hint, I'll understand. I'm so curious about everything that concerns you."

Polya threw him a guarded look, but there was no sign of his wanting to dissuade her or to pity her, as she so much feared. He kept on her level to such a degree that he made some of his conclusions dependent on her answers. A warm trustful wave swept over her, and for a while she felt perfectly at ease with her father, almost as much as she did with Varya.

"I see it this way," she began. "Now what are people out for? Some say happiness, but I think that's wrong. They ought to be out for purity. That's what happiness is—the chief reward of purity. And what is purity in this world? It's living without war, without wronging one another, without the little ones being killed, or the weak trodden on, because anyone can weaken on the long road, can't he? It's not locking the doors at night, and having a friend behind you always instead of an enemy, and having people go out of life with a smile and not a curse."

"All that's desirable, but hardly feasible," interposed Vikhrov. "But go on, go on."

461

"And also it's having everyone work, because a person without work is worse than a beast, he'd think nothing of blowing the whole world up. No one despises people so much as those who are themselves despicable. But that's as it should be, it would be a shame if it wasn't, don't you think so? They say people are living *there*, too, even listening to music and planting flowers."

"Where's that?"

"Well, in that what d'yer call it—that old world. I used to read treatises about it myself. One thing I can't understand, it's been rotting for so many centuries and it still stands. I wish I could take a peep at it to see what keeps it going, and why it hasn't busted and fallen to pieces ages ago from mere human pain."

"It *is* busting, bit by bit, Polya," laughed Vikhrov.

"I wish it would hurry up, life is passing, you know," Polya complained with childlike simplicity. "I'm a silly, funny girl, aren't I?"

"No, you're not very silly, and not funny at all," Vikhrov said agitatedly. "You say you would like to have a look at it.... Tell me, didn't they ever tell you anything about the Gorgon myth at school? I thought so, more's the pity. Unless you learn about these roots of humanity you'll never get to know the leaves in its crown. In Greek mythology there was a hellish monster with brazen claws, gold wings and serpent hair. I don't know whether it was due to horror, delight, or sorrow, but a glance from its eye turned into stone everyone who dared to look at it. The ancient poet placed its dwelling far away in the west, beyond the ocean."

"It's a country then?"

"No, it's much bigger and more formidable than that, Polya. It stands for the whole sum of base passions which ruled the conduct of the world of yesterday. And there was only one brave man among them—Perseus, who dared to challenge the monster."

Concern for the hero crinkled Polya's forehead.

"And did he conquer it?"

"He did."

"Good for him! And what happened next?"

Vikhrov paused over his words.

"The myth follows a rather complicated pattern. From the blood of the Gorgon were born poetry and a thundercloud, which, in hot climes, is identified with the idea of fertility. Not

462

a bad reward for victory, as you see. Even so, Perseus turned his face away when he raised his sickle over the Gorgon, although he had wisely provided himself with such new contraptions of the age as a magic mirror, winged sandals and a helmet of invisibility. He knew what he was letting himself in for."

Polya glanced uneasily at her father. The subject she had been so anxious to avoid seemed to be cropping up.

"I beg your pardon, I didn't quite catch you. Are you warning me against taking risks?"

"On the contrary. Besides, the Gorgon is not what she was—she has lost her teeth. The thing is, I never talked with you before, Polya, and I wanted to see how you were armed against this thousand-year-old evil."

"I'll tell you," Polya burst out, and in the girlish obstinacy with which she pressed her chin to her shoulder he recognised his favourite work of art—the Neapolitan Psyche. "Our armour is youth, purity, I think."

"Purity. Is that in the sense of not being contaminated with too much wisdom?" Vikhrov discreetly enquired.

"No, in the sense of our loftiness of purpose. In other words, the purity of our aims. But if the worst comes to the worst we could find something hotter. That's what a school friend of mine said—he's at the war now, but just the same those thoughts are mine too. What else do you think we need?" Polya said, darting a frowning glance at her father.

She did not like his protracted silence. Probably her father knew too much about life to rise above it to those fiery-winded heights of Rodion's.

"No, Polya, I didn't want to frighten you," her father said, reading her thoughts like an open book. "It's not important, anyway. Parents believe it to be their duty to stuff as much junk as possible into the travelling bag of their darling, who will chuck it out midway without regret. Those ridiculous people would think up wings for him on cotton wool to keep him from catching a cold."

A clatter of dishes came from the kitchen, where Taisa had returned from her queue. She came in at the appropriate time, carrying a tray with a saucer of caramels, a teapot and a plate of cold sliced beetroot on it. She sat down a little to one side without saying a word; she was either upset or simply did not dare to interrupt the learned talk. She merely asked her brother with her eyes whether they had hit it off, and he made a reassuring gesture, as much as to say, not quite yet, but things are going the right way. All of a sudden the door of the little sideboard opened with a low sigh, and Polya smiled, remembering her mother's stories. All this somewhat smoothed over the awkwardness of an incipient disagreement.

"There, Polya, try of your aunt's labours," her father said, apologising as it were for the humble fare. "She grows it herself in the front garden. Delicacies are best avoided in old age, but carbohydrates will do no harm—the more the better. Don't you think this beetroot flatters the palate?"

"Thanks, but I came here straight from the canteen," Polya said, and relenting at the sight of his obvious fear of losing her again, she stroked his hand. "I understand everything, Papa, but don't worry about me, please. I'm only going as a hospital nurse, and, besides, they say it's the quietest part of the front. Talk about Gorgons!"

Not to offend the old woman, she helped herself to a slice of beetroot, agreed that it was as sweet as sugar, and glanced at the wrist-watch under her sleeve, the very watch which Vikhrov had given his wife as a present shortly after their arrival in Moscow from the forestry division. Her military uniform safeguarded Polya against being pressed to stay for a day or two.

Vikhrov glanced at the photograph in the gilt frame.

"When did you see Mamma last?" he asked. "How is she?"

"I saw her just before I left. But I came here in June. I had only two letters, then we were cut off."

"Yes, so my sister told me. Please describe her last day before you left," he said, shutting his eyes the better to see what he wanted to see.

"There's nothing much to describe. She made her round of the patients, as her duties as feldsher required. After the death of Yegor Sevastyanich they sent us a young doctor who had no experience. The whole hospital lay on Mamma's shoulders. In the evening she received her constituents—she's a deputy, you know, and Saturday just happens to be her reception day. She came home tired, and there were also business accounts waiting for her to look through. Luckily the lights went out—our electric station doesn't work properly yet. We sat together in the dark for about half an hour, then went down to the railway station."

"That's good. We had no electricity at all when I was there," Vikhrov mused. "Does she feel cold any more, did you notice?"

464

Polya looked blank. Apparently this most important detail of Taisa's story concerning her mother had slipped her mind.

"Why should she, we have enough firewood, living on the Yenga."

Her father tried to explain as best he could.

"I meant, doesn't she feel miserable there, all alone. You have been living mostly in Loshkarev. Doesn't she feel lonely by herself?"

Polya still failed to understand the jealous question.

"She mixes with people all day, she has no time to feel lonely, really. It's different now perhaps. It's very bad that I haven't heard anything from her for a whole month. What she's doing now, at this moment, I don't know, I can't see."

"How can you see through the smoke of gunpowder," Taisa threw in by way of consolation.

"Oh, a mother like mine would find some way of letting me hear from her!"

It grew dark early, and Polya began to take her leave. After the usual parting words, advice to look after herself, and invitations to come and see them again before she left, the old couple saw her to the door. Polya allowed her father to do up the wooden buttons of her padded jacket; he did it fumblingly, simply to delay the moment of parting.

"Don't forget us, Polya. Write us when you get the chance, little defender of our!" said Taisa, bowing low to the departing girl with a sort of fierce intensity.

She was so reticent and absent-minded that evening that her brother could not recognise her. She had not even proposed sitting down before a journey according to the old Russian custom they had always observed in their family. She had not even noticed that the visitor had come with a package and was going away empty-handed. Now the street door was open, but Polya still lingered.

"If you need anything, Polya, say so," her father said. "Of course, a soldier doesn't pay for his keep, but I want you to know that everything here is yours down to the last nail, yours and Sergei's."

"I can tell by her eyes she wants something, but she's afraid to say so," said Taisa. "Maybe you'll take some money or some clothes? You're going out into the freezing cold. Don't be ashamed, Polya, we wouldn't grudge you a thing."

Indeed, she read in their faces such a willingness to make any sacrifice for her sake that she overcame her scruples.

"Well, you see, Papa," she began in a wheedling tone, "I have quite a few photographs of Mamma—I have even cut one picture out of the local newspaper after the elections to the district Soviet. But she has such a worried look on all of them, as though she were in a hurry to get somewhere even on the photographs. I've never seen her looking so jolly as in that picture of yours in the gold frame. You won't be angry if I ask you to give it to me, will you?"

It was the first favour she was asking of her father, and she was sure of success.

"Oh, I see. Just so," he said, taken aback. "I'll do it with pleasure, but ... to tell you the truth, your request has caught me unawares. Let us go back for a minute and put our heads together."

"I wouldn't have asked for it," Polya said, going back into the little study without noticing Taisa's embarrassed face, "but it's just standing on your desk doing nothing, and I'd so like to have it with me on the journey. True, I've never seen Mamma looking upset, but then I've never been able to make her laugh either."

"Don't make excuses, I understand you perfectly well, Polya," her father assented somewhat effusively, shuffling his feet uneasily. "I think I've found a way out. We have a photographer at the Institute, a very old man, but an expert at his trade—he photographs forest types, timber diseases, you know. He's not quite well just now, but he has a sister-in-law who does all the work for him. They have no telephone, worse luck, but I'll take this photograph down there first thing in the morning and have a copy made for you, two copies while we're at it. You're not going for another day or two, are you?"

While saying this Vikhrov displayed a remarkable mobility, now crossing to the window and holding the photograph up to the dim wintry light, now brushing the bronze garlands of the dusty frame with his sleeve, anything to be able to have an excuse for holding it in his hands a little longer.

"Our train is leaving this evening at ten o'clock," Polya said. He smiled bravely.

"In that case ... I won't even take it out of the frame. Take it as it is. It'll be safer under glass."

"Don't worry, nothing will happen to it," Polya said hurriedly.

She was beginning to understand her father's behaviour, and the realisation made her feel warmly happy. "I'll put it in my Komsomol card, that's the most reliable place for it. It's a beautiful frame, by the way, must be an old bronze one?"

"Oh, it's nothing much. Take it with the frame, but remember, I'm giving it to you in exchange for your letter. You'll write it as soon as you get there, four closely written sheets at the very least—will you? On second thought. . . ." He weighed the gift in his hand, mindful of the soldier's kit it was to go into, and this time without prompting, drew the photograph out of the frame through the slit on the underside. "Take it, it's yours, along with everything else here, Polya."

The photograph fitted neatly into the Komsomol card, and only the very edge had to be folded down. Polya left her father's house with a twofold sense of joy at a painful duty fulfilled at last and a long-wished-for acquisition made. In the half-empty Metro carriage she sorted out her crowded impressions. and first of all discovered with a light heart that she was taking away to the front with her neither shame for her father nor, what was still better, humiliating pity towards him. When all was said and done he lived no worse than her mother, who, it it true, continued to live in that cold rented room in the old maid's house through sheer obstinacy. The meagre fare which her father had put on the table for the occasion worried her a bit, and no doubt she had done the right thing, when, while waiting her turn in the kitchen, she had on a sudden inspiration thrust two tins of meat which she had just received for her rations into the little cupboard. The modest gift gave her a grown-up feeling, especially when she thought of it in connection with the test which her father had passed with such high marks.

5

She was walking up the dark stairs of her house when the anti-aircraft batteries started barking again; with the front so near the enemy air raids that month had become more frequent. The door of the flat was wide open and Natalya Zolotinskaya was out again. In the momentary flash of an ack-ack gun Polya caught a glimpse of the child's cot with its beaten pillows of an unnatural greenish whiteness. There was no need for her to hurry to her roof duties now, she was in the service and was going away soon. She slipped into her room without taking her coat off and gropingly found her things, which she had packed beforehand. But before leaving the place for ever, she pulled the balcony door open and looked out into the cold and darkness. The air raid was in full swing and resembled a storm, a low, angry wintry storm; it crouched over the city, which glimmered snowily below, and rummaged about, growling, in its vitals. The crash of explosions weaved themselves into the incessant barking of the anti-aircraft guns. Gigantic columns of smoke shot skyward here and there in the flitting searchlight beams; they looked like fan-shaped lines of force in a magnetic field, but no flames were visible—they were working somewhere inside the houses, close to people. At that moment Polya felt neither fear nor anger, only a cold cruel curiosity towards the invisible insect that was circling overhead, gambolling, dropping sharply with engines shut off, stinging, then zooming off to reachless heights. What a different Polya this was to the one who had first heard the ghastly howl of the air raid!

And then everything below—the snow-drifts around the little houses and the church façade looming through the bare branches of the trees—was lit up in a flickering rosy light. The fruit stall standing at the entrance to Blagoveshchensky Alley had caught fire. In the quivering light reflected from the ceiling Polya cast a last glance round Varya's room, trying to engrave upon her memory all the precious details, from the arrangement of the different objects to the pattern of the wallpaper; somehow, she could not leave her dwelling without a last tidying-up, although she realised that she would never return to that house, a very nice house even though it was not quite finished. Slowly, testing her strength of will in small things, she put her old "rusty-fusties" under the bed, straightened the crooked picture of Darwin on the wall, half opened Varya's box and saw her drawing on the top, then thought of Bobrinin, and guessing her friend's secret in a sudden flash of discovery, smiled at her, the darling, in her faraway "fiery-winded" gloom.

"Now goodbye everyone!" Polya whispered, getting up from her knees, and with no one to see her, bowing to Moscow from the window, to the city which had sheltered her before she left the quiet backwater for the great river.

By the time she ran downstairs the fire on the corner was going out. The storm rolled away westward amid a rumble and flashes as of summer lightning. The tenants of the house stood in the doorway with an air of patient boredom, like people taking refuge in gateways during a heavy downpour; they had got so used to it now that hardly anyone went down into the shelter during an air raid. They stood there silently watching two intrepid youngsters battling with the last big incendiary bomb in the roadway nearby. Having driven it into a hole, like a savage beast at bay, the boys were finishing it off with a mixture of sand and snow, and it snarled and snorted back at them to their evident delight, wreathing them in clouds of scarlet vapour. In answer to Polya's question, an old lady from flat No. 10 said that Natalya Zolotinskaya only a minute ago had run off to bandage somebody in the wooden little house across the road. Polya hastened there to say goodbye to the Queen of Clubs with an odd premonition that she would lift a corner of the veil over things which she had kept hidden from people. It was here that the closing incident of the day occurred.

A double whistle overtaking her from behind made Polya turn round. A fierce glare in the window of the room she had just left hurled her backwards; lying stunned on the back she saw the corner of her house heel over, hang poised in the air, then break up in chunks of various sizes, like an ice floe at high water, so slowly that the alabaster figure of the collective-farm woman seemed to be leaning over languidly from the pediment to pick up her sheaf, which had been torn away from her together with her arms. She dropped with a stony smile, increasing in size as she fell, and Polya shut her eyes tight in terror. Presently she was awakened by the cold liquid touch of thawed snow at the back of her neck. She sat up, licking the dirt from her lips, which tasted salty, and trying to understand where the boys with the incendiary bomb had got to. The house was still there, except for two stories sliced off the corner, and she herself was unhurt; only in her eyes yellow leaves floated away left and behind her. People were carrying something on a stretcher towards the entrance, and somebody shouted in a queer strangled voice that Natalya Zolotinskaya had been killed, and this meant the boys would be found afterwards under the debris; meantime they were taking away the woman she was to have given the key to Varya's room too, so that it shouldn't get lost. Then Polya got up without an effort, and walking unsteadily round a heap of still smoking rubble, overtook the stretcher. A woman's head in a crown of half-grey hair, not in the least disarranged, swayed in step with the stretcher bearers, the body below the waist having been hastily covered with a man's overcoat, the fur collar of which was trailing in the snow. Seeing this in the light of the still blazing incendiary bomb, Polya screamed, and Natalya turned upon her huge, terribly black eyes that were not like her own, and failed to recognise her.

"Keep order, please, keep calm. Very good. Thank you. It's so kind of you. I'll get up in a minute. It doesn't hurt at all, thanks," she kept speaking without a stop, answering questions that no one asked her, then suddenly, with an anguish that was more than human she said through clenched teeth: "Why, oh why doesn't someone stop them! My God, what scoundrels!"

Apparently excitement deadened the pain; she did not moan once while they were carrying her, but only tossed about protestingly because they were taking her down some steps to some place beyond recall, and Polya followed her down staring at her wide-eyed, walking as in a dream. And then the stretcher was set down in the middle of the basement, as if in a desert, and everyone went away, perhaps to telephone, or to dig up the boys, or simply to get away from the sight. And there was not a soul left with Natalya Zolotinskaya except a gentleman with a face of crumpled paper wearing a suit of extraordinary striped pyjamas, and there was something desperately familiar in his drooping chevelure and prickly gold-rimmed spectacles. But no, it was not the doctor of childhood memory, it was someone else whose name Polya couldn't for the life of her remember. And suddenly a sinister looking old woman cropped up, probably as dark within as she was without, who began to urge the gentleman in an earnest whisper to take his coat, which was lying on the stretcher, either because he was likely to catch a cold or because the coat itself would be spoiled and stained. Her son waved her off, begging her in the same tight-lipped hissing tone of longstanding hatred, for the sake of Almighty God, to leave him alone for once in his life. And the old woman vanished as if by magic, the way it always happens in dreams, but nevertheless the thing she saw there looking so blurred in the feeble glow of the electric lamp dangling from the ceiling was so horrifying, so hideously fascinating that Polya cowered in her corner, unable to tear herself away.

"God, what monsters! Where are the minds of humanity! No, you can't leave it like this. They've simply got to be killed off, one by one, with an axe. Who said they were capitalists? They're just scoundrels, they ought to be wiped out!" the wounded woman began over and over again in a vehement tone of sudden discovery. "Will somebody see what's wrong with my legs there. I want to get up, help me. I've got to go to my post, it's late." Then again, in a voice of unspeakable anguish: "And no one, no one asks Him sternly, in a man's way, what He needs such scoundrels in the world for!"

"Stop it, Natasha dear, lie still. The ambulance will be here soon, and then you'll have a long long rest..." the man in the pyjamas muttered over her, kneeling by her side. "Hold on with all your might, for the sake of our grandchild hold on. You are such a brave woman. Do you remember how you brought me that dynamite in a pillow-case? And I kissed your hand for the brave deed. And afterwards they deceived us both, made a laughing-stock of us, do you remember?"

"I don't see you, who are you?" Natalya said, shrinking back. "Shut the door there, it's draughty! Oh I see, there's only one half of me left ... the Queen of Clubs! No, it doesn't hurt, but it's terrible, I won't even be able to go for milk when Zoya comes back."

"Don't worry, I'll take care of her. I'll find her and give her a home," the man said in gasping haste, trying in vain through those dark fathomless eyes to reach her mind before it was too late, running, stumbling, hurrying to prostrate himself and beg her forgiveness. "It's me, Alexander. Don't you remember that evening on Sergiyevskaya, and later, how I taught you to skate?"

He succeeded at last. She grew quieter and began to understand.

"Ah, it's you again," Natalya murmured disappointedly in a tone of utter exhaustion. "How I loved you, Gratsiansky. Even when I saw you come out of the Daryal arm in arm with that whore, I still loved you. And how I tried all my life to keep away from you, but fate threw us together at every step, even now, now! You always clung to life ... you didn't even come to see our daughter in her coffin. How could you, how could you, Gratsiansky?"

"But I was ill then, my dear!" the one with the paper face groaned, and Polya realised that he was lying again.

"You didn't come even to see our grandchild off, although it involved no expense, Gratsiansky, beyond perhaps a bar of chocolate. How much I loved you and forgave you! But I forbid you to take Zoya from there, I will not have it. Don't snatch at

471

this straw, don't cause people any more harm. There, it's coming ... ah! Go away now, I'm going to die."

When, disturbed by the sudden silence, Polya peeped out
again from behind her hiding-place, Natalya was still alive. Her
fingers were moving over the coat, and the man in the pyjamas
was kneeling at her side, whispering last-minute excuses and
consolations; wisps of greyish hair hung down over his face.
Conscience and time forbade Polya to linger there any longer.
She stole out of the basement, wiped the sandy dirt from her
face with snow, then found her belongings under the stairs.

It was snowing heavily outside. The tramcars had started
running after the All-Clear signal. Luckily for Polya, the hospital
train was four minutes late in departing. Her new friends hoisted
her up into the truck by her arms. The coupled engine was hissing
nearby. The hospital chief and the commandant, thickly covered
with snow, were finishing their inspection round of the train.

"Well, girls, did you have a fright?" Strunnikov asked, stopping and playing his lantern over the faces of the girls in the
truck. He was referring to the furious air raid. "Never mind,
you'll get used to it!"

"We've got used to it a bit already," half a dozen subdued
voices answered him from behind Polya's back.

"Then what's the silence about? You can't do without a song
in war. Always keep it handy in your first-aid kit, never let
the camp-fire go out in cold weather, you know. All right, take
it easy."

Polya happened to be standing in the doorway, but, stunned
by the events of that day, she heard neither the words nor the
departing signal. There was no thought, no bitterness or pain
in her bruised body, only a feeling that she was already an old
woman. Leaning her head against the door jamb she gazed at
the sticky flying snow-flakes. The snow was so generous that
night, like every belated and therefore unwanted gift.

CHAPTER TWELVE

1

Let it be said in advance that for reasons beyond his control
Morshchikhin never finished the thesis he was writing. Thanks
to that thesis, though, he spent two hours in the immediate vicinity of a momentous discovery, whose publication would have

rewarded its author just as amply for the trouble he had taken. At the time Vikhrov had suggested to Morshchikhin that he should try his luck with Professor Gratsiansky the latter's name was already familiar to the thesis-writer not from his forestry articles, but from the very side that interested him most. He had not mentioned anything about this distant "acquaintance" of his with Gratsiansky, not through any desire to find out more about him than he already knew, but presumably not to belittle Vikhrov's services in his own eyes by an ill-timed confession. Actually, Morshchikhin's pre-war trip to the Leningrad archives had not been altogether barren of result. He had immediately stumbled upon a mysterious if short-lived youth organisation, which became known to the press already in those days under the name of Young Russia. Gratsiansky's name figured only three times in the dossiers of the Police Department—to judge by the vague context, in the capacity of a victim of subtle gendarme machinations. Morshchikhin had no hope of ever being able to open that secret lock, and since all legal time limits had expired he believed Gratsiansky to be dead. He was all the more astonished to learn therefore that the chief actor in this mystery drama was still alive, that he was moreover thriving on the soil of forestry with a flat in the adjoining neighbourhood, just a forty-kopek ride by bus. It was not very difficult in those days to still find surviving witnesses of the past, veterans of exile, or, say, participants of the barricade fights in the Presnya District, but such a figure, who had weathered the storms of tsarism and the vicissitudes of the revolution without a scratch, was a wonderful find indeed.

Morshchikhin was leaving at such short notice that he had no time to make a written request for an interview. He decided to go down to the address he had been given the next morning without any warning, and introduce himself as a research worker who wished to solicit the help of a distinguished colleague. The moment he turned into Blagoveshchensky Alley he realised why all his attempts to get in touch with Gratsiansky by telephone had failed. Everything here told its voluble tale of yesterday's upheaval: the charred remains of the stall covered with snow, from which women were picking out burnt potatoes; a heap of uncleared wreckage with stalactites of frozen ice; the church cupola, with a dent in its gilt surface, knocked sideways as if by a barbarian's club; the torn wires and the house itself with its corner chopped off, revealing surviving pieces of furniture in solemn-looking white covers. For an irresolute minute Morshchi-khin stood watching some daredevils from a bomb disposal squad removing an unexploded demolition bomb from a manhole. But such an opportunity, when he could call the day his own, might not occur for a long time. He managed to break through the cordon and enter the building. In answer to his knock, an old woman's voice sounding like Baba Yaga* out of a tree hollow, questioned him rigorously through the chained door as to who he was, where he came from, and what he wanted. At first it seemed as if he was in luck—the professor was in, but then the padded door was slammed to again, and a long humiliating in-terval followed after which about half a dozen bolts and locks were opened with a clang.

The mistress vanished with a celerity that was surprising in one of her age, and only the tail of her dressing-gown flickered for a moment at the bottom of the corridor like the ritual broom. Her son appeared in her place with his hand over his throat and a feigned sickly look on his face. Instead of the wreck of a man he had expected to see, Morshchikhin found himself confronted by a majestic figure standing securely on its own legs, and ob-viously fully conscious of its own outstanding role in human progress and resignedly shouldering the burdens of fame which it inevitably involved. Even if one did not know that this was the terror of the forest heretics he had a quality of presence that put him down as a man, who in his own particular province, vague though it may be, was not one to be trifled with by ordin-ary mortals. He emitted a short half-questioning sound, to which Morshchikhin replied that it was only sheer necessity arising from his speedy departure that gave him the temerity to intrude at such an early hour and under such deplorable circumstances; the clock through the half-open door showed eleven thirty. Gra-tsiansky heard his visitor out with an air of sourish disbelief. At first he seemed to be flattered by this recognition of his revolutionary services and wordly experience, but the next minute he took alarm, as it were. The flimsy excuse for the visit, and its suddenness, as if the visitor had been trying to catch him at something, and that too-new white sheepskin coat straight from the officers' storehouse aroused suspicions which not even a forced reference to Vikhrov could allay, the more so that the visitor had no letter of introduction.

---

* Baba Yaga—a Russian fairy-tale witch.—*Tr.*

On the other hand, it would have been unwise to turn the visitor away and then be tormented with doubt for a week afterwards as to the real reasons for that visit.

"Ah well, in spite of our ancient differences, I have always had a soft spot for that man, with whom er ... we shared a dish of skilly in a Greek eating-house on Karavannaya in the days of our political persecution," Gratsiansky said with a forced stiff smile. "I haven't seen him for ages, how is he getting on, still limping? Oh no, I don't mean ideologically. I've been intending to ring him up for years, but I just can't seem to find the time. Incidentally, I lost his telephone number—do you remember it?"

"Professor Vikhrov was complaining to me only yesterday that he hasn't had a telephone installed all this time despite his repeated applications," Morshchikhin answered pointedly, so as to leave no doubts about himself in the other's mind.

"Ah, that's just like Ivan. He never was capable of arranging his personal affairs," laughed Gratsiansky, as if he had never heard of Vikhrov having no telephone before. "I'd be glad to do him a favour, but I'm sorry you put this thing off so late. Pardon me for being inquisitive, but are you going away on business or just er ... going home?" he asked, jibbing at the last word, and explaining that owing to the state of siege people were leaving Moscow in all directions, and some were going home.

Not to complicate matters Morshchikhin had not mentioned his official posts, but he immediately understood from his host's question that he was curious to know how a young man of his age had avoided being called up.

"Oh, no, Professor, I'm going to the war," Morshchikhin reassured him without batting an eyelid.

The remark should have put Gratsiansky on his guard; already at that time he looked upon every visitor as a secret agent of criminal investigation, but his mental derangement had not yet reached its fatal pitch, and presumptuously confident of being able to beat his partner to it so long as the latter did not produce a trump card, he invited his visitor into his study with a wide gesture.

They went through the second door down the corridor on the right into a carpeted room lined with bookcases and hung with heavy curtains; the fresh snow outside the window was mistily reflected in the panes of the bookcases and the antiquarian knickknacks, whose modest looks would have deceived the inexperienced visitor. Seating Morshchikhin in an armchair and making him comfortable with an ashtray and cheap cigarettes in a dull silver holder, specially laid by for such an occasion, the host went over to the window and stood there for a long time watching the sappers reverently loading a drop-shaped bomb with a broken off stabiliser into a lorry.

"I must say, my dear comrade, that you have not chosen the best possible day for a talk on the subject that interests you," Gratsiansky's voice awoke with a soft rustle as soon as the sappers had driven off. "War has visited our quiet and peaceful alley. The fiery squall, the crash of stone, the roar of the er... yes, of the falling heavens, still ring in my ears. As a matter of fact last night I lost the dearest, if not the nearest person in my life, with whom many fond memories of my youth are associated. It is a bitter thing to have to admit in my declining years that despite a lifetime of endeavour to win the recognition of my contemporaries, this was the only creature in the world who loved me. She died in my arms, literally speaking, her legs crushed, and it is characteristic that her last dying breath was a curse to er ... capitalism. It is that which inspires me with profound faith in that—what do you call it?—the ultimate triumph of the cause to which you and I are dedicated. However, such shocks inevitably leave their marks, and I shall carry the memory of that bombing with me for the rest of my life, like a soldier who carries in his bosom—what's it called—oh yes, a splinter of enemy metal. No, don't go away, don't leave me," he added, noticing a slight movement in his visitor's chair, which was nothing more than an attempt to resist the paralysing pressure which was beginning to melt his will. "It wasn't a hint, it was just a natural search for sympathy. A man like you, who is going into battle for the advanced ideas of the century, has a right to claim attention for his urgent, if somewhat, hee-hee ... whimsical needs. Our only consolation is that grief of whatsoever kind only temporarily darkens our so-called soul, which is afterwards pierced anew in all directions by the beams of life with all its powerful and full-blooded contradictions—isn't that so?"

He was weaving his hypnotic web around his visitor, and a drowsiness began to steal over Morshchikhin, as if he were being put to sleep before an operation. The very chair in which he sat lent itself so obligingly to every position of the body that at first his thoughts began to wander, then his legs became numb, and finally he was obliged to feel his nose furtively to make sure that it hadn't stiffened. With the part of his mind that was still awake he reflected that only a man who was utterly unfeeling towards his fellows was capable of so liberally sharing his emotional experiences over the loss of a dearly loved creature, that all these lyrical effusions of his were merely a screen behind which he was deliberating the variants of a counter-attack, that actually, for all his outward garrulity, that gentleman was about as communicative as a gravestone. The exasperating duality of this impression made Morshchikhin take careful stock again of his companion against the background of his surroundings.

Gratsiansky's look of ascetic renunciation, particularly those hollow eye-sockets, the high forehead and sallow complexion, would have done well on canvas in the image of some foreign father of the church, a Saint Augustine, say, at the time of life when his eyes were shut to all things earthly and opened only to things divine, if such irrelevancies as a bright tie, bedroom-slippers with fur pompons, and a quilted eider-down jacket, somewhat too warm in such a well-heated flat, could be left out of the picture. Incidentally, Morshchikhin's eyes searched in vain for the source of that genial voluptuous warmth. The Gratsianskys kept no domestic help, and the furniture had about it a look of ostentatious moderation designed for the curious eye of the stranger, but one could not avoid the suspicion that an awful lot of good things lay hidden about in secret little closets and locked cupboards, while in the study itself there was a curtained niche from which dangled a telltale string of dried mushrooms. At any other time Morshchikhin would have been glad to see a master mind of the age enjoying the amenities of Soviet life, but now there was something almost indecent and repellent in this visible absence of war's austerities. In short, Morshchikhin had not yet come across such a snug sheltered home in half-besieged Moscow, a home in which all the window-panes, with strips of tracing-paper pasted over them for blast protection, were intact, in which there reigned a luxurious silence broken only by the ticking of the clock and the suspicious stirrings of a third person behind the half-closed door, and lastly with such a fragrant aroma of coffee hanging about it that the visitor, who had come down on an empty stomach, began to feel his mouth watering.

"I'm so sorry you're a bit late for breakfast and I can't offer you a glass of er . . . something," Gratsiansky tactfully apologised, noticing the slight twitching of his visitor's nostrils. "If you have the time, though. . . ."

"Don't bother, please, I had a splendid meal before I came here. If you don't mind, let us get straight down to business," Morshchikhin said, coming out of his stupefaction. "Unfortunately, all those who are going out to battle for the advanced ideas of the century, as you shrewdly put it, have little time to spare."

He was obviously getting angry, mainly with himself, for his unaccountable submission to the cold hostile will of the other man.

"Splendid then," acquiesced the host, and frowned slightly at the repeated rustle behind the door. "I trust that an hour will be quite enough for the er . . . conversation you are interested in? If you were to give me a fuller idea of your field of research we might be able to make better use of that hour."

Rubbing his stiff knees, Morshchikhin patiently explained the subject of his thesis, mentioned the inaccessibility of the Leningrad archives, omitted for brevity's sake any mention of either his pre-war trip or the Zubatov movement, and ended by sweetening the whole with flattering testimonials to the host's excellent memory and courtesy. The latter quite reasonably pointed out that for the given period of Russian history memoir literature had some classical works which covered the ground so thoroughly that it would be a sheer waste of time on Morshchikhin's part to go treasure-hunting off the track. Morshchikhin agreed with his appraisal of some of those books, but thought that memoirs written after the event and without the help of diaries, always bore the stamp of invention and a certain rounding off of reality, while the most brilliant historico-political researches, as he explained drearily with stiffening tongue, were mostly philosophical or statistical concentrates of unfortunately absent, although implied facts. "Those books, of course, are invaluable to educated men like you and me," Morshchikhin forced out of himself, remembering Vikhrov's advice, "as they bring into harmony an accumulated mass of knowledge, but the ordinary reader wants to learn about the past in all its workaday details, and these demands are justified to some extent, because an appeal to the heart is always more telling than to the mind; that, by the way, is the eternal meaning of art. And that's why the independent conclusions which the reader or spectator draws after having read a book or seen a play take much stronger hold than those which are offered to him ready-made from the page or the stage."

"Do you understand me now?" Morshchikhin concluded with a hopeless feeling.

"Yes, of course! The man who buys a ticket to the theatre for his hard-earned money is much more interested in feeling himself a witness or a judge of the events that are being shown him than a nitwit who is having socially useful truisms dinned into him," Gratsiansky lined up with him rather hastily as he settled himself in the chair opposite. He even cited as an example a number of well-known novels and plays of those days, which dealt quite intelligently with the problems of drainage ditch construction or the elimination of schedule violations on the railways. "I don't want you to misunderstand me," he caught himself quickly. "Personally, I think the spectator should be able to stand a show without an anaesthetic, and that the artistic fabric does not stand the weight of didactics, but then literature is a type of social thinking, which we simply cannot allow to be monopolised by private individuals, even if they are geniuses. No matter if this somewhat reduces the formal value of a work. Let it be even a bit worse so long as it is more in keeping with the epoch, more accessible to everyone."

"Excuse me, but who told you that our epoch aims at a lower level, a depreciation, so to speak, of art?" Morshchikhin countered. "On the contrary, we believe that art on the liberated planet will surpass all known models of the past."

"We shall continue our conversation then, hee-hee ... after the final liberation of our planet," Gratsiansky parried, putting an end to the discussion with a brilliant thrust. "From what I understand, then, you intend to give the world some highly artistic work?"

"No, but I should like to reproduce a number of sweeping and well-documented episodes of the youth movement. I intend to make use of diaries, biographies, court proceedings, even marginal notes concerning current prices of goods, newspaper reports, everything which moulded public feeling those days."

Gratsiansky nodded encouragingly.

"I see. And has the plan been approved by those who are in charge of this work?"

"Why yes, it was conceived at the outset as a reading aid to the history of the Party. I am interested in particular in certain obscure episodes of that period which I believe to be fraught with consequences for us."

"I see," Gratsiansky murmured smoothly, glancing at the door, behind which one of the floor-boards creaked rather betrayingly. Someone there was listening to their talk. "Well, what can I tell you? It's a splendid idea. True, it's none too novel, er ... attempts have been made before to reconstruct, say, monuments of archaic architecture by piecing the fragments together, but no one has yet tried publicly, on the square, to raise the familiar spirits of Endor and make them re-act their cruel spectacle for the er ... edification of posterity. Nevertheless, I perceive in your plan the sublime prototype of the literature to come, when the individual style of the author will have been done away with for good and all, when all people without exception will engage in literature, mutually correcting and supplementing each other, and when all different forms of work will have been levelled and the compositor at the linotype will make creative amendments in the works of his brilliant contemporaries. Please don't interpret this as an attack upon the trend of our splendid advanced, optimistic, shadowless, sterile-clean so to speak literature. It was only through innate revolutionary scepticism that my generation previously rejected the non-alcoholic lives of the saints. But then all the world's religions are nourished at first on this kind of unleavened bread until their followers get tired of it and develop a fancy for ham and peas. In the days of my free-thinking youth I too believed that the great art of the victorious epoch was to be inaugurated not by the *hopak* or jig on a planetary scale, but, if you don't mind me using a hypothetical image, by the portrayal of the tragic hero crucified er ... on the cross of his peculiar social and philosophical contradictions. The feat of Prometheus is directly proportional to the size of his vulture, don't you think so? I cannot boast of my views on art having changed drastically since then, but I have begun to understand that gold mining always begins with the erection of poor wooden structures; the dredges come afterwards. Dante, Dostoyevsky and Balzac will last out time, though. The future will take care of itself. Everyone chooses his food according to his teeth, doesn't he?"

"Excuse me, but I can't catch your drift," Morshchikhin put in, his anger rising steadily. "I must say there's something about your thoughts that I don't like. Why all this verbal froth of exasperation?"

"I'll gladly explain," Gratsiansky smiled, looking very pleased with himself. "On the one hand, I cannot but approve of your initiative, but on the other, I er ... never had any sympathy for these historico-philological exhumations, this graveyard curiosity towards disinterred relics; first towards rough copies and biographies, and from that towards the alcove secrets of the national heroes. Today they throw scientific light on Pushkin's family jars, savour Belinsky's letters and Dobrolyubov's diaries, turn the intimate life of Tolstoy inside out, tomorrow they take the skulls of Suvorov and Tsar Vladimir from the burial vaults in order to stick plasticine over them and admire them in whiskers, warts and other marks of identification. Napoleon was quite right to reprove his painter, saying, 'I want to see the grandeur of my soldier, and you show me the pimple on his nose.' The world is old, and wherever you dig you'll find the dead. So take my advice, young man, leave the dead alone, let them sleep in peace. Being an educated man you no doubt remember the sad tale of the Convent Deputy for the Department of Seine, who er ... full of hatred for the overthrown regime and the vices of the past, broke open the tomb of Agnes Sorel and threw out by the hair the skull of one of the most wonderful women of France, who rendered her country such great services. He paid heavily for it. And why should you drag out into that land of never-fading dawns our poor nasty old bones which you have dug up?"

"In a word, forgive and forget?" Morshchikhin said with narrowing eyes.

"On the contrary, I am for the real history. . . ."

"And a little against forensic medicine?"

The blow struck home. Gratsiansky glanced coldly at his visitor's feet.

"Oh, I didn't know you had such deep reasons for your visit, Comrade ... er ... Morshchikhin, I believe?" But he immediately changed his ground so as not to end the meeting on that sharp note. Besides, he could not dismiss the visitor now until he had discovered his mysterious intentions. "Oh no, I'm not against history, I'm for the truth as well. But there is such a thing as our own proletarian truth," he added didactically.

For some reason every pronouncement of Gratsiansky's now roused in Morshchikhin a violent desire to oppose him.

"I'm inclined to think, Professor, that every epithet limits the extent of a thing and implies the existence of another, but there is only one truth. Born in the very midst of the working people, the creators and guardians of all the world's values, our truth has long become the universal truth of the majority. Right now countless, as yet invisible armies are standing at the gates of the world's cities, ready to take them by storm. Ask them, 'Who are you?' and they will answer, 'Humanity!' So let *them*, the evil ones, dissociate themselves by epithets from all the toilers in the world. . . ."

Morshchikhin broke off, suddenly aware that he had become infected with the copious eloquence of his host, who was listening to him with all the more pleasure in that the time alloted for their conversation was trickling out in sheer "blether" while the main ticklish subject had not been touched on yet. It was clear to Gratsiansky, though, that he would not get rid of that simpleton without handing him out some trivial incident from the cellars of his rich reminiscences.

He spread his hands in a gesture of surrender.

"I say no more, you have almost convinced me," he said, bestowing on the visitor one of his proven smiles in which admission of defeat mingled with envy towards his young and simple-hearted victor. "I am ready to foot the bill."

Thereupon Morshchikhin, with a shade of respectful hatred, restated his request for the third time. Without a doubt Professor Gratsiansky kept copies or extracts of the Leningrad documents, which he had collected for his unwritten book; the mention of it brought a wince, even an ugly scowl to the face of his host. Morshchikhin would return the originals in two days, as soon as he had copied them, and promised in exchange to make due acknowledgements on the title-page of his thesis. There was a long minute of uneasy silence, after which Gratsiansky came forth with the statement that at one time, during his youth, he had indeed been confronted with the alternative of taking up either the society of men or the society of trees. Then, as now, there was no end of sociologists, but no one who could tackle the problems of theoretical forestry, which was tainted with bourgeois influences; that explains why his unfinished book did not see the light of day. As for the materials asked of him, he would gladly give Morshchikhin his whole archive as a gift together with the manuscript—"no, no, colleague, don't thank me for it, please don't"—but the trouble was that he had left the whole, really formidable, box of papers in the care of a relative when moving to Moscow from Leningrad some twenty years ago. Punctilious to a degree, that lady, who had graduated the famous Bestuzhev Courses and herself suffered no little harassment at the hands of the tsarist satraps, would naturally look after them ... but of course you could never be too sure. "I don't have to tell you that not only masterpieces of furniture but precious libraries, leave alone such trivial manuscripts as mine, become mere fuel reserves at crucial and stormy periods of social development."

"I'm sorry to hear it," Morshchikhin smiled without unclenching his teeth, although he heard only what he had been expecting to hear.

"Don't take it to heart, though, young colleague," Gratsiansky said patronisingly with a glance at the clock. "I would not like you to go away empty-handed myself, although our time *has* run out. At any rate, the archives of my memory are entirely at your disposal. Your unexpected visit, by the way, put me in mind of a very amusing incident—my first boyhood encounter with the Okhranka. The event had nothing of the heroic about it, nothing to suit the purpose of your thesis, but it will show you some of the mainsprings of life and help you to grasp the spirit of the times, the molecular tension, so to speak, of that epoch, when the militant minds of our generation were being formed. Will you risk it?"

"I have no choice," Morshchikhin said with a shrug, mentally sending his host to the devil. It was only intense curiosity towards the human enigma facing him that kept him in his chair. "I'd be much obliged to you, Professor."

Before the astonished gaze of Morshchikhin, Gratsiansky crossed to the half-open door, as if it were a magic cupboard, and came back with an aromatic nutritious beverage in a glass complete with sugar and a home-baked pastry, which he set before his visitor. Then he resumed his seat, squeezed his nose between his two palms as if making ready to plunge into a slumbrous pool of ghosts and memories, playfully cocked an eyebrow, then suddenly began to speak, now in a tone of natural resentment against the regime that had marred his youth, now with a touch of whimsical humour such as old men indulge in when looking back on the vagaries of long-buried years.

"Well, sir, this happened on the historical aftermath you are so interested in, when the first glimmer of the lingering and welcome dawn of the great revolution just broke after the Stolypin night," Gratsiansky began slowly. "Our generation matured early under the blows of tsarism. We young men of the capital challenged the autocracy, too, as best we could, that is, er ... we gathered secretly, posted patrols at the entrance, read lectures, criticised the Minister for Education, and even played about with print and more dangerous things, which I kept under my pillow to harden my will. Children! I remember even inventing a portable barricade which you could move about from place to place in a cab. You couldn't expect more of us. We scions of well-to-do families were not much better than those school-boys to whom the revolution meant freedom to smoke in the streets, wear their hair long, go to prohibited shows and make themselves an unmitigated nuisance to unpopular teachers. The workers shunned us, and we were a bit afraid of them ourselves, although as far back as 1909 I had occasion to wage a dogmatic fight with the anarchists in Lesnoy. A man by the name of Valery Krainov was with me at the time—do you know him? Not a bad fighter, either. That was when they tried to trap me. The thing started one morning with a visit from a queer little fellow in a brand-new army coat fresh from the store-room. He was in a terrible hurry as he had to leave urgently—only that one was going home, if I am not mistaken. See how interesting it all is. That one's name was Giganov, though."

2

If we were to correct certain unfortunate inaccuracies in Gra-tsiansky's fascinating story, which were quite excusable considering the remoteness of the event, the prolonged deficiency of haemo-globin and the prostration of soul caused by so recent a bereave-ment, the incident of which he spoke would have looked like this.

In 1911 the Gratsianskys returned to their town flat from the country rather early on account of the elder Gratsiansky's heart attacks, which had become more frequent. The family doctor intimated that in view of the state of the young man's respiratory tract it would do him good, too, to take a holiday on the Biscay coast together with his parents. Summer was drawing to a close and the Paris trip promised new impressions. Besides, the weather that morning was delightful, and there was a mysterious touch of haziness in the air following the previous night's rain. During breakfast Alexander was almost in excellent spirits but for a slight foretaste of the boredom and idleness that awaited him in the empty town. He was eating his ham and eggs and scanning the morning newspapers with an eye to the local news and gossip, which were the most interesting. They contained racy accounts about a suicide committed by a travelling businessman, about an aged countess who had been dismembered by her janitor-lover for the sake of the family jewels, and about the well-known giant Foss, who had disappeared without a trace after swallowing four dozen meat pies at a railway station buffet. In short, despite the dead season, life in the capital was in full swing. And then the parlourmaid came in and told the young master that a scared looking but otherwise quite nice soldier boy at the back entrance wanted to see him.

Picking his teeth, Alexander went into the kitchen. He had made it a practice never to refuse that pretty girl in small things by way of reward for her responsive nature. A long loose-limbed fellow of about thirty-five in a soldier's greatcoat jumped up from a stool at his entry and introduced himself as Mikhailo Giganov, private of the 146th Caspian Infantry Regiment stationed near St. Petersburg. He said he was leaving soon for the village and asked the young gentleman if he could have a private talk with him on a matter of some urgency. Asked what the urgency was, Giganov replied with a sigh that it was the same old thing, the sorrows of the people. There was something unclean and frowsy about his complexion, his shifty vice-rimmed eyes, his sleek hair greased to a high shine and combed down over a low forehead as if it were pasted on—not at all the regulation style of haircut for a common soldier. Everything about him warned Alexander. But his old chum Pavel Sleznyov had promised to call not earlier than dinner-time in order to make their plans for the evening's entertainments. Through sheer boredom Alexander told Giganov to follow him.

On second thoughts, though, it must have still been raining, because Alexander remembered throwing the windows wide open to get rid of that nasty smell of sodden army clothes, and Giganov had tried to protest for fear of being overheard, but Alexander had his own way. The window looked out on the street across an inaccessible front-garden with a high railing. Apparently the rain was petering out at last, because when Alexander threw the window open he remembered seeing the young maple outside with its foliage still quivering from the last drops. It somehow reminded him of a young jubilant animal shaking itself as it came out of its font of creation. Alexander was given to imaginative thinking ever since a youth.

He listened idly to Giganov's story, staring out of the window and breathing the water-dusted air which already had the bitter tang of autumn in it. He was thinking that the trees were more worthy of friendship than people, because they never lied in prosperity, never complained in adversity. But one had to possess an infinitely rich soul to fill the constant silence of such a companionship. And then Alexander caught a sound like a stifled sob, and glancing up in surprise at his visitor, met a look of tearful reproach in his eye, at which he coloured deeply. He felt a sense of obligation towards that poor downtrodden creature, who was ugly only because humiliation and want never made anyone attractive. Like the other members of his youth organisation, which had already taken shape by that time, Alexander had heard about the life of the people only by hearsay; he had never seen the inside of a factory or an army barrack, and preferred to show his respect for the underdog at a distance so as not to have his gentle poetical image of Russia marred by rude contact with reality. This was Alexander's first glimpse of the people's sorrow; there it sat on a chair within three paces of him, a squashed cigarette in its hand, wringing his conscience with its tale of woe.

Giganov began with a general complaint against the drudgery and hardships of a soldier's life, and was particularly sore with some officer with a Baltic name, his company commander to whom he was batman. He even wanted to let his trousers down to show Alexander the telltale signs of his woes and wrongs on the small of his back, but the young man would not let him do it—not for fear of offending the people's sorrow by a show of incredulity, but for fear of having to pay something for the looking, not to mention a feeling of physical loathing. It was only natural to enquire of Giganov what had made him carry his tears all across the town to the comparatively rich but outwardly unremarkable house in Sergiyevskaya Street. The visitor smoothed down a curl of hair on his forehead with the edge of his hand and said that he had often heard about the student's sympathy from their janitor, a fellow-villager of his from Kostroma, at which Alexander felt a bit hot and awkward, because he had really, on two occasions, discussed with that burly bearded fellow the causes of peasant poverty and certain radical means of doing away with it; to ensure secrecy and silence he had slipped half a ruble of his pocket money into the janitor's hand; the seed of truth which Alexander had planted in his slumbering soul seemed to have struck deep. This time, however, Alexander hesitated to show his sympathy for this new military species of the People's Sorrow, as it threatened to draw him into deep waters and poison the pleasure of the Biscay trip.

He told the People's Sorrow flatly that owing to the limited circle of his acquaintances in the student and ecclesiastical-professorial world, he was unable to help him, and warmly recommended him to report his case to the Minister for War, and if that did not yield results, directly to the State Duma, where the facts would be brought before the public and justice was bound to triumph.

"What's that, what place should I apply to?" Giganov said quickly, thrusting out his neck.

"I said, report directly to the authorities," Alexander said guardedly.

"Oh, that's a waste of time!" the other said with a disappointed gesture. "There's no truth in the authorities, it's all eyewash. Looks like the only thing left to me is the noose or a header in the ice-hole."

Naturally, being a cultured man, Alexander could not see a human life going down an ice-hole.

"You shouldn't give up the fight, you ought to love life more strongly, Giganov," the young man said sternly, and patiently explained to him in simple terms the ineffable charm and fascination of life. "Besides, it's so silly to do such a thing just when you are winning free. Didn't you say that you were going home?"

"What's the use of this life when there's no luck in it, and no one sympathises with our people's sorrow," Giganov persisted with baffled rage.

For one thing, Alexander felt flattered at thus having a full-weight human life put into his hand, but at the same time it seemed rather improbable for grown-up bayonet-wielding soldiers to seek the protection of a beardless first-year student of the Forestry Institute. But then, he argued with himself, the common people had such a childlike soul that they always stood in need of men of great heart and mind who could realise their most cherished dreams for them; besides, all the famous leaders of men such as Garibaldi, Pugachov or Wat Tyler didn't become rebels from their cradles; they, too, were children, until some trivial, perhaps ridiculous chance pushed them to the forefront, and then the popular wave swept them along on its crest into the glittering, so to speak, annals of history. A small voice had long been calling Alexander to some such deed that wasn't too dangerous, and at times he was not even averse to taking the lead in a venture of this kind, provided his name could be kept back for the time being. It should be said that even in those days Alexander Gratsiansky did not suffer from excessive naïvete, nevertheless he suddenly pictured himself in bronze, on a pedestal of a thousand years hence, draped in something ragged and bullet-ridden that fluttered in the breeze of history. His heart was softened and he shouted to Axinya to bring in some tea so that he could put his thoughts in order while the People's Sorrow was addressing itself to the refreshments.

"I really don't see how I can help you, Giganov," Alexander moaned, yielding shamefacedly, fulsomely. "Explain to me, what are your intentions?"

At this Giganov came into the open. Gazing somewhere over Alexander's shoulder, he said in a sneaky voice that to teach all the other enemies of the people a lesson he'd like to have his own back on that brute of a company officer, that is to say, to make a small but thorough attempt on his life. He undertook the execution of the deed himself, so that the young gentleman would not have to dirty his hands. All he had to do was to give him a little dynamite out of his supplies, and if he wanted to he, Giganov, would give him a note to the effect that he had not received anything of the kind from the student Gratsiansky.

A chill of discovery crawled up Alexander's spine. He said nothing; outside the window a cab drove past with a clatter of hooves on the wet roadway; still he was silent. The visitor waited patiently for his victim's consent with a look of canine devotion in his eye. Alexander was suddenly struck by the fact that in addition to his ears being peculiarly arranged for spying, the man's eye, too, was of a tubular listening kind with suckers at the end. Alexander looked down and tried to still the beating of his heart. The fact that they were after him meant that he had grown in physical and moral stature. Suddenly he felt an intense itching in his finger-tips, similar to that which makes an un-licked cub scratch when it begins to grow claws.

"But how are you going to carry out your sentence if you are going away to the village in a day or two?" Alexander asked in a low tone with the most innocent of airs as soon as Axinya had left the room. "You've got to have some plan, some alternative schemes, an alibi. This isn't like going to the baths, it's a terrorist act, Giganov."

"Don't worry about that, we'll manage the job fine," Giganov answered in the same blurred tone, sawing the air with his hand. "He's carrying on with a singer, and when he goes to the bitch in the evening after roll-call, we'll be waiting for him round the corner, the blighter, and let him have the works. All we need is the stuff."

Alexander shook his head ruefully.

"Besides," he parried, skilfully steering clear of anything that might startle the scoundrel, "I simply haven't got any of that er ... stuff handy just now. It's not the kind of thing you keep in a sideboard, and the chemists don't stock it either. In any case I can't decide these things without my comrades."

One could gather from this hint that he had no right to dispose of the organisation's property off his own bat.

"Just a handful or two would be enough to teach that bastard the lesson he deserves," Giganov went on urgently.

"I understand you, Giganov, but I just cannot share your impatience," Alexander said. He was enjoying the game. Then, as if taking pity on the man, he suddenly added: "If you're not a coward, though, and if your decision is not just the result of a momentary irritation, then er... I'd advise postponing your departure for a week or two. Come and see us next Wednesday, round about eight. Some of our members will be here, and we can then discuss your plan in detail."

For the sake of secrecy Alexander let his visitor out through the back door, and not until he had made sure that no one was shadowing him. At parting he made the People's Sorrow swear that it wouldn't say a word about their meeting to anyone in the company. For his part, he did not confide his plans to anybody, not even Sleznyov, so as not to spoil his enjoyment of what he considered at the time a quite safe and amusing game. On Wednesday they were celebrating his father's sixtieth birthday in the company of intimate friends and colleagues; the actual date of that jubilee fell on Sunday next, but it was decided to have the party earlier in view of their forthcoming trip abroad. Naturally, Alexander was keen to treat some of his friends to an entertaining spectacle, especially the late Natalya Zolotinskaya, with whom his love affair was at its height at that time. Strictly speaking, he had merely intended at first to play a practical joke on Giganov by sending him away with a cheese wrapped up in a newspaper, or better still, by making him dead drunk and then innocently phoning up to the Okhranka head-quarters and asking them to remove the prostrate body of their faithful servant who had collapsed in line of duty. As he entered into the spirit of the thing, however, his fanfaronade took on a still more frivolous shade.

Not being a thinker by profession, Giganov, anticipating a rich haul, presented himself at the Gratsianskys in good time. By way of observing the same secrecy technique, he was installed in a wall-cupboard containing winter clothes like a penned Madrid bull, who, after certain manipulations by Alexander, was to breathe his last, figuratively speaking, before the eyes of the assembled spectators. Every once in a while the doomed creature, half-choking under the fur coat of Gratsiansky senior, put its ear to the keyhole, in which the key had been prudently left inserted, but all it could hear were animated young voices punctuated by deeper ones and mingling with the pleasant tinkle of glasses, and it could but guess at the victuals of the élite by the gastronomical aromas that penetrated its foul naphthalinic den. After the lapse of two odd hours, Giganov was perspiring profusely and beginning to feel a bit out of sorts. He was wondering whether they hadn't forgotten him, or, still worse, whether the student's guests had gone away on the quiet to commit some foul deed upon the sacred person of His Majesty the Tsar, when suddenly a hush descended upon the company following the announcement of a funfair attraction. There was a sound of approaching steps, and a slit of light stabbed the darkness. Alexander Gratsiansky, with a dry click of his fingers, invited Giganov into the arena.

Licking his lips and blinking in the light, his long arms pressed to his sides, he stepped out into the corridor, glanced back suspiciously at Alexander, who was hustling him along, and the next minute found himself in the Gratsianskys' dining-room before the assembled guests. Seeing the trap, he stopped in his tracks with a muttered sound of annoyance. The company he saw looked like anything but a criminal association. There were hardly any young people there at all, except for two girls and a baldish student in a pince-nez, who stood up and stared at Giganov over the heads of their elders as if he were a freak of nature. At a bounteous table running the whole length of the spacious room sat some twenty-five elderly guests, the ecclesiastic

and other aristocracy of St. Petersburg in frock-coats, silk sur-
plices, and departmental uniforms, most of them with dignified
beards of assorted shapes and sizes or with shaven Roman-
Catholic jowls. On the host's right hand, peeling some longish
exotic fruit with nimble fingers, a gaunt-looking bishop was
laughing heartily in a genial falsetto, supported by a fat man
in a pongee jacket—no other than our old acquaintance, the
mystico-theologian Akvilonov—whose laughter shook the
flowers standing in a vase before him, while a large woman
decked out in rich furs despite the warm weather was trying to
prove something to them. The next minute all these well-fed
idle people were staring in distasteful surprise at the intruding
apparition in the long-skirted army coat. Akvilonov, wiping his
huge moustaches with a starched napkin turned round at the risk
of splitting at the seams. And although none of them, together
with the state system they stood for, would have lasted a week
without the Giganovs, no one stood up for him, because he was
really a toady, a police ear, a grovelling cur, the scum of the
nation. He knew it himself as he stood there squirming and fiddling uneasily with his sham army cap with its blue band. To
crown all, his retreat was cut off by the long-haired young master,
whose face had gone pale and even slightly drawn with the
excitement of the chase, and whose glance was full of the hauteur
of moral purity, as if he, smooth, sleek and well-kept, had the
sole right to judge Giganov for his loathsome deeds.

"If you don't mind, sir, I'd better go away," Giganov said
meekly amid utter silence. "Let me go, sir."

"Oh, no, Mr. Giganov, just one more minute please," Alexander
said in clipped tones with an almost cataleptic spasm, wagging
his finger in the man's face. "You were just boasting about our
political well-being, Mr. Akvilonov, and I wanted to show you
one of the means by which this has been secured in our God-
given empire since the beginning of time. Let me present to you
a Mr. Giganov, who has come to ask me for some dynamite to
be used on his company commander. It may interest you to know
that from enquiries made through a friend of mine, there is no
soldier by that name in that company. Consequently.... Well,
then, my dear man, tell us as coherently as you possibly can,
who sent you here and why, and we'll treat you to a glass for
it."

"Dear me, what a shame!" the bishop muttered in womanish
tones as he replaced the nibbled fruit on his plate. "Couldn't you

spare us this rude interruption of our polite conversation, young man?"

But Alexander was deaf to his father's commands, to Natalya's exclamation, sharp as a whiplash, to Sleznyov's remonstrances, uttered in his ear in a low voice. The words spluttered from his lips with foam. It was more than the fury of mere vengeance and animosity against the animal that had tried to bite him, it was the vindictive superiority of cowardly strength, the ungovernable outburst of an insulted young sahib on the one hand, and a now conscious need to gloat over the humiliation of an inferior creature on the other. There was no telling how this paroxysm would have ended had not a little black woman, his mother, approached and laid an imperious beringed hand upon his forehead, upon which he was instantly silenced, limp and submissive.

"You don't know how lucky you are, Giganov. Go away," he said wearily, then suddenly flared up again with only half his former heat. "Go and tell your captain, colonel, or whoever it is that he shouldn't send fools any more but should come himself if he feels like having a chat on er ... the subject that interests him. It's no good sitting around in gilded office-rooms like a fine gentleman. Let them work for their living, the good-for-nothing idlers. Yes, sir!" And suddenly, to his own surprise, he flicked Giganov's cheek with the end of his napkin.

An ugly look came into the man's eyes and he swung his arm back like a flail, but he controlled himself and merely grunted.

"You ought to be ashamed of yourself, sir! It's not as if I was doing this for myself!" he said with a loose mouth, breathing hard. "You didn't think, did you, why I was squirming before you like a worm that had been trod on, if you'll pardon me for saying so?"

And he went away, his head drawn into his shoulders, really looking like some revolting bent-backed insect that had been allowed to crawl out of its chink through a domestic oversight.

Everyone tried to drink, joke and laugh away the unfortunate incident. To be sure, the too impressionable boy had overdone it a bit, but when all was said and done, this was their own internal class misunderstanding. Only Sleznyov, on leaving, reproached Alexander for his too flippant behaviour and called him a Nietzschean, and Natalya, at their next morning's rendez-vous, remarked with distress that his conduct of the night before savoured of meanness rather than bravery; it was her unshaken belief that any contact with a vile wretch other than by a bullet

492

was defiling. Alexander himself regretted it a bit, not because yesterday's show had not been quite the success he had anticipated, but because the trick he had played on Giganov might lead the Okhranka to give tit for tat. There was all the more reason for anxiety in that Young Russia already existed and had even adopted the Rules drawn up by Sleznyov in which the aims and tactics of the organisation were elaborately set forth. The only hope was that Giganov would be ashamed to report the fiasco to his chiefs. Indeed, nothing more was heard about the incident right up to the time the Gratsianskys left for the seaside, and that was a good sign. It looked as if Alexander would get away with it.

He spent an excellent fortnight on the coast of Biscay; the disagreeable memory of that St. Petersburg incident was ousted by new impressions, and shallow sea bathing combined with Rouen ducks improved his health. He returned to St. Petersburg and his studies with so much surplus haemoglobin that he could well afford to squander some of it. His parents stopped over near Wiesbaden where they waited to be received by one of the local leading lights of medicine, and so the vast flat in Sergiyevskaya was at the complete disposal of Alexander and Sleznyov for their bachelor pleasures. Incidentally, after the scandalous disclosure of Young Russia, Alexander Gratsiansky took care to conceal his friendship with Sleznyov from Vikhrov and Valery, but he could not entirely give up the motley acquaintances which were the very zest of life to him.

3

His encounter with the Okhranka following the trick he had played on Giganov, Alexander Gratsiansky dated to September 1st, thus wrongly linking it with a historic act of country-wide significance. Actually, it took place a fortnight earlier, almost immediately upon his return from abroad, for September saw the second half of the adventure, which was not mentioned to Morshchikhin not only owing to lack of time.... It was during this period that, owing to unpardonable carelessness on the part of Axinya, sundry items of property were stolen from the professor's flat, to wit, grandmother's skunk cloak, an aneroid barometer presented to the professor by students of the Ecclesiastical Academy, and a washing-tub almost as good as new. Five days after the theft young Gratsiansky was invited to the police station to identify the stolen articles, which had been found. But instead of the usual formalities, the fat police officer began questioning Alexander caressively about the health of his parents, whom he knew personally, and wound up by informing him in an airy casual manner that an officer was waiting to see him in the next room; twice he called the student simply Alec, seeing that he was such an old friend of the family. What is more, the passport clerks were scratching away so irritatingly, and Gratsiansky had such a bad hangover after last night's bachelor spree with Sleznyov that he went to that chief encounter in a state of quiet fury, which tinctured his conduct in rather heightened tones.

Behind the door was disclosed a small stuffy room with blank peeling walls, used for bringing drunks to their senses and for interrogating ruffians. Despite the eagle-framed portrait of the Tsar and an open window giving on an inner court, the place smelt unbearably of hard-worked feet and that rank odour of prison and cheap tobacco which advertised these official institutions of the old regime from a distance. At a bare table covered with carved monograms and other efforts of nightly clerical inspiration sat the sinister thickset figure of a lieutenant-colonel, who was well known to the youth of St. Petersburg in those days. He was wearing a regulation officer's jacket with silver shoulder-straps, and the first thing one noticed about him was a skilful arrangement of the hair brushed over from the right ear to the left, and other signs of burnt-out passions disguised by the artifices of masculine cosmetics. Alexander could not help comparing him to a Roman Caesar who had burned the candle at both ends; indeed, his first impression tallied fully with what he had previously heard about this once brilliant officer of the guards, who had been forced to end his career in the gendarmery. His name was Chandvetsky. He was expelled from the privileged regiment for having failed to pay a card debt, his joining the game without having the cash being interpreted as an attempt to win at the expense of his partners. As a result of that scandalous affair the luckless gambler became known in St. Petersburg fashionable society by the ironic nickname of Herman;* his real name was Edward.

---

* Herman—a gambler, a leading character in Pushkin's story *The Queen of Spades*, to which Chaikovsky wrote his well-known opera.—*Tr.*

According to the same source of information—the all-knowing Akvilonov—this officer had intended, after the scandal, to complete the circle of his earthly existence as a recluse, since, in his youth, he had been interested in spiritual and ethical problems as well as gambling; for the sake of his dearly beloved wife, however, he did not retire from the world, but merely changed his department and his passion: his latest hobby was said to be carnations. At the Okhranka he was in charge of the youth movement, among other things, but owing to the growing resourcefulness of the revolutionary youth, he made blunders which impeded his promotion. The spoilt darling of doting parents, who always felt behind his back the influential connections of his father, Alexander experienced curiosity rather than fear in face of this luckless official.

Chandvetsky started the conversation by using the time-honoured methods of police seduction. He wanted to break in that unhandled colt by gentling.

"I cannot conceal my acute embarrassment, Mr. Gratsiansky, at having troubled you without sufficient reasons," he began with a Japanese smile. "I cherish a slender hope, though, that I have not dragged you away from your studies and other active pursuits."

"Unfortunately I must disappoint you," Alexander said with challenging directness, catching the hint. "Your kind invitation through the janitor has torn me away from a good book, and I doubt whether a conversation in such a place will make up for the pleasure and benefit I have lost."

How Chandvetsky managed it is a mystery, but it is a fact that Alexander knew whom he was dealing with long before the man showed his hand.

"Patience please," the lieutenant-colonel smiled, toying with his silver aiguillettes. "Giving pleasure to his patients is not one of the duties of a surgeon. Besides, you invited me yourself—none too courteously, it is true—to come and have a chat with you. Believe me, I could have found a moment to spare for that, or have arranged to see you in more congenial surroundings had I not been afraid to compromise you in the eyes of your friends. Unfortunately, we just cannot succeed in winning the sympathies of the young generation." He glanced round with a sigh at the stained filthy wallpaper, rested his elbows for a moment on the table, then brushed an invisible speck of something sticky from his sleeve. It was borne in upon Alexander that he knew everything there was to know about the Giganov scandal. "I wouldn't like you to think, Mr. Gratsiansky, that the assassination of an officer of the Caspian Regiment was my idea. I can assure you, we handle these things with greater subtlety than that. The fact of the matter is that Giganov, whom you made such game of, intends to take his promotion examination, and—of all the silly ideas!—he goes and thinks up a diploma work for himself so to speak, without the knowledge and consent of his superiors. Ah well, I don't blush. It's not a thing people would talk about in polite society, no more than they would about the town's sewerage, but it's nevertheless a thing which they have in all well-organised states. In the performance of my official duties I have long been watching Giganov and I quite agree with your appraisal of his intellectual capacities, but he is a plodding faithful worker with a large family, who is protecting you and your family from very unpleasant worries—very unpleasant, I assure you. Dogs are killed but not kicked, my dear sir. Naturally, he deserves disciplinary punishment for his unwarranted conduct, and we should certainly have punished him had he not felicitously succeeded in discovering a hornet's nest in the flat of a professor whose social position has always served us as a guarantee of his political loyalty. A professional flair is a gift, even though it is small coinage, don't you think so?"

"I would still prefer to finish my book," Alexander flared up, reddening slightly and beginning to feel anxious for Young Russia. "However, continue please."

"Never mind, you'll find it a bit more interesting in a minute or two," said Chandvetsky.

With the same look of utter boredom he bent down, picked up a package lying on the floor at his feet, and before the gaze of the astounded student produced therefrom a two-pound tea canister. It was Alexander's whole supply of dynamite, secured by dint of tremendous efforts, the criminal holy of holies of his secret society, which bound together a dozen and a half immature and reckless youths. Alexander made his own bed, and he could not understand how this piece of incontrovertible evidence came to be stolen from under his pillow. His legs became leaden, and church bells began ringing in his ears.

"There, you can't deny that he has a good nose, Giganov, can you?" the officer said reproachfully, staring hard at Alexander's nose. "I trust you recognise it?"

"Let's stop this ridiculous fencing, Mr. Chandvetsky," Alexander said with sullen desperation, his lips white. "What's this—an arrest?"

"For the time being just a desire to warn the son of a very respectable man, whose lectures I read during my leisure with invariable enjoyment. There's no need to thank me, I am just your unknown well-wisher and friend," Chandvetsky proceeded in a paternal manner. "You are young, and you do not even suspect what this stuff is. And yet you erroneously think there is enough of it to wash all the primordial sacred dirt off humanity."

His thoughts straying for a moment, the officer rested his elbows on the table once more. A volley of drunken oaths issuing from the courtyard made him turn round sharply towards the window. With a clumsy movement he swept the deadly package on to the floor. Alexander screamed and covered his face with both hands. He would have toppled over backwards in his chair had he not had the wall behind him. When he came to himself, which he did without help, the westering sun was still shining, gleaming in the officer's epaulets, but Chandvetsky was now smoking a cigarette and waiting. Alexander drew his breath noisily. Terror still gripped his heart.

"My God, what's the matter with you, Mr. Gratsiansky?" the officer said in a tone of kindly reproach without getting up from his chair. "Such a daring young man, and you act like a young lady. Fie!"

"Water, please," Alexander moaned, his head thrown back.

"That's all right, it'll pass. These fits of giddiness are peculiar to young men of your age," smiled Chandvetsky, pushing the canister, and together with it, Alexander's blighted dream, into the dirty corner with his boot. "What made you take fright, though? That tin of yours contains ordinary soap, just slightly coloured. We have nothing against people keeping household stores even in the poorest peasant hut. That's why I put your fainting fit down to overstrain. Still, you mustn't let your nerves go like that, young man. Let me give you a bit of advice from my own experience: learn to forget your enthusiasms, and regularly cleanse your stomach." And as if giving Alexander time to recover himself, he enlarged on the bracing effects of cold sponges and long hikes in the mountains as a necessary antidote to the over-indulgences of bachelordom.

Alexander was silent. Gradually the shock of his recent experience gave place to a wild exultation at his deliverance not unmixed with a grudging admiration for those who had so cleverly tricked him into buying soap for dynamite. He was left with a feeling of having just been whipped, but whipped in a civil manner, without the use of unwonted violence, and, most important of all, without pain, and with even a princely reward for his sufferings at the end of it. He looked up embarrassedly at his tormentor and thought gratefully that in addition to being a gendarme of the conventional pattern—cunning, slippery and urbane, this was a witty man of the world besides. He was struck by the professional structure of his skull with its almost complete absence of a nape and with a jutting double-tiered sort of forehead which apparently housed his detective and analytical laboratories. There, in one of those brain cells of his, like Giganov that time in the cupboard, now sat Alexander Gratsiansky, naked and pervious to light with all his childish secrets.

Suddenly there appeared in the officer's hands Alexander's cloth-bound private notebook, in which the Rules of Young Russia were copied out in a minute hand together with commentary, the assignment of roles after the uprising, and miscellaneous theses anent the organisation of the state. True, it was all written in cipher by the simple expedient of adding confusing letters after each letter of the text; thus the word "Russia" would read "Runvussinvia." But Chandvetsky, with his vast experience, would have no difficulty in taking this hurdle. In a word, this was a bit more serious than the dynamite, but at this point an idea came to Alexander. At any moment now his father would be returning to St. Petersburg, and that dried-up bishop, a schoolmate of his, was received at the house of a St. Petersburg lioness, who, in turn, was intimate with one of the highest officers of the state, who would think nothing of giving this bullying gendarme a rap over the knuckles, or even pack him off to the provinces, send him to hell to Siberia. The thought, like a gulp of lemonade in hot weather, helped Alexander to get back some of his mental poise.

"Frankly, this document worries me extremely," Chandvetsky proceeded, patting the notebook. "It reveals in you a dangerous tendency to give more thought to the good of your neighbour than to your own. Personally, I read it with absorbing interest. You certainly have the makings of a statesman, and that idea of propaganda among the troops and the military schools is worked up admirably. Oh, no, it's by no means foolish, I am not joking. The proclamations of the Decembrists and the social constructions of Fourier looked no less naive, but we know what effect they had on the coming generations. Men are always children, and the more unattainable the Rules, the more attractive and formidable they are. Some things in this amused me, of course, especially the Young Turk thesis concerning the immediate seizure of power. Life doesn't stand still, it is true, and we've got to hurry, most unfortunately. The handwriting is not bad either, although it is rather neurasthenic and cramped, which may, in time, affect your eyesight. You'd better think of that now. But what I can't approve of is your intention, as the future head of Russia, to appoint ministers only from among the members of your organisation. For one thing you simply won't have enough people to form a government with. Furthermore, what do you intend to do with the other parties, which, like you, have long been striving to inflict various substantial blessings upon mankind? You are appointing one of your friends, Sleznyov, to the post of Minister of Public Morals, while another no less distinguished philosopher, Cheredilov, you are putting in charge of the Arts, since destructive experiments in art are less expensive than in other fields of public life. But what are you going to do with—I forget his real name—Valery Krainov?" He paused for a moment tense-faced, waiting to be prompted, but at that time Alexander did not know Valery's secret. "Bear in mind, that man has serious people behind him, who do not take fright at a falling tin of soap and will hardly yield such big political game to a bunch of decadent good-for-nothings, as they call you among themselves. Will you have the courage to break the necks of your dangerous rivals? I am not going to offer you any assistance in this before the time comes, but, as an old well-wisher of your family, I would warn you against all three of these gravely reprehensible acquaintances. What use can you have for such suspicious companions, you, such a delicate and attractive youth?" There was a languid note of poorly disguised insincerity in his voice. "By what means are you going to change this country's history, you, who for all your charm, are an extremely unbalanced boy, in whose library the pamphlets of Ilyin stand side by side with Zarathustra? Like treasury notes, which are secured by the whole national wealth, so are the qualities of this country, which you now find so irritating, conditioned by her climate, geography and the very size of her territory. I foresee no spectacular changes in the future either, otherwise Russia would simply be torn asunder by monstrous centrifugal forces." Chandvetsky spoke in a flattering tone of equality, which neverthelss brooked no denial. It was as if he were appealing to the young man's outstanding intellect, erudition and vast fund of worldly experience. "My dear Alexander, don't you see that revolutionary valour implies a willingness to lose yourself in the mass, to merge with it completely, thus heightening its wisdom and strength, the way they increase the hardness of steel by adding a rare metal, or the resonance of a bell by adding silver to it. And I ask you again, will you be able, with your explosively touchy pride, to destroy yourself in a million strangers, who may never get to know your name? Look what lies at your feet, young man!"

The heat was abating, and together with the golden dust of sundown and the warm reek of garbage there trickled in from the courtyard the dismal notes of a barrel organ accompanying a street singer to the tune of "Marusya poisoned herself". The woman's voice was raucous and beery, but somehow it made Alexander's heart twitch with that pleasantly thrilling nostalgia one experiences when swinging safely at a dizzy height. By this time Alexander had recovered his composure enough to begin losing his temper at these police blandishments as well as at the bland irony, which dismissed him completely as an element of danger to the regime. Suddenly it occurred to him that Valery would have made a much better showing in his place, and he felt ashamed of his ambiguous silence. The worst was over, there was no new evidence, and what could they threaten him with here anyway—beatings, torture? Now such a saving remedy as pain—if not too prolonged!—would merely cover up the shame of his fainting fit, impart a touching grandeur to his puerile ridiculed notebook, not to mention a possible interpellation in the Duma concerning the brutal treatment of a student in a tsarist torture-chamber, after which the whole of Russia would learn of the existence of martyr Alexander Gratsiansky. Yes, it was time he put that loquacious serpent in his place.

"I beg your pardon, Colonel, I'm afraid I dozed off a bit. What was that you were saying about something at my feet?"

Chandvetsky shook his head with a barely perceptible gesture of annoyance.

"Standing on the brink, young man."

"Oh, I'm a bit too old for the bogyman, Mr. Chandvetsky. You'll have to take another line with me. The brink doesn't work."

"That's a pity. Only flies are not afraid of the chasm. But then, of course, they never crash."

Alexander stood up with an air of finality.

"Look here, Mr. Chandvetsky. I'm extremely flattered to have such a well-informed official personage waste so much of his precious time on me, but, unfortunately, I have to attend to various items of business this evening, and I have promised Mother that I would have my meals regularly, so that er ... unless you are going to use some more effective method of detaining me here, I shall take my leave, if you don't mind."

"I shouldn't advise it," Chandvetsky smiled grimly, drumming his fingers on the table. "I would have to take compulsory measures to ensure your attention, and that would mar our sincerity. To take a lesson standing is rather tiresome, so please sit down and stop being naughty, Gratsiansky. I am not asking you to tell me the secrets of that dangerous demon Sleznyov, or to confide to me the thoughts of that greatest blatherskite of all times and nations Cheredilov. I don't know why, but of all the bright boys who have passed through my hands, I like you best. Before we part as enemies, which you have so recklessly set your mind upon, I should like to air a few private opinions which coincide with your own. To begin with, modern youth does not like this regime, or rather its snobbish, conceited, gluttonous and so hopelessly impotent ruling class. Nor do I."

"But according to rumour, your reasons for hating it are a bit different from mine," Alexander said, and sat down hastily on the edge of his stool, aware that he had gone a bit too far.

Chandvetsky merely scowled, but controlled himself. He was used to the snags and setbacks of his profession.

He proceeded coolly as if nothing had happened. "It really is stupid for a society to idolise and tie to its neck all the descending generations of outstanding personalities who have at one time or another rendered some service to their country. Nature does not like to issue double rations of genius to one and the same family, and it is only creatures on the lower rung of development that seek treasures in old spots where others have already dug. On the other hand, with some of the 'subjects' I have interviewed, this deadly hatred of our regime is often accounted for by a sincere but carefully disguised conviction that they have been cheated out of some of the good things of life which are due to them as geniuses."

"That's sheer police slander!" Alexander burst out, for some reason immediately picturing to himself Valery Krainov.

"You needn't defend yourself, I didn't mean you. It's only natural for an outstanding personality who has failed to win recognition in one place to seek it in another. But tell me, Gratsiansky, did you take every possible step to achieve fame in your own country without destroying the existing foundations, which you had not built? The thing is, you and I would hardly survive the upheaval. The trouble with you is that despite your jumpiness at falling objects, in this case an ordinary tin of soap, you are much too cocksure. Young people are apt to believe that they feel, if not know, more than anyone else. Usually that mirage does not fade until the chief errors have been committed. Let us assume even that you are sincere in your desire for a revolutionary exploit, but why then are you so blinded by hatred? By a process of reasoning you may be able to draw up an abstract chart of social welfare, but it will not lead you to the barricade; you would need an incentive for that—despair, hungry wrath, an embittered mind. But did you ever rot in a prison, did you go blind from tears, or steal bread for your children? You flutter over your pleasures like a butterfly, a butterfly, if you don't mind me saying so, to which every flower it comes across is a scented palatial hall with delicious free rations. I'm worse off, I have a wife, a family, and an unpaid debt of twenty-eight thousand rubles. You are clambering up the face of a sheer cliff not to see the world from commanding heights, but for the world to see you in the heights above it. You are ambitious, but then so are most of *them*; a man like that wouldn't want to be in the chorus, the least he'd want to be is choir leader. You want *their* adoration, because you are so sensitive, because you have delicate white hands, an educated father, a grand piano for colour symphonies. Why, you would never succeed in creating that imaginary and perfect society in which you would be able to rest on your laurels, blessed by a grateful deeply-moved humanity. A revolution is a smelting down of everything, a race with a century compressed into a decade, an accelerated succession of the generations, a more frequent casting of skins, for only in that way will society be able to shed the scales of its old evils. Only a very clean person, that is, one with a hopelessly sterilised core, will be able to stand up to such a wind. Now try to imagine if suddenly *they* see through you, if on the very eve of perfect bliss they suddenly read all the thoughts which are now passing through your mind. Pretty awful, isn't it?" Imperceptibly, Chandvetsky's hand came to rest on Alexander's, and there flowed through it into his soul the Death Water of exhortation. For some reason Alexander did not remove his hand; it seemed now that it was not Chandvetsky speaking to him, but he speaking to himself in a low voice. "So what's the sense, my dear boy, deserting from a big comfortable house where your budding gifts would come in so useful? Although I smiled over this poetical notebook, the witness of your youthful visions of glory and nocturnal anxieties, I never for a moment underrated your possibilities. Peter once sailed toy ships on Lake Ladoga too. It's the bitter undoubted truth—our society is getting old, toothless, and ridiculous. Schoolboys now are teasing it and hanging scraps of school paper on its once formidable horns. An effete society does not usually give birth to great men, and only a spirit of effervescent youth, like yours, can save Russia. After all, if you are so keen on guillotining heads, we have a right to our own Bismarcks and Thiers. You are afraid of your own weakness, and not of the opinion of the mob, so hit it in the jaw, hit it hard, and you will have it licking your hands. Come with us, Gratsiansky, our glory is quicker and safer!"

The day was ebbing. Alexander gazed at the yellow glow of sunset across the roofs, which were low in this part of the city. He felt at once horrified and thrilled. But suddenly a fire brigade dashed down a nearby street with a clatter and a clang, and Alexander tried in vain to throw off the spell cast upon him by the gendarme; he first moved his head, swallowed the lump in his throat, then slowly withdrew his numb captive hand and hid it under the table. No one had ever read his innermost thoughts, his secret fears and intentions, with such uncanny insight, and he no longer could bring himself to go away without having heard the rest of it. . . .

"I never expected Giganov's colleague to offer me anything but the lowest scoundrelism," he said in a sneaky unsteady voice, prepared at any moment to apologise.

Chandvetsky threw himself back in his chair, his chin pressed to his chest; the veins on his forehead grew taut, the left side of his face had turned pink, as if it had been slapped, and his jaw dropped slightly. He unhooked his collar at the throat. Nevertheless, the victory he was out to win was near. The student did not go away, he sat there in front of him as if clamped to his seat. It remained to deal him the final blow by his own hand.

"You have the choice, young man, of either shooting at me or indoctrinating me, if you think, that is, that my poor policeman's brains are capable of assimilating your ideas, but whatever you do, please try to avoid foaming at the mouth. Abuse has always been a sign of faulty thinking, and I would advise you to run a lawn mower over your feelings from time to time; that's how the durable English lawns are made. The strong do not swear, they smile." The gendarme's face wore a bored look of superiority. "You've upset my train of thought, but if I remember rightly, I was going to ask what would happen to you if they ever found out, with their million eyes, what a sneaking egoistic nullity you were, and one suffering from mela-gomania at that. They would hardly pardon the spoilt boy from a good family the way I have overlooked your juvenile escapade with Giganov and your rude behaviour here. I have overlooked them because, for all your bluster you are nearer to me than Sleznyov or Krainov. You don't know how much success in life depends upon a proper estimation of one's own qualities. Let us look in the mirror together and I'll help you to distinguish your own features. Well then, you are hungry for life and want a lot of it, but your imaginary gifts are shallow to the point of non-existence, your knowledge of men is gleaned from novels, you know Russia only from your furtive talks with the house janitor and the water-carrier at your summer-place in the country. As for your shirts and parlourmaids, they are chosen for you by your mother. Isn't it true? Moreover, you are over-anxious about your health and would face any disgrace rather than undergo physical suffering. The sight of sorrow in others annoys rather than distresses you, not because it awakens painful civic sentiments—for you tolerate no obligations—but because it gives a bad taste to the joys of life, ice-cream included. Isn't that so? You like ice-cream, young man, don't you? No, you are no barricade fighter. In short, while having a perfect understanding of the way things work, of the logic of everything on earth, you will never learn anything and never accomplish anything in life, so that in your declining years the blood in you will go sour from sterility and envy towards your neighbour, towards his health, his talents, his sound digestion, even his mental travail from which are born not only masterpieces, but treasures still more sacred and beyond your grasp, such as the disappointment of genius. Failing to make good as Prometheus, you will probably attach yourself to one of them in the role of vulture, and in time you will come to like that lustful joy, akin to the throes of creation, of tearing at his liver, drowning his voice, and blackening him every minute of the day, if only to match up with him in the colour of your face. You don't make a pretty portrait! But insignificance, which is fully aware of itself, can be just as powerful as talent, only reversed. Those are just the people we need. Not that they have nowhere to escape from Russia and nothing to escape with, but because men like you hate the objects of their envy more than they do us. I'm not promising you a well-furnished philosophical peace, Gratsiansky, nor am I offering you Giganov's job. I'm calling you to join the archfiends, those who have left the deepest, the most memorable and still gloriously bleeding marks in the history of our ill-fated planet. Only a man with a long stride is capable of taking this ditch, which stands, perhaps, between you and real greatness—reversed, of course. So why not test yourself, take the plunge, show that you have the gumption, superman, as you call yourself in that book of posts. Don't be afraid to jump, we'll see that you don't fall. Well, which of them for a start—Krainov, Sleznyov, or even about yourself?"

Chandvetsky, with the stern eyes of the tempter, pushed his victim the last few inches that separated him from the brink.

"You are very shrewd, Colonel. What a pity you did not become a recluse after that adventure of yours," Alexander muttered, his face covered with blotches. He was overwhelmed by the list of misfortunes that awaited him, no less than by the amazingly accurate assessment of his character. "The only reason I do not bewail my fate is because I am utterly rotten. Apparently, it is left for you to hand me the pieces of silver and give me a nickname. Come on, undo the purse strings, Colonel!"

Chandvetsky eyed him coldly.

"I thought so—you're just a child of your degenerate age, a spiritual offspring of Zarathustra. And he was invented by philistine weaklings who are prepared to use a whip on a woman to avenge their enforced chastity. That type both adore and fear women, and cross themselves hurriedly in the dark gateway of the bawdy-house, praying heaven to send them half an hour of plebeian health free from the risk of infection. They marry, though, and are famed for the security of their domestic hearths, although they are tormented for the rest of their lives by the suspicious resemblance which their little ones bear to friends who happened to drop in on them at one time or another."

A sickening clammy weakness, like that of ptomaine poisoning, prevented Alexander from putting a stop to this cruel inquisition, but at Chandvetsky's last thrust he sprang to his feet with clenched fists and a swollen face.

"I agree with you, Herman, that I may turn out to be a failure, but as for the babies, I'd advise you not to leave your charming wife alone with me, Colonel."

Chandvetsky stood up, too, and slowly fastened the top hook of his tunic collar with one hand.

"It's improper to speak of respectable women in that tone, young man. I could punish you severely for that, but. . . ." He paused, and a cruel smile lurked under his short-trimmed moustache. "On second thoughts, try it, exercise your charms, Mr. Gratsiansky. You may go," he ended stiffly, puffing his chest out as men of his set did when challenging each other to a duel.

4

Abridged and touched up, the story omitted the fainting fit, the allusions to Young Russia and the least flattering of Chandvetsky's testimonials. Morshchikhin understood that the gendarme's intellectual powers had been deliberately exaggerated by Gratsiansky to give greater dignity to his own person. Instead of pausing here to savour the honey of posterity's admiration, he was tempted by the demon of senile boastfulness to link the affair with the historical calendar in order to lend greater colour to his story.

"This tweaking of Chandvetsky's nose cost me two days' arrest later on," said Gratsiansky, noticeably softened by his reminiscences. "I would have given that police panjandrum a proper dressing-down if I wasn't in such a hurry to go to my lecture at Countess Panina's People's House."

"Pardon me, I didn't quite catch you," Morshchikhin invented on the spur of the moment to gain time for thought. "Did you read a lecture yourself that day, or did you go to hear one?"

The question obviously pleased Gratsiansky.

"My own lecture, of course. I er ... started educational activities among the lower classes at a fairly early age," he answered, beaming.

"And how did your lecture pass off ... after such a jarring experience," Morshchikhin asked on tiptoe, in a voice not like his own.

"Splendidly. I lectured on the great Pushkin and I was never in such excellent form. By the way, all this happened on that memorable day, the first of September, when the most blood-thirsty monster of tsarism—Stolypin, er ... Pyotr Arkadyevich, was shot at in the opera house in Kiev, and you know how quickly such news spreads; I must say, though, that for all my aversion to acts of individual terror, I celebrated a double victory that evening. My audience had already heard something about the Kiev shot, so that the moment I mentioned the famous cat on the seashore, shackled in golden chains, everyone under-stood at once what that cat stood for, and what was meant by the thirty knights who stepped ashore, albeit with no red banner yet, and by the hero hanging on to the wizard's beard.* Naturally, I do not attribute that sensational success to myself alone. I always drew inspiration from the very thick of the masses, er ... and truly my words burned my own throat. I saw before me in the hall the manly excited faces of the workers, the future partisans, commanders and inspirers of the socialist five-year plans. I do not have to tell you, a people's tribune, about that noble feeling of kinship with one's people, who look to you er ... for the golden grain!" He brushed something from his eye, probably a speck of dust. "There, I've let my feelings run away with me. You do feel sometimes like wanting to warm your er ... chilled hands over the ashes of memory."

There was a good deal in his story that struck Morshchikhin immediately as being embroidered or rounded off, but not know-ing the whole, he was unable to compare what he had heard with the actual facts, like fitting a fragment to a broken saucer. It was at this point that there sprang to his mind Vikhrov's passing mention of the lecture of September the first, which, he had said, did not take place. One could excuse a person getting the date of so remote an event mixed up, but it was only by deliberate intention that so many lies could be spun around such a historical landmark as the assassination of the tsar's premier. Morshchikhin experienced the intense curiosity of the explorer. Confronting

---

* All these are allusions to characters from Pushkin's poem *Ruslan and Ludmila.—Tr.*

him sat a truly inspired, but so far blameless and unexposed liar.

The thing now was to look around him for further finds, since all great discoveries are preceded by a host of smaller ones. Gratsiansky had unwarily seated his visitor with his back to the light while he himself sat opposite, thus letting Morshchikhin see his whole face. It was a matter of surprise to the visitor that he had not until then noticed the telltale greyish strip of forehead where his host's greying mane geysered up from his brow. Owing to the disturbing events of the night before, Gratsiansky had not had time to complete his cosmetic toilet that morning, and it seemed strange to Morshchikhin, an ordinary Party man, that such a distinguished father of forestry, the national conscience of the forest service, so to speak, trimmed his forehead with a razor. One deceit followed logically from another; suddenly, all Gratsiansky's most estimable qualities, touched with the finger of doubt, fell away from his personality with the ease of crumbling plaster. Morshchikhin was holding the string of the man, as it were, and he could not resist the temptation of pulling a bit of it out carefully; he did so with an air of unconcern, as though he were brushing a stain from his knee and had no idea what would come of it.

"By the way, Professor, that organisation the colonel mentioned to you—was it the Young Russia?"

Gratsiansky's face stiffened; he had not suspected that his visitor was so well-informed.

"Yes ... it was really a passing childish amusement of ours, a test of strength rather than ..." he dragged out the words in a strangely jaded voice, and suddenly taking it into his head to start smoking in his old age, he thrust a Russian cigarette into his mouth with the tobacco end. "Who told you the er ... the name of the organisation—Ivan Vikhrov, I suppose?"

Morshchikhin looked up at his host with the clear eyes of innocence.

"No, but just before the war, in Leningrad, as a matter of fact, I thumbed through those papers myself ... you look surprised, Professor?" Morshchikhin himself was tingling with excitement by this time, which was quite unlike him. He had never been keen on that kind of treasure-hunting, but here the money-box just stuck out of the ground and was asking to be prodded with the spade. With the skill of a legal investigator he asked some irrelevant question, something about the social standing of

Countess Panina and her philanthropical establishment, not so much to divert Gratsiansky's possible suspicions as to map out the pattern of his further enquiries. Gratsiansky, with an air of obvious relief, began to describe the appearance and biography of that liberal lady, who had decided to atone for the sins of her ancestors by a career of enlightenment; he went out of his way to abuse her, and referred to her familiarly as Sofia Vladimirovna with the deliberate intention of leading Morshchikhin off on a false trail.

"I read doubt in your eyes as to the moral purity of my business connections," Gratsiansky proceeded. "But you shouldn't let the noble title of that philanthropic lady trouble you, colleague. In those days we used every legal means of propaganda that was available, and even Lenin addressed a meeting there in 1906 under the guise of a workman named Karpov. I therefore felt justified in doing so."

"Very interesting indeed. You ought to write your memoirs, really, you've had such rich experience!" Morshchikhin chimed in, and as if annoyed by a fly with an exasperatingly tricky flight, he swapped it as it wheeled with a last question. "By the way, as I was twice informed by people in the know, you worked on the police archives for over a year, enjoying what archeologists call the right of first excavation. I was wondering whether you noticed a blue file there containing the private correspondence of that very same Chandvetsky marked nineteen fourteen and stamped with the archive number 317a or 371b, I am not sure which? If you remember, the top edge was slightly burnt ... probably a result of the Okhranka having been set fire to during the early days of the revolution. If I am not mistaken you were in St. Petersburg at the time, too, weren't you?"

"Well, I paid flying visits there, but ..." Gratsiansky muttered vaguely, then it suddenly occurred to him that the fact that he had not dared to turn Morshchikhin out of the house for his impertinent and unaccountable manoeuvre could be used as deadly evidence against him. "In what way do these documents er ... interest you?"

"Well, in all kinds of ways," Morshchikhin retaliated with the same tantalising vagueness. "I wasn't thinking so much of the stylistic form of the correspondence as I was of its state of preservation...."

At this point the host showed signs of extreme uneasiness. For one thing, his glance became so slanted that it was rather painful to look him in the face. Something made Gratsiansky avoid a direct question as to the nature of the documents, which were capable, even on cursory examination, of exciting such a heightened interest. No, he could not recollect any file of Chandvetsky's correspondence in the Leningrad archives, which was not surprising, since no such file existed. Acting on the belief that in dealing with a liar he was justified in using the same weapon, Morshchikhin had invented the correspondence on the spur of the moment and used it as a probe to explore the dark corners of the mind without an anaesthetic. Gratsiansky, for his part, understood that if the file had contained any incriminating evidence against him, this conversation, of course, would have taken place elsewhere. All the evidences of his youthful indiscretions which were known to exist had been carefully studied, weighed and destroyed by him, especially one dangerous notebook of love lyrics; on the other hand, the presence of a spoon-bait pointed to the existence of an angler on the fringe of his quiet Moscow backwater. What was he angling for, that fellow in the military sheepskin, who was he trying to bait with that wobbly bit of iron with the deadly hook at the end of it?

"No, I know of no such file. It may have been sent to the archives after the twenties, when I stopped working on my book. And generally, from nineteen thirteen I wasn't allowed to live in St. Petersburg er ... under paragraph four clause sixteen of the Security Regulations."

"Oh, no," Morshchikhin gently insisted, refusing to give way in the face of such convincing testimony and data. "Judging by the inventory marks, that file was kept there from its first registration. It's not a question of chronology, but rather the nature of the damage. What I wanted to ask you was whether in *your* time page twenty-six, if I am not mistaken, dealing directly with the activities of Young Russia, had a stain of indelible ink all over the text?"

It was another random shot in the dark made in a spirit of sheer mischief, for he had been in too great a hurry that July to discover any irreparably damaged pages, although, under the circumstances, he might have done, in fact, he should have done considering how hard Gratsiansky had been at work on the archives in the course of a whole year. The only thing Morshchikhin had been lucky enough to stumble on was a police copy of a letter by a certain Kvaskova to her exile friend Weinbaum in Yeniseisk which referred directly to the existence in St. Petersburg of a society "for corrupting school babies" under the name of Young Russia; all the remaining information the hospitable host had supplied to him by his own story, and, still more, by his behaviour.

"It's so long ago, you know. You must make allowances for an old man's failing memory," Gratsiansky whispered, crying mercy.

So he did have something on his conscience, something that still remained to be discovered and was very near to the invented story about the ink-stained document, because a striking transformation had suddenly taken place in Gratsiansky's appearance. He looked like a man watching a police search in his apartment and seeing rummaging hands within half an inch of his hiding-place. And if the faded features of youth can always be dimly traced in an old man's face, that of Gratsiansky at that moment showed what physical changes would befall him on his deathbed. His sunken cheeks looked cadaverous, his jaw dropped and his nose became pinched; grey shadows lay in the hollows of his eyes, and his very fingers had a haggard look. It was a fit of deadly paralysing terror, fraught with grave consequences for a man of his age, and there is no knowing how it would have ended had not a dark old woman in an old-fashioned head-dress and with slightly squinting eyes slipped in through the door to her son's rescue. Imperturbably, she called him to the telephone. Gratsiansky walked out with a listless tread, and found the strength to carry on a long disjointed conversation, which was all the more curious because Morshchikhin knew that the line was damaged throughout the whole neighbourhood.

Morshchikhin had an impression that the old lady was looking through him at something outside the window.

"You have made the professor very tired. He'll be laid up now for two days at least. He gets very tired lately. There are so many tactless people about these days. Always coming and asking for things, sometimes only a recommendation, but mostly money. So let's put this talk off for another time, please," she said expressionlessly, now looking aside and moving away from the door for the visitor to pass.

She remained silent while the visitor, muttering apologies, struggled into his coat; the only sound was the clink of keys, which she fingered like a rosary. At that moment, however, Morshchikhin felt neither shame for his intrusion after such a trying night nor remorse for the odd manner of his gratitude for the coffee and pastry, not to mention the truly entertaining story about the St. Petersburg gendarme; neither did he feel them afterwards. On leaving Blagoveshchensky Alley Morshchikhin glanced back at the hospitable windows, weighed the consequences of his interview in the form of valerian drops and mustard-plasters, and shook his head ruefully, sorry that he had succumbed to the temptation of pulling at the mysterious string too soon instead of waiting for a more leisurely time, when he would have had a chance of discovering more missing clues.

Having heard of the much-talked-about forest controversy from Vikhrov at his evening sessions, Morshchikhin did not doubt that patient excavation on this site would yield valuable material not only for his thesis, but also for exposing an exposer who had been exposing all and everything around him in the course of a quarter of a century.

5

The grievous effects of Morshchikhin's visit were comparable to the direct hit of a demolition bomb. For three days thereafter Gratsiansky lolled about under his rug with hot-water bottles at his feet; only the sharp drop in haemoglobin caused by funerary agitation prevented him from attending the funeral of Natalya Zolotinskaya. In thought, however, he accompanied the poor woman in her imaginary hearse with its plumed jades to the cemetery gate, and that was far more in tune with his lyrical moods than the modern omnibus which rushed its citizens to their last domicile at a rattling pace—one wheel here, the other there. Lying on the sofa without movement, he gave himself up wholly to the melancholy of the moment: there he was, Natalya's one and only faithful friend, dragging himself wearily behind that ines-capable cart, his hand resting on the back, as befitted an old-fashioned knight of the golden days now gone for ever ... dragging himself at least twelve versts on foot, shunning the city's manifold temptations of transport, a lonely old man and with bared head, too, at the risk of catching a cold in the middle ear, if not being laid low with encephalitis and becoming a cripple for the rest of his life, but then with a sense of a duty fulfilled towards the mortal remains of one who had appreciated his qualities before all others. And so, his body luxuriating under the satin quilt while his mind strayed among wintry paths, he gazed with a dimming eye at the snow falling outside the window, and saw himself lying prostrate in a vast wilderness, deserted even by his closest Dizzy Doxies, while eagles of doubt circled over him; this would not have been so bad had not other more gruesome birds joined in the circling with the most unmistakable intentions.

The fact of the matter was that long before Morshchikhin someone else had been showing signs of unhealthy interest in this quiet nest in Blagoveshchensky Alley. One day it had been a queer plumber knocking uninvited at the door, the next a new domestic help supposedly from the top floor coming down to ask for some matches, or else a soft drilling sound under the floor-board had come trickling up from the cellar of an evening. The last sinister link in this chain of suspicious goings on was a visitation by someone who brought greetings to Gratsiansky straight from the world beyond the grave. The visitor did not come through the wall in the dead of night, as all respectable ghosts do, but in broad daylight and through the door. Not to attract the attention of the neighbours on the landing, Gratsiansky had been obliged to receive the visitor, albeit without coffee and pastries, after which the state of his health deteriorated to such an extent that his mother insisted on him visiting a celebrated specialist on haemoglobin. It so happened that on his way to the doctor he found himself at the Vikhrovs' at the other end of the city.

Extremely weighty reasons for this visit had piled up with Gratsiansky. Belatedly, rumours had reached him that Ivan Vikhrov had been awarded a high Order of Merit, of which no announcement was published for reasons of wartime expediency. Therefore, it was necessary to find out immediately whether this government act implied the recognition of Vikhrov's line in forestry with direct consequences for Gratsiansky and his followers, or whether it was due to some important wartime proposal of Vikhrov's on forest working. In either event he had a right to be interested for the sake of old friendship. Incidentally, owing to the absence of any fundamental research by Vikhrov, no murderous criticism of him had appeared in the press for a long time. As a matter of fact he always had a short memory for private grievances, and the war had pushed all differences, scientific among them, into the background. A more plausible excuse for reconciliation was hardly to be expected, all the more that it did not prevent Gratsiansky eventually from settling his score with Vikhrov on all counts. For one thing, the award was a splendid excuse for trying to find out something about Morshchikhin and his doubtful thesis.

With a bottle from the domestic wine cellar, he dropped in on the Vikhrovs at dusk and found his former friend by the window-sill, going through the letters and telegrams of congratulation from pupils from all over the country's forests, and, what pleased Vikhrov most of all, even from the front. The profession had been following all the phases of the famous controversy with such keen interest that every item of news quickly reached the hintermost corners of the country. The deputy of the forests was sitting in Taisa's shawl worn over a thick jersey of Yenga days; the chilliness of the unheated flat was more than compensated by the warmth of these messages, which were all the more precious for coming at such a time.

"Well, Ivan, you've won! Accept my verbal congratulations, too, the last in this long queue," Gratsiansky proclaimed from the doorway, then impetuously, before the other could collect his wits, he folded him to his heart and put his ear to both his cheeks in turn, generously offering himself for an answering kiss. "There, like a brother. Another one now. This is our common victory, you know. I've given half my life to make you still better, so I have a tiny share in your success!"

The attack swept Vikhrov off his feet, and delicacy made him half respond to the embrace of the congratulator, who was obliged to push him away gently lest he wetted him with an all-forgiving tear of senile joy.

"I'm sitting in the dark ... I'm sorry, they've switched the lights off in the whole district," Vikhrov muttered, touched by the congratulations of his chief opponent. "Don't take your things off, I'm afraid it's chilly here."

"Never mind, we'll pour some of these astringent Bordeaux calories into our old tanks and thaw that, what do you call it, er ... well, old ice." He hunted out a corkscrew in the host's sideboard. "Whose fault is it, about that ice, if not yours? Come on, have the courage to say it straight to my face. You're silent? God's your judge, Ivan, but it's a shame, really, a shame to forget the past. I remember that skilly we had in Karavannaya as if it were my first eucharist. There wasn't a fly-speck of fat in it, d'you remember? How's the health, old boy? You ought to take more care of yourself. If I had the power I'd take the ink away from you," he proceeded without waiting to hear Vikhrov's report about his health. And gratifying a strange need, he ran his fingers over the manuscript lying on the desk, as the next best thing to reading it. "How's your sister? Getting on all right? Standing in some queue, I suppose? Well, well, I *am* glad for your sake."

"You'd better sit over there, it's draughty by the window," Vikhrov said, drawing him away from the desk. "I'm glad you called. I've been wanting to prove to you I was right for a long time. Not only by the fact of having been awarded a medal, but by the very logic of forestry."

Not to lose time, he proceeded at once to expound the basic principles of rational forestry practice, but the other interrupted him in the middle of his discourse.

"Oh, come, Ivan, I never thought you'd start taking your revenge on me in your old age," Gratsiansky said in a tone of mild reproof as he did the honours with the bottle of wine. "Mind you, I always suspected that you don't like to be rubbed the wrong way, you love it sweet, criticism with some syrup in it, but I couldn't very well overlook your dangerous heresies, classical though I admit they are. Errors that are not corrected in time become a part of your soul. And here you are, already reaching for the dagger. It's cruel of you, you're not playing the game, old chap."

"Where do you see my dagger?" Vikhrov said, puzzled.

"Why, wasn't it you who sent that thesis-writer with a holster at his side to me? And about that old business, too, which has been cleared up ages ago. It was a clumsy and childish prank of mine, I admit, but Valery mended that long ago. At least, I hope this Morshchikhin of yours is a *decent* fellow?"

Vikhrov spoke at length about his attempt to help that young gifted man, who, he thought, held out great promise for the future.

"There seems to have been an unfortunate misunderstanding, Alexander. He wanted to drop in on me this evening, though. You'll be able to see for yourself what a charming and genial man he is. I'm really sorry you won't be able to get to know him better, he's going away to the front in a day or two. He's been appointed commissar of an armoured train. Just so."

Gratsiansky's face cleared. The news that Morshchikhin was soon leaving for the front made pleasanter hearing than all his listed virtues.

"Good, that's very good," he said, pursuing his own train of thought. "It's very nice to know that Moscow and our sacred progressive liberative cause are in such reliable hands. Well then, let's drink to those who are going into battle for the er ... for the advanced ideas of our century."

The relish with which that abstemious man tossed off his glass —he was not ashamed at ordinary times to toast the health of his own mother with a glass of lemonade—was a sight worth seeing. Indeed, he was quite unlike his usual self at that moment. He had a sickly washed-out appearance, and a depressing anxiety emanated from him like the odour of disease. The reference to Moscow touched Vikhrov. Like most warm-hearted and honest men, who are prone to endow people with their own thoughts, he decided that Gratsiansky was worried at the thought of the coming battle for Moscow.

"I don't recognise you ... are you well, Alexander?" he said with a sip at his glass, forgiving him all the heartache he had caused him in the course of twenty odd years.

"As a matter of fact, old chap," Gratsiansky said, the wine quickly going to his head, "the other day I lowered a generous heart into the grave, and now there is only half of me left. True, we lived apart all our life, not to be in each other's way, but the very existence of that great love was a sort of remission of my sins. You wouldn't understand that, being sinless. I accompanied her poor remains on foot to er ... her last home, and only when I threw a handful of cold clay into the chasm of death did I suddenly realise how lonely I now was. Yes, old chap, we are dwindling, getting fewer and fewer in this world. Those of us who remain should stick closer together. You must come and see me, just drop in whenever you feel like it."

"If it's Moscow that's worrying you," Vikhrov harped on, "you needn't be afraid—they won't surrender her. There are holy things which you couldn't even bear to think of being touched by unclean hands. And while you're about it, remember your history—how long it took us Russians to hit back, but when we did, we hit hard and sure. True, in my ramblings through the city I don't see any smiling faces, but nor do I see tearful ones. Ah, if I didn't have this game leg, and my heart wasn't getting a bit tricky!" He intercepted Gratsiansky's hand, which reached out again for the glass. "Wait a bit, this is strong stuff without a snack. My sister promised to bring some sausage."

"Oh, it'll go down without the sausage. So he's going on an armoured train? That's very good," Gratsiansky repeated in a voice sweetly bland, as he took another sip to strengthen his slender hopes. "Oh, yes, I nearly forgot the most important thing of all. A week or two ago I met a remarkably clever man ... he had some very flattering things to say about you, by the way. Would you believe it, in knowledge experience and profundity of scientific ideas, he considers you to be the world's leading forester. Frankly, I was a bit envious. But you needn't turn your nose up. With the present decline of capitalist culture, their high lights of forest science can be counted on the fingers."

"He comes from abroad, then, a visitor?"

"From Australia. He relates the most curious things. It seems that forestry practices with them are no better than they were here before the revolution. Just imagine, they simply ring-bark groves of gigantic red gum-trees to stimulate grass growth for stockbreeding. Can you imagine such a barbarous way of converting timber into meat and wool?"

"With the experience I've had I can imagine many things," said Vikhrov. "But that Australian of yours is a liar. The red gum-tree happens to be a comparatively short tree."

"Don't cavil at a word. I suppose he meant the size of the doomed area, not the height of the tree," Gratsiansky corrected himself. "Besides, er ... he's not quite a forester. He worked for a long time in the International Council for the Coordination of World Economy and came to Moscow on the question of supplies for our fronts. He's a great friend of ours. Drinks vodka like a fish, adores *shchi* and the balalaika, and knows your books er ... almost every one of them. He says a scientist of your standing would make a great name for himself out *there*, not to mention that he would enjoy proper conditions for his work."

"And what did you tell him?"

"I tried my best to persuade him that Soviet people adored their daily doze of sandpaper criticism and just couldn't live without it."

"I see," frowned Vikhrov. "And what did he say?"

"Oh, they're a sleazy lot. He just laughed. Such periodic shocks to my work desk, he says, would upset my thinking gear. He was very keen to meet you, by the way, in informal surroundings. I consented on your behalf."

"You shouldn't have. My thoughts are in my books. I have nothing to add to them."

Gratsiansky made a wry face at the sudden obstacle. He thought that long preparation through failures would have made Vikhrov more tractable and broad-minded.

"I can't make you out. Doesn't the forest interest you any more,

517

or do you intend to steer clear of it now that you've got that medal?"

"On the contrary, it's the forest that doesn't let me go, but...." Vaguely, so as not to hurt the feelings of the visitor from a friendly state, he hinted at the dangerous experiment of the Trojan horse and the gifts of the Greeks.

"Excuse me, Ivan, but it's rude," Gratsiansky remonstrated. "If it's a question of language difficulty, then I'll act as your interpretor, so be it. In the last resort, we could arrange the meeting at my place. When will we get another such chance of receiving detailed information about the Australian forests? Between us, we shall turn him inside out."

Vikhrov did not even take the trouble to express his dissent. Hurrying to have his say before Morshchikhin came, he bumbled on about the ways of obtaining the highest yield from the forest without ruining the source. Gratsiansky listened to him, his face twitching with a nervous tic, the while he stared at the falling snow outside the window; it had been snowing steadily for the last three days and nights; some of the snow-flakes pressed against the glass, as if trying to see what was going on within the darkened room. The effects of the liquor were wearing off, and Gratsiansky's one passionate desire at that moment was for utter peace in the wake of which everything would vanish—this humiliating sensation of an ageing, constantly poisoned, as it were, body; these ideas, which caused such a useless gyration of matter, and above all, his own slavish obligation to coax this forestial maniac into meeting the Australian. The last drop that made his cup run over was the host's pathetic apostrophe as to what cloak other than a green one posterity would wrap around their chilled and scorched planet.

"Look here, Ivan, all this, which you are repeating so tediously, is the ABC of simpletons. And it isn't a question of the forest at all. I'd like to tell you frankly what's on my mind, but ..." he looked round at a noise from the kitchen.

"That's my sister come back. That's all right, she wouldn't understand even if she heard."

"What has always surprised me in you, Ivan, is the provincial seriousness of your enquiring mind. For instance, why there isn't enough warmth in winter and so much of it in summer. Just look around you, why, Biblical times are coming! The sun is already hidden, everything has been sent flying. The mountains have slipped their age-old moorings, the seas are rising from their beds. The only way to survive now is to bury yourself deep in the ground or move along in step with the whole avalanche to the very end. And you stand right in its path, waving your arms about indecently. Who the devil cares for your forest at such a time!"

"Just a minute, what end are you talking about?" Vikhrov said in an icy tone.

"Well, that permitted one ... don't try to catch me. Passing from one state into another by the dialectics of development," Gratsiansky said, and his eyes flashed angrily in the darkness. "Posterity will want to seek and think for itself ... or do you intend to bequeath your old cloak to it without the right to have it altered?"

Vikhrov did not immediately grasp his drift, but the exultant ambiguousness of the question stung him to the quick. He told Gratsiansky that he had no fear for the future and his successors. Mankind could never give up Archimedes' screw or Mendeleyev's Table, still less the stern social boons which rid it of poverty and regular bloodshed, and saved it from the deplorable fate of the majority, whom capitalism kills if it is unable to corrupt.

"Truth to tell, these thoughts of yours are new to me, Alexander, I don't recognise you," he wound up. "You yourself wrote in one of my 'pogroms' that a person can desert from history only to the grave."

"Bah, history!" the other snapped. "Fortune-telling by the red ink of the nineteenth century, the dream of a sterile-clean world. You think *shchi* from the herbariums of blockaded Leningrad are made more filling by being sweetened with a humanistic dream. History is much too slow and naturalistic a narrator, with a bad taste for prolixities and crude effects. I'd prefer to read it all afterwards, in a primary school-reader, on three short pages with a suitable picture supplement showing, say, the taking of the Winter Palace." Unnerved by the ensuing silence, his face suddenly paled and he squeezed Vikhrov's hand desperately. "If you can, forgive me this rather unscrupulous argument, Ivan, but I couldn't help it. I had no other way of checking what a man like you, a distinguished man who had been knocked about so roughly, could think at a time when the enemy was at the city's gates. You don't know what an impressive answer was contained in your calm silence ... and that's why we shall win, we are bound to win in this battle of the worlds, Ivan. Without a doubt you would have been a great man out *there*, with them, but you ... you have refused even to accept praise from er ... from those unclean lips. Bravo! I'm so glad on account of your purity, your devotion to our banner,

Ivan! And don't be angry. Ever since Job, the higher faith has been tested at the price of cruel afflictions. But then from now on I am doubly your friend. You must come and see me on New Year's eve. We'll sit down and do some adding up, just the two of us, with no one to interfere."

"Have some water, Alexander," Vikhrov said, pouring some out of a carafe, and then lowered the black-out blinds.

"Yes, I'm simply drunk, forgive me. I'll have a pain now all day in the back of my head. I wonder what other things are there besides the hypophysis? There, I don't remember either. Oh no, don't put on the light yet, it's better like this. At least, will you let him drop in to leave you some magazines? Beautifully printed ... and with highly flattering comments on your researches. As a matter of fact he speaks Russian enough to get by. I wouldn't like him to interpret your refusal in a way that would reflect on our country ...."

"Wait a minute, who are you talking about?"

"That Australian. You're a funny chap, you haven't exactly been spoilt by praise, and here you have such a chance of er ... pouring fresh strength into yourself."

Vikhrov flatly refused to meet the man, and switching on the light, he cracked a poor joke about the ant, who, if it did give pleasure to the plant-louse, always calculated on getting something in return.

"You think so?" Gratsiansky said, as if a light of understanding had suddenly burst upon him. "It never entered my mind, old chap. In that case I'll make enquiries about him in certain quarters. But why don't you say anything about yourself? How's your sister?"

"My sister is so-so, not in the best of health, as I told you a moment ago. But there she is, you can ask her yourself."

Taisa came in with a plate of her saving remedy—beet, but Gratsiansky was unable to break down the barrier of previous mutual resentment. Her movements were uncertain, her answers irrelevant, and presently she went out to mend some underwear for her pet to take with him on his journey. She no sooner mentioned Sergei's name than he appeared in person in the company of another young man, not Morshchikhin, both covered with snow and faces flushed from the brisk walk. Sergei introduced his companion to his father as his future armoured-train mate, Kolya Lavtsov.

Sergei could hardly be expected to remember Gratsiansky from that night when, at the age of five, he had been carried into this house. But by his father's embarrassment, by the bottle with the mouldered foreign label, indicating, among other things, the importance of the occasion, by the cold curiosity towards himself on the part of the visitor and by a dozen other unmistakable signs Sergei recognised in him his old enemy, and he rather adroitly avoided shaking hands, confining himself to a distant bow.

It turned out that Morshchikhin was not coming. Previous plans had been cancelled and the armoured train was leaving at dawn the next day. Sergei had obtained permission to leave the send-off meeting in order to say goodbye to his people at home.

6

"Morshchikhin sends his warmest regards—he's conducting the meeting as a matter of fact. Please don't bother, Auntie Taisa, they've given us so much to take along that we'll need the tender to carry it. We've just popped in for a minute," Sergei said, nudging his friend in the ribs. "Well, Kolya, you wanted to see a real live professor—there he is, as large as life, and plump in the middle of his luxurious surroundings."

Lavtsov shuffled his feet uneasily, glancing reproachfully now at Sergei, now at the jerseyed professor, until the awkward silence was broken by Vikhrov seating the boys side by side at the table. Both, as if obeying a command, promptly lit up attenuated cigarettes after a preliminary tamping on the ashtray, and let out a puff of smoke both at once in the same direction, as like one another as twins. It was not only the tankman's uniform that made them look alike. Rather was it that shy awkward independence which betrays the striving of unfledged younglings not to disgrace themselves in the eyes of their elders at their first flight. Gratsiansky felt that he ought to withdraw now so as not to lay restraint upon the old couple in the matter of parting embraces and all kinds of absurd advice how to escape the calamities of war by means of simple circumspection. But he had so often whispered confidentially into people's ears about the origin of that boy to prove Vikhrov's connections with the hostile world, that a dark curiosity made him sit on listening and furtively studying Sergei and his friend, because they were going into battle for the advanced ideas of the century together with Morshchikhin and would consequently share his fate.

As often happens at parting, there was suddenly nothing to talk about. Taisa broke the lingering pause.

521

"It makes me sad to see you two children smoking soldiers' tobacco at such an early age," she said with a sigh, now waving her hand in front of her face to disperse the smoke, now brushing non-existent crumbs from the table-cloth. "And so, little by little, the war will get hold of you."

"Don't scold them, sister. They're soldiers now. Tomorrow they may be under fire," Vikhrov said agitatedly. "And it's only right, boys. It's time you harnessed yourselves to our old sacred plough. We're not yesterday's men, you know, we're ancients. We still remember the caveman's camp-fire, and the roar of the mammoth, and the glacial blizzard. Maybe for five hundred centuries running, man, the first crude model of him, tore the raw meat with his hands and wandered about a naked miserable creature, until he came out into the sunshine and saw his nakedness. It took him another thousand years to clothe himself, and don't let us be too modest about it—he provided himself with quite decent clothes, even with brass buttons on them. But one day he looked round upon himself under the new sun and found that he was not only naked again, but wallowing in blood ... and not in animals' blood, but in the blood of his own kind. Just so. Everything was steeped in it, even the songs and books, the bricks of his temples, the treasures of his galleries. And on top of it, all kinds of epidemics, soil erosion, exhaustion of the forestlands, food shortages, growing and more complicated demands, the coming into civilisation of new awakening races. And all this in the teeth of Nature's stubborn resistance, which stiffened with our advance into the microcosms, where she keeps her main ciphers and secrets. Even a healthy brain could barely cope with this, leave alone one corroded by the spirochaeta of social greed, which turns the thinking tissues into a jellied medium for the microbes of base passions. And so it was high time for humanity to be either dumped into the common grave or to seek a new trail, for sometimes we begin to feel a bit ashamed of ourselves before the cattle that we eat. That's why, absurd though it may seem, we ought to ask ourselves more often why it is that there is not enough warmth in winter when so much of it goes waste in summer. Childish doubts have always seemed naive to some people, but it is in them that there have ripened the seeds of the greatest storms that have ever shaken the world. Luckily for humanity, there is such a trail, the only one. That's why I often see some little factory of ours as a pyramid of immortality. Those were tombs of human impulses, but these the sacred cradle of joy itself.

That's why it does me good to look at your faces, enginemen of happiness and defenders of life." Suddenly Vikhrow looked round at his bored audience and fell silent. "That'll do, I've let my tongue run away with me. Come on, sister, fill the glasses!"

He stood up with his glass and leaned towards the boys, who were looking at each other nervously, not daring to accept the honour of the toast they had just heard.

"Damned strong stuff," said Kolya Lavtsov, emptying his glass and stroking the place which Nature had assigned for moustaches.

"You're making too much fuss of us, Father. We haven't earned it yet," Sergei said in a deep-chested voice.

Probably all would have gone about their respective businesses after that had not Gratsiansky suddenly given voice from out of his corner.

"I join you most heartily, Ivan. We're getting old ... there, you've wrung a tear from my eye. Ah well, at their age we, too, were the playing cards of grand history, but an armoured train, old chap, is not an eating-house in the Karavannaya, where, over a bowl of skilly and under the threat of tsarist jail, we exchanged forbidden dreams of a bright future for Russia. It's not even a military plane, which, risky though it is, is able to manoeuvre freely in three dimensions; an armoured train works in a straight line, you can't run away from it with another man's identity papers, nor can you jump off it with a parachute...." Evidently the thought of Morshchikhin did not leave him all that evening; realising suddenly that he was savouring his fugitive hopes too openly, he muttered something incoherently about heroes whose lives added up to the immortal glory of the age.

"Some heroes, sitting here in a clean flat and warming ourselves with wine," grinned Kolya Lavtsov, returning his glass to the table. "But once the Moscow Komsomol have promised the country to fight for the capital and all the rest of it, then we've got to keep our word."

"And what's more, Alexander, I strongly object to our people being compared to a pack of cards..." Vikhrov began.

"Allow me, Father, will you," Sergei interrupted him, barely able to control himself. "That was no accidental slip of the tongue, and since it applies to the two of us, in the first place, I'd like to deal with it myself. No, citizen Gratsiansky, in this fight between the two worlds we are not playing cards, anything but. I am my own master. But owing to a number of unforeseen circumstances we have had to fall back on Moscow, which is a bad business. Further retreat is out of the question, the future will be decided there. At the same time, the enemy has not been able to take the capital in his stride and we have not been able yet to push him back. Consequently, the scales are temporarily balanced, and a grain of sand can tip them. Isn't that so, Kolya? Well, that grain of sand, my own life, I, engine-driver's mate and Komsomol member Sergei Vikhrov, am quite consciously throwing into the scales."

"My, what a pity Comrade Morshchikhin can't hear you!" Kolya said admiringly. "Go it, Sergei, keep it up!"

"And secondly," the other proceeded with a boyish élan born of a long-cherished desire to come to grips with this Gratsiansky. "Secondly, I say, the war for us is not a game, and the people can't regard their blood as a gambling stake because every game can end in two ways. The war for us is a very tough, painful and sometimes dangerous job, which is justified by the noble purpose of defending humanity. That means working for a sure thing. Am I making myself clear, citizen Gratsiansky?"

"You're the youngest here, so please moderate your school-teacherish tone, Sergei," put in Ivan Vikhrov.

Sergei looked steadily at his father.

"I'm sorry. I'm sensible enough not to lecture an elderly and seemingly worthy man, seeing that he's your guest, but an armoured train, as has been correctly remarked here, moves only in a straight line, and I may never have the chance of stating my case on an equal footing with him."

At this point Gratsiansky himself put in a word for Sergei.

"Leave him alone, Ivan ... the young man's talking sense. But, goodness me, how swiftly the hands are running on the clock of history! It seems only yesterday that Taisa helped the little traveller off with his wet sheepskin in this very armchair, and now...." He noticed the pleading signs that Vikhrov was making to him from behind Sergei's back. "But, please go on, develop that er ... interesting thought of yours about the war, young man."

Sergei was disconcerted by the odd gleam from under his opponent's eyelids.

"I was going to say that if other social movements petered out in the fight for justice, we'd have guts enough to put it across. In a word, the war for us is not a gamble, not an adventure, as it is for our enemies, but a great public mission, the success of which first of all depends on the unselfishness of our contemporaries."

He meant moral purity, and his opponent pounced on this slip of the tongue.

"Unselfishness?" Gratsiansky said argumentatively. "I think that conception is more applicable to an animal or a machine than to a reasonable being. A thunderstorm, a cow, a bicycle are unselfish ... but, all right, explain what you mean by that word?"

For some moments Sergei stared down at his feet in silence.

"Well, a readiness to do something for one's fellow-creature without thought of personal gain."

Gratsiansky smiled.

"In that case, I daresay the most unselfish thing we do for our fellow-creature is to snore at night. . . . Oh, no, I don't mean to belittle your noble intentions, young man, far be it from me," he hastily inserted, perceiving Sergei's impatient movement. "But every intelligent act presupposes a purpose, the achievement of which promises us at least a moral satisfaction er ... proportionate to the efforts involved, that is, gain. I don't suppose you meant merely financial reward. But isn't the gratitude of the people nothing to you? Besides, *our* ethics do not rule out personal motives in a heroic deed. You just search your own soul, young man. Are you sure it's unselfishness that makes you throw the only treasure you have, your er ... grain of sand, on the scale?"

He stared at the young man so hard as if he would squeeze his thought into him.

"You mean that I am going to the front for the sake of personal glory, medals, or army rations?" Sergei said ironically with a slight break in his voice, gazing with hatred into the face of his opponent, which, but for the twitching of his eyelid, was perfectly calm.

"No, I believe you are doing it for the same reason that I have in mind and of which you are thinking at this moment," Gratsiansky said with pointed emphasis.

Of course, the question was also designed to rouse Kolya Lavtsov's curiosity towards the secret of Sergei's birth ... and then things would take their own course. But Lavtsov had not grasped the dark hint and therefore did not come to his friend's rescue. He merely egged him on with his eyes to hit hard once the thing had started. Sergei was silent, and his very silence contained an affirmative reply.

"I am greatly flattered," he said at last, his face pale, "that after going so deep into my father's biography you are now tackling my own, although it's really beginning only tomorrow. Very well, I'll answer you!" And suddenly he snatched a sheet of paper from the desk.

"It's time we went back, Sergei. Morshchikhin will be cross," Lavtsov gave a helping hand, clearing a way for possible retreat. "Let's be going, eh?"

"No, wait a minute. Don't be in a hurry to save me," Sergei muttered, dashing off some drawing or other on the paper. "I'll answer him to the point in a minute."

The pencil broke, and Sergei did not even notice who it was handed him another one, but then every cell of his body felt the presence of Gratsiansky, who had also risen from his chair and was looking over his shoulder. The longitudinal section of what was obviously a passenger locomotive began to take shape on the paper, more particularly, that small hidden space in the clearance between the bottom of the smoke-box and the leading bolster truck. The drawing was so accurate that one could identify the make of the engine.

"We call that the 'dog-box'," Lavtsov explained for the general benefit. "It's been on his mind all the week, he can't forget it." And while Sergei was finishing his drawing, Kolya related the story.

There was nothing much in it, really, he said. Just an ordinary thing that might happen anywhere. The driver of an engine which returned to depot after a night run was inspecting its underside in the pit with a torch when he noticed a pair of new boots sticking out in the dark. To the amusement of the depot boys, a free passenger, a sleepy-eyed man of about forty-five crawled out from under the engine with a face as sooty as a devil's. He was wearing just a thin raincoat in spite of the biting frost. The crazy fellow turned out to be a black-marketeer, who carried potatoes regularly to the market in Moscow. They took his bag of potatoes away from him and after checking his papers let him go scot free, not counting a couple of clips on the ear to teach him a lesson for next time.

"Attention, please," Sergei began, and explained how the profiteer had wriggled into his hiding-place. "He crawled in here with his clumsy load, between the pair of wheels during a snowstorm and a half-minute stop at a flag-station at the risk of losing his new boots. For two hundred odd kilometres he lay in that icy

526

draught, doing a shiver and shake, not daring to move in case he burnt himself on the pressure lubricator pipes over his head. Add to this the heat of the overheated cylinders, the din of the big wheels passing over the rail joints, the rattling of the leading truck wheels and you'll have some idea what his merchandise cost him. The same work performed for a worthier purpose could be qualified as a feat, but he went to all this trouble and risk for the sake of gain."

"He must enjoy robust health, that gentleman," Ivan Vikhrov remarked wonderingly.

"He would have got his goods to the market if he hadn't fallen asleep there from too much vodka, the baboon," Lavtsov said with a grin.

Meanwhile Gratsiansky had resumed his seat.

"Well, it remains for us to thank Sergei for a sound piece of advice—not to carry potatoes under an engine," he said with unaccountable irritation. His joke fell flat.

Ivan Vikhrov could no longer contain himself.

"From what I understand, the boy meant something entirely different," he interposed harshly, taking care to drive each word home. "He meant that if instead of trying to gain some private ends and doing senseless mischief to their fellows, people were to use their efforts towards a worthier end they would have achieved a happier state of affairs in the world long ago. Did I understand you rightly, Sergei?"

"Practically," Sergei nodded, tearing his drawing up into bits. "I was also going to ask what private ends Mr. Gratsiansky was pursuing when he reminded me, on the very eve of battle, that I was the son of a village shark, dekulakised in nineteen twenty-nine, and that I had to earn a new name for myself by washing it off with blood."

Only now, at last, was the hidden play revealed to Kolya Lavtsov, and when it dawned on him, he advanced on Gratsiansky with an ugly look on his face. Gratsiansky slid back, chair and all, and made swimming motions with his arms. Things were coming to a head and nothing could avert it, all the more that the situation gave this young stranger a full right to act as arbiter in this dispute.

"So that's your little game!" Lavtsov said mockingly, and looked Gratsiansky over from head to foot with distasteful curiosity. "You're a fine bird, aren't you, nosing about for carrion! No fear, we're not going to let you feed on this lad."

"Kolya, don't!" Sergei shouted warningly.

"Wait a minute. I haven't been taught good manners, but now I'm going to put in a word for you," Lavtsov continued, squaring his shoulders and reducing Gratsiansky to a state bordering on a swooning fit. "And I couldn't make out what he was driving at, tapping away like a hammer! Why, he's trying to drive a wedge into our armoured train, that's what he's doing. Right into the middle of our trio, so to speak, right in the works." Strongly tempted though he was to get even with that gentleman for the mean trick he had played, the young man nevertheless hesitated. It may have been because he was wearing the military uniform, or because of the difference in their ages, but he desisted from anything so drastic, and merely shook his head and turned away with a sigh. "We'd better be going, Sergei, before I cut up rough. I've got a sort of feeling that Comrade Morshchikhin's getting angry with us again."

Taisa managed somehow to detain the young men for another quarter of an hour, but the atmosphere, so recently charged with drama, was still uneasy and the conversation flagged. The boys began to take their leave, and Lavtsov pointedly thanked the hosts for an interesting evening well spent. All except Gratsiansky went out into the hall to say goodbye to each other without constraint and utter the usual words that are always said at parting. Soon afterwards Gratsiansky, who had recovered his poise, began to take his leave too. And here again Vikhrov displayed that excessive delicacy which had done him so much harm in the past. In the long run, Gratsiansky had the advantage over him in that he was always prepared to use the dastardly weapon of denunciation and slander from which Vikhrov would have turned away with loathing; it was Sergei now, not himself, that he was afraid for.

"The boys took it a bit too much to heart," he said, trying to smooth things over. "You can't blame them, they're being made to bear the brunt of the coming battle for Moscow."

"We all take things to heart, but none of us should draw hasty personal conclusions from an abstract argument."

"But you must agree, Alexander, that it wasn't right of you to say such things to a soldier, and just at a time when it really is the separate grains of sand that will decide the outcome of the fight."

"Haven't we too high an opinion of ourselves?" the other grumbled. "Neither he nor I count for much in the march of history. You ought to know that, Soviet professor that you are."

Vikhrov retorted by sharply reminding him of the striking example of 1835, when such an insignificant thing as the oak bark beetle killed thirty thousand oak-trees in the Vincennes forest. It could be pointed out that the bark beetle in question hardly acted in the singular, but then Gratsiansky himself realised his multiplicity. Suddenly he thawed, grumbled, forgave.

"Oh, I'm not angry. Children have always flung themselves upon the thorns of history, not knowing that similar attempts have been made in the past. They think Napoleon is a pastry, and Galliffet riding-breeches. But you should have stood up for your old and trusted friend, Ivan. Never mind, though. Don't forget about the Australian, think it over. In any case, come and see me on New Year's eve."

It occurred to him that he had placed too great reliance on Vikhrov's tractability; he would have done better to get him to come to his place on some pretext or other and then let the Australian know by telephone. It would look as if they had met by accident. The telephone connection in Blagoveshchensky Alley had been restored at the end of the next day.

That evening, as usual, the brother and sister held their before-bedtime session, talking about things which they both understood almost without words.

"We're all alone again, sister, just like in Pashutino. As if nothing had happened. Less expense, too. Just so."

"The war likes 'em young. What was *he* doing here?"

"Nothing. I'm afraid I'm no good for real fighting, Taisa."

"There are others to fight for the forest without you, Ivan."

"That's true, they've grown up. Next spring, when they've driven the Germans from the Yenga, you and I will go and see the old places, just a visit at first, and then.... I hear the Old Man calling me. He misses me."

"It would be lovely, if only we live to see the day," Taisa said and suddenly began to cry with such childlike despair that her brother's heart turned over within him. "Do what you like to me, Ivan.... I was afraid to tell you about it in front of Sergei. I lost all our ration coupons for the month, God knows what I did with them."

The news was nothing short of a disaster.

"Maybe someone stole them from you," he said, trying to make it easier for her.

"It's no use blaming anyone, it's my own fault. They were wrapped up in a bit of linen, and the firewood coupon was there too. I crawled all over the street on my knees, but I couldn't find them in the snow."

She was in despair. For a moment, her sense of responsibility for her brother's life overshadowed even Sergei's departure. Her brother made her sit down, and expounded to her a few controversial problems of feeding, with specific reference to the excessive consumption of calories by town dwellers and the hygienic value of temperance as practised in the fasts of ancient Russia, which enabled some zealots to achieve a titanic uplift of the spirit and sometimes extraordinary longevity on a daily diet consisting of a mildewed crust of bread and a handful of spring water.

He spoke until Taisa fell asleep. Neither of them suspected that night that the loss of their ration coupons would lead indirectly to further curious discoveries at the end of the month.

7

The boys got back to the club when the meeting was nearly over. The small gym-hall was packed to overflowing; the whole depot had come there in turns to give their collective offspring a send-off, and when one shift was due to start work, their places were immediately taken by others crowding round the doors. Important-looking railway, artillery and tank chiefs, limp with the heat, sat behind the platform table under a bunting slogan left over from the November parade; among the platform-party were guests from the local Communist Battalion, who were leaving for the front a day later. At the end of the second row sat engine-driver Titov, recognisable at a distance by his moustaches. As the boys squeezed their way towards the platform down the aisle he shook a fatherly finger at them, but Kolya Lavtsov immediately explained by gestures that they simply couldn't manage to get away earlier. As there was no room they had to sit down on the sport apparatus piled up in a corner, which could hardly be seen for the swarm of youngsters clinging to it.

"Now then, young rooks, make room for your elders," Kolya Lavtsov threw out, and they moved up with respectful envy for the heroes of the day, whose portraits hung side by side on the wall newspaper.

After a speech by the representative of the Moscow Committee of the Party Morshchikhin began answering the notes that had been handed up; they were all on one and the same subject— international politics. Confidence in victory enabled the speaker to talk about current events in retrospect, as if he were reading a page of history written a century later. The gist of his speech was that the old world had decided once more to test the intellectual and material maturity of its opponent. For that purpose a reliable and warlike organism had to be found which could safely be exposed to the dangerous fists of the Soviet giant. That country was found in Europe. It was Germany, shaken by previous military failures and convinced through its bourgeoisie that internal economic difficulties could best be ironed out at the expense of one's neighbour through the quenching of nationalist greed. By connivance and treacherous backstepping the old world had no difficulty in whipping up the stupid bluster of a convenient bully into a maniacal dream of world empire. Thus, in Morshchikhin's opinion, the war, which had been started that year, was perhaps the last reconnaissance in force before that decisive fight mentioned in the old revolutionary hymn. "Nevertheless," he said, "ordinary people always believed that this useless bloodshed could be staved off, that some time the obvious advantages of the socialist system would ensure a bloodless passing over of the nations to the side of perpetual peace."

The chandelier under the ceiling was burning faintly, but one could not help noticing that there was something essentially new about this workaday twilight, this calm hush in the hall, the readiness of all these citizens to make war the sole business of their lives from now on until victory. The enemy had lost for them his imaginary stupefying terrors, such as those inspired by some hideous outrage or the as yet undescribed details of a monster; in those six months Soviet people had seen him dead, and with upraised hands, and sobbing. Morshchikhin had a rare gift of persuasion, but that was not the reason why these orlinary people responded so warmly to his appeal for selfless deeds; it was because they realised that the personal civic reward for each of them depended upon their collective success. "So that's how the question stands!" Sergei thought, reminding himself of the unfinished dispute they had just had concerning socialist unselfishness.

On the way to the depot he gave Morshchikhin the details of his quarrel with Gratsiansky. The other made no comment; he merely scooped a handful of snow off a wooden fence in passing and squeezed it in his ungloved hand. The snowstorm was over, and its last dying sparks danced in the air, bringing a pleasant tingle to the face after the stuffy heat of the meeting.

Four of them walked down the middle of the street, straight through the virgin snow.

"I didn't want to make you look small, damn it, Sergei," laughed Kolya Lavtsov. "The trouble with you is you haven't swallowed enough of our engine soot yet, you're still green. What's new about a passenger riding in the dog-box? Why, when I was a waif, I hazed around half the country that way. It's as good as any compartment, except that it's sixth class, and a bit of a tight fit, and hot as hell. And then, of course, there's no window to look out at the scenery. I've seen worse things. On my third run out, after I'd passed my exams for driver's mate, I think it was, the exhaust pump started acting funny. I went out on the engine platform to give it a tap with the hammer, and I happened to look down. Did I catch a fright! Right down there, sitting on my fender in front of the engine was a gypsy! He wasn't an old man, round about forty I should say. Wearing a hat, too, and an ear-ring in one ear. . . ."

"Where did he rest his heels?" said Titov. He sounded doubtful, although he had had plenty of adventures of his own.

"That's just it, his only footrest was greed, it would seem. And he had a foal, too, the devil! Laid over his knees, with its feet hobbled. Travelling free."

"How did you manage to see the ear-ring under his hat?" Sergei asked, suspecting a leg-pull.

"I tipped his hat over with a stick to see what kind of chap he was. He couldn't very well fight me in that position, but I remember him using a lot of bad language, honestly!"

It was late and the world was asleep. But suddenly the moon swam out through a gap in the clouds and shed a brief blue light on the squat suburban structures, and all of them together, each in his own way, thought of the frailty of human dwellings, which were out of all proportion to the madness of modern war.

"Sometimes you do come across desperate fellows, it's a fact," Titov concurred, and it dawned on Sergei that for all the man's impressive manner he had a soul that was perhaps twice as young and naive as his own. "It happened to me soon after this topsy-turvydom started, the war I mean. I was outward bound with a full load from outside Riga. The countryside all round was in ruins, but thank goodness the night was dark and still, and you saw no women's tears or smouldering embers. It was pitch dark. My mate, a young fellow like Lavtsov here, suddenly sees a pair of legs dangling over the side of our cab. He says to me, 'Just look at those legs outside the window, Titov,' he says. And his voice was shaky, because he hadn't been properly run in yet, you know. I had a look, and sure enough, there was a pair of legs in good boots. 'Ask him who the devil he thinks he is, and where does he think he's going to,' I says. So my mate sticks his head out and tells him to come down out of it, as it wasn't right for any unofficial person to be travelling on top o' the cab. But by way of reply the fellow goes and tells him to do something to himself. 'Comrade Titov,' he reports back to me, 'that customer is acting very rude. What are we going to do?' We went into a huddle and decided to tie his legs to the post—luckily there was a piece of wire handy. At the station the militia took things in hand, and asked a few preliminary questions on the spot to find out who the fellow was. He tried to make out he was ill, but that was all eyewash. They found a lot of money on him, four thousand, and all kinds of army certificates, thirty-eight of 'em. He robbed the bodies of our officers on the battlefield. The sheepskin coat he wore was a stolen one too—it had a little hole on the stomach. Afterwards, on investigation, he turned out to be a very interesting customer."

"I don't understand, though," Sergei said after a pause, "why didn't he run away the first time you spoke to him?"

"The devil knows him," said Titov. "Maybe he was tired of running away from his fate, that's why he snarled at us, just to frighten it."

Titov's conjecture did not sound very convincing, and all looked at Morshchikhin to hear his decisive word. He said nothing for half a minute, and his silence could be taken as a sign of tiredness after the meeting.

"You see, Sergei," he suddenly began, "I heard that in certain dangerous professions there inevitably comes a period of what I'd call thread-wear, that is, when the screw thread gets worn and the nut doesn't hold any more. It's quite possible that constant fear of the future may give rise to a desire to challenge it to a duel, a temptation to defy it and goad it into action, to grapple with a still non-existent danger in order to secure a tiny respite for oneself in time to come. People of the plains are said to suffer from this malady in the mountain heights: they are drawn to the precipices!" After a pause he asked with a seeming irrelevance that surprised Sergei how his dispute with Gratsiansky had ended.

They reached the territory of the depot. The virgin hush following the snowfall blanketed all sounds of the night. Then there was a stir in the air, and a series of sharp thuds could be heard, as if something heavy was being shifted about somewhere far away, but much nearer than they had all imagined an hour before. It was the echo of the cannonade on the approaching front, a reminder of the war to those in Moscow. And all at once something new appeared in the relations between these men. The commissar went to the telephone in the Party committee's office, while the engine-driver led his mates to the armoured train which stood snow-camouflaged on the tracks.

They had to walk down the whole length of the train along a path that was deep in snow. The final preparations for departure were being completed, and no one slept that night. Some were fussing about at the anti-aircraft guns, others were checking the revolving gear of the turrets. The recently empty cars and armoured platforms looked bitter-cold and bleak, but as they became tenanted the chilled steel caught some of the human warmth of its occupants. The rear-end of the train rounded the workshops, and the workers took a minute off to drop in at the club-car—the depot's gift to the crew—which was hitched to the tail of the train. It was an ordinary passenger coach in which the partitions had been taken down; several men were sitting in the light of a candle, putting to good use the simple inventory of a soldier's entertainment.

"Ah, the drivers! Shut the door or you'll blow the electricity out," artilleryman Samokhin greeted Sergei, screening the candle on the table with his hand. "Why don't you start, what's wrong there?"

Sergei answered in the same jocular tone that they'd be off as soon as they had sharpened the wheels, and everyone laughed except two men, who were playing dominoes. Stepping down from the car, Sergei, who had dropped behind his mates, nearly knocked over the commander, who was passing by with Morshchikhin.

"Why aren't you at your station, Comrade Vikhrov?" Morshchikhin said sternly. "Did your team get an order not to leave the engine or did it not? You're making a bad start."

"I'm sorry, Comrade Commissar," Sergei said, jumping to attention with boyish gratitude for being strictly dealt with, and running to catch up with his friend who had slipped away unobserved in the dark.

At daybreak they got up steam. Blue gloom still lingered in the shadows of the buildings and the folds of the snow-drifts. The workers came out of the shops in the things they stood in to see

534

their comrades off. The roar of an aircraft engine could be heard, and all looked up anxiously at the smoke smudges of Moscow's dawn. Luckily it was one of their own planes. A representative from district headquarters congratulated the crew on their having been enrolled in the armoured division, and their answering cheer mingled with the hoot of the locomotive; its voice was anything but frightening and not very beautiful, but then it was not going to sing songs for them at the front!

The armoured train slowly pulled out, and Sergei, as long as he lived, would remember the momentary glimpse of his father's face in the crowd, of the cameraman on the oil drum, and the stooped figure of his examiner, old Markelich. The old man ran through the fresh snow-drift at the side of the track, stumbling and waving his left hand, while his right was stretched out towards the receding train as if he wanted to grasp the buffer, trying to catch up with the fighting days of his own youth.

CHAPTER THIRTEEN

1

Like most young people of his age, Sergei had been brought up to despise all moral uncleanliness, which thrived on the misfortunes of a fellow-creature. Komsomol valour meant for him a readiness to give all of himself to his socialist motherland. In addition, he had mastered to perfection the weapon that had been entrusted to him, and correctly understood the duty of a soldier to be the art of dealing and uncomplainingly taking blows. In short, he would seem to possess all that was necessary for speedy victory. Nevertheless, perhaps because the old world had not noticed him yet, had not taken away from him personally his life or health, his children, joys or work, or because he had heard of the vileness of fascism chiefly from the newspapers and by hearsay, while the Komsomol and that good woman Taisa had carefully protected him from all that was evil and likely to darken his bright faith in life, he still lacked that fine abandon of the warrior, provided for in no military regulations, which, in the long run, forms the stuff that charges the shells and primes the gasoline tanks of modern warfare.

He believed, for some reason, that it would take them at least a week to reach the front, and that would give him enough time to store up in himself some of that essential quality, if not to get really tough. However, they moved south by front-area tracks, and despite frequent delays on the way arrived at their destination towards the middle of the next day. The track, already faintly pink with the glow of sunset, brought the armoured train to a scrubby but enchanted-looking frost-bound wood within only half a kilometre of the wrecked station with the charred ruins on either side of it. The men tumbled out and stood about in the snow in small groups, taking stock of the unfamiliar front-line surroundings. Recaptured only a week before, the country bore the marks of heavy fighting, but apparently in order not to frighten the welcome guests at the outset, everything around them—the charred rafters, and the splintered telegraph-poles with their tangle of torn wires, and the very trees, slashed and raked by the artillery tempest—was now decked out in the fullest possible splendour of a brilliant sunset and a well-settled winter. Instead of the din of battle which he had expected, Sergei found here the fragile silence of a pinewood, broken only by the quick pants of the engine.

The infantry signalmen got busy at once, and presently a telephone report was received that the army commander himself was coming down to visit the armoured train later in the day. No doubt with the knowledge and consent of the higher authorities, if not on their direct advice, a limited number of volunteers was allowed to visit the nearby village, which had been in the hands of the enemy for over six weeks. Five men set off down the picturesque cut-through, which looked downy with hoarfrost. They were glad of the opportunity to stretch their legs, have a chat with the villagers, and satisfy a natural curiosity towards those mysterious tracks that are left on the beach after the ebb of an alien tide; at the request of driver Titov, Sergei took a bottle with him to buy some milk for him in the village.

It was only a short distance, and after all those jogging hours spent in the train it made a pleasant walk. The westering sun painted the crisp snow with changing colours, there was something exhilarating in the tingling glowing air, which had a peculiar smell of violets about it. They came across a very pretty ravine on the way, and they had hardly stepped down into it when Kolya Lavtsov, in a sudden spirit of mischief, pushed his friend off the trail and sent him flying headlong into the snow. Sergei was given no chance to retaliate. By the time he got out, shook himself, and ran to catch up with his friends, they had climbed the brow of the hill. A boundless central-Russian plain, all glittering with the same paschal frosting, unfolded before their gaze.

And again, except for the black gun emplacements in the snow and an elevator in the distance cut in two, there was nothing here to remind one of the war. Only once in a while soundless laceries flashed into being along the skyline and floated over that mysterious spot called the forward zone.

"Yes, there's a power for you!" artilleryman Samokhin said with a sigh, meaning Russia. A little further on, all five of them stopped in silence to admire the unfading, slightly bullet-ridden, as it were, beauty of that scene.

From here it was only a stone's throw to what was once a prosperous village, nestling picturesquely on the hillside. It was little more than a name now, but looking down upon the ruins from above one could still guess where the brick-built stables had stood, and where the girls used to dance during the Mayday club-revels. At the far end of the village, some soldiers, no more than a platoon, were pottering around the well-sweep. Apparently they were dismantling the well frame for firewood, a rather odd proceeding with such plentiful supplies of windfalls to be had in the nearby woods. They were laying the logs out neatly in a row. It struck Sergei that the frame was not getting any smaller. It would have been a shame not to go up and have a chat with the boys just to keep their spirits up, not to treat them to some Moscow tobacco. The five of them, of one accord, walked straight through the underbrush, descended the hill and passed down the main street of the village, which the motherland had powdered with a little light snow so as not to darken the meeting of the friends.

No one responded to the greetings of the newcomers, not because those grim tough men adopted an air of superiority towards these cheerful greenhorns in their brand-new uniforms, but rather because of the urgent nature of their task.

Some of them were in their tunics, and those were steaming slightly in the frosty air, because the well was a deep one, and the order had been to finish the job by nightfall. The sappers were recovering the bodies of shot villagers, which the enemy had thrown into the well when retreating; judging by the knack they showed, they had been working there for some hours in the tense inhuman silence of men defanging delay-action mines. Their ghastly finds, young and old, all looking alike now in the kinship of the grave, lay head to head, slightly on their sides, for a length of more steps than Sergei cared to count. Only with clenched teeth and bared head could one gaze upon that benumbing spectacle. What shook the soul was not so much those bodies stiffened into queer attitudes, some of them locked in frozen embraces, so that they had to be torn apart, not so much those staring wondering eyes of the mothers or the nakedness of the babies covered with the purplish down of hoarfrost and with the wisdom of old age in the straight line of their mouths, as the calm business-like air of those rank-and-file Soviet soldiers, who had sheathed their fury against the time they would need it.

"Make way there for grandpa, son," a pock-marked sapper said to the stunned Sergei, receiving from the well the stark corpse of an old man with a German trench-cap clutched in his hand.

He was laid at the side of an old woman, his wife, in all probability, and for lack of anything more handy to cover them up with, a few handfuls of snow were scooped up over their too well-remembered faces.

Artilleryman Samokhin was the only one who had the courage to peer down into the well.

"This is a stiff job you've got, boys. Enough to send a man out of his head. What a crime, eh? It hurts to look at with dry eyes!" he said, taking off his cap. The others bared their heads too. "How many are there down there?"

"That's all right, we'll be through by night, please God, and in the morning we'll start burying them," the sapper in charge said somewhat irrelevantly in the same low voice. "The worst of it is the boy down there is so cramped for room, they're all frozen, you know."

Samokhin got out a packet of expensive Moscow cigarettes and put them into the soldiers' mouths one by one. The air was still and one match made do for all.

"I wonder what made them go and kill the villagers? Was it just for fun?" Kolya Lavtsov said in a voice not like his own.

"Who can tell. I daresay it was just to frighten us. Sort of, see what we can do, you Soviet people wouldn't have the guts for it. It is a bit horrible," the pock-marked soldier said thoughtfully, glancing at the bodies. "Or maybe it's just out of curiosity, to see what comes of it. Afterwards they'll write a scientific work in six volumes. They're such a pernickety lot."

His neighbour merely shook his head as he greedily inhaled the heady tobacco smoke.

"Mind you, they shoved the bottom ones in there alive. It was only the top ones they spattered with a tommy-gun, sort of corked 'em up."

"What made 'em do that, did they stint the bullets or what?" Sergei said, trembling in all his limbs.

"Economising on ammunition, if you ask me. An interesting bunch, those customers. Never mind, there'll come a time when we'll examine them more closely."

The fourth in the line, a non-smoker and the oldest of them, wiped his hairy face with his sleeve.

"My God, what is the world coming to!" he said, glancing up at the turquoise shadowed sky.

He spoke in the impassive tone of a philosopher contemplating the foibles of human existence, and Sergei thought that it was these unsophisticated factotums of the new humanism who had the right to judge earthly civilisation with its leagues of nations—or whatever they were called!—with its academies, its societies, royal and others, of the most respectable sciences, its false gospels of brotherhood, its bland artful western politicians; the right to judge and deliver their lawful verdict, and if there was a god in the world, he would give his blessing to that sacred enterprise. Sergei also thought that the cap torn from the head of the murderer ought to be cast upon the altar of modern culture, and he wondered to what further depths naked villainy was capable of descending with the growth of technical facilities unless it were curbed at the price of no matter how much blood. His mind was confounded and nausea gripped his throat, but he forced himself again and again to look at and remember those peaceful defenceless tillers of the soil coming up from under the ground in order to return to it again on the morrow. Fury welled up in his heart, and with it, there grew and ripened within him that other thing which does not come with the mere throwing of drill grenades or the reiterating of lessons on the economics of capitalism.

The walk took them no longer than a couple of hours and was none too tiring, but they went back in silence, their feet sinking deeper into the snow as if they carried an extra weight. They came in time to fall in; presently the army commander rode up—he happened to be in the same area. After receiving the report, he and the assistant from artillery headquarters inspected the armoured train, and passed down the ranks of the newly arrived replacements, peering into the face of each man. Then, in the briefest of speeches, he congratulated the men on joining the army in the field, expressed his approval at finding them in such fine fettle, and complimented them on the excel-

lent matériel conditions. Sergei was expecting him to say something about the ghastly well in the gutted village, but apparently
the general did not want to weaken the indelible impression which
the crew had already received. He proposed there and then to
acquaint them himself with battlefront conditions; ordering his
car to wait for him at Divisional Headquarters, he joined the
engine-drivers in their cab and they rode down to the forward
lines, which were dotted off by smoke puffs. On his instruction
a successful raid was made on a small bridge, which the German
sappers had just repaired, and themselves came under the fire of
a mortar on their way back, thus receiving their baptism of
fire. They got back to their station at dusk; the colours had faded
and the frost was sharpening. Something flew overhead with a
snarling whine; there was a reverberating crash, and the wood
shuddered and shed its white finery.

The night passed without adventure, but also without sleep.
An enemy scout plane started circling over the station, but the
armoured train had already moved out on its first assignment.
It was starting its front life. It covered railway stations where
troops were detraining and patrolled stretches of the line which
were of special strategic importance. Restricted though its use
was in modern warfare, the mere appearance of the armoured
train at timely moments and the very clang of its approaching
weight with its bristling armament raised the fighting spirit of
the infantry.

During the first week the train crew went twice into fire action
on the forward edge, shooting at live targets and hearing the
patter of shell-splinters on their armour-plating with a ticklish
sensation, as if it were their own skin. More difficult was it to
get used to the air attacks and the shattering blasts of the 500
mm guns, which threatened to send the whole mass of iron
toppling down the embankment, but even this grew into a habit
in time. Battle dents now adorned the turrets, and machine-gun
fire stripped the battle posters off the sides of the engine despite Kolya Lavtsov's dogged attempts to paste the precious shreds
back into place. The motor-trolley "Death to Fascism" had
failed to return from reconnaissance, and when Morshchikhin,
standing under the colours, received the medals for the dead,
Sergei experienced the first thrill of a soldier's pride for his
comrades. Towards the end of the second week a stray shell
knocked Samokhin's forty-fiver off the tender—prejudiced in
favour of siege artillery, he called it deprecatingly "my wasp

killer"—and an hour later a direct hit tore a hole in the engine's side armour. The armoured train was withdrawn for repairs, and Sergei was given an opportunity to resume his conversation with Morshchikhin, which had been interrupted on the night of their departure.

It took place late in the evening, as he was returning from the canteen. It was a quiet little town in the rear, lost amid the snows and almost a stranger to bombings since it had nothing in it to attract enemy aircraft, not counting the railway workshops where the armoured train was undergoing repairs. Sergei was hurrying to his night work, and stepped aside into the snow in order to pass a man in front of him, when he heard his name called.

"It's me, what's the hurry?" Morshchikhin said in a hoarse voice. "We haven't had a talk for ages. How are you feeling, engine-driver?"

The town was famous for its widespreading century-old black poplars, and it was so dark under them that evening that Sergei recognised his chief by his voice rather than by his face or his stature. They walked side by side as much as the drifts caused by the two previous nights' snowstorm would permit them.

"I feel right up to the mark, Comrade Commissar."

"Have you thought up anything new about beauty? Do you still deny it, or are you magnanimously beginning to accept it? Maybe it's a good thing the museums are blazing and the world's ancient relics are going to smash together with the bugs that live in them, eh?"

The touch of irony in his chief's tone gave Sergei the right of informal address; he deliberately refused to avail himself of it.

"I've had time to think things over, Comrade Commissar," he said with something of his former boyish swagger. "I quite agree that smoking insects out of their holes would cost mankind cheaper than building everything anew on a bare site, but I still think, if I may be allowed to say so, that with the change in social aims there is bound to be a change in the conception of beauty. Some day we shall reach the highest curves, meantime I see it in the achievement of victory with a minimum of effort."

"I see, so we're back at geometry again? A bee line, eh?" Morshchikhin rallied him.

"Certainly not," he said, and Morshchikhin caught a familiar challenging ring in his boyish voice. "I understand beauty to be the most perfect, that is, economical form of organisation of matter, and grace—an ability to perform a rational movement with the least exertion."

But again, as that time in the museum in front of Venus, Sergei failed to shake his tutor.

"Your parent has overfed you on Spencer, I'm afraid. I have great respect for that infatuated old man, even though he is a bit too complaisant where his own personal discomforts are concerned. How is he getting on, by the way? I hear you received a letter from him?"

"As a matter of fact two letters, Comrade Commissar—the second one through the Komsomol Secretary," Sergei said, still playing up. "Everything's okay. Moscow still stands where she stood, and the depot is starting on the construction of another armoured train. My father also writes that his work never went better. He's in a hurry, and there's not so much interference now."

"Not so many air raids?" Morshchikhin asked in a casual tone.

The other pretended not to have heard.

"I'm going left now, Comrade Commissar. Have I your permission? I'm in a hurry to get to the depot."

Morshchikhin took his arm and piloted him down a side street in the opposite direction. Gradually, one word leading to another, he told Sergei about his visit to Gratsiansky, about their slippery conversation, and his host's unaccountable fright.

"You see how it is, Sergei. Without going into the details of what is a quite legitimate controversy on such a confused issue as the forest, I don't like the look of it somehow, it baffles me," he began with frequent pauses, as though inviting his companion to a free discussion, but the latter said nothing. "For instance, why has your father kept silent all these twenty-five years, well knowing that he was in the right? Or let's put it this way: who gave Gratsiansky the right to make such sharp political accusations as can only be brought against a person by a court of Soviet law and only after thorough investigation at that? Or why does Gratsiansky count Vikhrov as his personal enemy, and why should he want to overthrow a comrade who is better versed in forest affairs than he is? I read one of his articles—it's like a sniper's shot from round a corner except that it has the advantage of not leaving a hole in the victim. Only today I picked up a vile leaflet dropped from an enemy plane calling upon traitors to throw sugar into the petrol tanks. Not poison, mind you, nor acid, nor explosives, but just a harmless-looking product, and sweet at that, because it is capable of putting a thousand horsepower engine out of action. I love chess problems, and I'll certainly tackle this one when I have the time to spare. But what do *you* think about Gratsiansky?"

"Let me go, Comrade Commissar," Sergei said, quivering from head to foot. "I'll be late for work, and Titov, my chief, will grumble till the morning."

"That's all right, you can tell him I kept you. This is more important. Well, why don't you speak?"

"I happen to be a relative of Vikhrov's, and relatives can't be impartial witnesses. And so I know nothing about that man."

"I'm asking you as a member of the Komsomol—why don't you speak?" Morshchikhin said in a sterner tone, stopping to place a hand on his shoulder.

"I can't," Sergei said, breathing hard and glancing at the watch which glimmered like a star under Morshchikhin's sleeve. "You know yourself, luckily from me, who I am. I still have to earn my right to this conversation."

"You still can't forget the quarrel you had with Gratsiansky the night of your departure? He must have wounded you deeply!"

"A man doesn't forget such things until he dies—one or the other, Comrade Commissar."

Morshchikhin was silent; he was beginning to understand how potent, though technically undetectable, was the poison which had lawfully been instilled into the boy, who would seem to have had no ties whatever with the past.

"Don't worry, Sergei. I know who you are, and besides, you're my younger brother. Let's go into a quiet corner and you'll tell me what's on your mind."

"But I haven't thought things out myself yet, really," Sergei said, resisting to the last.

"It's just the beginnings of your thoughts that interest me. When a phenomenon can't be placed on the scale or heated in a retort, it's studied according to its place among similar things or by the effect it has on its surroundings. That was how Gallium and Neptune were discovered. I believe I am on the verge of a big discovery myself, but you could help me in it. Give me your arm, come along."

The station buildings and the uncoupled cars of the train on a side-track loomed darkly ahead of them. They wanted to go into the club-car, but musical rehearsals were in progress there. In the next car the boys were sitting around a packing case playing cards, but Morshchikhin took no notice of them that evening, although gambling was strictly forbidden by his own orders. At last they found room on a bunk in the end truck, and there, in complete darkness, without taking his eyes off the luminous dial of Morshchikhin's watch, Sergei unburdened himself to the commissar of all those trivial domestic details in regard to Gratsiansky which he had heard discussed in the family for years and which, as a rule, escape public attention. He found himself listening to a singer in the next truck while he was speaking; accompanied by an accordion, the man was humming an unfamiliar song with haunting words:

> *I know your custom, raven dread,*
> *To come with tidings from the dead;*
> *Today you fly into our village*
> *Carrying your gory pillage.*
> *Why do you hasten on this eve*
> *My sorrow-ridden heart to grieve?*
> *Tell me, bird, to whom do you bring*
> *That snow-white hand with a wedding ring?*

Oddly enough, Morshchikhin was quite unaffected by the harrowing nostalgia of the song with its burden of doom. Once in a while he interrupted his companion with questions, from which it was clear that Morshchikhin had used his time in the interim to make himself familiar with certain circumstances of which Sergei knew nothing. If this evidence were supplemented by all that Polya knew about Gratsiansky it would have made a curious indictment, but unfortunately without a scrap of material evidence to support it.

2

The same river of life carried Polya, together with her hospital caravan, to an abandoned front-line village. Around her moaned the nocturnal forest, and Polya did not recognise Pustosha, on the other side of which had flowed her childhood and the Yenga, and where now the old world had pitched its robber camp, and her mother languished all alone. It took them a long time, in that devastated countryside, to find a village abandoned by its inhabitants with a score of unscathed houses. Polya's friends, who remembered the autumn retreat, said that these frozen huts were incomparably better than the shacks covered with tent-capes and masked with fir branches, which were pitched on the wet ground. In compliance with orders they managed in two days to scrub the floors clean, knock together single-tier bunks, hang sheets over the smoky walls, and even brighten the windows with little curtains of linen dyed in rivanol. According to the experience of the head nurse, Maria Vasilyevna, even camp-life, with a little touching up, could be as good as medicine in some cases.

At midnight the next day the first party of wounded arrived. The train unloaded in utter darkness, without a shout or a groan, possibly in order not to attract the attention of the war, which was dozing nearby; until daybreak all were in a sweat and on their toes, while Polya, in addition, was tormented by nausea, a sense of her own inexperience, and pity. The seamy side of heroism, which often escapes the chroniclers, shocked her that night—the odour of festering wounds, the multiformity of human suffering and the heroic coolness of the surgeons, but above all the soldier's meek gratitude for the slightest act of kindness. Polya's hands were found to be steadier and more careful than many others, and she was better able to give pain-wracked bodies a posture that would make the sufferers forget their pain if only for a short while; and always she had ready an amusing incident to tell, the latest radio news, a word of sympathy by which she took on herself, as it were, some fraction of another's pain. She succeeded quickly in acquiring a sense of seniority over those unkempt long-bearded labourers of war, but never that saving impassivity which usually goes with the white gown. It was the combination of these qualities that accelerated Polya's transfer to the "heavy-duty" ward, where the hopeless and unconscious patients lay.

Strunnikov took her there himself; he stood with her at the foot of each man's bed and explained her duty to her, which was to pull them out of the black hole with all her might until she had them fit to slam dominoes; the agitation of an old man, perhaps the memory of his dead son, made him add that these men, after victory, would have to finish building the material base of communism. Polya threw herself into her work with enthusiasm, and at first Maria Vasilyevna couldn't praise her highly enough. Stern to the point of austerity, this masterful woman became attached to Polya for her tidy habits and her endurance, as well as for the colour of her hair, the reminiscent oval of her face and the cloudless serenity of her gaze. From the evidence of witnesses given during the investigation of an accident it later emerged that this woman had been grieving over the loss of her only daughter, a girl of Polya's age, who had died in childbirth shortly before the war, that Maria Vasilyevna had blamed the midwife for some medical oversight or other, that she had joined the army as a volunteer and had carried out at least a dozen soldiers under fire until she was given this quieter job at Strunnikov's hospital; for that matter, she still limped from the wound she had received.

With the towering mass of Pustosha standing between them and the enemy like an impenetrable wall, a safer place could hardly be found anywhere in the war. Only once in a while the German corps artillery far behind the enemy lines would open fire over their heads and draw an immediate response from our own side, and one day there was a dog fight. Four planes, joined together by an invisible thread, circled the mackerel sky with a gleam of wings, the whole hospital watching the fight from the doorsteps and windows, until one of them, with a black cross on it fled the scene, and the other, one of ours, traced a lethal downward curve with a trail of smoke. Maria Vasilyevna took advantage of the lull to show Polya the ropes in the hope of making an efficient nurse out of her by achieving a standard that raises a seemingly minor trade to the level of high art. Polya now ate her honest Soviet bread, to which she was entitled under Ration Schedule 4, with a clear conscience; the disease of doubt had passed without leaving hardly a trace, but a tiny scar, like a spot of measles, remained in her heart for ever. And so at last she came to know the bliss of dreamless fatigue, the essential seasoning to happiness, and the noble joy of the master who sees the wan smile of convalescence on the face of the soldier. But this did not last long.

Maria Vasilyevna noticed the change in Polya's behaviour immediately; not that she lost interest in her work, but she suddenly lost all her gaiety, which had made her as welcome as a sunbeam in the wards. The stronger wrath for people's sufferings waxed within her, the more powerful became the urge to give all of herself to assuage them; the more she read about girl snipers, pilots, and medical orderlies going into battle with the infantry, the deeper grew her conviction that the great river, by a thousand maternal wiles, had hidden her away again in the quiet backwater. At the same time an odd intuition, born of the proximity of the home of their childhood, told her that Rodion was somewhere near at hand—she just had to call him at sunrise for him to hear her voice. It was a selfless desire to share the danger with him, for no one else in the world, she believed, could ever need her help as much as he did. One and the same vision haunted her all the time, a vision of him lying in the snow with arms flung wide, like Varya's July dream of Bobrinin, with dimming mind and face upturned to the dimming sky. Polya would never forgive herself for dawdling.

Secretly and in violation of the rules, she wrote an application to the proper quarters asking to be transferred closer to the forward lines in any capacity; she mentioned her as yet unappreciated ability of doing much more for her country than running to the pharmacy, washing the wounded, and scrubbing the floors in the operating-room. "I'm giving satisfaction now as well, ask Maria Vasilyevna if you don't believe me," she complained, trying to knock at the door of someone's heart, "but a Komsomol girl has to keep on growing, and no matter how long I sit here, I'll never learn to make skin stitches." And further: "Not that I'm afraid of my pulse stopping in the prime of my life or my young blood congealing in my veins—I'm afraid of my conscience, if not my people, blaming me in time to come for having done so little compared with what I could have done." Several days later Strunnikov, during his round of the hospital, reproved her for going over the heads of her immediate chiefs, and she understood that her application had reached its destination. The conversation took place at the bedside of an artillery officer by the name of Dementyev, the most promising patient in her ward, whom Polya was helping to beguile the slow hospital time.

Dementyev had been taken off the train in an unconscious state due to a dangerous haemorrhage, the result of a hasty attempt to rejoin his unit before he had completed his cure. The nearest to the blink-eyed window, he lay listening intently to the snowstorm scratching at the panes, the quietest man in Polya's ward, fretting at the delay in his military activities caused through no fault of his own. Polya knew by this time that the lighter the wound the more capricious the patient was likely to be. But this one had no complaints or whims, and only at night, when there were none to witness it, Polya would get a rumpled envelope out from under his pillow and read out to him almost from memory the half-faded pencilled lines in the light of an oil lamp. It was a letter from his wife, now dead, written from the health resort she had been staying at on the eve of the war, an hour before a heavy German bomb dropped on the sanatorium. The woman described how beautiful and brilliant the sky had been that day, and what good the sea air was doing their baby who was convalescing after the scarlet fever, and what plans she had after finishing the conservatoire, and a hundred other details and sweet trifles which go to make up the music of a woman's prattle; between the pages there were petals, now discoloured by a soldier's sweat. The officer would listen to the letter with closed eyes, and only once did he dreamily let slip a remark about what he would do to the fascist Reich if they only gave him an old cannon, or just a blunderbuss, or even the broken blade of a cobbler's knife! And Polya thought at the time what terrible enemies the old world was making for itself by its crimes.

And just then Strunnikov and his retinue put in a sudden appearance. Strunnikov asked Dementyev why he was not sleeping, and the latter explained that somehow he couldn't fall asleep at night.

"And how do you feel?" Strunnikov said, reaching for the letter, in order to find out the reason for that untoward glitter and bitterness in the patient's eyes.

"On the whole, after you've pumped seven-hundred and fifty grams of girl's blood into me, I'm turning the corner," Dementyev said with restrained humour, refusing to give up the letter. "My head's none too good, though, nor are my legs—and I'll have to do a lot of walking. Pardon me, doctor, but we've done much better in the artillery than you have in medicine."

Strunnikov stroked his moustache good-naturedly.

"And now both of us have to pay for your contempt for medical science. You're in too great a hurry, Captain. So are you, for that matter, Vikhrova. I hear you want to leave us without your competent help and advice?"

"I want to be in the thick of things," Polya whispered guiltily.

"Aren't you in it here? Come to think of it, though, we're all idlers in comparison with what we ought to be doing. Never mind, we'll be pretty busy soon." The old man patted her kindly on the shoulder, gave orders for the room to be aired more often, and went away, accompanied by his rustling retinue.

He had good grounds for his prophecy. All that night the window-panes rattled from a not too distant cannonade. As a result of massed troop movements on the northern section of the front parties of wounded began to arrive towards dinner-time the next day. Most of the wards now were "heavy-duty" wards, but Polya received only two newcomers. They were in such a condition, however, that she dare not absent herself for a minute.

Practically speaking, the first one was as good as killed. A shell splinter had pierced his stomach together with a scrap of greatcoat. He had been forwarded from the regimental aid post in a state of profound shock and with a delay considerably in excess of the six-hour limit within which there was still hope of recovery and when a rapid septic process had started. Polya's assistant, Lea, told her, all in tears, that in the operating-room they had sewed him up quickly after taking a look inside, so as not to upset themselves, as she expressed it. During the three days he was there they never learnt his unit, his name, or his nationality, but every evening the grey wintry pallor of his face blazed into a flaming sunset, the momentum of battle jerked him up on to his elbows, and strange sounds burst from his swollen lips—now the exclamation "uszza!" such as highlanders use to whip themselves up when dancing the *lezghinka*, now hoarse passionate cries of "For'd! For'd!" as though rousing his comrades to the attack. Lea glanced fearfully at the dark corner, out of which the battle-heated enemy tanks rode down upon the dying man, and being a frail slight woman, she could neither soothe him nor bend his arm, which was thrown back cataleptically as though grasping an imaginary bunch of grenades.

"What are you looking at him like that for, Dementyev? You shouldn't! Really, I'll complain to the commissar about you," Polya whispered despairingly. "The man's feeling bad, that's all. He can't rest from the war even here. Come, turn away, pull the blanket up and go to sleep—it's night-time."

The other answered slowly with frightening gentleness and a dry glitter in his eyes.

"It can't be done, my adorable comrade, and no one dares to turn away from this sight. If I had my way I'd have a film made of this kind of thing and make everyone in the world go and see it under threat of a severe flogging." Apparently he counted on that natural and saving sense of indignation which comes over every living thing except the hardened brute at the sight of human suffering. "So please go on with your business and let me go on with mine, Polya!"

The place near the stove was occupied by another newcomer, the youngest of all Strunnikov's patients. Bending over the stretcher when he was brought in, Polya thought at first it was Rodion, who had come here himself from the forward lines without waiting for her. He had the same flying eyebrows, the same stubborn beardless mouth. She was even afraid to wipe the dirt mixed with the perspiration of anguish from his face. With every breath he took there came a gurgling sobbing sound from somewhere under his right shoulder-blade, and it seemed to the hospital girls that no orchestras, no guns could smother that hoarse tearing sound. While his lung and pleura were being sutured to stop the air from coming up through the puncture, Polya ran out into the passage several times to listen outside the door of the operating-room. This time her self-restraint deserted her. Besides a chest wound, the boy's thigh was badly damaged by a splinter, which was no less dangerous. Half an hour later the wounded man was carried into Polya's ward, clean and unconscious. Towards daybreak he opened his eyes, and Polya was satisfied at last that it was not Rodion. Rodion had brown eyes, but this one's were very blue—not quite as blue, say, as flowering flax at noonday on the Yenga, but rather the colour of snow in frosty twilight. No, it was not Rodion, it was a stranger by the name of Volodya Ankudinov, the liaison man of a partisan unit. A volley from a six-barrel mortar caught him as he was crossing the front with secret dispatches, which were no longer found on him when he was brought to the hospital.

In the morning, with Strunnikov's permission, an officer who had arrived from partisan headquarters had a private half-hour interview with Volodya. During the day his condition improved to such an extent that he was able to have a plaster cast put on his fractured thigh; the joy of being with his own people instead of a prisoner in the hands of the enemy helped him to endure the pain. He even found the courage to joke that he would no longer be able to dance the *barinya* in his club. With the earnest bedside manner of a professional physician Polya explained to him the importance of therapeutic exercises. Of course, at the beginning he would have to confine himself to light ball-room dancing without any frills in the way of dance squatting. She really believed that she would meet Volodya and his girl some day in Loshkarev at a dance party, and of course he wouldn't recognise his former nurse, and Polya would whisper to Rodion that that lieutenant had been a patient of hers, too, and she had nursed him to health. No, he was not Rodion, but he was a kind of younger brother of Rodion's.

She sat at his bedside for two days and nights running without a wink of sleep, and when, after five hours' sound sleep in the stuffy peasant hut (without undressing), Polya resumed her duties, she found the ward in semi-darkness—a frequent occurrence with the electric light failing so often. Sitting hunched up as if with cold in her corner, Lea was staring fixedly at the restless flame of the oil-wick. It may have been that ceaseless pendulum-like flicker of the flame over the snuff-brown wick which conveyed that sensation of alarm and peculiar jagged rasp-like silence which accompanies disaster. Volodya was lying insensible after a dose of morphine, and the highlander's place, as Polya noticed later, was now occupied by another man, who was also unconscious. Polya asked Lea in a whisper what had happened during her absence, but the latter, with a hopeless gesture, ran out of the room, pressing the end of her head-scarf to her mouth. There was no one else she could ask. Dementyev lay on his side with his knees pressed up to his chin and his head under the blanket, although he was not sleeping. She was not given time to ask, anyway. Volodya woke up three minutes after Polya had taken up her turn of duty and half an hour before night set in, the most hellish night Polya could remember, and nothing could blot it out, not even what happened to her in the course of that month.

Volodya was looking straight at Polya, but he did not see her, as he was looking at something else, something more important within himself. Suddenly, with a stiffening tongue, he uttered "the cranes are flying" and Polya thought it was a continuation of his dream. After some uncounted minutes, however, he complained in a quite lucid manner that his thigh felt hot under the plaster. Full of misgiving as to the splinter which was still left in the wound, she struck a match. A dark sinister pool glistened on the floor under Volodya's plank-bed; it spread slowly beneath the drops that fell with the regularity of a pendulum. Polya rushed out for assistance, and she was in luck. Outside the third hut down the row huddled a group of women in white hospital gowns—four of them, if she was not mistaken, but there may have been six.

"Oh, girls, Volodya is dying!" she cried as she ran, adding that Sergei Arsenich was to be called at once, because Volodya Ankudinov was dying in Ward 5 and the plaster had to be cut open immediately to stop the blood. She shouted also something about the splinter in his thigh having shifted.

During those four days the whole hospital population had become attached to Volodya for the grave unchildlike dignity with which he was going out of life. But no one responded to Polya's call, either because they did not grasp what it was about, or because something no less terrible had happened. For some reason they were standing there not on the path but in the deep snow, all dressed light despite the frost, which had sharpened towards night; they were all talking together, pleading with someone to take a grip on herself and not do anything to herself. In the centre, leaning against a willow, Polya saw Maria Vasilyevna with her head thrown back and a look on her white face that was more akin to madness than sheer despair. As soon as the women realised what Polya was shouting about, two of them hastily half-carried Maria Vasilyevna into the hut, and the others ran to look for Sergei Arsenich. As luck would have it, he was nowhere to be found. They wasted a lot of time, and when they returned, out of breath from running, all those they had been looking for were standing around Volodya's bed, all, that is, except Strunnikov, who had left for army headquarters the day before.

"Don't make such a noise for God's sake!" Lea whispered to them in the passage.

It was quiet enough in the ward. Volodya Ankudinov was still sitting up against the pillows, deep folds of maturity creasing his forehead and the corners of his mouth. No one was doing anything. Everything possible and useless had been done. Galya, the nurse from the dressing-room, was still holding a syringe, and the others, too, were holding something pink and glittery, while Sergei Arsenich, his sleeves rolled up, was wiping his glasses with the edge of his spattered gown. Together with the rest, Polya was experiencing the kind of feeling people usually have when they stand on the quayside in the dark, watching a big ship leave the harbour.

The head surgeon put his glasses on the moment the dying man opened his eyes. Volodya was listening to something. Lei-

552

surely, like a man who knows his time, he passed his eye searchingly around the people who stood before him. At that moment he was older, consequently stronger, than them all, including Dementyev, who had turned his face to the wall with the blanket over his head, so as not to see in Volodya's face that look of lucid awareness of what was happening. His lips stirred; he seemed to be groping in his mind for the parting word, which an older man was supposed to utter at such a moment. Polya afterwards swore to her new friends that she distinctly heard his last words: "Thank you all ... for our country's sake..."—words which only true heroism had the right to use.

This took place at about nine o'clock, and soon afterwards a deadly artillery squall started. It swept across Pnevka where Strunnikov's hospital was situated. Two hurricane-driven fires rushed towards each other, ripping the air. In Pnevka itself an errant shell smashed the dynamo set, which had been got going only that day and had broken down again in the evening. No one got a wink of sleep all night. In the morning, Polya, with a weary incredulous smile, heard the report of the enemy's attack, which had petered out; she stuck to the conviction all her life that there never had been any attack, and it was simply the whole war saluting the brave partisan soldier, who had not been given time in his brief span to perform the greater peaceful deeds for which he had come into this world.

3

Maria Vasilyevna's crime was that she had been in such a hurry to give the wounded highlander a blood transfusion that she had not checked the blood group and given him the wrong one, with fatal results. Strunnikov, who returned early in the morning, handed in his report and the investigations started at once. After that things began to happen so swiftly that Polya had no time even to see Maria Vasilyevna before she left. A young, very fluent and brisk captain, who introduced himself as the Divisional Jurist, arrived the same evening in a jeep. After a brief interview with the hospital management, during which he surprised the commissar by showing more interest in the character of nurse Vikhrova than he did in investigating the conduct of Maria Vasilyevna, the military jurist expressed a desire to meet Polya. She was not able to keep this interview a secret from her friends, and went to it full of the worst fore-bodings, largely on account of her father.

Despite the excellent character which the commissar gave her to her face and the captain's assurance that she herself had nothing to fear, Polya was miserable and silent. She was shivering, too, from the emotional strain of her recent experiences, if not from a bad cold, which had only just developed. The talk took place in the presence of several witnesses and in the light of a yellow petrol-and-salt flame over a flattened shell-case, which was a novelty in the way of lighting devices at that period of the war. The captain jotted down Polya's evidence, and particularly wanted to know when the accident occurred, whether it was before or after the electric station broke down; apparently, he thought one was more liable to make a mistake in the darkness and confusion and mix up the labels on the bottles and the figures in the case-record. It took a little time to clear up these circumstances.

"Don't be afraid, Polya, everybody has nothing but good to say of you," the captain reassured her once more. "From what I understand, though, you have no proper medical education, have you?"

"Just the same, it happened before I returned to the ward, when I was sleeping like a log. As for Maria Vasilyevna, she was a very knowledgeable and good woman," Polya said, and suddenly shuddered at having spoken about her in the past tense. "I'd vouch for her as I would for my own mother!"

"I see. But don't be in a hurry," the captain said. "By the way, your mother is somewhere in this neighbourhood, isn't she?"

"No, she's on the other side, in the Pashutino forestry range," Polya confessed, changing colour.

"With the Germans, eh? I see. Very good."

"There's nothing good about it, it just happened that way!" Polya flared up, ready to take the part and even share the guilt of these two absent women who were almost equally dear to her. "May I go now, or are you going to take me somewhere?"

"Please calm yourself, Polya, I beg you," the captain said, touching her hand lightly. "There is absolutely nothing against you."

He asked a few more questions concerning Maria Vasilyevna, particularly whether anything secretive had been noticed about her, and it emerged that she had very skilfully succeeded in concealing the fact that she was a chronic sufferer from heart disease, as she was afraid of being transferred to the rear. Then the captain told Polya that the chief inspector wished to meet her personally, but not here. He would receive her at headquarters, in the office of the Military Prosecutor, which was some twenty kilometres from Pnevka. Her face a shade paler, Polya enquired whether she was to take her things with her, but the captain explained that she had no need to, as she would be back at her job the next day unless she fell ill. While dressing to go out, Polya asked those who were remaining to take care that Dementyev didn't run away again to the forward lines before he was discharged from the hospital. She knew only too well that he would not stick it out. They all looked at each other, and Strunnikov went up to her embarrassedly and kissed her on the forehead, and she all but burst into tears at this unexpected caress.

Knowing the location of the surrounding villages, Polya was rather surprised, on riding out of Pnevka, when the car turned off in the opposite direction. But she was in no position now to ask any questions. Her companion, however, was so attentive that he even threw a fur rug on her feet, and by the time they reached their destination he had won her confidence to the extent of being told all about her hospital acquaintances, mostly about Volodya Ankudinov, who had been so keen on seeing the much-praised Moscow Metro and eating ice-cream in silver paper.

"It's a shame, though," Polya wound up, reverting to the subject of Maria Vasilyevna. "All this had to happen the day after headquarters mentioned us in dispatches. The commissar was so upset, he started shooting."

"Who did he start shooting at?" the captain asked, not half as interested now as he had been.

"At no one. He just let his gun off two or three times at the floor when they told him about Maria Vasilyevna. Letting off steam, I suppose."

It was a crisp star-bright night, but Polya did not recognise the familiar village. A huge ghostlike figure in a heel-length sheepskin and with a rifle shuffled its feet outside a large well-built cottage. Leaving his companion in a tiny anteroom in which a field telephone stood on a bench, the captain passed straight into the front room without taking his coat off. Through the half-open door Polya heard the words "send her in" uttered in a preoccupied manner, and then her companion went away, with an encouraging touch on her shoulder.

There was nothing remarkable about the overheated window-less room, except a mysterious curtain covering the whole wall, from under which could be seen the edge of a map. On an otherwise bare table lay a thin file, apparently Polya's dossier, suggesting that the two officers had been waiting for Polya all that evening. Obviously, they were giving special attention to that incident at Pnevka. Both had the same insignia, but she guessed at once that the man in charge was not that affable one with the natty moustache sitting at the desk, but that other one who sat smoking a little to one side; he was a man with a high forehead and a steady unflickering gaze from under narrowed eyelids, not the kind of man who was likely to make allowances for Maria Vasilyevna's former services. Polya gave her name in regulation style and fixed her eye intently on a bunch of sharpened pencils in a shortened shell-case on the desk.

For a start the younger officer asked her whether she had had her supper before leaving, whether she felt cold, and would she like a cup of tea after her journey. Polya said this was hardly the place for indulging in such a trivial pastime, even if she felt in the mood for it, which she did not.

"Just as you like, Vikhrova. Sit down then. Well, how is life treating you? You're a volunteer, I believe?"

Polya did not think an idle question like that of her having volunteered, asked merely for the sake of making conversation, required any answer.

"Life's nice and peaceful. It's like living out in the country. Yesterday we got a bit of a scare, otherwise it's quite all right."

"Yes, we *are* having it nice and peaceful here so far," the other said, glancing at his chief. "We thought you were one of the quiet ones, but you're pretty sharp, I see. Take your beret off and sit down, you're not at a cross-examination. That's right. Now take it easy and tell us all about it."

"Tell you all about what?" Polya said, passing her tongue over her lips.

"We're interested in everything. That's what we're here for."

Polya drew a deep breath, as though she were wading into icy water, then suddenly lost her nerve. Never had the fate of any person depended so fully upon her.

"All right. To begin with," she started off vehemently, "Maria Vasilyevna, for all her forty odd years, is a true daughter of our beloved motherland. In every way she has shown herself at work to be quite an advanced person, and has given us younger

556

members of the staff the full benefit of her experience. Not only us girls, but even the wounded—ask anyone you like—they all have nothing but good to say of her."

The major at the desk tapped impatiently with his pencil.

"Hold on, what's all the excitement about? You've cracked all your knuckles. You'll talk about Maria Vasilyevna in some other place. Tell us about yourself. And don't rattle away like a machine-gun. Express yourself in live simple language, like you do with your girl friends."

"Very well," Polya said and her voice sank.

She began talking about herself in the same words which she had used when joining the Komsomol, but broke off, dismayed by the now well-known aggravating details of her pitiful biography. And although she had never concealed them, it suddenly struck her that it was because of them and not only through her own magnanimity that she would have to share the guilt of Maria Vasilyevna.

"Shall I tell you everything from first to last, or only the main points," she whispered in confusion.

"Take your time, an hour if need be," the man in charge said with a friendly smile.

"Very well," she said, and felt the Komsomol card in her breast-pocket to make sure of herself. "I was born in our country's capital, Moscow, but I remember nothing about it because I spent all my conscious life first in the Pashutino forestry range with Mother, then in the town of Loshkarev, in the home of the local vet, Pavel Chernetsov—heard of him? Number twenty-two Kalinin Street, through the yard. He worked his way up from the poorest layers of the peasantry to that of an eminent specialist on cattle. My mother really did come from a home of the landed gentry, but she was abandoned there at the door when she was a baby and didn't understand what she does now— I mean, our progressive ideas, and, generally, class differentiation." Polya's eye travelled interrogatively from one major to the other, but they were listening to her without interruption and without looking up. "As to my father, he is a professor of forestry. He's fairly well known, because they've always been criticising him all his life ... in different newspapers."

"Did he deserve it?" the major in charge slipped in.

"No," Polya said with conviction. "He's terribly conscientious, you know, one of those who can't conceal their thoughts. And he has good ideas ... in his own line, of course. He wants the forest

557

to be taken proper care of, because it isn't only a green friend to man—"

She did not finish the sentence. The younger man was called to the phone by a knock on the door; he went out, shutting the door carefully.

"How's it to be taken care of? D'you mean it's not to be cut down, but to be fenced off from the people?" the one in charge probed.

"Of course not!" Polya said, amused to see how slow he was on the uptake. "You've simply got to use it wisely. Take our place, Pustosha—when they were felling the trees there, I saw two logs left behind to rot for every one they carted out. Yesterday they didn't think about the future, but we can't be like that. My father's name is Vikhrov, same as mine—never heard it? They've been going for him baldheaded for year, but he just doesn't give a sign. He's a hard-working man, my father is."

"I suppose you feel hurt on his account? I mean, because of what he has to stand from his own people."

The major pressed for an answer to this question with peculiar insistence. Then suddenly he asked whether there was any news about Yelena Vikhrova, her mother, from Pashutino. The question surprised Polya, because, for one thing, the Yenga was occupied, and for another, she had never mentioned her mother's name in any questionnaires. At this point the other major returned.

"You have some fine places here on the Yenga," he said, coming in. "I bet you miss them?"

"Rather!" Polya smiled, flattered. "I know every one of them. I could find my way about here blindfolded. Every little blade of grass is a friend of mine, if you know what I mean."

"Yes, wonderful places, I must say," the man in charge put in. "I used to roam about here with a gun quite a bit before the war, but I don't remember the Pashutino range somehow. How could I have missed it?" He glanced hesitatingly at the covered map, then spread another one on a smaller scale on the desk. "Come on, show me where it is, lass."

Her cheeks flushing with pleasure, Polya came over to his side.

"Cutting across here from Pnevka, straight through the thickets, you'll first come to Sudoviky," Polya said, boldly guiding the pencil through a maze of comb-like lines, "and then pass the Polushubovo Burn at this spot—"

"Why, I know Polushubovo well, I often drank milk there!" Polya paused, then went on:

"But there's a shorter cut to the old highroad by way of the forest track that brings you out to Shikhanov Yam. That's a beautiful village, too, only it has a bad name. The state poultry farm should be here somewhere, right next to it. Alexei Petrovich is the director there. It isn't here, this must be an old map. It was opened just before the war. From Shikhanov Yam you turn left by the chapel, where a merchant was murdered in the tsar's time, and you'll be only twelve kilometres short of Pashutino, there!" And with the point of the pencil she showed where her mother now was to within a metre of the place.

Exchanging glances and holding down the corners of the map, the two majors followed the route over Polya's shoulder. One of them asked how she knew the countryside so well, and she explained that she had been working as Pioneer leader in one of the schools of the neighbourhood during the last three years.

"I was something of a mass organiser as well," Polya said with shy pride. "I took the children on long excursions, collected medicinal and essential-oil herbs with them, and showed them sections of the soil...."

"And the constellations too," prompted the major in charge.

"Constellations come in the night, and children sleep at night," she judiciously explained.

They were all silent. The map rolled itself up.

"Well, Comrade Osminov, it's time we let her into the secret," the younger officer said, looking Polya over from head to foot once more with a searching glance. "Well, Polya, we read your application asking to be given a tough assignment, and we liked it very much, that letter of yours. There was a spelling mistake, it's true, but we liked it all the same. The reasons you give are most convincing, and we're glad to know that we haven't been mistaken in you. Major Osminov and I have decided to give you a chance to visit your native parts."

"But the Germans are there now!" Polya began in astonishment, then suddenly read everything in the respectful silence of these two experienced men. She caught her breath, and her heart became hard and small, probably like that of a young swift when it first learns to fling itself headlong into the cloud chasms of the sky.

"Excuse our clumsy manoeuvring, Polya," the man in charge said, patting her hand across the desk. "You'll soon see that it was for your own good. Well, what do you say about taking a stroll along the route you've just shown us, except that instead of turning left at the chapel where the murdered merchant was found you'll go straight on to Loshkarev, eh?"

Not to mention the obvious importance of the assignment, she was being offered a chance to test herself and decipher the meaning of those laconic words about heroism contained in the communiqués of Informbureau, where the names of her brave contemporaries flashed meteorlike from time to time. She kept some of those newspaper cuttings in her Komsomol card together with her mother's photograph and Rodion's letters.

"Am I to go there with someone else or alone?" Polya asked, not through faint-heartedness, but in order to steel herself for the decision.

"No, you are to go alone, at night. We'll drop you near the place by plane. You'll hardly meet with any wolves, they've all run away, but you won't be able to avoid meeting Germans, and the most dangerous ones at that. It's an urgent job. As a matter of fact, a good deal depends on the success of your expedition." He paused to let this sink in. "If you refuse you'll simply have to forget this conversation of ours, that's all."

Polya's answer could be read in her eyes. O, if her sole destiny in life was to stop the bullet that was flying towards her country with her own body, it was something well worth living for!

"Oh, no!" Poly flushed. "I look younger than my age, of course, but I don't want you to think I'm a coward. I'm not even afraid of dead people any more. Besides," she ran on, waxing inventive, "I acted a millionaire's daughter once in a play, and I have a pair of gold ear-rings—Father gave them to Mother on their wedding-day. I'll fluff my hair up fit to kill any fascist. And if I made my manicure and touched my lips up, why...."

Polya believed that only in that guise would it be safe for her to step into that sinful and dangerous world, and they listened to her without interrupting. The major in charge lighted a cigarette with a shaky hand and looked at Polya over his match, and the more gaily she rattled on, the sadder and grimmer his face grew.

"You can take the ear-rings with you, perhaps, but as to fluffing up your hair, that's quite unnecessary," the other by the name of Osminov said in clipped harsh tones. He thought it time to warn Polya of the chances she was taking in going for this walk among the familiar places of her childhood. "You see, Polya, there are all kinds of gentlemen there, in that old world, who fancy clean little Russian girls. I want you to know that all of us here, on this side, will be watching your every step, but there'll be no one there to stand up for you, so there's no need to use lipstick either. You'd better not."

He looked her full in the face with eyes that said what he dare not utter aloud because of her chastity, and Polya sustained his glance. Then they discussed certain technical details of the planned enterprise, but the real reason for sending her on this long and dangerous journey she did not learn until the eve of her departure.

"What will they think of me at the hospital if I don't come back in time?" Polya suddenly reminded herself.

"The worse they think the better. There'll come a time when good things that have had to be kept a secret will become known," Osminov said, inviting her to make her first sacrifice, soon to be followed by others.

She slept in a hut on the edge of the village, which was buried in snow and no one saw her go there. She left it several days later without having recollected the name of the village.

4

A small town both in population and industry, Loshkarev in recent years had become a railway junction and a crossing of improved highroads. Its capture would enable the Soviet troops to outflank the north-western group of the enemy, so that with the loss of Loshkarev all resistance on this patch of Russian territory would be rendered futile for the Germans. The December counter-offensive of the Soviet troops near Moscow was being mounted in force, and the Soviet command wanted to get more specific information about the enemy's defences and the nature of his troop transportations, the location of headquarters and dumps, and to what arms of the service the different units belonged, information without which the most victorious army would find itself in the position of a blinded warrior.

During those tense days the operative group left behind in Loshkarev during the autumn retreat failed to respond to call signals. The reason for this silence was not known. It could hardly be the result of treachery; more likely the radio set had been located with the help of a direction finder and destroyed. The last message from there had reported the arrival in the town of two important staffs of unestablished numeration, and a day later air reconnaissance had reported an intensive concentration of enemy tanks on the northern edge of Pustosha beyond Shikhanov Yam. The situation called for a close watch on the Loshkarev area, and first and foremost, a trusted person had to be sent urgently behind the German lines to re-establish the interrupted contact.

The choice had fallen upon Polya simply because she did not have to invent any story to account for her presence on occupied territory. But for the fact that she had a Komsomol card, the flight of such a silly girl, the daughter of an impoverished Russian noblewoman and a relentlessly persecuted professor, would be regarded as perfectly natural. Even those absurd ear-rings of hollow gold and enamel, their very metal, whose possession sets a value of merit and reliability upon a person in the eyes of capitalism, worked in her favour. Another advantage was that she was being sent to the very locality where her mother's history was known, and where any old inhabitant of the Yenga could corroborate these facts. Even Polya's volunteering to work in the front-line hospital looked like a trick to enable her to go over to the side of the old patron of the Soviets' enemies.

Polya was given several days to get used to this nasty but necessary variant of her biography. And as soon as she had persuaded herself that she was really running away from starving and besieged Moscow to the safety of her mother's wing, as soon as she had started to pity herself, the assignment seemed much easier and simpler to her. Under the circumstances, even such a childish fancy as dropping in at Loshkarev for a day to see her street, peep into the window of her old school, and pat the three little trees which she had planted in the Park of Youth, would seem quite plausible. In that event, willynilly, she would have to try to remember what the inhabitants spoke about in the registration or paraffin-oil queues, at what places the staff cars stopped most frequently, and from what places, as a rule, those swaggering Germans in smart general's uniforms emerged from. As a reward she might be allowed to go back by way of Pashutino, where she was sure to see her mother on the old maid's doorstep, but, of course, she would give no sign, and would even turn away, grateful that her mother was alive—alive!—even though she was lonely and looked so thin.

At first, all this was a bit of a muddle, but towards the end she had it stitched together with the threads of natural logic until it looked all of a piece, as if it were real. It was as if she had already come there and thrown herself at her mother's knees, dead frightened, and her mother had at first scolded her for such a mad prank, and then drawn the curtains on the windows and made tea for her to warm her up. And never had Polya dozed so sweetly, feeling warm and snug after the cold and fatigue, until she heard her mother saying in the voice of Osminov, "It's time to go, Polya. Get up."

It was getting dark in the hut. Polya stretched herself with a little shiver and sat up. She had fallen asleep on the bench by the table, with her head resting on her benumbed folded arms. She did not feel like eating, although she was a bit thirsty. Everything was ready. Osminov, dressed in his greatcoat, placed a bundle before her containing some underclothes with bread wrapped up in them. All that remained of Polya's personal property were a pair of gaily-coloured mittens which her mother had knitted for her, and another object concealed in her fist, a quite harmless object—not the ear-rings—which she had kept from Osminov only because it was so trivial. The ear-rings, as a piece of material evidence, had been rejected at the last conference as likely to arouse suspicion.

"You haven't got much left, poor girl, after the Bolsheviks have robbed you of your hereditary feudal latifundia," Osminov said with a laugh, while Polya was changing her felt boots for a pair of shoes worn down at heels but with new rubber overshoes to make up for it. "Mind you don't chaff your feet, you've still got time to change. How are you feeling?"

"I'm not feeling so bad, only...." She bit her lip, angry with herself for not being able to cope with those sickening cold ripples that kept running up her back. "I want you to send my letter to Rodion only in the event of my not coming back. The things I've written there will look funny otherwise."

"Yes, of course," Osminov answered with respect. "The thing is not to think of anything. Your line is clear. You're scared and are running away to join your mother. And after you've passed Sudoviky, keep to the highroad. The forest's all right—

the friend of man, and all that—but it's a blind friend, and may lead you out to Range 10. You'd better keep your eyes open so's not to run into that accursed German bunker. Come along now!"

Not a word was said all the way. The men sat at the back—two of them. The car started off in the direction of Pnevka, but half a kilometre short of it it turned off on to a cart-track, leaving the hospital with Dementyev on the right, behind the woods. Darkness gathered quickly. The last thing that Polya distinguished in a sudden lift of the gloom was the glimpse of an unfamiliar lake with a boat embedded in its frozen surface, and then snow-flakes covered the wind shield. Through a mist of drowsiness she saw a strange river ... it couldn't be her beloved Sklan, surely? Black and angry, as if after a drunken spree, it roared between its snowy eroded banks. The car, for some reason, did not go any further, although Osminov found the ford at once. The scout in a camouflage cloak lifted Polya in his arms without a by-your-leave so that she should not get water into her galoshes.

"I'm pretty heavy, you know," Polya warned him, although she wanted to say something else.

"That's all right, take it easy," the soldier said, cradling her carefully and gently.

"How quiet it is!" Polya whispered gratefully. She also wanted to hear that voice of her homeland again.

"Yes, the Germans are sitting quiet round here. They're letting hell pop near Moscow, but not round here, if I may say so. As a matter of fact they've piped down lately."

Through the underbrush a plane came into view in a forest clearing. Everything was ready here too. They took leave of each other with a matter-of-fact handshake, like equals. Osminov fastened the parachute harness down on Polya and helped her into the cockpit. A clattering wind whipped Polya's face. It was her first flight, but she had no thoughts or fears beyond a single fear—that the pilot would lose his way in the dark. And the single thought—"What would that famous fighter Rodion say if he saw me now?" Everything was going smoothly so far, although they had been flying over enemy territory for quite a time. It seemed rather odd at first that this military plane was flying specially for her, but that feeling passed too. She was a bit surprised that no one had spotted them. There hadn't been a single gunshot or rocket that night; you'd think it was just an ordinary winter's night with no war on. The pilot slowed down his engine and took a banked turn. It must have been the air itself that tore Polya out of her seat and sent her hurtling down into the stinging, whistling, indifferent unknown.

The first minute after landing was rather frightening, but even so, it was not half as bad as her terrors had painted for her. She lay in the snow for a while until the noise overhead had died away. She felt no pain anywhere, and looked round to take her bearings, checking back with the drawing she had memorised. It was a lonely spot, almost in the centre of Pustosha. The plane ride had halved the distance for her. A longish clearing, bearing slightly to the left, loomed through the bluish murk. Judging by the stunted birches, there was a swamp here, the starting-point of her route. There was to be another landmark in the shape of two hayricks, but there proved to be only one rick. If she found an old burn on the hillside on the right it would mean that the pilot had dropped his passenger with bull's-eye accuracy. Having disposed of her parachute in accordance with instructions, Polya crawled up the hill through the virgin snow and drew her breath with relief. A burnt-over area, oily-black to the touch, lay in her path. Consequently, the junction between the two German units of which Osminov had warned her lay somewhere behind. From here Polya was to start her walk through her native parts.

And as if guessing the state of mind of that young girl, who had been sent on a sacred and dangerous errand, all Nature there hurried to her aid. It hung a dark snowy veil over the whole Yenga, it sent forth a stiff nipping wind with sweeping drifts; it flung under Polya's feet the faint trace of tracks left by peasant sledges which had come here for hay in secret from the conquerors, and gave the forest strict orders not to lead her astray. And so the old pinewood put its arm round Polya's shoulders and guided her to valour by the shortest cut. The ground rose steeply, and the century-old pines grew more majestic at every step, while Polya dwindled to the size of a leaflet that was hardly noticeable on the mighty wave.

An hour later a goodly Russian snowstorm swept over Pustosha, blinding the German patrols, and closing up the peepholes of the shelters. But below it was quiet, save where the chilled trees rubbed against each other and whimpered puppy-like. The going was easy, although it was uphill, because there was less snow on the leeside, and in any case it was only six kilometres to Sudoviky, from where a well-trodden forest track ran straight out on to the main road. It was not a desolating sense of doom, but on the contrary, a buoyant confidence in the ultimate success of her errand that gradually took possession of Polya. After all, Osminov was not sending her to her death. And when the nimble, petrifying beam of an electric torch stabbed the snowy pall, lingered on a nearby stump, ran up a tree to the forking of the branches, then approached Polya again in groping zigzags, when a burst of machine-gun fire reverberated through the woods, and not one, but several flares hung poised overhead, she was terrified, not by lurking death, but at the thought that she had got the map wrong and forgotten Osminov's instructions. With an oblique glance she watched the shadows running round her in pretty rings, her mind in a tumult. She had thought she had done much more than five kilometres, and bypassed the German outpost, which according to reconnaissance reports, was located only at the third kilometre. If a leaning pine-tree had not screened Polya's shadow in the snow, and another had not received some of the machine-gun fire upon itself the story of her Loshkarev errand would not have been half as long.

In the spot-like flashes, like on a flickering screen, there swam into view through the trees a stockade with a wooden tower on the corner and other contrivances engineered by fear, running into the depths of the clearing. The shooting grew heavier; following the machine-gun, the more formidable iron dogs guarding the ill-starred advanced post of "great" Germany in the East, began to bark. One could easily imagine the man at the firing port blazing away crazily at his haunting vision of the night without ever hitting it, and how terrified he was here, in this vast unkempt Russian forest, and what dismal voices of widows lamenting their dead he heard in the moaning branches and the howl of the overhead wind, and with what a sharpened sense of fear bordering on insanity he divined the presence of a stranger, who stood nearby, outwardly almost unconcerned, waiting for his fit of hysterics to pass, as one waits under a tree until a flurry of rain has passed.

Probably the man's superior put a stop to this senseless waste of ammunition by pushing a fist into his chalky dithering face. The thing ended as suddenly as it had started. Polya had to wait for the longest minute of her life until the jittery soldier calmed down, and the clammy weakness that had seized her body passed; a handful of snow down her neck helped to master that

weakness. When her eyes got used again to the returning darkness, she tried to cross the clearing at a safe distance from the
block-house, but everywhere she ran into a blank hopeless wall
of blasted trees laid together crosswise. Memory frantically groped
amid snatches of military information overheard in the hospital
—how to dig oneself in under fire, lying on one's side, or not
to throw a hand grenade at a tank at less than ten metres so as
not to get hit by the splinters—but none of this was any use to
her at the moment. It was like picking up scraps that were no
good for a patch. Meanwhile, the whole army of the Loshkarev
front with its sleepless commanders and its silenced guns was
waiting for news from Polya Vikhrova. Thus she first learned
the responsibility that falls to the lot of a deep-rear scout.

The whole forest around was prompting something to her in
scores of voices, and one of them struck her as being more
sensible than the others. Indeed, no slashings could stretch from
pole to pole, and there must be a gap somewhere leading to the
other side of the globe. If this was Division Ten, of which
Osminov had told her, then she had been here a year ago, on
her winter vacation, together with her mother, when the forest-
ranger's son had been struck by a falling tree, and her mother,
who had been sent for, drove the horse herself and Polya had
never seen her look so beautiful and severe; they had lost their
way, too, in the falling dusk, until the crowing of a cock had
led them out straight to Sudoviky. Consequently, the cabin of
Pavel Omelyanich, the ranger, must be somewhere close at hand
with the shed behind it containing hay that smelt so sweet in
the frost. So there was nothing to get in a funk about yet. In
case of anything the local people could be relied upon to hide
the feldsher's daughter. And again, as if someone had pushed
her in the shoulder, she started off to the right, quite at random,
and after two-hundred paces came to the old cut-over area; at
first sight it looked very familiar and seemed to have recognised
Polya too: the snow there was warm and homelike, and didn't
sting at all as she crawled across it. There was no dwelling
there, however, not even a wattle fence, and wattles, she noticed,
never burned in the war. This then was her second mistake, and
a much more serious one. Now and again things faded around
her and began to shine instead with a mysterious inner light,
and then she seemed to see a forest glade, a summer glade in an
aspen grove, although she knew that there was none there.
Actually she was at the north-eastern and most remote edge of

567

Pustosha. Gigantic trunks buttressed the noisy whitish sky, and Polya thought how odd her father's talk about the thinning Russian forests was. She was too tired even to cry, and moreover, had lost one of her galoshes while crawling and gashed her knee on a twig buried in the snow. Driven by despair she managed somehow to cross a ditch, and immediately found herself on a goodly well-trodden road. A ground wind was sweeping the snow along it, and the feel of the ribbed tracks told her that tanks had recently passed here.

She was learning the first lesson of the scout—"Never say die." To fight on did not always mean to win through, but the lack of resistance to disaster always spells disaster. Indeed, Polya's diary recorded an outstanding thought of Rodion's to the effect that there was nothing a person could not achieve in this life if he willed it passionately enough, so passionately that he was prepared to sacrifice his very life for it. Polya had no notion on which side of the road the saving loophole was to be found. She stood there undecided. Suddenly, she seemed to see a black sleeve beconing to her from the roadside, and although she knew it was only the lower branch of a fir-tree swaying in the wind, she obeyed the call. Fifteen minutes later found her in the backyards of a forest village, and this was her first reward for the pluck and tenacity she had shown. The place itself bore little resemblance to Sudoviky. A poorer and blacker village than Sudoviky was hardly to be found in the whole district. It was nothing like the swaggering trading village of Shikhanov Yam, which vied with Loshkarev itself. In tsarist days all the tar for the Yenga shipbuilding trade came from this locality, and one couldn't grow very fat on tar profits. But here there was a bell-tower looming through the veil of snow, and the houses looked more prosperous, the street row straighter, although the place had a bleak desolate air about it. There were no trodden paths to the wells, as if all the inhabitants had gone East or had been killed off by the conquerors for super-strategic reasons. The moon obligingly provided light for a minute, and the virgin snows shone like a tawdry Christmas-card picture. It was with childlike gratitude that Polya then thought of the forest, which, avoiding the most dangerous circles of Osminov's route, had led her straight out to Maximkovo. It meant that she had done a full third of the way, and if she kept it up, by noon she would reach the turn of the road at the chapel marking the spot where the merchant had been murdered.

"We're as good as home now," Polya cheered herself up in an undertone, now absolutely sure of the place.

That nocturnal road passed through Maximkovo, but nothing in the world could make Polya break the snow trail under the cross-questioning glances of those dead cottage windows. As a result she lost half an hour battling with the snow wreaths on the edge of the village. Nevertheless, she came out on the straight road almost exactly on Osminov's schedule time. She could have pointed now unerringly to her location on the map. She had succeeded in crossing the north-eastern corner of Pustosha under the very nose of the block-house at Division Ten. Osminov would have been all the more horrified at her uncanny luck had he known that a fresh police unit was stationed at Sudoviky, which Polya had managed to avoid. Facing her now was the broad cut-through of the old highway.

"There, now you know what risk means in your business, but I was here," the forest said to her at parting in a branchy voice. "I'm sorry, but my service is ended."

"Thank you, you've been so kind. You can go back now," Polya answered mentally.

Bending low, crawling forward with its underbrush, the forest nevertheless accompanied Vikhrov's daughter as far as the embankment. When she looked back, after shaking the crusted snow from her stockings, she saw nothing but a misty haze, through which something big and shaggy seemed to be nodding to her from under a swinging paw.

The wind now blew in her back, and the going was easier and not so frightening. She even warmed from the walk, and still more from her own pleasing thoughts. It was good to know that while miners were cutting their coal, and engine-drivers driving their long trains through the snowstorm, and the soldiers doing what they had to do under army regulations, she, too, was marching forward in step with all of them on an errand of such national importance that she had neither the time to drop from fatigue nor the right to freeze half-way. However, the nearer she drew towards her goal the clearer she realised how far off it still was.

Despite the temporary lull in the fighting, this was the main street of war on the Yenga. Polya could not avoid running into a German patrol, or a liaison car, or last but not least, a traitor, prowling like a werewolf from village to village in search of another victim, who, if he overlooked him, might be his executioner tomorrow. And then Polya would be taken to a shallow cellar to be interrogated under torture. They would start to maim her body, spoil her face and eyes, not to mention other outrages. As a matter of fact, she did not mind suffering a bit for the sake of her country, provided it all happened after she had seen Rodion, and he had told her how badly he had missed her, and she had filled her eyes with the sight of him. She walked along all night, limping on the ungaloshed foot, following the trail of the snow-drift, which swept over the bared cobblestones of the highroad. She was lucky. Except for a tank-truck with a snow-blinded windscreen and three motorcyclists who streaked past her, no one met her or stopped her all through the night. She accounted for it in her own mind by the fact that war, despite the efforts of its generals, was above all a gigantic muddle, organised mutually for the sake of causing the greatest havoc, a muddle in which the incredible became possible because the logic of well-regulated and intelligent living had been upset.

5

Towards the morning the snow-fall abated, soft snow-dust hung in the air, and the road became alive. Women muffled up in rags were going somewhere with the customary gait of the disinherited, dragging sleepy children by the hands, and old men with the staffs of exiles trod the Russian land within their permitted radius. Mingling with the pedestrians were peasant carts and sledges, all of them empty, and no one asked himself what wheeled carts were doing on the winter road. All this trudged along with dreadful slowness, like currents in freezing water, but instantly fell back and slumped, all but dropping at the roadsides together with the miserable nags when a German Oppel or a Büssing shot out of the mist without warning or headlights. At such times Polya, too, floundering waist-deep in the snow, would gaze with interest at the "conquerors of Europe". They whizzed past geometrically erect, not seeming to notice these woebegone creatures of Nature, who had come into the world only through an oversight on the part of Great Germany, and their faces wore that expression of arrogant melancholy usually imparted to the dull-witted by the belief that they have the right to kill any living thing that crosses their path. It was not long before Polya had her first contact with the conquerors.

A black little mongrel had been tailing after her since the morning, lured by the bread which Polya was munching as she walked along. She did not want to drive it away, as it made company of a sort, and besides, the dog didn't beg for anything, it just hobbled along beside her, doing its best to show that its faith in human nobility was unshaken. An open staff car crept up silently behind Polya, and suddenly she stiffened, stunned by a shot, and looked round to see a smoking pistol close by. She didn't know exactly whether this was just a try-out before morning drill, or whether dogs were not allowed on occupied territory, but there lay the poor doggie, stretched out in the snow at Polya's feet, and not a soul left anywhere on the road for a hundred paces around her. She tried hard to remember the foreign words she had learnt at school, but it was no use, she couldn't make out what the man with the pistol was saying to her. He looked an officer, as he was wearing a high army cap, and he must have said something very funny and bawdy, because all the other occupants of the car guffawed in a coarse masculine way.

"*Sehr gut*," Polya said, just to be on the safe side. She meant his aim, of course, and was about to add something, but checked herself and merely smiled with the faintest twitch of an eyebrow, and had that shooter been a bit more farsighted he would have paled at that gentle Russian smile.

It should be said that all this time the forest had been closely watching Polya's progress westward; at the most dangerous moments the fringe of the woods crept up to the roadside as if by accident, and all she had to do was to plunge into it. The forest had never been so beautiful as it was that crisp morning, filled with fantastic arcades, columns and statues sculptured by the snowstorm the night before. The backdrop at the forest lanes glowed rosily; the sun shone with a wintry half-light, although it was twice its usual size. Polya easily overtook the crowd and let herself be swallowed up in it. That was more important than ever, because they were approaching the bridge across the Yenga. It was a temporary narrow wooden bridge put up by the Germans in place of the iron one, which had been blown up during the retreat and now lay a black tangled mass in the dazzling snow of the river valley. A freezing sentry shuffled about by the bridge under a roof of boards straight in front of Polya; he followed the passers-by with a lazy turn of the head, and Polya thought from a distance that it would be easier by far to cross a precipice by a shaky pole.

Polya's short experience of life told her that one had to think of something else in order not to betray one's thoughts. She dwelt upon the pleasant memory of a crêpe de Chine dress in the window of a Moscow fashion atelier almost next door to the Architectural Institute. Oh, Rodion would never stop loving her if he saw her only once in such a new dress. Luckily the sentry was busy lighting a cigarette, and to judge by the care he was taking to protect the flame in his cupped hands, it was his last match. Polya decided she was saved. She was already descending the steep path at the side of the bridge, when she heard a clicking sound behind her. The sentry was beckoning to her with a crooked finger. Polya had time to plunge into the snow bank in front of her at a single deer-like bound, and then the kindly Yenga snow would have received her riddled body in its embrace. The soldier had a tommy-gun and he could not have missed at that distance. Her heart stopped beating, but suddenly she remembered her mother's parting advice always to go forward to meet one's fear, and she turned back.

"*Guten morgen,* sir," she said with numb lips, summoning up a coquettish smile. "What cold raw weather. But then we get it pretty warm in spring here. *Es ist sehr kalt,* isn't it?"

The soldier did not answer. He looked a sorry figure in his shabby side-cap, tied down on his head with a stolen tea-cloth with red peasant embroidery on the hems. Pressing his gun under one arm and without even glancing at Polya, he undid her bundle. He was not looking for partisans' explosives or inflammatory Bolshevik leaflets, oh no. He was looking for spoils of war, something in the nature of a pearl-studded *kokoshnik** or some other valuable boyar object as a keepsake of the Moscow campaign. As he turned the darned lingerie over in his hands he seemed to be reflecting on the injustice of fate which had prevented him from rummaging about in the Russian ruins together with the advance units. The look of disappointment gave place to one of faint interest at the sight of Polya's colourful mittens.

He set his gun down against his leg and pulled them off Polya's outstretched hands one after the other.

"*Gut,*" he said, sticking them on to his chapped hands and

_____
* Woman's headwear.—*Tr.*

572

examining them from all sides with the grave air of a customer.

"Oh, *sehr, sehr gut*!" Polya laughed, faint with joy, and that maimed world in front of her, dearer now than ever, looked to her like a new-born flower with crimson, slightly turned down, petals. *"Bitte, bitte, es ist sehr kalt, aber dan Frühling kommt!"* she added with elation tinged with distress at the thought that she would have nothing to pay with next time.

She was flushed with victory. Now she had a twin experience in dealing with the enemy. There even came a daring fugitive thought that war was not half so terrible, and if you started young you could get used to its voice as easily as you did to the crowing of the cock that woke her in the mornings when she lived with Mother. Suddenly it all seemed child's play to her, all those armoured troop carriers and the stream of German lorries hastening to the forward lines chock-a-block with iron tanks, shell boxes, and droll mannequins in helmets who looked as if they had come out of the punching presses of war industry. After all, Polya had a lawful right to go in whatever direction she pleased on her native land, to go and smile at the open spaces of her winter, at the birds overhead, and those lonely white willows at the roadsides and in the hollows, which greeted the messenger from Moscow with a barely perceptible nodding of their branches. Even her knee stopped aching for such an occasion. True, there was something forbidding about this dear-beloved snowy beauty—for merely admiring it Polya could be hanged by a rope for such a length of time as would not con-travene the sanitary regulations in force on occupied territory. But then now, if she lived to have grandchildren, she would have something to tell them. To cheer herself up she vividly imagined them out there, sitting around a Christmas tree that had not grown yet, patiently waiting until Grandma got to them with the thrilling story of her errand.

The charred remains of Altukhov Pogost and the chapel raised to the memory of the murdered merchant were left behind; from here the road turned off to Pashutino. The columned smoke of Shikhanov Yam, lilac-tinted in the still air, came into view, and that meant she was half way. At last she entered the streets of the famous village with its gutted houses lying on either side, as if some sky-high giant bent on mischief had walked through it, laying about him left and right with an uprooted oak. And now she had almost reached the end of it without anything hap-pening, and was beginning to think the incident with the mittens would hardly make a story for that Christmas night to come; she would need details to fill it in with, and so she carefully made a mental note of everything she saw—the roofs of these once wealthy houses gashed by the shell splinters of anti-aircraft guns, and the horse lying in the snow, as if resting, with its mane tossed back pathetically, and the smoke curling over the hastily built peasant dugouts, and the military cemetery on the hillside charted out according to all the rules of German burial aesthetics, and the sudden spate of tank tracks running out fanwise from the birch grove on the left, and even that solitary man in the autumn overcoat who was sauntering through the new quarter of Shikhanov Yam with an idle air, as if there were no war on.

He passed her and glided over her with such a gloating look that after taking several more steps she threw caution to the winds and looked back to find that he was watching her too. It didn't look good, and as if to confirm her misgivings he insolently beckoned to her with his finger, and, unlike that shivering ragman on the bridge, came towards her himself to make doubly sure. A man of about forty-five with a bulbous nose, obviously a hard liver, he was chewing something, and there was nothing sinister in his appearance. In any case, Polya had nowhere to run away now.

"Did you call me?" she said.

He stood for a minute looking at her sideways in teasing silence.

"Where are you going to, my pretty maid?" he said caressively, chewing all the time.

"I was going to join Mamma," Polya intoned and crinkled her nose in a smile, but this time the charm didn't work. "Hunger's a good driver. How are you off for bread here?"

He never thought of answering.

"Fancy that!" he said, shaking his head sympathetically, and for the first time since she had started on her journey Polya felt desperately cold. "You don't say you've come here all the way from Moscow? That's the trouble with you Komsomol youngsters, you fool around and then, when things get hot, you come running to your mummy's skirt. You kids are all alike. And where does your mummy live?"

"She lives at the Pashutino forest range," Polya said in a plaintive voice, and her heart suddenly sank when she realised the slip she had made. The chapel was a long way behind her and in front there were no more turnings to the forestry.

574

The man gave no sign, however; the nose of a police-dog told him everything he wanted to know about her. He tossed something into his mouth under its grey moustache every once in a while as he listened to her confused description of Pashutino's geography to prove that she was a local girl.

"Oh, you haven't far to go, you'll be there by supper-time. I daresay it's pretty bad in Moscow, eh?"

"Well, yes, I should say it is. The people are having a rough time."

"Rough isn't the word. It makes your heart bleed to see the way they're suffering. I bet you must be frozen to the marrow. Now then, come into my cottage, girlie, I'll give you a warm up," he added in the cajoling tone of a hangman.

This was the only variant of failure Osminov's instructions had not provided for. Polya tried her hardest to cry, but the tears wouldn't come to her eyes.

"Oh, I can't, I'll be late to see Mamma. I'm afraid to walk in the forest at night."

"That's all right, girlie, we'll go straight from there. She'll have tea and cake ready for us. I bet she must have stared her poor eyes out, waiting for you."

He took Polya's arm in a sticky bony ring and led her back, stunned and unresisting. Now more than ever she should have remembered the details of her adventure, but her mind was blank and her grandchildren would never know how she walked those accursed three hundred paces in the opposite direction, what the traitor had been chatting about so amiably on the way, and what the local jail looked like from the outside, where she was handed over in the charge of an elderly German guard, who was sitting on the doorstep, a woeful figure in big straw galoshes.

"You've bungled the job, girlie, you're not cut out for it. This kind o' job needs clever handling," the traitor said, chewing without a stop.

"Let me go, let me go, you viper!" Polya whispered through bloodless lips, scratching at the bolted door. "Are you a Russian or not, you skulking beast?"

All she heard was the receding sound of crunching snow. The man in the overcoat had gone to report to his chief the capture of a suspicious girl, in order that she be given her deserts and he be rewarded with the rank of supernumerary ober-cur in the future world empire of Germany.

CHAPTER FOURTEEN

1

Demid Zolotukhin's late father had built his barn not so much for the storage of his stock in trade as to tickle his own fancy. He could have protected himself against thieves much more cheaply. It was a real bulwark of capitalism on the Yenga, with a low iron-banded door and without a single window, but with lots of corn bins and secret compartments in it. In his last years the old man had often wandered in there at sundown for the last pathetic pleasure of dipping his arm into the cool wheat, the prickly oats, and the oily buckwheat, and feeling, feeling the captive shoots of life in order to satiate that dim yearning for power, peace and deathlessness, which some people gratify by touching gold, holy objects, or a hot enthralled body. On a shelf above one of the bins there had once been a black coffin, the crown of Zolotukhin's meditations on the vanity of all human desires. Autumn water, which had eaten through the roof in the inclement year of nineteen seventeen, the frequent succession of thriftless heirs, and the nightly visits of thrifty neighbours who had not left a nail in the walls, had turned Zolotukhin's castle into a chinky shed with missing floor-boards here and there. Snowy noonday shone through the holes, and a low draught stirred the dry old litter on the floor.

For a minute Polya stood as if blinded, then groped her way into the far corner. Her fingers came in contact with a hoar frosted post and a horse collar on a hook from which some thief had already cut away the straps. Slightly to the right she felt underfoot a heap of husks and straw; she could take a rest here while awaiting her fate; only now did she realise how numb she was with fatigue. The place proved to be occupied. She stepped on somebody's hand, somebody who was sleeping there in sprawling abandon. She stamped down the blue snow which had trickled in through the rotting base-logs, and it grew lighter inside. It was a young man of military age, but he did not wake up. What struck Polya was not that he was sleeping only in a shirt, which had a torn collar, but that his face was blue. It was covered with hoarfrost.

A hoarse boyish voice behind her confirmed her guess.

"Don't touch him, let him lie there. He's dead."

The voice came from above, from one of the surviving corn

576

bins, and although she had got a bit used to the darkness she could not make anything out there.

"Who is it there, what are you doing there?"

"I'm waiting till they call me to tea." She realised now that the boy could not have been more than thirteen. "Come up here, you'll freeze on the ground. I've got a tarpaulin, it's warmer under here."

"All right," Polya said after a pause, and began to clamber up in the dark, clutching at what she could for support. "Where are you? You're a fine one, can't you give me a hand? I'll tear all my clothes."

"You talk less, otherwise you'll have nothing to sing with."

She struggled up and he let her in under the tarpaulin, shivering slightly as if he had touched a lump of ice. Polya learned by touch that he had no cap on either. With the tarpaulin pulled over their heads they lay there for a long time, breathing hard to make up for the escaped warmth. Whatever happened later, she was now in luck. Of course, it was bitter beyond words to think how she had disappointed them all—the Red Army and her people, her mother and Rodion included, but once she had stumbled, she had to face the thing out, as Osminov had taught her, and secondly, she had to take stock of her surroundings at once in order to try and find a way out.

She was so cold that she couldn't speak, but the boy came to her rescue.

"I bet you went to blow something up too, eh?"

"No, I was just going to see my mother," she said, and although it was a shame to reply to brotherly kindness and shared warmth with such ingratitude, she repeated her story of havoc wrought to the Soviet capital as picturesquely as she could.

The boy understood her, and did not take offence. He asked no more questions and merely sighed with the premature wisdom which children usually acquire in calamitous days.

"Never mind, our people will build Moscow up again when they get going," she hastened to comfort him, seeing how silent and dejected he was. "Want some bread? I have some with me." She broke off a lump. "Who is that down there?"

"He's not a local chap. Must have been going to see his mother, too, and lost his way," the boy said mockingly, but he took Polya's bread. "He didn't speak any more after they'd pushed him in here. Must have beat him up cruel. This is good bread, nice and warm!"

Polya was silent, her cheeks flushed. She suddenly pictured them doing the same thing to her.

"Have you been here long?"

"Yes, since yesterday."

"What have you done? Set something on fire?"

"No, I ran down Hitler."

"You don't say? Did you swear at him, or what?" Polya enquired with respect.

"No, I stuck papers on their tanks. If you spit on 'em they freeze on like glue. They guessed who it was because of the square-lined school paper."

Polya wanted very much to help him in his hour of trouble, if only by giving him the benefit of her advice as his elder.

"Don't you confess. You're not the only schoolboy in Shikhanov Yam."

"You can't fool them. Nobody else could have had the guts for it. I was considered the ringleader round here. Up to all kinds of tricks I was. Once I froze up a padlock with water, another time I painted a window with soot." He livened up. "But the funniest thing was lowering a feather down the chimney by a thread."

Although he bore himself in a manly fashion as far as the enemy was concerned, he was nevertheless younger than Polya, and therefore stood in need of her advice and instruction.

"That was wrong of you. A Komsomol boy should always show an example," she said in the voice of Varya, but curiosity got the better of her. "What happens when you lower a feather down a chimney?"

"What? That's where superstition comes in, well, you know, religious hangovers from the old regime. It makes a scratchy noise in the chimney, and they think it's the devil. You try it, it's a scream." He visibly shivered with cold. "I'm not in the Komsomol, anyway."

"All our family are non-Party people. Father's consumptive, so was mother—we buried her before the Germans came—and my sister's only just turned four. The women in Shikhanov hated the sight of me. I lowered a billet of wood down one of their chimneys, and would you believe it, they chased me for two hours." Suddenly he added with grim conviction, "Never mind, they'll like me now."

Polya felt the boy's hot breath upon her cheek all the time, and together with his breath his thoughts too communicated themselves to her. They were so black that Polya felt twice as cold from their blackness. In vain, then, had she dreamt of building bronze gates under communism, or planting forests upon the land—she had not quite made up her mind which. And that boy was the older, because he knew more about her future than she did herself.

Her heart was wrung, and she tried a childish ruse for the sake of verification.

"Did they beat you?" she asked.

"Don't be silly, they don't beat you for such things. I bet you thought they give you a caning and then let you go? No fear, they don't cane you for that," he said with bitter pride. He seemed to feel flattered at having a real good Nazi standing on guard over him this second day, even though he was an elderly second-rate specimen. "Shivering, eh? Scared I bet?"

"Of all the crazy ideas! I'm not shivering at all, I just can't get warm. I'm frozen to the marrow." She poked her head out from under the tarpaulin and twisted her stiff neck. "You think they'll shoot us?"

It was generous of him not to answer such a leading question at all, and it was borne in on Polya that he was not only older but stronger than her. She could not see his face, but there was something about him, something in the very way he spoke that reminded her of Rodion, and that Komsomol boy at her father's lecture, and Sapozhkov, and Volodya Ankudinov, except that this one was the youngest of all that big family. He probably had the same narrowed eyes, the same tired and slightly scornful mouth, for he, too, had reason to despise the thousand-year-old scheme of things in a world where nothing could be done without the shedding of children's blood. Through a dozen dim intermediate thoughts Polya was led to an equally vague conclusion that before the dawn was ushered in upon the earth there would have to be a succession of generations of builders and fighters, giants with hearts of iron, relentless to themselves and as persistent as a drill or a plough with a dream welded to its share.

"Was that the starosta, the man who brought me here?"

"No, the headman of our village is a different one." And in a whisper, the boy told her the remarkable story of the present starosta of Shikhanov, who was once a rich man in these parts. Polya listened absently to the tale of how he had run away from the Yenga and how the muzhiks had smashed up his rich house down to the last splinter and carried everything off for fear that if as much as a scrap of it was left standing he would come back again like a dog on the scent. While they were at it they chopped his garden down as well, so that the path that led to it was overrun with weeds during the past fourteen years. Then, suddenly, soon after the Germans came, he walked down the street as large as life with a stick in his hand and his grey head bared and the whole village, old and young, stared at him through the windows for over an hour, while he stood under the rain, looking at the site of his home, silent and sombre, as one would expect all those to be who return from the grave; he was terrible, too, not because of what you could read in his face, but because of what his return meant, according to the general rumour. He moved into a dugout, which he built himself on the same spot.

"No, the starosta's a different man. This rat you're speaking about is just laying himself out to give the police a hand. He'd been working here before as co-op manager, and ran away from the law just before the war. The mice ate up eight hundred kilos of his raisins. Now he goes nosing about, looking for something all the time—maybe the rope he'll swing on, the son of a bitch. He turned our cottage upside down. I had collected about two and a half kilos of vitamins, you know, those sweetbrier berries, and he went and crushed them with his boots. You're an accomplice of theirs, he says, you're hoarding that up for the Red Army, as if they've got nothing else to think of, the fool! I hope he doesn't start digging up the garden—my little sister will have no one to look after her then."

"He won't dig now, in this frost. What have you got there?"

"A munitions dump. I picked the stuff up along the roads—cartridge clips, starting handles for trucks, and at least forty hand grenades. I wish I had a couple handy now, I'd treat that rotter to them, I would—one of their officers."

A spasm of resignation, as it were, passed through Polya's body, as always happens with children after a fit of tears. She felt at peace, almost warm, and even forgot the pain in her knee, and seemed to have reconciled herself to the thought of dying not from a bullet.

"Is he a brute, too?" she said drowsily.

"You wouldn't say so by looking at him. He even plays on a mouth-organ, but he's kind of all broken up inside. He's terribly fond of killing cats. Mind you, he won't touch a bird, and if an old woman comes his way he'll let her go past, but he just can't stand the sight of a cat. As soon as it starts purring or rubbing against him he'll bash it with whatever he can lay hands on, and then he'll kneel down and stare at it—you couldn't drive him away with a stick. I thought maybe he was collecting the skins—the whole world these days is a rag-and-bone shop to these Fritzes. But no, he just gets a kick out of it. If you fall into the hands of a chap like that you're in for it. They were hanging a girl here, a Moscow girl, and he. . . ."

Luckily Polya did not hear the end of his story. She had never slept so soundly, and this time she had no dreams.

She awoke with a jerk, as if she had received an electric shock. An un-Russian soldier stood in the open doorway against a background of blue snowy evening. Suddenly she remembered everything and understood that he had come for her. Hers was the right of seniority after all. She crawled out from under the tarpaulin and patted her headscarf straight with a woman-like gesture. She had to do something before going away, like grown-ups did in similar cases. Her lips fumbled in the dark and touched the boy's eyebrow.

"Take the bread, it'll come in useful. As for the Komsomol, think it over," she said, clenching her teeth to keep them from chattering. "Now, behave yourself while I'm away."

He leaned over to her while she was climbing down from the corn bin, insensitive to the scratches and the splinters she got in her hands.

"Don't worry, I've got plenty of guts. Keep your own pecker up. And don't let 'em blindfold you, it's all the same to you, but it's worse for them, makes 'em jittery. Just show 'em the kind of stuff we're all made of."

The sun had long since set, and a crescent moon was riding the sky. Polya's escort led her between tall pale-blue snow-drifts. She did not know where she was going and why, all she knew was that the decisive inescapable moment was approaching when all preceding life seems to have been only a preliminary running start, after which comes the swift impetuous flight, the height and length of which is the measure of a person's worth. Now, when she had no need for it any longer, every little detail imprinted itself in her memory. From under the hillside came the roar of a lorry stuck in the snow; the engine would break off on a snarling note, take a breath, then start whining again, straining like a fly on sticky paper. Two of the conquerors, their taut-skinned faces nipped red by the frost, were leading a skinny cow to the slaughter; a third, a puny miserable *ersatz* of a man, was prodding her on from behind with a twig to show that he had his share there too. And not one of her own people did she meet on the way! They turned off into a deserted pinewood, and her escort looked round furtively while he gripped her shoulder. She happened to be scratching herself, tormented by a nervous itch that ran all up her body. This saved her from the guard, who, for all the soldiering he had been doing, still retained a panicky loathing for insects. Besides, the half-clad figure of a batman with a large thermos flask in his hands sprang out of a trench on the left, greatly to the guard's annoyance.

"Mach dass du fortkommst!" he growled.

She was in luck so far!

A deep passage led into a dugout. It was the most solid-built and comfortable-looking of all the dugouts they had passed. She scooped up a handful of snow as she entered so as not to go in alone! The spacious entry was partitioned off by a wall of thin unbarked birches. In the room on the left were two men. The younger one was lying on a cot by the wall in an unbuttoned tunic with his hands under his head, staring pensively at the low timbered ceiling. The other had a side growth brushed across his bald head and answered to the word *Langer*—he did look a bit longish, but whether that was his real name or a nickname there was no telling. He snapped at the guard over his shoulder, and the man vanished with a crunching turn on his heel. Silently, with unsparing hands, *Langer* searched Polya, who stood as if petrified. He even felt her teeth to see whether they unscrewed, and slashed her heels up with a screwdriver, then, assuming a glossy appearance as though he had been suddenly wrapped up in cellophane, he carried the remains of Polya's property out of the room. Not until he had gone did Polya feel a wave of anger mixed with bitter shame and hatred sweep over her, threatening to drown all caution. She did not know what words she would use, but she had enough fight in her now to give them a piece of her mind, which would make them remember the snub-nosed little Moscow girl for a long time!

As time flowed, however, a benumbing sense of disaster oppressed her. The peaceful sound of dreamy German music came from the earphones lying on the table. The snow, too, had long since melted in the palm of her hand. Then suddenly came the thought that *this thing* was not so simple, that between life and death there could be a pain of indefinite duration, and unless

582

a respite was granted, that long-drawn pain would stifle in her everything which she and her tutors had so carefully nurtured in her. In this way she came to the conclusion that it was easier to die running, and probably her plan would have succeeded; barefooted as she now was, nothing but a bullet could have overtaken her. So strong was her determination that the man on the cot suddenly raised himself on his elbow and looked questioningly at the prisoner. Presently Langer returned, and nodded the girl to follow him out, first into the entry, then into the next room.

Unless presentiment deceived her, the supreme inspirer of all human woes was waiting for her in that room in the person of the Old World, or rather its plenipotentiary. Truth to tell, Polya had long been wanting to have a peep at it, but had reckoned on doing so in safer conditions.

2

During the last six months Polya had gone over all the details of the coming encounter, but things worked out differently. *There* she had been interrogated in the summer and in the day-time, but *here* on the threshold of a winter night. Instead of the cheerful Russian cottage with sunbeams dappling the mats and a window offering escape, she found herself in a blind shelter flooded with the harsh light of an accumulator bulb, a tomb almost. A ray of hope, though, came with the thought that they would hardly want to spoil the soft expensive carpet on the floor with blood. *There*, in imagination, had been a multitude with toad-like faces, as the enemies of the human race were always depicted on Soviet placards, but here, in reality, sat a single man smelling of good perfume through the tobacco smoke. And there wasn't a sign of nickel-plated torture appliances in the corners or anything frightening like that—nothing but a bed behind a screen covered with a travelling rug, and on the wall above it, not anything lewd, but on the contrary, an oval portrait of a fine-looking sad-faced woman in mourning. On a large table, a sort of drawing desk with a map spread on it, stood a glass of coffee that had gone cold, and next to it lay a burnished steel pistol and the two objects which had been taken from Polya during the search, one of which was her mother's photograph. But what struck Polya as an ill omen and put her on her guard

583

was the fact that she had not been pushed in violently to fall at the feet of her tormentor the way it was described in many stories, but was merely told to sit down near the table on one of the wood blocks which was covered with a greenish military-looking fabric. The reason for this was not a desire to conduct the examination by gradual stages of severity according to the usual rules, nor lenience on the part of the examiner in consideration of the victim's sex and tender age—he had some experience in interrogating Russian girls—but a purely personal interest, which is worthy of note.

This officer held a rather important political post in his unit, the designation of which was as intricate and baffling to ordinary mortals as the ranks of the angels in the celestial hierarchy— something like Ober-Sturm-Banhof-Dienst-Führer, or maybe something still higher. His tank division had come to the Loshkarev sector of the front straight from France to deal the death-blow to Moscow from the north-west, and so the circle of his desires was completed, for despite the amenities of French life he had been feeling a bit bored in Paris. It was not the contempt of a soldier for an easy war, where the poetry of a mortal duel is prosified by the bribery of high-ranking personages or the convenient collusion of the bourgeoisie. No, it was not the sun of a contemporary Borodino with the protuberances of the Soviet *katyushas*, it was not the rare opportunity of hearing the magnificent "hurrah!" of the Russian attacks at close quarters that had attracted him here; he was not drawn by the lure of souvenirs and silver foxes, nor by the hazardous historical temptation of gazing down from the embattled Kremlin walls with a pensive air, nor by an estate in the Alazan Valley of the Caucasus promised him by the Führer, nor even by the chance of indulging in unlicensed joys in an occupied country in ways that would have been considered reprehensible even in the brothels of Western Europe. Unlike his less educated, often base-minded colleagues, he made it his aim to study Russian affairs scientifically.

Ever since he went to school he was stirred by geographical discoveries and colonial glamour, especially by the mysterious Eastern spaces with their imperceptible transition from dreadful snows to the blazing heat of middle Asia. He might have become an explorer, a distinguished collector of Tien Shan butterflies or Sarmatian antiquities, had not his mature years coincided with the birth in those spaces of a contagious idea of universal regeneration, which threatened to spill over into adjacent Germany.

Perhaps nothing influenced this refined and well-read youth in his choice of a profession so strongly as his hatred of socialism, a hatred born of the fear of losing his parent's little factory. It was only a button factory, but it meant more than just those round bits of stuff for fastening clothes in necessary places—it stood for the ideal German thing-in-itself, a tiny and serviceable masterpiece of capitalist civilisation. Compatriots and leading political thinkers from among the manufacturers or tradesmen fully shared the button-maker's feelings. Naturally, the wisest thing would be simply to sterilise all those spaces east of the Vistula by a process of what they called "soutanisation", that is, forcibly depriving of life every living thing that had had as much as breathing contact with Bolshevism, but it was doubtful whether the victims would voluntarily submit to such treatment. Thus arose the idea of the Moscow campaign, termed the pitched battle for liberty and culture, since it was rather awkward to ask the nation to shed its blood for a private button-making business.

In the eyes of this officer all previous failures to subdue Russia were due to the ignorance of the conquerors, who studied the calibre of her guns and the strength of her garrisons instead of infiltrating into her innermost spiritual rears. By a process of independent thought the officer arrived at the conclusion that what counted in a fortress was the morale of its defenders and not the thickness of the mortar behind which they lay hidden. Long before the war he made a thorough study of the earmarked country's historical past, the tenor of life of its people, even the form of its songs and the character of its rites, and had become so proficient in the Russian language that he was quite a match for some philologists of ours, who teach schoolchildren to maltreat their native language. He even traced the roots of Muscovite turbulence, which had come into the limelight after 1917, in the national predilection for fisticuffs as a form of relaxation necessitated by a surfeit of health and the rigours of a continental climate, and discovered the embryo of the idea of world unity among the toilers in the unifying policy of Muscovy in the Middle Ages. Nevertheless, the most important knowledge of all, contained neither in antiquarian editions, nor in the gossip of deserters, nor in the reports of reconnaissance, somehow eluded the inquisitive mind of the officer. Yet it pervaded the very air of the twentieth century and consisted not in a desire to annoy button manufacturers but in the everlasting yearning of the common people to live in peace, to plant trees and raise sons to comfort them in their old age instead of lying slumped on barbed wire, cursing God and the mothers that bore them.

For all his endeavours, Russia still remained a dense wild wood to that thoughtful and active officer. He would have thought nothing of blowing the whole country sky high; to a disappointed proprietor the whole globe was a comparatively cheap price for a button factory, and it should be said that although he had not spent much time at the gates of Moscow he had already accomplished something in this respect. However, in his desire to combine his harsh class duty with scientific benefit, he deemed it necessary to leave of Russia, besides her ruins, at least a cursory description, a sort of *Querschnitt*, as a gift to remote German licentiates, to save them the trouble of excavation and conjecture. For this purpose, he kept regular diary entries of his private impressions of people and buildings with photographs of how they looked before and after meeting him. Naturally, Polya was hardly interesting to him in the way of conversation, but then the cleverest spies have always preferred to ask children the way to hidden springs. That is why the officer did not want to frighten her at the outset or do anything that would cause impediment of speech.

He was over forty; the shadow of irremediable, and not only intellectual, fatigue lay in his sunken eye-sockets, so sunken that Polya to the very end was unable to distinguish his pupils. He made up for this by a fine head of hair the colour of beer froth, the athletic bearing of a staff officer, and a noble Aryan cranium of a type even superior to that required for a successful political career. He wore the winged emblem of the Wehrmacht on his narrow chest, and altogether there was something of the wilful spindle-legged bird about him, one of those who have the nasty habit of pecking you in the face without warning. In short, Polya realised that she would die that day unless she was able to deceive, divert, and coax him by aid of the meagre charms at her disposal.

Toying with his lighter, which he kept putting on and off, the officer looked steadily at Polya until he had her reduced to the required degree of pallor. The conversation started with mutual introductions.

"That's all right, be not afraid. Everything will be fine. Take a seat. What is your name?"

"Apollinaria," she said, licking her dry lips. "It's an uncommon name, really, but not so bad as some. Apollinaria Vikhrova."

"Apollinaria, so, so," he said, smacking his lips as if flavouring it. "How old?"

"Eighteen. I've entered the Institute already ... only I haven't quite made up my mind what to go in for. There are all kinds of private reasons."

"Very good. Thank you, Apollinaria. Who is your father, your mother?"

"Mamma is a feldsher, that is, a doctor's assistant. As for my father, he works in forestry, he's a professor, but he's not much of a success. They criticise him all the time. But then he who goes into the woods will have the cones dropping on his head, as the saying goes."

Besides a corresponding smile, she tried to win over the German officer by listing her father's misadventures under the Soviets. He heard her out with a visible strain, then tapped the desk impatiently with his lighter.

"You can tell me about that later. Very good. So you are coming from Moscow. Who are you?"

Polya nodded sympathetically.

"I was afraid of this misunderstanding myself, but I'll explain everything if only you have the least bit of patience. I won't be long, just three or four minutes will do for me ... may I?"

The officer looked at her and said nothing, as if giving his prisoner all the time she wanted. She felt the ground begin to tilt beneath her feet, and despair was so plainly written on her face that the officer saw fit to reassure her in order to achieve the best results.

"That's all right," he smiled. "Very good. I always had a desire to see Moscow with my own eyes, as well as the rest of Russia. Oh, these frozen rivers, that suffocating heat of the sandy steppes, where not so long ago the nomads built their camp-fires. The summer here gives us a dramatisch landscape of burning forests. Please, don't be afraid." Apparently, he understood the girl's nervous state, and to help her out he poked a finger at the winged badge on his chest. "I am Walter Kittel. I also have two sisters—Ursula and Lotta. They are pretty, like you. I often dream of them coming into the garden, singing, decorated with flowers. Quiet and tired."

Naturally, family information of this kind was to be received with gratitude as a token of trust and special favour.

587

"Oh, so you even have *zwei Schwestern? O, das ist sehr gut!*" Polya played up to him eagerly, as things seemed to be taking a good turn. "What lovely names. Do your sisters er ... go in for anything too?"

"Oh, *blagodaryu vas*—thank you!" Kittel said, turning the Russian syllables over in his mouth. "Ursula goes in for creating art. The chief feature of her paintings is the blending of the human body with thought, keeping a strict balance which is so favourable to the artist. At first she tried to balance the different trends in styles, then arrived at a search for harmonious colours like those to be found in Nature. Her painting is evocative, full of vibrating intensity, always brimful of chromatic chords, you understand? And then contemplative depth, the conveying of atmosphere. Oh, faithfulness to Nature has always warmed and influenced the world of German images!"

The German officer had a free evening for one thing, and was greatly attached to his sister Ursula for another, although he loved Lotta just as well, and last but not least, he simply got a kick out of spouting Russian with such audacious verve. Stirred to a companionable mood by his memories, he extended to his prisoner with a half-questioning gesture a packet of the best German cigarettes.

"Oh, no!" Polya said, embarrassed. "I haven't learnt to smoke yet. Mamma doesn't smoke either, though she is a medical worker. Nicotin. It's very bad for the blood vessels of the brain."

Walter Kittel smiled indulgently.

"In that case, then, perhaps a little vermouth, rum? It's so wintry today. *Nein? Na, dann nicht.*" Without getting up, he reached for a green gilt-edged box standing on a low bedside table, and pointed delicately with the tip of his little finger to a quaintly shaped sweet lying on the very top. "Take it. It's nutritious German chocolate."

"Thanks, I don't want anything, really," Polya resisted as best she could.

"Please. Take it. Apollinaria."

The box, held in mid air, began to tremble, and suddenly Polya seemed to see Osminov, stern-faced, nodding to her through the forests and walls from somewhere deep inland. She took the black square, and with an unfamiliar palpitating sense of treachery began nibbling it without noticing either its form or the taste of the filling.

"*Danke schön.* It's very nice. I never had any good German

588

chocolates," Polya said, trying to keep the strain out of her voice and manner. "Is your other sister an artist too?"

"Oh, Lotta is just a small child. A tender flower on the volcanic soil on which we live. But Ursula is a great artist of the new times." He lit the lighter and gazed for a long time at the smokeless flame. "Which art do you prefer, shading or high light?"

"Personally, I prefer high light," Polya said at random, swallowing at last with horror the bitten piece of fascist chocolate which had half-melted in her mouth.

Her preferences in pictorial art did not seem to fall in with the officer's, but fortunately, this threatened no serious consequences for the time being.

"Well yes, high light has always had a larger public, I suppose. Well, well. Everything will be fine. Don't be afraid," he said and extinguished the flame. "Now tell me please, Apollinaria, what were you doing in the positions of the German tank unit?" And because Polya maintained an uneasy silence, he leaned over to her across the table with a jubilant air. "Well, Moscow, tell me, eh?"

It was his first unexpected peck, and this time the phrase came easy to him; at times, though, Polya ceased to notice the incongruity of his Russian.

"Oh no, I just happen to be passing. It's true that I come from Moscow, but everyone now is running away from Moscow because of the air raids, no one's doing any work at all. It's simply *schrecklich*, just *schrecklich!* Ever since my own place was bombed out I've been sitting about in shelters for nearly a week. I nearly got ill. On top of it all, they haven't been issuing bread rations. I was knocked senseless by a blast and lay in the snow for two hours." Taking a deep breath she plunged into a long story about the blazing, besieged, devastated Soviet capital.

Her first-hand impressions of the direct bomb hit in Blagoveshchensky Alley now came in useful to her. The knowledge that it was for a good cause made her invent some highly coloured scenes of the Moscow debacle embellished with details that were capable of satisfying the most impatient imagination in Germany. She managed a very lurid description of how she had stumbled through the panic-stricken crowds of refugees amid the smoking ruins of the city. She did not spare even her favourite Kremlin belfry, lanky Ivan in the golden helmet, whom she toppled straight into the river, although she was not quite sure whether it would get that far in falling. Good God, why a stone would understand, if it had a heart, that the only thing left for her to do was to make a dash through snow-drifts and road-blocks straight for the Yenga, to the warmth of her mother's knees. Quite appropriately, she gave a little sniff towards the end that wasn't quite a sob yet, in case Kittel wanted to send her back to that hell again, then suddenly she felt upon herself his intent examining gaze—with the horror a tiny insect would feel, if it could, under a gleaming eye looking down at it through the tube of a microscope.

"That is not true, Apollinaria," Walter Kittel said in a sad sinister tone. "Now tell me. In what place is your mother?"

"She is quite near, she lives in the Pashutino range. Good God, fancy saying my mother isn't true! You can check it up if you like, everyone knows her here. There's her photograph on your table ... may I have it back?" Growing bolder, she stretched her arm out, not to take it, but to test his intentions in regard to herself by his refusal or permission.

Without answering, he moved the Colt aside on the table and groped about with a pencil amid the vastness of Pustosha until he found the tiny dot on the map that was Pashutino. Then he ran the point of the pencil up the road and looked up at Polya. She saw then with dismay what had been her undoing. This officer, too, knew that the turning to Pashutino, which she had left behind her, was a good quarter of an hour's walk from the place where she had been arrested. From this point of the road her legend was disposed of, and now, short of a miracle, nothing could save her.

"You must have got me wrong then, *Herr Offizier. Ich wollte zu meine Mutter kommen ... es ist so schrecklich dort in Moskau von deutschen Bomben. Und ich war schon in Walde, aber ein alter russischer Mann mit lange weisse Bart hat mir gesagt, dass sie hier, in Schichanow Yam, zu eine kranke Frau gefahren ist!*"* She got mixed up in the conjugations, and coming to the end of her tether, fell silent.

He listened to her with a grimace on his face, as if he had a toothache.

---

* I was going to see my mother. It's terrible there in Moscow from the German bombs. I was in the forest there already, but a Russian old man with a long white beard told me that she had gone here to Shikhanov Yam to visit a sick woman. (Spoken in school German.)

"*Nein*, Apollinaria. Better speak Russian."

Nevertheless, wishing to complete the investigations, he rang a bell; Langer, who had searched Polya, appeared at once. She shrank and drew her head into her shoulders, prepared for the worst, but nothing happened. The officer merely rapped out a short command, of which she could not make out a single word beyond the peremptory "*schnell!*" tossed off at the end.

"*Das ist nicht wahr*. It is not true. Speak not German, speak Russian, Apollinaria," Walter Kittel repeated with a bored air. "That is called leading a dance up the garden path."

He paused for about a minute while he examined the photograph of Polya's mother.

"Tell me, Apollinaria, is this your mother?"

"Yes, her name's Yelena Ivanovna."

"So. Why is she laughing?"

Polya shrugged her shoulders. "How do I know. I wasn't born yet."

"A handsome woman." Then suddenly he pecked again. "Well, where did you pass the front, show me."

Polya stood up and touched the map with her finger. Indeed, in the conditions of war and a blizzardy night, everything was possible in that impenetrable part of Pustosha.

"I went through the forest most of the time. I was afraid of meeting soldiers."

"How is it the soldiers let you through?"

"Well, I suppose they had heart enough to understand why and where a person was going to. I even gave one of them my mittens—you know, those things you wear on your hands in winter," she added, noticing the blank look on his face.

"You are a very young girl, Apollinaria. Bellona does not like children running about underfoot. Children should sleep when Bellona goes about her business. Now tell me the truth"—he pointed his finger at her like a pistol. "Where were you going?"

"Oh, heavens, there you go again!" cried Polya, on the verge of tears. "Haven't I been telling you that I was going to Mamma! I haven't made a secret of the fact that I come from Moscow, have I? I don't want to lose my life for nothing with *them*, not if I can help it! Why should I have to answer for the world mess they've been trying to make! Why, if it comes to that...."

The irritation with which he tapped the table with his lighter pulled Polya up dead in her tracks. Apparently he felt hurt in his best feelings. The sheer masculine soldierly pluck with which the Russian girls tried to slip through the narrow loopholes of the front under his eyes astonished the officer. Apart from the object for which they had undoubtedly been sent behind the German lines, he simply wanted to know what prize it was that drove them to certain and obscure death, what reward they received for their valour in a land where gold was despised and personal immortality was not believed in. Polya did not know then that two other Russian girls who had failed to break through to Loshkarev had sat in this same place before her on separate occasions. They were a bit older than Polya, and therefore, in Kittel's view, more hardened in the deadly sins of Bolshevism, which accounted for the interrogation having been a failure. He had put them, too, in the test tube of psychological investigation, testing them alternately with the syrups of hope and gratitude and the acids of terror and pain before splashing them out into non-being. But with those others he had shared neither his views about the gifts of sister Ursula nor the sweets which he had received as a present from the world's blondest Aryan angel, Lotta Kittel. Truly, one had to have a callous heart not to repay such trust by mutual frankness. He had had a feeling that this quiet winter evening would yield to him the most precious philosophic revelations about present-day Russia.

"*Nein!* Now listen to me. Apollinaria. You are a Russian *soldat*," he said, raising a hand to ward off possible protest. "*Dir ist aufgetragen hier durchzukommen, mir—dich nicht durchzulassen.* Fate will explain ... *das Schicksal wird entscheiden, wer von uns wichtiger ist für's Leben.** Yes, so. You want to light the torch of freedom all over the world, when the rich will not oppress the poor. And willingly undergo all hardships. Your aim is to spread working-class unity through the world. Mine is the enjoyment of shooting. Yes, so. I am an officer of Great Germany. The nations are quiet when she walks through Europe. I am full of my own restraint, but I am not limited by any er ... *predubezhdenie*—prejudices." He brought the barbarous word out with a manful effort. "My action is based also on the development of spiritual life, *aber, ich glaube,* people are drawn together *nur* by means of spiritual ties. Optical experience in this country is not enough for me. I want to read Russian people like a book.

---

* It is for you to come through here, for me not to let you pass. Fate will decide which of us is more life-worthy.

Now look. Night. Stars. A big Russian forest. No one else about. Here, er... well, *hier kreuzen sich unsere Wege.** Tomorrow we shall forget *unser Zusammensein*** for ever, you and I. *Die Wahrheit wird geboren, wo grosse Gegner offen miteinander streiten.**** Now we shall speak face on face, we shall have a heart on heart talk. Apollinaria. *Man muss den Gegner achten, der ja auch sein Leben aufs Spiel setzt. Verstehst du,***** Apollinaria?"

*"O, ja, ich verstehe,"****** she hastened to say in the most earnest tone, understanding absolutely nothing of his words or intentions.

Actually, it was nothing more than the desire of a fascist superman to subdue and logically crush her by his superiority, to put her on her knees, submissive, awed by the grandeur of his family and civic virtues, and then to crack her skull open when she least of all expected it. But the very fact that he had not done so at the outset, but tarried, consequently showing that he needed her for some reason, gave Polya a ray of hope, if not absolute confidence in a happy issue. The thing now was to attack without losing a moment, before she went under, borne down by his steady pressure, before he gave another death-dealing peck in a fit of birdlike fury.

"Well, quick, answer. Apollinaria. Don't swim in dog's fashion."

Some sudden force catapulted her from her seat, and she was no longer dismayed by the ironic glance from the other end of the black tube.

"I've been trying to tell you all the evening, but you won't let me get a word in! Why should I swim in dog's fashion before you?" she jumped down his throat, seized with a frenzy of lying inspiration born of sheer despair—a freak storm amid a brief shower of genuine tears. "I'd like to see what tune you would sing if you had to sit in an unheated cellar for a whole week with the bombs dropping all round you. If you want to know my mother was a Russian landowner, a boyar, if that means anything to you. She rode about in a gold carriage ever since a child. There! And he gives me a sweet and calls me

---

* Our paths cross here.
** Our meeting.
*** Truth is born from the clash of great adversaries.
**** One must have respect for one's adversary who is staking his life as well. Do you understand?
***** Yes, I understand.

names—Komsomol girl! If it wasn't for the Bolsheviks, maybe I'd be in Berlin now, drinking coffee with wafers. Maybe I'd be going about in furs and Valenciennes. And what am I now? Look at me!" And stepping back with fine abandon she hitched up her bit of skirt and showed her bruised swelling knee. "They've treated my father shamefully, too, he daren't raise his head, and I've cried my eyes out over him. They used to shun me even at school. Isn't it trachoma you've got, Polya, they'd ask me. Come on, then, shoot me!"

On the whole it was fairly convincing, occasionally, perhaps, a bit too plausible. Polya could have gone on reopening the festering wounds caused by Gratsiansky's insinuations, which had entered her soul like dirty splinters. If she suddenly fell silent it was not because she had run dry, but because she was struck dumb by the thought that the old world would believe her, would take pity on her, and spare her because of her unheard-of apostasy. She could vividly picture them all listening to her—not only Osminov, but the whole Great Patriotic War, from generals to privates, even the wounded in the hospitals, the irreconcilable Dementyev among them. And they all had sad fatherly faces, but did they understand that she was not doing this to save her own insignificant life, which had already separated from her, as it were, and now lay on Kittel's table next to that pebble, which was as precious to her as her mother's photograph.

3

Someone's heavy breathing behind her made her turn round. In the doorway, besides the bald Langer, there was a stranger—a broad-shouldered grey old man in a wind-breaker thrown over an ungirdled shirt; apparently, he had been dragged out of bed and rushed off to the officer's dugout at a smart trot. His chest was innocent of any burnished badges or medals awarded for treacherous deeds, but one could tell by his narrowed eyes and his cool grave mien that he was the starosta, who had been called out to check Polya's deposition. Beyond taking his cap off, he did not salute or bend before the officer, and merely stared down at his feet with sombre dignity.

"What's the matter?" he grumbled in the tone of a man who knows that he is needful. "Won't there be another day tomorrow that you have to start things at night! The sky's clearing up," he added, sustaining Kittel's scowling glance. "Mind the Soviet bombers don't start the music!"

As if to confirm this, the muffled thud of a distant explosion was heard, and simultaneously concentric circles began running in the glass on the table. For several moments all four of them, with different feelings, listened to the hush that ensued, but unfortunately or fortunately, nothing followed. It was simply the war stirring sleepily. Kittel took a sip at the foamy cap in the glass and made a sign to Langer not to go away. The interrogation proceeded.

It should be said that this officer did not agree with his Führer's tactics towards Russia, neither did he approve of Napoleon, who had underestimated the spontaneous significance of the peasant sea. All the more mistaken did he consider his Hauptführer to be in declaring the Slav multitude beforehand to be just a compost heap for the German race. In his opinion, the operation Barbarossa should have been launched with lulling political declarations, and afterwards, when the German garrisons would have been set on their legs locally, they could grip that multitude by the throat with an iron hand and rationally distribute them, some to be used as beasts of burden, others as fertilisers.

With this long-range objective in view, Walter Kittel did not tease the Russian muzhiks as other invaders had done, but, on the contrary, treated them rather leniently, joked with them, and never missed a chance to show off his garbled knowledge of Russian proverbs, such as "near is my shirt, but nearer is a skirt". It goes without saying, during his fortnight's stay in Russia he had not had time yet to win the heart of this stubborn people, but in his letters to his sister Ursula he already boasted of his intimacy with an old inhabitant of the Yenga—the present starosta of Shikhanov Yam—who had been a prisoner of war in Germany a quarter of a century ago and had suffered at the hands of the Soviets. In his turn, the starosta did not shun conversation with the high-ranking occupationist, although, more often than not, he did not air his views on politics, either because he was uncertain about the outcome of the war, or because he was understandably shy in the presence of his influential patron. At any rate, he had accepted the position of starosta after some hesitation, and Walter Kittel was all the more proud of his victory, since the harder it is to recruit a traitor the more he is worth.

"Ah, *bauer*!"* Kittel said in a friendly tone, waving his hand. "How goes it with you? What are people saying these days?"

"So, so, I can't complain," the starosta said, looking away and touching his grizzled beard. "There's a hitch with you, though, I hear. If you ask me, it doesn't look as if you'll be in Moscow by Christmas."

"Never mind. All is good. Thank you," Kittel said tight-lipped. "More haste less hay. Take a seat."

He motioned with his eyes to the second wood block by the desk and flipped a cigarette across the desk towards the old man. The latter declined it.

"I'd rather smoke my own, this is much too sweet for my tooth. As for what people are saying, what can you expect 'em to say nowadays. They don't say anything, they just think. Nowadays they've driven their thoughts deep inwards. Aye!"

He got out a patchwork tobacco pouch and coolly began to roll himself a thick makhorka cigarette, and although Kittel could fell any tree in that forest with impunity, he bore the stink and defiance without a word. Polya could not help recalling the fire hysteria of the German block-house at the Tenth Division the previous night.

"Here is a Russian girl. Apollinaria. She likes very much to look at German tanks. You are an old inhabitant. Take this. Who is it?"

The starosta took the photograph and began searching for his glasses.

"Ah yes, I heard about her kicking up a dust here ... they're such a sharp lot these days. Pasha Khromtsov boasted that he had caught another one. Well my girl, you're in for it. Rotten business. Why do you have to stick your heads right in the fire? Couldn't you sit at home in the chimney corner and wait till it all blows over? I don't know what's got into people these days." He managed at last to fit a missing glass into the frame of his spectacles, and although Polya was afraid to look at him, she saw out of the corner of her eye that the hand which held the photograph shook momentarily. "Well, well, what a place to meet!"

"Well, *bauer*, tell me, do you know that woman?"

"To be sure I do. She's our feldsher, Yelena Ivanovna, in her young days. This picture was taken in my presence, I had one

---

* Peasant.

like it at home. I was standing here at the side, but they've cut me out, it seems. I suppose I didn't fit into the frame. That's her all right, Yelena Ivanovna." Then, struck by a sudden thought, he ran his eye sharply over Polya. "You're not her daughter by any chance, lass?"

Polya turned away with a pained air. She could well afford to do so, as things had worked out in her favour. On the truth or falseness of any part of the evidence would depend whether Kittel, after the manner of all examiners the world over, would correspondingly believe or doubt the authenticity of the rest.

"So, so. Was she rich? Tell me."

"Well, as regards timberland they were considered the richest folks on the Yenga. It was a fine property, but the mistress let it go for a whistle to make ends meet. Oblog was cut down in my day—her father and I were kids at the time," he said jerking his head towards Polya, and keeping his eyes on the photograph all the time. "Yes, a lot of life has flowed since then, all of it, if you ask me. The lady herself was a German, and she didn't understand much about Russian ways ... a bit of a greenhorn, you know. Well, a merchant came down from St. Petersburg and just twisted her round his little finger. Cheated her out of a pretty big sum, he did. My old man was green with envy, couldn't forgive himself as long as he lived."

Kittel did not miss a word of all this, and gazed reflectively at the flame of his lighter. These new circumstances put a different look on things, and apparently he felt justified in putting all further questions in his own language.

"*Warum has du mir verheimlicht, dass du deutsche Angehörige hast?*"*

His voice sounded more gentle, and Polya felt a heady exhilaration. Things were adjusting themselves, and it occurred to her rather prematurely that no great harm would be done if she was half a day late in Loshkarev. From that moment, though, she had to press home her advantage without letting up.

"You would have believed me still less, then. It's your job to suspect people of all the vile things under the sun. Why, if I were to tell you everything I went through there, both of you would start blubbering over my poor life. There!"

"So, so, very good," Kittel drawled gently, rolling Polya's peb-

---

* Why didn't you tell me that you have German relations?

597

ble about in his fingers, *"Und was willst du tun, wenn du erst mal bei deiner Mutter bist?"**

"I'll find something to do. I'll start giving Russian lessons, if need be ... if only to you! Don't you worry, I'll make my living, I won't go abegging."

"That's so, yes. Thank you, Apollinaria. *Und wenn wir in Europa mit den Bolschewisten aufräumen, wirst du dann auch zu ihnen zurück schlüpfen?"***

"Pardon me ... *was, was sagen Sie?"**** Polya said, leaning forward with a puzzled air.

"I said that when we clean up the Bolsheviks, you will *bei Nacht und Nebel* slip back to them *wie ein Schmuggler?"*****

To show her independence, Polya shrugged her shoulders with a pained air.

"Why should I? I can stay with you, provided they treat me nicely. As it is, one made himself a present of my mittens, another went and ruined my shoes with a chisel. What am I going to show myself to Mamma in now? You can't blame a person for getting *zurück* ideas into his head! I'm a free bird. If I escaped from the Bolsheviks, I'll fly away from you too!"

"Very interesting, very. Apollinaria. Do you like our Germany? Tell me."

Polya's ruse was not to yield at once, but to keep up the pretence and thus rise in his estimation.

"How am I to know? How can I like her or dislike her when I've never been there? You're the first German I've ever spoken to."

"Oh, you will see it, Apollinaria. No, not Berlin, that is a young city. But the Rhine ... it is not a river, it is the home of the German spirit. All Germans have a deep love for the Rhine, where the boundaries of poetry and reality mingle together." The names of Rhine places burbled in his throat, the last of them accompanied by a wild gleam from the depths of his sunken eyes. "Oh, Boppard, Sankt Goar, Loreley ... and Köln. Its ancient name is Colonia Agrippina *weisst du? Und dann schlisslich—München, unsere Isar-Athen.* The Führer told me himself ... *hat mir mal persönlich gesagt: die Erschaffung der Welt hat mit Mün-*

---

* And what do you intend to do when you get to your mother?
** And when we clean the Bolsheviks up in Europe, you will run over to them again?
*** What, what do you say?
**** On a dark stormy night ... like a smuggler.

chen begonnen, als Gott noch nicht müde war.[*] The river Isar runs from the hills. It has a milky appearance. Oh, you will dizzy your head, Apollinaria! In Germany there are many enjoyments and a lot of fun from gay flirtations. In Germany also there are young people who get pleasure in each other. You may marry a businessman or a *Erbhofbauer, und sogar* a German *pension-berechtigten Beamten.*"[**] He laughed in a tickled sort of way at the mention of such a fascinating career, which no sensible girl in the world could resist. "Well, does that suit you? *Sagt dir das zu?* Apollina-aria!

"No it doesn't suit me," Polya said, forcing a wan smile into her face. "I'll find a boy myself, somehow."

She had special reasons for so defiantly rejecting the German happiness that was offered to her. At that moment the field telephone on the table began buzzing. Langer picked up the receiver, stood listening in silence, then without waiting for leave, went out quickly to issue orders. A violent flurry of anti-aircraft gunfire accompanied by a confused roar broke in upon the silence of the dugout through the open door. It was like the voice of the forest in a tempest, and although it did not yet mean salvation, the very feeling that a powerful friend was close at hand gave Polya a premature sense of confidence in the happy outcome of her adventure. First of all, she was borne down by the weight of the shameful motives for running away, which she had taken upon her shoulders, motives which put her on the same level as the starosta. He was sitting next to her, his huge idle hands with the unlighted cigarette dangling between his knees. It was more than simple aversion towards a traitor, rather was it a sense of superstitious revulsion at body-to-body contact with a corpse. She was seized with an urgent clamorous need to dissociate herself from him, even at the risk of her own life, to reassert her dignity. The opportunity was not long in coming.

Sensing perhaps the contempt of this defenceless Russian slip of a girl, or foreseeing the further course the interrogation would take, or from a sense of shame before Ivan Vikhrov, although his name had not been mentioned so far, the starosta got up to go away. The officer checked him with an imperious gesture.

"*Nein.* Sit here, *bauer.*" Then suddenly, he picked Polya's cher-

* And lastly Munich, our Athens on the Isar. The Führer told me himself that creation started with Munich, while God was not tired yet.
** ... a farmer, and even a pensionable civil servant.

ished pebble off the table between two fingers and held it up to her. "*Was soll das?*"*

"Oh, it's just ... just to make life easier. Don't be afraid, it won't explode," Polya said, smiling, when Kittel held the pebble over the flame of his lighter at arm's length for investigatory purposes.

"Oh, I understand. Apollinaria. A talisman?"

Any answer she gave now would have passed for the truth, but just then there came a shattering explosion, the most violent so far, and the earth around shuddered. Something fell down behind the screen. All this together goaded her to a piece of audacity that was to be her undoing.

"Not quite a talisman," she laughed. "I picked it up in the roadway in Moscow as a keepsake. I may be a runaway but I'm still a Russian a bit." And as if she had not said enough, she showed her teeth in a smile, showed slightly more of them than was permitted to one in her position.

The very thing Osminov had most dreaded happened. He had not doubted Polya's courage, he had doubted her ability to keep up a lie. Polya understood that she was likely to pay for this admission with her life, but then it took some of the weight off her mind. The starosta glanced at her sharply out of the corner of his eye, then rested his elbows on his knees and hung his head.

The officer looked very thoughtful. It was the first revelation that evening, a revelation about Soviet people of which nothing was mentioned in the supersecret circulars of the General Staff. Polya's pebble certainly weighed immeasurably more than its mere substance! Kittel had not seen such souvenirs among his soldiers during the war, and although he would never think of putting this girl on a level with his sister, he asked himself whether it would have occurred to that best girl of his class, Lotta Kittel, to carry away in her bosom a bit of plaster, say, from Munich's holy of holies, the Frauenkirche, even if she were leaving the country for ever.

At moments the bomb explosions sounded so near that trickles of sand oozed through the chinks in the timbered ceiling. Then the sounds of the air raid began to die away; having done their work, the Soviet squadrons were apparently returning to their base. Kittel's mocking eyes held hers as he dropped the pebble into his breast pocket with the intention of showing his amusing

_____
* What is this?

600

trophy when next reporting at the Reichskanzlei, to some of those who were prone to minimise the difficulties of the Eastern campaign. He gazed at her long and steadily, and Polya began to feel like a mouse under the eye of a big German cat with a university education.

The sinister silence was broken by the starosta, who stirred uncomfortably.

"Well, you two have it out between you, and I'll go and get some sleep," he said with an attempt to show his independence. It was meant for Polya Vikhrova, but he said this in the tone of one asking leave of Kittel.

The officer simply took no notice of the traitor's faint-heartedness, which was quite natural under the circumstances, and Polya remembered, through her terror, how that mountain of bone and flesh slowly sank back into its seat in obedience to a barely perceptible flick of the German finger.

"You are a good girl. You can be useful to Germany. Only cruel people could send you into the hands of Walter Kittel." His face grew sad and gentle before he took his next peck. "Now tell me, what headquarters sent you? Everything will be nice and quiet for you. *Aber* you must answer quickly when a German officer speaks to you. Apollinaria," he said, rapping on the table.

Polya looked up. She felt choky, and her shoulders sagged. She read in the face of the officer confronting her a promise of the most refined unpleasantness a Nazi superman was capable of inflicting with the aid of long experience and the achievements of medicine. With an inner eye, as if through a veil of darkness, she read a line and a half about herself in the as yet non-existent communiqué of Informbureau. "So this is what the real thing is like!" she thought, ready to get up and go barefooted wherever she had to go now, and then the whole world rocked around her, shaken by what was probably one of the biggest bombs used in modern warfare.

It was followed by other explosions, slightly muffled ones, which then started to move round the dugout like the footfalls of a giant groping blindly over the ground for some treasure he had lost. The Soviet planes, then, had not deserted Polya for a minute; maybe they had come only for her sake, come to salute an obscure Russian girl who was going out of life. All that Polya wanted now was a direct hit on the dugout. She could wish for no greater generosity than this from fate. And in that last minute that remained to her she had to give utterance to the unchosen exultant words which the magnificent fury of her people's weapon thundering up there in the skies awakened in her.

She would never have been able to remember them or repeat them.

"All right, try your teeth on our iron, and we'll see what kind of grinders you have," Polya began almost in a whisper, burning her bridges. "You just said that I was fighting for the Bolsheviks. Oh, I wish I was! But I'm no soldier. I'm just a spent bullet, I didn't have the strength to reach my target. No, it's they who are fighting for me day and night, day and night they are fighting for me while I am only taking lessons from them for the time being, and helping them as best I can, so that I won't feel ashamed of my youth afterwards in face of the dead. It's easy enough to kill me. You'll pluck one pine needle from the tree, but look how many will remain, how many, I tell you. You can't bury all of them! No, you can't smoke us off the planet now, it's too late— *zu spät, verstehen Sie?*"* Her moist row of teeth flashed in a turnip-white grin.

"Not so quick, please. Apollina-aria," said Kittel with the face of a researcher patiently accepting the vagaries of scientific experiment.

"Yes, there are more of us, because we are the human race. Ah, if you weren't here, if you weren't here at all! You've dirtied and polluted everything around you, even the water which the children drink . . . even the water! But never mind, we can wait . . . the world has lots of time! You just asked me who I am? I'm a girl of my epoch, and even though I'm only an ordinary one, I'm the world's future . . . and you ought to stand up when you speak to me, stand up, if you had the least bit of self-respect! But you sit there in front of me, because there's nothing human left in you. . . . You're just a horse trained by the head executioner. Well, what are you sitting there for, do your work . . . take me away, show me where you shoot Soviet girls here?"

At that moment she was older and wiser than her age. Rather was she ageless, like Volodya Ankudinov. And she was more beautiful than all the other girls of her age, was this snub-nosed little girl from Moscow. All the thoughts, which usually ripen with the years, swarmed round her before their appointed time. It was the same wild rapture, which made her army-coated contemporaries fling themselves under the enemy tanks with grenades

---

* It's too late, do you understand?

602

tied around their bodies, or draw the fire of their own artillery upon themselves. Her jerky agonised speech merged with the mounting tumult of the air attack, so that Kittel at first was quite unable to check it, all the more that things took a rather unexpected turn which completely altered the course of the interrogation.

Polya never knew what came first—the shot itself or the hoarse shout, like a command, "Run for it, lass!" Nor could she account for the behaviour of the Shikhanov starosta. Whether he had fired the shot because his conscience awoke, or because he had a grievance for the wrongs he had suffered as a prisoner of war in Germany, or maybe because he had decided to make his first instalment for some cherished blood of his own left on the Soviet side, Polya was never to know. All she remembered was that he snatched the Colt from the table, and immediately afterwards she saw a smoking hole in Kittel's eye-socket. It was the second revelation that evening for the educated and curious German officer, and it is to be hoped that before his inquisitive mind went blank he realised how much there was still unexplored in the Russian forest.

The sound of the shot mingled with a fresh rain of bombs which shook the roof, and all would have gone well probably if Kittel's assistant had not appeared in the doorway just then. Something about his commander's appearance—he was still sitting—must have struck him as odd. The starosta's second bullet missed Langer, and then they both grappled and rolled over the floor, while Polya dashed past them and out of the door, leaving them to fight it out between them.

4

The air raid was in full swing. The frozen ground was lacerated with vicious crashes, and the most ruthless timber-felling went on all round. In the thicket on the left a tank-truck with petrol was blazing, and in the gap between the black leaning trunks the licking flames could be seen rubbing cat-like against the sides of another paralysed truck. Stumbling, staggering at each step, Polya was returning to life. She could not remember how long she ran. All the world had hidden itself—stars and human beings alike. Only when she left the scene of battle and plunged for the last time under the black smoke fringe into a small clearing, was she nearly knocked over by a man, clutching his head and looking bloodier even than Kittel, unless it was the glow of the flames which he carried upon himslef. He dashed past without seeing her, moaning and screaming in a foreign tongue. This time it was given to Polya to witness his end, when, utterly exhausted, she leaned against a wattle fence and looked back. Suddenly the air above Shikhanov Yam burst like a steel drum and a falling pine struck down the occupationist, while a hot gust mixed with snow dust was driven into Polya's face. She retained no memory of that last half hour beyond an impression that the world was tumbling down, cut at the roots. During those minutes she felt neither fear nor the joy of deliverance. The pain in her knee, intensified by her fall, brought her awake to the present. She glanced first at her bare benumbed feet and her stockings, torn to shreds, then at her mother's crushed photograph in her hand, which she had automatically snatched up in running away. Her next thought was to continue on her way to Loshkarev, but now the timid human leaflet had known the ecstasy of movement on the very crest, outracing everything in the world, even time itself.

Nearby something stood out darkly under a heavy overhanging snow-drift. It was more like a manhole than a dugout. Polya went down the ice-covered slopped steps, pushed a squealing door with her knee, and bending her head peered into the stuffy peasant's dwelling. There seemed to be nothing there but an orange-tinted murk with a long flame at the edge swaying on a thread of sooty smoke.

"What living soul has God brought there now? Come in and shut the door. The baby will catch cold," a voice sounded from within the room, and Polya entered, yielding herself trustfully, like a leaflet to its wise and masterful river.

In the middle of the room, in fulfilment of life, an ancient woman was bathing a little girl in as ancient a wooden washing trough. She was performing it unhurriedly and gravely like a religious rite which no war dared to interfere with. All the rest was in keeping with it—the dented samovar with its lopsided burnished lid which stood smoking on the earthen floor, and an old man's smothered cough from under a sheepskin by the wall, responding monotonously, like amens, to the thunderclaps of the bombs.

"May I have a drink of water from the bucket, Grandma?" Polya began tentatively with chattering teeth.

She was not at all thirsty, and the old woman instantly caught in her voice that touch of humility, the countersign of sorrow by which the people, from time immemorial, recognise beggars, victims of fires, and wanderers. And after the manner of all peasants, the woman did not turn round until she had finished what she was doing and wrapped the child up in a warm piece of sack-cloth.

"Whose girl are you? Not a local, by the looks of it? I don't seem to remember your face," she said, handing Polya a dipper. "Where did you get your clothes torn like that? It wasn't the dogs, my child, surely?" the old woman added pityingly, glancing at Polya's feet, then looked away.

"I've come all the way from Moscow to see my mother," Polya said, forgetting about the drink and sinking on to a bench. "Do you mind if I sit here a bit? I'm so tired after my journey, Grandma."

Possibly the old woman had heard something about another passing girl having been caught. Everything about this one—her torn clothes, her bare feet, and stuttering speech—confirmed her suspicions. Without asking any questions, she seated the visitor at the table, warmed up a cup of hot water for her, shared her porridge scrapings with her, and never before or after had Polya received from her people such generous gifts. In between, Polya asked about her mother; the old woman had often been treated at the Pashutino hospital, and that drew her and Polya still closer together. No, nothing was known in Shikhanov Yam about the fate of the feldsher, who had disappeared from Pashutino a month and a half before. Maybe, Yelena Ivanovna had moved over to Chernetsov's for old time's sake, and so Polya now had a legitimate excuse for going to Loshkarev.

She asked to hold the baby, just for luck.

"What a sweet little girl, she's like a little carrot," Polya said, dandling the child, grateful for the hospitality. "Clever, too, she doesn't cry at all."

"They're all quiet these days, the children are. They're weak with hunger. They don't make a noise like they used to, and they don't run about ... they play sitting down. We were getting along so nicely till these wicked men came and took everything away from us down to the last chicken. Looks like it's your turn now, you poor girls," the woman said and cried a bit, but without tears and quite soundlessly, as if she were laughing.

Polya laid the baby in the cradle, sat down beside the old woman and took her hand in hers.

"Don't you worry, Grandma, we'll get the better of them, yet. You can't put out the sun!" This and a great deal more she said, putting all of herself into her whisper. "They'll answer for it all, you wait!"

"That's just the trouble, my dear. It's not just myself I'm worrying about. Look what they're doing—you'd think they had seven lives! They'll bring trouble upon themselves. Like as not they have little ones of their own." And then from her anguish was born that famous phrase, which was to reach the rotary press by way of hundreds of lips, about all the children in the world crying in the same language. "If only we old ones could have just a peep at that sun of yours!"

"You'll live to see it, Grandma. Nothing in the world happens before its time," Polya said, involuntarily falling into the tone of the common people. Her tongue barely obeyed her and drowsiness began to steal over her, for she was all soaked by now in the cosy warmth of the home. She gazed at the shadow of the cradle, slung from a pole, as it rocked hypnotically over the head of the old man lying by the wall. "Is Grandpa ailing, or just having a rest?"

As it happened she was sitting in his patched felt boots with his sheepskin over her shoulders, revelling in the flickering oil wick that did service for a lamp and the stuffy warmth of the primitive dwelling as if the world had no greater blessings to offer man. Polya did not hear the old woman's answer; her cheeks were flaming and the desire for sleep was overpowering, try as Osminov would to make her get up.

"You'd better go before it quietens down, or they'll start snooping around again," he whispered into Polya's ear in the voice of the old woman.

Polya stood up and rubbed her face with her hands as if she were washing it.

"I'll drop in to see you, Grandma, when it's all over ... if I'm still alive, that is," she said, and asked for an old pair of boots to go out in.

The old woman made her keep the clothes she had given her.

"My old man won't need 'em any more, he'll be going soon," she explained. "They kept driving him out to work in the forest, and you can't keep alive for long on skillygalee. First his eyes went bad with pus—nerves, they said it was—and then he got it in the legs. That's all right, he'd had his use of 'em. Don't turn off on the Shastirev cart-track, the Germans are taking hay there. You'd better keep to the autobahn, you'll be safe then. Ah, you poor lass!" And because she had nothing else to give her at parting, she made the sign of the cross over her a couple of times. "Come, go your way...take care of your neck, you poor little leaf!"

The words were like the breath of a searing flame to Polya, and she clearly pictured to herself the unwritten book of her Loshkarev adventure gradually contracting through the years first to the size of a page, then a paragraph, until it was reduced to this single line—this last parting word of her motherland. The tempest was still raging, smashing up the last remnants of enemy iron somewhere in the thickets. The local anti-aircraft guns were silent. The work was coming to an end. Anyone in Polya's place would have distinguished in the exultant purr of the engines, "Go, go about your urgent state business, Polya Vikhrova. Go without fear, even if something should whizz over your head, because the thing that is whizzing is ours, yours. Go without a backward look, and we'll hold them up in the meantime for an hour or so."

Blue gloom hung in front of her with nothing in it—neither the glow of fires nor the headlights of belated cars. The stars, at first timorously, lighted up in the rising wind, which at times could be seen blowing aside their prickly blue flame. Polya recollected Rodion's assertion, repeatedly made in his poems, that the biggest stars shone not in the desert, nor in the Arctic, but at home on the Yenga.

5

The last few miles were the hardest. Sometimes she dozed off, walking, no longer caring what happened to her. What with frequent stoppages and waits she did not reach her destination until the close of the next day. Faint with hunger and fatigue, she had to wait a long time for her opportunity, lying half-frozen behind a snowbank, while the sun sank behind the little town. It lay spread before her at the foot of the hill, and although the frost stiffened towards the evening no wisps of smoke, bluish against the sunset sky, could be seen anywhere to gladden the eye of the traveller. Luckily, the mobilised inhabitants were returning from their trench-digging work, each carrying a sheaf that had lain unthreshed since the autumn, while some of the bolder ones carried three. When the straggling procession drew level with the ditch, Polya joined the tail end of it. She offered one of the women to help her with her burden, and so a poor sheaf with glassy wheat ears served Polya as a pass in the eyes of the German sentries.

The little town was visible from end to end of its main street. At its far end the glow of sunset was fading in the sky. Curfew hour was approaching, bringing with it new troubles for Polya. She did not meet a living soul, and there was not a ray of light behind the shutters, as if to reassure the German town major that every living thing had submitted, died out, and at any rate had little to do with the job of living. She barely dragged herself along, reading the new street names at the corners with difficulty. The sky was darkening in the west when she came at last to Great Germany Prospekt. It used to be Pushkin Street, all gay with gardens, through which Polya ran countless times on her way to school. Now razed to the ground by fire, long and empty, it looked like a mine laid out flat. The secret address which Osminov had given her suspiciously coincided with the house Polya herself had lived in. It was queer to have to take precautions in entering the familiar courtyard and to knock at her own window after making sure that the fuchsia she had planted herself a year ago in an old can was still standing on the right where she had placed it.

A strange woman let Polya in. Drawing her torn shawl about her she listened in an unfriendly manner to Polya's request to see the bootmaker, then ushered her into a chilly dining-room, calling out to somebody down the corridor in a shrill voice that she hadn't hired herself out to open the door to every night bird that came flying in. A grey-haired man in spectacles with an unkempt beard sat bent over a boot, which he was stitching in the light of an oil wick. Polya had the impression that he had sat down at his bench only a minute before she came in. Nothing there contradicted the logic of wartime life, yet at the same time everything was extremely unusual, especially the expensive leather suitcase without its lid, which had been cut up for soles. Without straightening his back the bootmaker glanced at Polya over the top of his glasses with a wild look in his eyes. It was Chernetsov, looking as if he had been through ten years of hell since he had seen Polya off to Moscow. His face was set in hard stricken lines, and expressed anything but the joy of meeting.

"What do you want?" he said, although he must have recognised her at once; he then added, without looking up, that he was full up with work and couldn't take any more boots to mend.

Polya stood there, so disconcerted by the chill welcome that she felt like crying. Nevertheless she remembered to say, with a lump in her throat, that she wanted to order a pair of evening shoes with elk leather soles for the New Year. Chernetsov answered immediately, as Osminov had warned her when they parted, that he was not expecting to receive any elk leather until next spring. Then both were silent for a while, giving each other time to get used to this new relationship. Still without taking her things off, Polya gave him Osminov's message and the figures which she had memorised without understanding what they stood for. As was expected, the silence of the Loshkarev group was due to the death of the radioman, who had been caught transmitting. Chernetsov reported that judging by rumours and the absence of any consequences to his comrades, he had died well.

It seemed to Polya that this brave clever man, if not actually feeling nervous before her, a chit of a girl, a messenger from the homeland, was trying to justify himself in her eyes. He did not ask anything about her health or show her the kindness he usually did, but neither did he complain. He only looked into her eyes, which were red from lack of sleep, helped her to take her things off and seated her next to the unheated stove.

"Well, now I can greet you. I guessed at once what you came for from your disguise, but how you managed to slip through is more than I can understand," he began vaguely, squeezing her dry chapped hands in his own in order to check the password by their tremor. "Do you want something to eat? No? Well then, let's have the story of your ordeal."

"Do you mind if I have a nap first?" she said, drooping with fatigue. "My head is simply splitting."

"I'm sorry, but you and I are soldiers now. I've got to know what happened to you on the way. You see, this Shikhanov Yam has become the grave of many of our people, some of your closest friends among them."

There was something infinitely flattering in the persistence with which Chernetsov ignored her complaint. She was a real soldier now and no allowances were made for her. Chernetsov listened to her story, shaking his head from time to time. When she got to the starosta's shot, he let go her hand; he was not one to believe in miracles.

"It must be hell for you here," Polya said in dismay after a pause. "I mean, you've gone so grey ... I hardly recognised you from behind."

"Yes, it's quite recent, too, Polya." He turned away and prodded the rough bench with his awl. "You're in danger every minute of the day, even when you sleep. You never know where the shot may come from. But a man gets used to everything, even to the rumble of a volcano under his bed. Did he know you before, that starosta?"

"No, I don't remember him. He must have known Mamma. Why?" Luckily, her thoughts went no further through fatigue. "By the way, who's that woman here—a new lodger? She's so snappy and bad-tempered!"

"Yes, they're a rotten lot. Took two rooms. Her brother's working as proof-reader in the local newspaper. They were installed here through the town major's office. Not a day passes without a row," he complained, glancing at his visitor out of the corner of his eye to see how she took it. Apparently, he was still thinking of Polya's adventures in Shikhanov Yam. "Yes, you were lucky, luckier than most of them."

Polya smiled wryly. She would have been happy indeed had she not been worried about her mother. As if reading her thoughts, Chernetsov gave her the latest reassuring news about her. He had not seen Yelena Ivanovna himself, but he knew definitely that she was alive and well, and was with a partisan unit, which was formed on the Yenga soon after the war broke out. A more welcome reward for all she had been through could hardly have been thought of, and before Chernetsov could pull his hand away Polya's lips had touched it.

"Don't be angry . . . it's just meant for her."

To her surprise he had not yet mentioned a word about his daughter or asked about her, and Polya decided to ask him about Varya herself. At that Chernetsov got up and crossed over to a corner of the room for some tobacco.

"We know practically everything about her now, even the details, painful though they are to those who loved her," he began after a long silence. "I got some of the information directly from people who witnessed her death in order to report it when they got a chance. Her fame belongs to all of us now. Yes, that's exactly what happened, the thing that made you shudder just now. Varya died in that same Shikhanov Yam a week and a half ago . . . she died in the fascist noose." Chernetsov uttered this with death-like calmness, punctuating his story with short pauses. Polya could not remember how long he paused at this point. "That's what I meant by saying you were lucky, Polya, marvellously lucky; you chose such a dangerous route. Eyewitnesses reported that she bore herself very well, like the radioman. She started out with a friend to come here, but we don't know who the other girl was yet. Did you come here through the square?"

"Yes," Polya whispered with white lips.

"Then they must have removed the body already. So you're the only daughter I have now. You'll have to sleep here tonight, it's too late now. Come along, I'll put you up in the old room."

He took the oil lamp off the bench and led the way into Varya's room. Polya limped after him; she would have considered it blasphemy at that moment to ask for some iodine to paint her swollen knee with. He lingered for a long time that night, asking her questions about Moscow, not letting her fall asleep, and on one occasion calling her Varya by mistake.

Half the room was occupied by household utensils that had been piled together here, but Varya's bed stood in its former place. It was terrifying to lie between the same sheets under the familiar quilt, and afterwards to be left alone with the lilies-of-the-valley and the birds on the wallpaper, which had so often heard her confidential talks with Varya. Here, long before she entered the Pedagogical Institute, Varya used to narrate to her favourite passages from the famous book of Darwin's voyages. "Beagle, Beagle ..." Polya called, and there was only one person in the world who could understand and respond to her password. There were no tears yet, no acute realisation of her utter loneliness, but only jealous despair at someone else having shared with Varya her last journey. She lay for a whole hour with open eyes until a numbness that was not sleep spread through her limbs. Gradually the walls began to fade, and the darkness lifted, turning into a misty windless space at the ebb of day and summer. Slim-stemmed trees with flat crowns towering under the very sky stood scattered over sloping hillsides like rising columns of smoke, and it seemed as if Varya was waiting for her there, so imperturbable, real and alive that Polya went forward trustfully to pay her that debt of love and loyalty, which we never manage to pay during a dear one's lifetime. But search as she would, she could not find her, because everything around her was Varya. It was a sensation of nearness more gratifying than that of seeing. And it was not terror that seized her, not poignant yearning for the beloved, but a bright unwonted warmth, akin almost to a dawning light. From this, in turn, was born a calm awareness of her human duties upon earth, that is, maturity.

In the middle of the night the long-drawn creak of the door broke in upon her trance-like sleep. The place smelt strongly of dry wood, as untenanted buildings usually do. A whispering behind the partition made Polya sit up, fully awake. Judging by the voices there were three people there. The woman's voice, as Polya realised after a while with grateful astonishment, belonged to Chernetsov's lodger. She was telling the third person the story of Polya's capture in unexpectedly warm tones; now and again Chernetsov made corrections in the course of the narrative. Only now, when deciphered, did Polya learn the meaning of the secret instructions, which she had brought and which had already cost Varya her life. The respect with which these people spoke about Polya's expedition did not evoke in her the slightest pride in having succeeded. The third one, for his part, retailed the latest news—he must have been the proof-reader from that rag of a newspaper. He said that defensive works were hastily being built on the Yenga at the mouth of the Sklan, and that in Dergachovka the local partisans had tried unsuccessfully to burn fifty tons of grain intended for shipment to Germany. "A little petrol would do the trick," the woman lodger threw in regretfully. "They haven't got any, they haven't set up in business yet," the proof-reader said, adding a minute later that the Germans that morning hanged their starosta in Shikhanov Yam before a small crowd. The old man was said to have put the noose on his neck himself, crossed himself and cursed the invaders in terms whose exact import can only be guessed at. Thus Polya learned the outcome of his fight with Langer after she had run away.

"I suppose he was one of those whose patriotic feeling has got the better of his grudge," Chernetsov said, and switched over immediately to the subject of a certain Katya, who had come to see him that morning with a mending job in the Gauleiter's car. "It was quite an event. The whole street were at the windows."

"How is she?" the proof-reader whispered. "I met her in the street not long ago, she's gone so thin, poor girl."

"I shouldn't say so. On the contrary, I've never known her to look so beautiful," Chernetsov said. "She's keyed up to breaking point, though. I wanted to embrace her, but she wouldn't let me. Don't dirty yourself on me, she said. Complained that she was eating her heart out—you probably heard that Vasya Gladkikh spat in her direction before he died. Judith had plenty of guts, God knows, but even she was given a fair chance, she said. She put her man to sleep on a spring mattress then chopped his head off for him. Those were her very words. How she got to know that biblical story is beyond me."

"You ought to explain to the poor kid, Pavel, that the time hasn't come yet."

"I did. Stick it out, lass, my poor Judith, or I'll sit down and start crying with you. I told her that twice. 'All right,' she said with a proud bitter smile, 'I'm all frozen up inside as it is. If only I could take a peep at a Soviet star from a distance it would keep me going for another year'."

"My brave darling girl!" the woman lodger barely breathed. "What a generation has grown up unnoticed! Tell them to, and they'll fly without wings!"

At times their voices trailed off to a papery crackle. Polya began to feel ashamed of listening to secrets so sublime; at any rate, she understood that she would be ashamed now to tell even her mother, let alone her grandchildren, the story of the trivial dangers she had escaped in her expedition to Loshkarev. She pulled the quilt over her head and fell asleep.

Over their meagre breakfast Chernetsov asked her whether she felt rested, and his voice sounded apologetic and embarrassed.

"I looked in once or twice, but you were fast asleep. You must have taken a lot from the late Kittel, poor girl!"

"No, I wasn't. I heard the floor-boards creak under you, and it seemed as if I was a child again and was being wakened to go to school. I didn't want to get up. By the way, what are they doing now in the school?"

"They have frost-bitten Germans lying there. They're getting their lesson, too, the lesson of disappointment. Well, have you screwed up enough courage for the way back?"

And again, after what she had learned in Loshkarev, Polya could not bring herself to complain about her swollen knee. She simply decided not to look at it until she got back, but every step caused her a stabbing pain in the thigh."

"Oh, I could do twice the distance!" she said in as cheerful a tone as she could muster.

"That will be about the size of it. You'll go back by a round-about way. We've fixed you up overnight a splendid identity card, and even put the hen to it." He explained in passing that that was what they called the German imperial eagle in the underground. "Splendid. Now your lesson, Polya, and off you go!"

Only late in the day, after Polya had learnt the return message for Osminov by heart, did Chernetsov go to see her off as far as the outskirts. At a slight distance apart, she passed through the whole town with him. Not counting the ruins of the monastery on the sandy steep and the not-so-picturesque charred remains of the famous Loshkarev fire-tower, the town had hardly suffered, and looked more spacious, if anything, without the fences and the little wooden houses, which the inhabitants had pulled down for firewood. The deathly shadow of bondage lay even upon the brickbuilt villas of the former Yenga industrialists along the embankment, which had always been indifferent to human woes. In place of the Park of Youth, which had been cut down, brave ranks of squat German crosses were now drawn up under the command of a more imposing leader-cross with an iron helmet on its upright beam. Timid-looking snow-flakes floated in the air which was now noticeably warmer, and the streets with their bread queues and people lined up for some newly announced registration wore the same bleak air of squalor and slavish misery.

The market alone still hummed with life, no louder than a beehive after a cold snap. Polya, in passing, looked closely at the vendors and their wares, because one could best judge from them the level of life among the common people. An ancient woman with swollen legs—the widow of a tsarist government official—all hung about with the property of widowhood like a walking department store, held a handful of loose matches, which she sold by the stick. A thin little girl, who was offering the passers-by her textbooks for the sixth class, followed Polya with a despairing glance, while a greenish-looking man, evidently a local wood-goblin passing himself off as an old rustic, was trying to sell his birch switches for the Russian vapor bath, curtailed to the limits of wartime requirements. Here, with her eyes alone, Polya took leave of Varya's father.

No one stopped the poor slattern on the town's outskirts either; only a freezing sentry looked into Polya's bag, but when he saw the beggar's crusts, he dismissed her with a gesture of disgust and started a whining song about the Vaterland. Farther stretched the boundless Yenga water-meads; a keen breeze blowing into her face somewhat stimulated Polya and made her forget for a time the pain in her knee. Within an hour a strong ground wind was blowing, and the road began to lose itself in the drifts. Things would have gone bad with Polya had not a girl stepped out of the bushes at the crossroads, a beggar like herself, except that she was rosy-cheeked and sharp-eyed, and had come there specially to meet her. While the light lasted they managed to pass through the village by begging for alms at the most dangerous points from alien unsympathetic soldiers.

"What's your name?" Polya asked the girl.

"Varya. And what's yours?"

At any other time Polya would have been surprised at the coincidence.

"Then let's go slow, Varya, otherwise I'm afraid I'll drop."

"We've arrived in any case," the other said, pointing to a forest which projected darkly like a wedge in front of them.

In fact, they were presently hailed from behind a snowbank, and then men of the outpost patrol drove Polya down to the detachment headquarters in a low country sledge. According to the information of Varya's father, Yelena Ivanovna, her mother, was there now. Polya scarcely noticed the details of that trip; every now and then things became blurred in her consciousness. For some reason, all movements along the railway line that night were considered dangerous, but the partisan scouts undertook to get the Moscow messenger through early the next morning by way of the country roads and billet-free villages.

Unexpectedly, Polya got a short breathing-space.

6

For about an hour and a half she sat in a large well-heated dugout. They were expecting the commander back from one of his operations at any minute. A thin woman of indeterminate age in a padded jacket was tapping something out on a typewriter with one finger, while a huge man with a formidable collection of weapons strapped about his person was assiduously plying Polya with refreshments as per orders, particularly with white captured bread in oil-paper wrapping, and exhorted her to have another "go" at the curd cheese to put some "pep" into her; it was the best he could do to express his respectful solicitude for the important Moscow visitor. He was a giant of a man with mischievous eyes, like little ships in the broad stippled sea of his pock-marked face. Nature herself it seemed had moulded him for combat with the cosmic elements, and Polya pretended she was dozing in order to relieve him of such paltry and unaccustomed duties.

She woke up an hour later from the smell of makhorka smoke, to find the dugout crowded with men. Latecomers huddled round the door. The whole crowd stood patiently looking at the sleeping girl, and the general sigh of relief that went up showed how long they had been waiting. An old man of short stature went up to Polya. He was unarmed, and, but for his unwinking gaze from under beetling brows, was probably the homeliest-looking man there; a cloudlet of general silence preceded him. He had held some unbelievably peaceful post before the war, something within the brackets of a farm bookkeeper and an ordinary stableman, until one day, in the middle of the night, conscience and country, side-stepping the recruiting station, called him to arms, and he answered the call after the manner of all Russians, renouncing home and family, and his very body. He spoke quietly, but the links of his smooth, fluent and musical speech seemed to be threaded on a steel pivot.

"That's fine, little girl. My boys were beginning to get tired of waiting. Now let's get to know each other. We have our whole Soviet forest guard here. That one there is Petya Karaulov, stray mine we call him—everything he touches goes up in the air. God's gift that man has! And that one a bit nearer, the one with the Roman physique, who looks like a superbomber"—he pointed to Polya's recent companion—"he's Vasily Parfentyevich from Dergachovka. We call him S. B. on account of his size; and he does give the enemy a bad time and lots of aggravation, same as he does our cook, God bless him. By the way, I hope he fed you, lassie? And that one hiding over there in the corner with the bandaged head is a very interesting citizen who goes by the name of 'Nazi Death'. I bet you thought it was an old man with a scythe and empty eye-sockets? Nay, lassie. Something has snapped inside him, and no wonder, the way they treated him. You wouldn't forgive either if you were in his place. And this one is my commissar, and I'm their commander." He held out a small bony hand and gave his name, a name which later became synonymous with implacable popular vengeance against the invaders. "You look a bit done up, you didn't catch a cold, did you?"

"No, I'm all right, and I've had something to eat, too, thank you," Polya said. She understood the commander's ruse in trying to redouble his men's valour by generous public praise.

Polya searched the room with her eyes but could not find what she was looking for. The old man guessed what it was.

"What a pity Yelena Ivanovna didn't know you were here. She would have come flying on wings," he whispered into Polya's ear, and sighed, smacking his lips with a thoughtful air. "Maybe she wouldn't, though. She has so many children on her hands now, worse than babies, they are, although they do have long beards. She won't be here before the morning. And now, lassie, get up and warm the men's hearts for them. They can do with something hot to drink after their chilling journey. Well, can we begin?" he addressed the company at large, calling for silence, and before Polya realised what they wanted of her, announced to the partisans amid a hush that they had a visitor who had been lucky enough to attend the November parade in Moscow.

He led Polya out by the hand into the middle of the room so that everyone could hear her, and nodded to her encouragingly.

Pale with emotion, she listened to the hearty applause of the partisans until it occurred to her to join the handclapping herself, since it was the uncountable unity of the people and their own future they were applauding. She had actually attended the proud beautiful festival of her people, had heard its voice, as if she had spoken to it herself, and this helped her to get off to a good start. Everything is important in the chain of circumstances that accompany a never-to-be-forgotten event; from fear of missing any precious detail, Polya began with her meeting with Sapozhkov. Memory's sketchy record of this incident now expanded and unfolded under the emotional experiences which Polya had accumulated since then. They gave depth and significance to the character of that obscure Komsomol Secretary, they gave scope to his designs, which life was not to see fulfilled, and even warmth to his affected boyish insouciance. It was the most sincere if not exactly the most exhaustive report about the unprecedented parade of nineteen forty-one, without any of the explanations or colouring which tend to detract from the grandeur of a historical act. It was about how the clock struck, how the generals ascended the platform, and how the Kremlin looked at that grim hour, and how the snow crunched under the feet of the Soviet troops as they marched past. And what she had been unable to discern through the gloom of dawn that ushered in November 7th, she described from the picture which this Russian Komsomol girl of the middle of the century carried in her heart.

And she succeeded in conveying the grim solemnity of Red Square, the fusing heat of unity, and the foretaste of victory, which has swept breeze-like through the land on that morning. "There, lassie, thank you for so rare a gift. It means more to us than ammunition. That's a matter of bravery and human hands, but this thing of yours is passed on from eye to eye. Look, the men are crying!" the commander said after a long general pause, and kissed Polya on behalf of them all. "Bless me, I believe you're running a temperature! How will you go back, lassie?"

She did not answer. Her knee did not hurt her any more and she merely felt dizzy, but at moments she wanted to lie down just anywhere and continue her interrupted conversation with Varya. The woman in the padded jacket led her away to sleep, the partisans falling back to make way for them. Several pairs of hands reached out simultaneously to throw open the door. As soon as she shut her eyes Varya leaned over her, warm, misty and kind, like a spring rain.

By dawn she felt better. She was given some vodka and tucked in warmly in the sleigh. The trees stood dressed up in rime. The commander shook a crooked forefinger at the driver and touched his walrus moustache. Horsemen escorted her as far as the turning to Krasnovershya; there, a little way off behind the greying snow dumps of winter ran the front. They parted at the slope of a hollow containing a battered melancholy wood, which, like everything in misfortune, had a wild desolate look about it. But for the swamp in front, frozen though it was, and the number of enemy units which kept growing as she neared the forward lines, she was only an hour and a half's walk away from home, where Osminov was waiting for her. They gave her directions and asked her at parting whether she would make it; she answered through clenched teeth that she would make it now whatever happened.

"I'm light, I'll jump from mound to mound!" she said.

It was bare and desolate all round, without a single bird's track in the snow, and with a sky of ashen grey. A little heap of golden husks from a squirrel's meal gladdened the eye and remotely reminded her of the flowers along the banks of the Sklan where quite recently, only a hundred years ago, it seemed, she had roamed with Rodion hand in hand. She remembered every word of their conversation, which had ended with the usual tiff.

She had asked him, for one thing, whether he liked the way Kant wrote, and for another, whether he thought she deserved to be happy; as though sensing that war would soon part them, she pressed him to make his declaration. Children that they were, they avoided the word, the most sacred and immortal word in the human language, perhaps through a chaste fear of its mortal seamy side. A faint incautious breath, it seemed to them, would be enough to extinguish their mutual affection and tender awe. Polya's love for Rodion had not yet attained that degree of force when it takes the shape of wanting to possess the loved one for ever—owing to the war it started right away with a fear of losing him for ever.

She also remembered having expressed to Rodion her speculative surprise at the vast machinery that was set in motion to achieve the tiniest whims of Nature. She had in mind, for example, the host of potent physical laws, which, like surgeons, huddled over the buttercup to carefully open its corolla so as not to injure the petals and hurt the flower. She believed her remark would appeal to Rodion, but he had merely laughed by way of reply. He said that this was just one of the ordinary miracles of life, like the shadow of leaves on woodland pools, or the cry of a bird in sunset-gilded treetops, or like she herself, Polya. And he wound up, rather unfortunately, by saying that a miracle was measured by the amount of genius that went into an obvious, though charming and useless whimwham.

"So I'm a whimwham, then? Thanks for the compliment! It remains to be seen which of us will be ordinary and useless!" Polya had flared up, calling him the sorriest figure of our age. After that quarrel they had not met again right up to the time Rodion left for Kazan.

And so she went along, trying to think of anything under the sun except death, which lurked behind every tree. The three last hours proved to be the most exhausting of all the four days of her Loshkarev expedition. Limping along a little used forest road she emerged at last on the south-eastern edge of Pustosha; the error was not a serious one, Polya thought. She was to have come out to the wide sweep of the Yenga floodlands with the geodesic tower on a hillock half a mile away, where she was to meet Osminov's men. She could see nothing there through the pall of whitish mist, and would have to wait until it got dark. At nightfall the forest began to murmur, and although she strained her smarting eyes, swollen from the wind, and listened to her air, there was no sign of a plane.

During the past six months Polya and Sergei had been thrown together in different circumstances without suspecting their kinship. Following up Polya's childish thoughts about the machinery of things and leaving out the causes of the gigantic battle for the planet's future which was then taking place, it was a matter of no little interest to trace the unwieldy premises that led up to a friendship which was closer than the ties of kinship. After repairs the armoured train did not return to its former positions south of Moscow; in preparation for the big counter-offensive of that year, headquarters threw it over to the Loshka-rev section of the front as part of an armoured division, and the very next day the war guided the two young people towards each other.

It began at dawn, at the very beginning of the month, when it was reported to Army Headquarters that the German motorised infantry was concentrating in No Man's Land in the swampy stretch of the Yenga between Krasnovershya and the railway flag-station of the same name where the left flank of our army group curved parallel with the river. The enemy was not more than a battalion strong, but owing to the state of the roads and the terrain this area was not considered suitable for large-scale offensive operations. For twenty-four hours before this, a snowstorm had raged on the Yenga, so that our reconnaissance had not been able to discover the German river crossing—a flooring almost six metres wide secretly embedded in the ice. The stir of enemy activities at Krasnovershya was interpreted as a diversion cover-ing a more dangerous movement of troops north of Loshkarev. At the same time the German mobile battalion might have been the leading echelon of a march regiment, and if successful the whole division might surge forward through the gap which it made. To discover the enemy's intentions the best thing, under local conditions, was to send a heavy armoured train to the area to prevent any further crossing and, as the telephone mes-sage said, to keep the brown devils there "on edge".

It was not more than twelve kilometres from the base to Nizhny Bereznik, where our main line of defence ran. The armoured train would have started operations on time had not certain unforeseen circumstances occurred at the jump-off point while commander Tsvetayev went into the dugout to speak on the telephone about the object of the attack. In stopping, a sinister crunching sound came from under the wheels, and engine-driver Titov climbed down to see whether the rail had snapped; the track was badly battered and hastily patched up in places, and with a load of twenty tons on the locomotive axle, the team had to be particularly careful. Just then the engine-driver caught sight of a flock of about a score of German two-engined planes flying east down the track, and almost simultaneously Morshchikhin gave the order to prepare for air defence. The bombers were flying pretty high and occasionally came into the rifts of clouds in the paling sky. The puffs of shell bursts around them showed that they had come within range of our anti-aircraft batteries in the firing line.

Sergei was in the engine cab when his friend, reserve engine-driver's mate Kolya Lavtsov, dropped in a minute before to warm himself, although it was against the regulations. Kolya had been taken along in view of the importance of the assignment. The crew was fresh after a comparatively quiet night, and even shaved, where there *was* anything to shave, so that they were game for a scrap. They kept smoking without a stop, though. Fireman Grishin, one of the oldsters—in comparison with the callow youth—happening to mention that he had dreamt of apples, which was a bad omen in his view, Lavtsov casually remarked in an undertone that the planes were "ours", not in the sense of belonging to us, but in the sense of our being at the receiving end of their deadly loads. He let fall that remark not because he had any presentiments, but simply because he liked to tease a fellow, in this case no longer Sergei Vikhrov, but fireman Grishin, who was yet an unblooded "rooky". Incidentally, he was only about six years older than Lavtsov.

"You made a mistake not to finish your sugar this morning, Dad. It'll be wasted now. But don't worry, elderly professors of history will make a full scientific study of your poor life and experience."

"Mind you don't take a lead shower yourself," Grishin came back imperturbably.

"They're coming over to bomb the station," said Sergei Vikhrov, meaning the big railway junction behind the lines, where trains had been unloading night after night for the last week.

"Don't try to console him, you've got to be honest and truthful with a comrade," Lavtsov went on excitedly, without tearing himself away from the window. "You just wait, there's going to be some concert, I tell you. It'll take a Griboyedov to describe it. Look, there goes one of them, he's spotted Grishin, I bet you. That apple of yours is coming now, fireman. This one's 'ours' all right."

From the right side of the cab commander Tsvetayev could be seen running towards the engine straight across the snow. He ran hard, getting entangled in the long skirts of his army coat, and as luck would have it, stumbling over a tree-stump buried in the snow. By the way, he was that well-known Tsvetayev, famed for his courage and successes, whose name was later sung in poetry, and the boys watched their favourite commander with concern—would he make it? One of the planes dropped behind its flight formation and started coming down towards the squall of anti-aircraft guns.

"He's spotted us. Shut the windows, boys, otherwise the rain will start spitting," Titov, who had just returned, gave the order, while he held the plated door open for the commander.

The first bomb hit the ill-fated stump, which Tsvetayev had just left behind him. Death was always at his heels. He was half in the cab by that time, and the force of the blast slammed the door and flung him inside, cutting the heel of his boot clean off. The second followed immediately, and through the racket of the guns all heard a metallic moaning crash close by, somewhere in the tender. Tsvetayev had managed to shout to the engine-driver that he should open the injector, and since this trick had been mentioned the day before as a means of camouflage, Sergei sprang to the commander's order before Titov had time to bethink himself. While the latter was shutting off the water plugs, he dived under the armour plating on the left side and in utter darkness pulled the handle of the mud cock on himself. Nothing short of a direct bomb hit could have produced such a billowy roaring cloud of vapour, which was all the more effective in the frosty air. A two-minute discharge of ten-atmosphere steam was quite enough to deceive the air raider. He was a lucky man who could hit such a target on the nose at his first dive. After peppering the imaginary wreckage with his machine-gun the German pilot hastened to rejoin his fellows.

Luckily, this bad beginning did not prevent the assignment from being carried out. The tender tank was undamaged, and the running gear intact. But the flat car attached to the front for control purposes had been thrown across the track by the blast and stood wedged deep in the wooden sleepers; the resultant buckling made it impossible to uncouple it, as the screw coupling had not broken in the shock. The train could not move into firing position, but Tsvetayev, as always, was in luck. The hitch occurred under the eyes of our outposts, and the soldiers, under their lieutenant, were so bucked up by the arrival of this welcome aid that they lent a willing hand in helping to remedy the trouble. Such haste, incidentally, can be practised with impunity only in war, where the greatest muscular exertion is combined with faultless precision of movement. Nevertheless, by the time the coupling pin was knocked out and a hundred hands unloaded the damaged platform, by the time it was raised on jacks and tipped over the embankment with many a "heave-ho!", it was broad daylight.

From a conversation with the infantry lieutenant, it emerged in good time that for all his respect for the formidable-looking armoured train, which was compelled to move in one dimension, he regarded it with polite sympathy, as he would the old-fashioned machine-gun carts of the civil war period. A month ago, the lieutenant said, he had witnessed the destruction of an A.D. armoured train, caught at army supply base; he marked the spot on Tsvetayev's map with his finger-nail where a dozen and a half bombers in the course of half an hour had unloaded on the heroic steel Juggernaut, which, squeezed between two deep craters, continued to belch fire and thunder like a volcano until its last breath. Commander Tsvetayev had no time to argue about the vulnerability of armoured trains to air attacks, but he remembered the time and place of that tragic duel.

"Don't you think it's still more dangerous up in a plane, Lieutenant? There's always the additional risk of hitting the ground," Morshchikhin remarked to the lieutenant's embarrassment, and Sergei Vikhrov glanced at his commissar with gratitude for standing up for their weapon.

They proceeded stealthily, without smoke or sparks, tender foremost, taking into consideration all attendant circumstances, even down to the inconvenient gradient section of the line. To be able to get out of it more easily when withdrawing, engine-driver Titov ordered his crew to have an emergency supply handy in the shape of a couple of tins of mazut and an armful or two of dry wood to keep the furnace lively in the event of the soft Moscow coal letting them down. Taught by experience, Sergei shut off the gauge glass in advance. In short, the engine crew took precautions against every eventuality except the radical changes in the situation, of which nothing was yet known even at the command post.

Tsvetayev at the top had a much better view of things than those in the engine cab.

"There they are, my boys!" a voice came through the loudspeaker so distinctly that Titov involuntarily looked up, as if he could see the commander in his hexahedral hood.

The din of the moving train drowned out all other sounds. But as the forest on either side fell back the brisk skirmish on the firing lines became visible. Swaying and clattering over the joints the armoured train took the last dip, then suddenly a vast snowy plain swept into view before it, dotted with the black thawed patches of craters and subsiding plumes of upreared earth. The target lay spread in full view—in fact, there were two targets now. Besides the main target and slightly to the right of it there stretched the ruins of a brickworks; there, behind a surviving wall, the enemy motorised infantry were concentrating. Through the stereoscopic telescope one could see motorcyclists dismounting and small figures, almost merging with the morning mist, heaving out an armoured carrier that had got stuck in the snow. But the main target was the river.

The fact that the armoured train was late had its advantages. Under cover of the German field artillery, which was firing at our batteries from somewhere behind the river, two heavy tanks were crawling across the river, while two others were awaiting their turn on the bank; presumably there were many more of them hidden in the forest, which, in some places, came right down to the edge of the frozen water. Both of them, for different reasons, were unfavourably situated for defence; besides, the armoured train's fire power had been increased after repairs, whereas the guns on the German tanks did not exceed 37 mm at that time. The remarkable fact was that had the train arrived a minute earlier or later, when the tanks would have been standing on firm ground, the odds would have been against it, for having come out on the brow of a hill between two deep depressions, it would itself have made an excellent elevated target. One can well understand the ecstasy which such a born hunter as artilleryman Samokhin went into, if one forgot for a moment what would happen afterwards when the German artillery shifted its fire, and the tanks deployed for action, and the people at the Nazi airfield got wise to the trick that had led them to believe their pilot had made a direct hit on the engine. The loss of any fraction of this brief advantage just now would have looked like a military crime.

Time was now measured in its very smallest divisions, imperceptible in ordinary life; it therefore seemed ages while Tsvetayev was distributing the targets and handing out range setting data.

"Come on now, show them what's what, you god of war," the commander said as coolly as if he were about to shoot grouse from his lurking-place, addressing himself to both Samokhin and his famous rival Gnatsyuk, the gunner off the second armoured truck.

Naturally, the armoured train's first broadside volley with all its guns was the most effective; even the ack-ackers levelled their guns down, eager for a share of the booty. The target was straddled after the third shell, and the brown ruins on the right, under cover of which the German troops were being rallied, became Samokhin's first victim. His mine shells must have made a lucky hit there, because a cloud of reddish dust rose from behind the brick wall followed by a beautiful pink tree with a black dancing trunk, which suddenly became covered with crimson short-lived blossoms. And since there is nothing in the world more formidable—and vulnerable!—than fighting machines, the second armoured truck chose as its simultaneous target the two tanks that were crossing the river, or rather the bumpy blue-streaked ice under their treads.

Engine-driver Titov, with a darkened face, pressed his eye to the observation slit. Through the smoke pall that kept screening the river the shattered logs of the corduroy at the crossing could be seen heaving up on end on one side, while tiny springs sprang into gushing life in the crevices and holes on the other, and the leading tank began to side-slip to the edge of the submerged wooden causeway. The tank slid unwillingly into its icy wallow, like an animal forced to take an unwelcome bath. Owing to the distance, the smoke and the spray, it was difficult to make out the second tank, but it must have been jibbing and backing, its treads crunching the logs, while something went wrong with the engine, as always happens at a crisis, so that the crash of splintering timber and back-firing mingled with the explosions and the frantic cursing with which men usually try to deaden their minds before death. The tank was heeling over sharply, but the sappers had done a good job, and the corduroy twisted spirally without the logs coming undone. Samokhin had his wits about him; he intensified his fire and slashed away the cross-pieces. At last it was all over, and two fat bubbles floated up from the seething hole in the ice one after the other.

"Well done, Samokhin! Bravo, son! You're a wolf hunter all right!" the commander shouted through the roar and din of the shooting, and the gun crews afterwards swore that from that minute Tsvetayev gave his orders in a lilting voice. "That'll teach the blighters to monkey with Soviet fighters! Now full speed astern, back to cover!"

The first attack was followed by a second and a third, and each time they retired to the hollow with the gratification of the hunter after a wolf battue, when, having emptied his gun into a husky brute, he watches the limp bleeding body writhing in fury and death agony in the snow. As soon as the shell splinters began to kick at the plating or the falling earth to rain on the roof, the armoured train would crawl away to the other end of the hollow to spoil the enemy's sighting, then come out to return the fire and hide again like a boy playing snowballs. Each time, however, the attacker's preponderance kept falling off as more and more German tanks scuttled out of the woods and went straight into action. Twice already the armoured train had been obliged to beat off the attacking enemy infantry with case-shot; the whole plain was now pitted with shell holes; the turret on one of the trucks was put out of action, and the cut-up sleepers kept for emergency repairs on another were blazing with a dirty sooty flame. The armoured train, however, would not have made half the attack it did had not the heavy guns of our distant batteries come to its assistance. The local skirmish was even reported to front headquarters.

After fifteen minutes of fighting, engine-driver Titov, looking through the periscope, saw a smoky jet the size of a goodly pine-tree behind his rear platform, and simultaneously a booming tremor reached the cab along the rails. The track had been blown up behind them and retreat was cut off. Soon after this a second German demolition man was discovered right near the tender with a supply of grenades. It was amazing how he had managed to come up so close through all that shooting, so close that you could see the blood at the corners of his mouth after he had been shot down, and hear him screaming, almost without an accent, with the desperate fearlessness of the dying: "Go back, go on!" He laughed, and pointed backward to the blasted track, as though infected with the bravery of the Russians. He was rewarded generously for his daring—almost at the same instant black coal dust blotted out the peepholes and the whole cab shuddered from an explosion under the engine's belly.

The disaster occurred just as the train was moving into firing position, before the engine-driver had had time to put the engine into reverse. Titov threw the whole weight of his body on the handwheel, and no power on earth could tear him away from it. The enemy guns now had them bracketed, and a second more deadly hit could be expected any minute. Only in an extremity, therefore, could Tsvetayev issue the incredible order he did—"Blaze away at your own discretion!", without giving any targets even. Blaze away at the old world in general, at all the world's evil, which sears flowers, quenches childish laughter, and throttles human joys! Even so, his voice sounded calm, as usual, expressing a call to the soldier's last fine rapture rather than a farewell. In an attempt to stave off disaster, however, Titov opened the throttle, and the engine moved forward into No Man's Land with the speed of a moving target in a shooting range.

"What's going to happen now?" Grishin said with grey lips.

"What d'you expect? It's like a cocktail bar—you've had your drink and feed, kindly pay your bill and go home with you," Kolya Lavtsov said under sheer stress of excitement. Titov's stern glance silenced him more effectively than shouting would have done.

Considering their position, though, the terrain could not have been better. The ground shuddered all round, but here, under the high bank with the tiny firs on its brow, things seemed comparatively safe. On the other side of the track stretched the bottomland with a mysterious semicircular ridge losing itself in the distant darkling edge of the forest. The crew of the armoured train poured out to examine the damage, and all cast furtive glances at the sullen, as yet ominously empty sky. When Morshchikhin approached the engine, Titov was groping about in the shot-hole with his arm in it up to the elbow, while he grumbled to the commander about there being no gas-welding apparatus in the train.

"What are you going to weld, Dad? You'd better have a look first where the trouble is," urged Tsvetayev, thinking that his run of good luck would extend itself to the engine damage as well.

"H'm, it looks pretty serious this time," Titov said, continuing his examination. "I'm afraid we won't manage it before dinner," he added, smiling wryly at his own joke.

Tsvetayev's hopes were dashed. Through the fused edges of the hole could be seen the grainy clearage and dented end of the link block, jammed in top position. The bent valve rod could be straightened out after heating in the furnace, but unless the right-hand link were replaced there could be no question of the train going back under its own steam. Then it was that Tsvetayev recollected the story the infantry lieutenant had told them about the wrecked A.D. armoured train in the forest siding. This meant that the snowy ridge running into the forest, which they had first taken for an anti-tank scarp, was the railway branchline to the base. The branch-off was just two hundred metres from where they now stood. The decision suggested itself, and if only the lieutenant had not made any topographical error, if the man they sent managed to get back before the enemy aircraft arrived while the remaining crew started mending the track, if the Germans did not make scrap iron out of the crippled locomotive, and if, by chance, the spare link fitted, then. . . .

The commander glanced questioningly at Morshchikhin. The latter read his thoughts and nodded. When engine-driver Titov turned round to face them, his face showed that he had been thinking the same thing. In their position it was worth taking any chances to get the spare link block.

"We can try, at least," Morshchikhin said doubtfully, measuring the distance with his eye. "It won't be more than three kilometres. How heavy is it?"

"Fifty pounds at the most. One man could manage it under cover of darkness. It's a question of time," Titov said, glancing anxiously at the sky once more and diving into his pocket for his tobacco.

All three of them gazed long and steadily at Titov's two mates, trying to figure out which of them had more gumption and physical endurance for the job. The boys understood the significance of that examination. They stood silent, looking down at their feet, and their hearts stopped beating. Both were top-scale fitters, both were prepared to do anything for their Soviet country. Lavtsov looked the stronger, but suddenly Sergei realised that the choice was falling upon him, and a flush of agitation flooded his cheeks.

"Well then, Vikhrov, the wrecked engine is standing in that wood over there, and you've got to help out your comrades," Morshchikhin began slowly and not without hesitation. "Where did you burn those boots of yours?"

Sergei understood the question correctly.

"Don't worry about me, Comrade Commissar, I'm a Communist," he said quietly, and the word, used for the first time in application to himself, seared his throat, as it were. "Thank you for the trust, comrades."

Apparently he understood the urgency and importance of the task. His smile was the best argument in favour of sending him for the spare part.

"Take a carabine, just in case, and keep your eyes peeled," said Tsvetayev. "I don't have to tell you how impatiently we'll be waiting for you here."

"Give him the tools, Kolya," the engine-driver ordered Lavtsov. "Ease the thing on the shaft first, loosen it from inside. Don't use the hammer, you'll bend it. Well, that's about all. As for the rest, clear grit and coolness will do the trick!" he added, showing a clenched fist.

Sergei received from his comrade's hands a spanner, a punch, a chisel, and even a fair-sized oak bush, which Lavtsov fished out from some secret hoard. "That's to deaden the noise when you start knocking out the shaft," Lavtsov said. He also helped Sergei on with his camouflage cloak.

At this point a stray bullet snipped off the tip of a fir twig, which fell at the commissar's feet. Morshchikhin started.

"Go along, now!" he said, consulting his wrist-watch. "Don't run more risks than you can help. The working class needs heroes, not dead men. But hurry up. . . ."

Whether they hoped for a happy issue or not there was no telling, but, all three of them watched the messenger sadly until he disappeared in the snow around the bend of the branchline.

2

The first three hundred metres were the safest as regards enemy weapon emplacements. After that the going was harder. A narrow strip of dead space was under fire; occasional mortar bursts patrolled up and down it. The wind from the enemy's side drove eddies of dry snow across the field and blew out deep hollows in the drifts. One such dark patch in front of Sergei looking suspicious to the enemy, they played a machine-gun on it. Two short whistling rounds were fired into it, but it only turned out to be a horse's head, which had shrunk in the frost to the size of that of a wooden little horse at a merry-go-round. Excited though he was, Sergei could not help thinking that not even the most satanic brain could have invented a more joyless occupation for the lords of creation. Nevertheless, he was obliged to wait until the German machine-gunner had satisfied himself that no danger threatened him from that quarter. Meanwhile precious time was slipping away, and never before had Sergei been so acutely aware of how wastefully life was running out. He made the last stretch at a crawl, eyes shut tight, his strength ebbing fast, struggling through the snow with only the top of his head showing above the surface. Only forty more metres would bring him to the edge of the forest. He dived into the snow under a guelder rose bush, whose berries looked like frozen drops of blood, crawled on a little farther for safety's sake, then looked out of his trench.

A young luxuriant wood with a dense undergrowth crowded round him. The snowed-up railway track turned sharply left, and at the bend Sergei looked round, but saw nothing in the clearing behind him. The horizon was shrouded in ragged murk, from which white artificial cloudlets hung suspended. With the guilty sense of being an idler Sergei figured how much time he had spent getting there. He all but ran the rest of the way without pausing for breath, groping for the track with his foot. The forest there was droopy and dead, without even a tomtit in it; when it grew sparse and fire-blackened, with weals running from top to bottom of the trees where they had been barked, Sergei realised that he had reached the spot.

A wide clearing came into view through the forest slashings, looking like a gigantic shell hole with the underbrush on the margin swept clean away. Everything around told its tale of the bloody battle. The charred posts of railway cars, the hooks of trucks reared up on end, and all kinds of metal parts buckled and twisted out of all recognisable shape stuck out of the snow here and there. The worst lay hidden under the calm feathery snow. Even the trees there looked like men. Some lay sprawling, torn out by the roots, others, decapitated on the run, still tried to escape from the death trap, their shattered trunks leaning forward, while the tallest and sturdiest, themselves covered with glossy wounds and rents, seemed to be leading their wavering comrades. Merciful winter had covered up their injuries, padded them with snow until the spring.

Sergei wiped his wet face with the sleeve of his camouflage cloak and stood listening. Snowy peace reigned all round, and the only sound there was the beating of his own heart.

There was no time to speculate where the lieutenant had gone wrong. The black wreckage in the snow was just an ordinary work engine without armour, but fortunately of the same type. He had to stamp the snow down around it before he could start work. The engine had toppled over the embankment sideways with its main drive rod buried in the ground, stripped bare by the explosion like a visual aid. The light-weight bomb had hit it in its most vital spot—the steam dome; behind the torn plating could be seen the engine's slashed entrails, the fire and flue tubes with a yellow trotyl deposit on top of the scale forming a tiger-like pattern. The link proved to be undamaged, and but for the dangerous incline of the pair of wheels which were almost coming away, Sergei would have managed the job in half the time. Suddenly he heard an intermittent humming sound overhead. Enemy bombers were making towards the river from the north to finish off his armoured train. Time grew more precious and crowded than ever; he could not even spare any to glance up and see two flights of our own fighting planes going out to intercept the enemy. The air was filled with the whine of aircraft engines mingled with the discreetly subdued voices of the machine-guns. Not until ten minutes after the beginning of the dogfight did Sergei discover his mistake. He had been dismantling the left link instead of the right.

Not even three men in Sergei's place, with Titov himself at their head, could have managed the job in time. But that did not become known until much later. Meanwhile, it seemed to Sergei that a lifetime would never make up for that wasted quarter of an hour. It was not difficult, from the demonstrable damage of this wrecked engine, to imagine the consequences of this delay, and Sergei was thinking what was happening to his armoured train at that moment out there in the firing line. On top of all it came to him with a shock that Morshchikhin may have chosen him in order to save him from the hell of an air attack when he could have chosen Kolya Lavtsov who would never have made such a blunder.

"You've made a mess of it, professor's cub!" he whispered, licking a bleeding finger and gazing at the sky where the dogfight was in full swing.

Suddenly he realised that he had wasted another minute and a half of precious time on himself. Coldness and firmness flowed back into him. The work on the right side of the engine went much faster. His fingers stuck to the cold iron; they were crimson and sticky, but he did not feel his body; it was now merely the tool of his comrades, who had entrusted their lives to him.

Fortune smiled on the boy. A six-foot branch off a blasted fir-tree caught his eye just when he needed it. With this leverage, the link slipped off the shaft and buried itself in the snow. Sergei mentally consulted Morshchikhin's wrist-watch. The short winter day was drawing to a close, and this redoubled his energies and shortened the way back. The edge of the forest brightened in front of him when suddenly four enemy skiers emerged from the snow-covered hazel thickets. They glided across his path, and he could hear the swish of their skis, but he could not think of a pose natural enough to make him look like a dead man. Salvation came unexpectedly, as in a dream. Within forty paces of Sergei's old footprints the skiers unaccountably made a right-angle turn and plunged into the heart of the woods. The most difficult thing in war is to guess the logic of the enemy's intentions.

Sergei for his part darted away in the opposite direction, and he had not taken twenty paces when he came upon the fresh ski runs of another group of four skiers. The Germans must have split up into two parties before reaching the wrecked train, with the result that Sergei found himself caught between the two. While he lay hiding in a snowdrift the second group reached the edge of the forest, and had he reached the spot a minute before them he would have learned by experience how dangerous it was to loiter in a minefield. Stunned by the sight and shock of the explosion, steaming with perspiration, he made a dash back to the former path waist-deep in the snow, only to be checked by an intensive artillery bombardment of the flood meadow. He began to dart about, his heart heavier than the load of metal he was carrying. And so the site of the coming memorable meeting was outlined on all four sides; it remained but to mark the dot of time upon it. Sergei did not hear the ominous whistle; the blast struck him from behind with something big and flat, burying him in the snow together with his burden.

Heavy enemy bombers were circling over his armoured train—but that he knew not. Soviet fighters rocketed into the brightening blue, burning and stripping off their duralumin sheets—that he saw not. The fight petered out, the survivors returned to their bases, but Sergei still lay unconscious. Meanwhile, it was getting dark, and the stars began to shine through the frosty blue. A momentary sign of returning life made Sergei turn over on his back; he expended his last ounce of strength on the effort; after that he lay for a long time, staring up at the growing stars. And so Polya found him on her way back, when she strayed from her path.

For the moment she thought only Rodion could lie like that with his arms flung wide. Owing to the soot and clinging snow she could not make out the features for a while, but the familiar eyes were gazing calmly past her into the darkening sky; nothing in the world, it seemed, could now break the soldier's reveri. Polya raised his head and removed the icy crust from his face and eyelids; her fingers touched something sticky at the corners of his mouth. Yet he was warm, and his clothes had no tear in them; he did not answer to his name, however, as though he had forgotten who he was, and what he had come there for, and how old he was when they had killed him.

"Do you hear me? Wink your eye, I'll understand ... where have you been hit?" Polya whispered, and her only reply was the cold starry glimmer on the surface of his pupils. "Where does it hurt?"

It couldn't be Rodion, then. Rodion would have answered her from the deepest abyss!

"No. . . ." this one suddenly murmured irrelevantly and through that momentary loophole she succeeded in penetrating to his consciousness.

Her hospital experience with men in his state came in handy to her. She began to explain to him in baby language that it was night, and time to go home, that he would catch a cold there, and his chiefs would be cross with him if he was late at roll-call. Her efforts were crowned with success. Sergei sat up, and the first thing he did was to grope around him. Polya helped him to find the now unwanted treasure in the snow. It now remained to teach the shell-shocked man how to walk and speak.

They inserted Sergei's carabine in the opening of the link and dragged it along, leaving triple tracks in the virgin snow. They had to stamp down the snow every time before putting a foot down; the first steps were the longest. When their strength failed, they stopped to rest, leaning against each other, until the tiresome yellow blizzard faded from their eyes.

But their gruelling toil was all in vain. An emergency engine, sent down to the rescue, had long ago dragged Tsvetayev's battered armoured train back to its base, while these young people of the mid-twentieth century continued to struggle on through the snow and the most dreadful night of their generation. True, they only came under a desultory fire once, when they crawled up the embankment, but here the last disappointment awaited them. The armoured train was not there. There was nothing there now, neither the fir-trees, nor the railway track, nor the embankment itself in places. The charred remains of a plane with a white cross and a wrecked truck dangling over the edge of a bomb crater told their own story of what had happened there after Sergei's departure.

"It means they've gone away," said Polya. "Come along."

"Wait a minute. This is the very spot, I recognised it," said her companion. "Where have they gone to?"

"Home, I suppose," said Polya.

Something greenish glowed faintly in the darkness of the crater. The girl and boy slid down the crumbling slope of the crater to the bottom. Sergei bent down and picked the thing up. It was Morshchikhin's watch. It was still on his wrist, and it was still going. Besides frozen clods there was nothing else around. It was the absence of his friend's body, upon which he could throw himself with childish tears of anguish, that made the pain of this last meeting so poignant.

"Whose arm is it?" Polya whispered.

"Our commissar's," Sergei said with white quivering lips.

Both were silent. Their elders had not taught them what a person has to do when he finds only part of a friend instead of the whole. In their short lives these young people had already learned all the burial ceremonies, with their graveside speeches, their military honours and salutes, but after all, this was only a human arm.

"We ought to bury it, in the ground," Polya said, touching Sergei's shoulder with the tips of her fingers to stop the tremor.

"Yes. Hold it, have a rest. I'll manage it myself."

The earth was loose after the explosion and came away easily under the finger-nails, but Sergei wanted to make the hole as deep as he could. Polya laid the find aside and bent down to help him. Seen from the sky, they probably looked like a couple of children playing about in the sand.

"That's good now," said Polya, when the luminous dial faded from the sight beneath a mound of frozen earth about half a metre in diameter.

All the abstract knowledge of life and people acquired at school faded before that fresh unforgivable grave. At that moment the young people were united by a feeling of solemn, almost magisterial aloofness from the world, as if they were standing on a mountain and that world lay spread before them in the murk empty and dark, filled with the endless space of the future of which they had now, after Morshchikhin, became masters.

"Let's go now, or they'll kill us."

"No, it's too early. Let's sit down, I'm tired," said Sergei, still peering down from the scaled heights. "Don't you feel cold?"

"I do a bit and I don't a bit," Polya answered childlike.

They sat down on the edge of the crater, where it wasn't so windy.

"Why do they do it, do you know?" she asked.

"They're used to it, I suppose. What's your name?"

"Polya. And what is yours?"

"Sergei."

He was seized with a poignant yearning for his lost friend, who had given him so generously of his love, the stern proud love of a soldier. He began to cry, and the last vestiges of fun-loving carefree boyhood were washed away with his tears. It was a rough beneficent pain, inevitable to the process of forging or hardening, when the impersonal piece of metal acquires shape, strength and a purpose in life.

All of a sudden he rose to his feet, and Polya followed suit.

"May you be damned for ever more, murderer," he uttered quietly and distinctly into the night before him. "I'll never forgive you as long as I live, and even when I'm dead!"

"Nor will I," Polya said, stepping close to his side.

"And when we have killed the war and I'm happy, even then I swear to hate you for the sorrow we have suffered, for my friend Morshchikhin, for my comrades! And if my body should fail me through cowardice or fear, I swear to punish it with the cruellest punishment. . . ."

"And so do I," Polya echoed.

The lull that night was an unusual one for the front area. The whole world seemed to be sleeping after its recent frenzy, all except the stars, which lowered their silver threads into the depths of human eyes.

Neither Sergei nor Polya were aware of the burst of light that etched the skyline behind them; for a brief moment long shadows fell upon the pinkening snow. The air was filled with a multitudinous hum, and then a similar glare flowed over the horizon in front of them. Trainloads of artillery metal flew overhead in a thousand jets, wickedly jubilant. The subdued boy and girl listened to the uproar as if it were church bells ringing in the great change.

A month before that over fifty enemy tank, motorised and infantry divisions had been concentrated around Moscow; it was clear that the greatest battle of the year was going to be fought out there. The enemy armies had driven deep spearheads into the flanks of the Soviet defences, but were powerless to press home a converging attack upon the capital. At their last gasp, tragically far-removed from their bases, with rear zones utterly exposed and communications often severed, they continued to exercise pressure, not by the superior force of a strategic plan, but by the sheer momentum of metal and soldiers' flesh. They flung themselves on the Russian boar-spear and hung spitted on it. The deeper the Soviet front bent inwards the more energy accumulated in it, like a taut-drawn bow-string. By that time the Soviet armies had everything they needed for a powerful counter-attack to be developed into an offensive.

What Nazi Germany considered to be local skirmishes was really the beginning of her end. In the course of several days the bulk of her generation, lured by a world of loot, strewed the Eastern snow-fields. The curve of Nazi might began to drop, and the first crack, under the shock of further failures, turned successively into doubt, despair, and the panic terror of defeat.

Sergei and Polya knew nothing of this at the time, but in the sound of the rising tempest they caught the wrathful voice of their country, and they listened to it, subdued, with the trustful rapture of children welcoming the first storm of spring. It was here, on the edge of the bomb crater, that the Soviet scout party found them two hours later. The famous 6th of December on the Yenga came three days later, so that Polya was able to see her commission through to the end, even though she did it lying on a hospital bed.

3

It is rather difficult, at this time of the day, to ascertain what made Ivan Vikhrov drag himself off to Gratsiansky's to celebrate the New Year. To be sure, in the face of the common enemy, private grievances and natural traces of irritation caused by prolonged and unpleasant fricton, had been somewhat smoothed over. Nevertheless, it hardly seemed worth while clinking glasses on such a night with a man who had been tripping him up all his life. Vikhrov's excursion to Blagoveshchensky Alley, however, did not signify his surrender to the victor's mercy or a desire to put himself in his good books against future need; nor would it be quite fair to associate that visit with the recent loss of his food coupons. It would be more reasonable to assume a sudden resurge of intense curiosity, born at leisure, towards his mean, formidable and thrice unpunished enemy, a desire to trace the origin of his malign power; a curiosity similar to that which makes man spend the time allotted to him for contemplation of the eternal luminaries on studying short-lived microbes.

Indeed, beginning from the middle of December the Vikhrovs had been obliged to cut down their daily ration, which steadily dropped towards the end of the month. Against the background of Moscow's current difficulties, however, Vikhrov's personal needs looked so insignificant that he could never bring himself to apply for extra food coupons. In any case he spent most of his time at his work desk without physical exertion, and as for Taisa, she had been ailing for quite a time—the result of old age, she assured him—and during the last week had only got up to tidy the rooms.

It was she, who, at the risk of incurring her brother's anger, insisted on his making that New Year's visit.

"Why sit at home and freeze? A woodsman he calls himself! He can't get a bit of firewood for himself! Sitting there brooding all the time. Stop worrying about your pupils, they can't all be killed. Why don't you go down and see him, it'll take you out of yourself a bit. The old woman must have baked some pies, I'm sure, I can smell them from here," his sister coaxed. She was so small that evening. "They're well off. People in the know told me they've been raking it in hand over fist."

And again Vikhrov got angry.

"That's all gossip. It's a disgrace for you to repeat it and for me to listen to it," he said, carefully tucking the blanket around his sister in the absence of anything else to gladden her with. "It's late, anyway. How can I leave you now."

"Don't you worry your head about me, Ivan. I'm a worn-out body. But you should get some fresh air. You might bring me a home-baked bun." And she looked at him with such timid pleading that he yielded.

His consent was dictated by special motives, which for the time being were a secret. As a result of repeated failures Vikhrov found himself toying with the thought that his efforts were futile and that consequently he ought to retire from his scientific posts; in the course of time these vacillations hardened into an unalterable come-what-may decision. In the capacity of an ordinary forester at Pashutino, say, he would be unassailable to his opponent, and the reason he wanted to see Gratsiansky again before taking this most important step of his life was not to win him over to his way of thinking but simply to find out, in a heart-to-heart earnest talk, how far his detractor himself was sincere in the attacks he had been making upon him for so many years; the conclusion he would draw might somewhat soothe the disappointment of an old man. Lately, owing to certain premonitory signs perhaps, his friends and followers had begun to desert Gratsiansky, so that Vikhrov had little doubt that he would find him alone. The possibility of an undesirable meeting with the Australian did not occur to him until he was in the hall of the Gratsiansky's flat, and he was not sure he would have the strength for the return journey without stoking up on the New Year pie.

His doubts were immediately dispelled. Gratsiansky had guests —a nondescript old couple with an epileptic-looking daughter; with hands decorously folded in their laps they sat listening to a gramophone record of the Moonlight Sonata, and appreciatively eyed the viands on the table with which the hosts were going to reward them for their modesty and devotion.

Gratsiansky must have forgotten his invitation, because he frowned at the sight of Vikhrov, but the next minute became almost effusive in his welcome; he helped the visitor off with his things, and drew him into his study, stroking his back sinisterly as if he were luring him into a trap. Here an exact description of the conversation and circumstances is required if we are not to miss any of the expressive details of what followed.

"That's an excellent idea of yours, Ivan, coming to see me. It's the first time in twenty years, too. You ought to be ashamed of yourself! You need not have waited for my invitation at all if you felt like it. But never mind, I don't bear you any grudge—come in."

"It's awkward, your leaving your guests," Vikhrov feebly protested, halting in the doorway, but the Australian was not in the room.

"Oh, that's nothing, they're just our country-place neighbours. They took a fancy to me about eighteen years ago, and they haven't missed a single New Year party since then, worse luck! They can sit by themselves, damn it. Excuse me a moment while I change the needle, otherwise they'll spoil another good record for me."

While he was manipulating his machine out there the black old lady, his mother, joined Vikhrov in the study.

"Good evening," she said, looking at Vikhrov's sleeve without uttering his name, for all her life long she was always mixing up those beggarly, for ever hungry students who had burned holes with their cigarette ends in her table-cloths at their Sergiyevskaya flat. "Being an old friend, you love Alexander, of course, and rightly so—one would have to be a monster not to love him. Well, I wanted to warn you that on every New Year's eve he puts on the same record. It has certain memories for him."

"Pardon me, what record did you say?" Vikhrov asked, with a polite show of interest.

"Well, Braga's *Serenade* ... it's all the same to you, you'll know it at once. Well, you see, he gets so worked up towards midnight that he often cries ... so please don't laugh at his weakness. Alexander is so sensitive and impressionable that we all ought to be particularly careful and spare his health."

"You needn't worry, Madam, I'm not the laughing kind," Vikhrov reassured her drily, and was about to add something more when the host himself made a timely reappearance.

It was a full hour before the New Year, and so they had sufficient time to discuss the weather, the military plans of the Western powers in the matter of opening a second front and other current miscellanea.

"How are you getting on, generally, you forest brawler? I'm glad, very glad for your sake," Gratsiansky said, not waiting to hear the end of the other's provincially conscientious report. "You look fine, although you've lost some weight, but your eyes are shining—you're full of plans again, eh?"

"You've guessed right," Vikhrov concurred in a mysterious manner, getting out paper and tobacco. "I'm preparing to make a decisive step in life."

"Glad to hear it, tell me all about it. I've always been an admirer of your talent. Go ahead and smoke ... we don't allow smoking here, but never mind. I, too, have an urge towards a *final* step, but I just can't steel myself for it," he murmured, his eyes angling off, and his face looking peaked and stricken, as if at the memory of some incurable disease. He quickly recovered himself, however. "Well, what are you going to rejoice the freedom-loving peoples of this planet with, if it's not a secret?"

"It's no longer a secret, although I haven't handed in my application yet." For the first time Vikhrov was not afraid to disclose his plans to this man. "I want to leave the Institute. Just so!"

The other frowned mistrustfully.

"H'm, a rare event—the wood-goblin running away from his wood—where to, into the water? Explain yourself."

"On the contrary, I'm returning to the wood. It's not altogether pleasant to have to admit one's mistakes in one's old age, but it's still worse not to have any strength left to rectify them. I still have it. In short, I've come here today to tell you that you have won, Alexander."

"In what way have I beaten you?" the other said with an incredulous smile.

"Oh no, as far as my theoretical views are concerned I am still against the American nomadic system of forest utilisation with its clear fellings. In other words, I still stand for planned rational sustained yield forestry. But you have persuaded me of something else—that I have bitten off more than I can chew."

He looked his opponent squarely in the face while he spoke and suddenly became aware of an odd expression of evasive concern in his eyes. Considering Vikhrov's spartan needs and his well-known contempt for lucrative jobs, the man was quite capable of carrying out such a crafty and frustrating manoeuvre. It would bring Gratsiansky's little school with its negative attitudes face to face with the people, who would then judge the parties not by their declarations of loyalty or the noise effects they were capable of sustaining, but by the quantity of values which they produced—in this case the amount of timberland available for industrial use; the community would then give its strict attention to the victors, and that, for various reasons, was a prospect which Alexander Gratsiansky and his Dizzy Doxies viewed with misgivings.

"Truth to tell, Ivan, I never thought you were such a coward. It's not my business, but I don't think it's very noble to lie down on the ground in a duel when you can still stand on your feet. When do you intend to do this, after the war?"

"I don't know, but . . . our Institute has been evacuated and it gets along quite well without me. There are no indispensables in this world."

All the less reason, it seemed, did Gratsiansky have to fear the consequences of Vikhrov's retirement. There must have been a disturbing note of finality in the latter's voice and a precarious degree of insecurity in the former's position to call for such urgent persuasions.

"But this is desertion, Ivan. Nay more, I regard this step of yours as er ... a betrayal, an unconscious betrayal maybe, of the Russian forest. Your decision looks all the more unfortunate today of all days, when, after so many sleepless nights er ... I was just going to confess to you that theoretically you are quite right ... and I would have declared so in print if it wasn't for the strained war atmosphere. True, I still have to make certain statistical calculations ... I'm hard at work on them right now in fact." With a rather uncertain gesture he touched a writing-book in dark covers, which lay on his desk under a large photograph pasted together from corner to corner. Vikhrov could see the book from where he sat. "Why, damn it all, Ivan, you simply underrate yourself, when all is said and done, and you know I'm not one to throw compliments about. Man alive, with your knowledge...."

"Stop it, or I'll start giving myself airs," Vikhrov laughed at his wily tactics. He realised that this man was afraid, apart from everything else, of being left alone with the Russian forest. "No, really, stop it, or I'll go away!"

"But I can't let you go now in this unbalanced state of mind. Why, you've got cobwebs on the brain, Ivan. Wait a minute, I'll go and fetch a bottle of something to clear it." And he slipped out into the corridor, shutting the door behind him in case his guest took it into his head to run away.

He gave Vikhrov no time to tell him that he took no wine on an empty stomach. Soon after that there was a short ring at the front door announcing the arrival of a fifth belated guest. Taking a bottle from the table was the matter of a minute, but two minutes passed and the host had not returned yet. Vikhrov took a turn about the room, touched the cold radiator, and looked round to see where the delightful tropical warmth was coming from. Then he went up to the desk, and out of idle curiosity as to the nature of Gratsiansky's statistical calculations, he removed the glossy sheet of the aerial forest survey from the manuscript. It was an open writing-book covered with Gratsiansky's crabbed handwriting, which had a leftward slant. There were no figures in it at all. Vikhrov was dumbfounded when he read the first few lines, but he could not tear himself away from it, and even sat down on the arm of the chair for comfort. He had no twinge of conscience, as the writing-book bore no resemblance whatsoever to a diary—it had no dates, or entries, no intimate confessions or facts of private history, but it was a window into a strange hidden life for all that, and the impeccable Alexander Gratsiansky, that guardian of forestrial pure thinking and cutter-off of heads by bloodless means, appeared here in a somewhat unexpected aspect.

It was probably one of the fullest scientific selections of material for a treatise on suicide, supplemented with a list of references. The first two dozen pages gave the views of the ancients concerning a man's right to voluntarily cease his existence, and certain passages were heavily underlined with red pencil, namely, Seneca's death letter, Pliny's comments on the salutary comfort derived from timely departure from Nature, Joannes Stobaeus's testamentary advice to his son Septimius that life should be departed by good people in misfortune, and by bad in the height of good fortune, Lactantius's logical conclusion that the act of self-destruction simultaneously contains in itself both homicide and the punishment for it, Terence's advice to investigate thoroughly what life is before parting with it, and a good deal more that revealed the underside of Gratsiansky's wide and specific scholarship. There was a special table analysing the moral spectrum of such acts, from Judas and Sardanapalus down to their most up-to-date followers. This list of companions with whom Gratsiansky held nightly converse contained such names as Cleanthes and Chrysippus, Zeno and Democritus, Empedocles, who threw himself into the crater of Etna, and Cato the Younger, who stabbed himself after reading the *Phaedo*. All that was missing was the story of the Scythian steed and his mate, mentioned by Claudius Aelianus and others, who killed themselves after performing a certain reprehensible act. The margins of the book were filled with notes about the corresponding rituals in different ages, from the self-cremation of the Indian widows and the Russian Raskolniks to Valerius Maximus's testimony about Massilia, where, Vikhrov was surprised to learn, the cup of hemlock was handed publicly to the applicant by the ruling judges at the public expense if he could give sufficient reasons for their doing so. He conjured up at once the image of a man toying maniacally with a loaded weapon, already obsessed with his idea but still lacking the determination to take the final step. While professionally, as a forester, deploring the fact that human life was so short a span, Vikhrov had never suspected that powerful minds had been so long at work speculating on the meanest form of desertion from life. Nevertheless, it was with great interest that he turned over the page upon perusal.

A brief exposition of Hume's famous treatise on suicide was followed by Gratsiansky's own thoughts on the same subject, namely, on death as an instrument of cognition, on a person's right to do anything so long as it was not detrimental to his fellow-men, and on the seductive idea of a single all-absorbing loss beyond which there was nothing more to lose. Also, by way of consolation to the "departing", there were thoughts about the structure of the cosmos, about the rebirth of worlds, about spheres of existence passing through each other in the shape of rings, about millions of galaxies contained in the nuclei of atoms, and a good deal more of the same homespun stuff with an unpleasant moral flavour about it, like that to be found in wills drawn up in a tumult of soul. And yet it was absolutely frank, thoughtless of any risk of burning with shame or ruining one's career. Two ideas of Gratsiansky's impressed themselves particularly on Vikhrov's mind and showed him how little he knew this contemporary of his, although they had been such close neighbours in science and times. "The yearning for death is God's anguish over the failure of his creation," and then "*that* is the only thing in which man excels God, who could not do away with Himself if He wanted to." From the nature of these entries, it suddenly became clear that if their author had not tried to describe his malady as fully as possible in order to burn it afterwards together with the paper, then this was the statistical preparation Gratsiansky had been speaking about, his way of getting himself used to the final conclusive step.

And so Gratsiansky's belauded optimism was not worth a farthing, if he was already peeping into the black hole as the only way out of his difficulties. Vikhrov stepped away hastily from the desk and unconsciously wiped his fingers on his jacket lest a single letter of what was written there should stick to them. His first thought was that that man, with his twisted mentality, was quite capable of deliberately leaving his visitor alone with his writing-book in order to create around himself an atmosphere of sympathy and pity to cushion the fall, but the next minute he was ashamed of himself, and felt sorry for his comrade in distress. At that moment he did not know yet that it was merely an enemy soldier writhing before him on the field of an abstract lost battle. Gratsiansky, of course, knew too much about death to rush upon his fate so recklessly, otherwise Vikhrov would certainly have tried to restrain him from that dreadful step, and shake his resolve for self-destruction by quoting school-reader proofs about the beauty and value of life.

He had resumed his seat and was rolling himself a cigarette when he heard footsteps outside, and the old lady came in again.

"Alexander asks you to go away," she said simply, looking somewhere over Vikhrov's shoulder.

"I beg your pardon, you mean leave this room?" Vikhrov said, innocently believing that he was being invited to a New Year spread before settling down to listen to Braga's *Serenade*.

"No, I mean leave the flat," the old lady explained with a kind of virgin shamelessness.

Vikhrov thought at first that they had been watching him through the keyhole reading a stranger's thoughts, but in that event they would have turned him out immediately and not waited three minutes before punishing him; besides, the mistress had not even glanced at the writing-book, which the uninvited reader, in his haste, had not had time to cover up again. Linking this invitation to leave the flat with the ring at the door, Vikhrov decided that his host had been urgently summoned to some conference of state importance, but in that case the guests could have been kept waiting for an hour or so. It was unlikely that anyone would hold an all-night meeting on New Year's eve.

"Is he sending everyone er ... packing like this?" Vikrov asked in a full-chested tone, standing on his dignity. "Or is it only me?"

"Never mind, please go away," she said, opening the door to avoid further explanations.

The thing was so ridiculous and stunning that Vikhrov, with his innate delicacy, was completely at a loss. He could not make up his mind whether he should merely pass some uncomplimentary remark about his host before leaving, or smash up the New Year table, or at least slam the door and have the last word. He had it in him to do worse things than this, had he fortified himself a little before leaving home. At that moment, however, he felt nothing but a burning desire to cut short this humiliating procedure of his unmerited banishment. He struggled into his coat, snatched his hat, and rushed out into the street with such precipitancy as if two men, at least, were helping him at it. This resignation to fate did not by any means signify that he was impervious to insults; on the contrary, he was not one of those half-and-half natures who took things lying down, but he realised how complicated his private life and his work would become if he was in the habit of giving free rein to his feelings. Now that he thought of it, the rest of the guests, too, had stood huddled around the doorway of the dining-room with anxious-looking faces. The general character of the insult somewhat soothed his feelings and by the time he got home, this, combined with the influence of the lovely night, left nothing on his soul but a simple wonder as to what could have made Gratsiansky play such a strange, and, in any case, shabby trick.

Owing to the late hour he walked back, drinking in with pleasure the winy tingling air, filled with delightful snow crunchings and New Year hopes. As far as he could remember it had never been so lovely in Moscow since the winter began. The silhouetted bulks of the buildings loomed faintly through the bluish gloom, and the absence of lights and details gave them the chaste simplicity of a single ensemble. From the war and the brave people, who were making their historic leap into the future, his thoughts switched to Sergei and Polya and he walked with them mentally all the way to the suburb, his arms about their shoulders, trying, as it were, to make them friends forevermore. Knowing beforehand what he would find at home, Vikhrov was in no particular hurry, and thus fell into the inevitable error of those who underestimate the number of coordinates which life has to offer them.

A large black car stood outside his house; the tenants having been evacuated, the ground floor was now occupied by the local Air-Defence Headquarters.

"Where have you been all this time, we thought you would never come!" Taisa sang out cheerfully from the kitchen. She knew it was her brother from the noise of his stick which he tossed into a corner.

"I didn't bring you any pie, sister," Vikhrov answered apologetically.

"You just have a look who we have here, Ivan!"

Sitting at Taisa's bedside in the kitchen, stroking his grizzled moustache, was the smiling Valery. He looked a real giant to Vikhrov, for some reason.

4

Before embracing, they stood for quite a time each jealously regarding the other to see whether he had preserved the most precious traits of his youth.

"Well, old man, how goes it?" one of them—or was it both together?—asked.

"I had a feeling that you were here, and I got away earlier," Vikhrov quickly rose to the occasion. "Everything's fine, Valery."

"Yes, but the war."

"Never mind, we'll get there. Now how long is it since we saw each other, not fourteen years surely? Why, yes, Polya was getting on for five. Let me sit down, I'm rather tired. Walked both ways. Have you come for long? Or is it like last time, just to come up for a breath of Moscow's frosty air, then back again to the lower depths?"

"It's for good this time, at least I hope so. You didn't banquet long at Gratsiansky's, did you?" An amused twinkle came into Valery's eyes, as if he had guessed something.

"There's no place like home," Vikhrov answered evasively. "When did you arrive?"

"Yesterday, en route to Tashkent to see my family; straight from the Black Sea coast. I love the scrunch of the winter shingle under your feet! There's no better time for summing up an old man's life."

"I don't see any signs of creeping age, except for the spectacles, perhaps. You still look like an African baobab, Valery."

"You don't see it because we're all moving together in the same direction. But yesterday afternoon I went out to have a look at Moscow, and made the sad discovery that though the soul was still the same, the meat was getting tougher at dinner, the girls more respectful, the days shorter, and the stairs steeper. 'What can it be, Valery?' I asked myself. 'Do you remember the spring of nineteen twelve, when you were being exiled? The ice on the Volga was blue and thin, and we walked across it with the help of poles. A woman, one of our people, by the way, fell into the water. And you carried her across in your arms, Valery, all wet and freezing, with another fifteen hundred full-sized Siberian versts to go, but never had life's road seemed so light and beautiful.' Well, then, Ivan, when you begin to notice that the world around you is changing for the worse, have the sense of humour to put those changes down to your own account." He paused. "In about twenty years' time, if we're still alive, we'll be making the same speeches."

"Possibly. But come into my room. Taisa will get up and sit with us in honour of the occasion. The only trouble is though," Vikhrov hesitated, "I have nothing to give you for one reason and another. Never mind, the least I can do for you is to heat the stove. If I knew you were coming I would have met you and helped you with the luggage—I'm a free man now—and I wouldn't have gone visiting."

"Oh, we had an enjoyable evening here. Taisa told me some things I didn't know before. We spent quite a useful evening. By the way, why are you a free man? Have you left the Institute?"

Not to upset his friend, Vikhrov said nothing about his decision to go back to the Yenga.

"No, but my Institute has been evacuated." At this point he looked into his room and shook his head. "Oh, you magician from foreign lands! Look at the gifts he has brought!"

In the spaces between the manuscripts on the desk lay all kinds of food, packaged, boxed, and packetted—obviously the weekly ration. There was a smell of tangerine rind, and some bottles stood on the floor, there being no room for them on the desk. Before heating the stove, Vikhrov could not deny himself the pleasure of touching all these things.

"I counted on all the four Musketeers, but nothing came of it," Valery explained, and with the same thoughts in both their minds they looked at each other without airing them for the time being. "Come on, let me help you."

Kneeling before the stove, they began to build a fire in it. Valery split the kindlings with gusto, little suspecting that it was the last of the firewood in the house.

"I'd make a good furnace-man," he said, holding a lighted match to the stripped bark. "I fell in love with the smoke of the taiga ever since the days of my exile, and I missed this thing ever so much when I lived abroad. Once I called on Maxim Gorky at Sorrento. He treated me to a grand camp-fire in a hollow under the blossoming agaves, the old man did. It even brought the town's fire-brigade galloping down. What are you looking at the clock for, is it time?"

It was a minute to midnight. Vikhrov poured out the wine. They raised three glasses; Taisa got the smallest.

"Here's to victory, to our generous-hearted people, to our Party, which is performing an historic feat, to all the little springs of life, to the unclouded friendship of our contemporaries!" Valery reeled off. "Have I missed anything?"

"You've missed the Russian forest. You're a fine forester, aren't you?"

All three gazed at the spreading fire in silent gratitude.

"It's nice after a separation to start the conversation by summing things up," began Vikhrov. "Now you've been living abroad for a long time, how is it over there, especially on the other side of the 'big water'? I never could understand what makes things tick over there."

Valery searched among his impressions for an opening thread.

"Yes, that's about as easy as trying to make out what's going on inside a train by looking through the window of another one going in the opposite direction. Well, the first thing that strikes the eye when you come down the gangway is the deceptive smoothness of things. It makes you think of pebbles on a beach, where the surf has been at work for ages. The simpleton will also be struck by the rainbow-hued movement called bourgeois progress—the shots of the suicides usually ring out in the night in the suburbs when tourists are asleep in their hotels. Gradually, one begins to grasp the meaning of this active diffusion: everything preys on everything else in line of descent; everything is gear-toothed in a sort of mutual class guarantee, the way it should be in the jungle or the lower depths, as you called it. There are such insects with a voracious appetite—the praying mantis, you remember the entomological collection on the wall of our Institute? Well, it brings to mind a page from Fabre describing their habits, when one of them quietly eats away the belly of a colleague, who, in turn, is busy devouring his own prey. This is done to light pleasant background music under a cloak of respectability; up to a point both are polite—they prey, because he sometimes counts on a reward in the life to come, and the preying because it is good for his digestion."

"But there are human beings there, too, aren't there?" Vikhrov interposed.

"The majority, but as always in history, it takes more than ordinary misfortune to make a united army of humanity out of them. At the top you would meet only partners and accomplices, but the comrades and associates are only to be met at the bottom of the social ladder, among the class which has built up an immensely rich country ... but imagine a barn in which all the choicest bits go to the rodents. The only difference really between a robber and a capitalist is that the former plucks a single victim at one go, whereas the latter regularly wrings his profits out of tens of thousands of people, who are cowed by unemployment and depend upon him. The crime there, if any, is that of overstepping the prescribed speed limit of enrichment and the unscrupulous methods by which it is achieved. Their vaunted adjustment of the different parts amounts to just this ability to hit it off together—the gangster and the lawyer who defends him, the war manufacturer, the Christian preacher, and the unprincipled writer, who lends glamour to this planktonic existence and these imaginary bourgeois liberties. The thing is, Ivan, when this 'liberty' is given both to the sabre-toothed tiger and the ordinary defenceless working man, the latter quickly loses interest in it once and for all. In short, constantly racked as they are by greedy fear of the advancing new, they wouldn't mind gratifying their hatred if there was any guarantee that they could deal their opponent a smashing blow without crumpling up at his first retaliatory blow."

"Then what are they, soldiers or robbers?" Vikhrov interrupted.

"They're hucksters. A soldier is the noble title of a man who is capable of dying for an idea. But tell me of a single idea which that class has given to the world and put over in the name of life during the last century. They buy and sell; at best, a tradesman made a pirate. And since nothing is sacred to them, they are obliged, on the one hand, to convert all social education to the task of stimulating in the younger generation the money-making urge, a contempt for all things holy, chewing reflexes at the sight of a fellow-man, and a taste for everything that rots, crumbles, goes to earth and turns over, yielding a profit to the smart ones—that is, to breed their own supermen, who would not spare their own selves when in hot blood; on the other hand, to do their utmost to hinder the progress of the opposite camp by the threat of war, which diverts it from the business of peaceful construction, by slandering them in the eyes of wavering nations, and simply by dropping night men and mines in inland places where the traffic is heaviest. To be sure, these days history has slightly upset their plans."

Valery bent down to pick up a smouldering twig that had dropped out of the stove.

"Don't bother, I'll pick it up," Vikhrov said.

"No you don't," Valery answered, smelling the wisp of blue smoke that struggled through the dying flame with obvious relish. "I'm not boring you, am I?"

"On the contrary, I'm deeply interested."

"Well then, I've heard from people in the know that there are mines which go off at once, and God help the gaper who steps on one of them! There are also delayed-action mines; a lump of iron like that can lie about quite harmlessly for ten years, so that some old granny can even use it as a weight when salting cucumbers in a barrel, until one fine day you wake up to find no barrel and no granny. But the meanest of all, I think, are the periodic, repeated-action mines, those that let out a gas from time to time in small portions, which no recording apparatuses can detect."

"What gas is that, I wonder?"

"Well, let's call it the gas of suspicion, a gas that suddenly makes people mistrust one another. You just have to get them started, that's all." He glanced at Taisa, who was dozing in an armchair, and lowered his voice. "By the way, don't be angry, but I agree with some of your critics, who contend that your forestry theories are a bit premature. But your opinions about the forest are based on a legitimate and patriotic concern for the fate of this most important source of the nation's wealth. Now tell me, please, what makes your opponents declare your views to be hostile to the Soviet community—to me, for instance?"

Vikhrov shrugged his shoulders.

"Who can read another man's soul! Dokuchayev said that people only shake the tree that has fruit on it, they never shake an empty one. Besides, impotence in logical deductions always tries to make up for it by temperamental exuberance."

"Of course, envious malice has always been a source of inspiration to scoundrels, but. . . . No, it's not that! Tell me, has there ever been personal enmity between you and Gratsiansky?"

"I don't remember, unless it was . . ." Vikhrov began after a pause. "You see, he's rather stingy by nature, and back in St. Petersburg I once passed a humorous remark about a type of person, who, seeing pyramidon at a friend's place, will take a pill in advance so as not to have to buy one when he needs it."

"No, that's not it either. I'm asking because of a rather strange incident that occurred just now. I took it into my head this morning to get all you fellows together and crack a New Year's bottle, just the four of us. No matter how people may differ in opinion as they approach old age, we are nevertheless contemporaries, and the glow of one and the same banner lies upon our faces, isn't that so? To make a long story short, I packed the food in a bag and made the round of your homes, Father Christmas like. Cheredilov was away in Tobolsk, so I decided to park myself at your place and bring Gratsiansky along with me. I had some trouble finding him in that alley of his, and a black old lady studied me for a long time with the door on the chain."

"And she didn't let you in!" Vikhrov said with sudden animation. "Did you tell her who you were and where you came from?"

"Just for fun, and to make it a surprise, I introduced myself as Charles Dickens. After that she let me in, but ..." he chewed his moustache with a thoughtful air, "but there was no hugging of old friends."

"What time was it?"

"Round about eleven."

"That was soon after I left. It's very curious," Vikhrov said, and related how he had been expelled from the Garden of Eden. "To tell you the truth, I have never been extirpated in that way in all my life. I suppose he was called out urgently somewhere?"

"No," Valery shook his head, "he was at home, as it happens. He even came out of his room for a minute, not expecting to see me of all people there in the hall. I must say, I never saw a man so petrified. He avoided my eyes and muttered that I should have given him a ring before calling and that he just couldn't see me. Naturally, I was puzzled at such a reception. After all, I'm a general of a sort with an unblemished reputation, and I can hardly compromise anybody in this country. Didn't you say you heard a ring at the door? That's odd...." He half-closed his eyes, trying to piece things together into a logical pattern. "Evidently someone called on him during that hour, and called without warning, I take it. Consequently, it was on some urgent business, but what?"

"There were three other guests there beside myself," Vikhrov added. "Were they there when you came?"

"While the old lady was letting me in I saw the supper table from the hall, but there was no one sitting at it."

"Perhaps they went into the study?"

"That's unlikely, the hall-stand was empty."

"They have another stand for their own clothes at the bottom of the corridor," said Vikhrov.

"But this one was quite empty, although he had someone in his room, someone he did not want anybody to see, isn't that so?"

Vikhrov's suggestion that it might have been a "flame" was briefly dismissed by Valery, with the remark that he would never make a detective. Indeed, it was difficult to imagine such impatient passions at their age. The alternative assumption was the distinguished connoisseur of the forests of the Pacific, who had been so eager, for some unknown reasons, to make the acquaintance of Vikhrov, and who now, on the contrary, sought a confidential interview with Gratsiansky.

"That's more like it," Valery concurred after a thoughtful

pause. "Then let us try to figure out what made him hide the visitor's coat, a visitor on New Year's eve, who had such sudden need to discuss the problem of the eucalypts that old friends had to be sent packing."

They sat on for a while in utter silence.

"You just hinted at Gratsiansky being a long-delay mine of gas action," laughed Vikhrov, replenishing his friend's glass. "At this moment he is sitting quietly in his alley, while the gas of suspicion is noticeably floating about in the air. Doesn't that mean one of us is to blame for it?"

"Vigilance and suspicion are quite different things," Valery protested none too insistently.

Only now did it strike him how utterly absurd were his suspicions, which were tinctured with a sense of personal wrong. When all was said and done, Gratsiansky might have been taken ill suddenly or have received a letter that had cast a gloom upon his holiday mood. At any rate, the number of unknown quantities made Valery abandon any attempt to solve the equation there and then; he had no time to go deeper into the matter. The ticket to Tashkent lay in his waistcoat pocket.

5

The truth was that Gratsiansky had been making for the study with two bottles of excellent wine and would have assuredly caught Vikhrov in the act of reading the forbidden writing-book had he not heard behind him a delicate tap on the front door. All the guests were assembled and no one else was expected. This could mean one of two things, both equally unpleasant to contemplate, namely, that the nocturnal visitor was either unfamiliar with the position of the door bell, which was in good working order, or was none too anxious to advertise his arrival to all the occupants of the flat. Gratsiansky crept up to the door and heard the sound of a match being struck, followed by a short furtive ring, which seemed to him more ear-splitting than the recent demolition bomb. For the sake of gratifying an intense curiosity, Gratsiansky switched off the light, poked his head out of the door, then quickly slammed it to again, pretending not to have seen anything in the dark. But before he closed the door a voice distinctly uttered some-thing that made Gratsiansky tremble. It was the name of Chand-vetsky, the fugitive colonel of the St. Petersburg Okhranka.

Leave alone that it was physically impossible for him to turn up in Soviet Moscow of all places, it was quite unbelievable that that man could continue to exist anywhere upon this earth. It gave the whole thing a touch of not-of-this-world gruesomeness. Gratsiansky, nevertheless, would have preferred the most vulgar of New Year ghosts behind that door, all the more that there was nothing reprehensible or politically discreditable in a man now respectably dead and absolutely safe, feeling lonesome in his narrow earthy home, and deciding to pay a courtesy visit on New Year's eve. Unfortunately, it was not Chandvetsky himself, but apparently a confidential agent of his, since native ghosts, as a rule, seldom speak with a foreign accent. True, the visitor's foreign origin, barely detectable in his speech, was more pronounced than that of the Australian, who had also come with greetings from Chandvetsky three weeks before. Thus the name of the colonel of the gendarmes became a sort of password procuring access to a man with a guilty conscience.

Alexander Gratsiansky was now bound to the stranger at the door by an invisible thread, and no power on earth could break it. Breathless, he stood listening to the sounds behind the door and no doubt would have heard a speck of dust gliding in that stillness, but thank God there was no one there; it was inconceivable that any man, however patient and lacking in self-respect could have endured the humiliation of being kept waiting for fifteen minutes on a cold staircase. A slender hope was born that the man had gone away after having fulfilled his errand, but he could not go back to his guests now and drink himself drunk for joy to the accompaniment of Braga's *Serenade* without first making sure that there was no danger. He opened the door again noiselessly, and recoiled, breaking out into a clammy sweat.

"I have brought you greetings from Mr. Chandvetsky," the visitor repeated tonelessly, as though nothing had happened.

"But I had a visitor before with the same greetings," Gratsiansky said, stepping back to let his visitor pass. His heart beat so fast that he could scarcely speak.

"He has gone, but that doesn't matter. You kept me waiting, that's indiscreet. I am not sure you did right to keep me on the stairs for everyone to see." He spoke Russian fluently, but sounded as if he had something under his tongue. "We must discuss a matter of business in which you are interested."

The visitor shook a drop of thawed snow off his tall fur cap and began to take his things off without waiting to be invited.

"I have guests. . . . It's New Year's eve!" Gratsiansky began with a dead tongue.

The other smiled coolly, as if he had a pawn ticket for the soul of that elderly gentleman with the haggard face who stood before him holding two bottles in his lowered hands.

"I am sorry, try to get rid of them. I have plans for this night."

Again, there is no telling what would have happened to Gratsiansky had not his mother come out of the dining-room to his rescue, impelled by that inexplicable instinct which tells mothers all over the world when their children are in trouble.

"Show the visitor into my room while I clear the study, will you. Hang his coat on the other hall-stand, and don't forget to take your medicine," she said gravely and sadly, as if at a funeral; apparently, it was a prearranged signal advising him to take a grip upon himself while he still lived, breathed and was capable of independent movement. "I'm sorry, the room isn't tidied up."

"That's all right," the visitor said with a stiff bow. "That's awfully nice. I am sorry."

The circumstances show that the old lady had not deliberately intended to insult Vikhrov when she had asked him to leave their cosy flat. These details were not cleared up until six months later, when the flotsam of this remarkable shipwreck began to appear on the surface. This mucky refuse would hardly have been worth rummaging about in had it not contained some grains of supplementary information about Vikhrov's opponent.

CHAPTER SIXTEEN

1

While he was at the front Morshchikhin's thoughts kept returning to Gratsiansky; having nothing else to go by, he could merely run over their last conversation, particularly Gratsiansky's fictionised account of his courageous duel with the colonel of the gendarmes, who had tried to lure him to the path of treachery. To a Soviet young man, who had no personal experience of the tsarist Okhranka, Gratsiansky's story sounded plausible enough, if by plausibility we are to understand the authentic rendering of events. If there is the slightest admixture of a lie in such confessions, they are usually uttered glibly, without marks of punctuation, the easier to be able to skip the threshold of disturbed logical connection. But Gratsiansky, being a skilful narrator, had described the episode with the leisurely incisiveness of detail and genial good humour which always tincture the reminiscences of a winner. Inexperienced in the mysterious workings of the human mind, Morshchikhin never suspected that the better sort of lies are made out of half-truths.

Gratsiansky had rounded off the story of his clash with Chandvetsky with an effective pun about the colonel's wife, giving to his challenge—that of testing her constancy—the character of a slap in the face, as it were, to the old world. He had given a sufficiently transparent hint, by the way, that he eventually succeeded in carrying out that threat. He put significant dots here, so as not to compromise the lady whose favours he had enjoyed, whereas it should have been a comma with a no less interesting continuation after it. Seeing that so much space has been devoted to the life history of Vikhrov it would hardly be fair to limit it in the case of Gratsiansky. This second part of his story should be started by correcting a chronological inaccuracy. His first meeting with Chandvetsky took place at the beginning of August 1911, while the lecture at Countess Panina's People's House was actually fixed for September the first, when Stolypin, the well-known tsarist statesman, was assassinated. The interval of a month between the two dates was probably used to stage the spectacle which was to become the most piquant adventure in Gratsiansky's life. Hence he could not have gone to his lecture on Pushkin straight from the police station, and the lecture itself did not take place for the reasons given below.

As a matter of fact, student Gratsiansky was just about to leave the house when Sleznyov dropped in on him and persuaded him to give up the lecture and go with him instead to the very interesting but quite respectable house of a well-known St. Petersburg numismatist, that is a collector of coins, who had made a fortune on army contracts in the Russo-Japanese War, and was president of some board of trustees or other, although Sleznyov himself did not know exactly what board it was and who they were trustees of. He said that a mixed company gathered there every Thursday, from jobbers and stock-exchange speculators to the bastard son of a supposedly august personage. What, drag himself to the other end of the town for the sake of a glass of wine with the scions of dynastic blood—no, such an enterprise held little attraction for Gratsiansky! Why, this was the very society he was planning to blow up from within by means of intensive amateur schoolboy activities! For at that time he implicitly believed in the diabolical power of mimetism, invented by Sleznyov, who was awfully clever at that kind of thing.

"Unless you have a thorough knowledge of that set, their biologies, foibles and all the inside facts, there can be no question of blowing up the old world," Sleznyov said didactically without taking off his overcoat. "Your inflammatory gifts are not enough, you have got to acquire also a hatred, which comes only from direct dealings with the enemy. We've got to work, old chap, once we've taken on the job. In a word, I've called for you ... you needn't change. Take a handful of your governor's cigars with you. The cab's waiting outside."

Alexander hesitated.

"But a hall of workers is waiting for me, it's so awkward. I'm not going there for the applause at all, that's where you're wrong. But I suppose I can miss it for once, though, every man has a right to fall ill or twist an ankle, so why can't I, damn it all! What do they do at this numismatist's of yours—dance, gamble, drink?"

"I don't want to mislead you, but you have to take your chance. Sometimes you may run into a boring concert, when some celebrity or other blows in. But then, as in every puddle, you sometimes come across cute little toads," Sleznyov murmured insidiously into Alexander's ear, while the latter stood toying nervously with his glove. "And bear in mind, it's often in such places that the winds of high politics are born."

"Isn't it rather awkward going there without an invitation," Alexander fumbled, aware of a voluptuous tickling sensation around the knees.

"They're all uninvited guests there, they just drop in when they feel like it. The host's a sort of modern Famusov, a queer type of capitalist shark. His name alone speaks for itself— Tiberius Vonifatyevich Postny. Of course, this devil's den is not really a proper place for infants."

"Oh, all right," Alexander decided in a tone of fierce desperation, "let's go and see this Famusov of yours!"

A smart cab on inflated tyres stood at the curb. Sleznyov uttered the magic word, and the sleek animal harnessed to the elegant droshky seemed suddenly to have grown hellish wings. They arrived at their destination soon after sunset. It was an aristocratic suburb of St. Petersburg, and as they rode through it Sleznyov pointed out to Alexander the villa of Stolypin. The numismatist T. V. Postny lived nearby. His two-storey villa with a crunchy metalled drive running up to it stood buried in the depths of a park, riotous with autumn colours. Six months later Alexander recollected that several hired carriages with hearse-like nags stood lined up at the left wing. A middle-aged lackey in a striped convict-like waistcoat under his livery ushered the young men into a suite of rooms which had a neglected air about them; here and there, against a background of tapestried panels, scaffolding was set up for decorations, and Sleznyov took the opportunity to whisper again into Alexander's ear what such mansions had cost Russia in terms of soldiers' misery. The company, standing in attitudes of frozen expectancy, were about to sit down at a banquetting table. And scarcely had Alexander Gratsiansky cast his eye upon these strange phantoms, like the fairy-tale prince awakening the sleeping kingdom, when suddenly everything sprang into life and movement with a noise and a scraping of feet. Meanwhile, Sleznyov was telling his friend in a whisper that Postny, bloated with the people's blood, had taken a fancy to plain cooking. Indeed, alongside the luxurious cut-glass and dainty hors d'oeuvres, the main dishes had the rude appearance of a tosspot's repast—sun-dried and salted fish, mushrooms prepared in a variety of ways, and horse radish with kvass. In broad daylight this company would have looked monstrous, but here candles were burning all down the table.

"There he sits, the block of the universe; you'd smash the guillotine on such a neck!" Sleznyov said with inexpressible hatred, motioning with his eyes towards the host, who sat at the head of the feast, and leading Alexander up to him.

Postny patted Sleznyov on the shoulder in a fatherly manner without getting up, and caressed Alexander, too, with bloated little bear's eyes; immediately after this the company rustled down into their chairs, the backs of which they had all been holding. The newcomers got seats at the bottom of the table under a consumptive looking palm, so that Alexander found himself sitting next to an empty chair; he was the youngest of the company, though. He had the advantage of being able to study this collection of St. Petersburg types from where he sat without hindrance. There were about twenty-five of them together with the host, who remotely resembled both a mane-crested noble-man of Catherine's reign and a billiard-marker of a shoddy type, who had often been chastened with the cue in the small of his back. Despite his name (which comes from the word "lenten"), he was a massive old man with a set of chin folds like a creased boot top; nevertheless, there was a touch of mock respectability about him, perhaps the dignifying effect of age, which it is often the humour of an arrant knave to indulge in as the highest luxury. On the others Mother Nature had gone to work in a still more vindictive mood.

Sleznyov, who was sitting next to his friend, pointed out to him a dapper little fellow, who kept pulling down his jacket every minute as if he had a tic. It was a sport jacket in a yellow check pattern, and its wearer was the well-known daredevil adventurer Dorbin-Babkevich, who had taken a stroll on the floor of the Azov Sea in a diving-suit, had gone down in a submarine and up in a free balloon and even gone roller-skating in the building of the newly opened skating-rink in St. Petersburg, had invented a wall-drying apparatus where a metal box containing smouldering charcoal crawled over the doomed wall, and who, to crown a career of prodigious fame, threatened to open a factory of cinematographic films. Next to him, with shifty eyes gleaming, and without attempting to conceal his bad teeth spoilt by good living, a no less disreputable character—a journalist and sly dog by the name of Boris Shtrepetinsky, wearing a huge foulard tie and a stained morning coat—was pouring the latest town gossip into his ear. Everyone knew him as the man who, for a wager, had contrived to shave the horse of the Emir of Bokhara, and taken a photograph of the worthy Metropolitan Antonius in the arms of two aristocratic ladies of his congregation. His neighbour was a thoroughbred horsey-looking gentleman, apparently the illegitimate dynastic scion, who kept strictly to himself at the table so as not to impair his royal dignity. There was something about him, evidently the effect of the prolonged consumption of valuable food, which made him, if not quite human, at least somewhat akin to human beings. One of the guests, always to be found at shady gatherings, was the folklorist Panibratsev, who collected indecent ballads of an anti-government gist; he was a podgy man in a Russian blouse and a ring made from real manacle iron, by aid of which he was said to be catching trustful young souls in the Okhranka snare. "Undoubtedly a very talented agent provocateur, who hasn't been exposed yet," Sleznyov introduced him in an undertone. Variety was provided by a woman, an overripe beauty with a pearl necklace the colour of buck-shot on vast alabaster shoulders; by right of old friendship the host called her simply Neuralgia Zakharovna, which always sent her off into a titter that Alexander found most depressing.

"And who's that one sitting next to her, the scowling fellow with the ham complexion?" Alexander asked incuriously.

"You mean the one next to Benardaki? Why, that's Fridon Hajumovich Pappagailo, the nitrogen manufacturing shareholder, the rising star, Ryabushinsky's competitor. Do you see the emerald in his tie-pin? It's a gift from some wealthy Raja. There you are, old boy, that's called class solidarity among the vampires!"

"No, I mean the one opposite, the satanic-looking fellow. I shouldn't be surprised if he had a tail hidden under that frock-coat. Who is he?"

Alexander motioned his head at a gloomy gentleman with a narkish listening face.

"Oh, that's Brume."

"Who's he—an aristocratic blister or a stock-exchange grabber?"

"No, he's just Brume," Sleznyov murmured evasively, drawing his head into his shoulders and closing up.

So this then was the aristocratic underworld of the capital, and not the Ligovka, where the drunken ragged rabble held noisy court in those days. Alexander Gratsiansky thought it would be a good idea to lay a goodly charge under this villa, put a match to it, and view the results from a safe distance. At that moment, as if by concerted action, all turned their heads in his direction, as though suddenly feeling the icy chill of his determination to blow up the pillars of the old world; he was six months late in grasping the meaning of those glances. The company was waiting for a signal, and as soon as Alexander bent over his plate, they all attacked their food with the zest of people who had been driven down here from town on foot first thing in the morning. Having little reliance on the self-denial of her neighbours, Neuralgia Zakharovna took two bunches of grapes from a cut-glass bowl and put them on her plate for future use, stuffing a third into her already bulging handbag.

"Look at that lady putting the stuff away, Sleznyov," Alexander whispered maliciously to his friend, who, with his mouth full, advised him once again to study the ways of that evil class.

The company gorged itself fairly quickly, and when the clatter of knives on plates subsided it became possible to catch snatches of talk in various quarters. The main topics of conversation were the news of the autumn season—the chances of

Negus Menelik to the Abyssinian throne, the arrival in Russia of the Duke of Connaught, the intention of the popular brigand Zelim-Khan to proclaim himself the Imam of the Chechen, and the success of the drug "606"; two men nearby discussed the platinum market in cooing tones. It was getting quite dark outside, and one could no longer see how badly the windows had been cleaned; Alexander was beginning to feel bored to distraction, and was thinking that he could still manage to get to the House of Countess Panina in time for his lecture if he went to the expense of hiring a smart cab. To Sleznyov's great displeasure he folded his napkin with an air of decision, preparing to slip away, when suddenly the glass door opened and Chandvetsky appeared, greeted by a respectful murmur, and looking fresher and smarter than ever. With a curt guard-officer's nod he apologised to the host for being late, jokingly pleading urgent matters of state. Everyone moved up and Panibratsev drew a chair up into the breach that was thus formed, but it was not this natural commotion with its noisy castling that made Alexander Gratsiansky pale, forget himself, and stay on there to the end.

Chandvetsky had come in arm in arm with a tall beautiful woman in a long, high-necked, exquisitely simple gown; she could not have been more than thirty, and her name, as someone nearby murmured respectfully, was Emma. An ineffable sadness, like the shadow of a blossoming sprig, lay upon the pale Botticellian oval of her face, as Gratsiansky, who was well-read in art, immediately defined it. With himself and Sleznyov, she made the third human being there, and the young man at once felt a need to protect that lovely, slightly bewildered lady from the greedy sweating hands that were stretched out to her from all sides, offering to make way for her sake. She was about to join her haughty companion when everyone started protesting, saying it was a shame for the colonel to enjoy such bliss all by himself, that the husband and wife had to be separated for at least one evening. And since Chandvetsky had already occupied a seat next to Tiberius, she crossed straight to the empty chair at the corner of the table where Alexander Gratsiansky happened to be sitting, ignoring the eyes and hands that were directed towards her.

He stood up and waited on her, muttering words of high-flown gratitude for the honour of her choice; she did not glance at him once, and he saw only her profile. There was something irresistibly fascinating and entrancing in her intricate coiffure, which she wore slightly on one side, in the heavy ear-ring, which made one sorry for the rosy ear, which seemed as if it were chiselled out of evening glow, in the mysterious rustle of silks, which seemed to identify her with the Strange Lady of the then famous poem which was diffused in the very air of St. Petersburg. In addition, hidden music began to play something rather inapposite, Braga's *Serenade*, in fact, and all this, together with the violins, merged for Alexander Gratsiansky into an unforgettable fête, for participation in which one pays with one's life and thanks all the gods that be for having granted one a ticket of admission.

"Goodness me, we're always late, even at the theatre, because of his terrible job," Alexander's neighbour said to herself with a sigh, looking round at the company. "There are so many strangers here, I feel so nervous!"

Untaught in the language which angels speak, Alexander Gratsiansky would have been tongue-tied all the evening, had not his intimacy with Chandvetsky brought this heavenly vision down to earthly levels and made this woman an accessible object of admiration, so much so that Alexander was almost jealous of the dour-faced officer, who did not take his hog's eyes off him, and whom he now hated more fervently than ever.

"With your permission, these terrible strangers will now be one less," Alexander said, and immediately came to the conclusion that the hog, to be on the safe side, kept his bird in a golden cage, under lock and key. "My name is Alexander Gratsiansky. I am twenty. I am a student of the Forestry Institute."

He was wearing the regulation jacket, and the lady glanced at him over her shoulder.

"I don't like students, they're such a rowdy lot," she naively confessed, watching her plate being loaded from a German-silver dish out of the corner of her eye. "We had a student like that for a neighbour, I believe he went in for forestry too."

"Are there foresters in the groves of paradise?"

She missed the point of his confession, which raised her to the rank of an angel.

"I don't know about that, but he was a holy terror. Goodness me, you fellows are such a nuisance!"

Her ingenuous complaint, and the ugly narrowed look of Chandvetsky which he intercepted across the table pushed the young man over the restrictive edge of first acquaintance.

"Oh, if I had a ..." he put a rapturous meaning into his

pause, "a sister like you, you would have the quietest and best-behaved brother in the world! Your acquaintance with foresters, though, inspires me with daring hope. May I, with all humility and utter submission, call you simply Lady Emma ... as a paladin, as in poetry, as a sister?"

She looked at him in a startled manner and stopped eating. Obviously, no one had ever talked to her like that. Alexander did not see her eyes any more, and no more painful punishment could have been devised for him. It was more than he could bear to be deprived of them for even the brief space of time that her eyelashes shaded them.

Drops of moisture still gleamed in her hair. He asked her in the tone with which children beg forgiveness, "Tell me ... please ... is it raining outside?"

She forgave him at once.

"Yes, and there's a biting wind," she said with a little shiver brought on by the memory of the foul weather.

"It's autumn. Everyone knows that it will come one day, yet it always comes unexpectedly. And then we regret that summer has gone. It's the same in life. Would you like something to warm you, some wine?"

"No, don't. I'm a sight when I drink. Besides, he told me not to have anything today."

But Alexander insisted and filled her glass, relishing the fury which this roused in Chandvetsky, who was still watching them furtively from under his lowered eyelids. And Lady Emma yielded to Alexander's wishes and took three sips with the air of one committing an act of conjugal infidelity; then, thought-fully, she sighed and took a fourth. Her eyes darkened and her nostrils slightly distended and grew pink. Something new, some-thing he had never known before in his transient meetings with women and which young generous Natasha Zolotinskaya had never been able to give him, swept Alexander off his feet. Not daring yet to put it into that single word, in which entreaty mingles with obligation, he began to speak about other things; he spoke long and pompously, for already at that time he suf-fered from the gift of eloquence. He preferred to win the heart of his lady by a pyrotechnics of wit, a brilliant display of knowl-edge gleaned on the eve from books, and to compel surrender without perceptible retraints for himself. Possibly, he had some inkling of his destiny—that of the spider who jerks the web line at the other end of which sits the object of his love, his prey and his grave.

"Goodness me, what's it all about!" was all that Lady Emma said.

After dinner they passed into another room done in St. Petersburg-Moresque, with drinks, sweets and tobacco served on low mosaic stools. Some of the guests with the host and Chandvetsky at their head sat down at two card tables, still in the light of candles, as the chandelier barely allowed the light to pass through the coloured glass insertions. With the intention of continuing the assault, Alexander Gratsiansky arranged a cosy nest in the half-light behind the columns, but while he went to look for a second armchair for his lady, she was stolen by Dorbin-Babkevich. Surrounded by a crowd of admirers, he was describing, in the capacity of future knight commander, the route and possible calamities of the automobile race through Central Russia, which was to be held within a week.

"Aren't you afraid, Dorbin, that as a result of your escapades er ... you will have to spend the night in some er ... infected mountain village," the illegitimate one anxiously enquired with a slight stammer, examining the daredevil through his monocle.

"Sire!" the other cried fervidly, rushing towards him, not because that fossilised individual was entitled to that form of address, but because it raised him in his own estimation. "The elements were never kind to their conquerors, but your true sportsman, following in the tracks of his great predecessors Stanley and Miklukho-Maklai, is not daunted by hardships!"

"But, goodness me!" Lady Emma cried, horrified, and Alexander Gratsiansky started at the sound of her throaty voice. "What will you do if the motor busts up under your seat in the middle of the road?"

"Madame," that hero of our day said airily, crossing his feet in their inexpressible yellow gaiters and leaning his elbow on the beadwork fire screen, "in that case I shall lay my bones beneath the sod, remembering the mysterious light of your lovely eyes, Madame!"

For a whole hour Alexander suffered the agonising pangs of loneliness in his corner; he also felt a bit sick from the raw champignons served with hot goose fat, which was the last word in West-European cookery. He felt like getting drunk and going berserk in order to recover Lady Emma's attention, and doubtlessly he would have done so were he not afraid of upsetting his mother. After pondering at some length whether he should assault the innocent Dorbin-Babkevich or burn a hole in the carpet with a cigarette, he finally decided to smash a bottle of liqueur; no one except the lackeys, who immediately removed the rug, noticed this little revolt of his. Without a doubt, his next fit of jealousy would have taken a more quarrelsome and violent form but for an intervening incident which radically altered the whole situation.

At about eleven o'clock an excited butler called Chandvetsky out of the room to see a messenger who had come post-haste from town. Chandvetsky reappeared a few minutes later, frowning and getting into his coat.

"Ladies and gentlemen, no panic please. I have just received sad news from the telegraph office," he announced in an official impersonal tone amidst a deathly silence. "*Hofmeister* Stolypin has just been assassinated in Kiev."

All sprang to their feet and for some reason lined themselves up. All except Neuralgia Zakharovna, who collapsed in a heap on the ottoman.

"Who did it? Who fired the shot? Where was he hit?" voices were raised in alarmed inquiry.

"At 'Tsar Saltan'. Stomach and liver. His Majesty unharmed. About eighteen, wearing a dress coat. In the second interval. Name unknown. Damn it, where's my cap!"

"Goodness me, how awful!" Lady Emma almost moaned, and one would think the assassinated dignitary was some near relative of hers.

"Unfortunately the telegraph has no further details. Please carry on. I have to go away. May I hope that someone will see Emma home? The carriage will be waiting for you at the door, my child." His eyes pleaded with her to pull herself together.

He rushed out with an iron tread, forehead thrust forward, like a battering-ram getting ready to swing into action in the forthcoming battle for the empire's weal. Postny tried in vain to calm the guests. Forgetting Chandvetsky's request, they hastened away one after another on their various businesses—some to their editorial offices, others to the stock exchange, or simply to their homes to lock their coffers and shutters. It was not so much fear of the possible consequences which threatened in such cases; rather was it a bustling activity, a most pleasurable stir among these denizens of the lower depths like that caused by a dropped stone, which, together with the mud, throws up rich light food. Sleznyov, too, slipped away unobserved, and presently the only people left in the Moorish room besides the host and Gratsiansky were Emma and the royal bastard, who had drunk himself into a state of ignominious helplessness.

"It's time I went home, too," said Lady Emma, looking at no one in particular.

Her voice held a timid note, like that of a person overawed by fate, which was placing her in the keeping of this strange student. Gratsiansky bent his head, ready to serve, concealing his exultation beneath a mask of somewhat anxious and dutiful respect. The host, wheezing and grunting, went downstairs to see the guests off, helped them into the colonel's carriage and fastened the leather apron over their knees, which were joined at last.

On the evening of September 1, 1911 the weather in the capital was rainy, and a changeable wind blew. Towards the night the wind eased slightly and a yellow St. Petersburg fog blanketed the streets. As there was still an occasional drizzle, the carriage hood had to be raised.

"Come along, get a move on!" Lady Emma threw out impatiently to the dignified-looking coachman in his padded caftan girdled with a crimson sash, and they were engulfed in the scented maddening silence of autumn, broken only by the wet *clop* of the hooves.

Subdued by digestive sensations rather than rapture, Alexander Gratsiansky rocked on the seat beside his companion. After a while, under the effect of the regular swaying motion of the carriage, the champignon-induced malaise wore off, but the power of eloquent speech had not returned yet. After half a mile Alexander plucked up courage to glance at his companion. Her face was invisible, and only an ear-ring shone tantalisingly under her hat, quivering and disappearing now and again in her locks of hair or wreaths of mist which billowed around them. Owing to the late hour there was not a soul in the streets, and under the circumstances this ride was to be considered a great blunder on the part of Chandvetsky and a stroke of luck for his happy rival.

The only trouble was that the young man suddenly had a bad attack of the most ungentlemanly hiccups. It was not until they had gone another mile or so that it occurred to him to explain his regrettable silence by the obligation of nobility and deference imposed upon a lady's guide.

"I've been thinking of you, Lady Emma," he proceeded to his business with a voice of growing confidence. "It may be useful for angets to descend to lower levels from time to time for the sake of self-education, but in your husband's place I would never take you to such a den. It sullies. For my part I still feel a nasty taste in the mouth, don't you?"

"Oh, goodness me!" she sighed, and with a rustle of silk, moved away slightly, as much as the small space of the carriage would permit.

In those days Alexander Gratsiansky, the pampered darling, was accustomed to look upon his youth as a cheque book with which to pay for forbidden pleasures. There was an exquisite touch of depravity about this ride together, not because of the hot magnetic field that had formed between them from the very first minute, or, let us say, the sinful warmth which emanated from the knees of a strange woman; the depravity lay mostly in the very fact of Alexander's contact with the dark institution, where at that very moment her husband, by despicable methods, was making a living to keep her, the horse that carried them, and coachman who sat dozing on the box. Alexander's heart twitched with fear at the thought of Valery and Vikhrov ever getting to know of this extended circle of his acquaintances; Cheredilov was more complaisant. He had to seek off-hand a moral justification for his weakness, and most conveniently at this point an idea came to him that it would be abysmally stupid to miss such an opportunity of carrying out his threat, teaching the colonel a lesson, and testing in practice the security of his family hearth. The same imp of mischief goaded Alexander Gratsiansky into undertaking certain preliminaries, during which it immediately transpired that Lady Emma was curiously inexperienced in repelling such attacks. Towards the end of their journey Alexander even had the temerity to kiss her—not altogether successfully, because the carriage bumped over a pothole, and he scratched his cheek painfully against the ear-ring which had come undone.

"Goodness me!" whispered Emma, arresting his hand. "I'll tell him about you!"

And so from the very outset there was established between them that superstitious understanding peculiar to all lovers not to utter aloud the name of the third party so as not to court trouble.

"Oh, tell him, tell him!" reiterated Alexander Gratsiansky, greatly emboldened by the course of events. "Tell him, and let him send me down to the Siberian mines for it, ha-ha!"

During the next half-mile he succeeded in making up for his bungled first assault and having his revenge on Lady Emma for the pain she had inflicted.

"Goodness me, be sensible!" she said, feebly resisting and nodding at the powerful hemisphere of the coachman's back which served them as a fourth wall. "What will he think if he hears?"

"Nonsense! For one thing, Caesar's wife is above suspicion, for another—where am I to send the flowers tomorrow?"

"The man is mad!" she said, now thoroughly alarmed and prepared to stop the carriage.

She also resisted his attempt to see her to the door of the flat for fear that the neighbours would recognise Chandvetsky's turn-out. As there was nothing reprehensible in a well-bred student delivering a treasure to its home at the request of its owner, Lady Emma's resistance was interpreted by Alexander Gratsiansky as a quite natural fear for his fate on her part. This buoyed him up for a whole week, during which she promised to let him know the date and place of their meeting—he had finally succeeded in getting the promise.

But the letter from Lady Emma never came. Alexander had celebrated victory too soon; the worst of it was they had no common acquaintances and he might never have another chance of meeting her as long as he lived. He learned from Sleznyov, who knew all the backstage news and gossip, that Kulyabko, the chief of the Okhranka in Kiev, had been dismissed for negligence, and that by a special order of the Imperial Court, Colonel Chandvetsky, invested with special powers, had gone out to investigate the mysterious shot at the opera. Emma's silence was obviously the repentance of a woman inexperienced in amorous play, and so Alexander Gratsiansky neglected his lectures for a whole month and took to walking up and down in front of Chandvetsky's windows in every kind of weather until the house porters began to take him for a detective. That he could not stand. Nothing was left for him but to bank the fires of passion with an epigonous little poem about the intimate emotions of a pilgrim wandering barefoot on a thorny path in search of a fair and unkind lady. These pedestrian verses, wrapped in a symbolic mist, which was fashionable in those days, were received with enthusiasm by lovers of the art, first and foremost Sleznyov.

"Why, if you're not a Dante! Worse than that, a Casanova, damn it! Stop torturing me, tell me, who is she?" he tried, like others, to find out, while Natasha Zolotinskaya, preparing for the consequences of her girlish trustfulness, looked artlessly radiant, believing she was the cause, but Alexander Gratsiansky only smiled enigmatically. "True, this opus of yours, Alexander, reveals a psychological dissatisfaction that is quite understandable, but I can imagine what you're going to spring on us when you get to her boudoir at last!"

As he left the house at dusk one day early in the winter to take a stroll to restore his haemoglobin, Alexander Gratsiansky ran straight into Lady Emma.

2

She was returning from the skating-rink in a light squirrel coat, chilled and tired. Alexander thought it was rather odd, because Sergiyevskaya Street was out of her way, but Emma said she had looked up a girl friend to while away the time but had not found her in.

"Goodness me, this *is* a surprise!" was all she said, dropping her eyes and recoiling as if she had seen a ghost.

"I never thought you went in for that kind of sport, otherwise we could have.... But I go to that skating-rink too, how is it I never met you there?"

"I don't suppose you wanted to very much," she said, and her swinging skates clinked softly on their strap.

He plied her with questions—why did she look thinner, had *he* come back from Kiev, why had she so cruelly deceived her paladin. Lady Emma was silent; she dare not disengage her imprisoned hands, which had lost all will to resistance.

"Come, lift your veil now!" Alexander commanded peremptorily and bitterly, and Lady Emma realised that soon he would demand other balm for his soul's pangs.

In the yellow light of a gas lamp he peered eagerly into her sweet face, which looked all the more attractive with those slightly hollow cheeks and the glitter in her eyes, which, from his experience with Natasha Zolotinskaya, he attributed to his own irresistible charm; looking back, he remembered being curiously touched by the incipient wrinkles round her mouth. Alexander was swept by a gust of passion and puerile ardour.

"All this time I have been yearning madly for your eyes... every day, every minute. It's probably heaven's greatest miracle that you see me on my legs at all!" He considered he had a right to such poetic license. "So there, you owe me a debt, Lady Emma!"

"I know," she said faintly, and a curious little smile played about her down-shaded lips. "Oh don't, please don't!"

The more he looked at her the stronger did he find her resemblance to the Mona Lisa, the theft of which from the Louvre had served as a subject for speculation in the newspapers all through that year.

"You have been stolen from me, too, but I have found you. And findings are keepings, at least for this evening. I will not let you go, even if it cost me my life. We are going somewhere right away!"

Apparently Lady Emma did not read the newspapers, because a startled look flashed in her eyes at the mention of the theft. In a faint voice, she asked Gratsiansky, "But where, goodness me, where?"

"It's for you to choose, Lady Emma. Here are all the celestial delights of St. Petersburg," Alexander said with a courteous bow, more in love with her than ever for that charming grace of startled acquiescence, as he took the evening paper from his pocket and handed it to her.

It was almost magnanimous of him, that, realising the dismay of his victim, he granted her easy terms of payment instead of demanding cash down. Snow-flakes fell gently on the printed sheet with the theatrical notices, which looked yellow in the gaslight. and the snow turned into nothing in the frosty air. Emma was for going to the opera, where there were closed boxes. "Don't you see, Alexander, everyone knows me here," she explained, blushing, presumably on account of her husband's vocation. The young man answered vehemently that all the world's boredom, music included, he left in reserve for old age together with the gout. They began to look for something more entertaining, running their fingers along the lines and cooing like a couple of conspirators. In two small theatres in Nevsky two fashionable plays were running—*The Triumph of a Bacchante* and *The Drunken Corpse*; at the circus Moderne a daredevil was performing a hair-raising somersault over a real live izvozchik complete with cab and horse; at the Cabaret Intime, in the Fontanka, a human accumulator Alva Stanhom, capable of withstanding an electric current of eight-hundred thousand volts, was the hit of the season. In addition, that same evening the Negro Bambula was wrestling with Lurich, and at Villa-Rodé, on Stroganovsky Bridge, Mlle Lalya showed various tricks for grown-ups. In the end they decided to go to Comedians' Bivouac in Marsovo Polye. This was the most refined den in St. Petersburg in those days kept by the notorious businessman of the underworld Mitka Rubinstein.

Gaudy placards printed upside down to draw the public were posted at the entrance to the basement, which the magic spell of fashionable artists had transformed into a metropolitan Bohemia. The place smelt like a swamp under the vaulted ceiling, and the reeling walls had flaming firebirds on them, not to mention other less innocent subjects by no less a person than Boris Grigoryev. Together with the varied scum of the city some of the most celebrated writers frequented the place. Kuprin and Artsibashev dropped in with a retinue of admirers from the most surprising walks of life; Leonid Andreyev, in velvet blouse, stepped down here from his apartment to bask in the sunbeams of fame. When Alexander and his companion ran down the carpeted stairs Sleznyov was standing at the cloak-room counter. He suddenly disappeared behind a column, his face looking flushed and strained. To the student's great but insincere resentment, an elderly individual in a bowler—the hat of bankers and self-respecting detectives in those days—pawed Emma with oily eyes and stroked his moustache. Actually, Alexander was flattered to be seen in public with such a resplendent lady. Still, for the sake of self-preservation, it would be better for Lady Emma to remain in her hat and veil, so as not to attract the attention of tattlers and not to alert the absent jealous husband until the antlered appendages had grown properly on his forehead. Alexander Gratsiansky pretended to brush a speck of dust off his chest—his wallet was safe. The nocturnal swamp greeted them with a stench, with reeking vapours, gurglings, and a devils' racket, as always happens when human beings quit it.

They were given an inconvenient table in the passageway near an arch. It would have been better to occupy a recess behind one of the mysterious curtains from which Sudeikin's warty heavenly bodies looked down with a smirk, but Alexander Gratsiansky had only thirty rubles pocket-money which his mother had given him the day before, and outsiders who did not belong to the world of art and went here by the name of "pharmaceutists" were made to pay through the nose. Waiters scurried back and forth through a mist of kitchen fumes, carrying still lives raised aloft to the ceiling, while a sort of glass boy with painted cheeks, one of the poet Kuzmin's reciters, was scanning something about iris, incense,

670

and the icy volupty of ceaseless falls in a singsong voice. After him, as though performing a rite, a young woman with a fringe over the veiled eyes of a nun got up from a corner table and began to recite some verses about the fair Murgit who swore to consign her soul to the devil and eternal fires; someone next to her, who was pretty tight, beat time with a pair of castanets, his sniffling nose nodding drunkenly over the table-cloth.

Emma sat listening with her head bent over the table, and suddenly Alexander Gratsiansky, with the delight of a hardened sinner, detected a tear under her veil.

"What's the matter, Lady Emma?" he said, leaning forward. "You don't mean to say you're affected by those provincial verses without new rhythms or startling revelations? Do you call that an abyss—seven inches deep! Drink your wine, don't be afraid—*he*'s far away, *he* can't hear, *he* can't appreciate his Penelope's faithfulness."

"No, I'm just tired after the skating-rink," she murmured guiltily, drawing her head into her shoulders. "Will you please look who that is standing behind me in the pince-nez on a black ribbon, and why he dares to smile in that nasty way?"

Alexander Gratsiansky's eyes swivelled angrily towards the object.

"Oh, that's only Panibratsev, unquestionably a sycophant and an old swindler to boot. I'll go over and punch his nose if you like. He'll take it, just command me, Lady Emma!"

He had no desire whatever to roll over the floor with that bullock of a man, limp and sleazy though he was; he calculated on his companion's sensible moderation.

"Oh, it's not worth it, leave him alone! But, goodness me, how beastly it all is!" For a minute she looked round her, where everything was chewing, embracing, falsely swearing love and friendship, which art's votaries are always good at, drinking brandy and fixing dates, drawling obscenities through tobacco-stained teeth, concluding alliances and deals, laying bets, signing author's copies, and all together combining to make a noise of hopeless futility like that in a gigantic seashell held to the ear. Emma suddenly got up with an air of decision.

"I can't stand it. For God's sake let us go away quickly!"

He was startled for obvious reasons.

"But this is madness. Where are we to go, when we've only just come!"

"I don't care ... take me away from here, anywhere."

"But why, Lady Emma, why? At least, explain this whim of yours!" Alexander said coldly, for he had spent all his money on this almost untouched food and uncorked wine. He could not very well take the bottle away with him under his jacket.

Emma got her coat on while he was arguing with the waiter over the price of the veal steak. The inexplicable caprice of this woman raised her still higher in his estimation, if anything. He was even grateful to her for this forced extravagance, which gave him a chance to boast in his own set and put him on even terms with those above him, whom he hated and envied for being so free with their money. All that Alexander had left to carry him through a whole night of glamorous adventures was a gold coin and some small change for the cloak-room attendant.

"Well, what are we going to do now?" he demanded when they were outside, flinching at the thought of new whims which he now had no means of gratifying.

Fortunately, her only wish was to ride about at random for a thousand years. A sleigh with a shabby rug stiff from the frost stood waiting for a fare at the corner. The runners creaked, and the vast stone bulks of the buildings, half-buried in snow, floated past and behind them. Emma drank in the crisp pure air of early winter in uneasy silence, but Alexander Gratsiansky, after a minute or two, fully recovered from his regrets. Gripping the back of the sleigh behind his companion, he poured a string of ambiguities into her ear, for the most part historical anecdotes, which, like toothsome sweepings for the ragpicker, thickly litter the pedestals of the great. It sounded as if mankind had been playing its game of fire and blood for thousands of years merely to give Alexander Gratsiansky a chance to chase away the ennui of his Fair Lady and tickle his lips against the black lock over her ear-ring.

At this point he thought it opportune to turn over the dragging page.

"Don't you ever feed that jade of yours, you rascal!" Alexander Gratsiansky stood up and shouted hussar-like at the driver. The sleigh flew forward as if rushing downhill.

On a sudden mischievous impulse, and in order to disguise his next rude move, he asked Emma whether she was fond of Grieg. Brought up, no doubt, in an atmosphere of monastic ignorance biassed in favour of Bach and Haydn, she was rather at a loss, since she did not know who that man Grieg was—a lawyer, a civil servant, or a merchant. Taking advantage of her confusion,

Alexander Gratsiansky tried to squeeze his fingers into her fur-trimmed glove, and when nothing came of it, tried her sleeve.

"Goodness me, don't! You will be sorry for it yourself!" Emma feebly resisted, holding herself away from him and covering her face with her muff against the lumps of snow which flew up from under the horse's hooves.

"But can't you see the naughty boy has frozen his poor finger. Let him warm himself! He is not afraid, not a bit afraid of all the gendarmes in the world!"

"Aren't you really?" Emma queried, glancing at him oddly, then suddenly stopped the sleigh. "But first see who those people are over there. They must be victims of a fire. Poor things, go and find out, will you."

The scene was the Okhta Bridge, opened the year before, flung across the dark chilly waters. Motionless ghostlike figures huddled darkly against the cast-iron railings like a street sculptural group carved out of gloom and cold instead of bronze or iron. Unbroken snow lay white upon their shoulders and in the folds of their sheepskin coats. They were peasants, four of them: a spindly old man in an *armyak* and three ugly women of different ages in tight-fitting sheepskin coats done up on hooks. They had probably dragged themselves here from the farthest hinterland of Russia; the chill of boundless spaces hung about them. Alexander Gratsiansky shrewdly guessed what it was—the newspapers occasionally mentioned yet another crop failure on the Volga.

He went up closer to execute the commands of Lady Emma.

"Hullo, folks, er . . . what are you standing there for?" he said in a friendly tone so as not to frighten them. "You'll freeze to death. Why don't you go to some cheap hotel, or better still, to some inn or something . . . that's right. Where do you come from, who are you, why don't you speak?"

None answered him, but the woman standing nearest to him, the youngest of the three, started back at the sight of his uniform coat with the brass buttons; the old man alone continued bravely, without surprise or fright, to gaze at the student, or rather through him, as if he were just another hungry vision. And then Alexander Gratsiansky perceived a fifth figure, crouching at the knees of an old woman, the figure of a little girl in bast shoes and a shawl tied crosswise around her body; she woke up and stared at the student with the same dim eyes the colour of wintry gloom. The young man, with the best intentions, put a hand out to stroke the child, but the old woman pressed her head to her bosom wildly and jealously, as much as to say, don't touch her, she's ours. He felt hurt, because he had no intention of taking anything away from them; on the contrary, he wanted to cheer them up. Besides, the snow was so deep there, and Alexander, who was susceptible to colds, had left the house without his galoshes. The muzhiks' shyness and obstinacy suited him to a T, though, as it relieved him of both expense and pricks of conscience.

"No, they're not fire victims, just muzhiks. Come up from the country, I suppose," he reported vaguely, returning to the sleigh. "They're probably farmers from across the Volga. They've cut down all the forests, and now they're paying for it. Well, Lady Emma, let's be going."

"Give them something," Emma commanded in a strange bleak voice.

Alexander Gratsiansky hesitated, mentally turning his last gold coin over in his fingers. It wasn't that he stinted ten kopeks, he would have given much more than that for Russia to be able afterwards to describe his sacrificial emotions in well-cadenced verse, but somehow it was extremely humiliating to demand four rubles and eighty-five kopeks change from beggars, and he still had to pay the sleigh driver.

"Oh, that's all right, they're used to it. Things like that are always happening out there. Your poor boy has got his feet wet for nothing," Alexander dismissed the matter with a joke and got back into the sleigh.

For two days thereafter he was more annoyed than conscience-stricken at the thought that he had lowered himself in the eyes of a woman, although he believed he had spent quite enough on her that evening. It must have been his manly behaviour, though, which persuaded Emma that further resistance was useless. Things were going swimmingly. Alexander accompanied his lady love to her friend's house now almost every day, or carried trifling purchases for her the while he recited verses into her frost-nipped ear, all tending to shake conjugal fidelity. But she hurried along, as if anxious to run away from him into the flaky falling snow, to escape the fate which was overtaking her. The utter discomfiture of the colonel of the gendarmes took place in the Daryal rooming house on the corner of Nevsky and Vladimirsky. "Goodness me!" was all that Emma said that evening. She spoke very little, if she spoke at all, never asked any questions, agreed with everything by eyes alone, and possessed to perfection the gift of listening rapturously, which usually passes with women as a sign of intelligence in the eyes of their too talkative admirers. For a whole month Alexander Gratsiansky was in an ecstasy over his submissive victim, who was overwhelmed by his impatience, so much so that he ended up by wanting to marry her.

"Now look at me, Emma, and listen. Tomorrow you will file a petition for a divorce from that hog of yours," he told her, stupefied by the spells she had cast over him. "My father has a friend, an eminent lawyer, and if.... What are you laughing at?"

More and more often something twinkled in her eyes. It was not tears.

"For one thing, Alec, I'm older than you, and secondly...." She shook her head. "Why, goodness me, your father will simply kick you out if you bring a divorced wife into his house! Don't be in a hurry, everything will work out all right. Let it be the magical dream you've been wanting, and there's no need for you to wake up at all!"

In the professor's liberal family, of course, Emma would never be a success. So then Alexander Gratsiansky proposed eloping.

"I won't have anybody looking at you even, especially that hog of yours. Be ready tomorrow evening. Don't take anything with you except perhaps your favourite knickknacks. And wait for me outside the chemist's at the corner."

"You're silly and affectionate... affectionate, aren't you?" she said. There was something in the depths of her pupils she did not want him to see, and at times a sinister note crept into her voice, as though she felt like pitying him, but then reminded herself of something and fought down that feeling. "Where are we going to run away, we haven't any money? Show me, how much have you got left?"

"I don't care," he said, paling and biting his lips. "I'll rob a bank, I'll kill Benardaki, I'll borrow a loan from Postny—you have no idea what I'm capable of doing for your sake. I'll take the world by the scruff of its neck and bend it down to your feet like a dog."

Towards the end of the second month, though, Alexander Gratsiansky was very pleased that he had not carried out a single one of his threats and promises. Simultaneously with the cooling off there ripened in his mind a super-satanic plan for drawing Emma into the Young Russia organisation and thus start by planting one of their own people in the heart of the tsarist *Okhranka*. There was no doubt whatever that Sleznyov would approve the idea when he heard about it. On his way home after a walk,

Alexander passed the Winter Palace almost every day with the sardonic smile of an old bomber, whose whole aspect seemed to say, "You wait, you'll get soap for soap, tit for tat, an Azef for an Azef!" Oh, this would be such a blow at Chandvetsky that it would floor him like a bull on a Madrid arena.

Little by little Alexander Gratsiansky began to introduce his captive to some of the progressive ideas of the day, disclosing to her certain depths of political economy within the limits of his own plumbing, and teaching her the ABC of hatred, all the more that she herself had apparently suffered much from her husband, and had a very low opinion of the St. Petersburg aristocracy, especially the middle ranks of officialdom whom she knew personally.

On the other hand, she confessed to her lover one day, lying with her hands under her head, that she had no particular liking for revolutionaries either.

"That's because you've never seen them, you silly girl, and judge them only by your husband's slander. There are real fine people among them. I know one of them at the Forestry Institute, a senior student. He's like a sword blade on the stroke. Between you and me, that man transported a secret print-shop to the South in suitcases." Sleznyov had hinted to him about Valery's underground activities only quite recently, with a look of canine devotion in his eyes, and ever since then Alexander Gratsiansky considered he had a right occasionally to boast of his friend's heroism, since his intimacy with Valery cast a romantic reflection upon his own person. "I'm going to the theatre with him tomorrow, you can look at him from the box, but mind you don't fall in love with him!"

Emma flatly refused to go to the theatre both then and later, when, provoked by her disbelief, he told her Valery's real name, told her without fear of betraying a comrade, since, if the affair took a bad turn, Emma would be obliged to divulge to her husband the circumstances under which she received this information. Alexander Gratsiansky, by the way, had got it himself without making any effort during their first and only foursome visit to the Greek eating-house in Karavannaya. Krainov's aunt, who had just arrived in the capital, had indiscreetly hailed her nephew in the street. True, Krainov had not answered to his old name, but the sudden jerk of his stiffened arm and momentary hesitancy of speech had not escaped Gratsiansky nor Vikhrov, who was walking on the other side. Valery Krainov was arrested a fortnight later, so that the student had no suspicions of Emma having had anything to do with it.

Their meetings grew rarer, and Alexander Gratsiansky took skilful advantage of their very first tiff to break off the affair; the investigations in Kiev had been completed by that time, and Chandvetsky returned to St. Petersburg promoted in rank. The ice-drift had begun on the Neva when Sleznyov told his friend confidentially that his rival was going to Abhazia to take a cure. The colonel was going there with his wife, and Alexander Gratsiansky chose that day to deal his *coup de grâce*. Possibly, some remnant of decency would have kept him from committing so base an act of ingratitude towards the woman whose favours he had enjoyed, had not Lady Emma, during a tiff, made a nasty remark about his behaviour on the Okhta Bridge. Alexander Gratsiansky rushed off to the station in the morning, buying a bunch of expensive roses on the way; they had come straight from Nice, and he chose the reddest, the meaning of which was clear to a child. He strode down the platform with the defiant air of a dueller, carrying his unwrapped bouquet like a huge fire-brand for all to see and savour his vindictive triumph.

The train was about to leave. Official-looking types ran through the student's pockets with their eyes. Chandvetsky was walking up and down the passage of the sleeping car in an unbuttoned tunic.

"If you don't mind, I've brought some flowers for your charming wife," the student began ceremoniously without any greeting, but with the relish of a hunter who plunges a long jagged knife into the boar. "I'm sorry, I was afraid I'd be late, and I had no time to wrap it up in a newspaper."

"Oh, that's a very noble gesture on your part, Mr. Gratsiansky," the colonel said without the slightest hint of astonishment or anger. He smelt the fresh roses and looked into the compartment. "Are you busy, Elsa? A young man here wants to give you some beautiful roses. He has done us a service and apparently wants to cement our relations."

Before Gratsiansky could recover from the shock and utter a word a sickly looking woman in a hell-length skirt with a longish nose slightly blue from the cold weather came out of the compartment.

"Goodness, these are so pretty flowers!" she said, slightly maltreating the language and holding out her hands.

Alexander Gratsiansky experienced the sensation of a man who had been suddenly hit in the face with the flat of a two-inch board. Yellow circles and bloody sparks floated before his eyes. Someone uttered an exclamation, and one of the sleuths nearby laughed obsequiously when the student, dropping the bouquet on the floor, made a dash for the door. It was impossible to say yet what exactly had happened, but judging by Chandvetsky's hint, it was the worst of possible variants. Consternation drove Alexander to Sleznyov through the whole city.

Sleznyov was shaving his second cheek before a tiny mirror when Alexander Gratsiansky burst into the room wild-eyed and haggard.

"Things have taken a rotten turn, old boy, they couldn't be worse," Sleznyov agreed after he had heard his friend's hoarse confession. "People don't die from it, of course, but it's pretty rotten all the same. Tears won't help either . . . no, I'm afraid they won't. To tell you the truth, I simply couldn't make out what you found in that young lady, whom half the town knows intimately. Damn it, I've cut myself. Give me the spirits off the window-sill, old boy, will you."

"Why the hell didn't you tell me, why didn't you keep me away from the brink?" Alexander Gratsiansky said with a groan.

"But you never shared your secrets with me, old boy . . . and generally, you've become very reticent lately, now haven't you?" Sleznyov laughed, cauterising the cut pimple on his cheek with the burning wick saturated in methylated spirits. "You didn't even want to tell me what they arrested that friend of yours for . . . that fellow Valery. Besides, how was anyone to keep you back! Panibratsev complained that you almost burned a hole in him with your eyes when he dared to smile at the happy pair, that's it— the ram and the ewe. I even thought, simple soul, that you were out to save her, that Emma of yours. Lots of men are doing that now, it works out cheaper. But what was the use of trying to make you see sense. For God's sake, sit down, and stop fidgeting, I'll cut myself. As soon as I've finished we'll go and have lunch. They've opened a new restaurant on the corner, Nirvana they've called it. You'd give your soul for one of their *rasstegais*."

"Do you know where she lives?" Alexander Gratsiansky asked with white lips.

"Are you in a hurry to murder her?" Sleznyov laughed at him through the mirror. "Don't worry, things will come out all right. Just warn her she shouldn't babble, that's all."

"Give me her address, this very minute!" Alexander muttered.

It turned out that she lived in the same lodging-house where they had been meeting, only one floor higher up and two rooms nearer the staircase, so that she did not have far to go to keep her appointments. "All the frail sisterhood live there with their fancy men," explained Sleznyov, pushing his cheek out with his tongue and sticking a piece of paper on the cut. Alexander Gratsiansky flew thither on the singed wings of dream for no accountable reason other than perhaps a desire to ease the pangs of the heart by violent activity.

He sought his Lady Emma for a long time among the maze of rooms. At first he ran into a dark-skinned teacher of magic and Tibethan medicine straight from the Himalayas, and then found himself the visitor of a bored Swedish lady, who also practised fortune-telling by cards by the Japanese method. Emma came out to him in a flannel dressing-gown with a face of faded bloom, and not until the student had started trying to break the door down with his shoulder.

"Goodness me, is that you!" she exclaimed with ill-feigned joy, patting her rumpled hair. "Where have you been all this time, Alec, how are you getting on?"

He was choking, suffocated by the mingled stench of frying fat, singed hair, rancid face lotions and uncleaned carpets.

"I must speak to you!" he cried, pushing aside the dusty flame-coloured plush hangings.

"I can't see you now, you'll have to come some other time. I'm always engaged on Tuesday and Wednesday, so make it Thursday from three to five." She puckered her brow in thought. "No, Thursday won't do either. I tell you what, drop in on Saturday week."

"Oh, how cruelly you treated me, Lady Emma!" Alexander Gratsiansky moaned in the voice of a cracked violoncello. "People are killed on the spot for that sort of thing! At any rate, I am grateful to you for not having punished me still more cruelly."

Her eyes flashed with indignation.

"Keep your hair on, my young fellow-me-lad! Damn it, everyone plugs along as best he can. Didn't I give you a good time, did I beg any money from you or expensive presents? What's biting you there?" she turned round at a bass appeal from behind the screen. "I can't tear myself to pieces between you, gentlemen! Goodness me, what cads you all are. You go after your dirty bit of sweet, and then you come kicking up a row. Didn't you call it your magical dream?"

Alexander Gratsiansky heard her out with an air of hysterically exaggerated politeness.

"And how much do I owe you for that dream, all in all?" he said, failing to read in her eyes what it was she had drawn him down into this abyss with. "At least, I should like to get my poems back—those I wrote to you in my blindness."

She began to lose her temper.

"Poems? Ah, those! But that's impossible, you silly. They're in the file. Can't you understand, dearie, they'll never let me in there! Come, come, run along now, the floorman's getting angry. Mind you're not late on Saturday, or I'll go to the baths." She pushed him out and shut the door on the hook in the twinkling of an eye.

Only now did Alexander Gratsiansky feel the full impact of the smack in the face which Chandvetsky had dealt him with a gloved backdrawn hand. So that memorable dinner at Postny's had been merely the beginning of a diabolic game, the baiting of a hare, a play at cat-and-mouse. And that meeting in the street with Emma two months later had not been accidental either; she had probably been walking up and down Sergiyevskaya Street with her skates since early in the morning, cursing her miserable bitch's life. What she wanted that day was not dainty salmon, but a glass of strong gin! So he had spared no expense, had that Caesar of the Okhranka, to turn the young student inside out, to knock him out at a single blow, without, however, impairing his health or clothes. And unless the whole thing had been merely a noisome exhalation of the St. Petersburg swamp, then everything there had been specially hired—the villa, the Moorish church-lustre, Pappagailo and his Indian emerald. One would even think, in sheer desperation, that they had killed Stolypin only to lend colour to their cruel game in the eyes of their victim.

It was raining hard outside. Alexander Gratsiansky wandered about the city until evening, and when he grew tired, he went, drenched to the skin, to weep on the knees of Natasha Zolotin-skaya, who had once seen him come out of the lodging-house with Emma.

We could end here this never-disclosed episode had not another blow, the greatest of all, been awaiting Alexander Gratsiansky. A week after his return from Abhazia, Colonel Chandvetsky sent him an official summons to come and see him at the Mitninskaya headquarters. When the young man came into the private office, head drawn respectfully into his shoulders, he found Giganov there besides the chief. The police spy had smartened himself up for the occasion, and was sitting in an armchair turning over the pages of a blue magazine with a languid air. Every now and then he patted his sleek shiny hair and furtively smelt his hand after it.

Neither of them got up at Gratsiansky's entrance.

"The reason I have troubled you, Mr. Gratsiansky, is to thank you for the assistance you have given us," the colonel began without offering his visitor a seat. "That Valery of yours turned out to be a bird of high flight, and after giving the matter some thought we decided, Giganov and I, that your action could be taken as proof of your repentance. Oh, no," he added reassuringly, noticing the young man's pathetic condition, "I have no intention of putting our relations on an official footing. Have some water."

It was not concern for Alexander's condition, but a simple act of police courtesy. He knew only too well how strong the lust for life was in this well-cared-for, pampered young gentleman.

"That's all right, thank you," Gratsiansky nodded, holding on to the edge of the desk with one hand and wiping his clammy forehead with the other.

"I repeat, I do not intend to define the relations which have been established between us, but undoubtedly our annalists will inscribe your service in their scrolls. This will be the best recommendation for your future career, and will keep you from frivolous political enthusiasms. You realise, of course, what unpleasant consequences these annals will have for you should they happen to fall into the hands of our enemies at a bad turn in our country's history? I beg your pardon, did you want to say something?"

"I would ask you, Colonel," Alexander Gratsiansky began with a dry sob.

"You must call me Sir," Chandvetsky gently corrected him.

"I wanted to ask you, sir ... couldn't you arrange for me to be taken into custody for a month or two, at least."

"That's quite unnecessary," the colonel laughed. "No one will know anything about this talk we're having ... just you and I and Giganov here, but he's as silent as the grave. I repeat, he's no philosopher, but I should very much like you to be friends, or at least make it up between you. Well, let bygones be bygones, give him your hand like a good Christian, Giganov!"

Giganov all but purred demurely, tickled by a feeling of self-respect for which his profession gave so little grounds. He thought his chief was being much too generous, even though it was at someone else's expense. He would have been quite satisfied if this angry young gentleman had simply given him forty rubles or so for the privilege of abusing him.

Alexander staggered out into the street as if he had drunk deeply of the magic Death Water. He would have shot himself perhaps—indeed, he would have shot himself for certain that very evening were he not afraid of causing his mother such cruel pain. Incidentally, his adventure with Emma put him off women for a long time to come. He went about for a whole year with the crawlsome feeling of sitting in Chandvetsky's pocket, which was slightly more nasty than a prison cell in the Fortress of Peter and Paul. He would jump up in the middle of the night in a cold sweat of panic at the thought of being dragged forth by the collar and told: "Now, young man, that'll do lounging about. It's time you did some work!" But nothing happened. With the passage of the years a faint ray of hope that he had been forgotten began to struggle through the gloom of his dazed mind. After all, he was just a boy, who fully deserved to be taught a little lesson.

"My God!" he sometimes said to himself, contemplating the hand that remembered the grip of Giganov, then he would put on the Braga record and shed a romantic tear, which evoked the sympathy of the Dizzy Doxies and friends.

After some intensive historic research in the archives following the revolution, Alexander Gratsiansky succeeded in attaining a measure of security for himself in regard to certain undesirable documents, while the actual witnesses of his sin did not, for various reasons, survive the winter of nineteen forty-one. He was beginning to fall in love with life again when the connoisseur of Pacific eucalypts brought him a message of posthumous greeting from Chandvetsky.

Presumably, the fugitive gendarme, in his old age, was very hard up abroad. And when everything was sold—the personal souvenirs of the most august personages, his late wife's valuables, and various items of clothing—he reminded himself of Gratsiansky's elegant peccadillo, and like an old pair of trousers, took it to one of those establishments where they buy the rusty springs of scandal, the keys to skeleton cupboards, the wreckage of souls and other wordly junk that could be turned and used again.

Our descendants, from their eagle eyries, will better be able to see the heroism of the Soviet peoples in the battle for the great city. Its outcome did not yet mean that the campaign had been won. The most populated and economically important regions of the country with a third of all its industry and almost half of its arable land still had to be recaptured inch by inch. The enemy's fury, still unbroken, was directed south in a deep enveloping movement calculated to cut off the capital city's supplies of petrol and grain. Through the smoke of gunpowder two great fires advanced upon us—that of Stalingrad and the Kursk Bulge, but it was the December events at Moscow and the simultaneous blow at the enemy's strategic joints in the north-west that restored to all ordinary people in the world the hopes which had been dimmed in the early months of the war. By the spring of 1942 things were much more cheerful in Moscow, although the enemy air squadrons were still trying to get at it with a belated load of vengeance for their military disappointments; but few people now hid themselves in the bomb shelters; they preferred to look at the distant flashes of the defensive fire through the blacked-out windows and wait with patient boredom for the All-Clear signal.

Now, when the first breach had been smashed in the enemy's fighting spirit, the opening of a second front in Europe might have considerably hastened the defeat of the Nazis and saved many a million of soldiers' lives. However, those who were our allies at the time did not fulfil their sacred obligations either that year or in the three following years—for reasons of long-range significance. In this procrastination the inhabitants of Moscow bitterly recognised the cunning of that third person of the Latin proverb who rejoices at the sight of two opponents locked together in a death struggle and comes to the battlefield at the end of it together with the black birds. A hundred and seventy-nine of the two-hundred and fifty-six divisions which the Nazis disposed of were on the Eastern front, not counting the fifty divisions scraped up in vassal holes and corners. The Soviet people bore the brunt of the duel, and as one never forgets the behaviour of a friend in battle, so did the Vikhrovs always remember how, for three years, they and their neighbours discussed all kinds of variants of the second front, how eagerly everyone searched the morning papers for news of an Anglo-Saxon landing on the continent, and nine-hundred times running was their faith in soldiers' friendship deceived, until the nine-hundred-and-first, when, during the German offensive at Ardennes, Muscovites read with a smile the telegraphic appeal for assistance from their allies.

More and more often that spring did Ivan Vikhrov lay aside his pen to turn to the map of Europe, which hung behind him; it seemed blasphemy at such a time to write about the weight of dry pine needles per hectare of century-old stands. Remembering himself in 1914, he was thinking not of the furious battles that the spring would bring, but of the workaday things of war—the bogged down roads of the front area, his pupils in wet army coats, who were so badly needed for life and the Russian forest, marching through the drizzling mist. And although there was little chance of meeting them together because they belonged to different arms of the service, he recognised Sergei and Polya there, marching at the tail-end of the column, and he walked along with them in silent converse.

His eye wandered once more over the Atlantic coast on the map, as if expecting to find a transoceanic armada there, or the black smoke of an artillery attack, but he saw only a revived fly crawling from harbour to harbour and sunning itself in a slanting beam.

"What's the news from the front?" Taisa always asked as she laid the table.

"Everything's fine, sister. Our army will take Loshkarev back any day now, and we'll follow in their tracks," Ivan said, staring, fascinated, at the map.

Amid the vast little space of his country he found the blue vein of the Yenga, and from a barely perceptible bend in it unerringly divined the missing dot that was Krasnovershya. Brought up in the country, Vikhrov keenly felt the instability of city life, especially in stormy times; the older he grew the more fondly he recalled the simple peasant cart, the axe, the smoked pot over the hearth, and then he would try as much as he could to reduce the number of his needs and the things of daily use. The little village of his childhood on the Yenga hillside seemed to him more secure than all the citadels in the world. From here he set out on a mental walk to his sanctuary of Pustosha, and although he slackened his pace to miss none of the details he reached Shikhanov Yam in half an hour; it looked as if he was beginning to forget his native parts.

He understood that this growing nostalgia for the places of his childhood was an infallible sign of approaching old age, and he wavered in his decision all the winter. A painful conversation with a man whom he considered the direct successor of his forestry ideas decided him. Osminov was in Moscow on business and called on his teacher at the end of April. They whiled away a long Russian hour together, during which Vikhrov questioned his friend eagerly about front-line news and peered into his eyes to read the secret thoughts of the soldier in them. He was so grateful to Osminov for coming to see him that when the latter asked him about his plans he made no attempt to conceal his intention of moving to the Yenga for good.

To soften the impression, however, he made the admission in a casual way.

"Come and visit us after the war, I may be able to boast of more important accomplishments, we'll go after the wood-grouse, I'll treat you to pies with cloudberries," Vikhrov wound up in a careless tone. "Taisa used to be an expert at them in the old days."

The confession was meant to be a special sign of confidence, which he had not extended even to Valery at their last meeting, but instead of the sympathy and direct support which he had expected from Osminov, the latter's face and tone hardened rather unpleasantly.

"And how long have you been cherishing these ideas, Professor?"

"As a matter of fact I've had that intention for a long time. I miss the forest. At first I was kept busy finishing writing my books, which turned out to be useless, anyway, and then ... I kept waiting for our troops to cross the Yenga. So this news of yours has made me very happy. Just so."

"And you decided to run away under cover of the war? To make a quiet decent exit and shut the door behind you?"

Vikhrov frowned, as if he had been accused of an old man's ill-timed coquetry.

"There's no denying you a certain sagacity, Osminov. Yes, I didn't want my departure to give rise to any unnecessary talk. Besides, already before the war a noble urge was in evidence in all spheres of our life to get away from office ledgers into the big outdoors, into the thick of things. I'm tired of running in idle gear. The war has hit my Pustosha, I'll nurse it, do some underplanting. At any rate, I'll earn my bread, and mark my words, you'll read something nice about me in the papers yet, and not only abuse."

"You consider that the great battle for the Russian forest is over, then?"

"No, but a splendid new forestry generation has grown up and you are one of them. And if only they do not quit, like those who repudiated Morozov and Tulyakov in their time, then the main job is still to come. People have a weakness for the easy bread of life—Cheredilov is an example. Do you know where he is eating it now, by the way?"

The question was one of the ornamental kind that did not call for an answer.

"It's because I'm a loyal pupil of yours that I have a right to tell you frankly, Professor, that such desertion as yours would be looked on very severely with us at the front."

"It isn't true!" Vikhrov flared up. "The forest is my calling, not a mere profession. A man can't run away from his own soul. If I were given a second life I would live it the same way. I'm a gloomy simple man of the woods, and my tastes do not run to sweet bread. Like my father before me, I was sent to intercede for the forest. And I went and got myself a cushy job, and haven't done anything for the forest except scribble heaps of paper. So allow me, Osminov, to use my remaining strength and time as best I can."

Osminov laughed.

"But my dear teacher, you could have gone away without me knowing anything, and no power in the world could have stopped you buying a railway ticket, isn't that so? The reason you started this conversation was to get my opinion, wasn't it?"

"Inviting opinion doesn't mean accepting it beforehand," Vikhrov grumbled.

"Nevertheless, let me give it. I, too, reject the destructive American system of migratory lumbering. Having cleaned up some of their own territorial forests, they have already invaded Canada with the axe, and that country, too, will taste the bitter fruit of man's folly. I always liked your ideas about setting up a modern industrial timber works with a continuous supply of local raw material and without loss of a single ounce of organic matter in place of the present lumbering organisations which are engaged in logging. I even agree with you that with the development of more intensive income crops in the northern forestries the citric plants will move northward at a faster rate than by the long and doubtful process of training them to semi-arctic conditions. In a word, I unreservedly accept your main thesis about the northern Russian children being entitled to their Christmas tangerine."

"I highly appreciate your forebearance with an old man's peevish grumbling," Vikhrov said ironically. "I really didn't think it was quite fair to compare a century-old forest crop with the picking of cotton raised in a single season. All that I was demanding for the forest was economic citizenship, and I protested against systematic wastefulness, Osminov. Ah, if we could have this argument out in the cutting area! We cut down the forests, keep shortening the rotation period, and everything that is thinner than three inches at the top-end or is of a different species is left on the spot to become the prey of windfall, the bark beetle and fire. The work of the sun and mother earth was wasted. At Pustosha I'm going to try out in practice my excessive and danger-ous sympathies towards the Russian forest."

At the same time Vikhrov felt a change in his visitor's mood, and it worried him.

"We, your pupils, loved you as you are, prickly and impatient, and we always believed that your dream would come true some day."

"By the time the tundra meets the steppe?"

"Before that, I hope. But then didn't you teach us yourself that everything in the world, the forest included, was merely an instrument of human happiness. If man was happy the world around him would smile. If he was unhappy, then.... You ask a soldier what happens with Nature when a man feels out of sorts. Nothing in the world, therefore, dares refuse to take part in human progress and bear its share of the struggle. The breach has been made, and now everything is thrown into the gap—talents, the forest, the entrails of the earth. It's the law of all great offensives. The important thing here is the logic and consist-ency of social and economic transformations. You understand yourself what would happen if we were to put the forest first on the order of the day. And so politics for a real scientist inevitably becomes the top floor of his science. Only by having mastered everything will liberated mankind be able to make up for what it has missed through no fault of its own, and do it in a much shorter time than it will take to cure the virulent malady that is consuming its youth, its creative powers, its very faith in life."

"So that, if you had, say, to relight that torch of progress on a naked sterile-clean planet ..." Vikhrov began sarcastically.

"Oh no, I didn't say that," Osminov laughed coldly. "But I would say, in the words of Archimedes: free mankind from its shackles and it will, in a comparatively short time, turn any desert—I say, *any*—into a flowering garden."

"I think you are moving to the top floor of science a bit too soon; you haven't worked long enough on the ground floor yet," Vikhrov said coldly, strangely and sadly. "Ah well, you have grown up, you have grown up lately beyond recognition, Osminov."

"A soldier walks a lot and sees a lot, he's sort of completing his education day and night, that's why."

Things were heading for a break, and the yielding of an inch of ground would have meant for each of them renouncing his convictions. And then, as if through the wrong end of a pair of binoculars, Vikhrov distinctly saw a cheerless house in St. Petersburg, his own teacher in a ridiculous old-fashioned fur coat standing by the frozen window, and himself, then a young man, offering the older one advice of stupendous moral and ethical value. And suddenly he was tingling to know whether Osminov would start giving him the same sage advice which he had once given to Tulyakov.

"As far as I understand, you haven't said everything yet," he prodded.

"Yes," Osminov rose to the bait. "You were expecting my approval, but I can't approve of your flight from the battlefield, Professor. On the other hand, you've been working all through the five-year plans without holidays or days off, and that's no good either. Thinkers often become captives of their armchair creations, and then, more than anything in the world, are they afraid of someone, especially life, trampling on their drawings. Even with Archimedes they were traced in sand. Well then, Professor, why shouldn't you take a stroll through the Soviet land, travelling light? Just take an airing and a look at the places of your childhood, like the returning wanderer, to use a high-flown phrase. This contact with your native land is bound to awaken new thoughts."

Vikhrov heard out his aspiring pupil with a calm courageous smile, although, to tell the truth, he had always thought he would enter that inevitable closing cycle of evolution somewhat later. At any rate, he would have paid dearly for the privilege of being present at such a conversation of Osminov's with a similarly audacious unyielding stranger who was as yet sitting behind his school desk.

"Thank you for the gift of time, my dear Osminov. I shall certainly take your advice," Vikhrov said and shook his hand at parting with such warm gratitude that both were suddenly put at their ease.

In the hall Osminov reverted to the subject, but for a different reason.

"I almost forgot to tell you, I made the acquaintance of your daughter at the front. You can be proud of her. She's a brave clean girl. Don't you want to take advantage of her coming to get er ... sort of family advice on what you intend to do?"

In answer to the Vikhrovs' eager questions, he said that Polya had arrived in Moscow a day before him, mentioned that she had been awarded a medal, and added that he knew nothing about the object of her visit. Since his daughter now had no reasons to avoid the paternal home, Vikhrov volunteered to see Osminov off to the Metro in the hope of meeting her on the way.

2

Deeply agitated, he hung about the Metro station for over an hour, and even rehearsed a speech to the offspring in which he summed up the past, defined his attitude to the present, and peered across the threshold of the future. With the fall of dusk it grew more difficult to make out people's faces. Vikhrov turned to go home and ran into his sister; she couldn't sit at home either. April was running riot in the suburb that evening; torrents rushed underfoot, the wind puffed as it unwrapped the earth, and the rooks celebrated their housewarming among the bare trees of the Institute grove with shrill cries. Fearing to miss Polya in this weather, the old couple quickened their pace; indeed, at the bottom of the street they overtook the girl. She was wearing a new army sheepskin and walked with the aid of a stick.

Right there she received the first congratulations, embraces and rebukes.

"We were greatly touched by your detailed, though scant letters. Just so. And thank you for the information about Sergei...." Only the inconvenience of the place prevented Vikhrov from delivering the speech he had composed. "And it's most remarkable that you young people should have become related on the battlefield. Just so."

"We were in the same field hospital, but he wasn't able to write yet. He's better now. There's no need to take on like that, Auntie Taisa. It isn't as if I've lost an arm or been shell-shocked, like he was. I'm safe and sound," Polya said to the old woman, who buried her face in her shoulder.

"But you're limping," said her father.

"Oh, that's hereditary. After all, I'm a daughter of yours," Polya laughed it off.

They went up to the flat with their arms about each other, and this is where the remainder of Valery's wine came in useful. Taisa was so happy, she even called in some of the neighbours, who remembered Polya as a child; she wanted the whole world to sip a glass to her brave niece. Polya barely managed to answer all the questions, the first of which was, would she have many days to spare for her old people this time. No, she had to start back to join her unit on the Yenga the day after tomorrow. Taisa promptly suggested she should stay a week and go out together with her father on the grounds that it was easier for two people to get tickets and look after the luggage. Polya thanked her aunt with a light touch; unfortunately, Taisa's niece had business to attend to that very evening, not to mention the following days ... and all lapsed into a respectful silence at the hint of the top-secret plans which could not be confided even to a father.

Except that she was a bit thinner and taller, Polya looked her old self, but there was something strong-willed and unfamiliar in her steady gaze, in the patience with which she accepted the loving attentions of the old people, in the silent habit of passing her hand over her eyes from time to time, as if trying to shake off some haunting memory, and in the tired crease round her mouth. Taisa fussed around her, plying her with meagre wartime refreshments, and patting the new star decoration over the right pocket of her tunic; she could not get used to this new sensation of Polya's maturity and that look even of conscious superiority, which near ones find so striking in the startingly clear levelled eyes of the soldier home from the front.

"From what I could gather from your letter and what Osminov told me, you've been working in the hospital all the time?" her father enquired.

"Not all the time."

"You must have been helping to carry the wounded off the field, then, seeing that you've been hit?"

"Oh, that's nothing, I just scratched my knee. The doctors said there wouldn't be a mark left in six months. I think you'll find Sergei still at Mummy's place, if you should wish to look her up. Oh yes, I almost forgot to give that photograph of her back to you. It's crushed a bit, I'm sorry. But it helped me out of a tight corner on one occasion."

"Well, keep it, the war isn't over yet."

"I got myself another one; besides, your desk looks empty without it," she said with an arch smile, and deftly inserted the photograph in the empty frame.

Like Taisa, Ivan Vikhrov accepted Polya's hint as unmistakable proof of her well-informed mind and obvious superiority.

"You met Mummy?" he asked, examining the last mouthful at the bottom of his glass.

"Yes. A week ago she was quite well, she has a lot of work to do, and is quite happy." Polya also related that after working for nearly six months in the partisan detachment her mother returned to her hospital in Pashutino; at one time, during the westward drive it was used as a casualty clearing station, and all three of them lay there."

"Who was the third there with you?" Taisa asked timidly, patting Polya's decorations once more.

"An old school friend of mine, Rodion. He was wounded too on the first day of the offensive. Mummy pulled him through, though ... he was in the infantry, you know." A bitter unfamiliar note crept into her voice. "But it's worth it, so long as we can get rid of all this skum, and have our children at least come into a clean house."

From the tone of suppressed pain and pride for that unknown soldier Rodion, it was not difficult to guess the nature of her attachment. Ah well, let them build their nest, so long as they lived their allotted span in it in peace and love. The mention of children, however, disturbed Taisa.

"What children have you got, darling?" she asked gently, so as not to offend. "You're such a tiny leaf yourself, a wind could break you."

"I didn't say mine. I said ours."

Polya uttered this in a clear ringing voice, wondering, in her chastity, at the old woman's suspicion, and there was a light in her eye which could not be met without blinking. It became clear that if yesterday she owed everything down to the last scrap to her elders, today they depended entirely upon her courage and successes.

She glanced at the clock and rose.

"I'm sorry, but I have to go away on urgent business. I shan't be long. I'll be back before night in my old place!" She smiled and glanced at the next room with the guitar hanging over Sergei's bed. "I keep forgetting to ask, who goes in for music here?"

"I used to maltreat that instrument when I lived alone in Pashutino," Vikhrov said, and there was a new note of concern in his voice. "Is it official business you're going on?"

She hesitated.

"Not quite, Papa. I have a debt to repay. I went there once, but I didn't find them in. That's all right, I'll run down by Metro in a jiffy ... you won't have time to finish your tea."

"You borrow money from strangers, but you haven't an extra minute to spare for your own people. Always dashing about," Taisa rebuked her. "Isn't tomorrow a day?"

"It's a debt I simply can't put off, Aunt Taisa. I'm afraid I'll spend myself at the war and won't have anything to pay back with."

A long dreary silence ensued after her departure.

"That's the end of their childhood," sighed one of the neighbours, herself the mother of four soldiers on the most dangerous sections of the front, and added a word to the effect that the children had grown up and were assuming their official duties, the high official duties of a human being upon Earth.

3

As Polya's debt was not a pecuniary one, she had enough physical opportunities to repay it at an earlier date, beginning from September in fact, soon after the lecture at the Forestry Institute, but at that time, as she was sincerely convinced, she did not possess yet either the legal or moral right to follow her impulse. It was in such a mood that she had come to Moscow nearly a year ago, and truth to tell only the absence of her father during her first visit saved her from a dreadful and fatal mistake. Throughout that time Polya had been carrying on investigations, as it were, into Vikhrov's case, which had made slow progress on account of their checkered success, but with every day it grew bigger, did Polya's sad little debt, and during the last few months it had even begun to overshadow her life. Her acquaintance with Sergei and, through him, with Morshchikhin's conjectures, helped her to sort out the facts of the forestry controversy, so that by the spring of nineteen forty-two she had all the incriminating evidence against Alexander Gratsiansky collected in her heart, evidence, of which only detached fragments were known to some of his contemporaries.

To this should be added her own childish tears caused by a social inferiority complex, her long-standing humiliating envy of her coevals, whose fathers—airmen, builders, captains—had left a clean fiery stroke of the pen in the history of their country, and last but not least, the constant awareness of her own dishonesty, since she had kept things back even from Rodion. In short, it was the kind of debt that could hardly be repaid in a single instalment, and the curious thing about it was that all she had had to do to settle it in September was to go downstairs to the first floor. As it was, she had had to go a long roundabout way, through snow-drifts and deadly perils, to come one evening to the same place in Blagoveshchensky Alley and knock at the door with the handsome plate on it.

The small face of an old woman, hidden behind a hand, peeped through the door.

"Ah, it's you," said Gratsiansky's mother, recognising the morning visitor. She let her in, but the next minute was alert with suspicion. It may have been the new sheepskin coat, which created a resemblance between this girl and Morshchikhin. "Yes, the professor has returned from an important meeting, but he has lain down to take a rest. It would be better if you got in touch with him on the telephone or let me give him your message."

"Unfortunately, it's such a very personal matter," Polya insisted. "I shall not tire him, and I won't be long. I won't even take my things off."

The old woman kept looking backward—something was boiling in the kitchen; it had run over, and smoky fumes billowed out into the passage. Polya was nervously pulling thread after thread out of her torn mitten when suddenly the door opened and Gratsiansky himself peeped out of his ambush with one eye, anxious to put an end to the agonising suspense which the slightest sound in the passage now caused him.

"I do have a slight cold, but er ... who is it there?" he said, making his full appearance, holding the raised collar of his jacket at his throat. "My dear child, your attractive young face is so familiar to me, where could I have seen it?"

"I lived in this house before joining the army, with a friend of mine upstairs," she said, motioning at the ceiling with her eyes. "We met in the bomb shelter right at the beginning of the war. Don't you remember?"

Despite the army beret, worn at an angle, and the belted sheepskin coat, which was a bit too big for her, there was something infinitely homelike and restful about the girl, standing there at the threshold like a suppliant.

"Ah ... goodness me!" he graciously recollected, and the sound expressed an animal exultation at restored life which had all but slipped from his fingers. "Take off your warlike fleece, my dear. I am always at the service of our splendid, sensitive, progressive youth," he went on, rejoicing in the power of speech, which was still his, rejoicing in the reek of burnt fat that hung in the air, rejoicing in and sparing the life of a clothes moth when his hand mechanically reached out as it flew past, rejoicing in every single fraction of the wonderfully long minute while Polya was taking her things off. "Believe me, my child, this comforting knowledge of my modest usefulness is the er ... the sole delight of a poor old man whose health is shattered and who is no longer able to take a direct part in the gigantic combat er ... between the two antagonistic worlds."

"Oh, I'd never say your health was shattered. Quite the contrary!" Polya said, exultant too, but for a somewhat different reason, as, with a springy step, she followed the host into the room through the invitingly wide-opened door.

She looked round, and everything in her went cold, down to the tips of her fingers. Why, this was the very room which she had invented for her father while she was still at Pashutino; the same windows in their tapestried frames, the same smooth soft feel of something on the floor, which bespoke the occupant's profession without a single detail; a room crowded with expensive knicknacks, created by the inspiration of paupers for the pleasure of the disillusioned. A stack of paper lay in the middle of the desk guarded over by the bronze beast on the crystal inkwell which was half-filled with a dull fluid the colour of lies and of a consistency so thick that one drop of it would suffice to blacken anything in the world.

"Oh, no, I do not want flattery or pity, even if they came from the tenderest lips in the world," Gratsiansky continued coquettishly, warding off the protests that came not with both hands. "No, my good fairy, masters of matter though we are, we are completely in its power, and only at the cost of a terrible price shall we succeed in the end in breaking out of its orbit, and who knows er ... where that will bring us. But although even the wise man hopes that Nature will make an exception in his case, I thank all the gods that be for the cruel truth which is contained in the fall of the leaves, in the melting of the snows, in the unfinished drop left in the glass, damn it! Apparently Nature has a lot of wine and few vessels; let someone else fill the emptied one." Translated into human language, this merely meant: God, how good it is in your household even on this chilling spring evening, even though waiting for the next air raid to begin ... even though lying like a stone in the desert for all eternity, so long as I can look at that blue star twinkling in the gap between the curtains!

A distressing sense of captivity came over Polya, as though she were half immured, and all her body was numb, and she was already gasping for breath, while he went on bricking her up with sort of glass wool briquettes such as builders use for filling up empty spaces.

"But what urgency had brought you here, my dear?" she heard at last, and that might mean that having revelled in her oppressed silence, he was now permitting the girl to praise his generosity and quit the sanctum.

"Yes, I'll tell you in a minute.... I'll tell you everything. I am Polya Vikhrova, I am eighteen," she reeled off, nerving herself to the task in hand, then suddenly she looked up.

She saw a fear-stunned haggard face with cold, utterly implacable eyes in it ... eyes just like those of that other one, who had circled over her during the nights of the Moscow air raids and who had one day shot old Afanasyev in the open field instead of her, and had led her by the hand to the German dugout in Shikhanov Yam, and who later tried to worm out of her the most close-locked secrets concerning the Eastern spaces. She stared at Gratsiansky now as hard as she could to keep him from slipping away, because all of a sudden he began to look queerly blurred.

"I am Polya Vikhrova, I am eighteen," she repeated, coming closer. "I read in a book that walruses have lice on them which bite them both on land and under the water ... and the faster that powerful armless beast moves the more strongly do they stick to his skin."

Gratsiansky recognised the spectre that had been haunting him in his dreams and waking hours, recognised it by these eyebrows raised in wrath, by that mouth turned down at the corners with loathing, and by that slightly sorrowful cadence of the voice in which a verdict is usually uttered. Polya had nothing in her hands, though, and so nothing threatened him beyond a superficial unpleasant experience. Nevertheless, he gripped the arms of his chair and backed away from her in it by the few inches that separated him from the wall.

"What are you doing, I am an old man," he uttered in a parched voice.

She smiled without taking her eyes off him.

"Never mind, that puts us on even terms."

Whether it was because he was beyond her reach in any case, or because she bethought herself of the official ban on such arbitrary acts, but at the very last moment she changed her mind. She groped for the inkwell, and before he could cover himself, splashed the contents into his face.

"My God," was all he said.

"That's a deposit for the time being ... you'd better pray I shouldn't come back from the front," Polya said very quietly, and gave the postal number of her unit in case he wanted to lodge a complaint.

It now remained for her to straighten her beret and shut the door firmly behind her as she went out. A wild beady-bright pupil followed her from between wet blackened fingers. Thus began the end of Gratsiansky; this was not death yet, of course, but his whole being split in two, as it were, and the departed half of his soul seemed to be asking the other half, "Will you be long there?"

The old mistress found Polya in the hall drawing the belt of her sheepskin army coat.

"That's good. I was just going to warn you, my dear, not to tire him too much—his haemoglobin is so bad, you know...."

"Oh, we've finished," Polya said, and looked down at her boots. "I'm afraid I've dirtied the place a bit, excuse me please!"

"That's nothing, it'll dry up. It's damp out today, isn't it?"

"I think we'll have some frost tonight."

She hardly had the strength to go out. Leaning against a poplar at the open end of the alley, she looked back at the house which she was leaving for ever. Covered with camouflage plywood

696

sheets, the top floor melted in the spring dusk. She recalled her arrival in the city the year before, poor kind Varya, her own shattered dreams, and was astonished to find how swiftly the river was rushing its tiny leaf. In her excitement she did not even notice that her favourite evenings had set in, those evenings at the turn of winter, which, though still filmy and crisp, are already pervaded with the feverish languor of hope.

4

All those who had managed to run away from the enemy invasion surged back to the Yenga in the wake of the Soviet armies. Owing to heavy military shipments, passenger traffic on this line was held up by frequent stoppages. In some places it would have been quicker to walk. Peasant herds, sadly reduced after their winter wanderings, trudged homewards; the trappings of local government, or rather their bare necessaries, jogged along in carts; women led children by the hands, their heads covered with sack-cloth against the foul weather, and decrepit old men, with green in their beards, hobbled through the thick mud on crutches in order, before they died, to walk barefoot through some hallowed undried meadow out there. Instead of their native villages, they were greeted, as a rule, by the silence of desolation. Sitting down to rest by the charred ruins, they unwrapped their bundles with bread, and dabbing it in the salt of sorrow, partook of the funeral feast for their shattered lives, as they used to do at the cemeteries when visiting the graves of their parents.

Ivan Vikhrov was the lucky possessor of a paper certifying that he was going to the Yenga on official forestry business, and of a piece of cardboard enabling him to travel from Moscow to Krasnovershya. He came to the station long before the train was due to leave, and got the last remaining edge of a seat in the aisle. Feet could be heard walking on the roof of the carriage in search of a resting place. A baby was screaming in the corner, and a man of powerful physique, with a clatter of a tin cup against a travelling box, was trying to make himself comfortable at the feet of his more fortunate fellow-travellers.

"Well, that's fixed me up. A mug of tea would be just the thing now! I'd give anything for a drink."

"You don't say so!" a mocking voice answered out of the stuffy murk overhead for the mere sake of companionship and good cheer. "What will you be asking for next? Why, in the old days, my dear man, they used to build stone houses out o' tea."

"How's that?"

A match was struck, lighting up a bandaged head under a soldier's fur cap, with a heavy unshaven jaw and a pair of surprisingly mischievous eyes that looked interrogatively over the flame—probably a soldier out of hospital going back to join his unit.

"Quite simple. Some people, they say, didn't drink any tea, only water ... and they saved up fortunes!"

"You can't make a fortune out of tea," the soldier said in the tone of a man who knew, and a whiff of strong tobacco assailed Vikhrov's nostrils. "Hey, missus, what's the baby's name? What's it crying like that for?"

"Mitya," a woman's voice answered in the darkness. "I don't know what to do with him."

"Leave him alone, he's keen to get home, too. Cheer up, Mitya, you wait till the war's over! It'll be just about in time for your wedding."

The joke conveyed the calm cheerful force of a man who had all the time in the world at his disposal, and his neighbours closely followed his glowing cigarette in expectation of another sally, which was the best medicine for the discomforts of travel. At this point, however, there came an interruption in the form of a check-up of documents, and soon afterwards the train started off and all was drowned in the click of the wheels over the joints. It was a bright night and no one slept, not so much in anticipation of an air raid, as from the tremulous joyous excitement of going home after a long separation. Ivan Vikhrov now became one with the great deathless river; there was no greater security against possible woes than dissolving himself in it to last thought. When his ears got used to the din of the moving train he began to distinguish snatches of conversation in different parts of the carriage on the eternal themes of the people—on wealth and poverty, honour and dishonour, fame and infamy. Whether it was because human souls are more easily fused in the darkness or because the crowded carriage and the long journey made for mutual confidence it is difficult to say, but the thoughts that were voiced were the innermost thoughts of the people, which one would hardly ever hear in broad daylight. Immediately behind him they were discussing the life that would come after victory; would there still be fools *there* and bureaucrats—soulless official robots!

—and most important of all, how could life under communism be made safe against human greed, so that everyone should dip his spoon into the common pot in turn and fairness, without scooping up four times as much as others and make a hoard for himself. "Tut, tut, man, we haven't gone twenty versts, and you have lighted your eighth match—I've counted them. A box would last me a week. How are you going to level us?" All perplexities were immediately resolved by a young intelligent voice, so crystal-clear that it sounded like a brook from the foothills of communism.

In the next compartment, the mention of ill-earned wealth had started someone off on a train of reminiscences about an up-and-coming Orlov merchant. It was a long, sleep-inviting story of how the rascal had made a fortune during the Japanese war by mixing ordinary Belgorod chalk with the flour that went for the soldiers' bread, so that all the banks and safes in Russia were chock-a-block with his money.

"Such things did happen in Russia, it's a fact," the humourist confirmed out of the darkness. "My uncle knew one such blighter—he used to mix dry snow with the salt. Clever trick that! Would you believe it, he built himself a house of five storeys."

"Shut up, you silly ass," someone said inoffensively.

It was fully half a minute before the story-teller imperturbably resumed her narrative about the villain who was rolling in wealth, and how fate started knocking him about on account of his ill-gotten gains. First a drunken Cossack went and slashed his son in halves with his sword, and then his daughter, who had had the best of everything money could buy, went and threw herself under a train through betrayed love, after which the whole merchant's household went to rack and ruin; and how the villain, seeking to make it up with God and his fellow-men, set rich tables out in his yard, bowed low before passing beggars and wanderers and invited them to wine and dine at his expense, but the earth refused to accept his repentance, and when he died of a slow wormy disease he started to whistle like a hog in a high wind, it just gave you the creeps; and on the last night his grave caved in all of a sudden so's you couldn't reach the bottom with the longest of ropes, and they just chucked him in, and all the rest of his fortune went in filling in his wicked grave.

"That's how it is, folks; the apple ripens and blooms, and then it gets too heavy for the branch. I was only a bud of a flower at the time, but I remember it all...." And although everyone realised the incongruity of the details which the old woman had described, no one dared to laugh at her tale because of the atom of the people's truth which it contained.

The train made frequent long stops. The steel of war rolled westwards, overtaking all else in the world, leaving a deafness in the ears and a poignant hope in the heart; there were hardly any trains coming the other way. And while they were waiting to let through a military train, an enemy plane attacked the little railway station; for at least three quarters of an hour, so it seemed to everyone, he tried his damnedest to blast the carriage in which Mitya had woken up again, crying, and the soldier's cigarette was glowing in the dark. The airman was clumsy—he may have been just a beginner—and judging by the roar of the engine over the roof he was furious with himself for missing his target, but no one ran out for fear of losing his place, and all sat patiently silent, waiting for him to get in practice or spend his ammunition and zeal.

At one moment, when the explosions came nearer and splinters started scratching the walls, the passengers held their breath and stared before them into the darkness, as though they could see the luckless ace banking, coming in on his wing tips, as if crouching to spring, then climbing steeply again and swooping down on his prey if not to kill, then at least to frighten the baby with the screech of up-to-date military equipment. Suddenly he was silent.

"He's gone," the young voice broke the silence.

"Maybe his engine has stalled or he's run out o' petrol," the soldier said crunchily, as though he were treading on crisp snow. "You often get that at work; when things go wrong you can't even drive a nail in properly. Maybe he's young and raw, doing his training on us!"

"You'd better shut up, you heroes, or you'll have him back again," a quavery old voice sounded from above.

"Don't worry, Grandpa, nothing'll happen to you so long as I'm here. I've taken all the shooting that was coming to me, and now it's my turn to scare the pants off 'em!"

"Are you able to read the future, or have you got a charmed life? Was that revealed to you in a vision?" came simultaneously from two sides.

"No, I had no vision, but that's how things worked out." The evolutions of the night raider overhead could no longer be heard, and the train started creeping furtively out of the station. "It happened in the summer; we'd been driven off the Vyazma and hadn't reached Medin yet. Everything was topsy-turvy, you couldn't tell who was where. The sky was absolutely cloudless, and all the trains were going *that way* with all the black birds, no end of 'em, flying there for their prey. And coming *from there*, terrible to look at, old women and children trudged along through the bitter forest smoke. We'd just got out of encirclement, seven of us, with our rifles. As a matter of fact we had to crawl for it to save our lives, couldn't help it."

"Nothing surprising in that, fear will make anyone crawl on his belly. They're such horrible brutes, those parasites, they've got nothing human in them," a woman's voice joined in, apparently foreseeing a happy ending to this agonisingly frank soldier's confession.

"And another thing I'll never forget as long as I live was a stranger we met, an educated chap, who started to coax us," the soldier continued thoughtfully. "'You boys,' he says, 'made a good retreat the other day. Draw them on, the blighters, let 'em think we're not there at all. But now you ought to stand up to them for a day or two, and hit back, until you can take a good real smack at 'em.' 'There are only seven of us,' we said, 'we've escaped from encirclement, what can seven men do!' He got wild then. 'Ekh, I see all your sweethearts will have to be shot before it gets under your skin, if a mother's tears don't help,' he says. He couldn't understand that we hadn't got going yet. Anyway, we gave him a wide berth and went on our way. It's easy going downhill, you know! Mind you, it's not as if we were afraid of death or anything like that, but simply we didn't feel like saying goodbye to life; nor would anybody who was keen to know what communism was like and have a peep at it with just one eye. Look what a tremendous thing has been driven into the soil! It's like having to get up from a rich table without having touched the food."

"That's just it, we've been pampered and spoilt, we've forgotten what environment we're in. It's too early to live without locks yet," the young voice put in for clarity's sake. "Marx says...."

"Wait a minute there with Marx, don't interrupt. You'll always have him, but I've got to stick my head out again," the soldier coolly broke in. "Well, one evening after a rain we hit a deserted village. It lay in a mist like a sort of shroud. There wasn't a sound, not even a dog barking. We knocked at the first door and an old man came out; he'd seen his best days, but was still full o' beans, without a stick. 'Hullo, refugees,' he says. 'Why so late?'

He wasn't laughing, mark you. 'It's dangerous to go strolling here, they've dropped a landing party hereabouts, twenty-five men. Mind they don't give you an ear-wigging if they catch you. Two of 'em came for food this morning, and they shot a girl here. Have a look near the well if you don't believe me, she's lying there.' And he bolted the door in a twinkling, as if he'd never been there. Well, we went over and had a look. And there she lay in the path, a member of the female sex, something round about sixteen, in the prime of life. She was lying on her face and had a stone in her hand; didn't have the time to throw it. She put up a fight by the looks of it. We stood there, the seven of us, taking a rest. Then Fedyayev, the chap from Saratov, says: 'They deserve to be made potted meat of for that!' and I says yes, potted meat is right. That night five more men who had broken through joined us, and at daybreak we went after the enemy into the woods. This time I got one of 'em. He emptied his magazine, aiming straight at me, but all his bullets went wide. I realised then that I'd hunt them down to their lair without being killed. As luck would have it, I'd run out of cartridges, so I just had to use my hands. I must have looked a sight, all covered with blood, while he was kissing my knees. They say we're a warlike people. Warlike be damned! Who can love war? That's just the trouble that we're a peaceful people, there isn't a more peaceful people in all the world."

"How did you get hit in the head, then, if you're bullet-proof?" someone at the back asked after a pause.

"That's my own fault, I made a bloomer," the soldier laughed it off and rolled himself a cigarette. "My father—he was a lance-corporal in the Japanese war—taught me time and again: 'The main thing in a war, Pyotr,' he says, 'is not to act proud, but step out of the way when you see a bullet or a bigger thing coming for you.' Well, Pyotr forgot his parent's instructions and spent a month and a half in bed for his pains."

Everyone chuckled softly at this, highly pleased with the soldier and the way he bore himself—without flaunting his pain or concealing the truth from the people.

"Hey, soldier!" a voice called from above. "I've got some frozen apples I'm taking home with me. You wanted some tea, here, have some of these, come on." In the light of a match an old man's hand in a sheepskin cuff reached down from the luggage shelf.

And once more the people were pleased with it, and no one construed the old man's gift as a reward for being entertained.

Besides, the apples were small ones, and had the tart taste of forest apples, but that was not the point. While he was at it, the old man, in a burst of generosity, treated the others around him, and Ivan Vikhrov did not have the heart to refuse him. Someone on the top shelf warned the old man that he would have nothing left for his grandchildren, at which another voice in the next compartment started a no less instructive story about a soldier's wife in Mozhaisk, who, during the worst rumpus of the autumn retreat, went out to the refugees on the highroad every day with a basket of baked potatoes, and once folks heard her little daughter, who accompanied her mother, ask how it was that they were spending their supplies yet the bags never grew less.... The track had been hastily patched up on that stretch, and the old carriage rocked and creaked, threatening to fall to pieces, so that Vikhrov only caught snatches of the forgotten Russian legend, which was invariably revived in calamitous times.

Gradually he sank into a restful oblivion, induced by a sense of abundant travelling time and the companionable warmth of humanity. Uncertainty stretched before him in a green weary waste, through which, straight as an arrow, ran a sun-dappled clearance. The woman he loved was walking ahead with her arm slightly away from her body, as though she wanted to caress the little wayside firs, and he had to hurry and overtake her to look into her face for the last time before she disappeared through the gates of the Pashutino forestry, which looked oddly impressive.

When he woke up half the passengers were gone and everyone was asleep; sunny morning filtered through the slit at the bottom of the lowered blind. Shivering slightly from the cold, Vikhrov went out on to the platform of the car with his suitcase. They were approaching Krasnovershya. The nocturnal wit with the bandaged head was standing on the platform smoking, his feet braced and his back leaning against the open door. The wind whipped out whisps of smoke and the skirts of his army greatcoat. The soldier was a grim-looking man with a rough-hewn face—a fair copy of Perun.* His keen pale-blue eyes glided over the bleak ravaged land.

The broad bottomland of the Yenga ran past with dry greenish spots showing through the alluvial mud here and there. The river was back in its banks, and the powerful current, free from rafts,

---

* Perun—the thunder god of the ancient Slavs.—*Tr.*

looked oddly unfamiliar and idle. A balmy wind tore the foam from the watery crests. A familiar village on the hillside came into view behind the bend. Vikhrov recognised it by the quickened beat of his heart rather than by the dozen or so gutted cottages and chimney skeletons.

He asked the soldier whether he was getting off at Krasnovershya, and the man answered that he was going to look for a drink; they got off together. Their carriage, which was the last but one in the train, stopped just short of the wooden platform, which had been hastily knocked together. A girl of eight was walking along the embankment path, hugging a glass jar to her breast; she was so thin that even the wind down there blew more gently so as not to spill the contents of the jar. It was cranberry fruit-juice, a part of the wartime rations. Out of the corner of his eye Vikhrov saw the soldier descending the embankment.

"Wait a minute, ducky," the man called softly, so softly that Vikhrov would not have heard it had not the wind been blowing in his direction. "That's not kvass you have there, surely?"

"You can have some if you want," the girl said in a melodious local accent.

The soldier took the jar in both hands and took two manly gulps, meditated whether he should take a third, then wiped his lips with his sleeve, smiled to the girl and touched her head in a sign of benediction. Vikhrov realised that he had just seen his people at such close eye-searing range as seldom falls to the lot of anyone to observe in happy peacetime conditions.

5

He began his journey by making a round of Krasnovershya.

Ascending what used to be the main street, he looked down into the hollow, where the vernal torrent rushed on its way amid the basket willows and tangle of poles with barbed wire clinging to them; he prodded an old willow with his stick; it was a tree he had known when it was still a withe; and he stood for a long time on the brow of the hill to the suspicious wonder of the small boys who trailed after him. The dead had been removed from the fields, but no flax was to be seen anywhere yet. It all looked different from what he remembered. The village of Tomashevo on the skyline had moved closer to the Yenga, and a young woodlet of the second generation seemed to have been dragged out of the way towards the right, so as not to obstruct the view of the surrounding countryside, especially of the burnt German tank with its gun muzzle pointed at the sky. From here, more convincingly than ever was demonstrated the old truth that the most changeless things in the world were those very same changeful clouds that now raced through the blue clean-washed sky, the same except that they were now marshalled by another, more taut and imperious wind of time.

This was no shattering of a dream, it merely meant that yesterday's page had come to an end and the next one was being started. On the other side of the hollow stood a gleaming brick-built structure where the kolkhoz livestock used to be housed. The soldiers of a unit quartered in the vicinity were patching up the shingled roof over the charred beams. The smell of damp wood waste mingled with the smoke from the dugouts built in the hillside, and although an air of primal dearth hung over the scene, Vikhrov seemed to hear the measured soothing sound of milk fizzing into a pail. It would have been utterly useless to look for a cart here to take him to Pashutino, and besides, it was more befitting somehow to walk the twelve kilometres to Kalina's spring. And here Vikhrov was to learn by experience the inconstancy of distances. Unbridgeable in childhood, a third of its length during the years he served in Pustosha, it had now in old age resumed its former length again.

He accounted for his frequent stops on the way by a desire to greet the old, now deserted places. Not until he crossed the ridge of brush at Oblog did he discover a villager with a bast basket, scattering seeds, while a boy followed behind leading a cow hitched to a harrow; Vikhrov wished him luck in the old-fashioned way, and the man acknowledged the greeting with a sedate bow. A kilometre further on, just short of Pustosha, he heard a girl singing a popular song in a ringing voice; it was a paean to reviving life as delightful as the sudden trill of a lark overhead. A raincloud was gathering in the sky, but Vikhrov had practically reached his home; he was on the ancient road upon which, forty odd years ago, he and Demidka had set forth to discover the world. Kalina's kingdom began somewhere nearby. For fear of losing himself or tearing his coat in the thickets Vikhrov went a roundabout way, which saved him from the deadly surprises that lay hidden in the forest slashings.

Not counting the blithe days of midsummer, when thunderstorms lave the torrid heat of July and trace their fiery signatures across the sky, or the blissful emptiness of late autumn when the wood-skirts don their parting splendour, as if trying to stir the pity of the coming cold, not counting the fluffy winter twilights with their winy air, headier than vodka, strained through the needle-like filters of frost, and their entertaining stories of cunning foxes and loping wolves to be traced in the snow, treading in each other's tracks, there is no season in the Russian countryside more entrancing than these early hours of spring gloaming, when the nut-trees have pollened, and the birch, mistrustful of the early warmth, is still shy of budding, and the forest, entirely transparent and shadowless, rubs its eyes sleepily, afraid to tread on the small fry that is springing to life underfoot. Vikhrov pushed aside the unfriendly juniper guards and stepped into the thicket; the water squelched underfoot among the undried mosses and a light rain greeted him with a splutter. Suddenly a mysterious coolness drew from the depths, and then a huge wood grouse, as big as an event, fluttered from a bush, grazing the branches with its wing. "A patrol," Vikhrov said to himself with a reminiscent touch of boyish glee, and the faint gurgle of running water told him that he had reached his destination.

Before him lay the old familiar gully, now all overgrown, with the flat stone at the bottom. Not a flower nor a fallen twig was to be seen on the slopes; an open catkin hung down from a grey alder in the solemn stillness. Vikhrov went down, head bared, and as there was no one there to watch him, greeted Kalina aloud, and together with him the little angry deity that lived there under the ancient glacial rock.

"Greetings to you, kind and eternal one," he said, standing with lowered arms before the presence, than which none is more supreme. "It is me, Ivan Vikhrov, if you remember. I have come to visit you, to give you an account of myself...."

Briefly, for neither a deity nor a friend should be wearied with a tale of woes, he reported the main things that had happened to him in the last four decades, and the thing down there growled a bit, but what it acually said Vikhrov was unable to make out. The grass was still wet, so he sat down on the edge of his suitcase.

The retinue of trees around had grown taller and older, the lichen on the slab curlier and thicker. Enough light trickled through to enable him to distinguish the crystal knob pulsing in its crib and the tiny jets of sleepless water interlocking with each other. No, Kalina's spring was not complaining about the war having disturbed it, was not grateful at having been kept safe, it was simply murmuring its tale of recent misadventures.

It remained for Vikhrov to drink his fill of this Life Water to last him the rest of his days and to continue on his way while the light still held. He intended to spend the night in Pashutino. Under a ledge of the rock, as if someone had put it there for him to use, he found a birch-bark cup sewn together with bast.

"Leave it alone, it isn't yours!" a voice sounded from above the moment the newcomer put his hand out.

Vikhrov looked up with a start. Nothing stirred all round, and the fading light poured down through the bare treetops. But anxious eyes were watching the visitor out of the thickets, where a childish figure stood, blending with the hues of the April woods. So here was the explanation of the baby pines planted inexpertly round the spring, the path in front of it laid out with pebbles, and the whole tidy appearance of the gully tended by a loving hand. Obviously, the absence of toys from century to century made the peasant children invite the phenomena of Nature to share their games with them.

"I can't see you there! Who is it, come on out!" Vikhrov called quietly, himself tingling with excitement.

The bushes parted, and a boy of about ten in a forester's cap that sat on his eyebrows appeared on the slope.

"What d'you want here? This is *my* house," he demanded in a hostile tone, pulling up his top-boots, which kept slipping down.

This was not the first time Vikhrov had been caught trespassing, and so he wasn't scared at the sight of the master.

"I've come a long distance, old chap, all the way from Moscow. I was going to have a bite, you've turned up just in time. Would you like to join me? Sit down then," Vikhrov said, and began to open his suitcase with Taisa's tempting viands in it.

He was obliged to give further reassurances that owing to the state of his health and teeth he no longer dined off small boys. The trick worked better than the food bait, and the boy came and glanced into the suitcase with a studied lack of interest.

In a sudden burst of confidence he told the newcomer how he and his mother, the local forester, had gone down the track in the autumn to look for some food among the wreckage of a German troop-train, and all the folks in the neighbourhood had done the same because they were starving, and they had got away with it the first time, and it kept them in food all the winter, but after that a patrol had caught them in a pouring rain, and the boy had returned alone with empty bags to his grandfather's forest cabin. No, his father wasn't in the army, so they had no pension to live on, he didn't remember him at all. His voice took on a note of reticent gravity. Grandpa was an old man already, he was booked for the wooden box, and his name was Lisagonov. And difficult though it was to believe in such longevity, Vikhrov guessed that it was Minei, the ranger of the nearest beat, whose sixtieth birthday they had celebrated on the night the Sapegin manor was burnt down.

"You've been through the mill, I see, old chap," Vikhrov said a minute later, trying to keep the sympathy out of his voice so as not to reopen the child's wounds. "You're running quite a big household here, aren't you? I bet you've built a shack here too?"

"You bet I have!" the boy answered with legitimate pride. "I planted a bird-cherry tree outside it, such a curliewurly one."

He put so much tenderness into that local word that there could be no doubt as to his kinship with the Pashutino forester.

"The forest is my line of business too, old chap. We're sort of pals, then. What's your name?" He braced himself, knowing beforehand that he was going to hear that rarest of names, which had become almost sacred to him.

"Kalinka," the boy said softly, taking a patty that was offered to him.

It wasn't a miracle, not even a surprising coincidence, it was merely the continuation of life, a quite ordinary phenomenon of Nature. Nothing in the world could check it, blot it out—that torrent of gay, frothy, wise protoplasm. And if old Kalina was able to assume at will the shape of a tree or a mist, an autumn wind or a dozing cat, he would have no trouble at all in turning himself into a poor peasant boy. But however hard he peered into his face, Vikhrov could not trace the slightest resemblance to the lord of Pustosha, not counting a tiny scar at the temple, all that remained, after the resmelting, of Kalina's gashed eyebrow. Thus was completed the circle of Vikhrov's activities, with the new ring at the end of it clearly visible.

"We're kinsfolk then," Vikhrov said, getting up. "Well, take me to your grandfather if that's the case."

The weather was breaking. The lichen on the slab turned lilac, and the bare young birches stood shivering in the open spaces of the gully. The sun had hidden itself long ago, and a chilly ragged mist crawled out of its hole, as always happens when the celestial master's back is turned. Kalinka walked ahead, finding

trails and loopholes among the dense thickets by signs of his
own. Presently the ramshackle cabin came into view with the
reflection of the sky in its dark windows. The boy ran in first
and Vikhrov, wiping his feet on the doorstep, could hear him
trying to bestir his grandfather, telling him that a visitor had
arrived from Moscow. They took a long time lighting the lamp.
Contrary to expectation, the place did not smell of sour homely
dough or old honeycombs, like Kalina's cabin did, but of untenanted wooden emptiness. A very old woman swept imaginary
crumbs off the table with her sleeve and put a small lampion in
the middle. Minei, a long skinny old man, lay on the bench, his
head in the icon corner, where, in place of holy images there hung
an old pendulum clock.

At the sound of strange footfalls the old man sat up on his
elbow and peered into the flickering half-light with the intensity
of approaching blindness.

"Woodward Minei Lisagonov of the 16th beat reporting..."
he began, addressing himself to the flame, which somehow managed to reach his consciousness, then fell silent, since there was
nothing for him to report really.

He tried very hard to recover his former bearing, and the
visitor was obliged to curb his official zeal.

"Lie still, Minei, that's all right. I'm not a chief, not even
a press reporter. It's just Vikhrov who has dropped in to see
you—don't you remember him, a lame forester who was working
here before the revolution?"

"There's been so many of 'em here, lame ones, all kinds,"
Minei's wife said and hissed at Kalinka he should stop making
that rustling noise under the bunk with that bird of his and give
the visitor something to eat.

"We had one here by the name of Saksonov, a powerful man
he was," Minei put in in a quavery respectful voice. "He'd still
be here if that bear hadn't hugged him."

"You've got it all mixed up, Minei," the old woman said,
shaking her head ruefully. "It was Krutilov who the bear killed,
Saksonov was promoted to a bigger job."

"Don't you listen to her ... she's such an obstinate woman.
Saksonov, I said!" growled Minei, stirring under the patchwork
quilt.

Vikhrov had to explain at length who he was and remind him
how they had worked together on forest regulation in Pustosha.
Asked how they were living after the Nazis, the old woman said

they were living all right and were cared for, the soldiers had helped to put them back on their feet, and a fortnight ago the lady doctor from Pashutino had brought them some medicine powders, God bless her, but Minei's time was up, by the looks of it.

"He's been poorly all this winter. What can you expect—the leaves have fallen off our tree long ago, there are only two left now. But our Bread-winner doesn't let him go, you see, he still holds him!" She meant the forest.

"Aye, he still holds me," Minei repeated with dignity.

"It's too early for you to quit your green kingdom yet ... look how much life you've put into it," Vikhrov tried to comfort him.

"That's true, I've put a lot into it, and what I haven't suffered for it, mercy me! The forest's a thrifty master," Minei said solemnly and importantly. "To be sure, I wasn't looking for an easy job, yet I lived my life like a king. That's a fact! Eh, my, I remember the dawns ..." he said, revelling in the recaptured warmth of some sunny memorable dawn. "I could serve a bit longer maybe, but the trouble is my eyes are getting bad. There's not much use in a lantern that doesn't burn, is there? Mind you, lying here, I can hear every crackle in the woods. Hark, that's someone bringing down a tree in Svatkovsky Grove." He worked his hand free from under the quilt and commanded attention with an uplifted finger, but strain his ears as he would Vikhrov heard nothing but the crackle of the flame in the lampion.

"That's back of the Sklan, Grandpa," the old woman corrected him by force of habit.

"There she goes again! Svatkovsky I tell you!" Minei said in a peeved reedy voice. "It must be a maple they've felled ... we have mostly maples out there."

He talked fairly intelligently about the kinds of timber that would now be in demand for the peasants' needs; maple for axe helves and jack planes, aspen for large-size peasant utensils, and elm wood for fastening the cross-pieces of the runners in Russian sleighs. People would have to provide themselves anew with all kinds of trifles in the devastated countryside.

A little later the old woman heated up some water in a pot, and the visitor laid out his fairings on the table and got out a bottle of vodka, which Taisa had put in the suitcase as a remedy for a cold. Minei livened up at the pleasant table clatter, and Vikhrov took this opportunity of questioning the old man about forest affairs, chiefly, why they had so badly neglected the Bread-winner, and what improvident master had been running things lately at Pashutino, where things had come to such a pass that the famous Karavaikovsk compartments where the big eighty-year-old fir used to stand was now three-quarters overrun with asp and firewood birch, and even those were sprawling one on top of the other in some places. Frankly, and not without bitterness, Vikhrov ran over all the signs of negligence, so unpardonable in a forester, of which he had seen such ample proof on his way here, from the overgrown cut-throughs and silted up ditches to the bald patches caused by haphazard felling.

"I'll tell you, I've got nothing to hide from you," Minei said between pauses. "As long as I remember we've always been doing everything in life slapdash, in a hurry. To be sure, the road's a long one, and the horse is not a little one either. When it runs ahead you've got to whip the tail-end up to keep 'em together. When a compartment was allotted all you had to do was to go for it with the axe baldheaded. That's when all the wicked people pretended to be fools and cut everything, even what was not marked. Building work wasn't over when the war started. There again, it was no use kicking, if you didn't want the villains to put the kibosh on the lot of us. You get an order, say, to pile the timber on the roads without lopping it, and when things at the front start getting tight, to set fire to the whole bloomin' lot. And so we just hacked it down, our poor Bread-winner, and set fire to it, using our heart's blood instead o' matches. In Russia we always take it out of the forest!"

He fell silent, exhausted by the effort, and by his wheezy breath and the waxy reflection on his cheek-bones Vikhrov realised how bad Minei was.

"Never mind, Minei, have a rest. I've upset you."

"I'm all right now," the ranger continued after a while. "We did what we were told to do—we smashed through. Our conscience is clear, we earned our bread, we went into battle with babies at the breast. It's their turn now to get into harness and worry about our Bread-winner." Guided by unerring instinct, he glanced in the direction of Kalinka, who was fast asleep at the table, his head resting on his folded hands.

The evening cloudlet was still glowing faintly in the sky, but bedtime is early in the forest. Vikhrov led the boy to the sleeping berth behind the stove and smiled at himself; in the course of time he had developed quite a knack for dealing with such boys. He went outside. With his coat thrown over his shoulders he sat on the doorstep for about half an hour, sunk in thought, the burden of which was that, given other family circumstances, he would hardly be picking up orphans on the road of life, but would be sitting in his own home surrounded by a family of twelve, bonny stalwart foresters all. And he would scatter them throughout the country's forests, and once in every five years they would flock together to report back to him, and he would twit them with every forestial blunder they made. Another thing that occupied his mind at the moment was how to take his new foster-child back with him to Moscow without a travelling pass.

Pustosha was wrapped in a damp spring mist, and it was odd, at such a season, to hear the low rumblings of thunder, unaccompanied by lightning, which resembled distant earthquakes. Somewhere far away, from where the wind was blowing, another surrounded enemy army was being mopped up. In the adjoining cubbyhole there stood a chest with a sloping lid; for a pillow he used a bundle of tow left over from Kalinka's mother. If one forgot about legs that grew stiff by dawn and ignored the verminy drawbacks of such a shakedown, Vikhrov had not slept so sweetly for a long time. He was roused by the high-keyed roar of an engine outside. A woman with a medical bag slung across her shoulder was standing under a fir-tree, waiting for the skidding lorry to get out of the deep rut, but it was difficult to make out who she was through the dusty rain-smudged window. Kalinka explained that it was the lady doctor from Pashutino who had called on his grandfather. Vikhrov ran out just as she put her foot on the wheel hub to swing herself into the lorry.

Yelena did not turn round until it dawned on her that, short of a miracle, there could be only one person in the world who knew her by that old name of her childhood.

"Oh, it's you, Ivan? What a fright you gave me!" she said, clutching her heart, and Vikhrov thought he caught a faint note of disappointment in her voice.

6

He searched her face for an answer to the question which he dare not put into words, but he found little evidence of any change in her during the years of their separation. She stood there before him just as young, only slightly graver, a bit thinner, and even, as he first fancied, wearing the same cheviot overcoat which he had bought her three years after they moved to Moscow. Of course, it was a bit frayed at the cuffs and worn thin at the shoulders, and had acquired the uncertain colour of a weather-beaten peasant's *armyak*. But she herself was almost untouched by the flying years, except for the inescapable little wrinkles around the mouth and the crow's feet around the eyes, but these, as with most rural dwellers, came from a habit of screwing up the eyes in the breadth of dazzling horizons. But peer as he would at her severe features, now tranquillised at last, he could not detect beneath them the soft childish face painted in imitation of a Red Indian. The later image of the Moscow period, too, was somewhat faded, but that was no doubt due to the dull merciless light.

A cold slanting rain, the last before the buds blossomed, came down steadily.

"I'm very glad to see you too," Yelena said with restraint, disengaging her wet hands from his grasp; besides the boy on the doorstep, two other pairs of eyes were watching them from the driver's cab. "You were the last person I expected to meet in such a backwood, Ivan!"

She knew from Polya that he had been planning to come, and two urgent telegrams from Moscow were waiting for him at the office of the forestry division, but she had not thought they would meet so unexpectedly and in such an out-of-the-way place. Nevertheless, wishing to say something kind to him, she mentioned that only that morning she and Polya had been wondering where he could have got to.

"Is Polya still here?" Vikhrov asked, looking down at his feet.

"You're lucky, all three of them are still at my place. They're such charming boys. It's a pity they're going back to their units tomorrow morning." She started to put on a pair of old knitted mittens. "Well, I was glad to see you. Excuse me now, Ivan, this lorry is not ours, I can't keep it waiting any more."

"I'd like to talk to you, Lenochka."

"But won't you drop in this evening . . . to say goodbye to the youngsters?"

"You see, it will have to be a long talk, in private if possible. Don't be afraid, I'm not going to bother you with my misplaced confessions or belated regrets," he added quickly without looking up for fear of catching a grimace of annoyance on her face.

No, his former wife was not afraid of anything in the world now; she simply did not have the heart to cause him any further

713

pain. The cab door opened at this point, and a woman's indifferent voice reminded her that they had to be in Polushubovo before dinner-time and return the lorry to Loshkarev by the evening.

"I don't know what to tell you, Ivan," Yelena said, still hesitating. "Look here, you have to go to Pashutino in any case, and there are mines all over the place ... as a matter of fact I'm hurrying to Polushubovo, a poor woman trod on one of them the other day.... I'm taking an army surgeon down to see her. The war is still picking out its victims. If you haven't anything else to do and don't mind getting wet, we could have a talk on the way. You'd better hurry, though, I'm at work."

It took Vikhrov a minute to slip on his galoshes, snatch his coat off the chest, and shout to Kalinka, who did not tear his eyes off him all the time, that he should wait for him tomorrow morning to go to Moscow together. The lorry ride was as convenient as one could expect in those days; an empty crate served as a seat, and a bale of tow behind it as the back of a sofa. There was a drum of kerosene there, too, propped up with logs and braced with wire in the middle.

Yelena moved up to make room for him, and held up the edge of a wet weather-toughened tarpaulin.

"I'm used to it, but you're a townsman, I'd advise you to cover yourself up with it."

"I don't deserve such a low opinion, I'm as fit as a fiddle," laughed Vikhrov.

"Mind this rain doesn't tell on you, Ivan."

The lorry picked its way in second gear over a rickety wartime corduroy, and the squelch of the logs mingled with the splash of the kerosene in the drum. The water oozed through the gaps between the logs, and the rain turned into a downpour; willynilly the passengers were obliged to pull the ends of the tarpaulin over their shoulders, and this tended to draw them together. The conversation started with questions about the children. It appeared that Polya and Sergei had been admitted simultaneously into the same hospital, where, a day later, Rodion arrived suffering from shell-shock; Yelena had known him only from hearsay. "We all regarded them as children, we didn't notice that wartime experience had made them sometimes older than we are." It also transpired that since the end of the winter the field hospital had been housed in the Pashutino hospital building and the adjoining village, but had moved on westward a week ago in the wake of the advancing troops, leaving behind a small group of about a dozen wounded. After her return from the partisan detachment Yelena was given a job there, too, but not on the staff.

"A doctor from the field hospital is travelling with me, she's a splendid woman ... she consented to see my patients before she left. That Minei has done a good deal for me, you know."

"During the war?" Vikhrov said, surprised.

"No, before I married. When I felt bad I used to slip away from the manor and go to his cabin, and he used to hide me ... from myself. I think that simple woodsman understood my state of mind better than anyone else at the time."

"But are you happy now, at least?"

She hesitated.

"Of course. I've cured myself of the old complaint, I'm an accepted member of society now. If happiness comes from a knowledge of your being needed, then I daresay I'm happy."

Her reply naturally stirred hopes in Vikhrov which he had thought were dead. He stole a questioning glance at her, but apparently he was mistaken. This woman's eyes now shone with the steady unclouded light of utter fearlessness which comes from a sense of standing close to the eternal springs of life or from constant contact with clean ordinary people. The change left no room whatever for pity and the ludicrous designs of an old man, which he had brought with him from Moscow. The talk broke off long enough for him to adjust himself to the situation. Then Yelena in her turn asked about Moscow, about the Institute and Taisa.

The ride was a long one and gave them plenty of time. Vikhrov spoke at length about Moscow having changed considerably for the better in the last few years, so that if Lenochka thought of visiting them for at least a week she would hardly recognise it— not because it looked better, it was grim and fierce now, with barricades and rail obstacles in the streets and sandbags under the shop windows, a warrior with lowered visor ... but that was what made it doubly attractive in the eyes of those for whom the beauty of life is courage and movement towards a great historical goal. Despite the harsh conditions the Forestry Institute was returning from Central Asia in a few days, and there were rumours of sweeping forestry measures on a national scale to be undertaken in the next few years; as for the academic season, nothing was heard yet. Taisa sent her regards, would like to see Yelena, and felt miserable without anything to do; she was very keen on getting herself a job, but he had not let her.

"There are only two of us now. But never mind, I'm going

back with an addition; I've picked up a little boy here, an orphan; she'll have something to keep her busy now. No, really, Lenochka, come and spend your holiday with us," he almost pleaded. "I can imagine you coming home from work to find a cold stove, nothing to warm up yesterday's soup on. Taisa will be ever so glad."

"She's a good woman," Yelena said, mentally greeting her. "The number of times I've sat down to write her a letter. At first I thought it would be easier for you to bear our separation without getting letters from me, and then there didn't seem to be any more sense in it. I happened to be staying the week at Chernetsov's in Loshkarev when you came to visit Polya. I was sitting in the next room while you were drinking tea. I didn't come out for the same reasons."

"Yes, I knew you were there, my heart told me you were," Vikhrov said and turned away to look at the straight rows of young pines which he had planted himself years ago.

They were an ocular demonstration of the passage of time. They had long become mothers themselves, and their children could be seen running out into the road in their blue-green vests. They felt quite happy there, in the old clearing, standing under the rain and slowly turning round on their roots as the lorry passed to catch every drop in their leaves. No wonder the war had twice spared their lovely youth. Vikhrov himself would hardly have recognised the place but for the stream ahead of them, the gentle Veselukha, with its rickety bridge, which was memorable to him since his father's funeral. It was this way that the body of Matvei Vikhrov had been borne to the cemetery on that thundery mist-blurred noon, and Demidka had kept begging him to let him carry the icon as far as the river, until that charitable sparkling shower had poured down on the procession. The memory was so poignant that his nostrils were tickled by the savoury smell of the wet lasting from which his new shirt had been sewn.

"I may pay you a visit ... in the autumn, not now," Yelena was saying. "I miss Moscow myself. Of course, I treated you very cruelly. Ah Ivan, Ivan!" Suddenly her eye glinted with a suspicion of moisture. "But don't you see, I couldn't help it, I would have pined away there in six months, simply melted away like that patch of snow under the bridge there. You know, I was like a drop torn away from the sea. No matter where it rushes about it will always go back to it in the end, even at the risk of breaking in its fall from the heights. I feel all the more to blame in that I didn't very much believe that we could be happy."

"I'm not blaming you, Lenochka, but at least let me make sure for myself that you are happy now."

Apparently, he wanted proofs of the change for the better. Yelena did not like to indulge in reminiscences, perhaps because she had none to indulge in. She made as if she had not heard the question.

"Oh, how afraid I was of my sea, Ivan! And at the same time I hungered for peace of mind. And I achieved it."

"But it took a lifetime," Vikhrov sighed. "Here, let me wrap this tarpaulin round your legs. Your stockings aren't much good, I see, and we have a long way to go yet."

The rain, meantime, had stopped, but a side wind blowing from the open field was all but knocking the lorry over. Occupied with her own thoughts, Yelena submitted without protest.

"A life is not too high a price for such a thing. Besides, you are partly to blame for your own troubles, Ivan. I may have got used to it with you if you could have taught me to kill myself with fatigue. Happiness doesn't come to a person through his eyes, but through his restless hands ... and death, too, if you have noticed, comes from idle hands. Look how bleached Minei's have become, he hasn't been using them."

"No, that isn't true ... you have just thought it up," Vikhrov protested warmly, not daring to call her by her former name through superstitious fear of losing her for ever. "It was simply that I loved you for a lifetime, loved you to distraction. Just so. And the main thing, was my love wasted?"

They both knew they would be seeing each other again, and so the talk which Vikhrov had gone out to the Yenga for was not resumed. Following her own train of thought, Yelena suddenly asked gratefully and warmly about Valery, and Ivan, proud of his friend, described to her their last meeting without concealing the strange circumstances that preceded it. While he was at it, he gave the latest news, worthy of a brief mention, which had created a sensation in forestry circles, namely, Gratsiansky's decision to voluntarily quit the world in the prime of his creative powers, which he successfully executed a month ago by means of an ice-hole in the river.

"True," Vikhrov wound up, "such a vulgar method of committing suicide somehow doesn't fit in with his pampered nature—it's so long and cold! But then it has the advantage of not being messy, it leaves no traces and gives no grounds for conjectures. Valery and I even suspect that he left his hat and stick lying by the ice-hole specially for our simpletons, with the intention of twisting them round his finger again!"

Vikhrov also commented on Valery's new appointment, with which he had flown out to the Far East. "Ah, well, I'll send him a scrap of our spring in my next book, the way I used to send a handful of Russian snow in the old days."

They visited a number of villages during the day; Yelena was anxious to make full use of the lorry and the experience of an older colleague before taking over the management of the deserted Pashutino hospital pending the arrival of a new doctor. Vikhrov enjoyed a splendid airing, during which he discovered a hitherto unknown quality in his people: the greater the grief, the fewer the tears. Uncomplaining resolve shone in the peasants' faces together with a readiness, come what may, to break through to that unfading strip of evening sky, which, in the people's dream, betokens the peaceful work-imbued silence of the coming age.

Apparently Yelena Ivanovna was more to people than just their district deputy or local feldsher. From the way they met her and saw her off, young and old, with lingering gaze, and asked about her daughter—while one woman kept pushing three eggs into her pocket, perhaps the first to be laid in that bitter newly liberated land—Vikhrov gathered that Yelena had perhaps won greater recognition in life than he had done with his fat books about the Russian forest.

"What's the matter?" Yelena chaffed him on their way back. "Has something got into your eye?"

"It's much simpler than that, Yelena Ivanovna. Looking at my countrymen has upset me. The usual effects of age changes," he honestly confessed. He was glad to see that this woman was still graceful and young, although she was unlike her former self.

They had three more kilometres to go before they reached home. It had become windy, and the clear fringe of sky in the west promised a fair day for the morrow. They arrived in Pashutino at sundown. A long-legged cockerel in cotton-print breeches crossed the road in front of them—a good omen. Vikhrov read the telegrams from Moscow. The first asked his consent to be appointed to the post of Director of the Forestry Institute, the other two demanded his immediate presence in Moscow at what was hinted between the lines as being one of the most important conferences in the history of the Russian forest.

The scene was the spacious office of the Forestry Division, bathed in the afterglow of sunset. Repaired only yesterday, it was temporarily being used as living quarters. A man with a red beard and arms in clay up to the elbows was standing on a raised platform laying the stove, hurrying to finish the chimney before it grew dark. The setting sun, reflected in a puddle on the floor, played a streaming light for him on the fresh boards of the ceiling. While Yelena busied herself about the house, Vikhrov hung their wet clothes on the wall, listening at the same time to the young voices in the next room behind the chintz curtains, from which flowed the warmth of human tenancy.

"Don't be so hard on Rodion, sister. The poor chap's wilted completely!" he recognised the voice of Sergei.

"That's all right, he's getting his deserts! I was wilder than this with him once in Moscow," Polya laughed, as if there was no war, as if the great victory was an already accomplished fact. "Poor Varya and I went into the cinema, the newsreel showed a concert at the front. A crowd of soldiers were sitting on the grass and some artiste was singing. He was very funny, it looked as if he was showing the doctor his throat. And this soldier, Rodion, was there too, sitting under a tree with his back to me, paring a stick or something. I stared at him with all my eyes, used all my hypnotic powers, but he didn't even look round, the insensitive clot!"

"I haven't got eyes at the back of my head. Why didn't you yell, I'd have turned round then," the third said in an unfamiliar bass voice.

Just then Yelena came up behind Vikhrov with some aluminium plates and a steaming billycan.

"You're having dinner with us, of course, Ivan? We're throwing a farewell party today."

Vikhrov took her hand.

"Listen to their laughter. How much stronger than destruction and death youth and life are! By the way, who's that other one there? You don't mean to say...." He looked at her meaningly.

"Oh, you've grown terribly shrewd, haven't you!" she laughed. "Go along there, get acquainted."

It was an agitated Vikhrov, coughing nervously, who stepped across the threshold with his face set in that vague unfathomable expression which old fellows usually put on when they appear among the youth.

January 1950-December 1953

www.ingramcontent.com/pod-product-compliance
Lightning Source LLC
Chambersburg PA
CBHW011651010726
47499CB00010B/3209